Angélique

BOOK ONE

Angélique

The Marquise of Angels

Anne Golon

Translated by Rita Barisse

*Illustrations and maps by
Iva Garo, Nadja Golon and Regile*

G.K. Hall & Co • Chivers Press
Thorndike, Maine USA   Bath, Avon, England

This Large Print edition is published by G.K. Hall & Co., USA and by Chivers Press, England.

Published in 1995 in the U.S. by arrangement with Romance Consultants International, Inc.

Published in 1995 in the U.K. by arrangement with the author.

U.S. Hardcover	0-7838-1392-9	(Romance Collection Edition)
U.K. Hardcover	0-7451-7908-8	(Windsor Large Print)
U.K. Softcover	0-7451-3727-X	(Paragon Large Print)

The text of this Large Print edition is unabridged.
Other aspects of the book may vary from the original edition.

Set in 16 pt. News Plantin.

Printed in the United States on permanent paper.

British Library Cataloguing in Publication Data available

Library of Congress Cataloging in Publication Data

Golon, Anne.
    [Marquise des anges. English]
    Angelique : the marquise of the angels / Anne and Serge Golon.
      p.   cm.
    ISBN 0-7838-1392-9 (lg. print : hc)
    I. Golon, Serge. II. Title.
PQ2613.O476M313 1995
843'.914—dc20   95-9463

Contents

ℒetter

by Kathryn Falk, Lady Barrow

Dear Reader,

Welcome to the first book of the Romantic Times/Thorndike Press Classic Series.

A poll of *Romantic Times* magazine's readers resulted in a fascinating collection of out-of-print romances that Thorndike Press is interested in producing in large-print type.

Angélique headed my list of "keepers" as it did for many fans. When this book came out in the 1950's it became one of the bestselling historicals of its time, and the sequels went on to sell over 20 million copies in foreign languages around the world.

The first five books in the series were written in chronological order, which is why it is so important to start with Book One. The plot and adventures in *Angélique* are carefully planned and I hope you will read them as the author intended.

When *Angélique* was printed in a paperback edition by Bantam, in the mid-50's, the first two books, *Angélique: The Marquise of Angels* and *Angélique: On the Road to Versailles* were erroneously combined as Book I and some pages were eliminated from the beginning of Book II. We have rectified this in our Classic

Editions, and have returned the books to their original states. Book II will be available in December, 1995.

A classic endures. Recently, *Angélique* was a bestseller in Russia, and the books are still in print in France.

Sylvia Halliday, a French scholar in the romance genre, has penned a brief history of the Age of Louis XIV, to help readers more clearly understand this important era and to know the accuracy of the Golons' research.

A classic romance is one that not only is well written and contains bigger-than-life heroes and heroines, but should also educate and transform the readers. It can be reread and never loses its impact on the reader's imagination.

Through the years, many fans of *Angélique* have written to the author, Anne Golon, describing how her book has changed them and inspired them to take more control of their destiny.

I feel the same. It was a great influence on my teen years as it was for readers around the world. For women, this book has been a role model regardless of the culture or background.

As you will perceive when you become involved in this series, Angélique is a strong and resilient heroine who inspires readers to "survive."

In the turbulent times of the Golden Age of France and in our own chaotic period, Angélique stands as a role model for women who can overcome any difficulty.

Angélique is a woman — and a book — for all ages. I hope you will be both entertained and transformed as you enter a glorious period of French history when adventure and love knew no boundaries!

Kathryn Falk, Lady Barrow

Kathryn Falk is the founder and CEO of *Romantic Times* magazine and the author of *How to Write a Romance and Get It Published.*

Introduction

Remembering. . . . by Anne Golon

I remember the very first day, the first hour, when — with pen in hand — I chose the first words for the literary adventure before me — a big historical novel.

I remember it all quite clearly. A girl appeared in my imagination. She didn't even see me! She was lively, light and oblivious of her gracefulness and beauty. So full of curiosity. What interested her was life and the promises of life that were ahead of her.

I knew she would be the heroine of my novel!

What interested and surprised me also was the appearance of a landscape: a forest, a miscellany of green and hardwood shadows, the crenallated towers of an old castle peering through the tree tops, and below, black watery mirrors shining on a royal carpet of green lentils and gold ranonculus.

I once nearly experienced an amorous remembrance in a province of France! Although I was never there again it caught and stayed in my memory.

It was Poitou. A land of druids and forests that I had crossed on my bicycle at the age of 25, during the second World War, accompanied by my paint and brushes.

Poitou was beckoning to be the site for the beginning of the story about this carefree heroine. . . .

(Memories, you understand, do take possession of an author's imagination!)

This magical place would be the setting of her birth; the roots of her soul. . . .

For a long time I couldn't find her name.

Some were too sweet, others too antiquated. I refused to give her a trite name. I had to find a name to carry her into the future of her universe.

I thought of a bunch of flowers offered by Valentin or Nicolas. Lush yellow flowers and long stems that counterpointed her blond hair and green eyes. A marsh plant known as Angelica Sylvestre, Anges Weed, and Holy Spirit Weed.

Angélique! It came to me then.

That name suited her.

She began to exist for me.

My story began to develop into the adventure of a girl whose life careened from one edge to another. It would enlarge and become as eventful as many women's destinies in the 20th century. Those modern age heroines who experienced wars and tragedies.

Historical settings began appearing:

The pink city of Toulouse, the Mediterranean Sea haunted by pirates, Versailles, the revolts against a monarch whose strength and power evoked the name of the Sun King.

Social issues arose and confronted this woman, particularly the burning desire for freedom. The courage to fight for it.

What is an historical novel without eternal myths? Man and God, individual and society, love and destruction. I interlaced these and more with my characters.

I believed in the immortals: Ulysses, Tristan Isolde, Romeo and Juliet, Don Quixote . . . Angélique and Joffrey de Peyrac.

How does one explain that an imaginary character can live in one's heart and can express herself by someone's pen?

All I know is that I loved Angélique. For being different. For having the ability to astonish me by each new action and reaction. And I didn't know her before. . . .

This is what happens when you write. You receive a gift from the character, like a present to the author. She lived through me.

A strange feeling would often come over me as I started on the first book of my long story. I would tell myself: "It's funny, I know her . . . but she doesn't know me!"

Writing is mysterious, evolving from inspiration and imagination, thanks to God. Writing fiction is art. It cannot be merely made or fabricated. It is creation.

Anne Golon
Versaille
June, 1995

Preface — A French History

by Sylvia Halliday

Dear Reader of *Angélique*,

I hope this brief overview of French history will be useful. I tried to mention those personages and events that can help to clarify your understanding and enjoyment of this wonderful classic romance.

For those of you who are dedicated students of history, be assured that *Angélique* is scrupulous in its references and research, down to the last details of costume, custom, and personalities. Though Angélique's cousin, Philippe du Plessis, seems to be fictional, his mother, Mme. du Plessis-Bellière was a real person, a confederate of Fouquet and the Prince of Condé during the Fronde. (Incidentally, Philippe, as the son of a nobleman, is called a Knight — "Chevalier" in French.)

The details of King Louis's marriage to Maria-Theresa, the Infanta of Spain, are brilliantly captured in the book, down to the last formalities and rituals, and the descriptions of Paris and the Louvre are dead-on accurate.

A particularly ironic scene — for a lover of history — takes place when King Louis and his Queen return to Paris after their wedding. Angélique watches the procession from an actual house, and in the company of real personages who were there: the Queen Mother and Mazarin. However, her companions on that day are two historical women — Athénaïs and Françoise Scarron — destined to become, respectively, the King's mistress and the King's second wife.

A special note about the Comte de Peyrac and his Court of Gay Learning in Toulouse, an ancient city in the south of France. Though Peyrac seems to be purely fictional, the details of his existence are historically accurate. He and his friends in the Languedoc region are hot-blooded, and express their continuing resentment against the north of France, which had conquered it centuries before. They trumpet their pride in Toulouse and the Languedoc, and speak in soft, regional accents; their habits and manners betray the Spanish-Moorish influence on their culture.

As for the Court of Gay Learning — it seems to be patterned after the medieval Courts of Love, where troubadours sang of the ideals of gallantry and chivalry, and courtly, romantic notions of love were discussed and encouraged. Many of these ideas had come first to the Languedoc region by way of Moorish Spain. Indeed, there was actually such a Court of Love in Provence (in the south of France) during the days of the medieval troubadours. During the seventeenth century, there were attempts to revive the Courts of Love in France, to refine and civilize the still-rough culture. The last recorded revival of a Court of Love was held at the insistence of Cardinal Richelieu himself, in order to judge a question of gallantry that had been raised in one of the salons.

The Age of Louis XIV has been called the Splendid Century; it stretched from 1643, when Louis took the throne as a boy not quite five years old, to his death in 1715. Dominated by one man, it was one of the most influential periods of modern history. It saw the flowering of art, drama, literature, culture, science, philosophy, and architecture. It ushered in the Age of Reason and gave rise to great scientific discoveries. Its influence was felt for nearly a hundred years, and its reputation lingered in the rest of the world long after France had fallen into the decline that culminated in the French Revolution. The manners, the politics, the art, the architecture of Louis's France were copied by monarchs throughout Europe. The splendor of the Sun King's world served as a model for Peter the Great of Russia, who Westernized and modernized his still-feudal country, and built a palace at Peterhof in the style of Versailles. Mad Ludwig II of Bavaria built at Herrenchiemsee an exact replica (in reduced scale) of Louis's grand palace, and dozens of German princelings modeled their palaces and their Courts after Louis's example.

But, like most cultural upheavals, this great age was preceded by chaos and confusion, turmoil and transition, as the old ways grudgingly gave way to the new. The changes wrought by Louis XIV had been sparked by cataclysmic events that had swept France and the Continent in the previous century, and were changes that were affecting all of Europe. With a lesser king, France would perhaps have experienced the fate of England — the overthrow and execution of the Monarch (Charles I), the divided country, and the bloody civil wars. But France, owing in large part to her

great Prime Ministers, Richelieu and Mazarin —
and her brilliant King Louis in his maturity —
took a different turn. She prospered, she
blossomed, she grew into the greatest nation in
the world — but not without a difficult and painful
adolescence.

It is this earlier period — a period of insur-
rections and conspiracies, of unreasoning hatreds
and long-held prejudices, of clashes between the
old and the new — that forms the backdrop of
Angélique.

The strongest influence on France in the seventeenth century, and indeed in all of Europe, was
the Reformation of the previous century. The
Catholic Church had been challenged in country
after country, rejected and reformed.

The Church responded to these challenges by
digging in its heels and strengthening the Inquisition, rooting out Protestants, whom they viewed
as heretics, wherever they could be found. The
French Protestants, a minority in the country,
were called Huguenots; they were a branch of the
Calvinist sect.

The religious problem seemed to be resolving
by the end of the 16th century, when Henri IV
of France, a Huguenot, married a Catholic princess and united the country. (He did, however,
agree to convert to Catholicism in the interests
of peace — "Paris is worth a mass," was his famous
remark at the time.) He issued the Edict of Nantes
in 1598, which granted religious freedom and
equality to Huguenots.

When he was assassinated, his son, Louis XIII,
became king and ruled in tandem with his great

Prime Minister, Cardinal Richelieu.

At the same time, the Huguenots had fresh grievances of their own: the King's troops had been merciless in their conquest, raping and looting and pillaging. It was the first time that French troops had behaved in such a savage manner against their own countrymen. Moreover, the Catholic Church responded by increasing its pressure on the "heretics," and by trying to revive the power of the Inquisition. The Church was bitter about the loss of its position in affairs of State, the influence and riches it would never have again.

You will find in *Angélique* much of this religious animosity, fear of foreign influences, and suspicion of "new ideas." Angélique, though a Catholic, suffers mightily because of it. The character Joffrey is viewed as a danger to the Church because of his interest in science, his reading of the philosophy of Descartes, and his "modern thinking." Angélique's own grandfather had fought at La Rochelle; his reminiscences of Henri, his outmoded dress, and his resentment of Huguenots represent the thinking of the "old guard."

Another great force in France at the time was the dying out of feudalism. With the advent of gunpowder and modern warfare, the aristocrats — the great Nobles of the Sword — were becoming irrelevant to the Crown. No longer, as in feudal times, did the King depend on them to raise great armies and go to war for him; cannons and muskets could destroy an enemy fortress without a horde of mounted knights. Some nobles found positions in the King's government, but, by and large, they were ill-suited and poorly educated for the life of a bureaucrat. More and more, these positions were held by the untitled middle class (the bourgeoisie) who — having tasted poverty — thirsted for more.

Unless their families had unlimited wealth, the nobles had three choices: to stoop to trade, to truckle to the King and accept a meaningless post at Court along with a Royal "pension" (really only a form of patronage or welfare), or to sink slowly into proud ruin. Needless to say, this set of conditions didn't sit well with men who had been raised on the pride of their ancient family titles.

Some nobles plotted to regain their power; Angélique's father chooses to live peacefully in his crumbling castle, resigned to the decline of his family and his fortunes. As you will discover in *Angélique*, hard cash was required by a nobleman to send his daughter to a convent or to buy her a decent husband.

The discontents of the nobles and the ambitious, rising middle class burst forth in a series of internal wars called the Fronde (1649–1653). Louis was still a child during much of that time; his mother, Anne of Austria, ruled as his Regent, aided by the Italian Cardinal Mazarin, Richelieu's successor. The King was nearly dethroned half a dozen times during the Fronde, and he spent his childhood in a state of turmoil and near-poverty, fleeing from the armies of the nobles and Parliament. The fact that Mazarin was a foreigner, a shrewd and wily politician, and the rumored lover of Louis's mother, only added to the King's precarious position during those years. He never forgot the humiliation of the Fronde. When he reached his majority and took the reigns of office himself, he contrived to strip the aristocracy of its remaining power.

But in *Angélique*, he is still a young man finding his way, and under the influence of his mother and Mazarin. His youthful weakness spells trouble for Angélique. Moreover, that weakness allowed his enemies to plot against him. Fouquet, his sinister, ambitious, money-hungry Minister of Finance, is prominent in the book, though we never meet him. (Those of you familiar with Dumas's "Man in the Iron Mask" will recall how Fouquet ultimately met his downfall. He invited the King to his splendid chateau Vaux-le-Vicomte, and put on a great show of wealth. The Monarch wondered where Fouquet had found the money for such a lavish palace — presto! Farewell, Fouquet! Louis promptly hired the craftsmen responsible for Vaux to build Versailles.)

Other important historical characters you'll meet in *Angélique* are Prince of Condé, Monsieur, and La Grande Mademoiselle. Condé — a brilliant soldier — was the King's cousin, and not too many steps removed from the throne. His ambition led him to the *Fronde* and many other plots against his cousin. He changed allegiances constantly: he fought bravely for France, then allied himself with Spain. Ever the haughty aristocrat, he left others to pick up the pieces and lived a life of debauchery. For all his evil ways, he died peacefully in his bed in 1686, forgiven once again by his cousin. You will dislike him when you meet him in *Angélique*. You'll also meet Madame de Longueville, his sister and a confederate in his plotting. There's also mention of Turenne, another great general, who, early on, deserted the cause of the *Fronde* to do battle against Condé's army.

"Monsieur" (with a capital "M") was the King's younger brother, Philippe d'Orléans. ("Monsieur" was the title given to a King's younger brother; the King's son and heir to the throne was always called the "Dauphin," much as the title Prince of Wales is always used for the heir in England.)

Monsieur was a fascinating character — vain, frivolous, totally corrupt and morally reprehensible. He would be called "gay" today (his wife burned the perfumed letters from his male lovers when he died, and lived in shabby splendor because he was always giving money to his current favorites). But in the seventeenth century, a homosexual man was simply referred to as a man who had "inclinations." Indeed, Monsieur fulfilled his duties to his wife as he was obliged to — he impregnated her eleven times!

Incidentally, you'll notice that several times in *Angélique* there is reference to love "à l'Italienne" (in the Italian manner) — i.e. sodomy. It became so rife in Louis's court that he was urged to put a stop to it. He refused, on the grounds that he could scarcely begin by prosecuting his own brother. (I came across a wonderful quotation when I was writing my own book about Versailles — "Stolen Spring" by Louisa Rawlings. When a male visitor to the Court, approached for a homosexual liaison, expressed his horror, he was told: "But monsieur, don't you understand? In Versailles, the nobility; in Spain, the monks; in Italy, *everybody!*") "Monsieur" does not come off too well in this book.

La Grande Mademoiselle, Mademoiselle de Montpensier, was Louis and Monsieur's first cousin. Her father, Gaston d'Orléans, as younger brother to Louis XIII, had also been called Monsieur. (Indeed, while Gaston was still alive, Philippe was often called the Petit Monsieur. You will note this in the book.) Gaston had forever plotted against his brother, Louis XIII, hoping to overthrow him and win the throne for himself. Gaston was warm-hearted and ambitious, but stupid and muddle-headed, and he seems to have passed on those traits to his daughter. She was filled with a spirit of rebellion, but little common sense, like her father. (After every insurrection, Gaston's friends and confederates were executed, while he was spared. It never seemed to bother him that he led his supporters to disaster!)

Though she was eleven years older than Louis, La Grande Mademoiselle had hoped to marry her cousin. But the romance of the Fronde stirred her lively, rebellious spirit, and she sided with the Prince of Condé. When Condé's army was almost defeated by Louis's troops outside the gates of Paris, the hot-headed girl personally manned the cannon on the Bastille and prevented the young King and his army from following Condé into the city. She even directed the guns to be trained on Louis himself; he narrowly escaped injury. Mazarin was to say later: "That cannon killed her husband."

By the time we meet La Grande Mademoiselle in *Angélique*, she has become largely ineffectual — if still warm, kindly, and somewhat empty-headed — bypassed by Court and King because of her earlier activities. Condé, the brilliant soldier, could be forgiven again and again; France might have use of his services on the battlefield. But La Grande Mademoiselle (or "Demoiselle," as she is sometimes referred to in the book) was ignored.

The third strong influence on France at this time (after religion and the Fronde) was the Thirty Years' War. It had ended with the Peace of Westphalia in 1648, but it had left France drained of resources. (It was largely a religious war, with the German Protestants and others arrayed against Catholics.) When it ended, all of Europe was filled with discharged soldiers and mercenaries — hungry, homeless, rootless, ruthless after the savageries they had experienced in the war. Angélique's father's German servant, old Guillaume, is a veteran of that conflict, and her old nurse, Fantine, has a son who was the product of a mass rape by marauding troops. Early in the book, one of the local villages is overrun by a band of these brutal ex-soldiers.

The poverty of the peasants, the need for fresh taxes to restore the national treasury, the nobles whose finances had been depleted while they served in the war, the Church with its hunger for money to win back the faithful — all these contributed to an atmosphere of lawlessness and greed that pervaded the country. Disillusioned, people lost faith, and sometimes turned to magic, alchemy, and the Black Arts. It was a perilous time. You will see all of this very clearly in *Angélique*.

Sylvia Halliday is the author of 11 historical romances, written under the pseudonyms of Ena Halliday and Louisa Rawlings. She majored in Art History and French at Brown University. Her current publisher is Kensington Publishing and her latest title is *Summer Darkness, Winter Light,* using the name of Sylvia Halliday.

PART ONE

The Marquise of the Angels

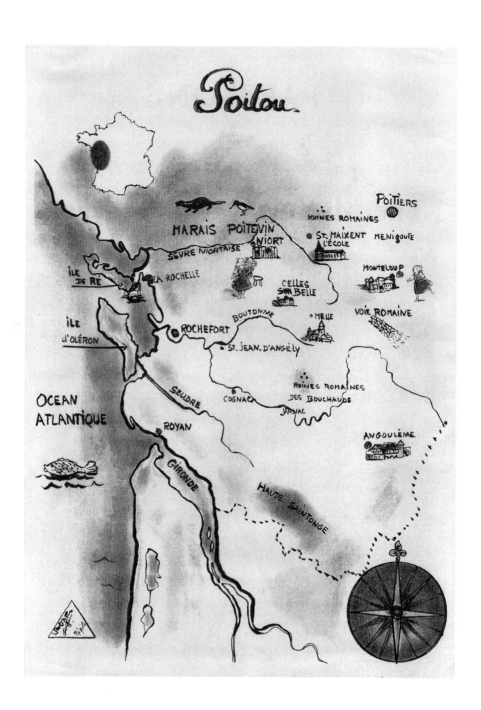

Poitou

POITIERS

RUINES ROMAINES

St. MAIXENT MÉNIGOUTE
L'ÉCOLE

MARAIS POITEVIN

NIORT

SÈVRE NIORTAISE

CELLES
SUR BELLE

MONTELOUP

ÎLE DE RÉ

LA ROCHELLE

VOIE ROMAINE

BOUTONNE

MELLE

ÎLE d'OLÉRON

ROCHEFORT

St. JEAN D'ANGÉLY

RUINES ROMAINES
DES BOUCHAUDS

OCEAN
ATLANTIQUE

SEUDRE

COGNAC

JARNAC

ANGOULÈME

ROYAN

GIRONDE

HAUTE SAINTONGE

Chapter 1

"NOUNOU," enquired Angélique, "why did Gilles de Retz kill so many children?"

"To please the devil, my child. Gilles de Retz, the Ogre of Machecoul, wanted to be the mightiest lord of his day. His castle was chock-full of retorts and phials and cauldrons brimming with scarlet broths and fearful vapours. The devil demanded that the heart of a little child be offered him as sacrifice. That's how his crimes began. And terrified mothers would point to the black turrets of Machecoul, around which the ravens circled continually, the dungeons were so full of innocent corpses."

"Did he eat them all?" asked Madelon, Angélique's little sister, in a trembling voice.

"Not all of them, he couldn't have," answered the nurse.

Bending over the stewing-pot in which the bacon and cabbage were cooking, she stirred the soup in silence for some moments. Hortense, Angélique and Madelon, the three daughters of the Baron de Sancé de Monteloup, waited anxiously for the rest of the story, their spoons arrested in mid-air beside their bowls.

"He did worse," continued the nurse at last in a bitter tone. "First he would send for a poor little mite, who would cry piteously for his mother. The lord reclining on his bed would revel in the child's terror. Then he'd have the child hung on the wall by a sort of bracket that squeezed his chest and neck and almost strangled him, but not enough to kill him. The child would struggle like a strung-up fowl, with choking screams and eyes bulging out of his head, till he turned blue. And the vast hall resounded with the laughter of cruel men and the groans of the little victim. Then Gilles de Retz had him taken down, sat him on his knees, propped the little angel's head against his chest, and talked to him gently, reassuringly.

"All this wasn't in earnest, he would explain. They'd only wanted to have fun, but now it was over. The child would have sweetmeats, a soft feather-bed, a satin costume like a little page. The child trusted him. A light of joy glistened in his tearful eyes. Then suddenly the lord would plunge a dagger into his throat.

"But even more frightful," the nurse went on, "was what happened to the very young girls he kidnapped."

"What did he do to them?" asked Hortense.

At that moment, old Guillaume, who had been sitting in a corner of the fireplace scraping a carrot of tobacco, intervened, grumbling into his yellow beard:

"Hold your tongue, old madwoman! I've been through the wars and yet you manage to make even my stomach turn with your nonsense."

Big Fantine Lozier veered round to face him angrily.

"Nonsense! . . . Easy to see you weren't born in Poitou, but a long way off, Guillaume Lützen. You need but go north towards Nantes and you'll soon come upon the accursed castle of Machecoul. Those crimes were committed two centuries ago, but the people still cross themselves when they pass close by. But you don't hail from here, you know nothing of the ancestors of this land."

"Fine lot of ancestors, if they're all like your Gilles de Retz!"

"Gilles de Retz did evil on such a vast scale that no country other than Poitou can boast of a criminal like him. And when he died, after being tried and sentenced at Nantes, but confessing his sins and beseeching God's forgiveness, all the mothers whose children he had tortured and eaten put on mourning."

"Now that's too much!" exclaimed old Guillaume.

"That's how we are, we people of Poitou. Great sinners, great forgivers!"

The nurse grimly set soup plates on the table and hugged little Denis with fervour.

"To be sure," she went on, "I didn't get much schooling, but I know the difference between fireside tales and true stories of bygone days. Gilles de Retz really did exist. Perhaps his soul is still roaming around Machecoul, but his body has mouldered in this earth. That's why you can't talk of him lightly, as of the fairies and goblins that frolic around the big stones set up in the fields. Though one shouldn't make too much fun of those evil sprites . . ."

"And may one make fun of ghosts, Nounou?" asked Angélique.

"Better not, my pretty one. Ghosts are not wicked, but they are sad and touchy, so why add

31

mockery to the torments of those poor creatures?"

"Why does the old lady weep, the one who wanders around this castle?"

"Who knows? Last time I met her, six years ago, between the old guard-room and the long corridor, I think she was no longer crying — perhaps because of the prayers his lordship your grandfather had said for her in the chapel."

"I heard her walk on the stairs in the tower," added Babette the servant-girl.

"It was a rat, more likely. The old woman of Monteloup isn't noisy and doesn't like to make a fuss. Maybe she was blind. That's what people think, anyway, because she always keeps her hands stretched out. Or else she may be searching for something. Occasionally she comes close to sleeping children and passes her hand over their faces."

Fantine's voice dropped and became lugubrious.

"She is looking for a dead child, perhaps."

"Your mind, good woman, is more gruesome than the sight of a charnel-house," protested old Guillaume again. "It may be that your Lord of Retz was a great man whom you are proud to call your fellow-countryman — across the distance of two centuries — and maybe the Lady of Monteloup was quite respectable, but I say it's wicked to frighten those pretty ones to such a point that they forget to fill their little bellies."

"Ha! You're a fine one to act squeamish, you brute of a soldier and devil's henchman! How many such pretty bellies did you run through with your pike when you were serving the Emperor of Austria in the fields of Germany, Alsace and Picardy? How many cottages did you smoke out, shutting the door on entire families to be roasted inside? Didn't you ever string up poor country folk? So many that the branches of the trees broke under the load. And didn't you rape women and girls till they died of shame?"

"Just like the rest of them, my good woman. That's a soldier's life. That's war. But the lives of these little girls are made up of games and pleasant tales."

"So long as the soldiers and brigands don't come darkening the countryside like a cloud of locusts. Then the life of little girls becomes the life of the soldier, a life of war, misery and fear. . . ."

The nurse grimly uncovered a big stone dish filled with hare-pie and started buttering slices of bread which she doled out.

"Listen to me, little ones — to me, Fantine Lozier."

Hortense, Angélique and Madelon, who had turned this argument to account by scraping their bowls clean, raised their noses again, and their ten-year-old brother Gontran left the dark corner where he had been sulking and came closer. This was the hour of war and looting, of robbers and drunkards, all mingling in the glow of fires, the clash of swords and women's screams. . . .

"Guillaume Lützen, do you know my son, who is a carter of our lord the Baron de Sancé de Monteloup in this very castle?"

"I know him; he's a very handsome fellow."

"Well, all I can tell you about his father is that he was in the army of Monseigneur the Cardinal Richelieu, when he moved down against La Rochelle to exterminate the Protestants. Personally,

I never was a Huguenot and I always prayed to the Virgin to keep me pure till my marriage-day. But by the time the troops of our Most Christian King Louis XIII had passed through the country, the best I can say is that I wasn't a virgin any longer. And I named my son Jean the Cuirass in memory of all those devils, one of whom was his father, whose cuirasses were so studded with nails that they tore to shreds the only skirt I owned at the time.

"As for the bandits and highwaymen whom hunger has so often let loose on the roads, I could keep you awake a whole night through with tales of what they did to me on the straw in the barns, while they were grilling the feet of my man over the hearth to make him spew up where he'd hidden his savings. And me thinking on account of the smell that they were roasting the pig."

Thereupon big Fantine burst out laughing, then poured herself a tumbler of apple-brandy to refresh her tongue which had become dry with so much talking.

In the nurse's veins flowed a little of the Moorish blood which the Arabs, in the eleventh century, had brought right up to the confines of Poitou. Angélique had suckled with her milk this compound of passion and dreams which had gone into the making of the ancient spirit of her province, a land of forests and marshes, opening like a gulf onto the warm ocean winds. She had imbibed willy-nilly a world of drama and fairy-tales. It had appealed to her and given her a sort of immunity against fear. She looked down with pity on trembling little Madelon or on her elder sister Hortense, sitting stiffly, prim-faced yet dying to ask Nounou what exactly the bandits had done to her on the straw.

Angélique, at eight, guessed pretty shrewdly what had happened in the barn. How many times had she led the cow to the bull or the goat to the billy? And her friend, the young shepherd, Nicholas, had explained to her that in order to have children, men and women did the same thing. And that's how Nounou had had Jean the Cuirass. But what troubled Angélique was that Nounou's voice, when talking of these things, alternated between langorous rapture and a very genuine horror.

However, there was no point in trying to understand Nounou, her silences, her rages. It was enough that she was there, vast and bustling, with her strong arms, her lap, beneath her dress of fustian, a wide-open basket where you could nestle like a little bird and hear her sing you a cradle-song or talk to you of Gilles de Retz.

Much simpler was old Guillaume Lützen, who talked slowly with a rough accent. He was said to be Swiss or German. It was nearly fifteen years since he had come limping and bare-foot along the Roman road that leads from Angers to Saint-Jean-d'Angély. He had walked into the castle of Monteloup, asked for a bowl of milk, and stayed on ever since, a jack-of-all-trades, repairing, tinkering, pottering about. The Baron de Sancé made him carry letters to neighbouring friends, or receive the *Sergent-des-Aides* when he came to collect taxes. Old Guillaume would listen to the sergeant patiently and then answer in his mountain dialect, either Swiss or Tyrolese, and the other would go away discouraged.

Had he come from the battlefields of the north or the east? And why had this foreign mercenary apparently been travelling south from Britanny? All that anyone knew of him was that he had been at Lützen under the command of the war-lord Wallenstein, and that he had had the honour of piercing the paunch of the stout and magnificent King of Sweden, Gustavus Adolphus, when the latter, losing his way in the fog during the battle, had fallen among the Austrian pikemen.

In the attic where he slept you could see the sunlight shine through the cobwebs on his old armour and his helmet, out of which he still drank his mulled wine or sometimes ladled his soup. His enormous pike, three times as tall as he, served to knock down the walnuts in season.

But above all Angélique envied him his little tobacco-grater, made of tortoise-shell and inlaid wood, which he called his *"grivoise,"* according to the custom of the German military in French service who were themselves called *"grivois."*

In the castle's vast kitchen, doors opened and closed all through the evening. Some led into the night, whence emerged, with a strong smell of compost, grooms and serving-maids and the carter, Jean the Cuirass, as swarthy as his mother. The dogs, too, slipped through — the two long greyhounds, Mars and Marjolaine, and the badger-dogs caked to their eyes with mud. From inside the castle, the doors opened to let through the sprightly Nanette who was training to be a chamber-maid, while hoping to acquire sufficient good manners to leave these hard-up masters and enter service with the Marquis du Plessis de Bellière, a few miles from Monteloup. To and fro passed also the two little footmen, with shaggy manes over their eyes, carrying logs for the big hall and water for the bedrooms.

Then the Baroness appeared. She had a kindly face, wasted by the country air and her numerous childbirths. She wore a grey serge dress and a black woollen hood, for the air in the main hall where she sat between her father-in-law and old aunts was damper than in the kitchen. She asked if the herb tea for the Baron would soon be ready and if Baby had given any trouble in feeding. She stroked Angélique's cheek in passing. The little girl was half asleep, and her long hair of burnished gold spread over the table and glowed in the light of the hearth.

"Time to go to bed, girls! Pulchérie will take you upstairs."

And Pulchérie, one of the elderly aunts, appeared with her usual docility. Since neither husband nor convent had been found to take her without a dowry she had decided to assume the role of governess to her nieces. And because she made herself useful instead of moaning and making tapestries all day long, she was treated with a little scorn and rather less consideration than the other aunt, fat old Jeanne.

Pulchérie assembled her nieces. The nurses would put the younger ones to bed, while Gontran, the tutorless boy, could retire to his straw pallet in the attic whenever he liked.

Following in the steps of the skinny old maid, Hortense, Angélique and Madelon reached the hall, where the hearth-fire and three candlesticks hardly dispelled the massed shadows that had accumulated through the centuries under the high medieval vaults. A few tapestries covered the walls, in an attempt to protect them from moisture, but they were so old and worm-eaten that the scenes they represented had become indistinguishable, except for the mournful eyes of some wan figures who seemed to stare reproachfully.

The little girls curtseyed before their grand-father, who was seated in front of the fireplace in his black greatcoat trimmed with mangy fur. But his white hands on the pommel of his cane were truly royal. He wore a huge, black, felt hat, and his square-cut beard, like that of the late King Henri IV, rested on a small fluted collarette, which Hortense secretly considered appallingly old-fashioned.

A second curtsey for Aunt Jeanne, whose sulking lips would not deign to smile, and then up the big stone staircase which was as damp as a cavern. The bedrooms were icy in winter but cool in summer. The bed in which the three girls slept loomed like a monument in the corner of a bare room, all the furniture having been sold by previous generations. The stone tiles, covered with straw in winter, were broken in many places. A short step-ladder of three rungs led up to the bed. After putting on their nightgowns and bonnets and getting down on their knees to thank God for His blessing, the three little damsels of Sancé de Monteloup clambered into their good featherbed and slipped under coverlets full of holes. Angélique promptly sought the hole in the sheet that corresponded to the one in the counterpane through which she could pass her rosy foot and wriggle her toes to make Madelon laugh.

The little girl was more fearful than a rabbit as a result of the stories that Nounou told. So was Hortense, though, being the eldest, she did not say anything. But Angélique relished her fear with a thrill of pleasure. Life was made up of mysteries and discoveries. The mice could be heard gnawing the woodwork, and the owls and fox-bats fluttering under the eaves of the two towers, with their shrill screeching. The greyhounds whimpered in the courtyard, and a mule scratched its hide audibly against the base of the walls.

And sometimes, on snowy nights, you could hear the wolves howling, as they came out of the wild forests of Monteloup towards the castle. Or again, beginning with the first spring nights there came floating up to the castle the songs of the villagers dancing a rigadoon in the moonlight. . . .

One of the walls of the castle of Monteloup gave on to the marshes. This was the oldest part, built under the Seigneur de Ridoué de Sancé, a companion of Du Guesclin's in the twelfth century. It was flanked by two stocky towers, with their rampart-walks in wooden tiles. When Angélique climbed up there with Gontran and Denis, they had fun spitting into the machicoulis, those openings through which the soldiers in the Middle Ages used to pour pails of flaming oil on their assailants. The walls were built on a small limestone promontory beyond which extended the marshes. In olden times this had been an inlet of the sea. The receding waters had left a network of rivers and canals and pools, now filled with verdure and willows, the realm of eel and frog, where the peasants could only get about in boats. The hamlets and huts were built on the former islands of the inlet. After roaming through this watery province when staying with the Marquis du Plessis one summer, the Duc de Tremoille, who prided himself on his exotic tastes, had called it "a green Venice."

This vast liquid meadow, the sweet marshes, stretched from Niort and Fontenay-le-Comte to the ocean. Just before Marans, Chaillé and even Luçon, it merged with the bitter marshes, the still salty lands. And finally there rose the white barrier of precious salt, for which Customs men and smugglers contended fiercely.

If the nurse disdained the stories of salt-tax collectors and smugglers, which thrilled the marshlands, the reason was that she sided with the firm ground and scorned all those who lived with wet feet and who were all Protestants, anyway.

On the landward side the castle of Monteloup presented a more recent façade, lightened by many windows. An old drawbridge with rusty chains, aflutter with chickens and turkeys, barely separated the main entrance from the meadows where the mules grazed. On the right hand was the seigneurial dovecot with its round-tiled roof and, beyond it, a farm. The other farms were on the far side of the moat. Still farther one could see the

40

steeple of the village of Monteloup.

And beyond that began the forest with its tight clusters of oak and chestnut. That forest could lead you without the least glade or opening to the north of Gâtine and the Bocage of Vendée, almost up to the Loire and the country of Anjou, provided you felt inclined to cross it from end to end and had no fear of wolves or bandits.

The nearest forest, that of Nieul, belonged to the Lord of Plessis. The people of Monteloup sent their pigs to root there, and this meant endless lawsuits with the Marquis's steward, the rapacious Monsieur Molines. In the forest, too, lived some clogmakers and charcoal-burners and an old witch, Mélusine. She would sometimes emerge from the wood in winter to come and drink a bowl of milk on the doorstep in exchange for medicinal plants. Following her example, Angélique picked roots and flowers, dried, boiled and ground them, then enclosed them in little bags in a secret hiding-place that only old Guillaume knew. Pulchérie could call her for hours without her reappearing.

Pulchérie cried sometimes when she thought of Angélique. The girl represented for her not only the failure of what she regarded as a traditional education but also the decline of her race and nobility, fast losing their dignity through poverty and want. No sooner did dawn break than the girl would rush off with flying hair, and hardly more clothes on than a peasant-wench: a shirt, a bodice and a faded petticoat. Her little feet, as dainty as those of a princess, were hard as horn, for she would send her shoes flying into the first shrub she came across so as to skip more freely. If she

41

was called, she would hardly turn her round, sun-tanned face, in which shone two eyes of a greenish blue, the colour of the plant that grows in the marshes and which bears her name.

"She'll have to be sent to a convent," sighed Pulchérie.

But the Baron de Sancé, taciturn and racked by worries, shrugged his shoulders. How could he put his second daughter into a convent, when he was not even able to end his eldest one there? His annual income amounted to not quite four thousand *livres,* out of which he had to pay four hundred for the education of his two elder sons, who were with the Augustine monks in Poitiers.

In the marshes, Angélique had a friend in Valentine, the miller's son. And in the forest, there was Nicholas, who was one of the seven children of a labourer, and was already working as a shepherd for Monsieur de Sancé.

With Valentine, she would go boating on the waterways bordered with forget-me-nots, mint and angelica. Valentine would pick whole branches of this tall, thick, exquisite-smelling plant. He would then go and sell it to the monks of the Abbey of Nieul, who used its roots and flowers for a medicinal liqueur, and its stalks for sweetmeats. In exchange, he obtained scapulars and rosaries which he would hurl at the heads of the Protestant village children, who would flee screaming, as if the devil himself had spat into their faces. His father, the miller, deplored this strange behaviour. Although a Catholic, he prided himself on his tolerance. And what business had his son, anyway, to peddle bunches of angelica when some day he'd inherit the miller's charge and could set himself up in the comfortable mill, built on piles at the water's edge?

But Valentine was a boy hard to understand. Of ruddy complexion and, despite his twelve years, already built like a Hercules, he was as silent as an oyster and had a vague stare, and people who envied the miller said the boy was almost a half-wit.

Nicholas, the garrulous, bragging mule-herd, would take Angélique along to pick mushrooms, blackberries and blueberries. She'd gather sweet chestnuts, and he'd cut pipes for her out of hazel-nut switches.

Those two boys could have murdered each other out of jealousy for Angélique's favours. She was already so pretty that the peasants regarded her as the living incarnation of the fairies who lived in the big dolmen on the witches' field.

She had ideas of grandeur. "I am a Marquise," she'd declare to whoever would listen to her.

"Really? How's that?"

"Because I've married a Marquis," she'd answer.

The Marquis would alternately be Valentine or Nicholas, or one of the other scamps, no more wicked than birds, whom she dragged along after her through fields and woods.

She would also say with a funny face:

"I am Angélique, I am leading my little angels to war."

From this she got her nickname: the little Marquise of the Angels.

Chapter 2

EARLY in the summer of 1648, Fantine began to anticipate the coming of bandits and armies. The countryside seemed peaceful enough, but the nurse, who divined so many things, "sensed" the brigands in the heat of that sultry summer. One could see her turning her face towards the north, towards the road, as if the dusty wind was carrying their scent to her.

It took very few signs to inform her of what was happening far away, not only in the district, but even in the province and right up to Paris.

After buying some wax and ribbons from a pedlar from the Auvergne, she was able to apprise the Baron of even the most important news concerning events in the kingdom of France. A new tax is going to be levied, a battle is being waged in Flanders, the Queen Mother no longer knows what to do to find money and content the greedier Princes. The Sovereign herself is ailing; and the King with the fair curls is growing out of his trunkhose, as is his younger brother, called the *Petit Monsieur,* since his uncle, King Louis XIII's brother, is called *Monsieur* and is still alive.

Cardinal Mazarin, meanwhile, is piling up knickknacks and paintings from Italy. The Queen loves him. The Parliament of Paris is not pleased. It listens to the cries of the poor people in the countryside, who are ruined by wars and taxes.

In rich coaches and fine ermine-lined coats, those gentlemen of Parliament drive up to the Louvre where the little King lives, clutching with one hand at the black dress of his mother, the Spanish woman, with the other at the red robe of Cardinal Mazarin, the Italian. They try to prove to these mighty ones who only dream of wealth and power that the people can no longer pay, the burghers no longer trade, that everyone is tired of being taxed for his least possession. Soon, no doubt, they'd have to pay tax for the bowl out of which they eat! The Queen Mother is not pleased. Nor is Monsieur Mazarin. So the great lords carry the little King to his seat of justice. In a well-modulated voice, though stumbling a little over the lesson learnt by rote, he replies to all those grave persons that money is needed for the armies, for the peace that will soon be signed. The King has spoken. Parliament bows. A new tax will be created. The provincial administrators will send out their sergeants. The sergeants will threaten. The good people will beg, cry, grab their sickles to kill the agents and tax-collectors, and leave their homes for the roads to join the disbanded soldiers, the brigands will come. . . .

Listening to the nurse, it was hard to believe that the single doltish pedlar could have told her so many things. She was accused of inventing things when she merely guessed them. A word, a shadow, the passing of a bold beggar, a troubled merchant, put her on the path of truth. She "sensed" the bandits in the thundery heat of that lovely summer of 1648. And with her, expecting them too, was Angélique. . . .

That evening Angélique had decided to go cray-fishing with Nicholas, the mule-herd. Without warning, she had dashed down to the cottage where Nicholas's parents lived. The hamlet of three or four hovels stood on the edge of the vast forest of Nieul. The ground that the Merlots cultivated, however, belonged to the Baron de Sancé. Recognizing their master's daughter, the peasant-woman lifted the lid of the cauldron on the fire, and threw in a piece of bacon to strengthen its flavour.

Angélique put on the table a chicken that she had just strangled in the castle farmyard. This wasn't the first time that she had invited herself to the peasant's table and she never failed to bring a small present, the seigneur being the only one, by feudal right, to own a dovecot and a chicken-coop in the vicinity.

The man sitting by the fireside was eating black bread. Francine, the eldest child, came to kiss Angélique. She was two years older than Angélique, but having had to look after her younger brothers for a long while already, she no longer went after crayfish or mushrooms with her vagabond brother Nicholas. She was sweet-tempered and polite, and her pretty cheeks were pink and fresh. Madame de Sancé wished to take her on as a chambermaid to replace Nanette, whose impudence disconcerted her.

When they had finished dinner, Nicholas pulled Angélique aside.

"Let's go round by the stables, I'll pick up a lantern."

Out they went. The night was very black; a thunderstorm was brewing. Angélique remembered afterwards that she had turned her face towards the Roman road which passed half a mile away, and that she had thought she heard a faint rumble.

It was even darker in the woods. They soon reached the brook, and set out their baskets baited with chunks of bacon on its bed. They would raise them from time to time, dripping and laden with clusters of blue crayfish, lured there by the light. They threw them into a pannier which they had brought for this purpose. Angélique did not think for a moment that the keepers of the Château du Plessis might come and catch them, and that there would have been a pretty hullabaloo if they'd discovered one of the Baron de Sancé's daughters poaching by lantern light with a young scamp.

Suddenly she sat up, and so did Nicholas.

"Didn't you hear something?"

"Yes, someone shouting."

The two children stayed motionless for a while, then returned to their fishing. But they were distracted and soon stopped.

"This time I heard it plainly. Someone's shouting over there."

"It came from the village."

Nicholas quickly picked up their fishing tackle and strapped the pannier on his back. Angélique took the lantern. Walking noiselessly, they returned over a mossy path. As they approached the edge of the forest, they stopped suddenly. A rosy light filtered between the trees and lit up the trunks.

"It . . . it isn't daylight?" murmured Angélique.

"No, it's a fire!"

"Good Lord! Perhaps it's your home burning. Let's hurry!"

But he held her back.

"Wait! There's too much shouting for a fire. There's something else."

They advanced cautiously towards the first trees. A long meadow sloped down to the nearest house, the Merlots', and five hundred yards farther the three other cottages huddled by the roadside. It was one of them that was burning. The flames from the roof lit a teeming throng of men who were yelling, running, dashing into the cottages, tottering out of them laden with legs of ham, or pulling cows and donkeys.

The mass of them, coming from the Roman road, flowed along the path like a thick, black river. Bristling with sticks and pikes, the stream passed by the Merlot farmstead, submerged it, rolled on towards Monteloup. Nicholas heard his mother scream. There was a shot. Old Merlot had had time to unhook his old musket and load it. But a little later he was being dragged out into the yard like a sack and assailed with sticks.

Angélique saw a woman in a chemise running across the yard of a house, fleeing. She was screaming and sobbing. Men were pursuing her. The woman tried to make for the forest but was caught by her pursuers, who were dragging her across the meadow.

"It's Paulette," whispered Nicholas.

Pressed against each other behind the trunk of an enormous oak, they watched the horrible scene, wide-eyed and gasping.

"They've taken our donkey and our pig," Nicholas again ventured.

Dawn came, paling the flames of the fire which was already dying down. The bandits had not burnt down the other shacks. Most of them had not stopped at this insignificant hamlet. They were sweeping on towards Monteloup. Those who had stopped to loot the four houses were now leaving the scene of their exploit. One could see their ragged clothes, their hollow, bearded cheeks. Some of them wore wide-brimmed, plumed hats, and one of them even had a kind of helmet. But most of them were clad in shapeless and discoloured rags. They could be heard calling to one another through the morning mist that was rising from the marshes. There were only some fifteen of them left. A little beyond the Merlots' hut they stopped to compare their plunder. Their gestures and tone indicated that they considered it pretty meagre: a few sheets and handkerchiefs rifled from the chests, some pots, coarse bread and cheeses. However, one of them was biting into a ham. The stolen cattle had gone ahead. The last looters collected their miserable haul in two or three bundles and wandered on without even a backward glance.

Angélique and Nicholas waited a long time before leaving the shelter of the trees. The sun was already bright and making the dew sparkle in the meadow when they ventured to descend into the hamlet which was now strangely silent.

As they approached the Merlot farmstead, they heard a baby cry.

49

"It's my little brother," whispered Nicholas. "He at least isn't dead."

Still fearing some bandit might be lingering, they crept noiselessly into the yard. They held each other by the hand, pausing at almost every step. They first came across the body of old Merlot, his nose in the dung-heap. Nicholas bent down, tried to raise his father's head.

"I think he's dead. Look how white he is, and him always so ruddy."

Inside the cottage, the baby was screaming. Sitting on the overturned bed, he was waving his little fists in distress. Nicholas ran towards him and picked him up.

"Thank you, Holy Mother, nothing wrong with the little mite."

Angélique was staring horror-stricken at Francine. The girl was stretched out on the ground, white and with closed eyes. Her dress was turned up to her stomach, and she was bleeding.

"Nicholas," murmured Angélique. "What . . . what have they done to her?"

Nicholas looked and a terrible expression suddenly aged his face. He turned his eyes towards the door and growled:

"The pigs! The dirty pigs!"

Abruptly he handed the baby to Angélique.

"Hold him."

He knelt down by his sister, modestly pulling down her torn petticoat.

"Francine, it's me, Nicholas. Answer me, you aren't dead?"

From the nearby stable came a groan. His mother appeared, moaning and bent double.

"It's you, son? Ah! my poor children, my poor children. What a calamity! They've taken the donkey and the pig and our meagre savings. Hadn't I always told my man to bury them?"

"Are you hurt, Maman?"

"Never mind about me. I'm a woman. I'm used to it. But my poor little Francine, she's such a tender little thing, it may well be the death of her!"

She was rocking her daughter in her big peasant arms, weeping.

"Where are the others?" asked Nicholas.

After a long search, they eventually discovered the three other children, a boy and two girls, in the bread-hutch where they had been hiding while the robbers had started raping their mother and sister.

Meanwhile a neighbour came for news. The wretched people of the hamlet gathered to take stock of their misfortunes. There were only two dead to mourn: Old Merlot and another old man who had also tried to use his musket. The other peasants had been tied to their chairs and beaten, but not to excess. None of the children had been throttled, and one of the rent-farmers had managed to unbolt the stable doors for his cows to take to the fields, where they were sure to be found later. But a lot of clothes and good linen had been stolen, all the fine pewter for the fireplaces had gone, and there was little food or hard-earned money left.

Paulette kept weeping and screaming.

"Six of them! Six of them!"

"Shut up," her father told her brutally. "Know-

51

ing the sort you are, always running after the boys in the bushes, I wouldn't wonder you enjoyed it. Whereas that cow of ours, which was with calf! I won't find her as easily as you'll find another swain."

"We must go away from here," said Madame Merlot, still clasping the unconscious Francine in her arms, "there may be others coming after them."

"Let's go into the woods with the cattle that are left. We did it before, when Richelieu's armies marched through."

"Let's go to Monteloup."

"Monteloup! That's where they'll be looting now!"

"Let's go to the castle," someone suggested.

They all approved at once.

"Yes, to the castle."

Their ancestral instinct sent them scurrying to the seigneurie, to their master's sheltering walls and towers which, for centuries, had cast a protective shadow over their labours.

"Yes," Angélique said, "let's go to the castle. But we mustn't take the road nor the short-cuts through the fields. If the brigands should still be around there, we'd never get as far as the gate. The only thing to do is go down to the dry marshes and approach the castle from the big moat. There is a small door that is never used, but I know how to open it."

She did not add that this little door, half-blocked by the rubble of an underground gallery, had served her as an escape more than once, and that one of the dungeons, whose existence the present

Baron de Sancé hardly suspected, was the hiding-place where she concocted her potions and philters like the witch Mélusine.

The peasants had listened to her confidently. Some of them only now noticed her presence, but they were so used to thinking of Angélique as a fairy come to life again, that her appearance in this hour of their misfortune hardly surprised them. One of the women took the baby from her arms. Then Angélique led her little troop by a long roundabout way across the marshes, under the broiling sun, along the steep bluff which had once dominated this gulf of Poitou, lapped by sea water. Her face grimy with dust and dirt, she urged the peasants on.

She let them in through the narrow opening of the abandoned postern-gate. The coolness of the underground passage gripped and refreshed them, but the darkness made the children cry.

"There, there," came Angélique's reassuring voice. "We'll soon be in the kitchen, and Nounou will serve out soup."

Following the daughter of the Baron de Sancé, the peasants climbed the half-crumbling stairs, moaning and stumbling, passed through the rubble-filled halls from which the rats scurried. Angélique moved without hesitation. This was her domain.

When they reached the large vestibule, the sound of voices alarmed them for a moment. But Angélique dared not imagine, any more than the peasants, that the castle might have been attacked. Nearing the kitchen, they were encouraged by the aroma of soup and hot wine. There were certainly many people there, but they weren't bandits, for the tone of the conversation was low, measured, and even sad. Other peasants from the village and the rent-farm had already come to put themselves under the protection of the old crumbling walls.

When the new arrivals appeared, there was a general shout of terror, for they were taken for brigands. But at the sight of Angélique, the nurse rushed forward and clasped her in her arms.

"My treasure! Alive! Oh, the Lord be thanked! And thank you, Saint Radegonde, Saint Hilaire!"

For the first time, Angélique stiffened against the fervent embrace. She had just led "her" people through the marshes. For hours she had felt this wretched herd behind her. She was no longer a child! Almost violently she freed herself from Fantine Lozier's arms.

"Give them something to eat," she commanded.

Later, almost as if in a dream, she saw her mother approach with tearful eyes, and fondle her cheek.

"You've caused us such anxiety, my daughter!"

Pulchérie came too, consumed like a burnt-out candle, her acne inflamed by crying, and her father, her grandfather. . . .

Angélique thought this procession of puppets extremely funny. She had gulped down a big bowl of mulled wine and was completely dazed, plunged into a blissful torpor. Around her, people were exchanging comments on the events of the tragic night: the village sacked, the first houses burnt down, the mayor hurled out of the window of the upper floor which he had been so proud to add

to his house only quite recently. Those looting hea-
thens had, moreover, invaded the little church,
stolen the sacred vessels, and tied the Curé with
his servant-girl to his own altar. They were surely
possessed by the devil! How else could they have
dreamt of doing such things?

In front of Angélique, an old woman was rocking
her granddaughter in her arms, a big girl with
tear-swollen face. The grandmother kept nodding
her head and repeating ceaselessly with a mixture
of awe and horror:

"The things they've done to her! The things
they've done! It's not believable! . . ."

There was talk of nothing but raped women,
beaten men, cows stolen, goats dragged away. The
sexton had held on to his donkey by the tail,
while two bandits were pulling it by the ears. And
the one who screamed loudest in the hubbub was
the wretched animal!

However, a good many people managed to escape — some to the woods, others to the marshes,
most of them to the castle. There was plenty of
room in the yards and halls to shelter the cattle
rescued with such difficulty. Unfortunately, their
flight had drawn some of the looters towards the
castle, and things might have turned out badly,
despite Monsieur de Sancé's musket, had old Guillaume not had a sudden inspiration. Pulling with
all his strength on the rusty chains of the drawbridge, he had succeeded in raising it. Like cruel
but frightened wolves, the brigands had shrunk
back before the miserable ditch of stagnant water.

Then there ensued a strange spectacle. Old
Guillaume was standing at the postern, shouting

insults in his native tongue and shaking his fists towards the ragged, fleeing figures in the darkness. Suddenly one of those tatterdemalions had stopped and answered him. It made a weird dialogue, across the fire-reddened darkness, in that Teutonic tongue that grated on your spine and gave you gooseflesh. Nobody knew exactly what Guillaume and his compatriot had been saying to each other. But it was a fact that the bandits did not return and left the village at dawn. Guillaume was considered a hero in whose military shadow it was good to rest.

The incident proved, at any rate, that the robber-band, which had seemed to be made up of country beggars and city paupers, also contained soldiers down from the north, disbanded after the peace treaty of Westphalia. These armies raised by the Princes in the King's service were made up of all sorts: Walloons, Italians, Flemings, men from Liége and Lorraine, Spaniards, Germans, a whole world that the peaceful people of Poitou could not even imagine. Soon some people asserted that among the bandits there had even been a Polack; one of those savages whom the *Condottiere* Jean de Werth had not so long ago led into Picardy, where they had throttled infants at their mothers' breasts. People had seen him. He had a perfectly yellow face, a fur bonnet, and no doubt an enormous amorous capacity, for by the end of the day all the women of the village declared that he had had his will with them.

The gutted houses of the village were being rebuilt. This was done quickly: mud mixed with straw and reeds made quite solid cob walls. The peasants set about gathering those crops that had not been sacked, and they were good, which was a consolation to many. Only two little girls, one of whom was Francine, did not recover from the violence they had undergone at the hands of the brigands. They both contracted a high fever and died.

Thus the brigands' incursion into the lands of the Baron de Sancé did not really much affect the normal life of the castle. Of course, the old grandfather grumbled more often about the insubordination of the Protestants and the misfortunes that had befallen the country after good King Henri's death.

"Those people personify the spirit of the country's destruction. I used to blame Monsieur de Richelieu for showing them such harshness. But he wasn't harsh enough."

Angélique and Gontran, who that day were the only members of the family to hear Grandfather's profession of faith, looked at each other with an air of connivance. Present-day events were completely beyond Grandfather's grasp!

All his grandchildren adored the old Baron, but rarely accepted his outmoded judgments.

The boy, who was now almost twelve, dared to remark:

"Those brigands, Grandfather, weren't Huguenots. They were Catholics who'd deserted from the famished armies, and foreigners who hadn't been paid, they say, or else peasants from the battlefields."

"They had no business to come here then. Besides, you can't make me believe that they weren't helped by the Protestants. In my time, the army, I admit, paid the troops badly, but regularly. Believe me, all this disorder is of foreign inspiration, English perhaps, or Dutch. They demonstrate and reassemble, all the more so since the Edict of Nantes was too lenient for them, allowing them not only the right to confess their beliefs, but also equality of civil rights. . . ."

"Grandfather, what is this right that has been left to the Protestants?" Angélique suddenly enquired.

"You are too young to understand, little girl," said the old Baron. He added:

"Civil rights represent something that you can't take away from people, without losing your honour."

"Then it isn't money," remarked the little girl.

The old gentleman complimented her:

"That's perfectly correct, Angélique, you really do understand things that are beyond your age."

But Angélique felt that the subject required still further explanation.

"So if the brigands loot us completely and strip us naked, they still leave us our civil rights?"

"Exactly, my child," answered her brother.

But there was irony in his voice and she wondered whether he wasn't making fun of her.

It was hard to make out Gontran. He spoke little and lived very much by himself. Unable to have a tutor or go to college, he had to make do, by way of studies, with the intellectual rudiments which he could glean from the schoolmaster and the village priest. Most of the time he withdrew to his garret to crush red ladybirds or grind coloured clay in order to execute strange compositions which he christened "pictures" or "paintings." Though very careless of his person like all the de Sancé children, he often reproached Angélique for living like a tomboy and not keeping to her station.

"You are not as stupid as you look," he added that day, by way of a compliment.

Chapter 3

*F*OR some moments the old Baron had been turning his ear towards the courtyard, from which rose shouts and cries, mingled with the clucking of frightened fowl. There was a brief scramble and then yet fiercer cries in which Guillaume's accent became recognizable. It was a glorious autumn afternoon, and all the other inhabitants of the castle were surely out of doors.

"Don't be afraid, children," said their grandfather, "they must be chasing some beggar. . . ."

But Angélique had already bounded towards the porch and was shouting:

"Old Guillaume is being attacked, they're trying to harm him!"

The Baron hobbled to fetch his rusty sabre and Gontran returned, armed with a dog-whip. They too reached the entrance-door and saw the old retainer armed with his pike and Angélique at his side. The adversary was not far off either. He kept out of reach on the far side of the drawbridge,

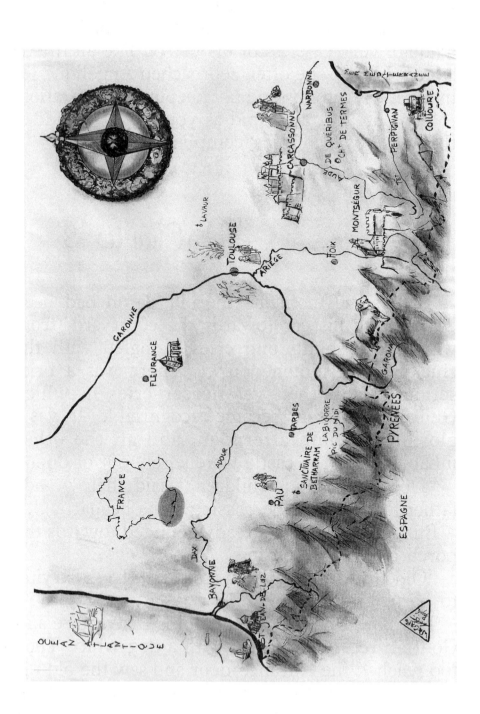

but was still facing them. He was a tall, half-starved-looking fellow, who seemed enraged. At the same time he was trying hard to recover a composed, official air.

Gontran immediately lowered his whip and tugged at his grandfather, whispering:

"It's the sergeant come for the taxes. He's been chased away several times already. . . ."

The bullied official, though still retreating slowly, without, however, turning his back, grew more self-assured as he saw the hesitation of the fresh reinforcements. He stopped at a respectful distance and, pulling out of his pocket a roll of paper that had been badly crumpled in the tussle, unrolled it lovingly. Then, wriggling and writhing, he began to read out a summons, according to which the Baron de Sancé was ordered to pay without delay a sum of 875 *livres,* 19 *sols* and 11 *deniers* in respect of rent-tax arrears, a tithe of the seigneurial tax, property tax, mare coverage tax, "dust dues" for the herds passing over the royal road, and fine for arrears in payment.

The old seigneur flushed with rage.

"Maybe you imagine, varlet, that a gentleman will pay out cash just for listening to revenue rigmarole!" he shouted furiously.

"You know very well that his lordship your son has hitherto paid his annual taxes fairly regularly," said the man, bowing. "I shall come back, therefore, when he is here. But I warn you, if tomorrow at the same hour he is not here for the fourth time and does not pay, I shall serve a writ on him at once, and your castle and all your furniture will be sold to pay his debts to the Royal Treasury."

"Get out of here, you State usurers' flunkey!"

"Baron, I would have you know that I am a sworn servant of the Law and can also be appointed executive agent."

"There's no execution without a judgment," fumed the old Baron.

"There'll be no trouble about getting a judgment, believe me, if you don't pay up. . . ."

"How do you expect us to pay if we have nothing to pay with?" shouted Gontran, seeing the old man was ruffled. "Since you are also a law-court officer, you can come and verify that the bandits have robbed us of a stallion, two she-asses and four cows. Moreover, the dues you claim are mainly owed by my father's rent-farmers. He's been willing to pay for them so far, because the poor farmers can't pay themselves, but he doesn't owe you anything on it. Besides, the brigands' last attack has damaged the peasants even more than us, and it certainly won't be after this last raid that my father'll be able to settle your bills . . . ."

The tax agent was more appeased by this sensible language than by the old Baron's insults. While cautiously glancing in Guillaume's direction, he came a little closer and explained, in a milder and almost kindly tone, but with firmness, that he could not do otherwise than receive and transmit the orders issued by the Revenue Administration. To his mind, the only thing likely to postpone legal action was a petition addressed by the Baron to the Tax Superintendent through the intermediary of the provincial administrator of Poitou.

"Between ourselves," added the law officer, making the old gentleman wince with disgust, "between ourselves, I'll tell you that my immediate superiors, such as the District Attorney and the Controller of Taxes, are not empowered to grant you derogation or exemption. Still, since you are of the nobility, you must know people in high places. So take a friend's advice: act through them."

"I don't propose to flatter myself by referring to you as a friend," remarked the Baron de Ridoué acidly.

"That's why I am telling you all this so that you can repeat it to his lordship your son. Financial straits are bad for everybody, after all! Do you think I enjoy being received by all and sundry as if I were a ghost? Or collecting more blows than a mangy dog? Well, a good evening to you all, and no offence!"

He put his hat back on his head and walked away with a limp and a sorrowful glance at the sleeve of his uniform tunic which had been torn in the scuffle. The old Baron disappeared, also with a limp, in the opposite direction. Gontran and Angélique walked behind him in silence. Old Guillaume, grumbling against imaginary enemies, carried his ancient lance back into his den of historical relics.

Down in the hall, when their grandfather started walking up and down, the children dared not speak for a long while. At last the little girl's voice rose out of the darkening shadows:

"Tell me, Grandfather, since the bandits left us

63

our civil rights, didn't that black fellow take them away with him now?"

"Go and join your mother," said the old man, whose voice was shaking all of a sudden.

He turned to sit down in a high, frayed, tapestry armchair and spoke no more.

With a bow and a curtsey, the children left.

When Armand de Sancé learned of the reception that had been given to the tax collector, he sighed and, for a moment, scratched the small tuft of grey hair that he wore under his lip in the fashion of Louis XIII.

Angélique had an almost protective affection for this good and quiet father, whose daily difficulties had carved deep furrows in his tanned brow. In order to bring up his numerous offspring, this son of impecunious noblemen had had to forgo all the privileges of his position: he rarely travelled, no longer even hunted, differing in this from the neighbouring seigneurs who, though hardly better off, consoled themselves in their poverty by spending their lives running after hare and wild boar.

Armand de Sancé devoted all his time to cultivating his small crops. He was hardly better dressed than his peasants and, like them, carried with him a potent aroma of horses and manure. He loved his children. He amused himself with them and was proud of them; they were his chief hold on life. For him, the children came first; after them, the mules. The seigneur had for some time been dreaming of setting up a small stud of these pack-animals, which are less delicate than horses, and sturdier than donkeys.

But now the bandits had taken his best stallion and two she-asses. It was a disaster, and he turned over in his mind selling his last mules and the plot of ground which had hitherto been earmarked for the stud-farm.

The day after the sergeant's visit, Baron Armand carefully pared a goose-quill and settled down at his writing-desk to draft a petition to the King in order to be exempted from the annual taxes. In this letter he explained the extent of a country nobleman's destitution.

He started by apologizing for not being able to mention more than nine living children, but that more were sure to follow for "both his wife and he were still young and made them gladly." He added that he had the charge of an invalid father without a pension, who had risen to the rank of colonel under Louis XIII; that he himself had held a captaincy and been recommended for a higher rank, but that he had been obliged to leave the King's service because his pay as an officer in the Royal Artillery at 1700 *livres* a year "had not provided him with the means of sustenance in the service." He also mentioned that his dependents included two old aunts "whom neither husbands nor convents had wanted for lack of a dowry, and who could only spend their remaining years in doing humble chores"; that he had four domestic servants, among them an old, pensionless soldier whose services he required. Two of his elder boys were at college and thus cost him 500 *livres* for their education alone. One daughter was to be placed in a convent but this required an outlay of 300 *livres*. He concluded by saying that he had for years been paying his tenants' taxes in order to keep them on the land, but that nevertheless he now found himself indebted to the revenue authorities who were claiming 875 *livres,* 19 *sols* and 11 *deniers* for just the current year. Yet his annual revenue amounted to hardly 4000 *livres* a year, while he had to feed nineteen people and keep up his rank as a country gentleman at the very moment when, to top his misfortunes, brigands had looted, killed and devastated his land, plunging his surviving tenants into even greater misery. Finally, he appealed to the royal kindness to grant him remission of the tax claimed, and aid or an advance of at least one thousand *livres,* and solicited the King's grace for the employment as ensign, on any ship commissioned for America or the Indies of his eldest son, the young "knight" at present being schooled in Logic by the holy fathers, to whom incidentally he still owed a year's school fees.

He added that he was personally always ready to accept any charge whatsoever that would be compatible with his standing, provided that it would enable him to feed his family, in view of the fact that his estate, even if sold, no longer did.

After scattering sand over this long epistle on which he had laboured for several hours, Armand de Sancé wrote one more line to his protector and cousin, the Marquis du Plessis de Bellière, whom he requested to transmit the petition to the King himself or to the Queen Mother, with accompanying recommendations to ensure its being favourably received.

He concluded courteously:

"I wish I may soon see you, sir, and find opportunities of being useful to you in this province, either with pack-mules, of which I have some very fine ones, or with fruit, chestnuts, cheese or pots of curds for your table."

A few weeks later, poor Baron Armand de Sancé could have added one more misfortune to his list.

One evening when the first frost was beginning to make itself felt, a horse was heard galloping up the road and over the old drawbridge which was as usual festooned with turkeys. The dogs barked in the courtyard. Angélique rushed to the window.

She saw a horse from which two tall, lanky riders, dressed in black, leapt down, while a trunk-laden mule appeared on the road, led by a little peasant.

The two girls and the old ladies hurried downstairs. They arrived in the drawing-room just as the schoolboys were greeting their grandfather and Aunt Jeanne. The servants came running from all directions. Someone had already gone to fetch the Baron from the fields and Madame from the kitchen-garden.

The youngsters responded rather ungraciously to the fuss made over their homecoming. They were fifteen and sixteen years old, but were frequently taken for twins. They had the same matt complexion, grey eyes and wiry black hair which hung down to the white collars of their crumpled and dirty uniforms. Only their expressions differed. Josselin's features showed more brutality, Raymond's more reserve.

While they answered their grandfather's questions in monosyllables, the delighted nurse spread a beautiful cloth over the table and brought dishes of pie, bread, butter and a cauldron full of the first chestnuts. The youngsters' eyes shone. Without waiting, they sat down to table and ate with such greed and slovenliness that Angélique was filled with admiration. She noticed, however, that they were thin and pale and that their black twill costumes were threadbare at the knees and elbows. They dropped their eyes when they spoke. Neither had seemed to recognize her, yet she remembered that she had formerly helped Josselin to raid bird-nests, just as Denis was helping her nowadays.

Raymond had a hollow horn at his belt. She asked him what it was.

"It's an inkhorn," he replied haughtily.

"I've thrown mine away," said Josselin.

Their father and mother arrived with torches. The Baron was a little alarmed despite his joy.

"How is it that you are here, my boys? You did not come home all summer. Aren't the first winter days an odd time for holidays?"

"We didn't come during the summer," explained Raymond, "because we hadn't a penny to hire a horse or even take the public coach from Poitiers to Niort."

"And if we are here now, it isn't because we're any richer . . ." continued Josselin.

". . . but because the fathers have turned us out," ended Raymond.

There was a constrained silence.

"By Saint Denis," cried their grandfather, "what

pranks have you been up to, gentlemen, that you should be treated so injuriously?"

"None whatever, but it's almost two years since the Augustine friars last received our fees. They gave us to understand that other students, whose parents were more generous, needed our places. . . ."

Baron Armand started walking up and down the room, which was a sign of great agitation in him.

"It hardly seems possible. If you haven't proved yourselves unworthy, the friars cannot turn you out so unceremoniously; after all, you're gentlemen! The fathers are well aware of it. . . ."

Josselin, the elder, said with a nasty smirk:

"They are indeed, and I can even repeat to you the words which the bursar gave us as our only refreshment for the journey: he said that the noblemen were the worst payers, and that if they hadn't any money they could very well do without Latin and sciences."

The old Baron straightened his stooping back.

"I find it hard to believe that you are telling the truth. Remember that Church and Nobility are as one, and that the students represent the future flower of the State. The good fathers know that better than anybody!"

Raymond, the second boy, who was preparing for the priesthood, answered with his eyes obstinately fixed on the ground:

"The fathers taught us that God will know how to choose his own, so perhaps we weren't considered worthy? . . ."

"Shut your album of household words, Raymond," said his brother. "I assure you this isn't the time to open it: if you want to become a mendicant friar, that's your concern. But I am the eldest and I agree with Grandfather: the Church owes us noblemen some consideration! If she now prefers commoners to us, sons of burghers and shopkeepers, let her. She'll have chosen her own downfall and she'll crumble!"

The two Barons protested in unison:

"Josselin, you have no right to utter blasphemies!"

"This isn't blasphemy: I am merely stating a fact. In my Logic class, where I am the youngest and the second out of thirty students, there are exactly twenty-five sons of merchants and officials who pay cash down, and five gentlemen, of whom only two pay regularly. . . ."

Armand de Sancé tried to grasp this slender straw to uphold his prestige.

"So two more sons of noblemen were sent down at the same time as you?"

"Not at all; the parents of those who can't pay are highly placed and the fathers fear them."

"I forbid you to talk like that about your educators," said the Baron, while his old father growled into his beard.

"Good thing the King is dead so he doesn't have to see such things."

"Yes, good thing, Grandfather, as you say," said Josselin with a sneer. "Even though it was a good monk who murdered Henri IV."

"Josselin, be silent," suddenly declared Angélique. "Talking isn't your strong point, and what's more, you look like a toad when you talk. Besides, it's Henri III who was killed by a monk, and not Henri IV."

The youngster started in amazement and stared at the curly-headed little girl who was thus rebuking him calmly.

"Why, who's there, little frog, the princess of the marshes, the 'marquise of the angels'! . . . And to think I even forgot to greet you, little sister."

"Why do you call me a frog?"

"Because you called me a toad. Besides, don't you always hop and disappear into the grass and reeds of the marshes? You haven't turned into a prim old prig like Hortense, by any chance?"

"I should hope not," said Angélique modestly.

Her interruption had relaxed the atmosphere. The two brothers, moreover, had finished eating and the nurse was already clearing the table.

The air nonetheless remained somewhat heavy. Amid the silence could be heard the screams of the youngest baby. The Baroness and aunts and even Gontran used this pretext to "go and have a look." But Angélique remained with the two Barons and her two elder brothers, who had come back from town in such a wretched state. She wondered whether this time honour wasn't lost. She would have very much liked to ask, but she didn't dare. However, her brothers inspired her with something that was rather like contemptuous pity.

Old Lützen, who had been away when the boys arrived, now brought new torches in their honour. He dropped a little wax while clumsily embracing the elder. The younger boy avoided the rough welcoming hug with some disdain.

71

But without being put off, the old soldier did not hesitate to proclaim his own point of view:

"It's not too soon that you two have come home. First of all, what's the use of your racking your brains with Latin when you hardly know how to write your own language? When Fantine told me that the young masters have come home for good, I said to myself straightway that Master Josselin could now at last go to sea . . . ."

"Sergeant Lützen, must I remind you of discipline?" bluntly remarked the old Baron.

The old retainer did not protest, and fell silent. Angélique was surprised by her grandfather's vexed and angry tone of voice. He turned to the eldest boy:

"I trust, Josselin, that you have forgotten your childish dreams of becoming a seafarer?"

"Why should I, Grandfather? It even seems to me that there is no other solution for me now."

"You won't go to sea as long as I am alive. Anything, but not that!" And the old man pounded the chipped stone floor with his stick.

Josselin was speechless at this sudden attack on the part of his grandfather concerning a project that was so dear to his heart and which had enabled him to bear his expulsion without too much rancour.

"That puts an end to the paternosters and Latin recitations," he had thought. "I am a man now and can sail before the Royal mast."

Armand de Sancé tried to intervene.

"Look, Father, why be so peremptory? It might be as good a solution as any. As a matter of fact, in the petition I recently addressed to the King,

I asked, among other things, for facilities to have my eldest son commissioned on a corsair or a man-o'-war."

But the old Baron writhed with anger. Never had Angélique seen him so furious, even on the day of his altercation with the tax sergeant.

"I don't like people whose feet itch to leave the soil of their ancestors. They never find the wonders of the world beyond the seas, but merely stark-naked savages with tattooed arms. The elder son of a nobleman must serve in the King's armies, that's all."

"I do want to serve the King, but at sea," answered the boy.

"Josselin is sixteen years old. It's time for him to choose his own destiny, after all," suggested his father, somewhat hesitantly.

An expression of pain flitted over the wrinkled face framed by the short white beard. The old man raised his hand.

"It is true that others before him in this family have chosen their own destiny. Must you too disappoint me, my son?" he added with deep sadness.

"Far be it from me to arouse painful memories in you, Father," apologized Baron Armand. "I myself never dreamt of exiling myself and I am more attached to our Poitou soil than I can say. But I recall how hard and precarious my situation was in the army. Even as a nobleman, you cannot reach the higher ranks without money. I was smothered in debts and obliged, at times, to sell my entire outfit, horse, tent, weapons, and even to hire out my own valet. Do you remember all the valuable land you had to sell to keep me in the service?"

Angélique followed the conversation with great interest. She had never seen mariners, but the mighty appeal of the ocean penetrated deep into the valleys of the Sèvres and the Vendée. She knew that along the coast, from La Rochelle past Sables d'Olonne to Nantes, there were fishing-craft that sailed for distant lands, where you met men as red as fire or striped like young wild boar. They even told of a Breton sailor, from around Saint Malo, who had brought savages back to France with feathers growing on their heads, like birds. Ah! if she had been a boy, she wouldn't have asked for Grandfather's advice! . . . She would already have gone, taking all her little angels along with her to the New World.

Chapter 4

NEXT morning, while Angélique was roaming in the courtyard, she saw a little peasant bring a crumpled piece of paper for the Baron.

"The steward Molines wants me to call on him. I shall probably not be back for dinner," said the Baron, motioning to an ostler to saddle his horse.

Madame de Sancé, who was just about to leave for the kitchen-garden, with a straw hat over her tied headkerchief, compressed her lips.

"Aren't the times we live in past belief!" she sighed. "To let a neighbouring commoner, a Huguenot steward, take the liberty simply to summon you, you, a genuine descendant of Philippe Au-

guste! I wonder what honest business a nobleman can transact with the manager of a neighbouring castle! It must be a matter of mules again. . . ."

The Baron did not answer, and his wife went away shaking her head.

Angélique, during this interlude, had slipped into the kitchen, where she knew she would find her shoes and cloak.

Then she joined her father in the stables.

"May I come with you, Father?" she asked with her most winsome smile.

He could not resist, and took her across his saddle. Angélique was his favourite daughter. He found her extremely pretty and sometimes dreamed of her marrying a Duke.

It was a bright autumn day, and the nearby forest, not yet shorn of its leaves, unrolled its russet foliage across the blue sky.

As they passed in front of the gate of the château of Plessis-Bellière, Angélique bent forward to try and glimpse, at the end of the chestnut avenue, the white vision of the exquisite building reflecting itself in a pool like a dream cloud. Everything was silent, and the Renaissance château, which its masters had abandoned to live at Court, seemed to slumber in the mystery of its park and gardens. The red deer of the forest of Nieul, which flanked it, passed through its deserted avenues. . . .

The house of steward Molines was two miles further on, at one of the park gates. It was a handsome pavilion of red brick with a blue slate roof, and stood, bourgeois and four-square, like a prudent guardian of the fragile edifice whose Italian grace still astonished the country folk, more used to medieval castles.

The bailiff was in the image of his house. Sturdy and austere, solidly entrenched in his rights and in his rôle, he seemed indeed the master of the vast Plessis estate, whose owner was constantly absent. Every other year or so, for hunting in the autumn or picking lilies-of-the-valley in spring, a swarm of lords and ladies would descend on Plessis with their carriages, horses, greyhounds and musicians. For a few days there would be a gay round of fêtes and entertainments, to the bewilderment of the neighbouring country squires who were invited to be made fun of. Then everybody returned to Paris and the château relapsed into silence, under the care of its stern manager.

At the sound of the horse's hooves, Molines stepped out into the yard of his house and bowed several times with a suppleness of spine that cost him little, since it was a requisite of his duties. Angélique, who knew how harsh and overbearing the man could be, did not care for this exaggerated politeness, but it obviously gratified Baron Armand.

"I had some time to spare this morning, so I thought I might as well not keep you waiting, Monsieur Molines."

"I am most grateful, Baron. I was afraid you might consider rather offhand my sending a footman to invite you."

"I did not take offence at it. I know you avoid calling on me because of my father, who persists in regarding you as a dangerous Huguenot."

"Your lordship is extremely perspicacious. I

77

have indeed no wish to displease Monsieur de Ridoué and the devout Baroness. I therefore prefer conversing with you here and trust you will do me the honour of sharing my meal, together with the little lady."

"I am not little any more," said Angélique sharply. "I am ten and a half, and there are Madelon, Denis and Marie-Agnès at home, all younger than I, as well as a new baby that's just been born."

"Mademoiselle Angélique will excuse me. Indeed, being an elder daughter requires judgment and maturity. I should be happy if my daughter, Bertille, were to see more of you, for the nuns at her convent assure me, alas, that she has a bird's brain with which nothing much can be done."

"You exaggerate, Monsieur Molines," protested Baron Armand courteously.

"For once I share Molines's opinion," thought Angélique, who detested the bailiff's daughter, a sly, swarthy little creature.

Her feelings towards the steward were more vague. While finding him rather unpleasant, she still had a certain respect for him, owing no doubt to the air of affluence about his person and his house. The steward's invariably dark clothes were of expensive material and were sure to be given away, or rather sold, before showing any trace of wear and tear. He wore buckled shoes with fairly high heels, in accordance with the latest fashion.

And the food at his house was excellent. Angélique's little nose quivered, as they went into the entrance hall, tiled and shining with cleanliness, next to the kitchen. Madame Molines plunged into her skirts in a deep curtsey, then returned to her cakes. The steward led his guests into a small office and ordered some fresh water and a flagon of wine to be brought.

"I am rather fond of this wine," he said, raising his glass. "It's the produce of a slope that has lain fallow for a while and from which I was able to gather grapes last autumn. The wines of Poitou don't compare with those of the Loire, but they have a rather subtle flavour."

He added after a pause:

"I cannot tell you, sir, how glad I am that you have come in person in answer to my request. It strikes me as a good omen for the success of the business I have in mind."

"In fact, you made me pass a sort of test?"

"May your lordship not hold it against me. I am not a well-educated man, I only attended a modest village school. But I confess that the arrogance of certain noblemen never seemed to me a mark of intelligence. Yet it requires intelligence to discuss business, be it even on a modest scale."

The Baron leaned back in his tapestry chair and observed the bailiff with curiosity. He was a trifle apprehensive of the propositions of his neighbour, who did not enjoy the best of reputations. Molines passed for a very wealthy man. In the beginning, he had been harsh with the tenants, but in recent years he had tried to become more amiable, even with the poorest peasants.

No one knew much about the reasons for this change of heart and this unwonted affability. The peasants distrusted it, but since Molines nowadays proved more amenable in matters of rent and other dues which the tenants owed to the King and the Marquis, he was treated with respect. Malicious tongues insinuated that he was acting thus in order to plunge his absentee master into debt. As for the Marquise and her son, Philippe, they were no more interested in the estate than the Marquis himself.

"If what people say is true, you're about to turn the entire Plessis estate over to your own account," said Armand de Sancé somewhat crudely.

"Sheer slander, Baron. Not only am I determined to remain a loyal servant of the Marquis, but I'd actually see no advantage in such an acquisition. To allay your doubts, I shall confide to you — and I am betraying no secret — that this property is already heavily mortgaged!"

"Don't offer to sell it to me, I haven't the means. . . ."

"I have no such idea in mind, Baron. . . . A little more wine . . . ?"

Angélique, for whom this conversation held no interest, slipped out of the office and returned to the big hall, where Madame Molines was busy rolling the dough for a huge tart. She smiled at the little girl and offered her a box, from which emanated a delicious smell.

"Here, taste this, my pretty one. It's candied angelica. You bear its name. I make it myself with fine white sugar. It's better than that of the abbey fathers who only use brown sugar. How do you expect the Paris pastrycooks to appreciate this condiment after it's lost all its flavour from being boiled in huge vats that haven't been scoured properly after being used for soups and black pudding?"

Angélique bit with delight into the slender, sticky green stalks. So that's what became of those big, strong marsh plants after you picked them! In their natural state, they had a more bitter tang. She looked around admiringly. The furniture had been polished to a high shine. In one corner stood a clock, that invention which Grandfather called diabolic. To get a better look at it and catch its ticking, she drew closer to the office where the two men were talking. She heard her father say:

"By Saint Denis, Molines, you puzzle me. All sorts of things are being said about you, though on the whole people agree in crediting you with a strong character and a flair for business. Yet here I learn from your own lips that in fact you indulge in the most incredible fantasies."

"In what respect does what I've just told you seem unreasonable?"

"Why, only think, man. You know that I am interested in mules, that I have produced a pretty fine strain by cross-breeding. You encourage me to enlarge this breeding-station and wish to handle the sale of its products yourself. So far, so good. But where I don't follow you is when you contemplate a long-term contract with . . . Spain. We are at war with Spain, my friend. . . ."

"The war won't last forever, Baron."

"We hope not. But we cannot found a serious business on a hope of this kind."

The steward had a faint, rather scornful smile, the meaning of which escaped the poverty-stricken nobleman. The Baron went on with vehemence:

"How can you expect to trade with a nation that's at war with us? First of all, it's forbidden, and rightly so, for Spain is our enemy. Furthermore, the frontiers are closed and the traffic and toll-barrier strictly watched. I'm willing to admit that supplying mules to the enemy is not as serious as supplying him with arms, especially since the fighting has moved from the district to foreign territory. And, last of all, I have too few animals to make any kind of trafficking worth while. It would require a lot of money as well as years of preparation. My financial circumstances do not allow such an experiment. . . ."

He was too proud to add that he was actually on the point of liquidating his stables.

"Your lordship will be gracious enough to consider that he already owns four exceptional stallions and that it would be far easier for you than for me to acquire many more from the neighbouring gentry. As for the she-asses, one can find hundreds of them at ten or twenty *livres* a head.

"A small additional amount of drainage work on the marshes might improve the pastures, and your draught-mules are, in any case, pretty sturdy. I believe that with twenty thousand *livres* this business could be put on a sound footing and begin to yield in three or four years' time."

The poor Baron felt his head reel.

"Upon my word, you do see things on a large scale! Twenty thousand *livres!* So you set such great stock by my wretched mules that everybody around here is laughing at? Twenty thousand *livres!* Surely *you* wouldn't advance me that sum?"

"And why not?" asked Molines placidly.

82

The Baron stared at him dumbfounded.

"You'd be crazy, Molines! I must make it plain that I have no surety."

"I'd be satisfied with a mere partnership agreement with equal shares and a mortgage on the stud-farm, but we would draw up the contract privately and in secret in Paris."

"If you must know, I may not have the means of going up to the capital for some time yet. Besides, your proposition seems to me too amazing and hazardous. I would like to consult some friends first. . . ."

"In that case, Baron, let's drop the matter here and now . . . for the key to our success lies in its utter secrecy. Otherwise, there's not a chance."

"But I can't rush unadvised into a business which seems to me, moreover, at variance with my country's interests!"

"It's my country, too, Baron. . . ."

"One wouldn't think so, Molines!"

"Then let's talk no more of it, Baron. Let's say I made a mistake. In view of your outstanding success, I considered that you alone in this part of the country would be able to set up a breeding-station on a large scale and under your name."

The Baron felt that the estimate was just.

"That isn't the question. . . ."

"In that case, will you allow me to point out, your lordship, how closely this question is connected with the one that causes you concern, namely that of bringing up your numerous family honorably. . . ."

"You deserve to be horsewhipped, Molines, for that is none of your business!"

"As you wish, Baron. Still, although my means are more modest than some people care to believe, I had thought of adding an immediate loan — by way of an advance on our future business, of course — amounting to the same sum as the initial investment: twenty thousand *livres,* to enable you to devote yourself to your estate without being harassed by worries about your children. I know from experience that work does not progress so well when the mind is distracted by worries."

"— and when you're hounded by the Revenue," added the Baron, flushing slightly under his tan.

"In order that these loans between us should not seem suspicious, I think we'd have no interest in divulging our agreement. I must insist, though, that whatever your decision may be, our talk should not be repeated to anyone."

"I understand. But you must realize that my wife will have to be informed of the proposition you have just made me. It concerns the future of our ten children."

"Excuse my asking you an improper question, Baron, but will the Baroness be able to keep this to herself? I have never heard it said that a woman can keep a secret."

"My wife is not a talkative person. Besides, we see nobody. She will not talk if I ask her not to."

At that moment the steward perceived the tip of Angélique's nose. She was leaning against the doorpost, listening without even trying to conceal herself. The Baron turned round, saw her, too, and frowned.

"Come here, Angélique," he said sternly. "I believe you are beginning to acquire the bad habit of eavesdropping. You always appear at inopportune moments and one does not hear you coming. These are deplorable manners."

Molines looked at her searchingly, but did not seem as annoyed as her father.

"The peasants say she is a fairy," he suggested with a thin smile.

She stepped forward unruffled.

"Did you hear our conversation?" asked the Baron.

"Yes, Father. Molines said that Josselin could leave for the army and Hortense for the convent if you produced a lot of mules."

"You have a curious way of summing up. Now listen to me. You will promise me not to speak to anyone of this matter."

Angélique raised her green eyes to him.

"I don't mind . . . but what will you give *me*?"

The steward stifled a chuckle.

"Angélique! . . ." exclaimed her father, astonished and dismayed.

The answer came from Molines:

"First prove to us that you are discreet, Mademoiselle Angélique. If, as I hope, our partnership materializes, we'll have to make sure the business prospers freely — and that nothing leaks out of our projects. In that case, as a reward, we shall give you a husband. . . ."

She pursed her lips, seemed to think it over, then said:

"All right, I promise."

Then she went out. In the kitchen, Madame Molines was pushing aside the serving-girls in order to put the cream-topped cherry-tart into the oven herself.

"Madame Molines, shall we be dining soon?" inquired Angélique.

"Not yet, my dear. If you're hungry, I'll give you a slice of buttered bread."

"It is not that. All I want to know is whether there is time for me to run down to Plessis."

"Plenty of time! We shall send a boy to fetch you when the table is laid."

Angélique ran off. At the turn of the first path, she took off her shoes and hid them under a stone where she could pick them up on her way back. Then she ran on again, nimble as a fawn. The undergrowth smelt of mushrooms and moss, and a recent shower had left small puddles here and there. She jumped across each in one leap. She was happy. Monsieur Molines had promised her a husband. She was not quite sure that this was a very remarkable present. What would she do with it? . . . Still, if he were as agreeable as Nicholas, he'd make an ever-present companion for crayfishing.

She saw the outline of the château rise at the end of the avenue, standing out white against the blue enamel of the sky. The castle of Plessis-Bellière was surely a fairy-tale house, for there was none like it in the whole region. All the country houses around were like Monteloup, grey, blind, moss-covered. Whereas here, an Italian artist of the last century had multiplied the windows, dormers, and porticoes. A miniature drawbridge crossed a moat filled with water-lilies. The corner turrets served only as decoration. Yet the lines of the building were simple: there was no overloading of its flowing arches, its supple vaults, but the natural grace of plants or garlands. Only above the main porch, a shield showing a winged monster thrusting out a tongue of fire recalled the more tortured decorations of the Middle Ages.

Angélique climbed with astonishing nimbleness onto the terrace; then, grasping the stone ornaments of the windows and balconies, she hoisted herself up to the upper storey where a gutter offered her a convenient support. She pressed her nose against the windowpane. She had often come here, and she never tired of gazing at the mystery of this closed room where one could see glimmering in the darkness the silver and ivory knick-knacks on the inlaid furniture, the fresh red and blue tints of new tapestries and the brilliant paintings on the walls.

In the far corner was an alcove with a damask counterpane. The curtains shone, heavy with the gold threads mingled in their weave. Above the fireplace, the eye was drawn to a big picture which filled Angélique with admiration. A world of which she had not even an inkling blossomed within its frame, a dainty world of Olympian dwellers, with their free, heathen grace; and you could see a god and goddess embrace under the eyes of a bearded fawn, their magnificent bodies symbolizing, like the château itself, Elysian grace on the edge of a wild forest. Emotion gripped Angélique so strongly that it almost overcame her.

"Oh!" she thought, "how I would like to touch all these things, stroke them with my fingers. I would like them to be mine some day. . . ."

Chapter 5

*I*N May the boys and girls of the region, the former with green ears of corn on their hats, the latter adorned with flowering flax, went dancing around the dolmens, those vast stone tables set up in the fields in prehistoric times. On the way back they paired off to enjoy themselves in the grasses and undergrowth.

In June, old Saulier married off his daughter, and there was a great feast. He was the only tenant-farmer of the Baron de Sancé, whose other farmers were all *métayers,* who had to turn over half their produce to the Baron. He was, moreover, the village tavern-keeper and very well off indeed.

The small Romanesque church was decorated with flowers and great thick candles. The Baron himself escorted the bride to the altar.

The meal, which lasted for several hours, was sumptuous with white and black pudding, chitterlings, sausages and cheeses, and there was wine.

After the meal, according to custom, all the village ladies presented their gifts to the bride.

The bride was in her new home, sitting on a bench behind a large table on which crockery, linen, copper and tin cauldrons were piling up. Her round, somewhat bovine face shone with pleasure under an enormous daisy-wreath.

Madame de Sancé felt almost embarrassed to be

bringing such a modest gift: some fine earthenware plates which she kept for such occasions. It suddenly occurred to Angélique that at Sancé they were eating out of peasant bowls. She was both indignant and pained by this lack of logic; people were odd! Wasn't it a safe bet that the village girl, too, would never be using these plates but would store them away carefully in a coffer and go on eating out of her bowl? And at Plessis there were so many marvellous things kept buried as if in a tomb . . . !

Angélique's face grew sombre and she kissed the young bride without feeling.

The young men of the village had meanwhile assembled around the wide conjugal bed and were making bawdy jokes.

"Oho! my wench," cried one of them, "one need take but one look at you and your bridegroom to guess that the caudle will be mighty welcome when it's brought to you at crack of dawn."

"Maman," asked Angélique as she was going out, "what is this caudle they always talk about at weddings?"

"It's a village custom, like dancing or bringing gifts," answered her mother evasively. The explanation did not satisfy her daughter, who promised herself she would not miss the "caudle."

The dancing had not yet started under the big elm on the village square. The men were sitting around the tables that had been placed on trestles in the open air. Angélique heard her elder sister sob and ask to be taken home to the castle, because she felt ashamed of her simple, patched frock.

"Bah!" cried Angélique, "how you complicate your life, poor girl! Am I complaining about my dress? Yet it is too tight and too short. My shoes really do hurt, though. But I brought my clogs along in a bundle, and I'll put them on for the dance — I have decided to enjoy myself!"

Hortense, however, insisted on being taken home, complaining that she felt too hot and was not well. Madame de Sancé went to tell her husband, who was sitting with the village notables, that she was returning home but was leaving Angélique with him. The girl sat down with her father for a moment. She had eaten a good deal and was drowsy.

Around them sat the vicar, the mayor, the schoolmaster, who was also an occasional cantor, surgeon, barber and bell-ringer, as well as several farmers who were called "smallholders" because they owned ox-driven ploughs and employed some farmhands, thus forming a small rural aristocracy. Also in this group was Arthemus Callot, the surveyor from the next hamlet, temporarily commissioned to help drain the nearby marsh. He fancied himself as a learned man and a foreigner, although he hailed from no farther away than the Limousin. And finally there was the bride's father, Paul Saulier himself, breeder of cattle, horses and donkeys.

This corpulent Poitou peasant was in fact the most substantial of the small farmers and though the Baron Armand de Sancé was "the master," his tenant was certainly a much richer man than he.

Angélique, watching her father's furrowed brow, had no difficulty in guessing his thoughts.

"One more sign of the nobleman's decline," he must be thinking sorrowfully.

Meanwhile, there was a commotion around the big elm in the square, where two men, each carrying under his arm a sort of inflated white bag, hoisted themselves on barrels. They were the bagpipe players. A flute-player soon joined them.

"We're going to dance," cried Angélique, and she rushed towards the mayor's house, where she had hidden her clogs.

Her father saw her emerge skipping from one foot to another and clapping her hands to the rhythm of the ballads and rondos. Her burnished gold hair was bobbing on her shoulders. Perhaps on account of her short, tight dress, he suddenly realized how much she had grown during the last months. She, who had always been rather frail, now looked all of her twelve years; her shoulders had broadened, her breasts strained gently against the worn serge of her dress. Under the golden tan of her cheeks her full-bloodedness shone with a rosy glow, and her moist lips were half-opened in a laugh which revealed her small perfect teeth. Like most of the young country-girls, she had slipped a big bunch of mauve and yellow primroses into the opening of her bodice.

The men seated around the Baron were also struck by the fire and freshness of her appearance.

"Your young lady is becoming a very beautiful girl," said old Saulier with an obsequious smile and a wink at his neighbours.

The Baron's pride was tinged with alarm.

"She's getting too big to mix with these yokels,"

he thought all of a sudden. "We should be sending her, rather than Hortense, to the convent. . . ."

Unconcerned by the glances and remarks she aroused, Angélique mingled gaily with the young men and girls who came running in groups or couples. She almost knocked against a youth whom she did not immediately recognize, so well was he turned out.

"Valentine, *mon doué*," she exclaimed in the dialect which she spoke fluently, "how handsome you look!"

The miller's son wore a coat that had certainly been tailored in town, and the grey broadcloth was of such fine quality that his coattails stuck out as if starched. Both coat and waistcoat were adorned with several rows of twinkling little gold buttons. There were metal buckles on his shoes and on his felt hat, and blue satin rosettes on the garters of his hose. The boy, who at fourteen was built like a Hercules, seemed rather gauche and ill at ease in his new clothes, but his ruddy face shone with satisfaction. Angélique, who had not seen him for some time, noticed that she hardly reached his shoulder and she felt almost shy. To dispel her uneasiness, she grasped his hand.

"Come and dance."

"Oh no!" he protested, "I don't want to spoil my beautiful costume. I'm going to have a drink with the men," he added importantly, as he headed towards the group of notables whom his father had joined at the table.

"Come and dance," shouted a boy, seizing Angélique by the waist.

It was Nicholas. His eyes, dark as ripe chestnuts, were full of gaiety.

They faced each other and started stamping the ground rhythmically to the shrill sounds and *ritournelles* of the flute and bagpipes. These dances, which might have been dull and heavy, had an innate sense of rhythm that lent them an extraordinary lilt. The main instrument, besides the bagpipes and flute, was the thudding clogs which beat the ground in unison, and the complicated figures which each dancer performed added grace and perfection to this pastoral ballet.

Dusk fell. The coolness of evening refreshed perspiring brows. Enthralled by the rhythm of the dance, Angélique felt elated, freed from her thoughts. Her partners followed one another in quick succession, and she read in their shining, laughing eyes a message that rather excited her. Dust rose like soft pink pastel in the setting sun. The pipers' cheeks were like balloons and their eyes bulged out of their heads with the strain of blowing.

It was time to stop and move to the tables which were laden with refreshments.

"What are you thinking of, Father?" asked Angélique, sitting down next to the still frowning Baron. She was flushed and breathless. He was almost vexed with her for being so carefree and happy while he was so worried that he could not even enjoy the village feast as he used to do.

"Taxes," he answered, staring glumly at the man facing him across the table, who was none other than Sergeant Corne, the Revenue agent whom they had so often sent packing from the castle gate. She protested:

"It's not right to have such thoughts when everyone is having fun. Do the peasants think of it, they who pay more heavily than anyone? Isn't that right, Monsieur Corne?" she cried gaily across the table. "Isn't it true that no one should think of taxes on a day like this — not even you?"

This evoked uproarious laughter. People began to sing, and old Saulier intoned the refrain of the "Tax collector-pilferer," which the sergeant deigned to listen to with a good-natured smile. But soon it was the turn of those less innocent rhymes which all weddings give rise to, and Armand de Sancé, more and more worried as he watched his daughter down one mug after another, decided to go home.

He told Angélique to take her leave and follow him. Raymond and the youngest children, accompanied by the nurse, had left long ago. Only the eldest son, Josselin, was still lingering, one arm around the waist of the prettiest wench. The Baron knew better than to call him to order. He was happy to see the thin, pale college boy recovering fresh colour and healthier ideas in the arms of Mother Nature. At his age, the Baron had long since tossed a sturdy shepherd lass from a neighbouring village in the hay.

Convinced that Angélique was following him, the Baron started saying good-bye to everyone. But his daughter had other plans. For several hours she had been seeking some means of attending the ceremony of the caudle at sunrise. So, taking advantage of all the jostling, she slipped out of the crowd. Then, taking her clogs in her hands, she began running towards the far end of the village

95

where all the cottages were empty, even of old people. She spied a ladder leading to a barn, climbed up nimbly and found the soft sweet-smelling hay.

The wine and the fatigue of the dance made her yawn.

"I'll sleep a little," she thought. "When I wake up, it'll be time for the caudle."

Her eyelids dropped, and she fell into a heavy slumber.

She woke with a pleasant feeling of well-being and contentment. The darkness in the barn was still thick and warm. It was still night, and from afar came the sound of the peasants' merry-making.

Angélique did not quite know what was happening to her. Her body was filled with a great sweetness and she felt like stretching herself and moaning. She suddenly felt a hand slowly passing over her breast, then moving down over her body, brushing her legs. Someone's hot breath seared her cheeks. Her outstretched fingers met a stiff cloth.

"Is it you, Valentine?" she whispered.

He did not answer but drew even closer.

The fumes of wine and the subtly intoxicating darkness hovered like a mist over Angélique's thoughts. She was not afraid. She had recognized Valentine by his heavy panting, his smell, even by his hands, scratched by reeds and marsh-grass. His rough skin made her shiver.

"You're no longer afraid of spoiling your beautiful costume?" she murmured with a naïveté that was not devoid of a subconscious cunning.

He growled and his forehead snuggled into the girl's graceful neck.

"You smell good," he sighed, "you smell like angelica in bloom."

He tried to kiss her, but she did not like the touch of his moist lips seeking hers, and she pushed him back. He gripped her more violently, his weight upon her. This sudden brutality awakened Angélique entirely. She struggled, tried to sit up. But the boy pinioned her, panting. She then started to pummel his face furiously with her clenched fists, crying:

"Let me go, you clodhopper, let me go!"

He released her at last, and she slipped down from the hay, then climbed down the ladder. She felt furious and sad, she knew not why. . . . Outside, the night was filled with shouts and light.

"The *farandole!*"

Boys and girls, holding hands, passed close to her, and Angélique was carried along in the stream. The dancers flowed through the lanes, jumped over fences, hurtled down the fields in the dim light of dawn. Drunk with wine and cider, they stumbled all the time, pulling others down with them amid roars of laughter. They wound back to the square. Tables and benches were knocked over as the *farandole* swept over them. The torches went out.

"The caudle! The caudle!" demanded the voices. They knocked at the mayor's house. He had gone to bed.

"Wake up, burgess! We're going to comfort the newly-wed!"

Angélique, who had managed to disengage herself from the human chain because her arms were hurting, now saw a strange procession approach.

In front marched two grotesque figures dressed in rags and bells, in the fashion of the King's jesters. Then followed two young men carrying on their shoulders a stick which was passed through the handles of a huge cauldron. Others surrounded them, carrying pitchers of wine and glasses. All the villagers who were still able to stand on their feet followed in their wake, making quite a crowd. Without standing on ceremony, they marched into the cottage of the newly-weds.

Angélique thought they were rather sweet, lying there side by side in their big bed. The young wife was quite flushed. Nevertheless, they both drank unprotestingly the mulled wine mixed with spices which they were served. But one of the visitors, more drunk than the others, tried to remove the sheet that covered them. The husband sent him flying with a blow of his fist. A scuffle ensued, during which could be heard the screams of the poor young wife clutching at her coverlet. Jolted by the sweating bodies, stifled by those peasant smells of wine and ill-washed flesh, Angélique was almost thrown to the ground and trampled on. Nicholas finally freed her and helped her outside.

"Phew!" she sighed, when she was at last breathing fresh air. "That caudle business of yours isn't very amusing. Tell me, Nicholas, why do they offer mulled wine to the newly-weds?"

"Well, one's got to fortify them after their wedding night."

"Is it as tiring as that?"

"That's what they say . . ."

Abruptly he started to laugh. His eyes sparkled, his black curls fell over his dark forehead. She saw that he was as drunk as the others. Suddenly he held out his arms and stumbled close up to her.

"Angélique, y're sweet, y'know, when y'talk like that . . . y're so sweet, Angélique."

He put his arms around her neck. She freed herself without a word and walked away. The sun rose over the devastated village square. The ball was definitely over. Angélique walked with unsteady steps along the path that led to the castle, a prey to bitter thoughts.

So Nicholas too, after Valentine, had indulged in strange behaviour. She had lost them both at the same time. She felt as if her childhood had died away, and at the thought that she would never again return to the marshes or the woods with her usual companions, she felt like crying.

This was how the Baron de Sancé and old Guillaume, who had gone to search for her, found her stumbling towards them with a torn dress and hay in her hair.

"*Mein Gott!*" cried Guillaume, stopping aghast.

"Where have you been, Angélique?" asked the Baron sternly.

But seeing that she was unable to reply, the old soldier picked her up in his arms and carried her towards the castle.

Armand de Sancé, deeply worried, told himself that he would very soon have to find a way, by hook or crook, to send his second daughter to a convent.

Chapter 6

ONE winter day, as Angélique was watching the falling rain at the window, she was amazed to see a host of riders and jolting carriages bumping along the muddy path that led to the drawbridge. Lackeys in livery with yellow facings preceded the carriages and a cart that seemed to be piled with luggage, chambermaids and valets.

The coachmen were already jumping down from their high boxes and leading their teams through the narrow gate. The lackeys posted at the back of the first carriage got off and opened the carriage-doors, whose lacquered wood set off a red and gold coat of arms.

Angélique flew down the stairs from the turret and reached the porch in time to see a magnificent lord stumbling through the dung in the courtyard; his plumed felt hat whisked to the ground, where-upon he aimed a violent blow with his stick at a lackey's back and let out a volley of curses.

Jumping from paving-stone to paving-stone on the tips of his elegant shoes, the nobleman finally reached the shelter of the entrance hall, where Angélique and some of her younger brothers and sisters were watching him.

He was followed by a youngster of about fifteen years, dressed with the same refinement.

"By Saint Denis, where is my cousin?" shouted the new arrival, glancing around him indignantly.

He noticed Angélique and exclaimed:

"By Saint Hilaire, the very image of my cousin de Sancé, when I met her in Poitiers at the time of her marriage! Suffer the old uncle that I am to give you a kiss, little one."

He lifted her up in his arms and kissed her cordially. Back on the ground, Angélique sneezed twice, so overpowering was the perfume that permeated the lordly clothes.

She wiped the tip of her nose with her sleeve, with a fleeting thought of Pulchérie who would have scolded her for it, but she did not blush, knowing neither shame nor embarrassment.

She curtseyed amiably to the visitor whom she had only just recognized as the Marquis du Plessis de Bellière. Then she stepped forward to kiss her young cousin Philippe.

The latter shrank back a step and threw a horrified glance at the Marquis.

"Father, am I really obliged to kiss this . . . er . . . this young person?"

"Why, of course, greenhorn, gather rosebuds while you may!" cried the noble lord with a burst of laughter.

The youth cautiously placed his lips on Angélique's round cheeks, then pulled a scented and embroidered handkerchief from his doublet and waved it over his face as if to chase flies.

Baron Armand, muddy to his knees, arrived at a run.

"My lord the Marquis du Plessis, what a surprise! Why did you not send me a courier to advise me of your coming?"

"To tell the truth, Cousin, I meant to go straight

to my residence at Plessis, but our journey has not been without mishaps: we broke an axle near Neuchaut. Time lost. Night is falling and we are frozen. Passing near your manor, I thought of asking for your hospitality without more ado. We have our own beds and wardrobe, our valets can set them up in whatever rooms you'll indicate. And thus we'll have the pleasure of chatting without waste of time. Philippe, greet your cousin de Sancé and his charming swarm of heirs."

Thus addressed, the handsome adolescent stepped forward resignedly and bowed his fair head deeply in a greeting that was somewhat exaggerated in view of the rustic look of the person for whom it was intended. He then went on to kiss obediently the grimy bulging cheeks of his young relatives. Whereupon he again pulled out his lace handkerchief and sniffed it with a haughty mien.

"My son is a jackass of a courtier, unaccustomed to the countryside," declared the Marquis. "He's only good at scraping the guitar. I had him attached as a page in the service of Monsieur de Mazarin, but I fear he may become an adept there of love *a l'italienne*. Doesn't he already look like a pretty girl? . . . You know about the Italian fashion in love?"

"No," said the Baron naïvely.

"I'll tell you one day, when we are far from these innocent ears. But one freezes to death in your entrance hall, dear fellow. May I greet my charming cousin?"

The Baron said he supposed that, at the sight of the carriages, the ladies had hurried into their

102

apartments to dress, but that his father the old Baron would be delighted to see him.

Angélique noticed her young cousin's contemptuous glance at the dark and decrepit drawing-room. Philippe du Plessis's eyes were of a very light blue but as cold as steel. The same glance that had brushed the faded tapestries, the sparse fire in the hearth and even the old grandfather with his old-fashioned ruff, now turned towards the door, and the fair eyebrows rose while a mocking half-smile hovered on his lips.

Madame de Sancé was entering, accompanied by Hortense and the two aunts. They had put on their best finery, but even this must have looked ridiculous to the young man, for he began to giggle behind his handkerchief.

Angélique, who could not keep her eyes off him, felt awfully like jumping at him and scratching his face. As if anyone could be more ridiculous than he with all those laces and flowing ribbons on his shoulders and those sleeves slashed from the armpit to the wrist to show his fine linen shirt.

His father, more soberly, bowed before the ladies, sweeping the stone floor with his fine curled plume.

"Forgive my modest attire, Cousin. I've come to ask for a night's lodging. This is my knight, Philippe. He has grown since you last saw him, but is no more agreeable to live with for all that. I shall buy him a colonel's commission shortly; the army will do him good. The pages at court have no discipline these days."

Aunt Pulchérie, cordial as always, suggested:

"Surely you will have some refreshment? Some

103

apple wine or sour milk? I see that you have had a long journey."

"Thank you. We shall gladly have a thimbleful of wine with fresh water."

"There's no more wine," said Baron Armand, "but we'll send a valet to fetch some from the vicar."

The Marquis meanwhile had sat down and, toying with his ebony cane tied with a satin bow, related how he had come straight from Saint-Germain, and how the roads were cesspools, and he again apologized for his simple outfit.

"What would they look like, had they come sumptuously dressed?" wondered Angélique.

Grandfather, whom so many sartorial protestations annoyed, touched the bucket tops of his visitor's boots with his stick.

"If I judge by the laces on your boots and band, the Cardinal's edict of 1633 banning all frills and furbelows has no more currency."

"Pah!" sighed the Marquis, "still too much so. The Queen Regent is poor and austere. There are several of us well-nigh ruining ourselves trying to maintain a little originality at this pious Court. Monsieur de Mazarin has a taste for luxury, but he wears the frock. His fingers are laden with diamonds, but he fulminates like his predecessor Monsieur de Richelieu against the paltry ribbons that the princes tie to their doublets. The boot-tops . . . yes. . . ."

He crossed his feet in front of him and scrutinized them with as much attention as the Baron Armand lavished on his mules.

"I believe this fashion of lace-trimmed boots will

suddenly be dropped," he declared. "Some of the young gentlemen have started wearing boot-tops as wide as torch-rims, and their circumference is getting so unmanageable that they have to walk with legs wide apart. When a fashion becomes dreadful, it dies out by itself. Don't you think so, my dear Cousin?" he said turning to Hortense, who blushed with pleasure.

She answered with a bold impulsiveness that was unexpected from this skinny girl.

"Oh, Cousin, I believe a fashion is always right until it disappears. However, I cannot venture an opinion on this point of detail, as I have never seen boots like yours. You are certainly our most fashionable relative."

"I congratulate myself, Mademoiselle, on the discovery that life in your remote province has not prevented you from being in advance of its spirit and etiquette. For if you consider me modern, you must know that in my time no lady would have deigned to be the first to pay a compliment. Yet that's exactly what they do in the new generation . . . and it's not unpleasant, far from it. What is your name?"

"Hortense."

"You must come to Paris, Hortense, and frequent the alcoves where our learned ladies, the *précieuses,* meet. Philippe, my son, watch out, you may find yourself up against powerful opposition during your stay in our good land of Poitou."

"By heaven," cried the old Baron, "though I'm familiar with some English, a little German and am a student of my own French tongue, I must confess, Marquis, that I don't understand a word of all you've been saying to these ladies."

"The ladies have understood and that's the main thing when talking of laces," retorted the Marquis gaily. "And my shoes? What do you think of them?"

"Why are they so long with such a square tip?" enquired Madelon.

"Why? Nobody can tell, little Cousin, but it's the latest fashion. And what a useful one! The other day, while Monsieur de Condé was holding forth with passion, Monsieur de Rochefort stuck a nail into the two ends of Condé's boots. When the Prince wanted to move, he found himself nailed to the ground. Just think, if his shoes had been less long, he'd have had his feet transfixed."

"Boots weren't created for the amusement of people to stick nails into other people's feet!" muttered the grandfather. "All this is poppycock."

"Do you know that the King is at Saint-Germain?" asked the Marquis.

"No," said Armand de Sancé, "and why is this such extraordinary news?"

"Why, dear fellow, on account of the *Fronde.*"

This verbiage amused the ladies and children, but the two Barons, accustomed to slow peasant talk, wondered whether their loquacious cousin was not making fun of them as was his custom.

"The *Fronde!* But that's a children's game!"

"A children's game! That's a good one, Cousin. What we call the *Fronde* at Court is no less than the revolt of the Paris Parliament against the King. Have you ever heard anything like it? Some months ago, those square-hatted gentlemen were bandying words with the Regent and her Italian

Cardinal — a matter of taxes that didn't even touch their privileges. But they pose as protectors of the people. And remonstrance follows on remonstrance. The Regent's temper is beginning to mount. You surely must have heard of the agitation last April?"

"Vaguely."

"It was the result of Broussel's arrest. He's a member of Parliament. The Regent had him arrested one morning while he was taking his medicine. The mob had been roused by the shouts of a servant, and Comminges, the guards' colonel, wouldn't wait till Broussel was dressed but dragged him in his dressing-gown from coach to coach. He finally succeeded in carrying him off, as he had been ordered to do, though not without difficulty. He later remarked to me that this cavalcade among the mutineers would have amused him, if he had kidnapped a pretty damsel rather than this wailing old fool who was in a complete dither.

"Nevertheless, the disappointed rabble started setting up barricades across the streets. It's a game the people dote on to cool their anger."

"And the Queen and the little King?" asked Aunt Pulchérie anxiously, who was sentimental.

"Not much to tell. She gave those gentlemen of Parliament a very haughty reception, then gave in. There have been no end of quarrels and reconciliations ever since. Believe me, though, these last months Paris struck me as a witches' cauldron seething with passion. It's a pleasant city, but in its bowels are hidden an incalculable number of beggars and bandits that one can't get rid of except by burning them in a bonfire like vermin.

107

"And I mustn't forget the pamphleteers and slum poets, whose pens prick more sharply than a bee's sting. Paris is flooded with lampoons in rhymes and prose: 'Down with Mazarin! Down with Mazarin!' So much so that they are called *mazarinades*. The Queen finds them even in her bed, and there is nothing more conducive to spending a bad night and spoiling your complexion than those innocent-looking scraps of paper.

"In fine, the storm broke. The gentlemen of Parliament had felt it coming for a long time; they always feared the Queen might take the little King away from Paris and three times they came to the palace after nightfall, a whole troop of them, asking to gaze at the beautiful sleeping child — actually, though, they wanted to make sure he was still there. But the Spanish woman and the Italian are cunning. On Twelfth Night, we were dining and wining merrily at Court, partaking of the traditional pancake, without an inkling of what was to come. In the dead of night I get orders to gather my men and horses and make for the gates of Paris. From there, off we go to Saint-Germain. There I find the Queen and her two sons, their pages and ladies-in-waiting, and all these great lords and ladies stretched out on the straw in the draughty old castle. Monsieur de Mazarin arrived too. Since then Paris has been besieged by the Prince de Condé, who's taken command of the King's army. Inside the capital, the Parliament is still waving the flag of insurrection, but they are uneasy. The coadjutor of Paris, Cardinal de Retz, the Prince de Gondi, who's maneuvering for Mazarin's position, has sided with the insurgents. As for me,

I am following Monsieur de Condé."

"I am well pleased that you are," sighed the old Baron. "Never in King Henri's times would there have been such riots. Parliaments and Princes in rebellion against the King of France! This is surely the pernicious influence of ideas from across the English Channel. Don't they say that the English Parliament also raised the banner of sedition against their king, even going so far as to imprison him?"

"They have even put his head on a block. His Majesty King Charles I was beheaded in London last month."

"How horrible!" cried everyone, appalled.

"As you can imagine, the news did not reassure anyone at Court, whither, incidentally, the King of England's inconsolable widow had repaired with her two children. That's why it was decided to act with utmost severity towards Paris. In fact, I have been sent, as second-in-command to Monsieur de Saint-Maur, to raise armies in Poitou and lead them to Monsieur de Turenne, who is the most valiant army commander in the King's service.

"It would be the very devil if on my lands and yours, dear Cousin, I could not recruit at least a regiment to offer to my son. Do despatch your lazy louts and other undesirables to my sergeants, Baron. We'll turn them into dragoons."

"Must there still be talk of wars?" said the Baron slowly. "We were hoping there would be a settlement at last. Didn't we sign a treaty in Westphalia last autumn, which sealed the defeat of Austria and Germany? We thought we'd have some breathing space. Though I daresay our province is not too badly off, considering that in Flanders and Picardy they still have to put up with the Spaniards after all that campaigning for thirty years. . . ."

"Those people are used to it," said the Marquis lightly. "Dear Cousin, war is a necessary evil, it's almost a heresy to ask for a peace which God evidently did not intend for us miserable sinners. The whole point is to try and be among those who wage wars and not among those who suffer them. For my part, I shall always choose the former, to which I am entitled by my rank. The trouble is that, in this particular case, my wife has remained in Paris, on the other side — yes, with the Parliament. Not that I think she has a lover among those grave and learned magistrates who are somewhat lacking in brilliance. But imagine, the ladies adore plotting and the *Fronde* enchants them. They have gathered around the daughter of Gaston d'Orléans, King Louis XIII's brother. They carry blue sashes and even tiny swords with lace shields. All this is very pretty, but I can't help worrying about the Marquise. . . ."

"She may run into trouble," moaned Pulchérie.

"No, I think she's excitable but prudent. My worries are of a different nature, and if trouble there is, I'm rather afraid it'll be for me. Do you see? Separations of this kind are fatal for husbands like myself who don't like sharing. . . . For my part . . ."

He broke off and had a violent fit of coughing, for the stable boy who had been promoted to the rank of valet for the occasion, had just flung an enormous bundle of damp straw into the hearth to kindle the fire. Nothing but coughing could be heard for a while amid the resulting blanket of smoke.

"By Jove, Cousin," exclaimed the Marquis, as soon as he had recovered his breath, "I sympathise with your desire for fresh air. Your insolent dolt deserves a sound thrashing."

He treated the incident as a joke, and Angélique found him likeable despite his condescending manner. His gossip had fascinated her. It was as if the old sleepy castle had woken up and opened its heavy doors on another world bristling with life.

His son, however, became ever more sullen. Stiffly seated on his chair, with his fair curls neatly falling on his lace collar, he was casting utterly horrified glances at Josselin and Gontran who, realizing the impression they were producing, exaggerated their slovenly behaviour, even poking their fingers into their noses and scratching their skulls. Their pranks appalled Angélique, who felt sick to the point of nausea. She had been ailing for some time. She had stomach-aches and Pulchérie had forbidden her to eat raw carrots as was her habit. But tonight, as a result of the various emotions and distractions provided by the extraordinary visitors, she felt on the verge of becoming ill. So she said nothing and remained quietly on her chair. Whenever she looked at her cousin Philippe du Plessis, something constricted her throat, whether from loathing or admiration she could not tell. She had never seen such a beautiful boy.

His hair, whose silky fringe curled over his brow, was of a brilliant golden hue which made her own curls seem a dull brown. His features were perfect. His fine grey broadcloth suit, trimmed with lace and blue ribbons, was becoming to his pink and white complexion. It was true that he could have been taken for a girl, had it not been for the hardness of his gaze which was quite unfeminine.

His presence turned the evening and the meal into an ordeal for Angélique. Every shortcoming on the part of the servants, every lack of comfort was underlined by a mocking glance and a sneer from the youngster.

Jean the Cuirass, who acted as butler, brought the plates, a napkin over his shoulder. The Marquis chuckled, remarking that this way of carrying the napkin was customary only at the table of the King and of Princes of the blood, that he was flattered by the honour thus shown him, but would content himself with being served more simply, that is with the napkin rolled around the arm. Full of good will, the carter endeavoured to twist the dirty cloth around his hairy arm, but his clumsiness and sighs merely increased the Marquis's hilarity, which was echoed by his son.

"I can see this fellow better as a dragoon than as a footman," said the Marquis, eyeing Jean the Cuirass. "What do you say, my lad?"

Intimidated, the carter uttered a bear-like growl which hardly honoured his mother tongue. The tablecloth, which had been taken out of a damp cupboard, steamed in the heat of the plates of hot soup. One of the servants, with excessive zeal, kept snuffing the candles, and repeatedly extinguished them.

To cap the disgrace, the boy who had been sent to the vicarage for wine returned and said, scratching his head, that the priest had gone to exorcise the rats of a neighbouring hamlet and Marie-Jeanne, his housekeeper, had refused to part with even the smallest barrel.

"Don't worry about this detail, Cousin," remarked the Marquis du Plessis gallantly, "we'll drink your apple wine, and if Master Philippe doesn't take to it, he can go without drinking. But, in exchange, will you explain to me just what that lad's been saying? I remember the dialect well enough from the time I talked it myself with my nurse, to grasp the gist of the fellow's speech. 'The priest has gone to exorcise rats.' What is this rigmarole?"

"Nothing very surprising, Cousin. The people of the next hamlet have been complaining for some time that they are invaded by rats which devour their grain reserves. The priest went there with holy water and will make the customary prayers so that the evil spirits that dwell in these animals will withdraw and cease to be harmful."

The Marquis stared at Armand de Sancé in amazement, then leaned back in his chair and laughed softly.

"I never heard a more amusing story. I shall have to write Madame Beaufort about it. So to destroy rats, you sprinkle them with holy water?"

"Why does that seem so funny?" protested the Baron, whose patience was beginning to run out.

"All evil is the work of demons that slip into the hide of beasts to harm mankind. Last year one of my fields was infested with caterpillars. I had them exorcised."

"And they disappeared?"

"Yes, hardly two days or so after."

"When there was nothing more to eat in the field."

Though Madame de Sancé adhered to the principle that a woman should humbly hold her tongue, she could not help speaking up in defence of her faith which she suspected was being attacked.

"I do not see, Cousin, why these sacred practices should not have an influence on malignant animals. Did not Our Lord himself send demons into a herd of swine, as the Gospel tells us? Our priests set great store by this kind of prayer."

"How much do you pay him for these exorcisms?"

"He asks but a small fee, and is always willing to oblige whenever sent for."

This time, Angélique caught the meaningful glance that passed between the Marquis du Plessis and his son: these poor people, it seemed to say, are really childish beyond belief.

"I'll have to talk to Monsieur Vincent of these rural customs," resumed the Marquis. "It'll make him ill, poor man, for he has founded an order specially to evangelize the country clergy. Those missionaries are under the patronage of Saint Lazarus, and are called Lazarists. They go out into the countryside in groups of three, preaching and teaching the village priests not to start Mass with a Paternoster and not to lie with their servant-girls. It's a somewhat unexpected enterprise, but Monsieur Vincent is a partisan of reform of the Church by the Church."

"Now there's a word I don't like!" exclaimed the old Baron. "Reform, always reform! Your words have a Huguenot ring, Cousin. Another step, and you'll betray the King, I fear. As for your Monsieur Vincent, clergyman though he be, from what I've understood and heard of him, there's something heretical about his ways and Rome would do well to watch him."

"Nevertheless, it had been His Majesty King Louis XIII's intention, when he died, to appoint him head of the Council of Conscience."

"Now what may that be?"

The Lord of Plessis lightly fingered his lawn sleeves to make them fluff.

"How can I explain? It's something enormous. The conscience of the kingdom! Monsieur Vincent de Paul is the conscience of the kingdom, no less. He sees the Queen almost every day, is received by all the Princes. This notwithstanding, he is as easygoing and gay as they come. His idea is that poverty can be cured and that the great ones of this world should help him to relieve it."

"Ravings!" exclaimed Aunt Jeanne acrimoniously. "Poverty, just like war, as you said a moment ago, is an evil that God has intended as a punishment for Original Sin. To rise against this necessity is tantamount to revolt against divine discipline!"

"Monsieur Vincent would reply, dear lady, that *you* are responsible for the evils that surround us. And he would send you, without more ado, to carry remedies and food to the poorest of your labourers, and remark that if you find them too coarse and earthy — these are his terms — you need but turn the medal over to see the face of the suffering Christ. In this way, this devil of a man has found a means of enrolling almost all the great personages of the kingdom in his charitable battalions. I myself, such as you see me," added the Marquis with a pitiful air, "I'd go to the hospital twice a week, when in Paris, to pour and serve soup to the sick."

"You'll never cease to surprise me," exclaimed the old Baron, much agitated. "Noblemen of your kind never seem at a loss to invent new ways of dishonouring their escutcheon. I am forced to conclude that the world is turned upside down: priests are being created to evangelize priests, and a shameless braggart like yourself, practically a libertine, must needs come and preach morals to an honest and wholesome family like ours. I can't stand any more of it!"

Beside himself, the old man rose, and as the meal was over, everyone followed suit. Angélique, who had not been able to eat anything, slipped out of the room. She felt inexplicably cold and shivers were running down her spine. All that she had heard kept swirling through her head: the King on the straw, the Parliament in revolt, the great lords pouring out soup, Paris — a world full of life and attraction. Compared with all this excitement and passion, it seemed to her that she herself was buried alive in a cave.

Suddenly she shrank back into a recess in the corridor. Her cousin Philippe passed by without seeing her. She heard him go upstairs and call his servants who, by the light of some tapers, were arranging their master's room. The youngster's treble voice rose in anger.

"It is incredible that none of you thought of buying candles for the last lap of the journey. You might have known that the so-called noblemen in these out-of-the-way holes are no better than their peasants. Did you at least heat the water for my bath?"

The man answered something that Angélique could not hear. Philippe went on resignedly:

"Ah well! I'll wash in a tub. Fortunately my father told me that there are two Florentine bathrooms at the castle at Plessis. I am in a hurry to get there. I feel as if the smell of the Sancé tribe would never leave my nostrils."

"This time he'll pay for it," thought Angélique.

She saw him come down again in the light of a lantern placed on a table of the anteroom.

When he was quite close, she stepped out of the shadow of the winding staircase.

"How dare you speak of us to the lackeys with such insolence?" She spoke in a clear voice that rang out under the vaulted ceiling. "Are you deprived of all sense of a nobleman's dignity? That's due no doubt to your descent from a King's bastard. Whilst our blood is pure."

"As pure as your skin is dirty," replied the young man icily.

With a sudden leap, Angélique jumped at his face, all fangs and claws. But the boy gripped her wrists with already manly force, and flung her violently back against the wall. Then he

117

walked away unhurriedly.

Angélique, dazed, felt her heart throb. An unknown sensation of shame and despair gripped her by the throat.

"I hate him," she thought, "some day I'll have my revenge. He will have to bow to me, ask my pardon."

But for the time being she was but a miserable little girl in the darkness of a dank old castle.

A door creaked and Angélique distinguished the massive figure of old Guillaume, who was carrying two pails of steaming water for the young lord. He stopped when he saw her.

"Who is there?"

"It's me," answered Angélique in German.

When she was alone with the old soldier, she always used the tongue which he had taught her.

"What are you doing there?" asked Guillaume in the same language. "It's cold. Why don't you go into the hall and listen to your uncle the Marquis telling stories? They'll keep you amused for a year."

"I detest these people!" said Angélique sombrely. "They are impertinent and too different from us. They destroy everything they touch, and then leave you lonely and empty-handed, while they go back to their beautiful châteaux crammed with marvellous things."

"What's the matter, little girl?" asked old Lützen slowly. "Can't your mind rise above a few mockeries?"

Angélique's malaise was getting worse. A cold sweat broke out on her temples.

"Tell me, Guillaume, you who've never been at the Court of princes: what do you do when you come across someone who is both wicked and cowardly?"

"That's a strange question from a child! But since you ask me, I'd say that one should slay the villain and let the coward run away."

He added after a moment's thought:

"But your cousin Philippe is neither wicked nor cowardly. A little young, that's all. . . ."

"So you, too, defend him!" cried Angélique sharply. "You, too! Because he's beautiful . . . because he's rich. . . ."

A bitter taste filled her mouth. She swayed, and sliding down the wall, she fell in a faint.

Angélique's sickness was no more than a natural occurrence. Madame de Sancé reassured the child, now a young girl, about the symptoms that had alarmed her, explaining that these would now recur every month until she reached an advanced age.

"Shall I also swoon each month?" enquired Angélique, surprised that she had not noticed the apparently necessary fainting of the women around her.

"No, that was an accident. You'll recover and get quite used to this state of things."

"Still, until an advanced age is a long time to go!" sighed the girl. "And when I'm old, I'll no longer feel like climbing trees."

"You can very well go on climbing trees," said Madame de Sancé, who showed much delicacy in bringing up her children and who seemed to un-

119

derstand Angélique's regrets. "But, as you yourself realise, it is indeed time to drop the manners which no longer suit your age and your rank as a noble young lady."

She added a little speech which dealt with the joy of bringing children into the world and the original punishment that weighed on women as a result of our mother Eve's sin.

"Add that to poverty and war," thought Angélique.

Stretched out under her sheets, listening to the rain falling, she experienced a certain feeling of well-being. She felt at once weak and grown up. She had the impression of lying on the deck of a ship moving away from a familiar shore to sail towards a new destiny. From time to time she thought of Philippe and clenched her teeth.

Put to bed and watched over by Pulchérie after her fainting fit, she had not been aware of the departure of the Marquis and his son.

She learnt that they had not stayed long at Monteloup. Philippe complained of the bed-bugs that had prevented him from falling asleep.

"And my petition to the King?" asked the Baron de Sancé when his illustrious relative was already about to mount into his carriage. "Did you present it to him?"

"My poor friend, I did, but I don't think you should nurse high hopes. The royal child is at the moment more poverty-stricken than you and hasn't even, so to speak, a roof to put over his head."

He added scornfully:

"I am told you are amusing yourself breeding

fine mules. Sell some of them."

"I'll think over your suggestion," said Armand de Sancé, for once indulging in irony. "It's certainly better for a gentleman these days to be toiling than to count on the largesse of his peers."

"Toiling! Pooh! what an ugly word," said the Marquis with a coquettish wave of his hand. "Well, goodbye, Cousin. Send your sons to the army, and your sturdiest yokels to my son's regiment. Goodbye, I embrace you a thousand times."

The carriage moved off with a jolt, while a delicate hand waved through the window.

There were no more visits from the Lords du Plessis. It was learnt that they had given some fêtes and, later, that they were returning to the Ile-de-France with a brand-new army. Recruiting sergeants had passed through Monteloup. At the castle, Jean the Cuirass and one farmhand let themselves be tempted by the glorious future in store for the King's dragoons. Nurse Fantine wept bitterly over her son's departure.

"He was not a bad boy and now he'll become an old ruffian like yourself," she said to Guillaume Lützen.

"A matter of heredity, good woman. Wasn't his supposed father a hardened old trooper?"

121

Chapter 7

*I*T became a habit, when counting days, to say it happened "before" — or — "after" — the visit of the Marquis du Plessis.

Then there was the incident of the "black visitor."

Angélique remembered him more deeply and more lastingly. Far from being destructive and harmful like the previous guests, he brought with him strange words of hopefulness that were to remain with her throughout her life; a hope so deeply anchored that in the moments of utter misery which she lived through later, she had only to close her eyes to recapture that murmuring, rainy spring evening when he had first appeared.

Angélique was in the kitchen as usual. Denis, Marie-Agnès and little Albert were playing near her. The baby was in his cradle by the hearth. For the children, the kitchen was the most beautiful room in the house. A fire burned there permanently and almost smokelessly, for the canopy of the vast fireplace was very high. The glow of this constant fire danced and was reflected in the russet copper pans and basins that decorated the walls. The shy and dreamy Gontran would often sit for hours watching these sparkling lights in which he saw strange visions, while Angélique recognized in them the household gods of Monteloup.

That evening Angélique was cooking a hare pie. She had already kneaded the dough in the shape of a tart and was mincing the meat. From outside came the sound of galloping hoofs.

"That's your father coming back," said Aunt Pulchérie. "Angélique, I think it would be proper for us to go into the drawing-room."

But after a short silence, during which the rider must have dismounted, the bell at the entrance rang.

"I'll go," cried Angélique.

She rushed out, heedless of the upturned sleeves that showed her bare arms white with flour.

Through the curtain of rain and evening mist she distinguished a tall, lean man whose cape was dripping with water.

"Did you put your horse under shelter?" she cried. "Animals catch cold so easily here. There is too much mist on account of the marshes."

"Thank you, Mademoiselle," replied the stranger, removing his wide-brimmed hat with a bow. "I made free, as travellers do, to take my horse and luggage straight to your stables. When I saw I was still too far from my goal and passing near the castle of Monteloup, I thought I'd ask his lordship the Baron for a night's hospitality."

His costume of coarse black material with only a white collar for trimming made Angélique suppose he was a small merchant or a peasant in Sunday dress. His accent, however, which was not the local one and sounded somewhat foreign, disconcerted her, as did his carefully chosen words.

"My father is not back, but come in and warm

yourself in the kitchen. We'll send a groom to rub down your mount."

As she returned to the kitchen, followed by the visitor, her brother Josselin was coming through the door from the outhouses. Covered with mud, his face red and dirty, he was dragging across the stone floor a wild boar which he had killed with a spear.

"Good hunting, sir?" inquired the stranger courteously.

Josselin threw him an unfriendly glance and answered with a growl. He then sat down on a stool and stretched his feet towards the flames. The stranger sat more modestly in a corner of the hearth and accepted a plateful of soup which Fantine brought him.

He explained that he was a native of these parts, his birthplace being near Secondigny, but that he had spent many years travelling abroad, so that eventually he acquired a strong accent in his mother tongue.

"But it'll soon wear off," he declared. He had landed at La Rochelle no more than a week ago.

At those last words, Josselin raised his head and looked at him with sparkling eyes. The children surrounded him and began pelting him with questions.

"Which country did you go to?"

"Is it far?"

"What is your trade?"

"I have none," said the stranger. "At the moment I think I'd rather like to travel through France and tell of my journeys and adventures to whoever will listen to them."

"Like the poets and minstrels of the Middle Ages?" enquired Angélique, who did after all remember some of Aunt Pulchérie's lessons.

"Something like that, although I can neither sing nor versify. But I could tell some lovely stories about the countries where the vine grows without being planted. The grapes hang from trees in the forest, but the inhabitants don't know how to make wine. It's better this way, for Noah inebriated himself and the Lord does not wish all men to turn into swine. There are still innocent peoples on earth. I could tell you, too, of those vast plains where, if you want a horse, you just wait behind a rock for the wild herds that gallop past. You fling a long rope with a running noose at the end and you capture your mount."

"Are they easily tamed?"

"Not always," said the visitor with a smile.

Angélique suddenly felt that this man must smile but rarely. He seemed to be in his forties, but there was a certain intensity and passion in his eyes.

"Do you at least cross the seas to reach those countries?" questioned the taciturn Josselin distrustfully.

"You cross the entire ocean. Over there, far inland, are rivers and lakes. The inhabitants are as red as copper. They adorn their heads with bird-feathers and move about in canoes made of stitched hides. I have also been to islands where men are quite black. They live on reeds that are as thick as a man's arm and are called sugar-cane — and that indeed is where sugar comes from. They also make a drink of this syrup that is stronger than corn-brandy. It makes you less drunk but gives you strength and gaiety. It's called rum."

"Did you bring this wonderful drink back with you?" asked Josselin.

"I have a flask of it in my saddle-holster. But I also left several barrels with my cousin, who lives at La Rochelle and who intends to make a good profit out of it. That's his business. I am not a tradesman. I am only a traveller who is interested in new lands, eager to know those places where nobody is hungry or thirsty and where man feels free. That's where I grasped that all evil comes from the men of white race, because they have not heeded the Lord's word but travestied it. For the Lord did not order us to slay or destroy, but to love one another."

"You are a Protestant, are you not?" Raymond ventured to ask bluntly.

"Yes, indeed. I am even a clergyman, though without a parish. And, above all, a traveller."

"You've come to the wrong place, sir," sneered Josselin. "I suspect my brother of being much attracted to the discipline and spiritual practices of the Company of Jesus, of which you doubtless disapprove."

"I have no thought of blaming him," protested the Huguenot. "Many a time I met Jesuit fathers over there who penetrated deep into those lands with evangelical courage and self-sacrifice. For certain tribes in Nova Francia there is no greater hero than the famous Father Jogues, a martyr of the Iroquois. But everyone is free to have his own conscience and convictions."

"Upon my word," said Josselin. "I am hardly

fit to argue with you on these subjects, for I'm beginning to lose my Latin. But my brother speaks it more elegantly than French, and . . ."

"That is precisely one of the greatest misfortunes of our country," exclaimed the pastor. "One can no longer pray to one's God, to the Lord of the Universe, in one's mother tongue and with one's heart, but must needs use these magic incantations in Latin. . . ."

Angélique was sorry there was no more talk of tidal waves and slave ships, of extraordinary beasts like snakes or giant lizards with pike's fangs which can kill an ox, or of whales as big as ships. She had not noticed that the nurse had left the room, leaving the door ajar. So she was surprised to hear whispers and to recognize the voice of Madame de Sancé, who did not think she was being overheard.

"Protestant or no, my girl, this man is our guest and will stay here as long as he pleases."

Soon after, the Baroness followed by Hortense came into the kitchen.

The visitor bowed very civilly, but he did not kiss their hands or make a display of courtly etiquette. Angélique thought to herself that he was surely a commoner, but a nice man all the same, despite being a Huguenot and just a trifle highly strung.

"Pastor Rochefort," he introduced himself. "I am on my way to Secondigny where I was born, but, as it is a long road, I thought of resting a little while under your hospitable roof, madam."

The mistress of the house assured him that he was welcome, that they were all practising Catholics but that this did not prevent their being tolerant, as had been recommended by good King Henri.

"That's what I dared to hope when coming here, madam," resumed the clergyman with a deeper bow, "for I must confess that friends of mine informed me that you have had an old Huguenot retainer in your service for many years. So I went to see him first and this Guillaume Lützen gave me to hope that I might be put up for the night."

"You may be sure of it, sir, for tonight and as many nights thereafter as you may wish."

"My only wish is to be at the orders of the Lord in the way that I can best serve Him. And I'm following His inspiration in avowing that I wish to see your husband most of all. . . ."

"You have a message for my husband?" asked Madame de Sancé, surprised.

"Not a message, but a mission perhaps. Allow me to keep the burden of it for him alone."

"Most certainly, sir. Besides, I hear his horse."

Baron Armand, in his turn, soon appeared. He seemed to have been apprised of the unexpected visit and did not greet his guest with his customary cordiality. He seemed constrained, almost anxious.

"Is it true, Monsieur, that you come from the Americas?" he enquired after the usual greetings.

"Yes, Monsieur le Baron. And I should be glad to have a few moments' private conversation with you concerning someone whom you know."

"Hush!" said Armand de Sancé, imperatively casting an anxious glance towards the door. He added rather hurriedly that their house was at

Monsieur Rochefort's disposal and that the latter need but ask for the men-servants if he wanted anything. Dinner would be served in an hour's time. The clergyman thanked him and asked for permission to withdraw in order to "have a wash."

"Wasn't that downpour enough for him?" wondered Angélique. "Odd people, those Huguenots! It was rightly said that they weren't like other people. I'll ask Guillaume if he, too, has a wash at odd moments.

"Must be part of their rites. That's why they so often look guilty or else are touchy like Lützen. Their skin must be quite thin with scrubbing, it must ache. . . . Like young Philippe who feels an urge to wash at all times! This constant concern with himself will probably lead him to heresy, too. Maybe they'll burn him and it'll serve him right!"

However, as the visitor was going towards the door to retire to the room Madame de Sancé was about to show him, Josselin caught him by the arm with his usual brusqueness.

"One word more, pastor. In order to work over there, in the Americas, I expect one needs to be very rich, or else to buy a commission as a navigator's ensign or at least some sort of craftsman's licence?"

"The Americas are free countries, my son. They ask nothing of you there, though it is necessary to work hard and also to defend yourself."

"Who are you, stranger, that you permit yourself to call this young man your son, and this in the presence of his own father and in mine, his grandfather's?"

The old Baron's voice had rung out with a sneer.

"I am the Pastor Rochefort, at your service, Monsieur le Baron, but I have no incumbency and am only passing here."

"A Huguenot!" growled the old man. "And one, moreover, who comes from those accursed lands . . ."

He stood on the threshold, supported by his stick but holding himself very straight. He had taken care to remove his vast black greatcoat that he wore in winter. His face seemed to Angélique as white as his beard. She felt afraid without knowing why, and hastened to intervene.

"Grandfather, this gentleman was completely drenched and we invited him in to dry himself. He has told us thrilling stories —"

"All right. I won't deny that I like courage and when the foe presents himself with his face uncovered, I know he is entitled to our consideration."

The clergyman picked up his damp coat from the chair.

"I had not come as an adversary. I had a mission to fulfill at the Château de Sancé. A message to bring from distant lands. I would have liked to speak of it with the Baron Armand alone, but I see that you are accustomed in your family to conduct your affairs in public. I like this custom. It was that of the patriarchs and also of the Apostles."

Angélique noticed that her grandfather had turned as white as the ivory pommel of his stick and that he was leaning against the doorpost.

She felt sorry for him. She would have liked

to stop the words that were to come, but the clergyman continued:

"Monsieur Antoine de Ridoué de Sancé, your son, whom I had the pleasure of meeting in Florida, asked me to go to the castle where he was born, to enquire after his family so that I can bring news on my return. My task is thus fulfilled. . . ."

The old Baron had slowly advanced towards him.

"Get out of here!" he panted hoarsely. "Never as long as I live shall the name of my son, who perjured his God, his King and his country, be pronounced under this roof. Get out, I say. I won't have a Huguenot in my house!"

"I am going," said the pastor calmly.

"No!" Raymond's voice rang out again. "Stay, Monsieur. You must not be out of doors on a rainy night like this. No villager of Monteloup will offer you a lodging and the nearest Protestant village is too far away. I ask you to accept the hospitality of my room."

"Yes, stay," said Josselin in a husky voice. "You must tell me more of the Americas and the sea."

The old Baron's beard quivered.

"Armand!" he cried, and the distress in his voice gripped Angélique's heart. "This is where your brother Antoine's rebellious spirit has taken refuge. In these two boys whom I loved. God has not spared me anything. I have lived too long indeed."

He tottered. Old Guillaume caught hold of him. He left, leaning on the old soldier and repeating in a shaking voice: "Antoine . . . Antoine . . ."

A few days later the old grandfather died, of what ailment no one ever knew. In fact he went out like a candle, when he was already supposed to have recovered from the emotion caused by the pastor's visit.

He was spared the grief of learning of Josselin's departure.

One morning, soon after the funeral, Angélique in her half-sleep heard herself being softly called:

"Angélique! Angélique!"

She opened her eyes, and saw with amazement Josselin at her bedside.

"I am leaving," he whispered. "You try and make them understand."

"Where are you going?"

"To La Rochelle first, and then I'll sail for the Americas. Pastor Rochefort told me of all those countries: the Antilles, New England and the colonies, too — Virginia, Maryland, Carolina. I'll end up in some place where I'm wanted."

"But you're wanted here, too," she said plaintively. She was shivering in her thin, threadbare nightgown.

"No," he said, "there's no room for me in this world of ours. I am tired of belonging to a class that has privileges but no usefulness. Rich or poor, the nobles no longer know what they are good for. Look at Papa. He's groping blindly. He lowers himself to breed mules, but dares not even exploit this humiliating position to lend fresh lustre to his title as a gentleman by means of money. He's finally losing on both counts. People point a finger at him because he toils like a horse-coper, and at us because we are nevertheless beggarly nobles. Happily, our uncle, Antoine de Sancé, has shown me the way. He was Papa's elder brother. He's become a Huguenot and left the continent."

"You won't recant your faith?" she implored, aghast.

"No. I am not interested in sanctimonious hocus-pocus. I want to live."

He kissed her quickly, walked down the few steps, then turned and looked at his half-naked young sister with shrewd eyes.

"You are becoming beautiful and strong, Angélique. Watch out. You too will have to leave. If not, you'll find yourself one of these days tumbling in the hay with a stable boy. Or else you'll become the plaything of one of our rich neighbours."

He added with sudden gentleness:

"You can take the word of one who has sowed more than his share of wild oats, my darling. It would be a dreadful life for you. You, too, should run away from these crumbling walls. As for me, I'm off to sea!"

And, bounding down the last steps, the young man disappeared from sight.

Chapter 8

"D O you realise," said Baron Armand to Angélique, "how much trouble all of you get me into?"

Strolling along a wooded path, she had come across her father sitting on a tree-stump, while his horse browsed nearby.

"Aren't the mules doing well, Father?"

"Oh yes, they are all right. I am just back from seeing Molines. You see, Angélique, Aunt Pulchérie has convinced your mother and me that it is impossible to keep you at home any longer. You must be put in a convent. So I decided on a very humiliating step which I had wanted to avoid at all cost. I've been to see Molines to ask him for that advance he had proposed to aid my family."

He spoke in a sad, gentle voice, as if something had snapped inside him, as if this latest blow was more painful than his father's death or his eldest son's departure.

"Poor Papa!" murmured Angélique.

"But it is not so easy," went on the Baron. "It would be hard enough if all I had to do was to hold out my hand to a commoner. But what worries me is that I can't fathom that fellow's secret intentions. He has made odd conditions for this new loan."

"What conditions, Father?"

He looked at her thoughtfully and caressed her

135

magnificent auburn-gold hair with his calloused hand.

"It's strange . . . I find it easier to confide in you than in your mother. You are a wild colt, but already you seem able to understand everything. Naturally I suspected that Molines was after a substantial profit in this mule business, but I couldn't understand why he'd come to me rather than to a plain mule-dealer. Actually, what interests him is the fact that I'm a nobleman. He told me today that he was counting on me to obtain, through my family or other connections, complete exemption from the Customs inspection and toll dues for a quarter of our mule production, from Fouquet, the Controller-General of Finance, as well as the guaranteed right to export this proportion to England, or to Spain when the war is over."

"But that's wonderful!" exclaimed Angélique enthusiastically. "This seems a very shrewd business deal. On the one hand there is Molines, a commoner and a clever fellow, on the other hand there you are, a nobleman . . ."

"And not very clever . . ." smiled her father.

"No, just not *au courant*. But you have titles and connections. You're bound to succeed. You yourself said the other day that sending the mules abroad seems impossible to you on account of all those tolls and taxes that increase the cost. And since you'll request exemption for a quarter of the output only, the Controller-General is sure to find the request reasonable! What will you do with the others?"

"The Quartermaster-General's department will

be entitled to an option on their purchase at the current price at the market of Poitiers."

"It's all taken care of then. That Molines fellow is a man of experience! You must see Monsieur du Plessis and perhaps write to the Duke de la Tremoille. But I believe all these great persons will soon be coming down here to have another try at their Civil War."

"There is talk of it, indeed," said the Baron, displeased. "Don't congratulate me too soon, though. Whether the Princes do come or not, it's not sure that I'll obtain their agreement. Besides, I haven't yet told you the most surprising part."

"What is it?"

"Molines wants me to start working that old lead mine which we own over at Vauloup," sighed the Baron. "I sometimes wonder whether that man has all his wits about him, and I admit I don't quite understand such devious business . . . that is, supposing it *is* business! In fine, he's asked me to entreat the King to renew the privilege granted to my ancestors of mining for lead and silver there. You know that abandoned mine at Vauloup? . . ." asked Armand de Sancé, seeing his daughter's abstracted look.

Angélique nodded.

"What can that infernal steward hope to get out of those old stones? . . . For, obviously, the mine will be re-equipped under my name, but at his expense. A secret agreement between us will stipulate that he will have a ten-year lease of the lead mine, with him taking over my rights as owner of the soil for the exploitation of the mine. But there again it's up to me to get from the Controller-

General the same tax exemption on a quarter of the future output, as well as the same export guarantees. All this seems rather complicated to me," concluded the Baron, getting up.

As he did so, his purse tinkled with the crowns which Molines had given him, and this pleasant sound cheered him.

He called his horse and looked at the thoughtful Angélique with what he hoped was a stern glance.

"Try and forget what I've just told you, and attend to your outfit. For this time it's final, my girl. You'll be going to the convent."

So Angélique prepared her outfit. Hortense and Madelon were leaving, too. Raymond and Gontran were to accompany them and, after leaving their sisters with the ladies of St. Ursula, would proceed to the Jesuit fathers of Poitiers, who were educators of great renown.

There was even talk of including nine-year-old Denis in this emigration. But Fantine rebelled. After loading her with the care of ten children, they were now going to deprive her of them "all." She detested these extreme measures, she said. So Denis remained. With him, in addition to Marie-Agnès, Albert and a last little boy of two whom everybody called "the baby," to look after, Fantine Lozier's "leisure" would be fully occupied.

However, a few days before their departure, an incident almost changed the course of Angélique's destiny. One September morning, Monsieur de Sancé returned, much agitated, from the château du Plessis.

"Angélique!" he cried, as he came into the dining-room, where the family was waiting for him to sit down to table, "are you there, Angélique?"

"Yes, Father."

He eyed his daughter critically. She had grown even more during the last months and her hands were clean and her hair well combed. Everybody agreed that Angélique was beginning to get some sense.

"That'll do," he murmured.

And turning to his wife:

"Imagine, the entire Plessis clan — Marquis, Marquise, son, pages, valets, dogs, have moved into the château. They have an illustrious guest, the Prince de Condé and all his Court. I ran into the lot of them and was quite ill at ease. But my cousin acted very amiably. He called me, inquired after you, and do you know what he asked me? To take Angélique to him, to replace one of the maids-of-honour. The Marquise had to leave behind in Paris practically all the girls who dress her hair, amuse her and play the lute. The Prince de Condé's coming has got her in a flutter. She says she needs a few graceful little maids-in-waiting to help her."

"And why not me?" exclaimed Hortense, scandalized.

"Because she said 'graceful,' " was her father's unequivocal reply.

"But the Marquis found I was very witty."

"But the Marquise wants pretty faces around her."

"Oh! that's too much!" cried Hortense, rushing to claw her sister.

But the latter had foreseen this move and dodged

it nimbly. With beating heart she went up to her room. She called one of the grooms through the window and ordered him to fetch her a pail of water and a tub.

She washed herself with great care and spent a long time brushing her beautiful hair, which she wore over her shoulders like a silken riding-hood. Pulchérie joined her, bringing the fine dress that had been made for her entry into the convent. Angélique admired the dress, although it was of a grey, rather dull hue. But the material was new, specially bought for the occasion from an important draper in Niort, and a white collar added a note of gaiety to it. It was her first long dress. She put it on with a thrill of delight. Her aunt clasped her hands with emotion.

"My little Angélique, one would take you for a young lady. Perhaps I ought to put your hair up?"

But Angélique refused. Her feminine instinct warned her not to diminish the splendour of her only adornment.

She mounted on a pretty bay mule that her father had had saddled for her and, in his company, set out on the road to the château du Plessis.

The castle had awakened from its spellbound slumber. When the Baron and his daughter had left their mules with Molines and walked up the main drive, strains of music wafted out to greet them. Long greyhounds and tiny griffons were gambolling on the lawns. Lords with curled hair and ladies in shimmering dresses were strolling in the avenues. Some of them stared with surprise at the Baron in his dark cloth and the adolescent girl in convent-school attire.

"Ridiculous, but charming," said one of the ladies, toying with her fan.

Angélique wondered whether the remark referred to her. Why was she ridiculous? She looked more closely at the sumptuous, gaudy dresses, trimmed with laces, and began to think her grey dress was out of place.

Baron Armand did not share his daughter's embarrassment. He was anxiously intent on the interview he meant to ask of the Marquis du Plessis. To obtain total exemption for a quarter of his mule and lead-mine production might have been easy enough for a nobleman of such ancient lineage as the present Baron de Ridoué de Sancé de Monteloup. But the poor gentleman realised that, after living for so long far from the Court he had become as awkward as a peasant among these people, whose powdered hair, perfumed breath and parrot-like exclamations utterly dazed him. In King Louis XIII's time, he seemed to remember, one made a show of more simplicity and roughness. Wasn't it Louis XIII himself who, shocked by the too bare bosom of a young beauty of Poitiers, had unashamedly spat into the indiscreet — and tempting — opening?

Having, on that distant day, been a witness to the memorable royal act, Armand de Sancé now thought back upon it regretfully as he and Angélique made their way through this beribboned crowd. Musicians perched on a small platform played instruments that produced frail, charming sounds: hurdy-gurdies, lutes, oboes, flutes. In a vast hall lined with mirrors Angélique perceived young people dancing. She wondered whether her cousin Philippe was among them.

Baron de Sancé, meanwhile, had reached the last of the rooms and bowed, doffing his old felt hat with its meagre plume. Angélique began to suffer for them both. "Poor as we are," she thought, "arrogance would be the only proper conduct." Instead of plunging deep into the curtsey which Pulchérie had made her rehearse three times, she remained stiff as a wooden doll, staring straight in front of her. The faces around her became a little blurred, but she knew that they were all dying to giggle at sight of her. A silence had fallen, mingled with stifled laughter as the footman announced:

"Monsieur le Baron de Ridoué de Sancé de Monteloup."

The face of the Marquise du Plessis grew quite red behind her fan, and her eyes sparkled with ill-contained merriment. The Marquis came to everyone's rescue by stepping forward affably.

"My dear Cousin," he cried, "you delight us by coming so soon and bringing us your charming daughter. Angélique, you are even prettier than when I last saw you at Monteloup. Isn't she pretty? Doesn't she look like an angel?" he asked, turning to his wife.

"Absolutely," the Marquise agreed, having recovered her self-control. "In another dress she'd be divine. Sit down on this stool, my pretty one, so that we can look at you at leisure."

"Cousin," said Armand de Sancé, whose rugged voice rang out oddly in this exquisite *salon*, "I

142

would like to talk to you without delay of some important business."

The Marquis raised his eyebrows in surprise. "Really? I am listening."

"I am sorry, but these matters must be treated privately."

Monsieur du Plessis threw around him a glance that was at once resigned and roguish.

"Very well, very well, Cousin. We shall go into my study. Ladies, excuse us. We shall join you presently. . . ."

Angélique on her stool was the target of a host of curious eyes. The awful emotion that had strangled her was receding a little. She could now clearly distinguish all the faces around her. All these ladies glittered from top to toe. They wore strange trinkets at their waists: small mirrors, tortoise-shell combs, comfit-boxes and watches. Never would Angélique be able to dress like them. Never would she be able to look at others with such haughtiness, or converse in such a high-pitched, precious voice which seemed perpetually to be sucking sweets.

"My dear," said one of them, "she has attractive hair but it's never had any care."

"Her breast is undeveloped for a fifteen-year-old."

"But, my dear, she's only thirteen."

"Do you want my opinion, Henriette? It's too late to refine her."

"Am I a mule that's offered for sale?" wondered Angélique, too amazed to take real offence.

"What do you expect?" cried another. "She has green eyes, and green eyes, like emeralds, bring bad luck."

"It's a rare hue," protested another.

"But charmless. Look at the child's hard expression. No really, I don't care for green eyes."

"Are they going to belittle my only good points — my eyes and hair?" thought the young girl.

"Philippe! Philippe!!" the Marquise at last called out. "Where is my son? Monsieur de Barre, would you be good enough to fetch the colonel?"

And when the sixteen-year-old colonel appeared:

"Philippe, here's your Cousin de Sancé. Take her along to the dance. She will find the company of young people more entertaining than ours."

Angélique had risen promptly. She was annoyed with herself for feeling her heart throb. The young lord looked at his mother with undisguised indignation. "How dare you," he seemed to say, "throw me into the arms of such a scarecrow?"

But holding out his hand to Angélique, he murmured through closed lips: "Do come, Cousin."

She put her little fingers into his open palm, unaware of their prettiness. Silently he led her to the entrance of the gallery where the pages and young people of her age were allowed to enjoy themselves.

"Make room! Make room!" he suddenly cried. "My friends, I introduce to you my cousin the Baroness of the Doleful Dress."

There was a general outburst of laughter, and all the young men rushed towards them. The pages wore odd little puffed trunks which stopped just below their thighs, and with their long, thin, boyish legs perched on high heels, they looked like stilt-birds.

"I am no more ridiculous with my doleful dress than they with those pumpkins around their hips," thought Angélique.

She would gladly have swallowed her dignity a little to stay on with Philippe. But one of the boys asked:

"Can you dance, Mademoiselle?"

"A little."

"Really? And what dances?"

"The *bourrée,* the rigadoon, the round dance . . ."

"Ha! Ha! Ha!" guffawed the young man. "Philippe, what an odd bird you've brought us! Come on, gentlemen, let's draw lots. Who's going to dance with the country-lass? Where are the volunteers for the *bourrée?* Plop! Plop! . . . Plop!"

Suddenly, Angélique wrenched her hand out of Philippe's and fled.

She ran through spacious rooms crammed with footmen and noblemen, through the entrance-hall paved with mosaics, where dogs were lying asleep on velvet squares. She was looking for her father and, above all, she was trying not to cry. All this wasn't worth a single tear. It was an incident to be wiped from her memory, like a rather mad and grotesque dream. It isn't wise for a quail to leave its thicket. Having absorbed some of Aunt Pulchérie's teaching, Angélique told herself that she had been justly punished for the upsurge of vanity that she had felt on hearing the Marquis du Plessis's flattering request.

At last she heard the somewhat shrill voice of the Marquis coming out of a small room.

"But not at all! Not at all! You're all wrong,

my poor friend," he was saying in a regretful crescendo. "You're only imagining that it's easy for us noblemen to obtain exemptions, weighed down as we are by expenses. Besides, neither myself nor the Prince de Condé is empowered to grant them."

"I am merely asking you to make yourself my spokesman with the Superintendent of Finance, Monsieur de Trémant, whom you know personally. The matter is not without interest for him. He exempts me from taxes and all transport dues solely throughout the province of Poitou as far as the ocean. This exemption to apply, moreover, to no more than one quarter of my mule and lead output. In exchange, the King's Quartermaster-General reserves the right to buy the rest of my mules at current prices, and the Royal Treasury is likewise free to acquire my lead and silver at the official rate. It's not a bad thing for the State to be able to count for various commodities on reliable producers at home rather than to have to buy them abroad. Thus I have some fine beasts for pulling cannon, sturdy and sound in limb. . . ."

"Your words reek of dung and sweat," protested the Marquis, putting his hand to his nose with disgust. "I wonder whether you aren't lowering yourself to some extent as a gentleman by launching into an enterprise which bears a strong resemblance — if you'll pardon the word — to trade."

"Trade or no trade, I have to live," retorted Armand de Sancé with a tenacity which was balm to Angélique.

"What about me?" cried the Marquis, throwing

up his arms. "Do you think I have no difficulties? Well, I'll have you know that until my dying day I'll reject all commoners' pursuits that would be detrimental to my rank."

"Your revenues, Cousin, don't compare with mine. In fact, I am reduced to plain beggary both as regards the King, who refuses me his assistance, and as regards the Niort money-lenders, who devour me."

"I know, I know, my good Armand. But did you ever ask yourself how I, a courtier with two important royal posts, manage to balance my budget? No, I am certain you didn't. Well, know that my expenses necessarily exceed my income. It's true that with the revenues of my Plessis estate, with those of my wife's in Touraine, my post as an officer of the Royal bedchamber — about 40,000 *livres* — and that of camp-master of the Poitou brigade, I have an average gross income of 160,000 *livres.* . . ."

"I'd be content with a tenth of that," said the Baron.

"One moment, Country Cousin. I have an income of 160,000 *livres.* But what with my wife's expenses, my son's regiment, my Paris house, my Fontainebleau pavilion, my travels to follow the Court on its journeys, the interest payable on diverse loans, plus receptions, clothes, carriages, servants, etc., I spend 300,000 *livres.*"

"So you're losing 140,000 *livres* per year?"

"Figure it out yourself, Cousin. If I have allowed myself to expatiate on this boring explanation, it's in order to make you see my point of view when I tell you that I simply cannot at present approach

Monsieur de Trémant."

"Yet you know him."

"I know him, but no longer see him. I keep telling you that Monsieur de Trémant is in the King's and the Queen Regent's service and is even said to be devoted to Mazarin."

"Well, precisely —"

"Precisely for this reason we do not see him any more. Don't you know that the Prince de Condé, to whom I am loyal, has fallen out with the Court . . . ? "

"How should I know?" asked Armand de Sancé, bewildered. "I saw you only a few months ago and at that time the Queen Regent had no more faithful servant than the Prince."

"Oh, times have changed since then," sighed the Marquis, exasperated. "I can't tell you the whole story in detail. All you need know is that if the Queen, her two sons and their red devil of a Cardinal have been able to move back into the Louvre in Paris, they owe it entirely to Monsieur de Condé. Yet by way of thanks this great man is treated most shabbily. The break occurred a few weeks ago. Certain offers from Spain seem interesting to the Prince. He has come down here to study them more fully."

"Offers from Spain?" repeated the Baron Armand.

"Yes, just between ourselves and upon your honour as a gentleman, imagine that King Philip IV is offering an army of ten thousand men each to our great General and to Monsieur de Turenne."

"To do what with?"

"Why, to reduce the Queen and especially that

thieving Cardinal! Thanks to the Spanish armies under his direction, Monsieur de Condé would enter Paris and Gaston d'Orléans, brother of our late King Louis XIII, would be proclaimed King. The monarchy would be saved and at last be rid of women, children and a foreigner who dishonours it. Now I ask you, with all these great plans afoot, what can I do? To keep up the style of life I've been explaining to you, I cannot afford to devote myself to a lost cause. The people, the Parliament, the Court, all hate Mazarin. The Queen keeps clinging to him and will never yield. It's impossible to describe the sort of existence which the Court and the little King have been leading for the last year or two. You can only compare them to gypsies, what with their flights, returns, quarrels, wars, and so forth.

"We've had enough of it. The cause of young King Louis XIV is lost. I may add that Gaston d'Orléans's daughter, Mademoiselle de Montpensier — you know, that big, loud-spoken girl — is a rabid *Frondeuse*. She was already fighting on the insurgents' side a year ago. She's clamouring to start again. My wife dotes on her, and her affection is returned. But this time I won't let Alice enroll in a different party from mine. Putting a blue sash around your waist and a wheat-stalk on your hat wouldn't matter much, if the separation of couples did not provoke other disorders. Now Alice is by nature cut out to be in the opposition. In opposition against garters for silk hose, against a fringe of hair for an uncovered brow, etc. She is quite a character. At present she is against the Queen Regent, Anne of Austria, because the latter

149

remarked that the lozenges Alice sucks for the care of her mouth remind her of a purging medicine. Nothing will induce the Marquise to return to Court, where she claims one's bored by the Queen's devoutness and the pranks of the little King and his brother. So I shall follow my wife, since my wife won't follow me. I am weak enough to find her stimulating and to appreciate certain amorous talents. . . . After all, the *Fronde* is a pleasant pastime. . . ."

"But . . . but you don't mean to say that Monsieur de Turenne, too? . . ." stammered Armand de Sancé, who felt the ground giving way under him.

"Oh! Monsieur de Turenne! Monsieur de Turenne! He's like everybody else. He doesn't like to see his services underrated. He asked to have Sedan for his family. It was refused him. He became angry, as is natural. It appears he has already accepted the King of Spain's proposals. Monsieur de Condé is in less of a hurry. Before making up his mind he is waiting to hear from his sister, Madame de Longueville, who has accompanied the Princesse de Condé to rouse Normandy. I must tell you that the Duchesse de Beaufort is here, too, and he is not indifferent to her charms. . . . For once, our great hero is not champing at the bit to go to war. You'll forgive him when you meet the goddess. . . . Her complexion, dear Cousin . . ."

Angélique, who was leaning against a screen, saw her father at a distance pull out his large handkerchief and wipe his forehead.

"He'll get nothing," she told herself, with an

aching heart. "What do they care about our mules and silver-lead mines?"

Chapter 9

AN unbearable pain constricted her throat. She walked away again and went out into the park, where the blue dusk was falling. The violins and guitar could still be heard in the reception rooms, but rows of lackeys were bringing out candelabra. Others, mounted on step-ladders, were lighting tapers placed in brackets on the walls, in front of mirrors that reflected their light.

"When I think," mused Angélique, slowly strolling through the avenues, "that my father had qualms about a few mules that Molines wanted to sell to Spain! Treason . . . ? A matter of complete indifference to all these Princes, though they live entirely off the monarchy. Can they really be thinking of fighting the King?"

She had walked right round the castle and found herself at the base of the wall which she had so often climbed in the old days to steal a glance at the treasures in the enchanted room. This part was deserted, for the couples who did not shun the chilly evening mist, preferred to remain on the lawn in front of the château.

Instinct made her slip off her shoes and, despite her long dress, she hoisted herself nimbly to the cornice of the upper storey. The night was black now. No one passing by could have seen her there, snuggled against the shadow of a small turret.

The window was open. Angélique bent forward. She guessed that the room was inhabited, for a small oil-lamp was shedding a golden glow, which only enhanced the glamour of the beautiful furniture and tapestries. She could see, shining like snowy crystals, the mother-of-pearl insets on the small ebony chest of drawers.

Suddenly, as she was gazing at the tall damask bed, Angélique had the impression that the painting of the god and goddess had come to life. Two naked white bodies were clasped amid disarrayed sheets whose lace borders were dragging on the ground. They were so closely mingled that at first she thought they were struggling adolescents, page-boys rather shamelessly tussling, before she made out that they were a man and a woman.

The brown tousled mane of the masculine partner almost entirely covered the face of the woman, whom his long body seemed to want to crush completely. Of the woman, Angélique could only make out certain details that melted into the shadows: a well-shaped leg raised against the virile body, a breast surging from beneath the arms that enveloped her, a frail white hand.

Angélique felt shaken, almost nauseated, and yet dimly wonderstruck, too. After having so often contemplated the picture of Olympus, savoured its freshness and its majestic impulse, she was finally left with an impression of beauty by this scene whose meaning she had grasped, with her peasant-girl intuition.

"So this is love!" she told herself, as a shudder of fright and pleasure coursed through her.

At last the two lovers unclasped. They were now resting side by side, like recumbent tombstone figures in the darkness of a crypt. Their breathing came slower in a felicity close to slumber. Neither of them spoke. The woman was the first to move. Stretching out her snow-white arm, she reached for the table near the bed, on which a flask shone ruby-like with a dark wine. She gave a contrite little laugh.

"Oh, darling, I'm shattered," she murmured. "We simply must taste this Roussillon wine which your thoughtful valet put here. Would you like a cup?"

The man answered from the depth of the alcove with a mutter that could be taken for assent.

The lady, who seemed to have recovered her strength, filled two glasses, held one out to her lover, while emptying the other with avid delight. Angélique suddenly thought that she would have liked to be in that bed, perfectly naked and relaxed, savouring the sunny wine of the south.

"So that is the Prince's caudle," she thought.

She was not aware of her uncomfortable position. She could now see the woman entirely, admire her perfect round breasts set off by ruby tips, her supple belly, the long legs which she had crossed.

There was fruit on a tray. The woman chose a peach and bit into it lustily.

"A plague on all importunates!" the man cried suddenly, leaping over his mistress to the foot of the bed.

Angélique, who had not heard the knocking at the door, thought she had been discovered and shrank back against the turret, more dead than alive.

When she looked again, she saw that the god had draped himself in a voluminous brown dressing-gown tied with a silver sash. His face, that of a young man in his thirties, was less handsome than his body, for he had a long nose and his hard, though flashing, eyes made him look rather like a bird of prey.

"I am with the Duchesse de Beaufort!" he cried, turning towards the door.

Despite this warning, a valet appeared on the threshold.

"If Your Highness will pardon me. A monk has just presented himself at the gate and insists on being received by Monsieur de Condé. The Marquis du Plessis thought it advisable to send him straight to Your Highness."

"Let him enter!" muttered the Prince after a moment's silence.

He went to the ebony bureau by the window and opened a few drawers.

From the back of the room, a lackey introduced another person, a cowled monk who approached while bowing several times with remarkable ease. When he straightened up, he revealed a swarthy face in which gleamed deep, languorous, black eyes.

The arrival of the ecclesiastic did not seem to trouble the woman on the bed in the least. She continued munching the succulent fruit with perfect unconcern. She had merely thrown a shawl over the top of her legs.

The brown-haired man, bent over the bureau,

pulled from it some large, red-sealed envelopes.

"Father," he said without turning round, "did Monsieur Fouquet send you?"

"He did indeed, Monseigneur."

The monk added a sentence in a melodious tongue that Angélique supposed to be Italian. When he expressed himself in French, his accent was rather lisping and had a childlike quality that was not devoid of charm.

"There was no need to repeat the password, Signor Exili," said the Prince de Condé. "I would have recognized you from the description I have of you and from the blue mark you have in the corner of your eye. So you are Europe's most skilful artist in the difficult and subtle science of poisons?"

"Your Highness does me too much honour. I have only perfected certain recipes handed down by my Florentine ancestors."

"The people of Italy are artists in all spheres," cried Condé.

He burst into a loud, neighing laugh, then his features abruptly resumed their harsh expression.

"You've got the thing?"

"Here it is."

The Capuchin extracted a carved casket from his wide sleeve. He opened it himself by pressing on one of the precious wood mouldings.

"You see, Monseigneur, all that's needed is to insert the nail at the nape of this charming figure who carries a dove on his fist."

The lid had sprung open. On a satin cushion gleamed a glass phial filled with an emerald-coloured fluid. The Prince de Condé picked up the flask cautiously and raised it to the light.

"Roman vitriol," said Father Exili gently. "It is a composition that acts slowly but surely. I prefer it to corrosive sublimate, which can provoke death within a few hours. From the indications Monsieur Fouquet gave me, I thought I gathered that you yourself, Monseigneur, as well as your friends, did not care for too precise suspicions to be aroused in the entourage of the person concerned. The person will feel a certain languor, resist a week perhaps, but death will have the natural appearance of a bowel-fever caused by gamey venison or not quite fresh food. It would be wise to see to it that the person is served with mussels, oysters or other shellfish which sometimes produce dangerous effects. To put the blame for such a sudden demise on them would be child's play."

"I thank you for your excellent advice, Father."

Condé was still staring at the pale green phial, and there was a gleam of hatred in his eyes. Angélique felt acutely disappointed by it: the god of love, in coming down to earth, had lost his beauty and now frightened her.

"Be careful, Monseigneur," continued Father Exili, "this poison must be handled with infinite precaution. To compound it, I am myself obliged to wear a glass mask. A drop falling on your skin could produce a gnawing disease which would not spend its power before it had devoured one of your limbs. If you are not able to pour this medicine yourself into the person's plate, do recommend to the valet charged with the task to use the utmost skill and precision."

"My valet who ushered you in is wholly trustworthy. Luckily, the person concerned does not know him. I think it will be easy to place him at his side."

The Prince cast a mocking glance down at the monk, from his great height.

"I presume that a life devoted to such an art has not made you overscrupulous, Signor Exili. Still, what would you say if I confided to you that this poison was destined for one of your compatriots, an Italian from the Abruzzi?"

A smile widened Exili's mobile lips. He bowed again.

"My only compatriots are those who appraise my services at their just value, Monseigneur. And at the moment Monsieur Fouquet, of the Paris Parliament, shows himself more generous towards me than a certain Italian from the Abruzzi, whom I also know."

Condé's neighing laugh rang out again.

"Bravo, bravissimo, Signor! I like to have people of your sort with me."

He gently replaced the phial on its satin cushion. There was a pause. Signor Exili's eyes rested on his creation with a satisfaction that was not devoid of vanity.

"May I add, Monseigneur, that this liquor has the merit of being odourless and practically tasteless. It does not alter the food it is mixed with. At most, supposing the person pays great attention to what he is eating, he could reproach his cook for having been a little too generous with spices."

"You are a precious man," repeated the Prince, who seemed sunk in thought.

He rather nervously picked up the sealed envelopes on the top of the chest of drawers.

"This is what I have to hand you to seal the bargain with Monsieur Fouquet. This envelope contains the declaration made by the Marquis d'Hoquincourt. Here are those by Monsieur de Charost, Monsieur du Plessis, Madame du Plessis, Madame de Richeville, the Duchesse de Beaufort, Madame de Longueville. As you see, the ladies are not as lazy — or as squeamish — as the gentlemen. I am still without the letters from Monsieur de Maupéou, the Marquis de Créqui and a few others. . . ."

"And yours, Monseigneur."

"That's true. Here it is. I was just finishing it and have not yet signed it."

"Would Your Highness have the extreme kindness to read the text out to me so that I can check the wording point by point? Monsieur Fouquet deems it essential that none of the terms be omitted."

"As you wish," said the Prince with an imperceptible shrug.

He took the sheet of paper and read aloud:

"I, Louis II, Prince de Condé, give my word and assurance to Monseigneur Fouquet never to pledge my loyalty to any other person but to him, to obey no other person without exception, to place at his disposal my strongholds, fortifications and other such whenever he shall so command.

"In assurance whereof I give this note written and signed by my hand, of my own volition even without his solicitation, he in his goodness trusting my word, of which he is assured.

"Executed in Plessis-Bellière this 20th day of September 1649."

"Sign it, Monseigneur," said Father Exili, whose eyes glistened in the shadow of his hood.

Quickly, as if in a hurry to have done with, Condé picked up a goose-quill from the bureau and sharpened it. While he initialled his letter, the monk had lit a small silver-gilt stove. Condé melted red wax in it and sealed his missive.

"All the other letters are similarly drawn up and signed," he concluded. "I think your master will be satisfied."

"You may rest assured, Monseigneur. However, I must not leave this castle without taking with me the other declarations which you promised."

"I warrant I shall obtain them for you before tomorrow noon."

"In that case, I shall stay under this roof till then."

"Our friend, the Marquise du Plessis, will see to it that you are made comfortable, Signor. I have informed her of your arrival."

"Meanwhile, I think it would be prudent to lock these letters up in the casket which I have handed to you. Its opening is invisible and nowhere else would they be so well shielded from indiscreet eyes."

"You are right, Signor Exili. As I listen to you, I'm beginning to understand that conspiracy, too, is an art and one that requires practice and experience. I myself am just a warrior and don't conceal the fact."

"A glorious warrior!" exclaimed the Italian, with a bow.

"You flatter me, Father. Though I confess I'd like to see Monsieur de Mazarin and Her Majesty the Queen share your opinion. However that may be, I believe that military strategy, though coarser and more all-embracing, still has some kinship with your subtle stratagems. One must always foresee the enemy's intentions."

"Monseigneur, you speak as if Machiavelli himself had been your master."

"You flatter me," said the Prince again. But he was visibly pleased. Exili showed him how to raise the satin cushion and slip beneath it the compromising envelopes. Then the casket was placed into the bureau. No sooner had the Italian withdrawn than Condé, like a child, took it out again and opened it.

"Show me," whispered the woman, holding out her hand.

She had not spoken during the whole interview, and had merely put her rings back on her fingers, one by one. But it was obvious that she had not missed a word of what had been said.

Condé went over to the bed and they both bent their heads over the emerald phial.

"Do you think it is really as terrible as he says?" murmured the Duchesse.

"Fouquet assured me that there is no cleverer apothecary than this Florentine. And, anyway, we must pass through Fouquet. He's the one who had the idea of the Spanish intervention — in Parliament, last April. An idea that displeased everyone, but it put him in touch with His Most Catholic Majesty. I shall be able to hold my armies only through his good offices."

160

The lady sunk back on the pillows.

"So Monsieur de Mazarin is dead!" she said slowly.

"To all intents and purposes, for his life is here within my hands."

"Don't they say that the Queen sometimes sups with him whom she loves so passionately?"

"So they say," said the Prince after a moment's pause. "But I don't approve of your plan, my dear. I am thinking of a cleverer and more effective move. What would the Queen Mother be without her sons? . . . There'd be nothing left for the Spanish woman but to withdraw to a convent and weep over them. . . ."

"Poison the King?" said the Duchesse, with a start.

The Prince whinnied merrily. He went back to the bureau and put the casket inside it.

"Just like a woman!" he exclaimed. "The King! You melt with tenderness because he is a handsome boy, stirred by adolescent emotions, who for some time now at Court has been making eyes at you like a fawning dog. That's how you see the King. For us he is a dangerous obstacle to all our plans. As for his brother, the little Monsieur is a perverse brat who already takes pleasure in dressing up as a girl and letting himself be petted by men. I consider him even less suitable for the throne than your virginal Royalty. No, take my word for it, we'll have in Monsieur d'Orléans, who believes in austerity as little as his brother Louis XIII believed in it too greatly, a King to our liking. He is rich and has a weak character. What more do we want?

"My dear," Condé went on, after he had locked the bureau and slipped its key into the pocket of his greatcoat, "I think it's time for us to present ourselves to our hosts. Supper will be announced soon. Do you wish me to call for your chamber-maid?"

"I should be obliged, my lord."

Angélique, whose bones were beginning to ache, had shrunk back a little on the cornice. She thought that her father must be looking for her, but she could not make up her mind to leave her ledge. Inside the room, the Prince and his mistress, with the help of their servants, were putting on their finery amid a great rustle of silks and some curses, for Monseigneur was not a patient man.

When Angélique looked away from the luminous screen formed by the open window, she saw around her only the opaque night, from which rose the murmur of the nearby forest as it swayed in the autumn wind.

At last the chamber was empty. The nightlight still glowed but the room had recaptured its mystery. Very softly, the girl crept close to the window-frame and slipped into the room. The scent of rouge and perfumes mingled strangely with the fragrance of the night — damp timber, moss and ripe chestnuts.

Angélique did not know exactly what she was going to do. Somebody might surprise her. She was not afraid. All this was but a dream. Like the mad lady of Monteloup, like the crimes of Gilles de Retz. . . .

With nimble fingers, she took out of the pocket

162

of the greatcoat, which had been thrown over a chair, the small key to the bureau, opened it, pulled the casket towards her. It was of sandalwood and gave off a pervasive scent. After locking the bureau again and putting the key in its place, Angélique found herself back on the cornice, the casket under her arm. She suddenly felt vastly amused. She imagined Monsieur de Condé's face on discovering the disappearance of the poison and the compromising letters.

"This isn't stealing," she told herself, "since it's a matter of preventing a crime."

She knew already the hiding-place in which she would conceal her theft. The corner turrets with which the Italian architect had adorned the four angles of the graceful château du Plessis were mere ornaments, yet they had been fitted with miniature battlements in imitation of the warlike decorations of medieval castles. These turrets, moreover, were hollow and pierced by small openings.

Angélique slipped the casket inside the one nearest to her. Anyone who would come and search for it there would have to be clever indeed!

Thereupon she slid adroitly down the façade and reached firm ground. Then only did she notice that her bare feet were icy. Putting on her old shoes, she returned to the château.

Everyone had gathered in the drawing-rooms. The dark and misty night held no more charm for them. As she came into the hall, Angélique's nose was pleasantly titillated by the most appetizing smells coming from the kitchens. She saw a row of little liveried valets go by carrying big silver platters. It was a solemn procession of pheasants and woodcock adorned with their own feathers, a sucking-pig crowned with flowers like a bride, several cuts of a very fine doe served on artichoke hearts and sprigs of fennel.

The tinkle of china and crystal-glass came from the halls and galleries where all the company was sitting around small lace-covered tables, some ten people at each.

Angélique stopped on the threshold of the largest room, and saw the Prince de Condé surrounded by Madame du Plessis, the Duchesse du Beaufort and the Comtesse de Richeville. The Marquis du Plessis and his son Philippe also shared the Prince's table, as did some other ladies and young lords. The brown frock of the Italian Exili struck a discordant note amid this glittering array of lace and ribbons, precious gold and silvery embroidery. Had the Baron de Sancé been present, he would have made a pair with the monk's austerity. But however carefully she looked around, Angélique could not see her father anywhere.

Suddenly one of the pages, carrying a silver-gilt flagon, recognized her in passing. He was the one who had mocked her most viciously on account of the *bourrée*.

"Oh! the Baroness of the Doleful Dress!" he jeered. "What do you want to drink, Nanon? Apple-wine or good sour milk?"

She stuck out her tongue at him and, leaving him agape, walked up towards the princely table.

"Good Lord, what's this coming over here?" exclaimed the Duchesse de Beaufort.

Madame du Plessis followed the direction of her

glance, saw Angélique and once again called her son to the rescue:

"Philippe! Philippe! Be good enough, my boy, to lead your cousin de Sancé to the table of the maids-of-honour."

The boy looked up at Angélique sullenly.

"Here's a chair," he said, pointing to the empty place beside him.

"Not here, Philippe, not here. You saved this place for Mademoiselle de Senlis."

"Mademoiselle de Senlis should have hurried. When she eventually deigns to join us, she'll find that she has been . . . advantageously replaced," he remarked with a brief, ironical smile.

His neighbours giggled.

Angélique had meanwhile sat down. She had gone too far to retreat. She dared not ask where her father was, and she was dazzled by the brilliant lights and their sparkling reflections in the glasses, decanters, silver-plate and the ladies' diamonds. Her reaction was to stiffen her back, throw out her chest, fling back her heavy golden hair. It seemed to her that some of the gentlemen were throwing not uninterested glances in her direction. Almost opposite her, the falcon eye of the Prince de Condé stared at her for a moment with arrogant attention.

"By the devil, you have some odd relatives, Monsieur du Plessis. Who is this grey duckling?"

"A young country cousin, Monseigneur. Oh, pity me. For two hours this very evening, instead of listening to the musicians and the charming talk of these ladies, I had to bear with the pleas of her father the Baron, whose breath still leaves me indisposed. As our cynical poet Argenteuil would say:

> I tell you most truly that
> the breath of a corpse
> Or a pensioner's wheeze
> would not smell so coarse."

An outburst of obsequious laughter shook the gathering.

"And do you know what he asked me?" continued the Marquis, wiping his eyelids with an affected gesture. "I challenge you to guess. He wants me to get him a tax exemption for some mules in his stable as well as — mark the unsavoury term — on his output of lead, which he claims he finds all molten in nuggets under the vegetable plots in his kitchen-garden. I've never heard such nonsense."

"A plague on these clodhoppers!" grumbled the Prince. "They cast ridicule on our coats-of-arms with their peasant ways."

The ladies choked with merriment.

"Did you see the feather on his hat?"

"And his shoes! There was straw still clinging to their heels!"

Angélique's heart beat so strongly that she thought her neighbour Philippe must hear it. She glanced at him and caught the handsome boy's hard blue eyes fixed on her with an indefinable expression.

"I can't let my father be insulted," she thought.

Angélique turned very pale and took a deep breath.

"It may be that we are paupers," she said very loudly and distinctly, "but at least we don't try to poison the King!"

The laughter died on the faces around her and the silence that fell was so heavy that it spread to the neighbouring tables. Slowly the conversations subsided, the convivial spirits slackened. Everyone looked at the Prince de Condé.

"Who? . . . Who . . . who?" stammered the Marquis du Plessis. Then he abruptly fell silent.

"These are strange words," said the Prince at last, at great pains to contain himself. "This young person is not used to society. She hasn't got beyond nursery tales. . . ."

"He'll ridicule me in another moment, and they'll throw me out with the promise of a thrashing," thought Angélique, in a panic.

She bent forward a little and looked towards the end of the table.

"I am told that Signor Exili is the greatest expert in the kingdom in the art of poisoning."

This new pebble hurled into the pool amplified the already violent ripples. There was a frightened murmur.

"Oh! this girl is possessed by the devil!" cried Madame du Plessis, furiously biting her little lace handkerchief. "She has covered me with shame. She sits there like a glass-eyed doll and then suddenly opens her mouth and utters such terrible things!"

"Terrible? Why terrible?" softly protested the Prince, whose eyes did not leave Angélique. "They would be terrible if they were true. But they are merely the ravings of a little girl who does not know when to keep silent."

"I'll keep silent when I want to," declared Angélique pertly.

"And when will that be, Mademoiselle?"

"When you stop insulting my father and grant him the poor favours he is asking for."

Monsieur de Condé's complexion suddenly darkened. The scandal was at its height. The people at the end of the gallery climbed on chairs.

"May the plague! May the plague . . ." choked the Prince. He suddenly got up, with outstretched arm as if flinging his troops into attack against the Spanish trenches.

"Follow me!" he roared at her.

"He'll kill me," thought Angélique. And the sight of the tall Prince towering over her made her shiver with fear and pleasure.

However, she followed him, a grey little duckling behind that huge, beribboned bird. She noticed that he was wearing wide starched lace flounces below his knees and, over his trunk-hose, a sort of short petticoat trimmed with countless braids. Never had she seen a man so extravagantly dressed. Yet she admired his walk, the way he placed his high arched heels on the ground.

"We are alone now," said Condé, abruptly turning round. "Mademoiselle, I don't want to get angry with you, but you will have to answer my questions."

This sugary voice frightened Angélique more than the outbursts of rage. She saw herself in this deserted boudoir, alone with this powerful man whose intrigues she was upsetting. She grasped that she too had become involved in them and was struggling as in a spider's web. She shrank back, stuttered, pretended to be a stupid country-girl.

"I didn't think I was doing any harm."

"Why did you invent such an insult at the table of an uncle whom you respect?"

She understood what he was trying to make her admit, wavered, weighed the pros and cons. In view of what she knew, a protestation of total ignorance would certainly defy belief.

"I did not invent . . . I repeated things I've been told," she murmured. "That Signor Exili was a very clever man at making poisons. . . . But that about the King I made up. I shouldn't have. I was in a temper."

She twisted a piece of her belt awkwardly.

"Who told you?"

Angélique's imagination worked fast.

"A . . . a page. I don't know his name."

"Can you point him out?"

"Yes."

He took her back to the door leading to the reception rooms. She pointed at the page who had mocked her.

"A pox on these eavesdropping ragamuffins!" growled the Prince. "What is your name, Mademoiselle?"

"Angélique de Sancé."

"Listen to me, Mademoiselle de Sancé. It's bad to repeat foolishly words that a girl of your age cannot understand. It might harm you, you and your family. I shall forgive your insolence this time. I shall even go so far as to study your father's case and see if I cannot do something for him.

But what guarantee have I of your silence?"

She raised her green eyes towards him:

"I can keep silent when I've obtained what I want just as well as I can talk when I am insulted."

"By the devil, when you've grown to womanhood, I'll wager that men will hang themselves for having met you!" said the Prince.

But a vague smile hovered over his face. He did not seem to suspect that she might know more than she had admitted. Impulsive and rather muddle-headed, Condé lacked insight. His first excitement spent, he decided that there was nothing more to it than backstairs gossip.

Being a man used to flattery and sensitive to feminine charms, he could not help noticing the emotion of this adolescent girl, whose beauty was already striking, and this helped to soothe his anger. Angélique tried to look up at him with eyes full of candid admiration.

"I would like to ask you something," she said with exaggerated naïveté.

"And what may that be?"

"Why do you wear a little skirt?"

"A little skirt? . . . But, my child, this is a 'rhinegrave.' Is it not supremely elegant? The rhinegrave conceals the graceless trunk-hose which only become a horseman. You can adorn it with braids and ribbons. It's a very comfortable garment. Have you never seen it in your countryside?"

"No. And those long frills under your knees?"

"They are called 'canons.' They emphasize the calf of the leg which emerges from it, arched and slender."

"It is true," approved Angélique. "All this is wonderful. I've never seen such a beautiful costume!"

"Oh! Women's talk of frippery will appease even the most dangerous fury," said the Prince, delighted with his success. "But I must return to my hosts. Do you promise me to be good now?"

"Yes, Monseigneur," she said with a cajoling smile that revealed her pearly teeth.

The Prince de Condé returned to the dining room, calming the party's agitation with sweeping gestures, as if he were blessing them.

"Eat, my friends, eat. Much ado about nothing. The impertinent little girl will apologize."

Angélique, without being asked, curtseyed to Madame du Plessis.

"I present my apologies, Madame, and ask you for permission to withdraw."

There was some laughter at Madame du Plessis's gesture for, unable to utter a word, she just pointed to the door.

But, before that door, another crowd had formed.

"My daughter! Where is my daughter?" clamoured Baron Armand.

"The Baron is asking for his daughter," cried an impish lackey.

Among the elegant guests and the liveried flunkeys, the impecunious nobleman looked like a big, captive bumble-bee. Angélique ran towards him.

"Angélique," he sighed, "you drive me mad. For more than three hours now, I've been looking

171

for you everywhere in the dark, between Sancé, Molines's house and Plessis. What a day, my child, what a day!"

"Let's go, Father, please, let's go quickly," she said.

They were already on the porch, when the voice of the Marquis du Plessis called them back.

"A moment, Cousin. The Prince would like to have a word with you. It concerns those Custom dues you were talking about . . ."

The rest was lost as the two men went back into the house.

Angélique sat down on the last step of the porch and waited for her father. She suddenly felt completely drained of all thoughts, of all willpower. A small white griffon came to sniff at her. She stroked him mechanically.

When Monsieur de Sancé reappeared, he gripped his daughter by the wrist.

"I was afraid you might have escaped again. You're really full of the devil. Monsieur de Condé paid me such strange compliments about you that I wasn't quite sure whether I oughtn't to apologize for having brought you into the world."

A little later, while their mules were stepping gingerly through the dark night, Monsieur de Sancé spoke again, nodding his head:

"I can't get the hang of those people. They listen to you with a sneer. The Marquis explains to me, with facts and figures, that his financial straits are much worse than mine. They let me go without even offering me a glass of wine to refresh my gullet, and then suddenly they run after me and promise to do all I ask. According to Monseigneur, I'll be granted the Custom dues exemption before the next month is out."

"So much the better, Father," murmured Angélique.

She listened to the nocturnal chant of the frogs which heralded the proximity of the marshes and the old fortified castle. She suddenly felt like crying.

"Do you think Madame du Plessis will take you on as a maid-in-waiting?" asked the Baron.

"Oh no! I don't think so," replied Angélique suavely.

Chapter 10

THE journey to the convent at Poitiers left Angélique with a jolting and rather unpleasant memory. A very old coach had been repaired for the occasion, and she had climbed into it with Hortense and Madelon. A groom drove the mules, while Raymond and Gontran were both mounted on fine thoroughbred horses, a present from their father. It was said that the Jesuits in their new colleges had stables reserved for the mounts of young noblemen.

Two heavy pack-horses completed the caravan. One carried old Guillaume, ordered to escort his young masters. Much bad news of trouble and war circulated in the countryside. There were rumours of Monsieur de la Rochefoucauld stirring up Poitou

on behalf of Monsieur de Condé. He was recruiting armies and requisitioning crops to feed them. And armies meant famine and poverty, bandits and highwaymen at the crossroads. So old Guillaume was there, his pike supported by the stirrup-holster, his old sword at his side.

The journey, however, was uneventful. Passing through the forest, they noticed a few suspicious figures among the trees. But no doubt the old mercenary's pike, or else the poor aspect of the carriage, discouraged brigands.

They spent the night at an inn, at a sinister cross-roads, where the wind kept whistling through the bare trees. The innkeeper condescended to serve the travellers a dish of hot water styled a broth and some cheese which they ate by the light of a dim tallow candle.

"All innkeepers are hand-in-glove with the highwaymen," Raymond informed his terrified young sisters. "It's in wayside inns that most murders are committed. On our last trip we stopped at a place where less than a month before they had cut the throat of a rich financier, for the sole reason that he was travelling alone."

Regretting these morbid reflections, he added: "These crimes committed by the lower orders are the direct outcome of the lawlessness of men in high places. Everyone has lost the fear of God."

There followed yet another day's travelling. Shaken like sacks of nuts on the frozen, rutted roads, the three sisters were aching in every bone. Only rarely did they roll over stretches of the old Roman road with its pavement of large, regular slabs. Most of the time the roads were plain clay ploughed up by the ceaseless passage of coaches and riders. At the bridgeheads they sometimes had to stop for hours until they were stiff with cold, because the toll-keeper was usually a slow and garrulous official, for whom each passing traveller was a happy occasion for indulging in a spot of gossip. The only ones to pass without slowing down were great noblemen who disdainfully tossed a purse out of a carriage window at the keeper's feet.

Madelon cried and clung shivering to Angélique. Hortense said through compressed lips:

"This is unbearable."

They were, all three of them, dog-tired and uttered a vast sigh of relief when, on the evening of the second day, Poitiers appeared, with its faded pink roofs rising in tiers on the slope of a hill skirted by the gay river Clain.

It was a bright winter day. You could have imagined yourself in one of those Southern landscapes to which Poitou is indeed the gateway, so gently shone the sky over the tiled roofs. The bells were ringing the Angelus. These bells were henceforward to regulate Angélique's days for almost five years. Poitiers was a city of cathedrals, convents and collegiate churches. The bells ruled the life of this frocked community, of the army of students, who were as noisy as their masters were soft-spoken. Priests and bachelor students met at the corner of sloping streets, in the shadow of courtyards, in the squares whose walls and steps offered a resting place to the pilgrims to the city.

The de Sancé children took leave of one another in front of the cathedral. The Ursuline Convent was a little to the left and towered over the river

Clain. The college of the Jesuit fathers was perched on the very top of the hill. With the awkwardness of adolescents, they parted almost without a word. Only Madelon embraced her two brothers tearfully.

Thus the gates of the convent closed on Angélique. It took her a long time to realise that the stifling feeling that oppressed her was due to a sudden exclusion from the open spaces. Walls, and more walls, and bars before the windows. Her companions did not much appeal to her; she had always played with boys, little peasants who admired and obeyed her. But here, among young ladies of high lineage and solid wealth, Angélique de Sancé was necessarily relegated to the lowest ranks.

She also had to submit to the ordeal of wearing a whalebone corset. This tightly laced garment, forcing a girl to hold herself straight, was meant to provide her with a disdainful, queenly deportment for the rest of her life and in all circumstances. Angélique, who was of vigorous build and supple sinews, and instinctively graceful, could have done without this torturing device. But the corset was an institution that extended far beyond the convent walls. Listening to the older girls, she could not doubt that the boned corset held an important place in the world of fashion. There was even talk of *busquières,* a sort of tongue-shaped bodice front stiffened with strong cardboard or iron struts and which was lavishly embroidered and adorned with bows and jewels. The *busquière* was meant to support the breasts, pressing them up under the lace until they looked as if they were about to burst out of their constraint at any moment. Naturally, the older girls discussed these details in secret, although the convent was specially entrusted with preparing young girls for marriage and life in society.

They had to learn to dance and curtsey, to play the lute and the harpsichord, to converse with two or three companions on a set subject, and even to handle a fan and apply cosmetics. Next in importance came housekeeping. In anticipation of reverses which Heaven might decree, the students had to attend to the most humble chores. Taking their turn, they would work in the kitchens and wash-houses, and clean and light the lamps, sweep and scrub the stone floors. Finally they were given the rudiments of an academic course: history and geography, dully presented; mythology, logic, theology, Latin. More attention was paid to stylistic exercises, the art of letter-writing being essentially feminine, and the exchange of letters between friends or lovers providing one of the most absorbing occupations for a woman of the world.

Without being an intractable pupil, Angélique gave little satisfaction to her teachers. She did what she was ordered to do, but did not seem to understand *why* she was obliged to do so many stupid things. Sometimes they would look for her in vain during lesson-time. She would eventually be found in the kitchen-garden, which was just a large garden which stretched away above the warm, quiet lanes. In response to the sternest reproaches, she would always answer that she had not realised she was doing wrong in watching the cabbages grow.

The following summer, there was a rather serious epidemic in the city, which was called the plague, because the rats came out of their holes to die and rot in the streets and houses.

The Princes' rebellion, led by Condé and Turenne, brought misery and famine to the western provinces, which had so far been spared by the foreign wars. No one knew any more who was for the King and who against, but the peasants, whose villages were burnt down, came swarming into the towns. This produced an army of paupers who congregated at the back doors with outstretched palms. Soon they had become more numerous than the priests and students.

The young ladies of St. Ursula distributed alms to the poor stationed before the convent, at certain hours on certain days. They learned that this formed part of the training of a future great lady.

Angélique came face to face, for the first time, with hopeless, ragged poverty, genuine poverty with leering eyes, full of hatred. She was neither moved nor upset by it, unlike her companions, some of whom wept or curled their lips in disgust. She felt as if she recognized a picture whose imprint she had always borne within her, a strange foreboding of what fate had in store for her.

The plague made ravages among these scum that crammed the steep lanes where the burning July sun dried up the fountains. There were also several casualties among the pupils. One morning, during recreation, Angélique did not see Madelon. She inquired after her and was told that the sick child had been taken to the infirmary. Madelon died a few days later. Before her pallid, shrivelled body

Angélique did not weep. She was even angry with Hortense for her spectacular tears. Why was this lanky girl of seventeen giving way to sobs? She had never loved Madelon. She only loved herself.

"Alas, my little ones," said an old nun to them gently, "it's the law of God. Many children die. I'm told your mother had ten children and lost only one of them. This makes two. That's not many. I know a lady who had fifteen children and lost seven of them. That's how it is, you see. God giveth; God taketh away. Many children die, it's the law of God. . . ."

After Madelon's death, Angélique became even more unsociable and no longer took kindly to discipline. She did only what she liked, disappeared for hours on end in forgotten crannies of the vast house. She had been forbidden to go into the garden and vegetable-plots. But she found ways and means of slipping into them, all the same. There was talk of sending her back home, but the Baron de Sancé, despite the hardships caused by the civil war, paid the fees for his two daughters very regularly, which many parents of other pupils did not. Moreover, Hortense gave promise of becoming one of the most accomplished girls of her class. Out of consideration for the elder, they kept the younger girl. But they gave up looking after her.

So it happened that, one January day in 1652, Angélique, who had just turned fifteen, found herself perched once again on the wall of the kitchen-garden, enjoying the sight of the bustling street below and warming herself in the gentle winter sun.

Poitiers was very animated in these first days of the year, for the Queen, the King and their supporters had just arrived there. Poor Queen, poor young King, tossed from revolt to revolt! They had come to the province of Guyenne in order to wage war against Monsieur de Condé. On their way back, they stopped at Poitiers to try to negotiate with Monsieur de Turenne, who held this province from Fontenay-le-Comte to the sea. Châtellerault and Luçon, former Protestant strongholds, had rallied to the Huguenot general, but Poitiers, which had not forgotten that a hundred years ago its churches had been sacked and its mayor hanged by the heretics, had opened its gates to the monarch.

All that stood by the youthful prince today was the black dress of the Spanish woman. The people, the whole of France had shouted for so long "Down with Mazarin! Down with Mazarin!" that the red-robed man had at last bowed out. He had left the Queen he loved and taken refuge in Germany. But his departure had not been enough to calm the rage. . . .

Leaning against the convent wall, Angélique listened to the murmurs of the seething town, whose excitement spread its ripples even to this remote district.

The curses of coachmen, whose carriages blocked one another in the winding lanes, mingled with the cries and laughter of pages and serving-girls, and with the neighing of horses. The pealing of bells floated above the hubbub. Angélique was now able to distinguish the different chimes, that of Saint Hilaire, of Sainte Radegonde, the great bell of Notre-Dame-la-Grande, the droning bells of the Tower of Saint Porchaire.

Suddenly, at the foot of the wall, a garland of pages passed like a swarm of birds of paradise in their silk and satin. One of them stopped to tie the ribbon of his shoe. As he straightened up, he raised his head and met Angélique's eyes watching him from the top of her wall. With a gallant gesture, the page swept the dust with his hat.

"I salute you, Mademoiselle. You don't look as if you are enjoying yourself up there."

He resembled the pages she had seen at Plessis, wearing the same little puffed-out pants as they did, the trunk-hose, a legacy of the sixteenth century which gave him long, spindly legs like a heron's. For the rest, he seemed pleasant enough, with a gay, tanned face and fine curly brown hair. She asked him his age. He said he was sixteen.

"But don't worry, Mademoiselle," he added, "I know how to pay court to ladies."

He cast a cajoling glance at her and then suddenly held out his arms.

"Do come and join me."

A pleasant sensation filled Angélique. The sad, grey prison, in which her heart was languishing, seemed to open its gates. This merry laughter floating up to her held the promise of something sweet and stimulating that she hungered for.

"Do come," he whispered. "If you like, I'll take you to the mansion of the Ducs d'Aquitaine where the Court is staying, and I'll show you the King."

She had hardly a moment's hesitation and adjusted her black woollen cloak and hood.

"Look out! I'm going to jump!" she cried.

He caught her almost in his arms. They burst out laughing. He quickly grasped her wrist and pulled her along.

"What will the nuns in your convent say?"

"They are used to my escapades."

"And how will you manage to get back?"

"I'll ring at the door and beg for alms."

He puffed with laughter.

Angélique felt intoxicated by the whirlwind that suddenly surrounded her. Among the lords and ladies, whose sumptuous finery amazed the provincials, passed merchants of all kinds. From one of them the young page bought two little sticks on which fried frog-legs were impaled. Having always lived in Paris, he found this dish extraordinarily amusing. The two youngsters ate with a hearty appetite. The page told her that he was called Henri de Roguier and was attached to the service of the King. The latter, a gay boon-companion, at times gave his grave councillors the slip to join his friends in strumming a guitar. Cardinal Mazarin's nieces, those charming Italian dolls, were still at Court, despite their uncle's forced departure.

While chatting away, the young boy was insidiously leading Angélique toward a less frequented part of the town. She noticed it but said nothing. Her body had suddenly awakened and was waiting expectantly for something which the page's hand about her waist seemed to promise.

He stopped and pushed her gently into a doorway. Then he began to kiss her with fervour. Between kisses his talk bubbled with amusing, commonplace trifles.

"You are beautiful. . . . Your cheeks are like daisies and your eyes as green as leap-frogs. . . . The frogs of your countryside. . . . Don't move. I want to open your bodice. . . . Let me. . . . I know how to. . . . Oh! I've never seen such sweet white breasts. . . . And as firm as apples. . . . I like you, my sweet. . . ."

She let him ramble on, caress her. She tossed her head back a little against the mossy stone, and her eyes automatically glanced up at the blue sky.

The page was silent now; his breath came more quickly. He fidgeted and several times looked around with annoyance. The street was fairly quiet but now and then some people passed. There was even a cavalcade of students who cried "Ho! Ho!" when they perceived the young couple in the shadow of the wall.

The boy stepped back, stamped his foot.

"Oh! this is infuriating! All the houses are crammed to bursting in this damned country town. Even the noble lords must receive their mistresses in anterooms. Now where could we go for a little quiet, I ask you?"

"We are all right here," she murmured.

But he was not satisfied. He glanced down at his chain-purse dangling at his waist, and his face brightened.

"Come on! I have an idea. We'll find a good-size drawing-room!"

He took her by the hand and pulled her along at a run, until they reached the square of Notre-Dame-la-Grande. Though she had now been in Poitiers for two years, Angélique was unfamiliar with the town. She looked with admiration at the façade of the church, as finely carved as an Indian jewel-box, flanked by fir-cone-shaped bell-turrets. The very stone seemed to have flowered under the sculptor's magic chisel. Young Henri told his companion to stay under the porch and wait for him. He came back after a short while, greatly pleased, with a key in his hand.

"The sexton has rented me the pulpit for a minute."

"The pulpit?" repeated Angélique, amazed.

"Bah! This isn't the first time he's rendered this service to homeless lovers."

He had gripped her waist again and was walking down the sunken steps that led to the sanctuary.

Angélique was impressed by the darkness and coolness of the vault. The churches of Poitou are the most sombre ones in France. Sturdy edifices, resting on huge pillars, they conceal in their shadows ancient mural decorations, whose vivid hues appear only gradually to the surprised eye. The two youngsters advanced in silence.

"I feel cold," murmured Angélique, pulling her cloak around her.

He put a protective arm around her shoulders, but her high spirits had subsided and she was frightened.

He opened the first door of the monumental pulpit, then climbed the steps and walked on to the round platform where the sermons were delivered. Angélique followed him mechanically.

They sat down on the floor which was covered with a velvet carpet. The church, with its deep gloom, its smell of incense, seemed to have calmed the page's enterprising mood. He put his arm again around Angélique's shoulders and gently kissed her temple.

"You are such a lovely little sweetheart," he sighed. "I do like you so much better than the great ladies who tease me and make fun of me. That doesn't amuse me, but I must try and please them. If you only knew. . . ."

He sighed again. His face had recaptured its boyishness.

"I'll show you something very beautiful, something exceptional," he said, rummaging in his chain-purse.

He pulled from it a square of white linen, edged with lace and rather grimy.

"A handkerchief?" asked Angélique.

"Yes, the King's handkerchief. He dropped it this morning. I picked it up and have kept it as a talisman."

He gazed at it dreamily for some time.

"Shall I give it to you as a love-token?"

"Oh do!" said Angélique, quickly stretching out her hand.

Her arm knocked against the massive wooden balustrade, and a booming echo resounded under the dome.

They sat quite still, amazed and a little alarmed.

"I think someone's coming," murmured Angélique.

With a wretched look the boy confessed:

"I forgot to close the pulpit-door downstairs."

They both fell silent, listening to the approaching footsteps. Someone was mounting the stair to their refuge, and the black-capped head of an old

186

priest appeared above them.

"What are you doing here, my children?" he asked.

The resourceful page already had his story ready:

"I wanted to see my sister, who is in boarding-school at Poitiers, but I didn't know where to meet her. Our parents . . ."

"Don't speak so loudly in the house of God," said the priest. "Get up, and your sister too, and follow me."

He led them into the vestry and sat down on a stool. Then, his hands propped on his knees, he looked slowly from one to the other. The white hair emerging from his priestly cap made a halo around his face which, despite his age, had retained its fresh peasant colouring. He had a large nose, small lively, keen eyes, and a short white beard. Henri de Roguier suddenly looked scared and lapsed into silence with unfeigned confusion.

"Is he your lover?" the abbé suddenly asked Angélique, his chin motioning in the direction of the young boy.

A blush spread over the girl's face, and the page cried quickly and frankly:

"I wish she were, sir, but she's not that sort."

"I congratulate you, my daughter. If you had a beautiful pearl necklace, would you amuse yourself by throwing it into a courtyard full of dung, where the hogs would nuzzle it with their wet snouts? Eh? Answer me, child. Would you do that?"

"No, I wouldn't."

"You mustn't cast pearls before swine. You must

not squander the treasure of your virginity which should be reserved until your marriage. And you, callow lout," he continued softly, "whence comes the sacrilegious idea of taking your girl friend to the pulpit of a church to dally with her?"

"Where else could I take her?" the page protested sulkily. "You can't talk quietly in the lanes of this town which are as narrow as cupboards. I knew that the sexton of Notre-Dame-la-Grande sometimes rents the pulpit and the confessionals so that one can whisper secrets far from indiscreet ears. You know, Monsieur Vincent, that in these provincial towns there are many damsels so strictly kept by a grumpy father or a nagging mother that they never have an opportunity to hear sweet secrets, if . . ."

"How well you instruct me, my boy!"

"The pulpit cost thirty *livres* and the confessionals twenty. It's a lot for my purse, believe me, Monsieur Vincent."

"I do believe you," said Monsieur Vincent. "But it costs even more in the scales in which the devil and the angel weigh up the sins in front of Notre-Dame-la-Grande."

His face, which had so far retained its serene expression, now grew stern. He held out his hand.

"Give me the key that was entrusted to you."

And when the boy had handed it to him:

"You will go to confession, will you not? I shall wait for you tomorrow evening in this same church. I shall absolve you. I know only too well in what sort of an environment you live, poor little page! And it is better for you to play the man with a child of your age, than serve as a plaything to ripe ladies who debauch you in their alcoves. . . . Yes, I see you're blushing. Before her, so fresh, so new, you are ashamed of your sordid loves."

The boy hung his head, his impudence had vanished. He finally stammered:

"Monsieur Vincent de Paul, I beg of you, don't tell this to Her Majesty the Queen. If she sends me back to my father, he won't know where else to establish me. I have seven sisters who need a dowry, and I am the third youngest of the family. I was able to obtain the signal favour of entering the King's service thanks only to Monsieur de Lorraine who . . . who likes me," he concluded with embarrassment. "He paid the commission for me. If I am thrown out, he will probably demand that my father reimburse him, and that's impossible."

The old churchman looked at him gravely.

"I shall not name you. But it is well that I should once again remind the Queen of the turpitudes that surround her. Alas, she is a pious woman, devoted to good works, but what can she do against so much rottenness? You cannot change souls by decree. . . ."

The vestry door opened, and he broke off. A young man, with long curly hair and dressed in a rather smart black suit, came in. Monsieur Vincent straightened up and looked at him sternly.

"Vicar, I hope I am right in assuming that you know nothing of that trafficking that your sexton indulges in. He has just pocketed thirty *livres* from this young gentleman to allow him to meet his lady friend in the pulpit of your church. It is time that you watched over your clerics a little more carefully."

To regain his composure, the vicar took a long time in closing the door. When he turned round, the twilight in the room ill-concealed his embarrassment. As he remained silent, Monsieur Vincent went on:

"I notice, moreover, that you are wearing a wig and a lay gown. This is forbidden to priests. I shall be compelled to bring these lapses and traffickings to the notice of your parish beneficiary."

The priest tried to conceal a shrug.

"It will leave him quite indifferent, Monsieur Vincent. The beneficiary is a canon in Paris. He bought the living three years ago from the previous incumbent who retired to his estate. He has never come here, and as he has a chapter-house on the apse of Notre-Dame-de-Paris, I wager that Notre-Dame-la-Grande of Poitiers must seem quite paltry to him."

"Oh, I tremble," suddenly cried Monsieur Vincent, "lest this damnable trade in parishes and incumbencies, sold like asses and horses on the market place, drag the Church down to perdition. And who are the people appointed nowadays as bishops in the kingdom? Great war-lords and libertines who sometimes have not even received Orders but, being rich enough to acquire a bishop's see, dare to clothe themselves in the robe and ornaments of ministers of God . . . ! Oh, may the Lord help us to overthrow such institutions!"

Glad to see the lightning strike elsewhere, the vicar ventured:

"My parish is not neglected. I do look after it

and give it all my care. Do us the great honour, Monsieur Vincent, of attending our service of the Most Holy Sacrament tonight. You will see the nave packed with the faithful. Poitiers has been preserved from heresy by the zeal of her priests. Poitiers is not like Niort, Châtellerault and . . .”

The old man glowered at him.

“The vices of the priests were the primary cause of heresies!” he said bluntly.

He rose and, taking the two young people by the shoulder, pushed them out in front of him. Despite his great age and stooping back, he seemed full of vigour and briskness.

Evening was descending on the square in front of the church, where the pale winter light lent life to the stone flowers.

“My lambs,” said Monsieur Vincent, “my little children of God, you have tried to taste the green fruit of love. That's why your teeth are on edge and your hearts full of sadness. Let the sun of life ripen what has always been destined to blossom and mature. You must not stray in your quest of love, for if you do you may never find it. What crueller punishment is there for impatience and weakness than to be condemned for ever to bite only into sour, savourless fruit?

“You will now go each your separate ways. You, boy, to your service, which you must attend to conscientiously. You, girl, to your nuns and your work. And at the rise of day do not forget to pray to God, who is the father of us all.”

He left them. His glance followed their graceful figures until they parted at the corner of the square.

Angélique did not look back until she had reached the convent gate. A great peace had settled within her. But her shoulder still felt the imprint of a warm, old hand.

"Monsieur Vincent," she thought. "Is he the great Monsieur Vincent? The one whom the Marquis du Plessis called the Conscience of the Kingdom? The one who compels the noblemen to serve the poor? He who each day has private talks with the King and the Queen? How simple, how gentle he seems!"

Before lifting the knocker, she cast a glance back at the town, which was shrouded in darkness. "Bless me, Monsieur Vincent," she murmured.

Angélique accepted unrebelliously the punishments inflicted on her for this latest exploit. Indeed a change came over her fractious conduct. She applied herself to her studies, showed friendliness towards her schoolmates. She seemed at last to have adapted herself to the strictness of convent life.

In September, her sister Hortense left the convent-school. A distant aunt called her to Niort as a lady companion. In actual fact, that lady, who was of very lowly nobility and had married a rich magistrate of obscure origins, was anxious that her son should add lustre to their dull escutcheon by an alliance with a noble name. The young man's father had just offered him the office of *procureur du Roi*, a King's proctor in Paris, and it was desirable that he should seem at ease among people of high rank. It was an unhoped-for opportunity for both sides. The marriage was promptly arranged.

At the same time, the young King Louis XIV returned victoriously to his great capital.

France emerged bled white from a civil war, in the course of which armies had trampled her soil, seeking, and not always finding, one another: there had been the Prince de Condé's army, the King's led by Turenne, who had suddenly chosen not to turn traitor after all, Gaston d'Orléans's army allied with the English and opposed to the French Princes, the Duc de Beaufort's army at odds with everyone but helped by the Spaniards, the Duc de Lorraine's, which operated on its own account, and finally the army of Mazarin, who had wanted to send reinforcements to the Queen from Germany. Mademoiselle de Montpensier came close to being appointed a general of the army for the initiative she had taken one day in firing the cannon of the Bastille against the troops of her own royal cousin. It was a gesture that was to cost the Grande Demoiselle dearly, for it frightened off a good many suitors among the princes of Europe.

"Mademoiselle had just 'slain' her husband," Cardinal Mazarin had muttered in his soft Abruzzi accent, when he learned of it.

The latter remained the great victor of this mad and horrible crisis. Less than a year afterwards, his red robe could be seen again in the corridors of the Louvre, but there were no more lampoons against him. Everyone's strength was exhausted.

Angélique had turned seventeen when she learned of her mother's death. She prayed a great deal in the chapel, but did not weep. She could not realise that she would never again see the grey-clad figure with the black shawl, which in summer was covered by an old-fashioned straw-hat. Assiduously concerned with the orchard and kitchen-garden, Madame de Sancé had lavished more care and caresses, perhaps, on her pear-trees and cabbages than on her numerous offspring.

On the occasion of her mother's death, Angélique saw her brothers Raymond and Denis again, for they came to announce the news to her. The young girl received them in the parlour, behind the cold grille required by the Ursuline order.

Denis was now at college. In growing up, he had begun to look so much like Josselin that she sometimes thought she was seeing her eldest brother again, with his black schoolboy uniform and the inkhorn at his belt. She was so struck by this resemblance that, after greeting the clergyman who accompanied her brother, she paid no more attention to the former and he had to give his name.

"I am Raymond, Angélique. Don't you recognize me?"

She was almost intimidated. At her convent, which was stricter than most, the nuns considered priests with a devout servility, from which an instinctive female submission to the male was not wholly absent. To hear herself familiarly spoken to by one of them troubled her. Now, she was the one to drop her eyes, while Raymond smiled at her. With much tact, he told her of the misfortune that had befallen them and spoke very simply of the obedience that was owed to God.

Something had changed in his long face with its sallow complexion and clear, ardent eyes.

He also told her of their father's disappointment at the fact that Raymond's religious inclinations had become strengthened during the recent years spent with the Jesuits. With Josselin gone, he had hoped that Raymond would assume the rôle of heir. But the young man had renounced his inheritance in favour of his younger brothers, and had taken his vows. Gontran too was a disappointment to poor Baron Armand. Far from wishing to join the armies, he had gone to Paris to study no one quite knew what. So they would have to wait for Denis, now aged thirteen, to see the name of Sancé recapture the military lustre that was traditional in families of high lineage.

While talking, the Jesuit father kept looking at his sister, this young girl who was leaning her rosy face against the chill bars as she listened to him, and whose strange eyes seemed, in the shadow of the parlour, limpid as sea water. He felt a kind of pity as he asked:

"And you, Angélique, what are you going to do?"

She shook her heavy hair with its golden lustre, and answered indifferently that she did not know.

A year later, Angélique de Sancé was again called into the parlour. Here she found old Guillaume, looking exactly as she remembered him. He had carefully propped his trusty pike against the wall of the cell.

He told her that he had come to fetch her back to Monteloup. Her education was now finished. She was an accomplished young lady, and a husband had been found for her.

PART TWO

Marriage in Toulouse

Chapter 11

THE Baron de Sancé looked at his daughter Angélique with undisguised satisfaction.

"Those nuns have made a perfect young lady of you, my little tomboy."

"Perfect! Oh! Wait and see," protested Angélique, shaking her locks back in a familiar gesture.

The air of Monteloup, with its sweetish scent rising from the marshes, gave her a new spurt of independence. She straightened up like a wilting flower under a pleasant downpour.

But Baron Armand's parental vanity would accept no rebuff.

"Anyway, you are even prettier than I dared to hope. Your complexion is perhaps a little darker than your eyes and hair call for, but the contrast is not unattractive. Besides, I've noticed that most of my children have the same dark complexion. It's the last vestige, I fear, of a drop of Arab blood that the people of Poitou, in general, have kept in their veins. Have you seen your little brother Jean-Marie? A real Moor, one would say!"

Then, abruptly, he said:

"The Comte de Peyrac de Morens has asked your hand in marriage."

"Me?" said Angélique. "But I don't know him!"

"That doesn't matter. Molines knows him, and that's the main thing. He assures me that I could not dream of a more flattering alliance for any of my daughters."

Baron Armand was beaming. He mowed down some primroses with the tip of his stick on the sloping bank along the narrow path where he and his daughter were strolling on this warm April morning.

Angélique had arrived at Monteloup the night before, accompanied by old Guillaume and her brother Denis. As she expressed surprise at seeing the schoolboy on leave, he explained that he had obtained a holiday to attend her wedding.

"What is all this about a wedding?" thought the young girl.

She had not taken the matter seriously, but the Baron's assured tone now began to alarm her.

He had not aged much during the past years; a few grey threads showed in his moustaches and in the small tuft of hair he wore beneath his lip, in the style fashionable during the reign of Louis XIII. Angélique, who had expected to find him depressed and unsure as a consequence of his wife's death, was almost surprised to see him in good spirits and smiling.

As they reached the sloping meadow that overlooked the dry marshes, she tried to change the subject which threatened to create a conflict between them just when they had begun to find each other again.

"You wrote and told me, Papa, that you had serious losses with your cattle due to army requisitioning and looting during the last years of the terrible civil war."

"Sure enough, Molines and I lost practically half our livestock, and without him I'd be in prison for debts by now after selling all my estates."

"Do you still owe him much?" she asked anxiously.

"Unfortunately, out of the forty thousand *livres* he lent me long ago, I have been able to pay him back only about five thousand in the course of five years of desperately hard work. And even those Molines refused to accept, pretending he paid them over to me outright and that they were part of the agreement. I had to get quite angry to make him accept them."

Angélique observed very shrewdly that since the steward himself considered he did not require reimbursement, her father was wrong to persevere in his generosity.

"If that fellow Molines suggested this business in the first place, he was sure to gain by it. He is not the type of man to make you a present, but he has a certain integrity, and if he leaves those forty thousand *livres* to you, he must consider that the trouble you took and the services you've rendered him are well worth it."

"It is true that our little commerce in mules and lead, exempted as it is of taxes on transport to the sea, works fairly well, and in the years free of looting, when one can sell the rest of our output to the State, we cover our expenses, that is true."

He cast a perplexed glance at Angélique.

"But how shrewdly you talk, my daughter! I wonder if such practical and even vulgar speech becomes a young girl who has just left the convent."

Angélique started to laugh.

"It seems that in Paris women manage everything: politics, religion, literature, even sciences. They are called *précieuses*. They meet every day at one another's homes, together with wits and wise men. The mistress of the house lies on her bed, and the guests crowd the narrow passages of the alcove, and there they discourse. I wonder, when I'm in Paris, if I'll create an 'alcove' to discuss commerce and trade."

"What a horror!" cried the Baron, frankly shocked. "Angélique, surely the Ursulines in Poitiers did not give you such ideas."

"They claimed I was extremely good at figures and arguments. Even too good. . . . On the other hand, they were upset about not being able to turn me into a model of devoutness — and hypocrisy, like my sister Hortense. Hortense let them hope she might take the vows, but the attraction of marrying a *procureur* definitely proved more potent."

"My child, you must not be jealous, since Molines, whom you judge severely, has managed to find you a husband who is certainly very much superior to Hortense's husband."

The young girl stamped the ground impatiently.

"Molines really exaggerates! Hearing you talk, wouldn't one think I was his daughter, not yours, that he should take such care of my future?"

"You would be quite wrong to complain of it, my little mule," said her father smiling. "Listen to me. Comte Joffrey de Peyrac is a descendant of the ancient Counts of Toulouse, whose noble heritage goes back even farther than those of our King Louis XIV. Moreover, he is the richest and the most influential man in the Languedoc."

"That may be, Father, but after all I cannot

marry a man whom I don't know, whom you yourself have never seen."

"Why not?" asked the Baron, genuinely surprised. "All young girls of quality get married in this fashion. It can't be left to them or to the accidents of fortune to decide upon alliances that are advantageous to their families, and on establishments that involve not only their future, but their name."

"Is he . . . is he young?" inquired the girl with some hesitation.

"Young? Young?" grumbled the Baron, out of sorts. "What a futile question for a practical-minded person to ask! As a matter of fact, your future husband is twelve years older than you. But the thirties are the age of strength and attraction in a man. Heaven can still grant you numerous children. You will have a palace in Toulouse, castles in Albi and in the Béarn, carriages, fine clothes . . ."

Monsieur de Sancé stopped, his imagination exhausted.

"For my part," he concluded, "I consider that a proposal of marriage by a man who has not seen you either is an extraordinary, unhoped-for stroke of luck."

They walked on a few steps in silence.

"Exactly," murmured Angélique, "I consider this chance rather too extraordinary. Why should this Comte, who has everything that's needed to choose a rich heiress for his wife, go out of his way to seek a girl without a dowry in the depths of Poitou?"

"Without a dowry?" repeated Armand de Sancé,

and his face brightened. "Come back with me to the château, Angélique, and get dressed for an outing. We shall take our horses. I want to show you something."

In the castle yard, at the Baron's order, a groom led two horses out of the stables, and harnessed them quickly. The young girl, much intrigued, asked no more questions. While mounting her horse, she told herself that after all she was destined to marry and that most of her companions got married in this way to suitors whom their parents chose for them. Why, then, did this project revolt her so much? The man who was intended for her was not an old man. She would be rich.

Angélique became aware suddenly that she was experiencing a pleasant physical sensation and it took her a few moments to realize its cause. The hand of the groom who had helped her into her sidesaddle had slid down her ankle and was caressing it softly in a way that, with the best will in the world, could not be taken for absent-mindedness.

The Baron had disappeared into the château to change his boots and put on a fresh neck-band.

Angélique fidgeted nervously and the horse shied a little.

"What's come over you, peasant?"

She felt flushed and furious with herself, for she had to admit that the brief caress had filled her with an exquisite thrill.

The groom, a broad-shouldered Hercules, raised his head. Brown locks of hair fell over dark eyes that glowed with a familiar malice.

"Nicholas!" cried Angélique, while the pleasure

204

of seeing her old playmate and confusion at his having permitted himself so daring a gesture struggled within her.

"Oh, you've recognized Nicholas!" said the Baron de Sancé, coming towards them with long strides. "He's the most mischievous devil in the whole region, nobody can keep him down. Neither tilling the land nor tending mules interests him. Lazy and a touser of wenches, that's what your former companion's become, Angélique."

The young man did not seem at all ashamed of his master's judgment. He continued to gaze at Angélique with a broad smile that disclosed his white teeth, and a boldness that bordered on insolence. His open shirt revealed a broad, dark chest.

"Hey, boy, take a mule and follow us," said the Baron, who had noticed nothing.

"Very good, Master."

The three mounts passed over the drawbridge and set out on the road to the left of Monteloup.

"Where are we going, Father?"

"To the old lead quarry."

"Those crumbling furnaces over by the lands of the Abbey of Nieul?"

"Those very ones."

"I don't know why that bit of barren ground . . ."

"That plot of ground, which is no longer barren and which is now called Argentière, represents, quite simply, your dowry. You remember that Molines had asked me to renew our family's mining rights, as well as to petition for tax exemption on one quarter of the output. After duly obtaining these, he sent for some Saxon workers. Seeing the importance he attached to this hitherto useless ground, I told him one day that I intended to give it to you as a dowry. I believe it's from that day onward that the idea of your marriage to the Comte de Peyrac sprang up in his fertile mind, for that gentleman of Toulouse would indeed like to acquire this land. I do not quite understand the type of business he is up to with Molines. I think he is more or less the consignee of the mules and metals that we send by sea to their Spanish destination. Which proves that there are far more gentlemen than is commonly believed who take an interest in trade. Still, I should have thought that the Comte de Peyrac had enough land and properties not to demean himself to such commoners' practices. But perhaps it amuses him. He's said to be quite an original person."

"If I understand you correctly," said Angélique slowly, "you knew that someone coveted this mine and you made it clear that your daughter had to be taken with it."

"You do present things in a peculiar light, Angélique! I think that this solution of giving you the mine as dowry was excellent. The desire to see my daughters well established has been my principal concern, as it used to be your poor mother's. But in our family, we do not sell our land. Despite the worst hardships, we have succeeded in keeping our patrimony intact, even though du Plessis more than once has cast an envious eye on my famous dry marshland. But to marry my daughter off not only honorably, but weathily, is something that really pleases me. The estate will not leave the family, it will not go to a stranger, but to a new branch of the family, a new alliance."

Angélique fell a little behind her father. Thus he could not see the expression on her face. The girl's small white teeth were biting her lip with impotent rage. She could not explain to her father how humiliated she felt by the way in which this proposal of marriage had been brought about, even less so since he was so obviously convinced that he had very astutely assured his daughter's happiness. She tried, however, to keep on fighting.

"If I remember rightly, didn't you rent this quarry to Molines for ten years? So there'd still remain four years to run. How can you give this plot in dowry when it is rented?"

"Molines is not only agreeable, but he will continue to work the mine for the Comte de Peyrac. We're almost there."

After an hour's ride they reached the place. Angélique formerly thought that this black quarry and its Protestant villages were situated at the end of the world. But now it seemed quite close. The well-kept road confirmed this new impression. A small hamlet had been built for the workmen.

Father and daughter slipped down to the ground and Nicholas approached to take the horses' reins.

The desolate-looking place that Angélique remembered had changed completely. A system of water-mains brought running water and worked several upright millstones. Cast-iron pounders were crushing stones with a dull thud, while heavy blocks of rock were split by manual sledgehammers. Two furnaces were glowing and enormous leather bellows made the flames kindle. Black mountains of charcoal rose next to the furnaces, and the rest of the mining-site was occupied by heaps of stones. Into the wooden spouts through which the water flowed, the workmen shoveled the sand from the rocks as they left the grindstones. Others, with hoes, raked the contents of the pipes against the current.

A fairly tall building, set farther back, had gates with fences and iron bars and was locked with big padlocks. Two men armed with muskets stood watch nearby.

"The reserve of silver and lead ingots," said the Baron.

He added very proudly that he would ask Molines some time in the near future to show the contents to Angélique.

He then took her over to the adjacent quarry. Enormous tiers, each four yards high, now turned it into a sort of Roman amphitheatre. Here and there, black underground passages burrowed into the rock, from which emerged small donkey-driven carts.

"We have ten Saxon families living here — professional miners, metal-founders and quarrymen. They and Molines together have set up this mine."

"And the business yields how much profit per year?" asked Angélique.

"Why, that's a question I never asked myself," confessed Armand de Sancé, a trifle shamefaced. "You see, Molines pays me his rent regularly. He's paid the whole cost of installation. The furnace bricks come from England and perhaps even from

Spain, brought by smugglers' caravans from the Languedoc."

"Through the intermediary, I presume, of the man you intend me to marry?"

"That is possible. It appears he has his finger in no end of pies. Besides, he is a scientist and actually designed the plan of this steam machine."

The Baron led his daughter to the entrance of one of the low galleries cut into the mountainside. He showed her a sort of enormous iron cauldron under which a fire was kept burning, and from which protruded two thick pipes, wrapped in cloth, that led into a well. At regular intervals a jet of water spurted from it on to the surface of the ground.

"It's one of the first steam machines that have ever been built. It serves to pump out the subterranean water from the mine. It's an invention which the Comte de Peyrac perfected during one of his stays in England. You see that, for a woman who wants to become a *précieuse*, here's a husband as learned and brilliant as I am slow and ignorant," he added, making a pitiful face. "Ah; good morning, Fritz Hauer."

One of the workmen who stood near the machine removed his bonnet and bowed deeply. His face looked as though it had been turned blue by rock dust encrusted in his skin in the course of his long career in mining. Two fingers were missing from one of his hands. Stocky and hump-backed as he was, one would have said that his arms were overlong. Strands of hair fell into his small, sparkling eyes.

"I think he looks rather like Vulcan, the god

of Hell," said Monsieur de Sancé. "It seems there's not a man alive who knows the entrails of the earth better than this Saxon workman. That's perhaps why he has such an odd appearance. All these mining problems have never seemed quite clear to me, and I don't know to what extent witchcraft may be involved in it. It is said that Fritz Hauer knows a secret process for transforming lead into gold. Now that really would be extraordinary. However that may be, he's been working for the Comte de Peyrac for several years and was sent by him to Poitou to set up Argentière."

"The Comte de Peyrac! Always the Comte de Peyrac!" thought Angélique, exasperated.

She said aloud:

"Perhaps that's why he's so rich, this Comte de Peyrac. He turns the lead this Fritz Hauer sends him into gold. Next thing we'll know he'll turn me into a leap-frog. . . ."

"You really pain me, my child! Why this sarcastic tone? One would think I was seeking to cause you misfortune. Nothing in this project can in the least justify your distrust. I expected shouts of joy and hear nothing but taunts."

"That's true, Papa, forgive me," said Angélique, contrite and grieved by the disappointment she could read in the seigneur's honest face. "The nuns often said that I wasn't like the other girls and that my moods were disconcerting. I won't conceal from you that this marriage proposal, far from delighting me, strikes me as extremely unpleasant. Give me time to think it over, to get used to it. . . ."

While talking, they had returned to where the

horses were tethered. Angélique quickly mounted into the saddle, in order to avoid Nicholas's too eager assistance, but she could not prevent the groom's brown hand brushing her arm as he handed her the reins.

"This is very embarrassing," she thought to herself, annoyed. "I shall have to put him severely in his place."

The narrow paths were flowering with hawthorn. The exquisite scent, which reminded her of the days of her childhood, somewhat appeased the girl's restiveness.

"Father," she said suddenly, "I gather that, with regard to the Comte de Peyrac, you would like me to come to a decision soon. I have just had an idea. Will you allow me to ride over to Molines? I should like to have a serious talk with him."

The Baron glanced at the sun in order to guess the time.

"It is almost noon. But I imagine Molines will be delighted to receive you at his table. Go ahead, my daughter. Nicholas will accompany you."

Angélique was about to refuse this escort, but she did not want to appear to attach the slightest importance to the peasant boy, and after waving a gay goodbye to her father, she rode off at a gallop. The groom, who was riding a mule, was soon left far behind.

Half an hour later, Angélique, passing in front of the gate of the Château du Plessis, stooped forward to see if she could make out a white apparition at the far end of the chestnut avenue.

"Philippe," she thought and was surprised that

this name should have arisen again in her memory as if to add to her melancholy.

But the du Plessis were still in Paris. Although a former supporter of Monsieur de Condé, the Marquis had managed to ingratiate himself with the Queen and Cardinal Mazarin again, whereas the Prince, the victor of Rocroi, one of the most glorious of France's Generals, had, to his disgrace, gone to serve the King of Spain in Flanders. Angélique wondered whether the disappearance of the poison-casket had played some part in Condé's destiny. At any rate, neither Cardinal Mazarin nor the King and his young brother had been poisoned. And it was said that Monsieur de Fouquet, the leader of the plot against His Majesty, had just been appointed Controller-General of Finances.

It was amusing to think that a little, unknown country-girl had perhaps changed the course of history. One day she would have to make sure that the casket was still in its hiding-place. And the page she had accused, what had become of him? Bah! that was of no importance.

Angélique heard the gallop of Nicholas's mule behind her. She spurred her horse on and soon arrived at the steward's house.

After the meal, Molines ushered Angélique into his small study, where some years before he had received her father. It was here that the mule trade had first started, and the young girl suddenly remembered the ambiguous answer the steward had given to the question of the practical-minded child she had then been:

"And what will you give *me?*"

"We'll give you a husband."

Had he already thought of an alliance with that strange Comte from Toulouse? It was not impossible, for Molines was a man who thought far ahead and whose mind entertained a thousand schemes at once. Actually, the steward of the neighbouring château was not unlikeable. His somewhat wily demeanour was inherent in his subordinate station, for he was a subordinate who knew himself to be more intelligent than his masters.

For the neighbouring seigneur's family, his intervention had been a real godsend, but Angélique knew that the steward's self-interest alone was at the root of his generosity and his aid. That pleased her, removing as it did any scruple of considering herself under an obligation to him or owing him any humiliating gratitude. She was surprised, however, by the genuine sympathy that this calculating Huguenot commoner inspired in her.

"It's because he is creating something new, something solid, perhaps," she thought suddenly.

On the other hand, she was far from ready to form a part of the steward's projects, like a she-donkey or an ingot of lead.

"Monsieur Molines," she said flatly, "my father has spoken to me seriously of a marriage that *you* appear to have arranged for me with a certain Comte de Peyrac. In view of the very considerable influence you have acquired over my father during the last years, I cannot doubt that you too attach great importance to this marriage, that is to say that I am called upon to play a part in your business dealings. I should very much like to know precisely what part."

213

A cold smile stretched the steward's narrow lips.

"I thank Heaven that I have found you as you promised to become when the people hereabout called you the Little Fairy of the Marshes. In fact, I promised the Comte de Peyrac a lovely and intelligent wife."

"A rash commitment. I might have turned out ugly and stupid, and that would have greatly harmed your trade as a procurer."

"I never commit myself on a mere presumption. I had news of you repeatedly through contacts I have in Poitiers, and I myself saw you during last year's procession there."

"So you had me watched," cried Angélique furiously, "like a melon ripening under glass!"

At the same time, the picture struck her as so funny that she burst out laughing and her anger subsided. At heart, she preferred to know where she stood rather than to let herself be trapped like some silly little goose.

"If I wanted to indulge in the language of your society," said Molines gravely, "I might confine myself to traditional considerations: a girl, a very young one, too, has no need to know why her parents choose this or that husband for her. The lead and silver business, trade and Customs, do not come within the province of women, especially of noble ladies. . . . Even less so does the business of animal breeding. But I know you, Angélique, and I shall not talk to you in this fashion."

She was not shocked by this familiar attitude.

"Why do you think you can talk to me differently than to my father?"

"That is difficult to put into words, Mademoiselle. I am not a philosopher, and my studies have consisted above all in practical experience. Forgive me for being very frank, but there's something I want to tell you. The people of your world will never be able to understand what spurs me: it's *work*."

"Peasants work even harder, I should have thought."

"They drudge, that's not the same thing. They are dull, ignorant and don't realize their own interests, just like the nobility who, for their part, *do not produce anything*. The latter are useless creatures, except when it comes to waging destructive wars. Your father is beginning to do something useful but, if you will forgive me, *he will never understand the meaning of work*."

"You think he will not succeed?" said the girl, suddenly alarmed. "I thought his business was doing nicely, and that your interest in it was the proof of it."

"Proof of it would be, more than anything else, that we produced several thousand mules a year, and the second and most important proof would be that the enterprise yielded a substantial and *increasing* income: that is the real sign of a business that's doing well."

"Well, isn't that what we'll achieve some day?"

"No, because stock-breeding, even on a large scale and supported by capital for bad times — sickness or wars — still remains stock-breeding. It's like husbandry, a tedious business that yields little. Besides, neither tilling nor breeding has ever really produced riches for anyone: remember the example of the enormous herds of the shepherds

215

in the Bible, who yet lived most frugally."

"If that is your conviction, I fail to understand, Monsieur Molines, why you, who are so cautious, have thrown yourself into this slow and relatively unprofitable business."

"That, Mademoiselle, is where your father and I have need of you."

"I surely cannot help to make your she-donkeys foal twice as quickly."

"You can help us to double our income."

"I cannot see how."

"You will easily grasp my idea. What matters in a profitable business is quick returns, but since we cannot change the laws of God, we must turn to account the feebleness of the mind of man. Thus it is that the mule business is mere window-dressing. It covers our expenses, puts us on excellent terms with the Quartermaster-General's department to which we sell hides and pack-animals. Our mules enable us above all to travel freely, exempt from Customs or toll dues, and to put heavily laden caravans on to the roads. We thus despatch, with a quota of mules, lead and silver for shipment to England. On their way back the mules carry sacks of black slag which we christen 'flux,' necessary products for mine-working, but which are in fact *gold* and *silver*, and come straight from warring Spain via London."

"I no longer follow you, Monsieur Molines. Why do you send silver to London if it is to be brought back afterwards?"

"I bring back double or triple the quantity. As for the gold, the Comte de Peyrac owns a gold-mine in Languedoc. When the mine of the

Argentière is his, the exchanges I shall transact for him on these two precious metals will no longer seem in any way suspicious, since both gold and silver will be coming officially from the two mines he owns. Therein consists our *real* business. For, understand this: the gold and silver that can be mined in France amounts to very little; on the other hand, we can get into the country, without tax, toll or Customs dues, a great quantity of Spanish gold and silver. The ingots I present to the money-changers do not talk. They cannot confess that instead of coming from Argentière or Languedoc they actually come from Spain by way of London. Thus, while passing on a legal profit to the Treasury, we can, under cover of mining work, import a substantial quantity of precious metals, without paying labour or taxes, and without ruining ourselves by extensive installations, for no one can guess how much we produce here and they must trust the figures we declare."

"But if this traffic is discovered, isn't there a risk it may send you to the galleys?"

"We don't manufacture counterfeit coins, nor have we any intention of ever doing so. On the contrary, we regularly supply the Royal Treasury with good, sound gold and silver bullion which the Treasury checks, stamps and mints. But once the mines of Argentière and Languedoc are united under the same name, we shall then be able, under cover of these tiny national extractions, to make rapid profits on the precious metals from Spain. That country is crammed with gold and silver shipped from the Americas; Spain has lost all taste for work and lives entirely by bartering its raw materials with other countries. The banks of London serve as their intermediaries. Spain is both the richest and the most wretched country in the world. As for France, these commercial transactions, which poor economic management prevent her from carrying out in the open, will enrich her almost in spite of herself. And they'll enrich us, too, for the sums invested will bring a quicker and more substantial return than the marketing of the she-asses which require ten months for gestation and don't yield more than ten per cent at most on the invested capital."

Angélique could not help being fascinated by these ingenious plans.

"And what do you plan to do with the lead?"

"Lead has a very good yield. It's needed for warfare and for hunting. It has grown even more valuable these last years since the Queen Mother sent for Florentine engineers to complete the installation of bathrooms in all her residences, as her mother-in-law, Catherine of Medici, had already done before her. You must have seen a model of one of those rooms at the Château of Plessis, with its Roman bath and all its lead pipes."

"Does your master, the Marquis, know of these various projects?"

"No," said Molines with an indulgent smile. "He would not understand anything about them, and the least he'd do would be to remove me from my office as steward of his domains, even though I perform my duties to his complete satisfaction."

"And how much does my father know of your trafficking in gold and silver?"

"I thought that the mere fact of knowing that

Spanish metals travel over his estates would displease him. Is it not preferable to let him believe that the small revenues that ensure his living are the fruit of honest and traditional toil?"

Angélique felt shocked by the somewhat disdainful irony that pierced through the steward's tone of voice. She said dryly:

"And why am I entitled to hear you disclose your underhand schemes?"

"I know that you will kick against the traces as long as you cannot understand the reason for them. The problem is a simple one, in fact. The Comte de Peyrac needs Argentière. And your father won't give up this plot unless it serves to establish one of his daughters. You know how obstinate he is. He will never sell a scrap of his patrimony. The Comte de Peyrac, on the other hand, being desirous to marry into a family of good nobility, had found the combination to his advantage."

"And if I refuse to share his views?"

"You do not wish your father to be imprisoned for debts," said the steward slowly. "It wouldn't take much to reduce you all to even greater poverty than was once your lot. And what would be your own future? You'd grow old in squalor, like your aunts. . . . For your brothers and younger sisters it would mean lack of education, and later the need to go abroad for a livelihood. . . ."

Seeing the girl's eyes sparkle with anger, he added in an ingratiating voice:

"But why force me to sketch such a black picture? I thought you were made of a different stamp than those noblemen who are content with a coat

219

of arms for their only sustenance and who live off the King's alms. . . . You can't get out of difficulties without grasping them resolutely and doing your share. That means you must act. That's why I have not concealed anything from you, so that you shall know how to apply your efforts."

No words could have touched Angélique more directly. Nobody had ever spoken to her in a way more closely in line with her character. She straightened up as if under the lash of a whip. She recalled Monteloup in ruins, her young brothers and sisters wallowing in the dung, her mother with fingers reddened by the cold, and her father seated at his small desk, carefully writing a petition to the King, who had never answered. . . .

The steward had pulled them out of their wretchedness. Now the time had come to pay.

"Very well, Monsieur Molines," she said in a toneless voice. "I shall marry the Comte de Peyrac."

Chapter 12

ANGÉLIQUE rode back through the fragrant paths, absorbed in her thoughts, seeing nothing.

Nicholas followed on his mule. She no longer paid heed to the young groom. She tried, however, not to examine too closely the feeling of fright that kept stirring in her. Her mind was made up. Whatever happened, she would not look back. So

the best was to look forward and grimly reject anything that might cause her to waver in carrying out such a well-planned programme.

Suddenly a male voice called out to her:

"Mademoiselle! Mademoiselle Angélique!"

She pulled on the reins mechanically, and her horse came to a stop.

Turning round, Angélique saw that Nicholas had dismounted and was motioning to her to join him.

"What's the matter?" she asked.

Rather mysteriously, he whispered: "Get down, I want to show you something."

She obeyed, and the groom, after tethering both mounts to the trunk of a young birch-tree, preceded her into the shelter of a small wood. She followed him. The light of spring shining through the tender leaves was the color of angelica. A chaffinch whistled ceaselessly in the thicket.

Nicholas walked with lowered head, carefully looking around. Finally he knelt down and, as he got up again, he held cupped in his open palms some fragrant red fruit.

"The first strawberries," he murmured, while the malice of his smile lit a flame in his chestnut eyes.

"Oh, Nicholas, this isn't right," protested Angélique.

But emotion made tears rise suddenly to the edge of her eyelashes, for with this gesture he was proffering her all the charm of her childhood, the charm of Monteloup, the races through the woods, the dreams scented with hawthorn, the coolness of the canals where Valentine used to take her, the brooks in which they fished for crayfish —

Monteloup which resembled no other place on earth, because in it mingled the sickly-sweet mystery of the marshes, the pungent mystery of the forests. . . .

"Do you remember," he murmured, "what we used to call you? Marquise of the Angels . . ."

"You are silly," she said in a brittle voice. "You oughtn't to, Nicholas . . ."

But already she was picking, with an old familiar gesture, the small delicious berries out of his offering hands. Nicholas stood quite close to her, as in the old days, but now the lithe, lean boy with his squirrel face towered over her by a head, and through his open shirt-front she breathed the rustic smell of manly skin, tanned and covered with black hair. She saw his powerful chest slowly rise and fall, and she felt so stirred she did not dare to raise her head, certain that, if she did so, she would meet his bold, burning eyes.

She continued to taste the strawberries, concentrating on this delight, which for her was priceless indeed.

"For the last time Monteloup!" she thought. "I am savouring it for the last time! All that I ever loved best is contained in these hands, in Nicholas's brown hands. . . ."

When she was finished, she suddenly closed her eyes and leaned her head against an oak-trunk.

"Listen, Nicholas . . ."

"I am listening," he answered in dialect.

She felt his hot breath, with its tang of cider on her cheek. He was so close, almost pressed against her, that the radiance of his massive presence enveloped her entirely. Yet he did not touch her and, looking at him, she suddenly saw that he had put his hands behind his back to resist the temptation to seize her. She met the shock of his steady gaze, in which there was no trace of a smile, but only a brooding prayer that left no room for doubt. Never had Angélique sensed so strongly the attraction of the male; never had she heard a clearer confession of the desire aroused by her beauty. The whim of the Poitiers page-boy had been but a game, an astringent experiment by two young animals testing their claws.

This was something else, something powerful and hard, as old as the world, as the earth, as the storm.

The pure young girl took fright. More experienced, she would not have been able to resist so potent an appeal. Her flesh stirred, her legs trembled, but she shrank back like a doe before the hunter. Fear of the unknown that awaited her, of the peasant's contained violence, held her back.

"Don't look at me like that, Nicholas," she said, trying to make her voice firm, "I want to tell you . . ."

"I know what you want to tell me," he interrupted her moodily. "I can read it in your eyes and in the way you hold your head. You are Mademoiselle de Sancé and I am a farmhand . . . and now it's all over with us two, even looking each other in the face. I've to keep my head lowered! Very good, Mademoiselle, yes, Mademoiselle. . . . And your eyes will pass over me, without even seeing me. . . . No more than they see a rock, less than a dog. There are some noble ladies in their châteaux who let themselves be washed by their lackey, because what's a lackey? What matter if you show yourself naked before him? . . . A lackey isn't a man, he's a thing . . . a thing that serves. Is that how you are going to treat me from now on?"

"Be silent, Nicholas."

"Yes, I shall be silent."

He breathed violently, but with closed lips, like a sick animal.

"I want to tell you just one last thing before I am silent," he resumed. "And that is that there's never been anyone but you in my life. I understood it only after you had gone, and for several days I was as though mad. It's true that I'm lazy, a touser of wenches, and that I loathe the land and beasts. I am like something that's not in its place and that keeps wandering here and there without knowing why. My only place is you. When you came back, I couldn't wait to know if you were still mine, if I'd lost you. Yes, I am bold and speak freely. Yes, if you'd been willing, I would have taken you, here on the moss, in this little copse that is ours, on this earth of Monteloup that is ours, ours alone as it used to be!" he cried.

The frightened birds had fallen silent in the trees.

"You're raving, my poor Nicholas," said Angélique gently.

"Don't," said the man, growing pale under his tan.

She shook her long hair and a spark of anger flashed in her.

"How do you expect me to talk to you?" she said, also speaking in dialect. "Whether I wish it or not, I am no longer free to listen to shepherd's gallantries. I am shortly to marry the Comte de Peyrac."

"The Comte de Peyrac!" repeated Nicholas, dumbfounded.

He stepped back and considered her in silence.

"So it's true what they say in the village?" he breathed. "The Comte de Peyrac. You! . . . You are going to marry that man?"

"Yes."

She did not want to ask any questions. She had said yes, that was enough. She would say yes, blindly, to the very end.

She took the little path that led her back to the road, and her whip lashed the tender shoots along the roadside nervously. The horse and mule were browsing together at the edge of the forest. Nicholas untied them. With lowered eyes he helped Angélique to mount. Suddenly she gripped the groom's rough hand.

"Nicholas, tell me . . . do you know him?"

He raised his eyes and she saw in them a gleam of vicious irony.

"Yes . . . I've seen him — he's been to these parts a number of times. He is so ugly that the girls run away when he passes on his black horse. He's lame like the devil and just as wicked. . . . People say that he lures women to his castle in Toulouse with philtres and strange songs. . . . Those who follow him are never seen again, or else they go mad. . . . Ha! Ha! Ha! What a fine husband, Mademoiselle de Sancé!"

"You say he's lame?" repeated Angélique, whose hands were growing ice-cold.

"Yes, lame! lame! Ask anyone and they'll tell you: The Great Lame Devil of Languedoc!"

He began to laugh and walked towards the mule, imitating an exaggerated limp.

Angélique whipped her steed which flew into a gallop. She fled through the hawthorn bushes away from the sneering voice that kept crying: "Lame devil! Lame devil!"

She arrived in the courtyard of Monteloup just as a rider crossed the old drawbridge behind her. His perspiring dusty face and his hide-bottomed trunk-hose showed at once that he was a messenger. At first no one understood what he was asking for. His accent was so extraordinary that it took some time to grasp that he was actually speaking French. To Monsieur de Sancé, who arrived at the run, he handed an envelope that he pulled out of a small iron box.

"Good Lord, Monsieur d'Andijos is arriving tomorrow!" cried the Baron, greatly excited.

"And who may that be?" inquired Angélique.

"He's a friend of the Comte. Monsieur d'Andijos is to marry you. . . ."

"What, he too?"

". . . by proxy, Angélique. Let me finish my sentences, child. *Ventre Saint-Gris,* as your grandfather would have said, I wonder what those nuns have taught you, if they haven't even instilled into you the respect you owe me. The Comte de Peyrac is sending his best friend to represent him at the first marriage ceremony, which will take place here in the chapel of Monteloup. The second blessing will be given at Toulouse. That one, alas, your family will not be able to attend. The Marquis d'Andijos will escort you on your journey to the Languedoc. These southern people are awfully quick. I knew they were on their way but I did not expect them so soon."

"I can see it was high time I accepted," murmured Angélique bitterly.

Next day, a little before noon, the courtyard filled with creaking carriage-wheels, neighing horses, resounding shouts and garrulous voices.

The south had come to Monteloup. The Marquis d'Andijos, very swarthy, his moustache trimmed to "dagger-points," with glowing eyes, wore petticoat-breeches of yellow and orange silk which gracefully concealed the paunch of a *bon vivant*. He introduced his companions who were to be witnesses of the marriage, the Comte de Carbon-Dorgerac and little Baron Cerbalaud.

They were ushered into the dining-room, where the de Sancé family had set out, on trestle tables, their greatest riches: honey from their hives, fruit, curdled milk, roast geese, wines from the hills of Chaillé. The new arrivals were dying of thirst. But the Marquis d'Andijos had hardly taken a sip before he turned round and spat with precision on the tiled floor.

"By Saint Paulin, Baron, your Poitou wines revolt my tongue! What you've poured out is a tooth-grinder as tart as they come. Ho, Gascons! Bring in the barrels!"

His forthright simplicity, his singsong accent, the smell of garlic on his breath, far from displeasing the Baron, actually delighted him.

As for Angélique, she had not even the strength to smile. Ever since the night before, she had worked so hard with Aunt Pulchérie and Fantine to give the château a presentable appearance that she felt stiff and aching in all her bones. It was better that way: she could not even think any more. She had slipped into the finest dress made for her in Poitiers, which, though still grey, was enlivened with little blue bows at the bodice. She did not know that her warm face, firm but soft like a fruit that is not yet fully ripe, emerging from the wide stiff lace collar, was in itself the most dazzling ornament. The eyes of the three gentlemen turned continually towards her with an admiration which their temperament was unable to conceal. They began to pay her countless compliments. She grasped only half of them on account of their rapid talk and that incredible accent which made even the flattest words ricochet in a shower of sunbeams.

"Shall I have to hear this kind of talk all my life?" she wondered with annoyance.

Meanwhile, the lackeys were rolling into the hall huge barrels, which they hoisted onto trestles and which were promptly tapped. Hardly had a hole been made than they stopped it with a wooden spigot. But the first jet left big puddles on the floor which shone with a transparent pink and golden-brown light.

"Saint-Emilion," commented the Comte de Carbon-Dorgerac, who came from Bordeaux, "Sauternes, Médoc. . . ."

Used to their apple wine or sloe-juice, the inhabitants of the castle of Monteloup tasted these

229

different wines with circumspection. But soon Denis and the three youngest boys became very gay. The exhilarating aroma went to their heads. Angélique felt pervaded by a stronge sense of well-being. She saw her father laugh, open his old-fashioned jerkin without bothering about the threadbare linen underneath. And the southern gentlemen were already unfastening their short sleeveless waistcoats. One of them even removed his periwig to wipe his brow; he put it back somewhat askew.

Marie-Agnès, gripping her elder sister's arm, was shouting into her ear with a piercing voice:
"Angélique, do come! Angélique, come and look, up in your room, such marvels! . . ."
She let herself be dragged upstairs. Into the vast room, in which she had slept for so long with Hortense and Madelon, had been carried big iron-and-leather coffers which were called *"garde-robes."* The maids and man-servants had opened them and had spread their contents out on the floor and on some rickety armchairs. On the enormous bed Angélique saw a taffeta dress of the same green tint as her eyes. An exquisitely fine lace trimmed the boned bodice, and the front of the *busquière* was entirely covered with diamond and emerald embroideries in the shape of flowers. The same flower pattern was reproduced on the cut velvet of the mantle which was deep black. Diamond clasps kept it in place at the sides of the skirt.
"Your wedding dress," said the Marquis d'Andijos, who had followed the two girls. "The

Comte de Peyrac searched for a long time among the dress materials he had ordered from Lyons, for a colour to match your eyes."

"He has never seen them," Angélique protested.

"Monsieur Molines described them to him with care: the sea, he said, as it looks from the beach as the sun plunges into its depths."

"Molines be damned!" cried the Baron. "You won't have me believe that he is such a poet. I suspect you, Marquis, of embellishing the truth in order to bring a smile to the eyes of a young bride, flattered by such attention on the part of her husband."

"And this! And this! Look, Angélique!" repeated Marie-Agnès, whose shrewd little mouse-face shone with excitement.

Together with her two young brothers, Albert and Jean-Marie, she lifted up the dainty lingerie, opened boxes in which lay ribbons and lace ornaments, or parchment and feather fans. There was a delightful travelling-case of green velvet lined with white damask, mounted with silver gilt, and fitted with two brushes, a gold box with three combs, two small Italian mirrors, a square pin cushion, two bonnets and a fine linen nightgown, an ivory candlestick and a green satin bag containing six candles of virgin wax.

There were also some simpler but very elegant dresses, gloves, belts, a small gold watch and no end of things whose use Angélique could not even guess at, among them a small mother-of-pearl box which contained a selection of black velvet patches lined with gummed taffeta.

"It's considered good form," explained the

Comte de Carbon, "to affix these little beauty-spots to certain parts of your face."

"My complexion is not white enough to need stressing," Angélique declared, closing the box.

Overwhelmed, she wavered on the verge of childish joy, of feminine delight as, with an instinctive taste for ornaments and beauty, she became aware of them for the first time.

"And this," asked the Marquis d'Andijos, "does your complexion refuse to share its sparkle, too?"

He opened a flat jewel-case, and in the room thronged with maids, lackeys and farmhands, there rose a cry followed by murmurs of admiration.

On the white satin gleamed a triple row of pearls of a very pure, slightly golden hue. Nothing could have been more becoming for a young bride. Earrings completed the set, along with two rows of smaller pearls that Angélique at first took for bracelets.

"They are meant to adorn the hair," explained the Marquis d'Andijos who, despite his plumpness and his warrior's manners, seemed very well up in ladies' fashions. "You put up your hair. But to be frank, I can't exactly tell you how."

"I shall dress Madame's hair," broke in a tall, sturdy maid-servant, stepping forward.

Though younger, she strangely resembled the nurse, Fantine Lozier. The same Saracen flame had burnished her skin. She and Fantine were already casting hostile glances at each other out of the same dark eyes.

"That's Marguerite, called Margot, the Comte de Peyrac's foster-sister. This woman has served the great ladies of Toulouse and for many years followed her masters to Paris. She will henceforward be your chambermaid."

The maid skilfully lifted up the heavy auburn hair and imprisoned it in the interlacing pearl ornament. Then, with an unrelenting hand, she removed from Angélique's ears the modest little stones the Baron de Sancé had offered his daughter for her first communion, and fastened the sumptuous jewels instead. Then it was time for the necklace.

"Oh! this calls for a more low-cut neckline," cried little Baron Cerbalaud, whose eyes, as dark as wild blackberries after rain, tried to divine the young girl's graceful form.

The Marquis d'Andijos hit him lightly on the head with his stick.

A page rushed forward, holding a mirror.

Angélique saw herself in her new splendour. Everything about her seemed to shine, even her smooth skin, faintly tinted pink at the cheeks. A sudden glow of pleasure rose in her, flushed her lips, which opened in a delightful smile.

"I am beautiful," she said to herself.

But then everything grew hazy, and from the depth of the mirror seemed to rise the horrible sneer:

"Lame devil! Lame devil! And as ugly as sin. What a fine husband, Mademoiselle de Sancé!"

The marriage by proxy took place a week later, and the festivities lasted three days. There was dancing in all the neighbouring villages, and on the wedding-night there was a display of fireworks and rockets at Monteloup.

In the courtyard of the château and in the surrounding fields large tables had been set up and covered with pitchers of wine and cider and all sorts of meats and fruit, which the peasants came to eat, making merry at the expense of the noisy Gascons and Toulousans, whose drums, lutes, violins and nightingale voices mocked the village fiddlers and pipers.

On the eve of the bride's departure for the distant land of Languedoc, a great dinner was laid out in the courtyard of the castle. Among the village notables and the neighbouring gentry who attended were Molines and his wife and daughter.

In the large room where Angélique had so often listened to the creaking of the huge weathervane at night, Fantine helped her to dress. After lovingly brushing the gorgeous hair, she held out to her mistress the turquoise bodice and fastened the bejewelled centre-piece.

"How lovely you are, oh! how lovely, my little treasure!" Fantine sighed, as if regretfully. "Your breasts are so firm, they won't need all those stays to support them. Mind those bodice fronts don't flatten them. Let them be free and easy."

"Isn't the neck cut too low, Nounou?"

"A great lady must show her breasts. How beautiful you are! And for whom, good God!" she sighed under her breath.

Angélique saw that the face of the old Poitou woman was streaked with tears.

"Don't cry, Nounou. You will take my courage away."

"Alas, you will need it, my child. . . . Bow your head so that I can fasten your necklace. As for the pearl headdress, we'll leave that to Margot: I can't make head or tail of that tangle! . . . Ah, my treasure, what a heartbreak! When I think that this big gawk of a woman, who stinks of garlic and the devil from a hundred metres away, will wash and pluck you on your wedding night! Ah! it breaks my heart!"

She knelt down on the floor to arrange the long train of the dressmantle. Angélique heard her sob. She had not expected such despair, and the anguish that gripped her own heart increased a hundred-fold.

Fantine Lozier, still bending on the floor, murmured:

"Forgive me, my child, that I was not able to defend you, I who suckled you. But I've heard of that man for too many days now; I can no longer close my eyes."

"What do they say of him?"

The nurse straightened up. She had assumed her seer's black, fixed gaze.

"Gold! Crammed with gold is his castle. . . ."

"It's not a sin to possess gold, Nounou. Look at all the presents he has given me. I am delighted with them."

"Make no mistake, my child. This gold is cursed. He creates it with his retorts, his philtres. One of his pages, Henrico, the one who plays the long drum so well, told me that in his palace at Toulouse, a palace red as blood, there is an entire building where no one is allowed to set foot. Its entrance is guarded by a pitch-black man, as black as the bottom of my cooking-pot. One day, when the guardian was away, Henrico saw through the

half-opened door a big hall full of glass-bowls, retorts and pipes that whistled and boiled! And suddenly there was a flame and a clap of thunder.
Henrico ran away."

"That boy is full of imagination, like all the people of the south."

"Alas, there was a note of truth and fear in his
voice that one could not mistake. Oh, he's paid
the devil's own price for his power and wealth,
has the Comte de Peyrac. A Gilles de Retz, that's
what he is, a Gilles de Retz who doesn't even hail
from Poitou!"

"Stop babbling nonsense!" said Angélique
harshly. "Nobody's ever said that he eats little children."

"He lures women by weird spells," whispered
the nurse. "There are orgies in his palace. It seems
the Archbishop of Toulouse denounced him publicly from the pulpit, and spoke of the scandal and
the Evil One. And that heathen of a groom who
told me of it last night in my kitchen roared with
laughter, and said that after that sermon the Comte
de Peyrac gave orders to his men to thrash the
Archbishop's pages and porters, and that there had
been battles right in the cathedral. Can you imagine
such outrages taking place here? And all this gold
he owns, where does he get it? His parents left
him nothing but debts and mortgaged lands. He
is a gentleman who never pays court to the King
or to the great lords. They say that when Monsieur
d'Orléans, the governor of Languedoc, came to
Toulouse, the Comte refused to bend his knee before him on the pretext that this fatigued him,
and when Monsieur pointed out that he might ob-

tain great benefices for him in high places, the Comte de Peyrac answered that —"

Old Fantine broke off and busied herself with pinning up the girl's skirt here and there, although there was no need for it.

"What did he answer?"

"That . . . that stretching out his arm wouldn't make his leg less short. Such insolence!"

Angélique looked at herself in the small round mirror of her travelling case, ran a finger over her eyebrows, which had been carefully plucked by the maid Margot.

"So it's true what they say about his limping?" she asked, trying to keep her voice level.

"Alas, it's true, my baby. Oh Holy Mother, how beautiful you are!"

"Be quiet, Nounou. You tire me with your moaning. Go and fetch Margot to dress my hair, and don't speak of the Comte de Peyrac any more in the way you just did. Don't forget that from now on he is my husband."

At nightfall, torches were lit in the courtyard. The musicians, grouped on the steps in front of the castle in an orchestra of two hurdy-gurdies, a lute, a flute and an oboe, softly accompanied the noisy conversations. Angélique suddenly asked that the village fiddler be sent for so that the villagers might dance in the vast meadow at the foot of the castle. Her ear was not yet accustomed to the daintier music written for the Court and its lace-clad lords. She wanted to hear once more the gentle *musettes* of Poitou and the bold sound of the pipes keeping time with the muffled rhythm of the peasant clogs.

The sky was starry but veiled by a light mist that put a golden halo round the moon. Dishes and fine wines passed unceasingly. A basketful of warm round rolls was placed before Angélique and stayed there until the young woman raised her eyes to the one who was offering it. She saw a tall man dressed in stout cloth of a light grey that identified him as a miller. Since flour cost him little, he had powdered his hair as plentifully as any member of the landed gentry. His collar and canons were of fine linen.

"Here is Valentine, the miller's son, who's paying his respects to the bride," cried Baron Armand.

"Valentine," said Angélique with a smile, "I have not seen you since my return. Do you still go up the canals in your boat, to pick angelica for the monks of Nieul?"

The young man bowed very low, but did not reply. He waited till she had helped herself, then lifted the basket and passed it on. He was soon lost in the crowd and the darkness.

"Taste this, you simply must," said Marquis d'Andijos into her ear.

He was offering her a dish that looked unprepossessing but had a most subtle smell.

"It's a *ragoût* of green truffles, Madame, freshly come from Périgord. You must know that the truffle is divine and magical. There is no dish more sought after to prepare the body of a young bride to receive her husband's homage. The truffle warms the body, enlivens the blood and makes the skin more receptive to caresses."

"Well, I see no necessity for tasting them to-night," said Angélique coldly, pushing the silver bowl away. "Considering I shall not meet my husband for several weeks . . ."

"But you should prepare for it, Madame. Believe me, the truffle is the best friend of Hymen. On this delicious diet you'll be all tenderness on your wedding-night."

"In my country," said Angélique, looking him full in the face with a little smile, "we cram geese with fennel before Christmas to make their meat tastier for the night when they'll be eaten as a roast."

The Marquis, slightly tipsy, roared with laughter.

"Oh! How I'd like to be the one who'll gobble up the little goose that you are!" he said, bending down so close that his moustache brushed her cheek. "May God damn me!" he added, straightening himself, his hand over his heart, "if I let myself be carried away to utter any more unseemly words. Alas, I am not entirely to blame, for I have been deceived. When my friend Joffrey de Peyrac asked me to fulfil the rôle and formalities of a husband at your side without enjoying his delightful rights, I made him swear that you were humpbacked and cross-eyed, but I can see that once again he took no trouble to spare me torment. You really won't try these truffles?"

"No, thank you."

"Then I shall eat them," he said with a pitiful grimace which, in any other circumstances, would have made the young woman laugh, "though I am a bogus husband, and a bachelor to boot. And

I hope that nature will favour me by bringing me on this festive night some ladies or damsels less cruel-hearted than yourself."

She made an effort to smile at his follies. The candelabra and torches were producing an unbearable heat. There was not a breath of air. People sang and drank. There was a heavy smell of wines and sauces.

Angélique passed a finger over her temples and found them moist.

"What's the matter with me?" she thought, "I feel as if I were going to burst all of a sudden, shout words of hate at them. Why? . . . Papa is happy. He's marrying me off in almost princely fashion. The aunts are jubilant. The Comte de Peyrac has sent them big necklaces of Pyrénées stones and all sorts of frippery. My brothers and sister will be well educated. And why should *I* complain? They warned us, at the convent, against romantic day-dreams. A rich and titled husband, is not that the first aim of a woman of quality?"

A shiver seized her. Yet she was not tired. It was a nervous reaction, a physical revolt of all her being, which was yielding at the most unexpected moment.

"Am I afraid? Those tales of Nounou's again, gleefully seeing the devil everywhere. Why should I believe her? She always did exaggerate. Neither Molines nor my father concealed the fact that the Comte de Peyrac is a scientist. It is a far cry from that to imagining goodness knows what devilish orgies. If Nounou really believed that I might fall into the clutches of such a creature, she would not let me go. No, I am not afraid of that. I don't believe it."

The Marquis d'Andijos, at her side, a napkin under his chin, was raising a juicy truffle in one hand, a glass of Bordeaux in the other. He declaimed in a slightly raucous voice while his accent occasionally subsided into a contented hiccup:

"Oh divine truffle, lovers' boon! Pour into my veins the joyous rapture of love! I shall caress my mistress till dawn. . . ."

"That's what I refuse," thought Angélique suddenly, "that's what I'll never bear."

She visualized the horrible, misshapen lord to whom she would be delivered up as a prey. In the silent nights of remote Languedoc, that unknown man would have every right over her. She might cry for help, shout, implore. Nobody would come. He had bought her; she'd been sold to him. And that's how it would be to the end of her days!

"That's what they all think but won't say, what they whisper perhaps in the kitchen, among the grooms and maids. That's why there is a sort of pity for me in the eyes of the southern musicians, of that handsome, curly-haired Henrico who beats the long drum so cleverly. But hypocrisy is greater than pity. Only one person sacrificed and so many people contented! Gold and wine flow in torrents. Does it matter what will happen between their master and me? God, I swear it, he'll never put his hands on me. . . ."

She rose, for she felt a terrible rage within her, and the effort to try to control herself almost made her sick. Amid the general hubbub nobody paid

241

any heed to her departure. Noticing the steward whom her father had engaged at Niort, a man named Clément Tonnel, she asked him whether he had seen the groom Nicholas.

"He is in the barn, filling up the bottles, Madame."

The young woman walked on. She moved like a mechanical toy. She did not know why she was looking for Nicholas, but she wanted to see him. Since the scene in the wood, Nicholas had never again raised his eyes to her, confining himself to his duties as a lackey, which he accomplished with care mingled with nonchalance. She found him in the storeroom, where he was pouring wine from the vats into the jugs and decanters which little grooms and pages were constantly carrying to him. He was wearing the yellow house-livery with braided lapels that Monsieur de Sancé had hired for the occasion. Far from seeming ill at ease in this costume, the young peasant was not lacking in style. He straightened up as he saw Angélique, bowed deeply in the manner in which Clément had instructed all the house-servants during the last forty-eight hours.

"I was looking for you, Nicholas."

"Your ladyship . . ."

She glanced at the little pages who were waiting their turn, pitchers in hand.

"Bid a boy take your place for a moment and follow me."

Outside, she once again passed a hand over her brow. No, she had no idea what she was going to do, but excitement filled her and intoxicated her, as did the heady scent of the pools of spilled

242

wine on the floor. She pushed open the door of a nearby barn. Here too there hovered the wine's heavy fragrance. During part of the night the bottles had been filled here. Now the vats were empty and the barn deserted. It was dark and hot.

Angélique put her hands on Nicholas's strong chest. Suddenly she broke down against him, shaking with dry sobs.

"Nicholas," she moaned, "my playmate, tell me it isn't true. They are not going to take me away, they won't give me to him. I am afraid, Nicholas. Hold me, hold me tightly!"

"Your ladyship . . ."

"Stop it!" she cried. "Oh, don't be nasty, not you too!"

She added in a hoarse, panting voice which she hardly recognized as her own:

"Hold me! Hold me tight! That's all I am asking you!"

He seemed to hesitate, then his powerful peasant's arms closed around her tiny waist.

The barn was dark. The warmth of the piles of straw gave off a sort of quivering tension, similar to that of a thunderstorm. Angélique, half-mad and drunk, rolled her forehead against Nicholas's shoulder. Once more she felt surrounded by man's fierce desire, but this time she abandoned herself to it.

"Oh, you are kind," she sighed. "You are my friend. I want you to love me . . . just once. I want to be loved just once by someone young and handsome. Can you understand?"

She linked her arms around his sturdy neck, forced him to bend his face towards her. His breath was scented with hot wine. He sighed:

"Marquise of the Angels . . ."

"Love me," she whispered, her lips against his. "Just once. Then I'll go. Don't you want to? Do you no longer love me?"

His answer was a low growl and he lifted her up in his arms. He tottered through the darkness and flung himself down with her on a pile of straw.

Angélique felt strangely lucid and freed from all human ties. She had entered another world: she was floating above what had always been her life till then. Dazed by the total darkness of the barn, by the oppressive heat and smells, by the novelty of those brutal yet adroit caresses, she tried above all to overcome her natural modesty which caused her to shrink back in spite of herself. She ardently wished that it be done and done quickly. She kept repeating to herself through clenched teeth that the *other* would not be the first to take her. She would thus be avenged. This was the answer she hurled at the gold that thought it could buy everything.

Carefully following the urgings of the man whose breath was now coming ever faster, she gave herself up, accepting everything from him, ready to offer herself obediently under the weight of the body that seemed to be crushing her. . . .

She was on the verge of realizing her vengeance when there was a sudden lantern-flash across the barn, and the horrified shout of a woman by the door. Nicholas, with one leap, had thrown himself aside. Angélique saw a bulky shape rush against the groom. She recognized old Guillaume and grabbed at him as hard as she could as he passed.

Nimbly, Nicholas had already reached the rafters and opened a window. She heard him jump out and run away.

The woman on the threshold kept on shrieking. It was Aunt Jeanne, holding a flagon in one hand, the other placed over her ample, trembling bosom. Angélique let go of Guillaume and threw herself upon her aunt, digging her nails, like claws, into her arms.

"Will you shut up, old madwoman? . . . Do you want a scandal, do you want the Marquis d'Andijos to pack his bags, with his gifts and promises? No more Pyrénées crystal rock and other sweet trifles for you. Shut up or I'll shove my fist into your toothless old mouth!"

From the nearby barns peasants and servants approached, agog; Angélique saw her nurse come, then her father who, despite somewhat uncertain step, continued to watch over the festivities like a good host.

"Was it you, Jeanne, who was shrieking as if the devil were tickling you?"

"Tickling!" yelped the old spinster, out of breath. "Oh Armand, I believe I am dying."

"Whatever for, my dear?"

"I came here to get some wine. And in this barn, I saw . . . I saw . . ."

"Aunt Jeanne saw an animal," broke in Angélique. "She doesn't know if it was a snake or a stone-marten, but really, Aunt, there's no need to get so frightened. You'd better go back to the banquet, they'll bring you some wine."

"That's right," approved the Baron in a thick

voice. "For once in your life try to be of help, Jeanne; it upsets everybody."

"She didn't try to be of help," thought Angélique. "She spied on me, she followed me. During all these years that she's been at the castle, sitting before her tapestry like a spider in its web, she's come to know us all better than we know ourselves; she feels us out; she guesses our secrets. She followed me here. And she asked old Guillaume to hold the lantern for her."

Her fingers still dug into the jelly-like forearm of the fat woman.

"You understand me?" she whispered. "Not a word to anyone before I leave. Otherwise I swear to you I'll poison you with the special herbs I know."

Aunt Jeanne produced a final gurgle and her eyes rolled upward. But the allusion to her necklace, even more than the threat, had already broken her resistance. Compressing her lips, but in silence, she followed her brother out.

A rough hand held Angélique back. With no attempt at gentleness, old Guillaume removed from her hair and dress the wisps of straw that still clung to them. She looked up at him, trying to make out the expression on the bearded face.

"Guillaume," she murmured, "I would like you to know . . ."

"I have no need to know, Madame," he replied in German, with a haughtiness that was like a slap in the face to her. "What I saw was enough for me."

He shook a fist towards the darkness and

growled a curse. She straightened her head and walked back to the feast. As she sat down, her eyes sought the Marquis d'Andijos and found him crumpled up under his stool, blissfully asleep. The table looked like a tray of church-candles when the last wax is melting. Many of the guests had gone or fallen asleep. But there was still dancing in the meadow.

Stiffly, unsmilingly, Angélique continued to preside over her wedding feast. Exasperation at her unfinished act, at the vengeance she had promised herself and had been unable to complete, made her ache to her fingertips. Rage and shame tore her heart. She had lost old Guillaume. Monteloup was rejecting her. There was nothing left for her but to go to her lame spouse.

Chapter 13

THE following day, four carriages and two heavy wagons took the road to Niort. Angélique was at pains to believe that all this display of horses and coachmen, of shouts and creaking axles was in her honour. So much dust raised for Mademoiselle de Sancé, who had never known any escort other than an old mercenary armed with a pike, was hard to believe. The grooms, maids and musicians were piled up in the heavy carts together with the luggage. Along the sunny road, amid the flowering orchards passed this procession of brown faces. Laughter, songs and guitar-scraping left in their wake (with a smell of horse-dung) a feeling of carefree joy. The children of the south were returning to their broiling lands, perfumed with wine and garlic.

Amid this gay party, Master Clément Tonnel alone struck a note of stiff formality. Hired merely for the week of the wedding, he had asked to be brought along as far as Niort, so as to save the expense of an escort. But on the evening of the very first stage, the steward came to see Angélique. He offered to remain in her service, either as major-domo or as valet. He explained that he had served several lords in Paris. However, after returning to his native Niort to settle the inheritance of his father — a butcher — he had learned that his last place had been taken by a scheming footman. Since then he had been looking for a respectable house of rank, in order to resume his former functions.

With his discreet and knowledgeable air, Clément had worked his way into the good graces of Margot the maid, who asserted that a new valet, so well-mannered, would be cordially welcomed at the palace of Toulouse. His Lordship the Comte surrounded himself with people of too many types and colours who did not provide proper service. They all lolled in the sunshine, and the laziest of the lot was undoubtedly Alphonso, the steward set up as their overseer.

So Angélique engaged Master Clément. He frightened her, though she could not say why. But she was grateful to him for talking like everyone else, that is to say without that insufferable accent that was beginning to exasperate her. This cold, pliant, almost too obsequious man, this servant who only yesterday was still unknown to her, would at least remind her of her own province.

As soon as Niort, capital of the marshes, had been left behind, with its great dungeon, black as iron, Madame de Peyrac's equipage hurtled on towards the sunlight. Almost without noticing it, Angélique found herself at grips with an unfamiliar landscape, treeless and striped with vineyards in all directions. They passed not far from Bordeaux. Then the green maize alternated with the vines. As they approached the Béarn, the travellers were received in the castle of Monsieur Antonin de Caumont, Marquis de Péguilin, Duc de Lauzun. Angélique gazed in surprise mingled with amusement at the dapper little man, whose grace and wit, according to Andijos, made him the "most idolized boy at court." The King himself, though affecting gravity in his youth, could not resist Péguilin's sallies, which had made him guffaw even during council meetings. But Péguilin had been exiled to his home lands in punishment for some impudence towards Monsieur de Mazarin. He did not, however, seem particularly depressed and told no end of funny stories.

Still little used to the gallant verbiage that was then fashionable at Court, Angélique understood barely half his stories, but this stage of the journey was a gay and lively one and helped to relax her. The Duc de Lauzun grew ecstatic over her beauty and complimented her in verse that he improvised on the spot.

"Ah! my friends," he cried, "I wonder if the

Golden Voice of the Kingdom won't lose its highest note on her account."

It was the first time that Angélique had heard mention of the Golden Voice of the Kingdom.

"He is the greatest singer in Toulouse," they explained to her. "Since the great minstrels of the Middle Ages, the Languedoc has known none like him. You will hear him, Madame; you'll find you can't help succumbing to his spell."

Angélique tried hard not to disappoint her hosts by a glum face. All these people were pleasant, sometimes a little coarse, but always kindly. The excessively warm air, the tiled roofs and the plane-tree leaves had the sparkle of white wine, and the southerners' wit had its levity.

But Angélique, as they were drawing close to their goal, felt her heart grow heavier.

On the eve of their entrance into Toulouse, they stayed at one of the residences of the Comte de Peyrac, a château of white stone in Renaissance style. Angélique was delighted with the comfort of one of the rooms, which contained a mosaic bath. Margot busied herself nearby. She was afraid lest the dust and heat of the journey might have further darkened her mistress's complexion, of whose warm tint she secretly disapproved.

She rubbed her with various ointments and ordered her to remain on the divan, while she massaged her with much energy, and then plucked all the hair from her body. Angélique was not shocked by this custom which, when there had been Roman bath-houses in every town, was common even among the people. Nowadays, only young girls of high birth were subjected to it. It was most improper for a great lady to conserve any superfluous down upon her. While everything was being done to make her body perfect, Angélique could not repress a feeling of horror.

"He will not touch me," she told herself again, "I'd rather throw myself out of the window."

But nothing impeded the dizzy course, the whirlwind that swept her along.

Next morning, sick with apprehension, she climbed for the last time into the carriage that was to take her to Toulouse. The Marquis d'Andijos sat down beside her. He was jubilant, he sang and babbled. But she was not listening. She had been noticing for some minutes that the coachman was holding back his horses. A little ahead of the carriage, a crowd of people and riders were barring the road. When the carriage had come to a stop, she could hear more distinctly the songs and shouts, which were punctuated by the rhythmical beat of the drums.

"By Saint Séverin," cried the Marquis, jumping up, "I believe this is your husband coming to meet us."

"Already!"

Angélique felt herself go pale. The pages opened the carriage-doors. She had to step down to the sandy road under the implacable sun. The sky was a deep azure blue. A torrid breath rose from the yellow maize fields on both sides of the road. A scintillating *farandole* was approaching. A swarm of children dressed in quaint costumes with big green and red diamond patches, was bouncing, somersaulting and finally stumbling amid the horses and riders, who were themselves dressed in extravagant liveries of pink satin with white plumes.

"The princes of love! The Italian comedians!" exulted the Marquis, spreading his arms in an enthusiastic gesture that spelt danger for his neighbours. "Ah! Toulouse! Toulouse!"

The crowd had opened to make a passage-way. A tall, loose-limbed, swaying figure appeared, dressed in crimson velvet and leaning on an ebony cane.

As the limping figure approached, one could distinguish, framed by an abundant black wig, a face as displeasing to the eye as was his gait. Two deep scars ran from his temple to his left cheek and across one half-closed eyelid. The lips were strong and clean-shaven, which was not the fashion and added to the strangeness of this weird scarecrow.

"It isn't he," prayed Angélique. "Please God, don't let it be he!"

"Your husband, the Comte de Peyrac, Madame," said the Marquis d'Andijos.

She dropped into a well-learned curtsey. Her mind at bay recorded absurd details: the diamond bows on the Comte's shoes, the fact that one of them had a higher heel than the other to lessen his limp; the pleated stockings with stitched silk pipings, the sumptuous costume, the sword, the huge, white lace collar.

Someone spoke to her; she answered she knew not what. The drumbeats mingling with the blaring trumpets dazed her.

As she sat down in the carriage again, a bunch of roses and posies of violets landed on her knees.

"Flowers are the principal joys," said a voice. "They rule over Toulouse."

Angélique became aware that it was not the Marquis d'Andijos who sat at her side. In order not to see the horrible face, she bent over the flowers.

Soon after, the city appeared, bristling with towers and red steeples. The procession drove through the narrow lanes, deep shadowy corridors in which lingered a crimson light. At the palace of the Comte de Peyrac, Angélique was quickly clothed in a magnificent white velvet dress, adorned with white satin. The clasps and bows were studded with diamonds. While the girls were dressing her, they served her iced drinks, for she was dying of thirst. At noon, amid the jingle of bells, the procession moved off towards the cathedral, where the Archbishop was awaiting the couple in the square outside.

When the blessing had been given, Angélique walked down the aisle alone, according to princely custom. The hobbling lord preceded her, and this tall, red, fidgeting shape suddenly seemed to her as extraordinary as the devil himself under those vaults hazy with incense. Outside, the whole town seemed to have gathered to celebrate. Angélique could not relate all this hubbub to the very personal event which was her marriage to the Comte de Peyrac. She unconsciously sought the spectacle that produced the broad smiles of the crowd and their urge to frolic. But all eyes were turned towards her. It was to her that the fiery-eyed lords, the sumptuously dressed ladies bowed.

To return from the cathedral to the palace, the newly married couple mounted on two magnificently caparisoned horses. The road along the banks of the Garonne was scattered with flowers and the cavaliers in pink whom the Marquis d'Andijos had called the "princes of love," kept flinging down more baskets full of petals. On the left, the river shone golden, the mariners in their small boats cheered loudly.

Angélique became aware that she was smiling somewhat mechanically. The intensely blue sky and the scent of the flowers they trod on intoxicated her. Suddenly she stifled a cry; she was being escorted by little pages with liquorice-faces which she had at first believed to be masks. But now she understood they really were black-skinned. It was the first time she had seen negroes.

There was definitely something unreal about everything she experienced. She felt terribly alone, in the heart of an ambiguous dream which she would try to remember, perhaps, on waking. And always at her side, she saw in the sunshine the disfigured profile of the man they called her husband and whom they acclaimed. Gold pieces tinkled on the pebbles. Pages were flinging them among the crowd and people were scuffling for them in the dust.

In the palace gardens, long white tables had been set up in the shade. Wine was flowing from the fountains in front of the gates, and the people of the street could drink from them. The gentry and the leading townspeople were admitted inside.

Angélique, seated between the Archbishop and the man in red, and incapable of swallowing a morsel, saw an incalculable number of courses and dishes parading past. Potted partridges, fillets of duck, pomegranates in blood, fried quail, trout, rabbits, salad, lamb tripes, *foie gras*. The desserts were innumerable — fried cream garnished with peach fritters, all kinds of jams, honey pastries, and pyramids of fruit as high as the little black-amoors who were carrying them. Wines of all types, from the darkest red to the clearest gold, followed one another.

Angélique noticed at the side of her plate a kind of small golden pitchfork. Glancing around, she saw that most people used it to impale their meat and carry it to their mouths. She tried to imitate them, but after a few fruitless efforts preferred to revert to a spoon, which had been placed beside her when they saw that she did not know how to use the odd little instrument. This ridiculous incident added to her confusion.

Frozen with apprehension and resentment, Angélique felt exasperated by so much noise and plenty. Her native pride did not allow her to show this, and so she smiled and found a friendly word for all. The iron discipline of the Ursuline Convent enabled her to sit erect with a regal bearing despite her fatigue. She was, however, quite unable to turn her face towards the Comte de Peyrac and, re-alizing how odd this attitude must seem, she con-centrated all her attention on her other neighbour, the Archbishop. The latter was a very handsome man, in the prime of life. He had much eloquence, the graciousness of a man of the world, and very cold blue eyes.

Alone among all those present, he did not seem to share in the general merriment.

"What profusion! What profusion!" he sighed, gazing around him. "When I think of all the paupers who crowd outside the gates of my palace every day, of the uncared-for sick, of the children of the heretical villages that cannot be wrested from their beliefs for lack of money, my heart bleeds. Are you devoted to good works, my daughter?"

"I've only just left the convent, Monseigneur. But I should be happy to devote myself to my parish under your guidance."

He lowered on her his lucid glance, and smiled faintly as he puffed himself up beneath his rather flabby chin.

"I thank you for your obedience, my daughter. But I know that the life of a youthful mistress of a house is full of novelties that demand her attention. Therefore I shall not divert you from them until you expressly wish it. Isn't a woman's greatest work, the one to which she must devote all her care, the influence she must learn to exert over her husband's mind? A loving, skilful wife, in our day, can be all-powerful over her husband's mind."

He leaned towards her and the *cabochons* of his episcopal cross flashed with a mauve sparkle.

"A woman can be all-powerful," he repeated, "but between you and me, Madame, you have chosen a rather odd husband."

"I have chosen . . ." thought Angélique ironically. "Did my father even lay eyes on this horrid jumping-jack? I doubt it. My father loves me dearly. On no account would he have wanted to cause me unhappiness. But here we are: he wanted

256

me to be rich; I wanted to be loved. Mother Sainte-Anne would warn me again that one mustn't be romantic. . . . This Archbishop seems a good man. Could it have been with the men of his entourage that the Comte de Peyrac's pages had come to blows in the cathedral? . . ."

Meanwhile, the crushing heat had yielded before the oncoming dusk. The ball was about to begin. Angélique uttered a sigh.

"I shall dance all night," she said to herself. "Nothing on earth will make me consent to remain alone with him for even a moment. . . ."

She glanced nervously at her husband. Whenever she looked at him, the sight of his scarred face whose black eyes glowed like coal, made her uneasy. The left eyelid, half-closed by the weal of a scar, gave the Comte de Peyrac an expression of malicious irony.

Leaning back in his tapestry armchair, he had just carried to his mouth a sort of small brown stick. A servant hurried forward with a piece of burning coal at the end of tongs, which he held close to the end of the little stick.

"Oh, Monsieur, the example you set is deplorable!" exclaimed the Archbishop, with a frown. "I consider tobacco the dessert of hell. That it be consumed as a powder for the sole purpose of curing the humours of the brain and on doctor's advice, I grant with difficulty, for it seems to me that snuff-takers take an unhealthy enjoyment in it and too often give their health as a pretext for grinding tobacco whenever they please. But pipe-smokers are the scum of our taverns, besotting themselves for hours with this accursed plant. I never knew that a gentleman consumed tobacco in such a vulgar fashion."

"I have no pipe and I do not take snuff. I smoke the rolled leaf as I saw certain savages of America do. No one can accuse me of a musketeer's coarseness or a Court fop's affectation. . . ."

"When there are two ways of doing a thing, you must always choose a third," said the Archbishop sourly. "I just noticed another oddity that is peculiar to you. You put neither toadstone nor a piece of unicorn into your glass. Yet everybody knows that these are the best precautions against poison that an enemy hand is always capable of pouring into your wine. Even your young wife employs this prudent custom. For toadstone and pieces of unicorn do indeed change colour when in contact with dangerous beverages. Yet you never use them. Do you deem yourself invulnerable . . . or without enemies?" added the prelate, and there was a flash in his eyes that impressed Angélique.

"No, Monseigneur," answered the Comte de Peyrac. "I merely hold that the best way of preserving oneself against poison is to put nothing into one's glass and everything into one's body."

"What do you mean?"

"I mean this: absorb every day of your life an infinitesimal dose of some powerful poison."

"You do that?" exclaimed the Archbishop, horrified.

"Ever since my tenderest childhood. You are not unaware, Monseigneur, that my father succumbed to a Florentine beverage, although the toadstone he had put into his glass was as big as a pigeon's egg. My mother, who was an unprejudiced woman, sought for some *true* means of preserving my life. From a Moorish slave she learned the method of protecting yourself against poison by the use of poison."

"Your arguments always contain some paradox that alarms me," said the Archbishop, seemingly worried. "It is as if you wished to reform everything, yet nobody can fail to realise how much harm and disorder this word 'reform' has brought to the Church and the kingdom. Once again, why employ a method of which you have no guarantee, when other methods have proved their worth? Naturally, you must have genuine toadstones and genuine unicorn horns. Too many charlatans have set up a trade in them and sell you goodness knows what instead of the real article. But my monk Bécher, for instance, a very learned Franciscan friar, who does work in alchemy for me, could get you some excellent ones."

The Comte de Peyrac leaned forward a little to look at the Archbishop, and as his abundant black locks touched Angélique's hand, she shrank back. She noticed at that moment that her husband was not wearing a wig, but that his great shock of hair was natural.

"What intrigues me," he declared, "is how he himself obtains them. When I was a boy, I took an interest in killing countless toads. Never did I detect in their brains the famous protective stone which is called toadstone and which apparently should be found there. As to unicorn horns, I may say that I have travelled all over the world and my conviction is unshakable; the unicorn is a

259

mythological, imaginary animal; in short, it does not exist."

"You can't assert things like that. You must allow room for mysteries and not claim to know everything."

"What is a mystery to me," said the Comte slowly, "is how a man of your intelligence can seriously believe such . . . fantasies. . . ."

"Heavens," thought Angélique, "I've never heard a high-ranking ecclesiastic treated with such insolence!"

She looked from one to the other, as each stared into the other's eyes. Her husband was the first to notice her emotion. He directed a smile at her that crinkled his face curiously but disclosed very white teeth.

"Forgive us, Madame, for arguing thus before you. Monseigneur and I are intimate foes!"

"No man is my foe!" cried the Archbishop, indignantly. "Do you forget the charity that must dwell in the heart of any servant of God? Perhaps you hate me; I do not hate you in the least. But with you I feel the shepherd's concern for the straying lamb. And if you won't listen to my words, I shall at least know how to separate the wheat from the chaff."

"Ah!" cried the Comte, and his laughter was rather frightening, "you show yourself to be the true heir of Foulques de Neuilly, bishop and right arm of the terrible Simon de Montfort, who burnt the Albigeois at the stake and reduced to ashes the refined civilization of Aquitaine! Languedoc still mourns after four centuries its ravaged splendours and trembles to hear the description of those horrible crimes. I who am of the most ancient Toulouse lineage, who bear Ligurian and Visigoth blood in my veins, I quiver when my eyes meet the blue eyes of you northerners. Heirs of Foulques, heirs of the uncouth barbarians who implanted here your sectarianism and your intolerance, that's what I read in your eyes!"

"My family is one of the oldest in Languedoc," exclaimed the Archbishop, half rising. And at that moment his southern accent rendered his speech practically unintelligible to Angélique's ears. "You know very well, insolent monster, that half of Toulouse is mine by heritage. For centuries our lands have been in Toulouse."

"Four centuries! Four miserable centuries, Monseigneur," cried Joffrey de Peyrac, rising in his turn. "You came in the chariots of Simon de Montfort, with the hated crusaders. You are the invader! Man of the North! Man of the North! What are you doing at my table? . . ."

Angélique was beginning to wonder, horrified, whether they were not going to fight then and there, when a roar of laughter from the guests punctuated the Comte's last words. The Archbishop's smile was less sincere. However, when Joffrey de Peyrac's tall body twisted itself in a deep bow of apology to the prelate, the latter graciously offered him his pastoral ring to be kissed.

Angélique was too disconcerted to share in this exuberance. The words these two men had been hurling at each other's heads were by no means trifling, but for southerners, it is true, laughter is often the sparkling prelude to the blackest tragedies.

"Does the tobacco smoke offend you, Madame?" asked the Comte suddenly, bending towards her and trying to catch her eye.

She shook her head. The subtle smell of tobacco stressed her melancholy, recalling to her mind the presence of old Guillaume at the fireside in the big kitchen of Monteloup. Old Guillaume, Fantine, all the familiar things had suddenly become remote.

In the wooded groves violins started to play. Though tired to death, Angélique eagerly accepted the Marquis d'Andijos's invitation to dance. The dancers had gathered in the large tiled courtyard which was cooled by fountains. Angélique had learned enough fashionable dance-steps at the convent not to feel embarrassed now among the lords and ladies of a very up-to-date province. She was dancing for the first time at a real ball and she was beginning to enjoy it, when there was a sort of commotion. Couples broke apart under the pressure of a crowd that was running towards the tables. The dancers protested, but someone cried: "He's going to sing." Others repeated: "The Golden Voice! The Golden Voice of the Kingdom! . . ."

Chapter 14

A discreet hand touched Angélique's arm. "Madame," whispered Margot the maid, "this is the moment when you should leave. His Lordship the Comte has charged me to lead you to the pavilion on the Garonne where you will spend the night."

"But I don't wish to leave!" protested Angélique. "I want to listen to that singer whom everyone praises so. I have not even seen him."

"He will sing for you, Madame. He will sing for you in private, the Comte has promised it," the big woman assured her. "But your sedan chair is waiting."

While speaking, she had thrown a hooded cloak over her mistress's shoulders and held a black velvet mask out to her.

"Put this over your face," she whispered. "Thus you won't be recognized. Otherwise the tin-kettle musicians might well run all the way to the pavilion and upset your wedding-night with the terrific din they make on their pots and pans."

The maid giggled behind her hand.

"It's always like that in Toulouse," she explained. "The young couple that doesn't manage to steal away like thieves in the night must pay a heavy forfeit in coins or else put up with the infernal row of those devils. Monseigneur and the police have tried to suppress this custom in vain. . . ."

She pushed Angélique into a sedan chair, which two sturdy footmen promptly lifted on to their shoulders. A few riders emerged from the darkness to form an escort. After passing through a maze of narrow lanes, the small party reached the countryside.

The pavilion was a modest building surrounded by gardens that sloped down to the river. As she alighted, Angélique was startled by the profound silence, which was disturbed only by the chirping of crickets. Margot, who had ridden pillion behind one of the horsemen, slipped to the ground and showed the young bride into the empty house. With sparkling eyes and a smile on her lips, the maid apparently relished all this love-mystery.

Angélique found herself in a room tiled with mosaics. A small lamp burned near the alcove, but its light was wasted, for the moonlight shone so far into the room that it lent a snowy sparkle to the lace sheets on the big bed. Margot threw a last critical glance at the young woman, then hunted in her bag for a flask of angel-water for purifying the skin.

"Leave me," protested Angélique impatiently.

"Madame, your husband will come, you must . . ."

"I must nothing. Leave me."

"Yes, Madame."

The maid dropped a curtsey.

"I wish Madame a sweet night."

"Leave me!" cried Angélique angrily for the third time.

She remained alone, annoyed with herself for not having been able to control her feelings in the servant's presence. But she did not like Margot. Her sure and skilful manners intimidated her, and she feared her mocking black eyes.

She remained motionless for a long time, until the great silence of the room became more than she could stand.

Her fear awoke afresh. She clenched her teeth.

"I am not afraid," she told herself almost aloud.

"I know what I have to do. I shall die rather than let him touch me!"

She walked towards the French window that opened out on the terrace. Only at Plessis had Angélique seen these elegant balconies that Renaissance architecture had made fashionable.

Toulouse was hidden by a turn of the river. There were only gardens and gleaming water in sight, and farther away maize-fields and vineyards. Angélique sat down on the edge of a green velvet couch and let her forehead rest against the balustrade. The pearls and diamond pins of her intricate hairdress had begun to hurt her. She tried to undo it, not without difficulty.

"Why didn't that big fool undo it and undress me?" she thought. "Does she imagine my husband will do it for her?"

Inwardly she gave a mocking, sad little laugh.

"Mother Sainte-Anne never failed to lecture us on the docility a woman must show to all her husband's desires. And when she said *all,* she'd roll her eyeballs, and we'd stifle our giggles for we well knew what she was thinking of. But I've no taste for docility. Molines was right to say that I cannot bow to something I don't understand. I've obeyed them to save Monteloup. What more can they ask of me? The Argentière mine belongs to the Comte de Peyrac. He and Molines can go on trafficking. My father can continue to breed mules to carry the Spanish gold. If I died by throwing myself off this balcony, nothing would be changed. Everyone's got what he wanted. . . ."

She had finally managed to undo her hair. It spread over her bare shoulders, and she shook it out with a toss of her head, in the wild familiar way of her childhood.

Just then it seemed to her that she heard a faint noise. Turning round, she stifled a cry of terror. Leaning against the frame of the French window, the lame one was gazing at her.

He was no longer wearing his red costume, but was dressed in breeches and a very short black velvet doublet.

He advanced with his uneven step and bowed deeply.

"Will you allow me to sit beside you, Madame?"

She nodded her head in silence. He sat down, rested his elbow on the stone balustrade, and gazed out nonchalantly.

"Several centuries ago," he said, "under these very stars, ladies and troubadours would mount the walks on the walls of their castles, and there Courts of Love would be held. Have you heard of the troubadours of Languedoc, Madame?"

Angélique had not foreseen this kind of conversation. She was taut with defensive tension, and could only stammer with difficulty:

"I . . . I think so. . . . That's what they called the poets in the Middle Ages."

"The poets of love. *Langue d'oc!* The soft tongue! So different from the uncouth speech of the north, the *langue d'oïl*. In Aquitaine people learned the art of love for, as Ovid said: 'Love is an art that can be taught and in which you can perfect yourself by studying its laws.' Have you as yet taken an interest in this art, Madame?"

She did not know what to reply; she was too

wary not to sense the slight irony in the other's voice. From the way the question was put, both yes and no would have been equally ridiculous. She was not used to elegant dallying. Dazed by so many happenings, her gift for repartee had deserted her. She could only turn her head away and gaze mechanically out at the slumbering plain.

She realized that the man had moved closer to her, but she did not move.

"Do you see," he went on, "in the garden, the little fish pond into which the moon is dipping like a toadstone into a glass of anisette? . . . That water has the same colour as your eyes, my sweet. Never, in the whole wide world, have I come across such strange, such alluring eyes. And you see these roses which cling in garlands to our balcony? They are the same tint as your lips. No, truly, never have I met such lips . . . and such tightly-closed ones. As for their sweetness . . . I shall judge."

Suddenly two hands had seized her waist. Angélique felt herself bent backward by a strength she had not suspected in this tall gaunt man. She found her neck thrown back into the hollow of an arm whose pressure numbed her. The horrible face loomed over her. She cried out with horror, writhed, sick with revulsion. Almost instantly she found herself free. The Comte had released her and was looking at her laughingly.

"It's just as I thought. I scare you to death. You'd rather jump down from this balcony than be mine. Isn't it so?"

She stared at him, with beating heart. He rose and his long spidery silhouette lengthened under the moonlit sky.

"I shall not force you, poor little virgin. I have no taste for that. So you've been delivered up brand-new to the Big Lame Man of Languedoc? What a terrible fate!"

He bent down and she hated his mocking smile.

"I want you to know that I have possessed many women in my life: white, black, yellow, red. But I've never taken one by force nor seduced one with money. They have all come to me freely, and you too will come some day, some night . . ."

"Never!"

The word had shot out violently, but the smile did not fade from that strange face.

"You are a young savage, but I don't dislike that. An easy conquest renders love worthless, a difficult one lends it value. Thus spoke André Le Chapelain, master of the art of love. Goodnight, my pretty one, sleep well in your big bed, alone with your graceful limbs and your enchanting little breasts that will be so sad to have gone uncaressed. Goodnight!"

When Angélique woke up the next morning, the sun stood high in the sky. The birds, already dazed by the heat, were silent in the trees.

She could hardly remember how she had undressed and got into this bed with its emblazoned sheets that smelt of violets. She had wept with fatigue and disappointment, perhaps with loneliness. This morning she felt more clear-headed. The assurance her peculiar husband had given her that he would not touch her unless she herself desired it put her mind at rest for a while. "Does

268

he imagine that I shall find his game leg and seared face irresistible?"

She toyed with the idea of a pleasant life at the side of a husband with whom she would be on terms of friendship. After all, life might not be lacking in charm. Toulouse offered so many attractions.

Margot came in to dress her, discreet and impassive. At noon Angélique returned to town. Clément presented himself and announced that His Lordship the Comte had instructed him to advise Her Ladyship that he was working in his laboratory and would not be back for lunch. Angélique felt relieved. The man added that the Comte had engaged him as his major-domo. He was well pleased with his new post. People hereabouts were loud and lazy but cordial. The house seemed to be rich and he would do his best to satisfy his new masters.

Angélique thanked him for his little speech, in which a hint of condescension mingled with obsequiousness. She was not displeased to keep near her this fellow whose manners contrasted strongly with the exuberance of her environment.

During the next days Angélique learned that the palace of the Comte de Peyrac was certainly the most frequented place in town. The master of the house took an active part in all the festivities. His tall ungainly figure passed from one group to another, and Angélique was astonished by the animation aroused by his mere presence.

She was getting used to his appearance and her revulsion lessened. No doubt the thought that she owed him submission in the flesh had accounted for much of her violent resentment as well as for the fear he had inspired in her. Now that she felt reassured on this subject, she had to admit that the man attracted people, with his sparkling talk and playful, curious disposition.

Towards her he affected a casual indifference. While lavishing upon her the attentions due her rank, he hardly seemed to see her. He greeted her every morning, and, seated opposite him, she presided over the meals, at which there were always at least a dozen guests; thus she avoided a *tête-à-tête* with him.

Not a day passed, however, without her finding in her room a present — a scarf or a jewel, a new dress, a piece of furniture, even sweets and flowers. Everything was in perfect taste, and of a luxury that dazzled and enchanted her — but embarrassed her too. She did not know how to show the Comte the pleasure these presents gave her. Whenever she was obliged to address him directly, she could not make herself raise her eyes to his slashed face and she became gauche and started stammering.

One day she found in her room a red morocco-leather case with iron mountings. When she opened it, she found the most magnificent diamond necklace she could have ever dreamed of.

She was gazing at it tremblingly, convinced that the Queen herself surely had nothing comparable, when she heard her husband's peculiar step.

Impulsively she ran towards him with shining eyes.

"What a beauty! How can I thank you, Monsieur?"

Her enthusiasm had carried her towards him too fast. She almost knocked against him. Her cheeks met the velvet of his doublet, while a steely arm was grasping her. The face that terrified her seemed so close that her smile faded, and she drew back with an uncontrollable shudder of fear. Joffrey de Peyrac's arm promptly fell away, and he said with a somewhat scornful casualness:

"Thank me? Why? . . . Don't forget, my dear, that you are the wife of the Comte de Peyrac, last descendant of the illustrious Counts of Toulouse. In this capacity, you must be the most beautiful, the most exquisitely adorned woman. Hereafter do not consider yourself obliged to thank me."

Joffrey de Peyrac did not remind her of his prerogatives, except on very rare occasions: for instance, when there was a ball at the Governor's or at the house of one of the higher city officials, which demanded that Madame de Peyrac indeed be the most beautiful and the most bejewelled woman in the gathering. On these occasions he would come in unannounced, sit down near her dressing-table and watch attentively as the young woman dressed. He would guide Margot's and the waiting-maid's skilful hands with a word here and there. No detail escaped him. Feminine adornments held no secrets for him. Angélique marvelled at the acuteness of his observations, at his carefully studied elegance. As she was most willing to become a great lady of distinction, not a word of these lessons escaped her. In those moments she forgot her grudges and apprehensions.

But one evening, as she was looking at herself

in the tall mirror, dazzling in an ivory satin dress with a high lace and pearl collar, she saw at her side the sombre figure of the Comte de Peyrac, and sudden despair weighed down on her shoulders like a leaden cape.

"What good is wealth and luxury," she thought, "in face of this dreadful fate: to be tied for life to a horrible, infirm husband!"

He suddenly realised that she was looking at him in the mirror, and as suddenly drew away.

"What is the matter? Don't you find yourself beautiful?"

She turned a mournful gaze back to her own image.

"Yes, Monsieur," she said obediently.

"Well, then? . . . You might at least smile. . . ."

She thought she heard him sigh very softly.

In the months that followed, she came to realise that Joffrey de Peyrac lavished far more attention and compliments on other women than on his wife. His gallantry was spontaneous, gay, elegant, and the ladies strove to provoke it with obvious enjoyment. They were playing at being *précieuses*, as the Paris fashion decreed.

"This is the Palace of Gay Learning," the Comte said to her one day. "Everything that contributed to the grace and courtesy of Aquitaine, and hence of France, must be found again in these walls. Thus, Toulouse has just celebrated its famous Floral Games. The golden violet has been awarded to a young poet of the Roussillon. From all parts of France and even of the world rhymesters of rondeaux come to Toulouse to be judged, under the aegis of Clémence Isaure, who so brilliantly inspired the troubadours of the past. So don't be frightened, Angélique, by all the unknown faces that come and go in my palace. If they disturb you, you can always retire to the pavilion on the Garonne."

But Angélique felt no desire to isolate herself. She gradually let herself be won over by the charm of this life of song. After first scorning her, several ladies found she had wit and welcomed her in their circles. The success of the parties the Comte gave in this house, which after all was hers as well, had roused in the young woman a desire to help in planning them properly. She could be seen running from the kitchens to the gardens, from the garrets to the cellars, followed by her three little blackamoors.

She had grown accustomed to their funny, black, round faces. There were many Moorish slaves in Toulouse, for the ports of Aigues-mortes and Narbonne were gateways to the Mediterranean, which was but one vast pirate lake. To sail from Narbonne to Marseille was a real expedition! At that time everyone in Toulouse was laughing uproariously at the misadventures of a Gascon gentleman who had been captured by Arab galleys. The King of France had promptly bought him back from the Sultan of Barbary.

But of the Comte's negro servants, really only Kouassi-Ba impressed Angélique. When she saw this dark colossus with white camel eyes loom before her, she had to check an urge to shrink back. Yet he seemed very gentle. He never left the side of the Comte de Peyrac except when he kept watch over the door to a mysterious apartment at the farthest end of the palace. The Comte withdrew there every evening and sometimes in the daytime. Angélique had no doubt that this forbidden domain sheltered the retorts and phials which the page Henrico had mentioned to Fantine. She felt a great curiosity to enter it, but did not dare. It was to be one of the visitors to the Palace of Gay Learning who would finally enable her to discover this hidden facet of her husband's strange personality.

Chapter 15

THE visitor arrived covered with dust. He was travelling on horseback and had come from Lyons by way of Nîmes. He was a rather tall man of about thirty-five years. He started to talk Italian, changed to Latin, of which Angélique had little knowledge, and finished by speaking in German.

In that tongue, which was familiar to Angélique, the Comte introduced the traveller.

"Professor Bernalli of Geneva is doing me the great honour of coming to talk to me of the scientific problems which for many years now have been the subject of correspondence between us."

The stranger bowed with a very Italian flourish and protested profusely. His abstract arguments and formulas were certain to bore a charming lady whose mind surely ran to more light-hearted topics. Prompted neither by bravado nor genuine curiosity, Angélique asked to be allowed to be present at their discussions. However, to be discreet, she sat down in the corner of a casement window that overlooked the courtyard.

It was winter, but the cold was dry and the sun was shining. From the yard came the scent of copper braziers, around which the footmen were warming themselves. Angélique, with a piece of embroidery work on her knees, strained an ear towards the conversation of the two men, who were facing each other across the fireplace, where a small log-fire was smouldering.

They spoke of people whose names were completely unknown to her: the English philosopher Bacon, Descartes, the French engineer Blondel, who seemed to arouse both men's indignation, for, they said, he had treated Galileo's theories as sterile paradoxes. From all this Angélique eventually gathered that the new arrival was a fervent supporter of Descartes, whom her husband, on the contrary, was attacking.

Seated in the depths of his tapestry armchair in the casual pose he liked best, Joffrey de Peyrac seemed as nonchalant as when he was discussing the rhymes of a sonnet with some ladies. His insouciant attitude was a contrast to that of his interlocutor, whose passionate interest in this dialogue kept him bolt upright on the edge of his stool.

"I'd be tempted to regard you as a madman," said the Italian at one point, "and yet something deep within me approves of what you say. Your theory would be the climax of my studies on liquids in motion. Ah! I certainly don't regret this perilous

275

journey which has afforded me the priceless joy of talking to a great scientist. But take care, my friend! If I myself, whose words never compared with yours for boldness, am considered a heretic and am forced to exile myself to Switzerland, what may happen to you?"

"Pah!" said the Comte, "I do not seek to convince anyone, unless they have minds versed in science and are able to understand me. I have not even the ambition to write down and publish the results of my work. I devote myself to it for pleasure, as I take pleasure in versifying songs with lovely ladies. I am living quietly in my palace at Toulouse, so who would want to come and harm me?"

"The eyes of power are everywhere," declared Bernalli, looking disillusioned and glancing round the room.

At this very instant, Angélique thought she heard a very slight sound not far from her, and it seemed to her as if the hangings over one of the doorways had moved. It gave her a disagreeable feeling. From then on she listened to the men's conversation with only one ear. Her eyes fastened unconsciously on the face of Joffrey de Peyrac. The darkness that filled the room in the early winter dusk softened the nobleman's disfigured features. His black eyes alone shone with a passionate glow, and his teeth sparkled in the smile which accompanied even his gravest words. Angélique felt her heart stir.

When Bernalli had retired to dress for dinner, Angélique closed the window. The footmen placed torches on the table while a maid was stoking up the fire. Joffrey de Peyrac rose and went over to the window-recess where his wife was sitting.

"You are very silent, my dear. Did you fall asleep listening to us talk?"

"No, on the contrary, I was very much interested," said Angélique slowly, and for the first time her eyes did not shrink away from her husband. "I don't pretend I understood everything, but I confess I care more for this kind of discussion than for the verses of those ladies and their pages."

Joffrey de Peyrac placed a foot on the step of the embrasure and leaned down to consider Angélique with attention.

"You are a curious little woman. I believe you are beginning to become more tractable, but you haven't ceased to surprise me. I've used all sorts of seductions to conquer the women I desired, but it never before occurred to me to make use of mathematics."

Angélique could not help laughing, while a blush rose to her cheeks. She lowered her eyes to her needlework in some confusion. To change the subject, she asked:

"So you devote yourself to experiments in physics in that laboratory which Kouassi-Ba guards so jealously?"

"Yes and no. I have some measuring instruments, but I use my laboratory principally for chemical research on metals such as gold and silver."

"Alchemy," repeated Angélique with awe, and the vision of Gilles de Retz's castle passed before her eyes. "Why do you always want gold and sil-

277

ver?" she inquired with sudden fervour. "It is as if you sought them everywhere, not only in your laboratory, but in Spain, in England and even in the little lead-mine my family owns in Poitou. . . . And Molines told me that you also have a gold-mine in the mountains of the Pyrénées. Why do you want so much gold?"

"Much gold and silver is needed, Madame, in order to be free. And note what Master André le Chapelain says at the head of his manuscript *The Art of Love*: 'To occupy yourself with love, you must have no worries about material subsistence.' "

"Don't imagine you'll win me with gifts and wealth," retorted Angélique, recoiling fiercely.

"I don't imagine anything, my darling. I am waiting for you. I sigh. 'Every lover must pale in the presence of his beloved.' I pale. Do you think I have not paled enough? I know that it is recommended to minstrels to kneel to their lady, but that's a position my leg finds inconvenient. Forgive me. Oh, you can be sure I may say like Bernard de Ventadour, the divine poet: 'The torments of love which the beauty whose slave I am causes me will surely make me die.' I am dying, Madame."

Angélique shook her head, laughing.

"I don't believe you. You don't look as if you're dying. . . . You shut yourself up in your laboratory, or else you hasten to the homes of the precious ladies of Toulouse in order to guide their poetic compositions."

"Can it be that you miss me, Madame?"

She hesitated, a smile on her lips, anxious to

maintain the tone of light banter.

"I miss distractions, and you are distraction and variety personified."

She resumed her needlework. She no longer knew whether she liked or feared the way in which Joffrey de Peyrac sometimes looked at her during these jocular jousts for which their life in society gave them numerous occasions. All at once he dropped his irony, and in the ensuing silence she had the impression of falling under a strange, enveloping, all-consuming influence. She felt naked, her small breasts pressed against her lace bodice. She wanted to close her eyes.

"He is taking advantage of my disarmed distrust in order to cast a spell over me," she thought to herself with a little shiver of fear and delight.

Joffrey de Peyrac was attractive to women. Angélique could not deny it, and that which had been a cause of amazement to her during the first days, was becoming more understandable. Certain troubled expressions, certain flutterings among her pretty women-friends as the faltering step of the limping nobleman could be heard approaching in the corridors, had not escaped her. He had only to appear for a thrill to pass through the feminine gathering. He knew how to talk to women. He found caustic and gentle words, knew how to address a lady in a way that made her feel that she had been singled out among all the others. Angélique bridled like a restive horse under the cajoling voice. With a feeling of light-headedness, she recalled the confidences of her old nurse: "He entices young women with strange songs . . ."

When Bernalli reappeared, Angélique rose to meet him. She brushed against the Comte de Peyrac in passing and had a fleeting regret that his hand had not reached out to take her by the waist.

Chapter 16

A burst of hysterical laughter rang through the empty gallery.

Angélique stopped short and glanced around. The laughter persisted, rose to its highest pitch, then fell off in a sort of sob only to rise again. It was a woman's laugh. Angélique could not see her. This wing of the palace into which she had ventured in the heat of day was very quiet. April with its first spell of warmth produced a sultry heat in the Palace of Gay Learning. The pages were drowsing on the staircase. Angélique, who did not care for a midday siesta, had decided to wander through her still unfamiliar home. There were innumerable staircases, halls, and passages opening into galleries which she had yet to explore. Through the casements and dormer-windows the city was visible with its high open-work belfries through which shimmered the blue sky, and with its wide red quays along the Garonne.

Everyone was asleep. Angélique's long skirt rustled like leaves on the stone-floors. Then the piercing laughter had rung out. The young woman noticed a door ajar at the end of the gallery. There

followed a sound of splashing water and the laughter stopped abruptly. A man's voice said:

"Now that you've calmed down, I'll listen to you."

It was the voice of Joffrey de Peyrac.

Angélique approached softly and peeped through the slit of the door. Her husband was seated. She saw only the back of his armchair and one of his hands placed on the arm-rest and holding one of those little tobacco-sticks which he called cigars.

Before him on the tiled floor, in a pool of water, knelt a very beautiful woman whom Angélique did not recognize. She was richly dressed in black but was apparently soaked to the skin. An empty bronze basin at her side showed clearly what had become of the water which was usually served to cool the flagons of fine wine. The woman, whose long black hair was sticking to her temples, was staring with horror at her crumpled lace cuffs.

"You dare to treat me in this fashion?" she cried, in a stifled voice.

"I had to, my beauty," replied Joffrey in a gently scolding voice. "I could not let you go on losing your dignity before me. You would never have forgiven me. Come on, get up, Carmencita. Your clothes will soon dry in this torrid heat. Sit down in this armchair opposite me."

She struggled to get up. She was a tall woman, whose opulent beauty was of the type which the painters Rembrandt and Rubens celebrated. She sat down in the chair the Comte had indicated. Her black eyes were staring straight ahead with a wild expression.

"What's the matter?" said the Comte, and Angélique shuddered, for the detached voice of that invisible figure had a charm which she had never noticed before. "Look here, Carmencita, you left Toulouse more than a year ago. You were going up to Paris with your husband, whose high position held out an assurance of a brilliant life. You have even carried your ingratitude towards our poor little provincial society so far as never to send us any news. And here you suddenly appear in the Palace of Gay Learning, screaming, clamouring . . . for what exactly?"

"For love!" she answered in a hoarse, gasping voice. "I cannot live without you. Oh, don't interrupt me! You don't know what an ordeal this long year has been for me. Yes, I thought Paris would stanch my thirst for pleasure and entertainments. But in the midst of the most beautiful Court festivals lassitude gripped me. I thought of Toulouse, of the pink Palace of Gay Learning. I found myself talking of it with shining eyes, and people made fun of me. I had lovers. Their uncouth ways revolted me. Then I understood: you were the one I was missing. At night I would lie wide-awake and I would see you. I saw your eyes, alight with the flame of your smithy, your gaze so afire that I swooned, your white, knowing hands . . ."

"My graceful gait!" he added with a little laugh. He got up and went over to her, exaggerating his limp.

She looked him in the face.

"Don't try to put me off through disdain. What do your lameness and your scars matter in the eyes of the women you have loved, compared with the gifts you've bestowed upon them?"

She stretched out her hands to him.

"You give them utter rapture," she whispered. "Before I knew you, I was cold. You lit in me a flame that devours me."

Angélique's heart throbbed violently. She feared she knew not what, perhaps that her husband's hand would drop on the lovely, gold-skinned shoulder that offered itself voluptuously.

But the Count was leaning against a table and smoking impassively. She saw him in profile, the ravaged side of his face turned away. Suddenly another man was revealed to her, with features as pure as those on a medal under that shock of thick black hair.

"He who burns with too much lust does not really know how to love," he said, and he negligently blew a wisp of blue smoke away. "Remember the precepts of courtly love that the Palace of Gay Learning taught you. Go back to Paris, Carmencita, it's a refuge for people of your kind."

"If you turn me away, I shall retire to a convent. My husband wants to shut me up in one, anyway."

"An excellent suggestion, my dear. I hear a great number of pious asylums are being founded in Paris where devoutness is very much the fashion. Hasn't Queen Anne of Austria just bought the magnificent convent of Val-de-Grâce to shelter the Benedictines? And the Visitation de Chaillot is very much frequented too."

Carmencita's eyes flashed.

"So that's all the impression it makes on you?

I am ready to bury myself under a veil, and you do not even pity me?"

"My reserves of pity are exceedingly small. If there's someone to be pitied in all this, the only one I can see is your husband, the Duc de Mérecourt, who was imprudent enough to bring you back from Madrid in his embassy carriages. Don't try to involve me again in your volcanic existence, Carmencita. Let me recall to you other precepts of gallantry: 'A lover should not have more than one mistress at a time.' And this one, too: 'A new love chases the old one'!"

"Are you speaking for me or for yourself?" she asked.

Beneath her black hair, against her black garments, her face had turned as white as marble.

"Do you talk like this on account of your wife? I thought you had married her to satisfy your greed. Something about a piece of land, you told me. But you've chosen her as your mistress . . .? Oh, I have no doubt she'll turn out a remarkable pupil in your hands. But imagine your letting yourself fall in love with a girl from the north!"

"She is not from the north, she is from Poitou. I know Poitou for having travelled through it: it is a gentle land which was formerly part of the kingdom of Aquitaine. Our southern tongue is still alive in the dialect of their peasants, and Angélique herself has the colouring of the girls of our lands."

"I see you no longer love me," cried the woman. "Ah! I can see through you better than you think!"

She sank to her knees, clinging to Joffrey's doublet.

"There is still time. Love me! Take me! Take me!"

Angélique could not bear to hear any more. She fled. She dashed through the gallery, ran down the winding stairs of the tower. At the bottom of the steps she knocked into Kouassi-Ba, who was plucking at a guitar, while humming one of his native tunes in his rich, velvety voice. He grinned at her with all his teeth and lisped:

"Bonzou, Médême."

She did not answer but continued in her headlong flight. The palace was waking up. A few ladies had already gathered in the main hall and, with trays on their knees, were sipping cool drinks. One of them called out to her:

"Angélique, my love, do find your husband for us. Our imagination is languishing in this heat and we need . . ."

Angélique did not stop, but made an effort to smile at the gossiping ladies in passing.

She finally reached her room and flung herself down on the bed. "This is too much!" she kept saying to herself, but gradually she had to admit to herself that she did not know why she was so profoundly upset. Anyway, it was intolerable. It could not go on.

Angélique bit furiously into her lace handkerchief and looked around sombrely. Too much love, that's what exasperated her. Everyone talked of love, argued about love in this palace, in this city, where the Archbishop sometimes thundered from his lofty pulpit against the rakes, the libertines and their bejewelled mistresses in their finery, consigning them to hell-fire, if not to the flames of the Inquisition. Words that were specifically aimed at the Palace of Gay Learning.

Gay learning! What did it mean? Gay learning! Sweet learning! The secret of it made lovely eyes shine, lovely throats coo, inspired poets, gave voice to musicians. And the master of this mad and tender ballet was the now mocking, now lyrical cripple, the magician who had enslaved Toulouse with wealth and pleasure! Not since the days of the troubadours had Toulouse enjoyed such glory, such triumphs! The town had thrown off the yoke of the northmen, had found again its true destiny. . . .

"Oh, I hate him! I loathe him!" cried Angélique, stamping her foot.

Violently she shook a small silver-gilt bell, and when Margot appeared, she ordered her to call for a sedan chair and an escort, for she wanted to leave without delay for the pavilion on the Garonne.

When night fell, Angélique remained for a long while on the terrace of her room. Gradually the silence of the riverside scenery soothed her nerves. All alone, she tried to meditate and see clearly within herself.

She rubbed her forehead against the balustrade. "I shall never know love," she thought with melancholy.

When, at last, listless and tired she was about to withdraw to her room, a guitar struck a chord beneath her window. Angélique leaned out but could see no one amid the black shadows of the shrubs.

"Can it be Henrico who's returned to keep me company? He's a nice young boy . . ."

But the invisible musician began to sing. His deep, male voice was not that of the page. From the very first notes the young woman felt her heart stir. This voice, with its inflections, now velvety, now sonorous, its perfect diction, was of a quality which the gallant amateurs who invaded Toulouse by nightfall did not always possess. Fine singers are not rare in Languedoc. Melody springs naturally from lips used to laughter and verse. But here was a true artist. His voice had an exceptional volume. It seemed to make the garden ring, the moon vibrate. He was singing an old ballad in that ancient *langue d'oc* whose subtlety the Comte de Peyrac so often praised. He brought out every shade of it. Angélique could not grasp all the words, but one word recurred constantly: *"Amore! Amore!"*

Amour!

A certainty grew in her: "It is he, the last of the minstrels, the Golden Voice of the Kingdom!"

Never had she heard anyone sing like this. She had often been told: "Oh, if you could only hear the Golden Voice of the Kingdom! He doesn't sing any more. When will he sing again?" And people would look at her slyly, pitying her for not having known their local celebrity.

"To hear him once and then die!" said Madame Aubertré, wife of the city governor.

288

"It's he! It's he!" Angélique said to herself. "How can he be here? Has he come for me?"

She saw her reflection in the large looking-glass. Her hand was lying on her bosom and her eyes were open wide. She scoffed to herself: "How foolish I am! It may be just Andijos or some other would-be lover who's sent a paid musician to serenade me! . . ."

Nevertheless, she opened the door. With both hands clasped over her bodice to contain her heart's throbbing, she slid through the anterooms, slipped down the white marble stairs, emerged into the garden. Was life going to begin for Angélique de Sancé de Monteloup, Comtesse de Peyrac? For love is life!

The voice came from an arbour which sheltered a statue of the goddess Pomona. As the young woman approached, the singer fell silent but went on softly strumming his guitar. The moon was the shape of an almond that night. It was bright enough to light the garden, and Angélique could vaguely distinguish in the arbour a black silhouette seated against the base of the statue.

At the sight of her the unknown man did not move.

"He's a negro," thought Angélique, disappointed.

She quickly noticed her mistake. The man wore a velvet mask, but his snow-white hands resting on the instrument left no doubt as to his race. A black satin scarf tied over the nape of the neck, Italian fashion, hid his hair. As far as she could make out in the darkness of the bower, his rather threadbare costume was an odd mixture of a valet's and a comedian's. He wore heavy beaver boots, yet lace frills peeped out under the sleeves of his jacket.

"You sing wonderfully well," said Angélique, "but I should be curious to know the name of him who sent you."

"No one, Madame. I've come here knowing that this pavilion shelters one of the most beautiful women of Toulouse."

The man spoke in a very slow bass voice, as if he were afraid of being overheard.

"I arrived in Toulouse tonight and went to the Palace of Gay Learning, where there was a carefree and numerous gathering, in order to sing my songs. But when I learned that you were not there, I came to find you, for your beauty is so renowned in our province that I have desired to meet you for a long time."

"Your talent too is renowned. Are you not the one who is called the Golden Voice of the Kingdom?"

"I am, Madame. And your humble servant."

Angélique sat down on a nearby marble bench. The scent of climbing honeysuckle was intoxicating.

"Sing again," she said.

The warm voice rose once more, but more softly and as if muffled. It was no longer a ballad, but a song of tenderness, a confidence, an avowal.

"Madame," said the musician, breaking off, "forgive my boldness, I would like to translate into the French tongue a refrain prompted by the charm of your eyes."

Angélique inclined her head. She did not know how long she had been here. Nothing mattered any more. The night belonged to them. He strummed for a long while, as if trying to find the thread of the melody, then heaved a long sigh and began:

> Green eyes the colour of the ocean,
> The waves have closed over me,
> And shipwrecked by love
> I wander in the deep ocean
> Of her heart.

Angélique had closed her eyes. Even more than the ardent words, the voice numbed her with a delight she had never experienced before.

> When she opens her green eyes
> The stars are reflected in them
> As at the bottom of a pool in spring.

"He must come *now*," Angélique thought, "for this moment will never recur. One cannot live twice through such moments. It's so much like the love stories we used to tell each other at the convent."

The voice had grown silent. The unknown man slipped on to the bench. The firm arm that seized her, the hand that lifted her chin with an imperious gentleness made Angélique realise instinctively that here was a master who must have made more than one tender conquest. She felt a twinge of regret, but as soon as the singer's lips touched hers, she became light-headed. She did not know that a man's lips could be of such petal-like freshness, so meltingly tender. A muscular arm was gripping her but the mouth was still breathing charming words, and this charm and strength swept Angélique away in a whirlwind in which she tried vainly to recapture her reason.

"I oughtn't to do this . . . It's evil . . . If Joffrey found us . . . ."

Then everything was engulfed. The man's lips forced hers half open. His burning breath filled her mouth, sent coursing through her veins a delicious sense of well-being. With closed eyes she abandoned herself to the endless kiss, to the voluptuous possession which already foreshadowed and called for yet another. Waves of pleasure surged through her, a novel pleasure for her girlish body, so that she suddenly had a feeling of irritation and pain and recoiled with a violent shudder.

It seemed to her that she was either going to faint or weep. She saw the man's fingers caressing the naked breasts which he had artfully freed from her bodice while he was kissing her. She stepped back a little and rearranged her dress.

"Forgive me," she stammered, "you must find me very forward, but I did not know . . . I did not know . . . ."

"What did you not know, my love?"

And as she kept silent, he whispered:

"That a kiss could be so sweet?"

Angélique rose and went to lean against the entrance to the bower. Outside, the moon was setting, aglow with a golden tint as it fell towards the river. It must have been hours since Angélique had come into the garden. She was happy, marvellously happy. Nothing mattered any more, except to be able to re-live hours like these.

"You are made for love," murmured the minstrel. "One can feel it at the touch of your skin. The man who will know how to awake your enchanting body will lead you to the heights of passion."

"Be quiet! You must not speak that way. I am married, as you know. Adultery is a sin."

"It is an even greater sin that such a lovely lady accepts such a lame lord for her husband."

"I did not accept him: he bought me."

She immediately regretted these words for they disturbed the hour's serenity.

"Sing again," she begged. "Just once and then we must part."

He rose to pick up his guitar, but there was something unusual about his manner which troubled Angélique. She looked at him more closely. She did not know why, but she suddenly felt afraid.

While he was singing an air of strange longing very softly, she studied him sharply. Just now, when he kissed her, she had had the fleeting impression of a familiar presence and now she remembered: in the singer's breath mingled with the scent of violets a peculiar aroma of tobacco. . . . The Comte de Peyrac sometimes chewed violet pastilles, too. . . . He also smoked. A dreadful suspicion stirred in Angélique. . . . When he got up, a moment ago, to take his guitar, he had faltered strangely. . . .

Angélique uttered a cry of fear, followed by a cry of anger, and she started to tear the honey-

293

suckle off the arbour, stamping her foot all the while.

"Oh, this is too much! This is too much. . . . It's monstrous. . . . Take off your mask, Joffrey de Peyrac. . . . Stop your masquerade or I'll tear your eyes out, I'll strangle you, I'll . . ."

The song stopped abruptly; as if cut with a knife. The guitar uttered a mournful wail. The white teeth of the Comte de Peyrac gleamed under the velvet mask as he laughed.

He approached her with his uneven gait. Angélique was terrified but also utterly beside herself with outrage.

"I shall tear your eyes out," she repeated through clenched teeth.

He gripped her wrists, still laughing.

"What will the dreadful lame lord have left if you tear his eyes out?"

"You have lied with unspeakable impudence. You've made me believe that you were the . . . the Golden Voice of the Kingdom!"

"But I *am* the Golden Voice of the Kingdom."

And as she stared at him, dumbfounded:

"What is there so extraordinary about that? I had some talent. I studied with the greatest maestros of Italy. Singing is an art that is much practised in society these days. Frankly speaking, my dear, don't you like my voice?"

Angélique turned away and quickly wiped away the tears of rage that were running down her cheeks.

"How is it I never guessed you had this gift, never suspected it?"

"I asked them not to tell you. And perhaps you

weren't over-eager to discover my talents?"

"Oh, this is too much!" cried Angélique again.

But after the first moment of rage, she suddenly felt rather like laughing. To think he'd pushed his cynicism to the point of encouraging her to deceive him with himself! He really was the devil . . . ! The devil in person!

"I shall never forgive you this odious comedy," she said, compressing her lips and wrapping herself in dignity as best she could.

"I love playing comedies. Life, you see, has not always been kind to me, and people have so often sneered at me that it gives me infinite delight to make fun of them, in turn."

She could not help gazing gravely at the masked face.

"Were you really making fun of me?"

"Not entirely, and you well know it," he answered.

Without a word, she turned and walked away.

"Angélique! Angélique!"

He was softly calling her back.

Standing on the threshold of the arbour in the mysterious pose of an Italian harlequin, he put a finger to his lips.

"For pity's sake, Madame, do not tell anyone this story, not even your favourite maid. If it's known that I leave my guests, disguise and mask myself to go and steal a kiss from my own wife, I'll be a laughing-stock!"

"You are insufferable!" she cried.

She gathered her skirts and ran up the sandy avenue. When she reached the stairs she realised she was laughing. She undressed, tearing off fastenings and pricking herself with pins in her haste. She tossed from side to side between the sheets, feverish and unable to find sleep. The masked face, the injured face, the profile with the pure lines, passed in turn before her eyes. What was the enigma of this deceptive man? Suddenly she rebelled, and then the memory of the pleasure she had felt in his arms made her go weak and soft.

"You are made for love, Madame."

At last she fell asleep. In her slumber, Joffrey de Peyrac's eyes appeared to her "all alight with the glow of his smithy" and she saw a flame dance in them.

Chapter 17

ANGÉLIQUE was sitting in the Venetian gallery of mirrors in the palace. She did not yet know what she was going to do and what her attitude would be. Since her return that morning from the pavilion on the Garonne, she had not seen Joffrey de Peyrac. Clément informed her that the Count had shut himself up with Kouassi-Ba the Moor in the laboratory. Angélique bit her lips angrily. Joffrey might not appear again for hours. But then she didn't want him to anyway. She did not care one way or the other. She was still too annoyed by the hoax he had played on her the night before.

She decided to go to the pantry where today the first liqueurs of the season were being bottled.

The table set at the Palace of Gay Learning was reputed to be the most exquisite in the province. Joffrey de Peyrac took great personal pains with the menus offered to his guests, and Clément, who had undeniable talents in this respect, had assumed an important rôle in the palace ménage.

Hardly, however, had Angélique reached the kitchens, which today smelt of oranges, aniseed and aromatic spices, when a breathless little blackamoor came to announce that the Baron Benoît de Frontenac, Archbishop of Toulouse, asked to pay his respects to her and to her husband.

Morning was not the usual time for visits, which were normally made in the cooler hours of the evening. Moreover, for several months now, after goodness knows what new quarrel over precedence, the Archbishop had not set foot in the palace of the Comte de Peyrac, whom he accused of challenging his own influence over the minds of the Toulousians.

Intrigued and vaguely disturbed, Angélique removed the apron she had just pinned to her dress and quickly smoothed her hair. She wore it rather long and falling in curls over her lace collar as was the fashion. She arrived in the entrance hall and saw the tall figure of the Archbishop in red robe and white cape-collar at the top of the flight of stairs. Down in the gardens, Monseigneur's escort, his lackeys with swords at their sides, his pages and grandees on horseback, made a great deal of noise around the carriage and its six bay horses.

Angélique dropped down on her knees to kiss the pastoral ring, but as she rose again the Archbishop kissed her hand, to indicate by this worldly gesture that his visit was devoid of solemnity.

"Please, Madame, don't let your genuflexions make me measure the weight of my age compared with your youthfulness."

"Monseigneur, I only meant to show you the respect I feel for an illustrious man clothed in the dignity conferred on him by His Holiness the Pope and by God Himself. . . ."

Meanwhile the prelate had removed his hat and gloves and was handing them to one of the young abbés in his retinue, whom he motioned to leave.

"My suite will wait for me outside. I would like to talk to you, Madame, far from frivolous ears."

Angélique cast a mocking glance at the little abbé who was being accused of having frivolous ears, and who was blushing.

In the salon, the young woman, after ordering refreshments, apologized for her husband's absence. She would have the visitor's presence announced to him.

"I am sorry to have kept you waiting myself. I was in the pantry supervising the confection of our liqueurs. But I am wasting your time, Monseigneur, in talking of these trifling details."

"Nothing is trifling in the eyes of Our Lord. Think of the servant Martha. It is rare in our days to see a great lady busy herself with household affairs. Yet the mistress of a house sets the example of dignity and diligence for her servants. And when, as in your case, the grace of Mary mingles with the goodness of Martha . . ."

But the Archbishop's voice sounded preoccupied, and the worldly banter did not seem an art

298

he relished. Despite his fine bearing and the deliberately forthright gaze of his blue eyes, there was something suspicious about him that always struck one. Joffrey had observed one day that the Archbishop was a man who excelled at making people feel guilty.

After rubbing his hands thoughtfully, he repeated that he was very happy to see again the young woman, who had made so few appearances at the episcopal palace since that already distant day when he had officiated at her marriage at the cathedral.

Suddenly he asked her:

"Do you, Madame, know anything about your husband's work as an alchemist?"

"Indeed I don't," replied Angélique, unruffled. "The Comte de Peyrac has a taste for the sciences. . . ."

"He is even said to be a great scientist."

"I believe it. He spends long hours in his laboratory, but he has never shown it to me. No doubt he considers that this sort of thing is of no interest to women."

She opened her fan and made use of it to conceal a smile or perhaps a sense of discomfort which she felt under the prelate's piercing eyes.

"It is my duty to sound the hearts of men," he said as if he had detected her confusion. "But do not be perturbed, my daughter. I can see in your eyes that you are upright and, despite your young years, of outstanding character. And there may still be time for your husband to repent of his faults and abjure his heresies."

Angélique uttered a little cry.

"But I swear to you that you are mistaken, Monseigneur. It may be that my husband does not conduct himself like an exemplary Catholic, but he has no concern whatsoever with the Reform or other Huguenot beliefs. I even heard him mock those 'sad beards of Geneva' who, he says, have been commissioned by Heaven to deprive all mankind of their love of laughter."

"Deceptive words," said the prelate sombrely. "Are not notorious Protestants constantly seen visiting his home, your home, Madame?"

"They are scientists with whom he discusses science, and not religion."

"Science and religion have intimate bonds. I have been informed recently that the famous Italian Bernalli paid him a visit. Do you know that this man, after being in conflict with Rome over his impious writings, has taken refuge in Switzerland, where he became converted to Protestantism? But let us not tarry over these significant signs of a state of mind I deplore. The question that has intrigued me for many years is this. The Comte de Peyrac is a very rich man and getting ever richer. Whence comes this vast profusion of gold?"

"But, Monseigneur, does he not belong to one of the oldest families in Languedoc, related even to the ancient Comtes of Toulouse, who had as much power over Aquitaine as the Kings in the Ile-de-France?"

The prelate gave a little scornful laugh.

"That is correct. But titles of nobility don't signify riches. Your husband's very parents were so poor that the magnificent palace where you reign today was falling to ruin, and this no more than fifteen years ago. Did Monsieur de Peyrac never talk to you about his youth?"

"N . . . no," murmured Angélique, surprised by her own ignorance.

"He was the youngest of the family and so poor, I repeat, that at sixteen he sailed to distant lands. He wasn't seen again for many years and was believed to be dead, when he suddenly reappeared. His parents and his elder brother had died. Their creditors had split up the estate among themselves. He bought back the lot and ever since his fortune has grown constantly. He happens, moreover, to be a nobleman who is never seen at Court, he even makes a show of keeping away from it and he is not in receipt of any royal pension."

"But he has land," said Angélique, who felt oppressed. "In the mountains he breeds sheep from which he obtains wool. He has a big cloth factory to weave the wool, olive groves, silkworm-breeding farms, gold and silver mines. . . ."

"Gold and silver, you say?"

"Yes, Monseigneur, the Comte de Peyrac owns numerous quarries in France from which he claims he extracts quantities of gold and silver."

"How appropriate a term, Madame," said the prelate in a suave voice. "From which he *claims* he extracts gold and silver! . . . That's what I wanted to hear. The dreadful assumption is getting stronger."

"What do you mean, Monseigneur? You alarm me."

The Archbishop of Toulouse again fixed upon her his clear gaze, which grew as hard as steel.

He said very slowly:

"I do not doubt that your husband may be one of the greatest scientists of our time; that's why I believe, Madame, that he has actually discovered the Philosopher's Stone, that is to say Solomon's secret of manufacturing gold by magic. But what path has he taken to reach this goal? I greatly fear he has acquired this power by a pact with the *devil!*"

Once more Angélique held the fan before her lips in order not to burst out laughing. She had expected an allusion to the real pact in which the Count was involved and of which Molines and her father's confidences had given her some hint; she was not without apprehension, for she knew that such activities on a nobleman's part represented a stain that could throw discredit on his house. Therefore the odd charge made by the Archbishop, who was said to be a man of great intelligence, struck her at first as being extremely funny. Was he speaking seriously?

In a sudden flash she recalled that Toulouse was, of all the cities of France, the one where the Inquisition had still maintained a headquarters. The dreadful medieval institution of the tribunal against heretics preserved powers in Toulouse that even the King's authority did not dare to contest.

The laughing city of Toulouse was also the red city which had massacred the greatest number of Huguenots in the course of a century. It had seen, long before Paris, its own bloody St. Bartholomew's Night. Religious ceremonies were more numerous here than anywhere else. It was a real "ringing island" with its bells perpetually calling the faithful to service, a city quite as much submerged under crucifixes, holy pictures and relics, as under flowers. The Spanish flame smothered the pure Latin clarity, inherited from former Roman conquerors. Side by side with the brotherhoods of pleasure, such as the "Princes of Love" and the "Abbots of Youth," famous for their pranks, one could meet in the streets processions of flagellants, their eyes glowing with mystical passion, slashing themselves with switches and thorns till the pavement ran with their bloody traces.

Angélique, caught up in the whirlwind of a life of pleasure, had never given much thought to this aspect of Toulouse. But she was aware that it was the Archbishop himself, this man seated in front of her in the tall tapestry armchair and raising a glass of iced lemonade to his lips, who was still the Grand Master of the Inquisition.

Therefore it was in a sincerely disturbed voice that she murmured:

"Monseigneur, you cannot possibly level a charge of witchcraft against my husband. . . . Is not gold-making a current practice in this country which God has endowed with His richest gifts, scattering in its soil gold in a pure state?"

She added shrewdly:

"I have been told that you yourself employ teams of gold-washers who rinse the gravel of the Garonne in baskets and often bring back a booty of gold sand and nuggets with which you relieve much poverty."

"Your objection is not devoid of common sense, my daughter. But it's just because I know something of the working of the soil's gold that I maintain that were one to wash the gravel of all the rivers and brooks of Languedoc, the yield would still not amount to half of what the Comte de Peyrac appears to possess. I am well informed, believe me."

"I do not doubt it," thought Angélique. "It's true the Spanish gold traffic on mule-back has been going on for a long while. . . ."

The blue eyes watched her hesitation closely. She snapped her fan shut rather nervously.

"A scientist is not necessarily a henchman of the devil. Aren't there supposed to be scientists at Court who have set up a glass lens to look at the stars and the mountains of the moon, and doesn't the King's uncle, Monsieur Gaston d'Orléans, indulge in these observations under the guidance of the Abbé Picard?"

"Yes indeed, and I know Abbé Picard personally. He is not only an astronomer, but the King's Grand Geometrician."

"So you see . . ."

"The Church is broad-minded, Madame. She has authorized all sorts of researches, even the most daring, like that of Abbé Picard whom you mentioned. I go even farther. I have under my command, at the Archbishopric, a very learned monk, of the Franciscan Order, Friar Bécher. He has been doing research work for years on the transmutation of gold, but with my authorisation as well as with Rome's. I confess it has cost me a great deal so far, particularly in special materials which I have to import from Spain and Italy. This man, who knows the most ancient traditions of his art, asserts that, in order to succeed, one must have a higher revelation which can only come from God or Satan."

"And has he succeeded?"

"Not yet."

"Poor man. He must be on bad terms with both God and Satan, despite your high protection."

Angélique bit her lips, immediately regretting her malice. She thought she was going to stifle and felt obliged to blurt out any kind of foolishness to free herself from this constraint. The conversation seemed to her as silly as it was dangerous.

She turned towards the door, hoping to hear her husband's uneven step approaching in the gallery and gave a start.

"Oh! you were here all the time!"

"I've just come this moment," said the Comte, "and it is unforgivable, Monsieur, to have kept you waiting so long. I must admit that your visit was announced to me almost an hour ago, but it was impossible to interrupt the very delicate handling of a certain retort."

He was still dressed in his alchemist's smock which touched the ground. It was a sort of wide shirt on which the embroidered signs of the zodiac mingled with vari-coloured acid stains. Angélique had no doubt that he had not changed his clothes out of a certain obstinacy, just as he made a point of calling the Archbishop of Toulouse "Monsieur," thus putting himself on an equal footing with the Baron Benoît de Frontenac.

The Comte de Peyrac motioned to a footman in the anteroom, who helped him to take off his garment. He then approached and bowed. A ray of sunlight made the heavy lustrous locks of his dark mane glisten.

"He has the most wonderful hair in the world," thought Angélique.

Her heart beat faster than she cared to admit. The scene of the previous night rose again before her eyes.

"It can't be true," she told herself again. "Someone else must have been singing. Oh, I'll never forgive him!"

The Comte de Peyrac had meanwhile pushed forward a high stool and sat down close to Angélique, though a little behind her. He was thus out of her sight but she felt the warmth of his breath, whose scent reminded her all too strongly of an intoxicating moment. Moreover, she was conscious of the fact that Joffrey de Peyrac, while exchanging banalities with the Archbishop, was availing himself of the opportunity to caress his young wife's neck and shoulders with his eyes, even plunging boldly into the soft shadows of her bodice, seeking the young breasts whose perfection he had ascertained the very night before.

He deliberately played this game in front of the prelate, whose strict sense of virtue was common knowledge.

Indeed, though the Archbishop of Toulouse had inherited his office from one of his uncles, he had insisted on receiving orders and of assuming his responsibilities not only as an administrator of the most important see in France but also as a shepherd of souls. His exemplary life offered no grounds for criticism and had rendered him still more redoubtable.

Angélique felt an urge to turn to her husband

and implore him: "I beg of you, be cautious!"

Yet, at the same time, she was relishing his silent homage. Her virginal skin, starved of caresses, was longing for a more direct contact, for those knowing lips that would waken her to voluptuousness. Sitting very straight and a little stiffly, she felt a flame rising to her cheeks. She told herself that she was being ridiculous, that there was nothing in all this to irritate the Archbishop since she was, after all, the wife of that man and belonged to him. She felt invaded by the desire to be his, to surrender herself, gravely, with closed eyes, to his embrace. Her discomfort could certainly not escape Joffrey de Peyrac and he must be amused by it. "He is playing with me like a cat with a mouse, he's avenging himself for my having spurned him," she thought with dismay.

To dispel her confusion, she called one of the little blackamoors who was drowsing on a cushion in a corner of the room, and ordered him to fetch a comfit-box. By the time the child had brought the ebony and mother-of-pearl case containing nuts, comfits, spiced sugar almonds and rose-sugar, Angélique had recovered her self-control and was following the two men's conversation more attentively.

"No, Monsieur," the Comte de Peyrac was saying, as he casually munched a violet-flavoured lozenge, "don't think that I have gone in for science for the purpose of learning the secrets of power and might. I've always had a natural taste for these things. Had I remained poor, for instance, I should have tried to obtain a post as water engineer to the King. You cannot imagine how back-

307

ward we are in France in all these matters of irrigation, pumping, and so on. The Romans knew ten times more than we do, and when I visited Egypt and China —"

"I know that you have travelled widely, Comte. Have you not been to those countries of the Orient where the secrets of the Three Magi are still known?"

Joffrey started to laugh.

"I went there but I did not come across the Three Magi. Magic is not my concern. I leave this to your good gullible Bécher."

"Bécher always asks when he may be allowed the pleasure of seeing one of your experiments and becoming your pupil in chemistry."

"I am not a schoolmaster, sir. And even if I were, I know I'd keep narrow minds at arm's length."

"Yet this friar is regarded as having a subtle mind."

"In scholastics, no doubt, but in sciences of observation he is worthless. He does not see things as they are, but as he *believes* they are. I call such a man unintelligent and narrow-minded."

"Well, that is your point of view. I am too ignorant in lay sciences to judge the merits of your antipathy. But don't forget that Abbé Bécher, whom you treat as an ignoramus, published in 1639 a remarkable book on alchemy for which, incidentally, I had some difficulty in getting the imprimatur of Rome."

"The Church's approval or rebuke has no bearing on a scientific writing," said the Comte somewhat dryly.

"Allow me to differ. Does not the spirit of the Church embrace the whole of nature and its phenomena?"

"I don't know why it should. Remember, Monseigneur, Our Lord's words: 'Render to Caesar what is Caesar's.' Caesar is the external power over men, but also the external power over things. In speaking thus, the Son of God meant to affirm the independence of the realm of the soul, the religious domain, from the realm of matter, and I have no doubt that abstract science is included in the latter."

The prelate nodded several times, while a bland smile split his narrow lips.

"I admire your dialectics. They are worthy of the great tradition and show that you have well assimilated the theological teaching you received in the University of our city. Nevertheless, that is where the judgment of the high clergy intervenes to settle arguments, for nothing looks more like reason than unreason."

"Monseigneur, that phrase of yours delights me. For I hold that, unless it is a question of strictly Church matters, that is of dogma and morals, I must draw my arguments from *observed facts* alone, and not from logicians' quibbles. In other words, I must trust the methods of observation exposed by Bacon in his *Novum Organum* published in 1620, as well as the indications given by the mathematician Descartes, whose *Discourse on Method* will remain one of the monuments of philosophy and mathematics. . . ."

Angélique could see that the names of the two savants were practically unknown to the prelate, who was considered a learned man. She was fearful lest the discussion take a harsher turn, and especially lest Joffrey do nothing to placate the Archbishop.

"Why must men argue over the respective merits of pin-heads?" she wondered. But more than anything she feared that the Archbishop's skilful digressions were meant to lead Joffrey de Peyrac into a trap.

The churchman's susceptibility seemed to have been wounded. His pale, carefully-shaven cheeks flushed, and he dropped his eyelids with an expression of haughty cunning which frightened the young woman.

"Monsieur de Peyrac," he said, "you speak of power: power over men, power over things. Did it ever occur to you that the extraordinary success of your life might seem suspect to many, and particularly to the watchful attention of the Church? Your wealth increases daily, your scientific work brings to you scientists who have grown grey over their studies. I talked to one of them last year, a German mathematician. He was amazed that you had solved, as if they were child's play, problems on which the greatest minds of our day have pondered in vain. You speak a dozen languages . . ."

"Pic de la Mirandole, in the last century, spoke eighteen."

"You have a voice that makes the great Italian singer Maroni go pale with jealousy, you versify delightfully, you carry to its highest point — forgive me, Madame — the art of attracting women. . . ."

"And this? . . ."

Angélique guessed, with an aching heart, that Joffrey de Peyrac had raised a hand to his disfigured cheek.

The Archbishop's embarrassment resolved itself in an angry grimace.

"Ah, you manage, goodness knows how, to make people forget it. You're a man of too many parts, believe me."

"Your charges surprise and shake me," said the Comte slowly. "I had not yet realized that I was the butt of so much envy. It seemed to me, on the contrary, that I was burdened with a cruel disadvantage."

He leaned forward, and his eyes shone as if he had just discovered the point of a good joke.

"Do you know, Monseigneur, that I am, after a fashion, a Huguenot martyr?"

"You a Huguenot?" exclaimed the horrified prelate.

"I said 'after a fashion' Here's my story: my mother entrusted me, on birth, to a woman she had chosen, not according to her religion but according to the size of her breasts. It so happened that this wet-nurse was a Huguenot. She took me to her village in the Cévannes, which was dominated by the château of a Protestant seigneur. Not far from there, as could be expected, there was another seigneur and some Catholic villages. I don't know the exact order of what happened next. I was three years old when Catholics and Huguenots started fighting. My nurse and the women of her village had taken shelter in the château of the reformed seigneur. The Catholics took it by storm towards the middle of the night. They cut everyone's throat and then set fire to the house. As for me, after having my face slashed by three sabre-cuts, I was flung out of the window and fell two storeys into a snow-covered courtyard. The snow saved me from the shower of flaming debris that fell all around me. In the morning, one of the Catholics who had come back for loot, and who recognized me as the child of Toulouse nobles, picked me up and put me into a basket on his back together with my foster-sister Margot, the only other one to have escaped the slaughter. The man passed through several snowstorms before reaching the plains. When he arrived in Toulouse, I was still alive. My mother carried me to a terrace in the sun, undressed me and forbade the doctors to come near me, for she said they'd finish me off. I remained like that, stretched out in the sun, for years. It was only towards the age of twelve that I was able to walk. At sixteen I sailed away. That's how I came to have leisure enough for studying. Thanks to my illness and lying motionless first, thanks to my voyages afterwards. There is nothing suspicious about it."

The Archbishop remained silent for a moment, then said musingly:

"Your story explains a good many things. I am no longer surprised by your sympathy for the Protestants."

"I have no sympathy for Protestants."

"Let's say then, your dislike of Catholics."

"I have no dislike for Catholics. I am, Monsieur, a man of the past and am ill-accommodated to our intolerant age. I should have been born a century or two ago, in the days of the Renaissance, a gentler name than that of the Reform, when the French knights discovered Italy and, in its wake, the luminous heritage of Antiquity: Rome, Greece, Egypt, the lands of the Bible . . ."

Monseigneur de Frontenac gave an imperceptible start which did not escape Angélique.

"He has got him where he wants him," she told herself.

"Let us talk of the Bible lands," suggested the Archbishop gently. "Does not the Scripture say that King Solomon was one of the first Wise Men and that he sent vessels to Ophir where, far from indiscreet eyes, he had cheap metals changed into precious ones by transmutation? History says that he brought back his vessels laden with gold."

"History also says that Solomon doubled taxes on his return, which proves he cannot have brought back much gold and, especially, that he had no idea as to when he would be able to replenish his stock. Had he really discovered the process of making gold, he would not have levied taxes nor gone to the trouble of sending his ships to Ophir."

"He might have chosen, in his wisdom, not to let his subjects into a secret which they might have put to bad uses."

"But I should go further: Solomon cannot have been familiar with the transmutation of metals into gold, for such transmutation is an impossible phenomenon. Alchemy is an art which does not exist. It is a sinister farce come down to us from the Middle Ages and which will founder in ridicule anyway, for nobody will ever be able to per-

313

form this transmutation."

"And I tell you," cried the Archbishop, growing pale, "that I have with my own eyes seen Bécher dip a tin spoon into a mixture of his own composition, and raise it again transformed into gold."

"It was not transformed into gold, it was coated with gold. If the good man had only bothered to scrape off this slight film with a chisel, he would have found the tin immediately underneath."

"That is correct, but Bécher asserts that this was only the beginning of transmutation, the starting-point of the phenomenon itself."

There was a silence. Joffrey de Peyrac's hand slipped over the arm-rest of Angélique's chair, and lightly touched the young woman's wrist.

The Comte said casually:

"If you are convinced your monk has found the magic formula, whatever have you come to see me about this morning?"

The Archbishop did not bat an eye.

"Bécher is convinced that you know the supreme secret which permits the completion of the transmutation."

The Comte de Peyrac burst into ringing laughter.

"I have never heard a funnier assertion. To think that I would throw myself into such childish research! Poor Bécher, I gladly leave him to all the excitement and hopes of the false science he practises and . . ."

A dreadful noise, like that of a thunderclap or a cannon, interrupted him.

Joffrey started up and blanched.

314

"That's . . . that's the laboratory. I hope to God Kouassi-Ba hasn't been killed!"

He hurried towards the door.

The Archbishop had sat up as straight as a judge. He gazed at Angélique in silence.

"I am leaving, Madame," he said at last. "It seems that Satan is manifesting his fury in this house on account of my presence. Allow me to withdraw."

And he strode away. The crack of whips and the coachman's shouts could be heard as the Archbishop's carriage drove away from the great porch.

Chapter 18

ALONE and stunned, Angélique passed her little handkerchief over her perspiring brow. This conversation, to which she had listened with fascination, left her disconcerted. She was sick and tired of all these stories of God, Solomon, heresy and magic. Then, reproaching herself for these irreverent thoughts, she made an act of contrition. Finally she decided that men were insufferable with their squabbles and that God Himself must be exasperated by them.

Angélique could not decide what to do. She was dying to go into the wing of the castle from which the thunderous din had come. Joffrey had seemed genuinely alarmed. Had anyone been hurt? . . . Yet she did not move. The mystery in which the Comte wrapped his studies had made her understand more than once that this was the only realm in which he did not tolerate a layman's curiosity. The elucidations he had deigned to give the Archbishop had been offered reluctantly and solely out of regard for the visitor's position. But even these had not sufficed to allay the prelate's suspicions.

Angélique shuddered. Witchcraft! She threw a glance around her. In this delightful setting the word seemed a sinister joke. But there were still too many things Angélique knew nothing about.

"I shall go and have a look," she decided. "So much the worse if he is vexed."

But at that moment she heard her husband's step and soon after he came into the drawing-room. His hands were black with soot. He was smiling, though.

"Nothing serious, thank goodness. Kouassi-Ba got a few scratches, but he hid himself so well under the table that I thought for a moment that the explosion had volatilized him. The material damage, however, is serious. My most precious retorts of special Bohemian glass are in pieces; there is not a single one left."

At a sign from him, two pages stepped forward, carrying a basin and a golden ewer. He washed his hands, then straightened his lace cuffs with a flick of his finger.

Angélique screwed up her courage.

"Is it necessary, Joffrey, for you to devote so many hours to this dangerous work?"

"It is necessary to have gold in order to live," said the Comte, indicating with a sweeping gesture the magnificent drawing-room. "But that isn't the question. I find a pleasure in this work that nothing

316

else can give me. It's my life's purpose."

Angélique felt a twinge at her heart, as if those words deprived her of a precious treasure. But noticing that her husband was watching her attentively, she strove to assume an air of indifference. He smiled.

"It's the only purpose in my life, except to conquer you," he concluded with a chivalrous flourish.

"I do not set myself up as a rival to your phials and retorts," said Angélique a little too quickly. "However, I must confess that Monseigneur's words have perturbed me."

"Really?"

"Did you not sense a hidden menace in them?"

He did not answer immediately. Leaning against the window, he was gazing thoughtfully out at the flat roofs of the city, closely grouped so that their round tiles formed a vast carpet of mingled hues of clover and poppies. To the right, the high tower of Assézat with its lantern proclaimed the glory of the pastel traders, whose fields still covered the surrounding countryside. Pastel, a plant abundantly cultivated, had for centuries provided the only natural colouring matter and had made the fortune of the burghers and traders of Toulouse.

Angélique returned to her armchair and a little blackamoor placed at her side the basket-work box in which the shimmering silk threads of her tapestry were entangled. The palace was quiet. Angélique reflected that she would be lunching alone with the Comte de Peyrac, unless the inevitable Bernard d'Andijos happened to invite himself. . . .

"Did you notice," the Comte said suddenly, "the Grand Inquisitor's art? First he talked of morals, stresses in passing the 'orgies' at the Gay Learning, alludes to my voyages, and thence leads us on to Solomon. In short, one discovers all at once that the Baron Benoît de Frontenac, Archbishop of Toulouse, is asking me to share with him my secret of the manufacture of gold, failing which he will have me burned as a sorcerer on the Place des Salines."

"That is the threat I thought I divined," said Angélique, frightened. "Do you think he really imagines that you have dealings with the devil?"

"He? No. He leaves that to his credulous Bécher. The Archbishop has too positive a mind and knows me too well. But he is convinced that I have the secret of scientifically multiplying gold and silver. He wants to know it in order to be able to make use of it himself."

"He's a vile creature!" cried the young woman. "And yet he seems so dignified, so full of faith, so generous."

"He is. His wealth goes into his good works. He holds open table every day for impecunious officers. He has taken in charge the fire service, the foundlings' home, I know not what else. He labours for the good of souls and the greatness of God. Still, his private demon is the demon of domination. He hankers after the days when the sole master of a city and even a province was the bishop who, crozier in hand, rendered justice, punished, recompensed. Therefore, when he sees across from his cathedral the growing influence of Gay Learning, he rebels. If things go on in this

318

way, then in another few years it'll be the Comte de Peyrac, your husband, my dear Angélique, who will rule over Toulouse. Gold and silver give power, and thus power will fall into the hands of a henchman of Satan! So Monseigneur does not hesitate. Either we share the power, or else . . ."

"What will happen?"

"Don't be afraid, my dear. Although the intrigues of an Archbishop of Toulouse might be disastrous for us, I don't see why it should come to such extremes. He has shown his cards. He wants to have the secret of gold-making. I shall gladly let him have it."

"So you do possess it?" gasped Angélique, opening her eyes wide.

"Let's not confuse things. I possess no magic formula for *creating* gold. My aim is not so much to amass wealth as to put the forces of nature to work."

"But isn't this a somewhat heretical idea, as Monseigneur would say?"

Joffrey burst out laughing.

"I see you have been well catechized. You are beginning to struggle in the cobwebs of all those specious arguments. Alas, I admit it's difficult to see through them. Yet the medieval Church did not excommunicate millers, who used wind and water to turn the blades of their mills. But today's Church would go to war against me, if I tried to build on the heights around Toulouse the same steam-pump of condensed water that I have set up in your mine at Argentière. Yet it isn't because I place a glass or stone receptacle on the fire of a smithy that Lucifer will suddenly drop into it. . . ."

"I must admit the explosion just now was very impressive. Monseigneur was greatly troubled by it, and I think this time he was sincere. Did you do it on purpose?"

"No, it was sheer carelessness. I let a preparation get too dry — fulminant gold obtained from rolled gold and royal water and then precipitated by ammonia. There was no spontaneous generation involved in this operation."

"What is it that you call ammonia?"

"A product which the Arabs manufactured centuries ago, calling it *volatile alkali*. A learned Spanish monk, who is a friend of mine, recently sent me a demi-john of it. I might manufacture it myself, but it's a tedious business, and in order to advance my research I prefer to buy my products whenever it is possible to find them ready-made. This manufacture of pure ingredients greatly delays the progress of a science which fools like that monk Bécher call chemistry, as opposed to alchemy, which is for them the science of sciences, that is to say an obscure mixture of vital fluids, religious formulas and Heaven knows what else. But I am boring you. . . ."

"No, I assure you," said Angélique with shining eyes. "I could listen to you for hours."

He responded with a smile, which was rendered even more ironical by the scars on his left cheek.

"What a funny little mind! Never would I have dreamed of talking to a woman of such things. I, too, enjoy talking to you. I have the impression that you can understand anything. And yet . . . weren't you on the brink of crediting me with sinister powers when you first arrived in Languedoc? Do I still frighten you?"

Angélique felt herself blush, but she bravely returned his gaze.

"No! You are still a stranger to me and that is, I think, because you are not like anybody else, but you no longer frighten me."

He hobbled over to where he had sat during the Archbishop's visit in the chair just behind her. Although he did not fear, at certain moments and with provocative insolence, to show his disfigured face deliberately in the glare of light, he sought, at others, the shadow of darkness. His voice then took on new intonations, as if the soul of Joffrey de Peyrac, delivered from its fleshly envelope, could at last express itself freely.

So Angélique could feel near her the invisible presence of the "red man" who had so terrified her. This was certainly the same man, but she had changed. She was on the point of putting the anxious womanly question: "Do you love me?"

Suddenly her pride rebelled, for she remembered the voice that had said "You'll come. . . . They all come."

In order to dispel her confusion, she led the conversation back to the scientific field where their minds had met so strangely.

"Since you see no reason for not yielding up your secret, why do you refuse to receive this friar, Bécher, of whom Monseigneur seems to think so highly?"

"Well — I suppose I could satisfy him to that extent. What troubles me is not the matter of revealing my secret but of making people understand it. I would exhaust myself in vain to prove that matter can be transformed but not transmuted. The minds of these people are not ripe for such revelations. And the pride of those sham scientists is such that they'd cry havoc if I assured them that my two most valuable assistants in this research have been a black-skinned Moor and a rustic Saxon miner."

"Kouassi-Ba, and the old hump-backed Fritz Hauer, at Argentière?"

"Yes. Kouassi-Ba told me that when he was still a child and free, somewhere in the heart of his wild Africa, he saw gold being worked according to the ancient methods learned from the Egyptians. The Pharaohs and King Solomon had gold mines even in those parts; but I ask you, my dear, what will Monseigneur say if I confess to him that King Solomon's secret is in the keeping of my negro Kouassi-Ba? Yet he it is who guided me in my laboratory work, and gave me the idea of treating certain rocks containing invisible gold. As for Fritz Hauer, he is a miner thoroughly at home underground, a mole who breathes in the bowels of the earth. These Saxon miners have handed down their knowledge from father to son, and thanks to them I can at last find my way through Nature's odd mystifications and employ successfully all the various ingredients: lead, silver or vitriol, corrosive sublimate and others."

"Did you ever manufacture corrosive sublimate and vitriol?" inquired Angélique, for whom these words were vaguely familiar.

"I did indeed, and this helped me to demonstrate the ineptitude of all alchemy, for from corrosive sublimate I can extract at will either quicksilver or yellow and red mercury, and these latter bodies, in turn, I can transform back into quicksilver. The original weight of mercury will not only undergo no increase but, on the contrary, it will diminish, because there is loss through evaporation. In the same way I can, by certain processes, extract silver from lead, and gold from certain ostensibly sterile rocks. But if I were to inscribe over the door of my laboratory the words 'Nothing is lost, nothing is created,' my philosophy would seem very daring and even in opposition to the spirit of Genesis."

"Doesn't a process of this type enable you to send to Argentière Mexican gold ingots that you buy in London?"

"You are a clever little minx, but I find Molines rather garrulous. Never mind, if he's talked to you, he must have judged that he could. Yes, the Spanish ingots can be melted down again on a smithy with pyrites or lead ore. They then assume the appearance of a grey-black dross, which even the most finicky Customs officer cannot possibly suspect. And it's this matte which your father's good little mules transport from England to Poitou, or from Spain to Toulouse, where it is once again transformed, by me or by my Saxon Hauer, into fine, glistening gold."

"That is a 'fiscal fraud,' " declared Angélique rather sternly.

"You are adorable when you talk like that. This fraud in no way harms either the kingdom or His Majesty, and it makes me rich. Anyway, I shall soon call on Fritz to start work in a gold mine I have discovered at a place called Salsigne, not far from Narbonne. With the gold from that mountain and the silver from Poitou, I shall no longer need precious ore from America nor have to resort to this fraud, as you call it."

"Why haven't you tried to interest the King in your discoveries? There may well be other parts in France that could be worked according to your methods, and the King would be very grateful to you."

"The King is far away, my pretty one, and I'm not cut out to be a courtier. Only people of that sort can hope to exert some influence over the destinies of the kingdom. I don't deny that Monsieur de Mazarin is devoted to the Crown, but he is above all an international intriguer. As for Monsieur Fouquet, who is instructed to find silver for Cardinal Mazarin, he is a financial genius, but to make the country rich by a well-planned exploitation of its natural wealth is, I believe, a matter of complete indifference to him."

"Monsieur Fouquet," exclaimed Angélique, "that's it! I remember now where I heard of Roman vitriol and corrosive sublimate! It was at the Château du Plessis."

The whole scene rose again before her eyes. The Italian in his rough homespun gown, the naked woman among the laces, the Prince de Condé and the sandalwood casket in which gleamed the emerald flask.

"What are you thinking of?" asked the Comte de Peyrac.

"Of a curious adventure I had a long time ago."

And then, although she had kept silent for so long, she told him the whole story of the casket, all the details of which had remained etched in her memory.

"Monsieur de Condé's intention," she added, "was no doubt to poison the Cardinal, and perhaps even the King and his young brother. Less understandable to me were those letters, a sort of signed oath which the Prince and the other lords were to hand to Monsieur Fouquet. Wait! The wording escapes me. . . . It was something like this: 'I pledge my loyalty solely to Monsieur Fouquet, place all my possessions at his disposal. . . .'"

Joffrey de Peyrac had listened to her in silence. Then he laughed scornfully:

"A fine lot indeed! And when you think that Fouquet at that time was merely an obscure member of Parliament! But with his financial skill he was already able to have princes do his bidding. Now he is the richest man in the kingdom, apart from Mazarin, of course. Which proves that there was room for both of them in His Majesty's warm sun. So you were bold enough to get hold of that casket? You concealed it?"

An instinctive prudence suddenly sealed her lips.

"No, I threw it into the water-lily pond in the big park."

"And do you think anyone suspected your part in this disappearance?"

"I don't know. I don't think they attached much importance to my small person. Still, I did hint at the casket to the Prince de Condé."

"Did you? But that was foolhardy!"

"I had to, in order to obtain exemption of transport taxes for my father's mules. Oh, that's quite

325

a tale," she said laughingly, "and I know now that you were indirectly mixed up with it. But I'd gladly start this sort of rashness all over again, were it only to see the ashen faces of that arrogant crowd."

When she had finished telling the story of her skirmish with the Prince de Condé, her husband nodded.

"I am almost surprised to find you still alive at my side. Actually you must have seemed too innocent to them. But it's a dangerous thing to get tangled as a pawn in courtiers' intrigues. Making away with a little girl wouldn't embarrass them, if the need arose."

He got up as he talked and Angélique saw him advance towards a door-hanging, which he quickly pulled aside. He returned with a vexed air.

"I am not nimble enough to catch eavesdroppers."

"Someone was listening?"

"I am certain of it."

"This isn't the first time that I have had the impression that we are being spied upon."

He sat down behind her again. The heat was getting more oppressive, but the city suddenly began to vibrate with a thousand bells ringing out the Angelus. The young woman crossed herself devoutly and murmured an orison to the Virgin Mary. The mighty wave of sound broke over them and for a long while Angélique and her husband, who were seated by the open window, could not exchange a word. So they remained silent, and the intimacy which was growing between them stirred Angélique deeply.

"Not only does his presence not displease me, it actually makes me happy," she thought to herself with surprise. "If he kissed me now, would I find it unpleasant?"

Once again, she became conscious of her husband's eyes on her white neck.

"No, my darling, I am not a magician," he murmured. "Perhaps I have received some power from nature, but above all I have wanted to *learn*. Do you understand?" he said in that cajoling tone that charmed her. "I thirsted to learn all that was difficult: sciences, letters, and also women's hearts. I applied myself with delight to this charming mystery. One thinks there is nothing behind the eyes of a woman and then one discovers a new world. Or else you imagine a new world and discover there's nothing . . . except a jingling bell. What is there behind your green eyes, which evoke fresh meadows and the tumultuous sea? . . ."

She heard him move, and his luxuriant black hair flowed over her naked shoulder like a warm, silky fur. She quivered at the touch of the lips which she was unconsciously yearning for. Savouring, with closed eyes, this long, ardent kiss, Angélique felt the hour of her defeat approaching. Then she would come trembling, still restive but submissive, like the others, to offer herself to the embraces of this mysterious man.

Chapter 19

SOME days later, Angélique was returning from a morning ride along the banks of the Garonne. She liked to spend a few hours on horseback just after sunrise, when it was still cool. Joffrey de Peyrac accompanied her infrequently. Unlike most noblemen, he had little taste for riding and hunting. One might have thought he feared violent exercise, if his fame as a swordsman had not been almost as great as his renown as a singer. The flying leaps he executed despite his crippled leg were said to be little short of miraculous. He practised every day in the palace armoury, but Angélique had never seen him fence. There were many things she still did not know about him, and sometimes, with sudden melancholy, she recalled the words the Archbishop had whispered to her on her wedding day: "Between you and me, you have chosen a rather odd husband."

The Comte appeared again to have adopted towards her the respectful, but distant, attitude which he had displayed in the early days. She saw but little of him and then always in the presence of guests, and she wondered if the fiery Carmencita de Mérecourt did not to some extent account for this new estrangement. The lady had, in fact, after a journey to Paris, returned to Toulouse, where her hysterics put everyone on edge. It was being seriously said that this time Monsieur de Mérecourt would shut her up in a convent. If he had not yet carried out this threat, it was for diplomatic reasons. War with Spain still continued, but Monsieur de Mazarin, who had for some time been trying to negotiate a peace, recommended that nothing be done that might inflame Spanish susceptibilities. The beautiful Carmencita belonged to a great Madrid family. The ups and downs of her conjugal life were thus more important than the pitched battles in Flanders. Everything was reported to Madrid, for despite the breaking off of official diplomatic relations, secret messengers were crossing the Pyrénées constantly in a variety of disguises as monks, pedlars or merchants.

Carmencita de Mérecourt flaunted her eccentric way of life, and this perturbed and offended Angélique. Despite the worldly elegance she had acquired from contact with this brilliant society, she had at heart remained as simple as a flower of the field, rustic and over-sensitive. She did not feel strong enough to fight Carmencita, and she sometimes told herself, her heart gnawed by jealousy, that the flamboyant Spanish-woman was better suited than herself to the Comte de Peyrac's unusual character.

Only in the sphere of science was she sure of being the woman who came before all others in her husband's eyes.

That morning, as she was riding back towards the palace with her escort of pages, gallant noblemen and some young girl friends she liked to have with her, she saw once again, in front of the gate, a carriage with the Archbishop's crest. From it she saw alight a tall figure austerely dressed in homespun, followed by a beribboned nobleman, sword at his side, and loud-mouthed, for even at a distance she heard the echo of his voice shouting orders or abuse.

"Upon my word," exclaimed Bernard d'Andijos, who continued to be one of her most faithful followers, "that looks like the Chevalier de Germontaz, Monseigneur's nephew. Heaven preserve us! He is an oaf and the biggest fool I know. If you will take my advice, Madame, we shall pass through the gardens to avoid meeting him."

The small party veered to the left and, after dismounting at the stables, made for the orange grove, which was a very pleasant place surrounded by fountains.

But no sooner had they settled down to an assortment of fruit and iced drinks than Angélique was informed by a page that the Comte de Peyrac was asking for her. In the entrance hall Angélique found her husband in the company of the nobleman and the monk she had seen a moment earlier.

"This is the Abbé Bécher, the distinguished scientist of whom Monseigneur has told us," said Joffrey. "And I also wish to present to you the Chevalier de Germontaz, His Excellency's nephew."

The monk was tall and lean. His prominent eyebrows concealed rather close-set, restless eyes, which glowed with a feverish, mystical light. A long scrawny neck with protruding sinews emerged from his homespun frock. His companion seemed to serve as a foil to his appearance. As boisterously *bon-vivant* as the other was consumed by self-mortification, the Chevalier de Germontaz had a ruddy complexion and, for his twenty-five years, an already estimable *embonpoint*. An opulent fair wig cascaded over his blue satin costume trimmed with flowing pink ribbons. His rhine-grave was so ample and his laces so plentiful that his nobleman's sword seemed incongruous among such a surfeit of frippery. With the ostrich-feather of his wide felt hat he swept the ground before Angélique, then kissed her hand but, as he straightened up again, he gave her such a daring glance that she was outraged by it.

"Now that my wife has joined us, we can proceed to the laboratory," said the Comte de Peyrac.

The friar gave a start and looked down on Angélique with surprise.

"Am I to understand that Madame will enter the sanctuary and be present at the discussions and experiments to which you are good enough to invite us?"

The Comte grimaced ironically and eyed his guest with insolence. He knew how impressive the expressions of his face were for those who saw him for the first time, and he relished the moment with malice.

"Father, in the letter I addressed to Monseigneur in which I consented to receive you in accordance with the desire he had frequently expressed, I told him that this would in a sense be a visit at which only persons of my choosing might be present. Now he has elected to have you accompanied by the Chevalier, in case your eyes might not see all that which is desirable to see."

"But, Comte, you as a scientist know that a woman's presence is in complete contradiction with the hermetic tradition according to which no results can be obtained among contrary fluids. . . ."

"In my science, Father, results are invariably consistent and do not depend on the mood or quality of the persons present. . . ."

"Personally I think that's excellent!" cried the Chevalier, obviously delighted. "I won't conceal that I fancy a pretty lady more than phials and old pots. My uncle insisted upon my accompanying Bécher in order to instruct myself in the duties of my new office. Yes, my uncle is going to buy me the benefice of a grand vicar over three bishoprics; but he is a terrible man. He'll grant it to me on the sole condition that I take Holy Orders. I confess I'd have been content with the benefices."

While talking, the party had moved towards the library, which the Comte wished to show them first. The monk Bécher, for whom this visit was a long hoped-for opportunity, asked a stream of questions to which Joffrey de Peyrac answered with a resigned patience.

Angélique followed them, escorted by the Chevalier de Germontaz, who lost no opportunity to touch her in passing and cast provocative glances at her.

"He really is an oaf," she thought. "He looks like a fat sucking-pig garnished with flowers and laces for a New Year's Eve banquet."

"What I fail to understand," she said out loud, "is in what way a visit to my husband's laboratory has any connection with your new ecclesiastical office."

"So do I, I confess, but my uncle explained it

to me at length. It seems that the Church is less wealthy and less powerful than she appears to be and especially than she ought to be. My uncle also complains of the centralization of royal power to the detriment of the rights of the states such as the Languedoc. It seems there is an attempt to whittle down more and more the prerogatives of Church assemblies and even of the local Parliament of which, as you know, he is the president. They are to be replaced by the authority of the provincial Administrator and his henchmen, the police, the financiers and the army. He would like to combat this growing invasion by irresponsible delegates of the King by an alliance of the great personages of the province. Yet he sees your husband amassing a colossal fortune with neither the city nor the Church getting anything out of it."

"But, Monsieur le Chevalier, we give to charity."

"That's not enough. What he would like is an alliance."

"For a pupil of the Grand Inquisitor, he is somewhat lacking in finesse," thought Angélique, "unless this happens to be a well-learned lesson!"

"In brief," she resumed, "Monseigneur considers that all the wealth of the province should be handed over to the Church?"

"The Church must be at its head."

"With the Monseigneur at *its* head! You preach very well, you know. I am no longer surprised that you are destined for sacred eloquence. Convey my compliments to your uncle."

"I shall not fail to do so, kind lady. Your smile is ravishing, but I believe your eyes lack tenderness for me. Do not forget that the Church still remains the foremost power, especially in our Languedoc."

"What I see most of all is that you are a convinced vicar-to-be, despite your ribbons and your laces."

"Wealth is a convincing means. My uncle has known how to make use of it in my case. I shall serve him to the best of my ability."

Angélique shut her fan abruptly. She no longer marvelled at the trust the Archbishop put into his fat nephew. Despite their different characters, they shared the same ambition. In the library, where screens maintained a semi-darkness, something moved and bowed at their approach.

"Why, what are you doing here, Master Clément?" asked the Comte with a hint of surprise in his voice. "Nobody comes in here without my permission. I do not think I gave you the key?"

"May your Lordship excuse me; I was tidying up this room myself, not wishing to entrust the care of these precious books to uncouth servants."

He zealously gathered up his duster, brush and step-ladder and retired, bowing deeply.

"I am beginning to understand," sighed the monk, "that I shall see very strange things here: a woman in a laboratory, a valet in the library, touching with unclean hands the books that contain all of science! . . . However, I find that your reputation has not suffered thereby! Let's see what you have here."

He recognized the richly-bound classics of alchemy: *The Principle of the Conservation of Bodies or Mummies*, by Paracelsus; *Alchemy*, by Albertus Magnus; *Hermetica*, by Hermann Couringus; *Ex-*

plicatione 1572, by Thomas Erastus; and finally, what pleased him most, his own book, *Of Transmutation,* by Conan Bécher.

Thus greatly cheered and put at his ease, the monk followed his host. The Comte ushered his guests out of the palace and led them to the wing which housed his laboratory.

The visitors saw smoke rising from a huge chimney on the roof, which looked like the beak of some apocalyptic bird. When they came quite close, the device, with a creaking noise in their direction, revealed a gaping black mouth from which sooty smoke was pouring.

The monk jumped back.

"It's just a chimney-vane to make the wind activate the draught of the furnaces," exclaimed the Comte.

"At my place, the draught is very poor on a windy day."

"Here it is the other way round, for I use the lowering of pressure caused by the wind."

"And the wind does your bidding?"

"Exactly. Just as it does for a windmill."

"In a mill, Comte, the wind makes the millstones turn."

"Here the furnaces don't turn, but the air is sucked in."

"You can't suck air in, since it is a void."

"Yet you'll see that I get a devilish draught."

The monk crossed himself three times before passing over the threshold behind Angélique and the Comte, while the negro Kouassi-Ba saluted them solemnly with his curved sabre and returned it to its sheath. At the far end of the vast room two furnaces were glowing. Still a third one remained dark. In front of the furnaces were strange machines made of leather and iron, as well as earthenware and copper pipes.

"These are the bellows for my forge. I use them when I need a very hot fire, as when I have to melt copper down, or gold or silver," explained Joffrey de Peyrac.

Wooden shelves ran the length of the main room. They were packed with pots and phials bearing labels marked with cabalistic signs and figures.

"I have a stock of various products here: sulphur, copper, tin, lead, borax, orpiment, realgar, cinnabar, mercury, lunar caustic, blue and green vitriol. Opposite, in those glass jars, I have oleum, aqua fortis and spirit of salt. On the top shelf you can see tubes and receptacles of glass, iron, glazed stone, and still farther on, retorts and alembics. In the small room at the back are rocks containing invisible gold, like this arsenical ore, and diverse stones that produce silver by fusion. Here you have some cerargyrite, or horn silver, from Mexico, which I got from a Spanish nobleman who has been there."

"The Comte wishes to mock my poor monkish learning by pretending that this waxen stuff is silver, when I can't detect a trace of it."

"I'll show you presently," said the Comte.

He picked up a big chunk of charcoal from a pile beside the furnaces. He also took from a jar a tallow candle, lit it from the flame of the glowing embers, dug a little hole in the charcoal with an iron pin, inserted into it a blob of the "horn silver" which actually was of a dirty yellow-grey in colour and semi-translucent and added to it a little borax. Then he grasped a curved copper tube, brought it near the candle-flame and adroitly blew the latter against the little hole filled with the two saline substances. They melted, blistered, changed colour; there then appeared a series of metallic drops which the Comte, by blowing harder, merged into a single gleaming globule.

He removed the flame and held up the small sparkling ingot on the tip of a knife.

"Here you have melted silver that I've extracted from this odd-looking rock."

"Do you perform the transmutation of gold just as simply?"

"I perform no transmutation of any kind. I merely extract precious metals from ore that already contains them, but in a non-metallic state."

The monk did not look very convinced. He cleared his throat and glanced around. He nodded and cautiously approached a roaring furnace in which several crucibles were simmering, some at red heat.

"This is certainly a very fine laboratory," he said, "but I see nothing that in any way resembles the 'athanor' or the famous 'House of the Sage's Chicken.' "

Peyrac laughed till he almost choked, and then, calming down, he apologized:

"Forgive me, Father, but my last collection of those venerable idiocies was destroyed when the explosive gold blew up the other day while Monseigneur was here."

Bécher assumed a deferential expression:

"Monseigneur did in fact mention it. So you manage to make an unstable gold which bursts?"

"I even manage to make fulminating quicksilver, to conceal nothing from you."

"But the Philosopher's Egg?"

"It's inside my head!"

"That's blasphemy!" cried the monk in great agitation.

"What's all this about chickens and eggs?" exclaimed Angélique. "Nobody has ever told me about them."

Bécher gave her a scornful glance. But seeing that the Comte de Peyrac was suppressing a smile and that the Chevalier de Germontaz was yawning openly, he had to content himself with this modest audience for lack of a better one.

"It's inside the Philosopher's Egg that the Philosopher's Stone comes into being," he said, drilling his fiery gaze into the young woman's candid eyes. "The firing of the Philosopher's Stone is effected on purified gold, Sun, and fine silver, Moon, to which must be added quicksilver, Mercury. The alchemist subjects them inside the sealed matrass or philosophical egg to the increasing and decreasing ardours of a well-regulated fire, Vulcan. This helps to develop in the compost the seminal powers of Venus, the visible product of which is the Philosopher's Stone, the regenerating substance. From this point on, the reactions will develop within the egg in a definite order: they make it possible to control the baking of the substance. It is especially important to watch for the three colours black, white and red, which indicate the putrefaction, ablation and rubefaction, respectively, of the Philosopher's Stone. In short, the alternation of death and resurrection, through which all vegetating matter must pass, according to ancient philosophy, in order to reproduce itself.

"The spirit of the world, the compulsory intermediary between the soul and the universal body, is the active cause of generations of all kinds and vitalizes the four elements. This spirit is contained in gold, but alas it remains inactive and imprisoned there. It is left to the Sage to release it."

"And how, Father, do you go about releasing this spirit which is at the basis of the world and yet a prisoner of gold?" Peyrac asked suavely.

But the alchemist remained insensitive to irony. His head thrown back, he pursued his old dream.

"To deliver it requires the Philosopher's Stone. But even that is not enough. One must supply the initial impulse by means of a projecting powder, starting-point of the phenomenon which will transform *everything* into *pure gold*."

He remained silent for a moment, deep in his thoughts.

"After years and years of research, I think I may say that I have arrived at certain results. Thus, joining the philosopher's quicksilver — the female principle — with gold — which is male — but carefully choosing pure gold-foil, I put the mixture into the 'athanor' or 'House of the Sage's Chicken,' which is the sanctuary, the tabernacle that every alchemist's laboratory must possess. This egg, which is a retort of perfect oval shape and hermetically sealed so that none of its matter can exhale, is placed by me in a bowl filled with ashes and put into the oven. Thereupon, this mercury, whose heat and inner sulphur, excited by the fire, I keep constantly at the necessary degree of heat and in the necessary proportions — this mercury succeeds in dissolving the gold without violence and reducing it to the state of atoms. At the end of six months I obtain a black powder which I call the Cimmerian Darkness. With this powder I am able to transform certain parts of objects of vile metal into pure gold, but unfortunately the vital germ of my *purum aurum* is not yet strong enough, for I have never been able to transform them completely."

"But you certainly tried, Father, to fortify that moribund germ?" inquired Joffrey de Peyrac, an amused twinkle in his eyes.

"I did, and twice I think I was very close to my goal. This is how I proceeded the first time: for twelve days I let the juice of garden mercury, purslane and fig-wort digest in manure. Then I distilled the product and obtained a red liquor. This I put back into the dung. From it were born worms that devoured one another, except for one that survived. I fed this single worm with the three preceding plants until it had fattened. Then I burned it, reduced it to ashes and mixed this pow-der with vitriol oil as well as with the powder of Cimmerian Darkness. But the latter was scarcely fortified by it."

"Ugh!" said the Chevalier de Germontaz with disgust.

Angélique cast a bewildered glance at her hus-band, but he remained expressionless.

340

"And the second time?" he asked.

"The second time I had great hopes. That was when a traveller who had been shipwrecked on an unknown beach brought me back some virgin earth which had never been trodden on by man, or so he assured me. It is a fact that completely virgin earth contains the seed or germ of metals, that is to say the true Philosopher's Stone. But probably this particle of earth was not absolutely virgin," concluded the learned friar with a crestfallen air, "for I never obtained the hoped-for results."

Now Angélique too felt a strong urge to laugh. To conceal her hilarity, she hastened to ask:

"But didn't you tell me, Joffrey, that you yourself were shipwrecked on a desert island, that was fog- and ice-bound?"

The monk Bécher started up and seized the Comte's shoulders with shining eyes.

"You were shipwrecked on unknown soil? I knew it, I was sure of it. So you are the one of whom our hermetic writings speak, the one who comes back 'from the posterior part of the world, where one hears the thunder growl, the wind whistle, hail and rain come down.' That's the place where one will find the thing if one looks for it."

"It was somewhat as you describe it," the nobleman remarked carelessly. "I shall even add a mountain of fire amid ice that appeared to be eternal. Not a single inhabitant. It was somewhere near the Tierra del Fuego, the land of fire. I was rescued by a Portuguese sailing-boat."

"I'd give my life and even my soul for a morsel of that virgin soil!" exclaimed Bécher.

"Unfortunately, Father, I confess it never occurred to me to bring any back."

The monk cast a gloomy and suspicious glance at him, and Angélique could well see that he did not believe her husband.

The young woman's clear eyes gazed, in turn, at the three men who were standing before her in the weird setting of tubes and jars. Leaning against the brick-post of one of the furnaces, Joffrey de Peyrac, the Great Lame Man of Langue-doc, dropped a haughty, sarcastic glance on his interlocutors. He did not trouble to disguise the poor esteem in which he held their old Don Quixote of alchemy and his beribboned Sancho Panza. Opposite these two grotesque figures, Angélique saw him so tall, so free, so extraordinary that an overwhelming feeling swelled her heart till it ached.

"I love him," she suddenly thought. "I love him and I am afraid. Oh! if only they won't harm him. Not before . . . Not before . . ."

She did not dare conclude her wish: "not before he has clasped me in his arms. . . ."

Chapter 20

"LOVE," said Joffrey de Peyrac, "the art of love is that most precious characteristic of our race. I have travelled across many lands and it was acknowledged everywhere. Let us rejoice over it, gentlemen, and you, ladies, preen yourselves, but let us all be wary. For nothing is more fragile than this reputation, if a discerning heart and a skilful body do not help to sustain it."

His face, masked in deep black velvet and framed by his luxuriant mane, was thrust forward and revealed his sparkling smile.

"That is why we have gathered here in the Palace of Gay Learning. However, I did not invite you for a return to the past. No doubt, I shall recall the teaching of our master in the art of love who once roused the hearts of men to feelings of love, but we shall not overlook what the ensuing centuries have added to the perfection of this art: the art of conversation, of entertainment, of sparkling wit, or even those simpler enjoyments which also serve to foster an amorous disposition — good food and good drink."

"Ah! this suits me better!" bellowed the Chevalier de Germontaz. "Sensibilities can go hang! I eat half a wild boar, three partridges, six chickens, I down a bottle of Champagne wine, and hop! to bed, my pretty one!"

"And when the pretty one is called Madame de Montmaur, her story is that you are a very good and loud snorer, but that's all you can do in bed."

"She says that? Oh, the traitress! It's true that one night, feeling a bit heavy —"

A general burst of laughter interrupted the fat chevalier who, assuming a brave front, lifted the silver lid of one of the dishes and seized a chicken-wing between two fingers.

"When I eat, I eat. I'm not like you who mix up everything and who try to use refinement where there's no need for it."

"You oafish hog!" said the Comte de Peyrac

softly, "how pleased I am to contemplate you! You so well personify all that we banish from our customs, all that we hate. Look, gentlemen, and you, ladies, here you have a descendant of the barbarians, of those crusaders who came in the wake of their bishops to light a thousand stakes between Albi, Toulouse and Pau. They were so fiercely jealous of this delightful land where everyone sang of ladies' love that they reduced it to ashes and turned Toulouse into an intolerant, suspicious city, with the ruthless eyes of fanaticism. Let's not forget it. . . ."

"He should not talk like that," thought Angélique.

Everyone laughed, but she could see a cruel gleam in certain black eyes. It was something that always surprised her, this bitterness of the southerners over a past four hundred years old. But the horrors of the crusade against the Albigeois had been such that even now, in the countryside, mothers would threaten their children with the terrible Montfort. Joffrey de Peyrac liked to stir up this rancour, not so much from a provincial fanaticism as out of his horror of all narrow-mindedness, stupidity and coarseness.

Seated at the other end of the table, Angélique looked at his crimson velvet costume studded with diamonds. His masked face and dark hair set off the whiteness of his high collar of Flanders lace, of his cuffs and of his long, lively hands, each finger of which was ringed. She herself was dressed in white, and this reminded her of her wedding-day. As on that day, the noblest lords of Languedoc and Gascogne were present and sat at the two big banquet tables that had been set up in the gallery of the palace. But today there were neither old men nor ecclesiastics in this brilliant gathering. Now that Angélique was able to put a name to every face, she recognized that most of the couples around her that evening were not man and wife. Andijos had brought his mistress, a flamboyant Parisian, Madame de Saujac, whose husband was a magistrate in Montpellier. At the moment she was bending her brown head coquettishly over the shoulder of a captain with a golden-hued moustache. Some lone cavaliers drew closer to those bold and independent ladies who had come without a chaperone to the famous Court of Love.

An impression of youth and beauty rose from these sumptuously dressed men and women. Gold and precious stones sparkled in the torch-light. The windows were wide open to the warm spring evening. To keep the mosquitoes at bay, lemon balm leaves and incense were being burned in perfume pans, and their intoxicating scent mingled with the smell of wines.

Angélique felt awkward and out of place like a wild flower in a rose-bed. Yet she was in the full bloom of her beauty, and her manner could stand comparison with that of the noblest ladies. The hand of the little Duc de Forba des Ganges brushed her bare arm.

"How sad, Madame," he whispered, "that such a master should possess you! For I have eyes only for you tonight."

She gave him a playful little tap on the fingers with the tip of her fan.

"Do not be in too much of a hurry to put into

practice what you are being taught here. Listen rather to the words of experience: shame on him who rushes and veers with every wind that blows. Have you not noticed what a pert little nose and rosy cheek your right-hand neighbour has? I have been told that she is a little widow who asks only to be comforted for the death of a very old and cantankerous husband."

"I thank you for your advice, Madame."

" 'A new love chases the old,' says Monsieur le Chapelain."

"Any teaching from your charming lips must needs be followed. Allow me to kiss your fingers and I promise you I shall look after the little widow."

At the other end of the table a discussion was in progress between Cerbalaud and Monsieur de Castel-Jalon.

"I am as poor as a beggar," the latter was saying, "and I'm not hiding the fact that I sold an acre of vineyard to rig myself out decently to come here. But I claim that I don't have to be rich to be loved for myself."

"You'll never be loved with refinement. Your idyll will resemble, at most, that of a devout man who fondles his bottle with one hand and his mistress with the other, while sadly musing over the hard-won coins he'll have to pay out for both."

"I claim that sentiments —"

"Sentiments don't grow in penury. . . ."

Joffrey de Peyrac extended his hands with a laugh.

"Peace, gentlemen, listen to the old master

whose humane philosophy should settle all our disputes. Here are the opening words of his treatise on the Art of Love: 'Love is aristocratic. To concern yourself with love, you must have no material cares and not be harassed by them to the point of counting the hours of every day.' So be rich, gentlemen, and deck your beautiful ladies with jewelry. The sparkle of a woman's eye at the sight of a bauble will soon turn into a sparkle of love. Personally, I adore the glance which a bejewelled woman casts at her mirror. Do not protest, ladies, and do not be hypocritical. Do you appreciate a man who so disdains you that he does not seek to enhance your beauty?"

The ladies laughed and murmured.

"But I am a poor man," cried Castel-Jalon sadly. "Peyrac, don't be so harsh, give me some hope!"

"Get rich!"

"Easy to say!"

"It's always easy for him who wants it. Or, failing it, at least don't be mean. 'Avarice is love's worst enemy.' Since you are a beggar, don't count your time, nor your prowesses; commit a thousand follies and above all make people laugh. 'Boredom is the worm that gnaws at love.' Is it not true, ladies, that you prefer a buffoon to a solemn pedant? . . . And finally I give you this last consolation: 'Merit alone makes you worthy of love.'"

"What a beautiful voice he has and how well he speaks," thought Angélique to herself.

The little duke's kiss had left a burning sensation on her fingers. Obediently he had turned away and was leaning towards the rosy little widow. Angélique was lonely, and her gaze, across the long table and the blue, perfumed smoke, never left the crimson silhouette of the master of the house. Did he see her? Was he sending her a mute appeal from behind the mask with which he had veiled his wounded face? Or was he merely savouring, casually, indifferently, the subtle joust of words, like a contented Epicurean?

"Do you know I am much bewildered," cried the young Duc de Forba des Ganges, half-rising. "This is the first time I've attended a Court of Love, and I was expecting, I confess, a pleasant libertinage and not words of strictness such as I have just heard. 'Merit alone makes you worthy of love.' Do we have to turn into saints to win our ladies?"

"Heaven preserve us, Duc," said the little widow laughingly.

"That's a serious challenge," said Andijos. "Would you care to see me wearing a halo, my dearest?"

"Certainly not."

"What makes you think there is merit in altars?" cried Joffrey de Peyrac. "There's merit in being wild, gay, swashbuckling, cavalier, rhymester and — that's where I have my eye on you, gentlemen — a skilful and ever-ready lover. Our fathers opposed courtly love to Gallic love. But I'll say to you: let's partake of one and the other. One must love truly and completely, and that means carnally."

He fell silent for a moment, then continued in a lower voice:

"But let us not despise the exaltation of feelings which, though not alien to desire, transcend and

348

refine it. That's why I hold that he who wants to know love must submit to the discipline of heart and senses which Le Chapelain recommends: 'A lover must have but one mistress. A mistress must have but one lover.' Choose each other, love each other, part when fatigue overtakes you, but do not be like those flighty lovers who indulge in the drunkenness of passion, who drink from all the cups simultaneously, and thus transform the courts of the kingdom into barnyards."

"By Saint Séverin!" exclaimed Germontaz, emerging from behind his plate. "If my uncle the Archbishop were to hear you, he'd lose his wits. There's no sense in what you say. I've never been taught anything of the sort."

"You've been taught so few things, Monsieur le Chevalier! . . . What is there in my words that shocks you so?"

"Everything. You preach faithfulness and libertinage, decency and carnal love. And then, as if you were suddenly in the pulpit, you attack the 'drunkenness of passion.' I shall pass this term on to my uncle the Archbishop. He'll probably refer to it next Sunday in the cathedral."

"My words are those of human wisdom. Love is the enemy of excess. In loving, as in dining and wining, let's prefer quality to quantity. The bounds where pleasure ends, are those where the strain and nausea of profligacy begin. But can a man savour a knowing kiss, if he guzzles like a hog and drinks like a fish?"

"Am I to recognize myself in that description?" growled the Chevalier de Germontaz, with his mouth full.

Angélique thought that he was good-natured enough. But why did Joffrey seem to go out of his way to provoke him? He knew full well, after all, the dangers of this disagreeable presence.

"The Archbishop has sent us his nephew to spy on us," he had declared to his wife on the eve of the banquet.

And he had added airily:

"Do you know that there is open war between us now?"

"What happened, Joffrey?"

"Nothing. But the Archbishop wants the secret of my fortune, or else my fortune itself. He won't let go of me."

"You'll defend yourself, Joffrey?"

"As best I can. Unfortunately the man isn't born yet who can stamp out human stupidity."

The footman had removed the plates. Eight little pages came in, some carrying baskets of roses, others pyramids of fruit. Before each guest was placed a plate full of spiced sugar-almonds and various sweetmeats.

"I am glad to hear you speak so simply of carnal love," said the young Cerbalaud. "Just imagine, I am madly in love and you see me all by myself at this gathering. I don't think I lacked fervour in my declarations, and without boasting I may say I had the impression at times that my flame was shared. But my lady-love is a prude, alas! If I venture a daring gesture, I harvest cruel eyes and a marked coolness for days. For months now I've been circling on this diabolical carousel: winning her by proving my ardour, and losing her whenever I attempt to prove it! . . ."

350

Cerbalaud's misadventures amused everybody. A lady seized him with both arms and kissed him on the mouth. When the hubbub had subsided a little, Joffrey de Peyrac said with kindness: "Be patient, Cerbalaud, and remember that it is the shy ones who are able to reach the greatest heights of sensual pleasure. But they need a skilful lover to release in them whatever scruple it is that makes them confuse love with sin. Distrust those damsels, too, who so often confuse love with marriage. Now I shall quote you certain precepts: 'In devoting yourself to the pleasures of love, do not go beyond the desire of your beloved; whether giving or receiving the pleasures of love, always observe a certain modesty.' And finally: 'Always heed a lady's commands.'"

"I think you unduly favour the ladies," opined a gentleman who, for his pains, received several sharp cracks from a fan. "To hear you talk, one would constantly have to die at their feet."

"But that's as it should be," approved Bernard d'Andijos's mistress. "Do you know what we *précieuses* in Paris call the young men who woo us? We call them 'the dying.'"

"I don't want to die," said Andijos glumly. "It's my rivals who will die."

"Must we allow women all their whims?"

"Naturally."

"They'll despise us for it —"

"And deceive us —"

"Must we allow ourselves to be deceived?"

"Certainly not," said Joffrey de Peyrac. "Fight a duel, gentlemen, and kill your rival. 'He who

351

is not jealous cannot love.' — 'Suspicion of my beloved makes love's ardour grow.' "

"That infernal Chapelain thought of everything!"

Angélique raised a glass to her lips. Her blood was throbbing in her veins, and she began to laugh. She liked the end of a meal among these southerners, when their accent suddenly rang out with a flourish, challenges and quips were tossed about, and one nobleman would draw his sword while another tuned his guitar.

"Sing! Sing!" a voice clamoured. "The Voice of the Kingdom!"

On the balcony that overhung the gallery the musicians started to play softly. Angélique saw that the little widow had put her head on the shoulder of the young Duc. She was picking up sweetmeats with dainty fingers and slipping them between his lips. They were smiling at each other.

Round and limpid, the moon appeared in the velvety sky. Joffrey de Peyrac motioned to a footman who went about snuffing the candles. It became very dark, but eyes gradually grew accustomed to the soft moonlight; voices had lowered their pitch and in the sudden tranquillity could be heard the sighs of couples in each other's arms. Some of them had already risen from the table. They were roaming through the gardens or in the open galleries pervaded by the balmy breath of night.

"Ladies," said the grave, harmonious voice of Joffrey de Peyrac, "and you, gentlemen, be welcome in the Palace of Gay Learning. For a few days we shall converse together and dine at the same table. Apartments have been prepared for you here. You will find there good wines, pastries and ices. And comfortable beds. Sleep there alone if your mood is morose. Welcome there a friend of an hour . . . or of a lifetime, if that be your wish. Eat, drink, make love . . . but be discreet, for 'love must not be told if it is to retain all its flavour.' One more bit of advice for you, ladies. Remember that laziness, too, is one of love's great enemies. In those lands where woman is still the slave of man, in the Orient and in Africa, it is most often her task to exert herself to lead her master to enjoyment. Under our civilized skies you've indeed been unduly favoured. Too often you respond to our ardour with a languour that is not far from listlessness. Learn therefore to give of yourselves lavishly, and your efforts will be rewarded by the delight of your senses: 'Hasty men, passive women, make pleasureless lovers.' I shall finish by confiding to you a gastronomical hint. Remember, gentlemen, that the wine of Champagne, of which you will find bottles to refresh you at your bedside, is endowed with imagination rather than with constancy. In other words, it is better not to drink too much of it to prepare yourselves for combat. But no other wine can vie with its glory for celebrating victory, refresh a happy night and sustain ardour and strength. Ladies, I salute you."

He pushed back his armchair, abruptly propped his feet on the table, and, taking his guitar, began to sing. His masked face turned towards the moon.

Angélique felt dreadfully alone. A bygone world was rising again from its ashes tonight in the shadow of the tower of Assézat. Hot-blooded Toulouse had found her soul again. Sensual pleasure had the run of the city, and Angélique's youthful vigour could not remain insensitive to it. Almost all the guests had left the room by now. Some of them, still in the window-recesses, with a glass of rosolio in their hands, were indulging in playful flirtation. Madame de Saujac was kissing her captain. The long, warm evening, mellowed by fine wines, by dainty dishes accented with select spices, by music and flowers, completed its course by surrendering the Palace of Gay Learning to the magic of love.

The man in red continued to sing, but he, too, was alone.

"What is he waiting for?" Angélique thought. "For me to throw myself at his feet and cry to him: 'Take me!'?"

A long shiver went through her, and she closed her eyes. Within raged confusion and contradiction. While only yesterday she had been ready to surrender, she rebelled against seduction tonight: "He entices young women with his songs." It had seemed so terrible from afar, but from close by it was so wonderful. She rose and, in her turn, went out, telling herself that she was "escaping temptation." But immediately afterwards, reflecting that this man was her husband before God, she shook her head in despair. She felt lost and afraid. Strictly brought up, she shied from too free a life. She belonged to a time when scruples and remorse were the price of weakness.

Many a woman who would surrender herself to-night with a sob to her lover's embrace, would run weeping to confession tomorrow, clamouring for convent bars and the veil to expiate her sins. Angélique knew very well that the power to which Joffrey de Peyrac wished to subjugate her was not marriage, but love. Had she been married to another, he would have acted likewise. Had not her nurse been right in saying that this man was serving the devil? . . .

Walking down the wide staircase, she passed a couple in a close embrace. The woman was murmuring something like a plaintive little prayer. In the palace filled with sighs, Angélique in her white dress wandered through the garden. She perceived Cerbalaud alone too, walking, through the avenues, no doubt musing over the speeches he would make to his prudish lady-love. She smiled.

"Poor Cerbalaud. Will he remain faithful to his love, or jilt her for a more cruel girl? . . ."

With faltering steps, the Chevalier de Germontaz was coming down the stairs. He stopped before Angélique, breathing noisily.

"A plague on these southern mummeries and simperings. My little lady-friend who had shown great willingness up to that point, has just struck me across the face. It appears I'm no longer delicate enough for her."

"It is true that ribaldry and religiosity seem to be the only means at your command. The trouble with you, perhaps, is that you have not yet really made up your mind about your future vocation."

Very red in the face, he came close to her and

she felt his wine-soaked breath full in the face.

"The trouble with me is that I let myself be prodded like a bull by little frippets of your kind. Women! This is how I treat them."

Before she could make a move, he had rudely grabbed her and planted his moist, fat mouth on her lips. She struggled wildly, sickened with disgust.

"Monsieur de Germontaz," said a voice suddenly.

Maddened with fear, Angélique saw the scarlet figure of the Comte de Peyrac at the top of the stairs. He raised his hand to his mask and flung it back. She saw the fearsome face which could cause even the most hardened to shudder when he convulsed his disfigured features. Slowly and with an emphatic limp, he came down the stairs; on the last step she saw a metallic flash as he drew his sword.

Germontaz had recoiled, reeling a little. Behind Joffrey de Peyrac, Bernard d'Andijos and Monsieur de Castel-Jalon appeared. The Archbishop's nephew cast a glance towards the gardens and saw Cerbalaud, who was also drawing closer. He panted hoarsely.

"This . . . this is a trap," he stammered. "You want to murder me!"

"The trap is within yourself, you swine," answered Andijos. "Who asked you to dishonour the wife of your host?"

Tremblingly Angélique tried to gather up her torn bodice over her bosom. It wasn't possible! They were not going to fight! Someone must intervene. . . . Joffrey was risking his life with this strapping big brute! . . .

Joffrey de Peyrac continued to advance; and suddenly it was as if a juggler's agility had entered the long, misshapen body. When he stood before the Chevalier de Germontaz, he pressed the tip of his weapon against the other's stomach and said simply:

"Defend yourself."

Responding to the reflexes of a military education, the other drew his sword, and the weapons crossed. It was an equal fight for a few moments, and so heated that twice the hand-guards clashed and the duellists' faces were within a few inches of each other.

But, each time, the Comte de Peyrac broke away nimbly. His swiftness made up for the handicap of his game leg. Once Germontaz forced him back against the stairs and compelled him to mount a few steps, but he vaulted the balustrade, and the Chevalier barely had time to wheel round to face him again. Germontaz was beginning to tire. He was well versed in all the subtleties of fencing, but this rapid play bewildered him. The Comte's sword slashed his right sleeve and scratched his arm. It was only a surface wound, but it bled profusely; the wounded arm which held the sword soon grew numb. The Chevalier fought with increasing difficulty. Panic appeared in his great, popping eyes. Joffrey's, burning with a sombre fire, were unrelenting. Angélique read in them the death sentence.

She bit her lips till she almost cried out with pain, but she dared not make a move. She closed her eyes. There followed a sort of deep, raucous cry like a woodcutter's grunt of strain. When she looked again, she saw that the Chevalier de Germontaz was sprawled out on the mosaic tiles with the hilt of Joffrey's sword protruding from his side. The Great Lame Man of Languedoc bent over him with a smile.

"Mummeries and simperings!" he said softly.

He gripped the hilt of his sword and pulled it up with a jerk. There was a crimson spurt, and Angélique saw her white dress splashed with blood. She almost fainted and had to lean against the wall. Joffrey de Peyrac's face loomed over hers. It was streaked with sweat, and she could see his lean chest rise and fall under the red velvet coat like the bellows of a forge. But the watchful eyes kept their mordant, merry light. The Comte smiled quietly as he met her emerald glance, still dim with emotion.

He said imperiously:

"Come."

Chapter 21

THE horse slowly followed the river bank, raising the sand from the small, winding path. Three armed lackeys escorted their lord from a distance, but Angélique was not aware of their presence. It seemed to her that she was completely alone under the starry sky, alone in the arms of Joffrey de Peyrac, who had thrown her across his saddle and was now carrying her away to the pavilion on the Garonne for their first night of love.

At the pavilion, the servants, well-trained by a strict master, remained invisible. The chamber was ready. On the terrace an assortment of fruit had been placed near the couch, and flagons of wine were cooling in bronze basins, but the room seemed empty.

Angélique and her husband did not speak. The hour was meant for silence. Yet when he drew her towards him with brooding impatience, she murmured:

"Why don't you smile? Are you still cross? I assure you I did not encourage this incident."

"I know, darling."

He took a deep breath and said in a muffled voice:

"I cannot smile for I have waited too long for this moment, and it grips me so that it hurts. I have never loved any woman as I do you, Angélique, and it seems to me I loved you even before I knew you. And when I saw you. . . . It was *you* I had been waiting for. But you passed haughtily by, within reach of my hand, like a fairy of the marshes, unattainable. So I made amusing conversation, for fear of mockery or a gesture of horror. Never have I waited for a woman so long nor displayed so much patience. And yet you were mine. Twenty times I was on the verge of using violence, but I wanted not only your body, I wanted your love. So when I see you here, mine at last, I can't forgive you all the torments you inflicted upon me. I can't forgive you," he repeated with a burning passion.

Bravely she met the look on his face, which no longer frightened her, and smiled.

"Take your vengeance," she murmured.

He quivered, smiled in his turn.

"You are more of a woman than I thought. Ah, don't provoke me! You will beg for mercy, beautiful enemy!"

From that moment onward, Angélique stopped belonging to herself. As she found again the lips that had already intoxicated her once, she also recaptured the whirlwind of unknown sensations, whose memory had left a dim yearning deep in her flesh. Everything came alive within her. With the promise of a fulfilment which nothing would hinder, her pleasure rose gradually to such a height that she was frightened by it.

She threw herself back, gasping, trying to escape from those hands whose every gesture brought to her new springs of rapture, and then, as if emerging from a well of oppressive sweetness, she saw the starry sky and the mist-veiled plain, through which the Garonne was weaving its silver ribbon, swirl around her.

Sound of body and glowing with health, Angélique was made for love. But the abrupt revelation she had of her own body overwhelmed her, and she felt buffeted and jostled by a violent assault, which came more from within her than from without. Only later, when her experience had grown, was she able to judge how very much Joffrey de Peyrac had restrained the violence of his own desire in order completely to assure his conquest.

Almost without her being aware of it he undressed her and laid her on the couch. With untiring patience he would bring her back to him, each time more yielding, warm and moaning, with fever-bright eyes. She struggled and surrendered in turn, but when the emotion she could not control had reached its peak, she felt utterly relaxed. It seemed to her that a sudden feeling of well-being, mingled with a delicious, throbbing excitement, permeated her body. All prudery discarded, she offered herself of her own accord to the most daring caresses; with closed eyes she let herself flow, unresisting, along the stream of voluptuousness. She did not rail against the pain, for every particle of her body was furiously calling for domination by her master. When he took her, she did not cry out, but her green eyes opened wide and reflected the stars of the spring sky.

"So soon!" murmured Angélique.

Stretched out on the couch, she was coming to life again. A soft Indian shawl protected her perspiring body from the gentle breeze of the night. She looked at Joffrey de Peyrac who, standing very black against the moonlight, was pouring cool wine into the cups. He began to laugh.

"Gently, my sweet. You are too new to allow me to pursue the lesson farther. The time will come for long delights. Meanwhile, let's drink! For we have both laboured tonight and our work deserves a reward."

Her enchanting face raised towards him, she gave him a smile which possessed a seductiveness of which she was not yet aware, for a new Angélique had been born in a matter of minutes, a free, fulfilled Angélique. He closed his eyes as if dazzled.

When he opened them again, he saw an anxious expression on the exquisite face.

"The Chevalier de Germontaz," murmured Angélique. "Oh, Joffrey! I had forgotten. You've killed the Archbishop's nephew!"

He soothed her with a caress.

"Think no more of it. There were witnesses to the provocation. To have overlooked it would have exposed me to blame. The Archbishop himself, being of noble blood, cannot do otherwise than bow before the fact. Oh, darling," he whispered, "your body is even more perfect than I guessed."

With one finger he followed the firm, white curve of the youthful body. She smiled and breathed a long sigh of contentment. She had always been told that men, after love, were brutal or indifferent. . . .

But Joffrey would certainly never resemble any other man.

He came and nestled close to her on the couch and she heard him chuckle softly.

"When I think that the Archbishop is this minute looking down from the high tower of his bishopric on the Palace of Gay Learning and damning my licentious life to hell! If he knew that I was at this very hour savouring those 'guilty delights' with my own wife, whom he has joined to me himself with his own blessing! . . ."

"You are incorrigible. He is not wrong to regard you with suspicion, for when there are two ways of doing a thing, you always think up a third. You could either commit adultery or else perform your conjugal duties soberly and sensibly. But no! You surround your wedding-night with such violent circumstances that I practically experience a feeling of guilt in your arms."

"A very pleasant feeling, is it not?"

"Be quiet! You are devilish! Admit, Joffrey, that though you yourself have adroitly by-passed sin, most of your guests tonight are not in the same position! How skilfully you have flung them into what Monseigneur calls disorderliness. . . . I am not quite sure that you are not a . . . dangerous man! . . ."

"And you, Angélique, are an adorable stark-naked canoness! And I have no doubt that my soul will obtain forgiveness in your hands. But let us not frown on the sweet joys of life. So many other peoples live according to other customs, and are none the less generous or happy for it. Faced with the coarseness of heart and senses that we hide under our fine clothes, I have dreamed of women and men becoming more refined and bestowing more grace on the name of France. I rejoice in it, for I love women, as I do all things of beauty. No, Angélique, my jewel, I am without remorse and I shall not go to confession! . . ."

Angélique could be completely herself only now that she had become a woman. Before, she was but a rosebud, cramped within a body which a drop of Moorish blood had spiced with a longing for carnal ardour.

In the days that followed, she felt as if she had been transplanted into a new world, in which everything was ripeness and enchanted discoveries.

It seemed to her as if the rest of her life had faded away, as if time had suspended its flight. She became more and more amorous. Her complexion had a rosy flush, her laughter a new boldness. Every night Joffrey de Peyrac found her more eager, more avid, and even when, like a young Diana, she would brusquely refuse to submit to his new fancies, she would as quickly give way to a rapt abandon.

Their guests seemed to live in the same relaxed and buoyant climate. They owed it partly to a miracle of organisation, for the genius of the Comte de Peyrac never overlooked a detail when it was a question of the comfort and enjoyment of his guests. He was everywhere, to all appearances airily detached, yet Angélique felt that he thought only of her and sang for her alone. Sometimes a twinge of jealousy would come over her when she saw his black eyes plunge into the bold ones of a coquette who begged his advice on some subtle point of the lover's art. She pricked up her ears, but she had to acknowledge that her husband always extricated himself loyally by some pointed sally disguised as a compliment.

With a mixture of relief and disappointment, she saw at the end of a week the heavy crested carriages turn in the palace courtyard and set out on their way back to distant country houses, while beautiful, lace-cuffed hands waved through the carriage-windows. The gentlemen saluted with a flourish of their plumed hats. Angélique, at her balcony, waved them a gay farewell.

She was not sorry to recover some calm and to have her husband all to herself for a while. But secretly she was sad to see the end of those exquisite days. Never — Angélique suddenly felt it with foreboding — never would those rapturous times return. . . .

On the very first evening after his guests' departure, Joffrey de Peyrac shut himself up in his laboratory where he had not set foot since the beginning of the Court of Love. This infuriated Angélique, who kept tossing with rage in the big bed where she waited for him in vain.

"That's men!" she said to herself bitterly. "They deign to grant you a little time in passing, but nothing can hold them back when their own pet obsessions are involved. For some it's duels, for others it's war. Joffrey's mania is retorts. I used to like him to tell me about it, but now I detest his laboratory!"

She sulked, but eventually she fell asleep.

She awoke in the flickering light of a candle and saw Joffrey at her bedside. She sat up with a start and folded her arms around her knees.

"Is it really worth while?" she inquired. "I hear the birds already wakening in the garden. Don't you think you'd do better to finish the night, so well begun, in your apartment, hugging a nice, plump glass retort in your arms?"

He laughed without any sign of contrition.

"I am so sorry, darling, but I was in the middle of an experiment I could not drop. Do you know that our terrible Archbishop is to blame for it? Yet he took his nephew's death in a very dignified way. But this is the point: duels are forbidden. It's one more trump up his sleeve. I've received an ultimatum to reveal to that fool of a friar the secret of gold-making. And as I cannot in decency explain to him my Spanish traffic, I have decided to take him along with me to Salsigne, where I'll let him be present at the extraction and the transformation of the gold-bearing rock. I shall recall the Saxon Fritz Hauer and also send a courier to Geneva. Bernalli longed to witness these experiments, and I am sure he'll come."

"All this doesn't interest me," interrupted Angélique, moodily. "I'm sleepy."

With her hair veiling half her face and her little chemise, whose lacy frills were slipping over her naked arm, she was aware that her appearance somewhat belied her stern words.

He caressed the soft, white shoulder, but with a sudden movement she dug her pointed teeth into his hand. He slapped her lightly and with feigned anger flung her back across the bed. They grappled for a moment. Very soon Angélique succumbed to Joffrey de Peyrac's strength. Her mood, however, remained rebellious, and she struggled in his embrace. Then her blood began to course more quickly through her veins. A spark of desire flashed deep within her and spread through her whole being. She kept on fussing, but sought with breathless curiosity the surprising sensation she had just experienced. Her body tingled with fire. Waves of pleasure swept her from summit to summit in an ecstasy she had never known before. Her head thrown back over the edge of the bed, with half-open lips, Angélique recalled the shadows of an alcove in the golden light of a lamp. She heard again the soft, plaintive moan, she thought she heard it with extraordinary sharpness. She suddenly recognized her own voice. Above her, in the grey light of dawn, she saw the sparkling, half-closed eyes, and faun-like face that smiled and listened to the chant it had aroused.

"Oh, Joffrey," sighed Angélique, "I feel as if I were going to die. Why is it more wonderful each time?"

"Because love is an art in which one progresses towards perfection, my little beauty, and because you are a wonderful pupil. . . ."

Sated, she now sought sleep, snuggling against him. How brown Joffrey's torso seemed against the laces of his nightgown! . . . And how intoxicating was this scent of tobacco!

Chapter 22

*A*BOUT two months later, a small troop of horsemen followed by a carriage with the coat-of-arms of the Comte de Peyrac clambered up a road along a rocky ledge towards the hamlet of Salsigne in the Aude.

Angélique, whom this journey had at first delighted, was beginning to feel tired. It was very hot and there was a lot of dust. Moreover, the regular motion of her horse had lulled her into a pensive mood; with distaste she had watched Conan Bécher astride his mule, with his dangling, skinny legs and sandal-shod feet, and then pondered over the consequences of the Archbishop's stubborn grudge. Then she had thought of her father's letter which the Saxon, Fritz Hauer, had brought her when he arrived in Toulouse with his cart, his wife and his three fair children who, despite the years spent in Poitou, still spoke only a rugged Germanic dialect.

Angélique had wept a great deal when she received this letter, for her father announced in it the death of old Guillaume Lützen. She had gone and huddled in a dark corner and sobbed for hours. She had not been able to explain even to Joffrey what she felt and why it broke her heart to recall the bearded old face with its severe pale eyes, which used to shine with so much gentleness on the little Angélique of long ago. The past was the past, but Baron Armand's letter had brought back to life barefooted little ghosts with their hair full of straw, pattering through the icy corridors of the old castle of Monteloup where the chickens sought the shade in summertime.

Her father was complaining, too. Life continued to be hard, although everyone's needs were taken care of, thanks to the mule traffic and the Comte de Peyrac's generosity. But the country had been ravaged by a dreadful famine; this, added to the plaguing of the salt-smugglers by the salt-tax collectors, had led the inhabitants of the marshes to revolt. Emerging from behind their reeds, they had looted several hamlets, refused to pay tax and killed tax-officers and collectors. The King's soldiers had to be sent for to pursue them as they slipped like eels through the waterways, and many of them had been hanged at the crossroads.

Angélique now realised what it meant to be one of the wealthiest people in the province. She had forgotten that oppressed world, haunted by the fear of taxes and exactions. Had she not become very selfish in the ecstasy of her happiness and her luxury? Perhaps the Archbishop would have harassed them less if she had known how to win him over by busying herself with his charities?

She heard poor Bernalli sigh. "What a road! Worse than in our Abruzzi! And your lovely carriage on it! There'll be nothing but firewood left of it. It's a real crime!"

"I begged you, though, to get into it," said Angélique. "At least it would have been of some use."

But the gallant Italian protested, while he rubbed his aching back.

"Fi, Signora, a man worthy of the name would not loll in a carriage while a young lady was travelling on horseback."

"Your scruples are old-fashioned, my poor Bernalli. Nowadays one stands less on ceremony. However, knowing you as I'm beginning to, I am sure that the mere sight of our hydraulic machinery moving and driving water will be enough to cure you of your aches and pains."

The scientist's face beamed.

"So you really remember, Madame, my passion for this science I call hydraulics? Your husband did indeed lure me here by hinting that he had set up in Salsigne a mechanism for raising water from a torrent flowing at the bottom of a gorge.

369

That is all that was needed to make me take to the road again. I am wondering whether he may not have discovered perpetual motion."

"You're mistaken, my dear Bernalli," said Joffrey de Peyrac's voice behind them. "It's merely a model of the hydraulic rams which I saw in China and which can raise water a hundred and fifty fathoms or more. Ah, have a look down there. We've almost arrived."

They soon found themselves on the bank of a small mountain torrent and could see a sort of tiptank which would pivot on its axis and toss a fine parabola of water to a very great height. This jet of water dropped into a sort of basin situated on a raised platform, whence it then fell gently into a series of wooden drains. An artificial rainbow cast an iridescent halo round this machinery, and Angélique found the water-ram very pretty, but Bernalli seemed disappointed and said resentfully:

"You are losing nineteen-twentieths of the torrent's output. It has absolutely nothing to do with perpetual motion!"

"I don't care at all if I lose output and power," remarked the Comte. "For me it means that I get water at the height where I need it and the small output is enough to concentrate my pounded gold-bearing rock."

The visit to the mine was postponed till the morrow. Modest but adequate lodgings had been prepared by the local magistrate. A wagon had brought up trunks and bedding. Peyrac left the dwelling-houses to Bernalli, Friar Bécher and to d'Andijos who, naturally, was one of the party. He himself preferred the shelter of a vast, double-roofed tent which he had brought back from Syria.

"I think I inherited the camping habit from the crusaders. In this heat and in these parts, which are the driest in France, you will see, Angélique, that we'll be far more comfortable than in a stone-and-mud construction."

When evening came, she did indeed savour the cool air that came down from the mountains. The lifted flaps of the tent revealed a sky reddened by the setting sun; from the banks of the torrent could be heard the sad, solemn songs of the Saxon miners.

Joffrey de Peyrac seemed worried.

"I don't like that monk!" he exclaimed with violence. "Not only will he understand nothing, but he'll interpret everything according to his devious mind. I'd even have preferred to explain things to the Archbishop, but he wants a 'scientific witness.' Ha! Ha! What a joke! I'd prefer anyone to this rosary-manufacturer."

"Still," protested Angélique, slightly shocked, "I've heard that many a distinguished scientist is also a religious man."

The Comte could ill conceal a gesture of annoyance.

"I don't deny it, and I'd go even further. I'd say that for centuries the Church preserved the cultural heritage of the world. But in our day she is being desecrated by scholastics. Science is at the mercy of fanatics who, whenever they can't find some theological angle to attach to phenomena that have but a natural explanation, are ready to deny facts that are self-evident."

He fell silent and, pulling his wife towards him,

he said to her something that she was to understand only much later:

"I have also chosen you as a witness."

Next day, Fritz Hauer came to conduct the visitors to the gold-mine. It consisted of a deep excavation which formed a quarry at the bottom of the foothills of Corbières. An enormous section of ground, about a hundred metres long by thirty metres wide, had been scraped, and its grey mass had been cut up by means of wooden and iron wedges into small blocks, which were then loaded on to wagons and transported to the grindstones.

Other hydraulic pounding devices particularly attracted Bernalli's attention. They were made of wooden blocks faced with sheet-iron, which tipped over when a caisson full of water lost its balance.

"What a loss of water-power," sighed Bernalli, "but what a beautifully simple installation from a labour-saving point of view. Is this another of your inventions, Comte?"

"I merely imitated the Chinese; out there, I was told, such installations have been in existence for three or four thousand years. They use them mainly for hulling rice which is their staple food."

"But where does gold come into all this?" remarked Friar Bécher judiciously. "I merely see a grey and heavy powder which your workmen extract from this pounded rock."

"You'll get a demonstration in the Saxon foundry."

The small party passed along a lower level where covered Catalan furnaces were set up in an open hangar. Bellows worked by two youngsters each sent out a burning, stifling breath. Livid flames, exhaling a pronounced smell of garlic, spurted at times from the open mouths of the ovens, leaving a sort of heavy, smoky steam which settled all around in the form of white snow.

Angélique took some of this snow and raised it to her mouth on account of the intriguing garlic aroma. Like a gnome emerging from Hell, a human monster in a leather apron violently struck her hand away.

Before she had time to react, the gnome rasped:

"*Gift, gnädige Dame* (Poison, noble lady)."

Puzzled, Angélique wiped her hand, while Friar Bécher's eyes bored down on her.

"In our laboratories," he said softly, "alchemists work with masks."

Joffrey too had heard him and broke in:

"In ours, there *is* no alchemy, although not all these ingredients, of course, are fit to eat or even to touch. Are you distributing milk regularly to all your company, Fritz?" he asked in German.

"Six cows were driven here before we came, Your Highness!"

"Good, and don't forget it's to be drunk, not sold."

"We are not needy people, Highness, so we mean to stay alive as long as possible," said the hump-backed old foreman.

"May I know, Comte, what is that pasty, molten stuff I can perceive in this oven of Hell?" asked Bécher, crossing himself.

"It's the same heavy sand, washed and dried, that you saw being extracted from the mine."

"And according to you this grey powder contains

gold? I did not see the slightest spark of gold-dust, not even in the belt when it was rinsed just now."

"And yet it's gold-rock. Bring me a shovelful, Fritz."

The workman dug his shovel into an enormous pile of greyish-green grainy sand that had a vaguely metallic look. Bécher cautiously spread some out in the hollow of his hand, sniffed it, tasted it and, spitting it out, declared:

"Vitriol of arsenic. Violent poison. But nothing to do with gold. Anyway, gold comes from gravel and not from rock. And the quarry we just saw contains not an atom of gravel."

"That's perfectly correct, my distinguished colleague," confirmed Joffrey de Peyrac, who then added, addressing himself to his Saxon foreman:

"If it's the right moment, add your lead!"

They had to wait a little longer, however. The mass in the oven grew even redder, melted and bubbled. The heavy white fumes continued to smoke, settling everywhere, as a white, powdery coating. Then, when there was practically no more smoke and the flames had dwindled, two Saxons in leather aprons rolled up several nuggets of lead on a cart, and dipped them into the pasty mass.

The bath liquified and settled down. The Saxon stirred it with a long stick of green wood. Bubbles escaped from it, then the scum rose. Fritz Hauer skimmed it off repeatedly with enormous sieves and iron hooks. Then he stirred again. Finally, the foreman bent down to an opening which had been cut below the shaft of the oven. He pulled out the stone-stopper that blocked it, and a silvery trickle started to flow into the previously prepared ingot moulds.

The monk approached inquisitively, then said: "All this is still only lead."

"So far we still agree," assented Monsieur de Peyrac.

But suddenly the monk uttered a strident cry: "I see the three colours!"

He gasped and motioned towards the iridescence of the cooling ingot. His hands shook and he stammered:

"The Philosopher's Stone! I have seen the Philosopher's Stone!"

"The good monk is going mad," observed Andijos, no respecter of the Archbishop's confidential agent.

Joffrey de Peyrac explained with an indulgent smile:

"Alchemists still set their heart on the apparition of the 'three colours' in seeking the Philosopher's Stone and the transmutation of metals. And yet it is only an unimportant phenomenon, comparable to that of a rainbow."

Suddenly the monk fell on his knees before Angélique's husband. He thanked him, stuttering, for having allowed him to watch "his life's work."

Vexed by this ludicrous demonstration, the Comte said curtly:

"Get up, Father. So far you've seen exactly nothing, as you'll be able to judge for yourself in a minute. There is no Philosopher's Stone, I am sorry to say."

Fritz Hauer had followed the scene with an air

of repugnance on his dust-stained face.

*"Muss ich das Blei vor allen diesen Herrschaften durchbrennen?"** he asked.

"Act as if I were the only one present."

Angélique saw the still lukewarm ingot being gripped with wet rags and shoved into a cart. It was transported to a small oven set up above an already blazing forge. The bricks of the oven's central chamber, which constituted a sort of open crucible, were very white, light and porous, and were made of animal bones. Their aroma, together with the smell of garlic and sulphur, rendered the atmosphere very unpleasant.

Bécher, who had been red with heat and excitement, turned livid at the sight of the pile of bones, and he began to cross himself and mumble exorcizing prayers.

The Comte could not refrain from laughing and said to Bernalli:

"Just look at the effect our work produces on a modern scientist. When I think that assaying over bone-ash was child's play in the days of the Romans and the Greeks!"

However, Bécher did not shun the terrifying spectacle. Very pale and continuing to reel off his rosary, he kept his eyes fixed on the preparations that the old Saxon and his assistants were making. One of them was putting more glowing embers into the forge, the other was operating a pair of pedal-worked bellows. All at once the lead seemed to melt in the middle of the round chamber created by the bone-dust brick of the oven. When

*"Must I assay the lead in front of all these lords and ladies?"

376

it had all been smelted, the fire was brought to even greater heat and the lead began to smoke.

At a sign from old Fritz a boy appeared carrying a pair of bellows whose end was inserted in a piece of fire-proof piping. He placed the tip on the edge of the chamber and began to force a cold draught on to the dark red surface of the cake of molten lead. Suddenly, with a whistling noise, the air blown against the liquid metal ignited. The luminous spot increased in intensity, turned a dazzling white and spread over the whole bulk of the metal.

The young assistant thereupon quickly removed all the incandescent embers below the oven. The big bellows stopped too. The process continued unaided: the metal was bubbling and dazzling to the eyes. Now and then it was shrouded by a dark veil, then the veil split, forming dark flakes that danced on the surface of the incandescent liquid. Whenever one of these floating islands reached the edge of the bath, it adhered to the bricks, as if by magic, and the surface reappeared purer and more sparkling.

Simultaneously, the disc of metal was visibly dwindling. It finally shrank to the size of a large pancake, became darker, and blazed up with a flash. At this moment Angélique saw clearly that the remaining metal shivered violently, solidified and became very dark.

"This is the lightning-phenomenon described by Berzelius, who did much work on cupellation and onset," said Bernalli. "But I am very glad to have watched a metallurgical operation that I knew of only from books."

The alchemist did not say anything. His gaze was vague and distracted.

Meanwhile, Fritz had seized the pancake with a pair of tongs, dipped it into water and presented it to his master, yellow and sparkling.

"Pure gold," murmured the friar respectfully.

"It is not absolutely pure," said Peyrac. "Otherwise we should not have seen the lightning phenomenon, which reveals the presence of silver."

Recovering from his emotion, the monk asked if he could have a small sample of this product to hand to his benefactor, the Archbishop.

"Go and take this nugget of gold drawn from the entrails of our Corbières hills," said the Comte de Peyrac, "and make it quite clear to him that this gold comes from a rock which contained it already, and that he need only discover some such deposits on his estates to make himself rich."

Conan Bécher carefully wrapped the precious cake, which weighed at least two pounds, in a handkerchief, and did not reply.

One morning after the return from Salsigne, upon entering the palace library together with her husband, Angélique discovered Clément Tonnel, the major-domo, engaged in inscribing on wax tablets the titles of books. He seemed embarrassed and tried to conceal his tablets and his engraving point.

"By Jove, you do seem to take an interest in Latin!" cried the Comte, who was more surprised than angry.

"I've always been drawn to studies, Your Lordship. My ambition would have been to become a notary's clerk, and it is a great joy for me to belong to the household not only of a noble lord but of a distinguished scientist."

"My books on alchemy won't be able to instruct you on the subject of law," said Joffrey de Peyrac with a frown, for the man's obsequious manners had never appealed to him. Tonnel was the only man on his staff whom he did not call by his Christian name.

When he had left the room, Angélique said with annoyance:

"I have no reason to complain of the services of this Clément, but, I don't know why, his presence irks me more and more. Whenever I look at him, he brings back to my mind something indefinable but unpleasant. Yet I brought him with me from Poitou."

"Pah!" said Joffrey with a shrug, "he is somewhat lacking in discretion, but so long as his thirst for knowledge does not lead him to forage in my laboratory . . ."

But Angélique remained inexplicably troubled, and several times in the course of the day the pockmarked face of the major-domo came to trouble her thoughts.

Some time later, Clément Tonnel asked for leave to return to Niort in order to deal with a legacy. "He never seems to stop inheriting," thought Angélique. She remembered that he had left a previous post for the same reason. Master Clément promised to be back the following month, but Angélique had the presentiment that she would not see him again so soon. She had been on the point of entrusting him with a letter for her family, but thought better of it.

When he had gone, she was gripped by an unreasonable urge to see Monteloup and its countryside again. Yet she did not miss her father. Though she had become very happy, she bore him a dim grudge for her marriage. Her brothers and sisters were scattered. Old Guillaume was dead and, from the letters she received, she guessed that her aunts were becoming acrimonious and garrulous, and Fantine Lozier more and more domineering. Her thoughts dwelt for a fleeting moment on Nicholas, who had disappeared from the district after her marriage.

Angélique realised finally that she was haunted by the idea of going back in order to pay a visit to the Château du Plessis and to find out if the famous poison-casket was still shut up in its hiding-place in the sham turret. There was no reason why it shouldn't be. No one could discover it without pulling down the château. Why was this old business coming back to harass her all of a sudden? The antagonisms of that period were already remote. Cardinal Mazarin, the King and his young brother were still alive. Monsieur Fouquet had obtained power without resorting to crime. And wasn't there even talk of the Prince de Condé's return to favour?

She shook off those speculations and soon regained her peace of mind.

Chapter 23

*T*HERE was rejoicing in the air, in Angélique's house as well as throughout the kingdom. The Archbishop of Toulouse, busy with more important matters, called off for a while the suspicious watch he kept on his rival, the Comte de Peyrac.

In fact, Monseigneur de Frontenac had just been summoned, together with the Archbishop of Bayonne, to escort Cardinal Mazarin on his journey towards the Pyrénées.

The whole of France echoed with the news: with a display of pomp fit to make the world tremble, the Cardinal was proceeding towards an island in the Bidassoa, in the Basque country, to negotiate peace with the Spaniards. So at last there would be an end to that eternal war which sprang up every year with the flowers in spring. But even more than this, an unbelievable project filled even the humblest craftsman in the kingdom with joy. As a peace token, haughty Spain had agreed to offer her Infanta as spouse to the young King of France. In consequence, in spite of reticence and jealous glances, everyone preened himself on both sides of the Pyrénées, for in the Europe of the day, which consisted of England in revolt, a multitude of tiny German and Italian principalities, and those common "seafaring" Flemings and Dutch, only these two royal descendants were truly worthy of each other.

Upon what other king could the Infanta, the only daughter of Philip IV, that pure pearly-skinned idol, brought up in the austere shadow of sombre palaces, be bestowed? And as a bride for this young prince of twenty summers, the hope of one of the greatest nations, what princess offered so many guarantees of nobility and so many advantages by alliance? . . .

The provincial Courts commented on these tidings with passion, and the ladies of Toulouse said that the young King wept a great deal in secret, for he was madly in love with a little childhood friend, the dark-haired Marie Mancini, the Cardinal's niece. But reasons of State were imperative. Under the circumstances, the Cardinal demonstrated, in striking fashion, that, as far as he was concerned, the glory of his royal pupil and the good of the kingdom came first and foremost. He desired peace as the crowning accomplishment of the intrigues that his Italian hands had woven for years. His family was mercilessly set aside; Louis XIV would marry the Infanta.

So it was that with eight carriages for his person, ten carts for his luggage, twenty-four mules, one hundred and fifty servants in livery, one hundred riders and two hundred foot-soldiers, the Cardinal travelled down towards the emerald banks of Saint-Jean-de-Luz.

On his journey, he required the presence of the Archbishops of Bayonne and Toulouse with all their retinue, in order to add to the lustre of the delegation. Meanwhile, on the other side of the mountains, Don Luis de Haro, the representative of His Most Catholic Majesty, countered this great display with lofty simplicity and crossed the table-land of Castille, carrying in his coffers only rolls of tapestries depicting scenes that recalled — to whom it might concern — the glory of the ancient kingdom of Charles V.

Nobody was in a hurry, neither of the two wishing to be the first arrival, reduced to the humiliation of waiting for the other. Finally they advanced yard by yard, and by a miracle of etiquette the Italian and the Spaniard reached the banks of Bidassoa on the same day and at the same hour. A long time passed in indecision. Who would be the first to launch a boat onto the water to set out for Pheasant Island in the middle of the river where the meeting was to take place? Each found a solution that was to safeguard his pride. The Cardinal and Don Luis de Haro sent word to each other simultaneously that they were ill. The stratagem having miscarried from excess of concord, there was nothing to do, in decency, but wait for the "illnesses" to be cured; but neither of them wished to be cured.

The world was on tenterhooks. Would peace be made? Would the marriage take place? The slightest gesture was commented on.

In Toulouse, Angélique followed matters from afar. She was absorbed in the joy of a private event, which seemed to her far more important than talk of the King's marriage.

In fact, as her love for Joffrey grew each day, she began ardently to wish for a child. Then only, it seemed to her, would she really be his wife. However much he assured her that he had never loved a woman to the point of showing her his laboratory and talking to her of mathematics, she remained skeptical and had fits of retrospective jealousy which made him laugh and, incidentally, secretly delighted him.

She had come to know the sensitiveness of his bold personality, to measure the courage he had displayed in mastering his ugliness and his infirmity. She admired him for having won such a battle. It seemed to her that, had he been handsome and invulnerable, she would not have loved him nearly so passionately. She wanted to give him a child to make him perfectly happy. As the days passed, she began to fear that she was barren.

When, finally, in the early winter of 1658, she found herself with child, she cried with happiness.

Joffrey did not hide his enthusiasm and his pride. That winter, while there was a great general fuss over the preparations for the still unannounced royal wedding, life was very quiet at the Palace of Gay Learning. Between his research and his young wife, the Comte de Peyrac called a halt to the life of fashion at his residence. Eventually, without mentioning it to Angélique, he turned the Archbishop's absence to account by again taking in hand the public affairs of Toulouse, to the great satisfaction of a good many members of the Parliament and the population in general.

For her confinement, Angélique moved to a small château that the Comte owned in Béarn, in the foothills of the Pyrénées where it was cooler than in town. Naturally, the parents-to-be discussed at great length the Christian name they would give their son, heir to the Comtes de Toulouse. Joffrey wanted to call him Cantor, after the famous troubadour of Languedoc, Cantor de Marmont, but as his birth came in the midst of the festivities which accompanied the Floral Games being held in Toulouse, they called him Florimond.

He was a dark-complexioned little boy, with plenty of black hair. For several days Angélique bore him a grudge for the anguish and pain of childbirth. The midwife assured her, though, that for a firstborn things had gone very well. But Angélique had rarely been ill and did not know physical pain. During the long hours of waiting she had gradually felt engulfed in this elemental suffering, and her pride had rebelled. She was alone on a road on which neither love nor friendship could help her, ruled over by an unknown child who already claimed her entirely. The faces around her became those of strangers.

This hour foreshadowed for her the dreadful solitude that she was to face one day. She did not know it, but her being had a premonition of it, and for twenty-four hours Joffrey de Peyrac was worried by her pallor, her silence and her constrained smile.

Then, on the evening of the third day, as Angélique was bending curiously over the cradle in which her son slept, she recognized the finely chiselled features which the unmarred side of Joffrey's face had occasionally revealed to her. She imagined a cruel sabre coming down on this angel face, the graceful body hurled out of a window, crushed in the snow on which flames rained down. The vision was so clear that she cried out in horror.

Seizing the new-born baby, she clasped it convulsively against her bosom. Her breasts ached, for the milk was rising and the midwife had tightly bandaged them. Ladies of quality did not suckle their children. A sturdy, healthy young wet-nurse was to take Florimond away to her mountains, where he would spend the first years of his life.

But when that evening, the nurse entered Angélique's room, she threw up her arms in horror, for Florimond was already sucking heartily at his mother's breast.

"Madame, you're out of your mind! Now how shall we get rid of your milk? You'll have a fever and your breasts will harden."

"I shall feed him myself," said Angélique fiercely. "I don't wish him to be thrown out of a window!"

There was scandalized talk of a noble lady acting like a peasant-woman. Eventually it was agreed that the nurse would nevertheless be part of Madame de Peyrac's household. She would supplement Florimond's feeding, for he had a voracious appetite.

While this question was still the talk of the neighbourhood, Bernard d'Andijos arrived in Béarn. The Comte de Peyrac had finally appointed him first gentleman of his household and had sent him to Paris to prepare the Comte's residence there in expectation of the journey he proposed to make to the capital.

On his way back Andijos had gone straight to Toulouse to represent the Comte at the Floral Games. He was not expected in Béarn and seemed much agitated. Flinging his horse's reins to a lackey, he dashed up the stairs four steps at a time and strode into Angélique's room. She was lying in bed, while Joffrey, propped against the window-seat, was strumming his guitar and singing softly.

Andijos had no eyes for this family picture.

"The King is coming!" he cried breathlessly.

"Where?"

"To your palace, the Gay Learning, in Toulouse! . . ."

Then he dropped into an armchair and wiped his face.

"Come, come," said Joffrey de Peyrac, after playing a little air on his guitar to let the newcomer recover his breath, "don't get excited. I have been told that the King, his mother and his Court have set out to join the Cardinal at Saint-Jean-de-Luz, so why should they be passing through Toulouse?"

"It's quite a story! Don Luis de Haro and Monsieur de Mazarin are, it seems, wasting so much time in courtesies that they have not yet got down to broaching the subject of the marriage. It is said, moreover, that their relations are getting strained; there is trouble over the Prince de Condé. Spain wants him to be welcomed back with open arms and wishes that not only his treason during the civil war be forgotten, but also the fact that this Prince of French blood has served for several years as a Spanish General. It's a bitter pill that is hard to swallow. The King's arrival under these circumstances would be inappropriate. Mazarin advises him to travel. So they travel. The Court is going to Aix, where the King's presence will doubtless appease the revolt that has just broken out there. But all these great lords will pass through

Toulouse. And you won't be there! Nor will the Archbishop! Parliament is in an uproar! . . ."

"It's not the first time, though, that they'll have received a great personage."

"You must be there," begged Andijos. "I have come myself to fetch you. It seems that when the King learned that they'd be passing through Toulouse, he said: 'So I'll at last meet the Great Lame Man of Languedoc whom everyone's been telling me about!' "

"Oh! I want to go to Toulouse!" cried Angélique, jumping up in bed.

But she fell back with a grimace of pain. She was still too stiff and weak to be able to undertake a journey over the bad mountain roads and withstand the fatigue of a princely reception. Her eyes filled with tears of disappointment.

"Oh, the King in Toulouse! The King at the Gay Learning, and I shall not see him! . . ."

"Don't cry, my darling," said Joffrey. "I promise you I shall be so deferential and courteous that they won't be able to do other than invite us to the wedding. You will see the King at Saint-Jean-de-Luz in all his glory and not as a dust-covered traveller."

When the Comte had left the room to give orders for his departure next morning at dawn, Andijos tried good-naturedly to console her.

"Your husband is right, dear friend. The Court, the King! Pah! What does it matter! A single meal at the Palace of Gay Learning is worth all the balls at the Louvre. Believe me, I have been there, and I felt so cold in the anteroom of the council chamber that the drip at the end of my nose turned into an icicle. You'd suppose the King of France hadn't any forests to cut down for firewood. As for the officers of the royal household, they had such holes in their hose that I saw even the Queen's ladies lower their eyes, though goodness knows they aren't bashful."

"Don't say the Cardinal did not wish his royal pupil to get accustomed to a luxury that was not in keeping with the country's means?"

"I don't know what the Cardinal's intentions were. All I know is that he never stinted himself when it came to buying diamonds, rough or cut, paintings, libraries, tapestries, engravings. But I have an idea that, for all his timid airs, the King is anxious to rid himself of this tutelage. He is sick of bean-soup and his mother's remonstrances. He is sick of taking upon himself all the misfortunes of plundered France, and that is easily understood, for he is a handsome youngster and a King to boot. The time isn't far off when he will shake his lion's mane."

"What is he like? Do describe him," demanded Angélique impatiently.

"Not bad-looking. Not bad! He has presence and majesty. But because of chasing from town to town at the time of the *Fronde*, he has remained as ignorant as a farmhand, and if he weren't the King, I'd say that I believe him to be a bit underhanded. Moreover he's had smallpox and his face bears the marks of it."

"Oh! You're trying to discourage me!" cried Angélique. "And you talk like those Gascon, Béarnais and Albigeois devils who still wonder why Aquitaine has not remained an independent king-

389

dom, separate from the realm of France. For you there's nothing like Toulouse and its sunshine. But I'm dying to know Paris and see the King."

"You will see him at his wedding. Maybe that ceremony will inaugurate the true coming-of-age of our sovereign. But if you do go up to Paris, you must stop at Vaux on your way to greet Monsieur Fouquet. He is the true king of the day. What luxury, my dear! What splendour!"

"So you, too, have been to pay court to that ill-bred, shady financier?" enquired the Comte de Peyrac, as he came in.

"I had to, my dear fellow. Not only is it necessary if you want to be received anywhere in Paris, for the Princes are devoted to him, but I confess I was consumed with curiosity to see the King's great banker in his own setting, for he is certainly the outstanding figure in the kingdom at present, after Mazarin."

"You might as well come right out and say 'before Mazarin.' It's common knowledge that the Cardinal has no standing with the money-lenders, even when it's a question of the country's needs, whereas that fellow Fouquet enjoys everyone's confidence."

"The nimble Italian isn't jealous, though. Fouquet brings money into the Royal Treasury to keep the wars going, and that's all they ask of him — for the time being. He doesn't worry whether the money is borrowed from usurers at twenty-five or even fifty per cent interest. The Court, the King, the Cardinal, all live off these malpractices. Heaven knows when they'll stop him, and meanwhile he'll go on displaying his emblem, the squirrel, everywhere, as well as his motto *Quo non ascendam?* — Whither will I not rise?"

Joffrey de Peyrac and Bernard d'Andijos continued discussing Fouquet's unwonted ostentation for a while. Although he had made his start as Master of Petitions and then as a member of the Paris Parliament, he still remained the son of a mere Breton privateer. Angélique became pensive for, whenever there was mention of Fouquet, she recalled the poison-casket, and the memory always left her with a disagreeable feeling.

The conversation was interrupted by a little serving-boy who was bringing a tray to the Marquis.

"Humph!" said the latter, burning his fingers on the hot brioches which miraculously enclosed a nut-sized piece of iced *foie gras.* "Nowhere but here does one eat such marvels. Here and at Vaux, as it happens. Fouquet has an outstanding chef, a certain Vatel."

He exclaimed suddenly:

"Oh! that reminds me of a . . . curious encounter. Guess whom I ran into at that very place, deep in conversation with Monsieur Fouquet, Lord of Belle-Isle and other places and all but Viceroy of Brittany. . . . Guess?"

"Hard to guess. He knows so many people."

"Guess all the same. It's someone of your household . . . if one may say so."

Angélique suggested it might perhaps be her brother-in-law, her sister Hortense's husband, who was a man of law in Paris, just as the famous Superintendent of Finances had been long ago.

But Andijos shook his head.

"Ah, if I weren't so afraid of your husband, I'd bargain my information for a kiss, for you will never guess."

"Well, take the kiss, for it is good manners to kiss a young mother when you see her for the first time, and do tell me, for you make me impatient."

"All right then. I caught your former major-domo, that Clément Tonnel whom you had in Toulouse for a couple of years, in secret conclave with the Superintendent."

"You must have made a mistake. He only left us to go to Poitou," said Angélique very quickly. "And there is no reason why he should be in touch with important people, unless he was trying to enter service in Vaux."

"That's what I think I understood from their conversation. They mentioned Vatel, Fouquet's cook."

"You see," said Angélique, with a sense of relief she could not explain to herself, "he is merely looking for work under the direction of this Vatel who is supposed to be a genius. Still, I think he might have told us that he was not coming back to Languedoc. But what's the use of expecting deference from such common people when they don't happen to need you?"

"Quite so! Quite so!" agreed Andijos, though his mind seemed to be elsewhere. "Still, there was one detail that seemed odd to me. It so happened that I entered, unexpectedly, the room where the Superintendent was in conversation with that fellow Clément. I was one of a party of gentlemen whom wine had made rather gay. We apologized to the Superintendent, but I noticed that our man was talking to Monsieur Fouquet in a rather familiar way and quickly sat up in a more servile attitude when we came in. He recognized me. As we were going out, I saw him say a few quick words to Fouquet. The latter gave me a snake-cold stare, then said: 'I don't think it's of any importance.' "

"Was it you who were considered to be of no importance, my friend?" enquired Peyrac, who was casually plucking at his guitar.

"It seemed to me . . ."

"What a judicious opinion!"

Andijos made as if to draw his sword, and the conversation was resumed on a bantering note.

"I simply must remember," thought Angélique. "It is there, in my head, buried deep down among my memories. And I know that it is very important. I must try and remember!"

She cupped her cheeks in both hands, closed her eyes, concentrated. The thing was far distant. It had occurred at the Château du Plessis: of that she was certain, but beyond that everything was shrouded in mist.

The fire in the hearth warmed her. She picked up a hand screen of painted silk and fanned herself mechanically. Outside in the darkness a storm was raging, without lightning, but hurling packets of hail which, now and then, drummed against the windows. Unable to sleep, Angélique had sat down in front of the fireplace. Her back ached a little, and she was vexed with herself for not recovering her strength more quickly. The midwife kept hinting that her weakness was the result of her stubborn insistence on feeding the child, but Angélique turned a deaf ear; each time she pressed the baby against her breast and watched it suck, her joy increased. The sight entranced her. It touched her heart, filled her with a feeling of gravity. She already saw herself as a solemn and indulgent matron, surrounded by toddling infants. Why did she so often recall her own childhood, just when the little Angélique seemed to be fading away within her? . . . It wasn't a dim, inexplicable uneasiness she felt. The question gradually grew more precise: "There is something I simply must remember!"

Tonight she was waiting for her husband's return: he had sent a courier to announce his coming, but the storm was holding him up so that he would probably not arrive before the next day. This thought almost made her weep with disappointment. She was looking forward so impatiently to his account of the reception for the King. It would have distracted her. The banquet and the ball, it was said, had been magnificent. What a pity she had not been able to attend, instead of staying here racking her brain to retrieve a wisp of her memories.

"It was at Plessis. In the room of the Prince de Condé . . . while I was peeping through the window. I must try and visualize again everything from that moment onwards, point by point. . . ."

A door slammed and there was the sound of voices in the hall of the little château.

Angélique leaped to her feet and rushed out of the room. She recognized Joffrey's voice.

"Oh, dearest, you at last! I am so happy!"

She raced down the stairs and he received her in his arms.

Sitting at his feet on a cushion, she nestled against him. When the servants had left, she demanded impatiently:

"Now, tell me about it!"

"It went very well," said Joffrey de Peyrac, munching some grapes. "The town outdid itself. But, without boasting, I believe that the reception at the Palace of Gay Learning carried the day."

"And the King? The King?"

"The King, why, he is a handsome young fellow who seems to enjoy the fuss that's made of him. He has round cheeks, caressing brown eyes and a good deal of majesty. I believe he's suffering from heartbreak: the little Mancini has inflicted on him a wound of love that is not likely to heal very soon, but as he has a lofty idea of his kingly office, he bows to reasons of State. I have seen the Queen Mother, who is beautiful, sad and a little on her dignity. I also saw the Grande Demoiselle and Little Monsieur bickering over questions of etiquette. What else can I tell you? I saw many beautiful names and ugly faces! . . . As a matter of fact, nothing gave me as much pleasure as seeing little Péguilin again, the Chevalier de Lauzun, you know, the nephew of the Duc de Gramont, who is Governor of the Béarn. He used to be my little page in Toulouse before he went up to Paris. I still can see his cat-face when I instructed Madame de Vérant to make a man of him."

"Joffrey!"

"But he has fulfilled his promise and put into practice the teachings of our Courts of Love. I could see for myself that he was the rage among all those ladies. And his wit has earned him the friendship of the King, who cannot do without his buffooneries."

"And the King? Tell me about the King! Did he express his satisfaction at the way you received him?"

"He did, and very graciously. And he regretted your absence several times. Yes, the King was satisfied . . . too satisfied."

"How so, too satisfied? Why do you say that with a wry grin?"

"Because the following was reported to me: when the King was mounting into his carriage, a courtier remarked to him that our fête could vie in splendour with those given by Fouquet. And His Majesty replied: 'It could indeed, and I wonder whether it won't soon be time to make these people disgorge a bit.' The good Queen cried out: 'What a thing to say, my son, amidst all these rejoicings to please you!' To which the King replied: 'I am tired of seeing my subjects crush me with their display of wealth.' "

"Well, really! What an envious boy!" exclaimed Angélique, indignantly. "I can hardly believe it. Are you sure he said that?"

"My faithful Alphonso, who was holding the carriage-door, reported it to me himself."

"The King couldn't entertain such mean thoughts on his own. The courtiers must have biased his feelings and set him against us. Are you quite sure you did not show too much insolence towards some of them?"

"I was all sugar and honey, I assure you. I

humoured them as much as I could. I even went so far as to leave a purse filled with gold in the room of every lord who was lodged at the palace. And I assure you none of those gentlemen forgot to pocket it."

"You flatter them, but you despise them and they feel it," said Angélique, thoughtfully shaking her head.

She rose and went to sit on her husband's knees. Outside, the thunderstorm was still raging.

"Whenever the name of that man Fouquet is mentioned, I shiver," she murmured. "I see that poison-casket again which had been out of my thoughts for years, and it comes back to haunt me."

"You are nervous, my sweet! Am I to have a wife who trembles at the slightest breeze?"

"I must remember something," moaned the young woman, closing her eyes.

She rubbed her cheeks against the warm, violet-scented hair, whose locks were curling from the damp.

"If only you could help me remember . . . but that's impossible. If only I could remember, I feel I would know where to look out for danger."

"There is no danger, my darling. Florimond's birth has shaken you."

"I see the room. . . ." continued Angélique with closed eyes. "The Prince de Condé has just jumped out of bed because someone's knocked at the door . . . but I hadn't heard the knocking. The Prince has wrapped himself in his dressing-gown and shouted: 'I am with the Duchesse de Beaufort. . . .' But at the far end of the room, the valet has opened the door and introduced a hooded monk. . . . That monk was called Exili. . . ."

She broke off and suddenly stared in front of her with an intensity that frightened the Comte.

"Angélique!" he cried.

"Now I remember," she said in a toneless voice. "Joffrey, I remember. The valet of the Prince de Condé was . . . *Clément Tonnel.*"

"You're raving, darling," he said with a laugh. "That man's been in our service for several years, and only now do you notice this resemblance."

"I only caught a glimpse of him in the darkness. But his pockmarked face, his obsequious manners. . . . Yes, Joffrey, I am certain it was he. I understand now why, all the time he was in Toulouse, I could never look at him without a twinge of displeasure. Do you remember what you said one day, 'The most dangerous spy is the one whom one does not suspect,' and you began to sense that he was roaming around the house? That unknown spy was he."

"You are becoming inordinately romantic for a woman who's interested in science."

He caressed her forehead.

"Aren't you a little feverish?"

She shook her head.

"Don't make fun of me. I am tortured by the idea that this man has been watching me for years. On whose orders was he acting? Monsieur de Condé's? Fouquet's?"

"You never spoke of this affair to anyone?"

"To you . . . once, and he overheard us."

"All this is bygone history. Calm yourself, my treasure, I am sure you're fretting needlessly."

However, several months later, when she was weaning Florimond, her husband said to her casually one morning:

"I wouldn't like to force you to, but it would please me to know that you were taking one of these with your breakfast each morning."

He opened his hand and she saw a small white pill gleaming in it.

"What is it?"

"Poison . . . an infinitesimal dose."

Angélique looked at him.

"What are you afraid of, Joffrey?"

"Of nothing. But it's a practice I've always found useful. The body gradually becomes accustomed to it."

"Do you think someone may try to poison me?"

"I don't think anything, my love. . . . It's simply that I don't believe in the powers of the unicorn's horn."

In the following month of May, the Comte de Peyrac and his wife were invited to the royal wedding, which was to take place in Saint-Jean-de-Luz, on the banks of the river Bidassoa. King Philip IV of Spain would personally give away his daughter, the Infanta Maria-Theresa, to the young King Louis XIV. The peace was signed — or practically so. The French nobility crowded the roads en route to the little Basque town.

Joffrey and Angélique left Toulouse early one morning before it grew hot. Florimond also made the journey, together with his nurse, his cradle-rocker and a little blackamoor whose duty it was to make him laugh. He was now a healthy though not a fat baby, with the black eyes and locks of a delightful little Spanish saint.

The indispensable Margot watched over her mistress's wardrobe in one of the carts. Kouassi-Ba, for whom three liveries had been made, each more dazzling than the one before, looked like a grand vizier on a horse as black as his skin. There was also Alphonso, the Archbishop's ever-faithful spy, four musicians, to one of whom, little Giovanni, the fiddler, Angélique had taken a special fancy, and a certain François Binet, barber and wigmaker, without whom Joffrey de Peyrac never travelled. Valets, maids and lackeys completed the entourage, which was preceded by the suites of Bernard d'Andijos and Cerbalaud.

Absorbed in the excitement and details of their departure, Angélique hardly noticed that they were leaving the environs of Toulouse. As the carriage was passing over the bridge on the Garonne, she uttered a little cry and pressed her nose against the window-pane.

"What's wrong, my dear?" asked Joffrey de Peyrac.

"I want to see Toulouse once more," answered Angélique.

She gazed at the rosy city spread on the banks of the river, with the tall arrows of its spires and the stiffness of its towers.

A sudden anguish gripped her heart.

"Oh, Toulouse!" she murmured. "Oh, the Palace of Gay Learning!"

She had a premonition that she would never see them again.

PART THREE

The Corridors of the Louvre

Chapter 24

*E*NOUGH! I am bowed down with grief, and yet I must also suffer stupid people around me. If I weren't conscious of my rank, nothing would stop me from jumping off this balcony to put an end to this existence!"

These bitter words, uttered in a piercing voice, brought Angélique running to the window of her own room. She saw a big woman in night attire, her face buried in a handkerchief, leaning from a neighbouring balcony. A lady approached as the sobbing continued, whereupon the woman started flailing her arms like a windmill.

"Idiot! Idiot! Leave me, I tell you! Thanks to your stupidity I'll never be ready. Not that it matters, anyway. I am in mourning and need but shroud myself in my grief. Who cares if my head looks like a scarecrow!"

She ruffled her abundant hair and showed a face speckled with tears. She was a woman in her thirties with fine, aristocratic but somewhat sagging features.

"If Madame de Valbin is ill, who will dress my hair?" she cried dramatically. "You all have clumsier paws, the lot of you, than a bear at the fair of Saint-Germain!"

"Madame . . ." broke in Angélique.

The two balconies were at arm's length in this narrow street of Saint-Jean-de-Luz, with its courtier-crammed hôtels. Everyone knew what was going on at his neighbour's. Though dawn was just breaking, a pale, rosy dawn, the town was already buzzing like a beehive.

"Madame," Angélique repeated, "can I be of any help? I hear you're in trouble over your hair. I have a wigmaker who is clever with his irons and powders. He is at your disposal."

The lady dabbed her long red nose and uttered a deep sigh.

"You are very kind, my dear. I accept your proposal. I can't get anything out of my servants this morning. The Spaniards' arrival puts them in as much of a frenzy as if they were on a battlefield in Flanders. And yet, I ask you, who's the King of Spain?"

"He's the King of Spain," answered Angélique, laughing.

"Pah! His family, after all, does not approach ours in lineage. They're wading in gold, that's a fact, but they are turnip-eaters and more boring than crows."

"Oh, Madame, don't deflate my enthusiasm. I am so delighted at the prospect of meeting all these princes. They say that King Philip IV and the Infanta, his daughter, will reach the Spanish shore today."

"That's possible. I, at any rate, shall not be able to greet them for I'll never finish dressing at this rate."

"Have patience, Madame. Give me time to dress myself and I'll bring you my wigmaker."

Angélique hurried back into her room, which was in a most appalling state of disorder. Margot

404

and the maids were putting the finishing touches to their mistress's sumptuous dress. The trunks were wide open, so were the jewel-boxes, and Florimond, bare-bottomed and on all fours, was crawling blissfully among these splendours.

"Joffrey must tell me what jewels I should wear with this gold cloth dress," thought Angélique, removing her dressing-gown and slipping into a simple dress and a cloak.

She found Master François Binet on the ground floor of their lodgings, where he had spent the night curling the hair of the ladies of Toulouse, Angélique's friends, and even of the maids who wanted to look their best. He picked up his copper basin in case there were gentlemen to be shaved, and, his case filled to overflowing with combs, irons, ointments and false switches and, accompanied by a boy who carried his small stove, followed Angélique into the neighbouring house.

This dwelling was even more crowded than the one in which the Comte de Peyrac had been put up by an old aunt. Angélique noticed the beautiful livery of the servants and surmised that the tearful lady must be a person of high rank. To be on the safe side, she dropped a deep curtsey when she found herself in front of her.

"You are charming," said the lady with a doleful face, while the wigmaker was arranging his instruments on a stool. "If it weren't for you, I'd have ruined my face with tears."

"This isn't a day for weeping," protested Angélique.

"What can I do, my dear? I don't feel up to all this rejoicing."

Her lower lip drooped in a sad pout.

"Did you not notice my black dress? I have just lost my father."

"Oh! I am so sorry. . . ."

"We detested each other and quarrelled so much that this very thought doubles my grief. But how annoying to be in mourning just during the celebrations! Knowing my father's spiteful character, I suspect him . . ."

She broke off to bury her face in a cardboard cone which Binet was holding out to her while he sprinkled his client's hair copiously with a scented powder. Angélique sneezed.

". . . I suspect him of having done it on purpose," concluded the lady as she emerged.

"Having done it on purpose? Done what, Madame?"

"Why, died, of course. But never mind. I forgive and forget. I am always a generous soul, whatever they may say. And my father had a Christian death — that is a great comfort to me. But what vexes me is that they should have taken his body to Saint-Denis with only a few guards and almoners, no pomp, no expenses. . . . Don't you think it's intolerable?"

"I certainly do," agreed Angélique, who was beginning to fear she might make a blunder. This lord who was buried at Saint-Denis must have belonged to the royal family. Unless she had misunderstood . . .

"If I'd been there, things would have been handled differently, believe me," the lady went on, with a proud jerk of her chin. "I like pomp and keeping one's rank."

406

She fell silent and examined herself in the mirror which François Binet offered her, kneeling, and her face lit up.

"Why, this is very good," she cried. "What a becoming and flattering coiffure. Your wigmaker is an artist, my dear. I am quite aware that I have difficult hair."

"Your Highness has fine, but supple and abundant hair," said the wigmaker with a learned air. "It's with hair of this quality that one can compose the most beautiful hairstyles."

"Really! You flatter me. I shall give you a hundred crowns. Ladies! . . . Ladies! This man simply must frizz the little ones."

From the adjoining room, where ladies-of-honour and chambermaids were chattering, the "little ones," two adolescent girls of an awkward age, appeared.

"These are your daughters, I presume?" inquired Angélique.

"No, they are my younger sisters. They are insufferable. Look at the little one: the only good thing about her is her complexion, and she managed to get herself bitten by those flies they call gnats, and now she's all swollen. And on top of it she cries."

"No doubt, she is sad too about her father's death?"

"Not at all. But she's been told too often that she would marry the King; they called her nothing but 'the little Queen.' Now she is vexed that he is marrying another."

While the wigmaker was busying himself with the girls, there was a stir on the narrow staircase, and a young nobleman appeared on the doorstep. He was very small with a doll-like face that emerged from a frothy lace ruffle. There were several lace frills, too, at his cuffs and knees. Despite the early morning hour he was very carefully dressed.

"Cousin," he said in a mannered voice, "I've been told that you have a wigmaker who's doing absolute wonders."

"Ah, Philippe! You're more wily than a pretty woman in picking up rumours of this sort. Tell me at least that I look beautiful."

The young gentleman pursed his lips which were very red and full and scrutinized the hairstyle with half-closed eyes.

"I must admit that this artist has made the most of your face, more than one could hope for," he said with insolence tempered by a coquettish smile.

He went back into the anteroom and leaned over the balustrade.

"De Guiche, my dearest, do come, it's the right place."

Angélique recognized the gentleman who came in — a handsome, very dark and well-built lad — the Comte de Guiche, elder son of the Duc de Gramont, Governor of the Béarn. The man called Philippe seized the Comte de Guiche by the arm and bent tenderly over his shoulder.

"Oh, how happy I am! We shall certainly have the most elegant hairstyles at Court. Péguilin and the Marquis de Humières will blench with jealousy. I saw them tearing after their barber, whom Vardes had snatched from them by means of a well-filled purse. These glorious captains of the *becs-de-corbin* household guard will be reduced to appearing before the King with chins as bristly as chestnut-husks."

He broke into somewhat shrill laughter, passed his hand over his freshly-shaved chin, then with a graceful gesture also caressed the Comte de Guiche's cheek. He leaned against the young man with much abandon, and raised lovelorn eyes towards him. The Comte de Guiche, with a fatuous smile, received this homage without embarrassment. Angélique had never seen two men indulge in such behaviour and it made her feel ill at ease. It did not seem to the liking of the mistress of the place, either, for she suddenly cried:

"Ah! Philippe, don't come and parade your fawning ways here. Or else your mother will again accuse me of encouraging your perverse instincts. Ever since the ball at Lyons where you, I and Mademoiselle de Villeroy dressed up as peasant-women of the Bresse, she's been reproaching me on your account. And don't tell me that little Péguilin is in trouble or I'll send a man to bring him here. Let's see if I can't get a glimpse of him. He is the most remarkable fellow I know, and I adore him."

In her noisy and impulsive manner, she rushed out on the balcony again, then recoiled with a hand over her vast bosom.

"Oh, my God, here he is!"

"Péguilin?" inquired the little nobleman.

"No, the gentleman from Toulouse who frightens me so."

Angélique too went out on the balcony and saw her husband, the Comte Joffrey de Peyrac, coming

409

down the street followed by Kouassi-Ba.

"Why, it's the Great Lame Man of Languedoc!" exclaimed the young lord, who had joined them. "Why are you afraid of him, Cousin? He has the most gentle eyes, a caressing hand and a brilliant mind."

"You talk like a woman," said the lady with disgust. "It seems that all the women are crazy about him."

"Except you."

"I never stray into sentimentality. I only know what I see. Don't you think this sombre, hobbling man with his hell-blade Moor has something terrifying about him?"

The Comte de Guiche was throwing agonized glances at Angélique and twice was about to open his mouth. She motioned to him to keep silent. This conversation amused her greatly.

"That's just it: you don't know how to look at a man with a woman's eyes," said young Philippe. "You remember that this nobleman refused to bend his knee before Monsieur d'Orléans, and that's enough to put your back up."

"It's true that he did, at the time, show rare insolence. . . ."

At this moment Joffrey raised his eyes towards the balcony. He stopped, then doffing his plumed hat, bowed very deeply several times.

"You see how unfair public rumour is," said the young lord. "This man is said to be full of arrogance and yet . . . could one possibly salute more gracefully? What do you think, my dear boy?"

"The Comte de Peyrac de Morens is certainly

well-known for his courtesy," the Comte de Guiche hastened to reply, "and remember the marvellous reception we had in Toulouse."

"Yes, it's still rankling in the King's memory. This doesn't prevent His Majesty being most impatient to know if the lame man's wife is really as beautiful as they say. It seems to him inconceivable that such a man can be loved. . . ."

Angélique withdrew on tiptoe and, taking François Binet aside, lightly pinched his ear.

"Your master is back and will be asking for you. Don't let your head be turned by the crowns you get from all these people, or I'll have you soundly thrashed."

"Don't worry, Madame. I shall finish attending to this young lady and then I'll slip away."

She went downstairs and returned to her own house. She was thinking that she liked this Binet, not only for his good taste and skill, but also for his shrewd cunning, his underling's philosophy. He used to say that he addresses everyone of the nobility as a "highness" to be sure of not offending anybody.

In her room, which was in even worse disarray than before, Angélique found her husband with a napkin tied around his neck, waiting for the barber.

"Well, little lady," he cried, "you're losing no time. I leave you, fast asleep, to gather news and learn the order of the ceremonies, and an hour later I find you leaning over a balcony elbow-to-elbow with the Duchesse de Montpensier and Monsieur, the King's brother."

"The Duchesse de Montpensier! The Grande

Mademoiselle!" exclaimed Angélique. "By all the Saints! I should have guessed it when she talked of her father being buried at Saint-Denis."

As she undressed, Angélique related how, quite by chance, she had made the acquaintance of the famous lady rebel, the old maid of the kingdom, who now, after the death of her father, Gaston d'Orléans, was the richest heiress in France.

"So her young half-sisters, the Mesdemoiselles de Valois and d'Alençon are those who will carry the Queen's train at the wedding. Binet has dressed their hair too."

The barber appeared, out of breath, and started lathering his master's chin. Angélique was in her chemise, but propriety hardly mattered at this stage. What mattered was to make haste to join the King, who had asked that all the nobles of his Court come and greet him that very morning. Afterwards, with all the excitement of the meeting with the Spaniards, there would be no more time for presentations.

Margot, with her mouth full of pins, handed Angélique a petticoat of gold cloth, then a second one of gold lace as fine as filigree, with a pattern outlined in precious stones.

"And you say that effeminate young man is the King's brother?" inquired Angélique. "He behaved strangely with the Comte de Guiche; one might positively think he was in love with him. Oh, Joffrey! do you really think that . . . that they . . ."

"That's what is called the Italian fashion of love," said the Comte, laughing. "Our neighbours beyond the Alps are people of such refinement that they are not content with the simple pleasures of nature. We owe to them the birth of letters and the arts, to be sure, as well as a rascally Minister whose cleverness has at times been useful to France, but we are also indebted to them for the introduction of those peculiar ways. It's a pity the King's own brother should have taken to them."

Angélique frowned.

"The Prince said that you had a caressing hand. I'd like to know how he found out."

"My word, the Petit Monsieur is so fond of rubbing up against men, he may have asked me to help him straighten his cuffs. He never loses an opportunity to get himself petted."

"He spoke of you in terms that almost roused my jealousy."

"Oh, my darling, if you start to get ruffled, you'll soon be submerged in intrigues. The Court is one immense, sticky spider's web. You'll get caught up in it if you don't look at things from a high point of vantage."

François Binet, who was as talkative as all men of his profession, spoke up:

"I've been told that Cardinal Mazarin encouraged the Petit Monsieur's taste so as to avoid any clash between him and his brother. He ordered him to be dressed as a girl and had his little friends put on the same disguise. As the King's brother, there is a constant fear that he might start plotting, like the late Monsieur Gaston d'Orléans, who was so insufferable."

"You judge your Princes rather harshly, barber," said Joffrey de Peyrac.

"The only thing I own, your lordship, is my

tongue and the right to wag it."

"Liar! I made you richer than the King's wig-maker."

"That is true, your lordship, but I am not boasting of it. It's imprudent to arouse envy."

Joffrey de Peyrac dipped his face into a bowl of rose water to cool it from the razor's smart. His scar-seamed face always turned shaving into a long and delicate operation, to which Binet's remarkable lightness of touch was essential. He slipped off his dressing-gown and started to dress with the help of his valet and Alphonso.

Angélique, meanwhile, had put on her cloth of gold bodice and stood motionless while Marguerite fastened the front, a genuine work of art of filigree gold interlaced with silks. A gold lace put a sparkling froth around her bare shoulders, giving her flesh a pale shimmer, a porcelain translucency. With the soft pink glow of her cheeks, her blackened eyebrows and lashes, her wavy hair that reflected the same glints as her dress, the startling transparency of her eyes, she saw herself in the mirror like a strange idol made entirely of precious stuffs: gold, marble, emerald.

Margot suddenly gave a cry and rushed towards Florimond, who was about to put a six-carat diamond in his mouth. . . .

"Joffrey, what jewels should I wear? Pearls seem to me too demure, diamonds too hard."

"Emeralds," he said, "in harmony with your eyes; all this gold is insolent, it is rather heavy. Your eyes lighten it, make it come alive. You need earrings and the gold and emerald choker. You can slip in a few diamonds with your rings."

Bending over her jewel-box, Angélique concentrated on the choice of trinkets. She was not yet blasé, and this profusion still enchanted her. When she turned around, the Comte de Peyrac was fastening his sword to a diamond-studded belt.

She gave him a long look and an unfamiliar shiver ran through her.

"I believe the Grande Demoiselle wasn't altogether wrong when she said there was something terrifying about you."

"It would be vain for me to try and hide my deformities," said the Comte. "If I tried to dress like a fop, I'd be ridiculous and pitiful. So I attune my costume to my face."

She looked at his face. It belonged to her. She had caressed it, she knew its slightest furrows. She smiled and murmured: "My love!"

The Comte was clothed entirely in black and silver. His cloak of black watered silk was veiled with silver lace fastened with diamond studs. Underneath the cloak could be seen a silver brocade doublet trimmed with black lace of a very intricate needle-point. The same lace fell in three frills from his knees below the dark velvet petticoat-breeches. The shoes had diamond buckles. The cravat, which did not take the form of a band but of a large bow, was also embroidered with very small diamonds. His fingers wore a multitude of diamonds and one very large ruby.

The Comte put on a hat with white plumes and asked if Kouassi-Ba had taken care of the presents that they would offer the King for his fiancée. The negro was outside, in front of the door, an object of admiration for all the sightseers, with his cherry-

red velvet doublet, his ample Turkish-style pan-
taloons and his turban, both of white satin. People
pointed to his curved sabre. He was carrying, on
a cushion, a very beautiful red morocco case with
gold studs.

Two sedan chairs were waiting for the Comte
and Angélique.

They quickly reached the mansion where the
King, his mother and the Cardinal were staying.
Like all the residences in Saint-Jean-de-Luz, it was
a house in Spanish style, garlanded with balus-
trades and twisted gilt-wood banisters. The courtiers overflowed into the square, where the plumes
on their hats fluttered in the wind, which carried
with it the salty tang of the sea.

Angélique felt her heart beating fast as she
crossed the threshold.

"I am going to see the King," she thought, "the
Queen Mother, the Cardinal!"

How close to her this young King had always
been — assailed by hostile Paris crowds, fleeing
through a France ravaged by civil war, driven from
town to town, from château to château, at the
mercy of the princely factions, betrayed, deserted,
and eventually victorious. Now he was harvesting
the fruit of his struggles. And even more than the
King, the woman whom Angélique perceived at
the far end of the room — her black veils, her
matt Spanish complexion, her distant yet affable
air, her perfect little hands lying on her dark dress
— the Queen Mother was relishing this hour of
triumph.

Angélique and her husband moved across the

chamber with its shiny parquet floor. Two little blackamoors held up Angélique's court mantle, which was of curled and chiselled gold cloth in contrast to the gleaming gold lamé of her skirt and bodice. The giant Kouassi-Ba followed them. It was hard to see, and it was very warm because of the heavy tapestries and the throng.

The First Gentleman of the King's Household announced:

"Comte de Peyrac de Morens d'Irristru."

Angélique curtseyed deeply. Her heart was in her throat. Before her loomed a black mass and a red mass: the Queen Mother and the Cardinal.

She thought:

"Joffrey ought to bow more deeply. He bowed so beautifully to the Grande Mademoiselle. But in front of the mightiest, he affects merely to move his foot a little. . . . Binet is right . . . Binet is right. . . ."

It was silly to be thinking of Binet and to keep telling herself that he was right. What made her do it?

A voice was saying:

"We are pleased to see you again, Monsieur, and to compliment . . . to admire the Comtesse, of whom we had already such favourable reports. But contrary to the rule, we find that for once the fame falls short of the reality."

Angélique raised her eyes. They met a brown, bright pair of eyes that rested on her very attentively: the King's eyes.

Richly dressed, and of medium height, he held himself so erect that he looked more imposing than any of his courtiers. Angélique found his skin rather pitted from smallpox and his nose too long, but his mouth was strong and sensuous under the lightly traced brown line of his moustache. His abundant, chestnut-coloured hair fell in cascading curls that owed nothing to the artifice of a wig. Louis had fine legs and graceful hands. Under the laces and ribbons, one sensed a supple, vigorous body, used to hunting and horsemanship.

"Nounou would say: 'He is a handsome male.' They are wise to marry him off," thought Angélique.

She again upbraided herself for having such vulgar thoughts at such a solemn moment of her life.

The Queen Mother asked to see the inside of the case which Kouassi-Ba had just presented, kneeling, his forehead touching the ground, in the attitude of one of the Three Wise Men. There were exclamations of delight at the sight of the little travelling-case of trifles, with its boxes and combs, scissors, crochet-hooks, seals, all in massive gold and island tortoise-shell. But the portable shrine particularly delighted the devout ladies who composed the retinue of the Queen Mother. The latter smiled and crossed herself. The crucifix and the two statuettes of Spanish saints, as well as the night-light and censer, were of gold and silver-gilt. Joffrey de Peyrac had commissioned an Italian artist to paint a gilt-wood triptych representing the scenes of the Passion. These miniatures were beautiful and their colours exquisitely fresh. Anne of Austria declared that the Infanta, who was reputed to be very pious, was sure to be delighted with this present.

She turned towards the Cardinal to show him

the paintings, but he was lingering over the dainty instruments in the case which he was gently turning between his fingers.

"It is said that gold flows from the hollow of your hands, Monsieur de Peyrac, as a spring of water flows from a rock."

"The image is correct, Your Eminence," the Comte answered softly, "as a spring from a rock indeed . . . but a rock that had first been mined by dint of quantities of fuse and powder, dug out to unbelievable depths, a rock blown to bits, crushed and ground down. Then indeed, by labour, sweat and effort, gold may well gush forth, and even in abundance."

"This is a very fine parable about toil that bears fruit. We are not accustomed to hearing people of your rank talk in this way, but I confess it does not displease me."

Mazarin was still smiling; he raised to his face a small mirror from the dressing-case and cast a quick glance at it. Despite the paints and powder with which he tried to conceal his yellow complexion, a moisture of exhaustion glistened on his temples and dampened his curls under the red cardinal's cap. For long months he had been worn down by illness; he at least had not lied when he had given his failing health as a pretext for not being the first to appear before Don Luis de Haro, the Spanish Minister. Angélique caught a glance from the Queen Mother towards the Cardinal, the glance of an anxious, worrying woman. She was probably dying to say: "Don't talk so much, you're tiring yourself. It's time for your herb-tea."

Was it true that she had loved her Italian, this Queen who had for so long been spurned by her too chaste husband? . . . Everybody said so, but nobody was sure. The hidden stairs of the Louvre kept their secret well. Only one human being, perhaps, knew, and that was this fiercely protected son, the King. In the letters which the Cardinal and the Queen exchanged, did they not call him the Confidant? Confidant of what? . . .

"I should like to discuss your work with you some time," said the Cardinal.

The young King added with spirit:

"So should I. What I have heard arouses my curiosity."

"I am at the disposal of Your Majesty and Your Eminence."

The audience was over.

Angélique and her husband went to greet Monseigneur de Frontenac, whom they noticed in the Cardinal's immediate entourage. Then they made the round of the great personages and their relatives. Angélique's back ached from all the curtseys, but she was in such a state of excitement and pleasure that she was not aware of her fatigue. The compliments addressed to her convinced her that she was admired. It was certain that she and Joffrey formed a couple that attracted a good deal of attention.

While her husband was conversing with the Maréchal de Gramont, a young man of short build but pleasant features planted himself before Angélique.

"Do you recognize me, Goddess just descended from the Sun's chariot?"

"Why, of course!" she cried, delighted. "You are Péguilin."

Then she apologized:

"I'm being very familiar, Monsieur de Lauzun, but I can't help it: I hear everyone speak of Péguilin. Péguilin here, Péguilin there! Everyone has so much affection for you that, without having seen you again, I fell in with all the rest."

"You are adorable, and you delight not only my eyes, but my heart. Do you know that you are the most extraordinary woman in this gathering? I know of ladies who are about to break their fans to pieces and tear their handkerchiefs with jealousy over your dress. How will you look on the day of the wedding, if you appear like this today?"

"Oh! on that day I'll keep in the background before the pageantry of the processions. But today it was my first presentation to the King. I am still so thrilled."

"Did you find him gracious?"

"How can one fail to find the King gracious?" said Angélique, laughing.

"I see that you are already well primed on what to say and what not to say at Court. I myself, goodness knows by what miracle, am still at Court. I have even been appointed captain of the company that is called 'the gentlemen of the *becs-de-corbin.*'"

"I admire your uniform."

"It is not unbecoming. . . . Yes, indeed, the King is a charming friend, but look out! You must not scratch him too hard when you play with him."

He bent over her ear.

"Do you know I was almost sent to the Bastille?"

"What did you do?"

"I no longer remember. I believe I hugged the little Marie Mancini a bit too closely, and the King was madly in love with her. A *lettre de cachet,* the King's private warrant of arrest, was ready; I was warned in time. I threw myself in tears at the King's feet and made him laugh so much that he pardoned me. So instead of sending me to the dark prison, he made me a captain. You see, he is a charming friend . . . when he is not your enemy."

"Why do you tell me this?" Angélique asked.

Péguilin de Lauzun gazed at her disarmingly with his bright eyes.

"For no reason at all, my dear."

He took her arm familiarly and pulled her along.

"Come, I want to introduce you to some friends who are dying to meet you."

The friends turned out to be young members of the King's suite. She was delighted to find herself thus on an equal footing with the foremost persons of the Court. Saint-Thierry, Brienne, Cavois, Ondedei, the Marquis d'Humières, Louvigny, the Duc de Gramont's second son, all seemed very gay and gallant and were dressed magnificently. She also saw de Guiche, to whom the King's brother was still clinging. The latter cast her a hostile glance.

"Oh! I recognize her," he said.

And he turned his back.

"Don't take offence at his manners, my dear," whispered Péguilin. "The Petit Monsieur sees all women as rivals for de Guiche, and de Guiche made the mistake of giving you a friendly glance."

"You know, he no longer wishes to be called the Petit Monsieur," remarked the Marquis d'Humières. "Since his uncle, Gaston d'Orléans died, one has to address him as just 'Monsieur.'"

There was a commotion in the crowd, followed by a jostling, and several eager hands reached out to steady Angélique.

"Be careful, gentlemen," cried Lauzun, raising a schoolmasterly finger, "remember a famous sword in Languedoc!"

But the crush was such that Angélique, laughing and a little confused, could not avoid being pressed against some precious, beribboned doublets that smelled pleasantly of iris powder and amber. The King's officers were making room for a procession of lackeys carrying silver platters and pots. Word went round that Their Majesties and the Cardinal had just retired for a few moments to have a bit to eat and to rest after the ceaseless presentations.

Lauzun and his friends departed to return to their duties. Angélique looked about for her friends from Toulouse. At first she had been apprehensive of running into the fiery Carmencita, but she had just learned that Monsieur de Mérecourt, having drunk his bitter cup to the dregs, had suddenly decided, in an upsurge of dignity, to send his wife to a convent. He was being repaid for this ill-considered move with a smarting disgrace.

Angélique began to wend her way through the various groups. The smell of roasts, added to that of perfumes, was giving her a headache. The heat was stifling. She had a good appetite. She told herself that the morning must be far advanced and that, if she did not find her husband within the next few moments, she would return to their house alone and have some ham and wine.

The people from her province must have foregathered at one of their own lodgings for a meal. She saw around her nothing but unknown faces. Those accentless voices produced an odd impression on her. Had she herself, during these years spent in Languedoc, perhaps caught that quick-fire, singsong way of speech? The thought was a little humiliating.

Eventually she found herself in a recess under the stairs and sat down on a bench to catch her breath and fan herself. It was definitely no easy matter to find one's way out of these Spanish houses with their hidden corridors and false doors.

A few steps away, the tapestry-covered wall revealed a narrow opening. Angélique glanced through it and saw the royal family gathered around a table in the company of the Cardinal, the two Archbishops of Bayonne and Toulouse, the Maréchal de Gramont and Monsieur de Lionne. The officers serving the Princes were coming and going through another door.

The King shook his hair back several times and fanned himself with his napkin.

"The heat in this part of the country spoils the most festive occasions."

"It's pleasanter on the Pheasant Island. There the breeze blows in from the sea," said Monsieur de Lionne.

"I won't have much opportunity to enjoy it, since I won't be allowed, by Spanish etiquette, to see my fiancée before the wedding day."

"But you'll be going to the Pheasant Island to

424

meet your uncle, the King of Spain, who will become your father-in-law," the Queen told him. "And then the peace will be signed."

She turned towards Madame de Motteville, her lady-in-waiting.

"It all moves me very much. I was very fond of my brother and often corresponded with him. But imagine, I was twelve years old when I left him on this very shore, and I have never seen him since."

There were exclamations of sympathy. Nobody seemed to remember that this same brother, Philip IV, had been France's greatest enemy, and that his correspondence with Anne of Austria had caused Cardinal Richelieu to suspect her of conspiracy and treason. Those events were now far away. Hope in the new alliance was as strong as it had been fifty years ago, when on this same river Bidassoa, the two countries had exchanged little round-cheeked princesses, wedged into their stiff, fluted ruffs: Anne of Austria, to marry the young Louis XIII, and Elizabeth of France the little Philip IV. The Infanta Maria-Theresa who was expected today was the daughter of Elizabeth.

With passionate curiosity Angélique watched the great ones of the world in their privacy. The King was eating heartily, but with dignity; he drank little and several times asked for water to be mixed in his wine.

"Upon my word," he cried suddenly, "the most extraordinary sight this morning was, beyond doubt, that odd black and gold couple from Toulouse. What a woman, my friends! A marvel! I'd been told so but couldn't believe it. And she seems sincerely in love with him. In fact, that Lame One bewilders me."

"He bewilders all those who meet him," said the Archbishop of Toulouse acidly. "I, who have known him for several years, have given up trying to understand him. There is something diabolical beneath it all."

"There he goes, drivelling nonsense again," thought Angélique sadly.

Her heart had throbbed pleasantly at the King's words, but the Archbishop's remark aroused her worries again. The prelate was unrelenting.

One of the gentlemen of the monarch's suite said with a little laugh:

"To be in love with one's husband! It really is ludicrous. This young person would do well to spend a little time at Court. She'd soon lose her silly prejudices."

"You seem to believe, sir, that the Court is a place where adultery is the only law," sternly protested Anne of Austria. "As though it were not good and natural for husband and wife to love each other. There is nothing ludicrous about it."

"But it is so rare," sighed Madame de Motteville.

"That's because it is rare for a couple to marry for love," said the King in a resigned tone of voice.

There was a moment's constrained silence. The Queen Mother exchanged an anxious glance with the Cardinal. Monseigneur de Frontenac raised his hand with unction.

"Sire, do not distress yourself. If the ways of Providence are unfathomable, the ways of the little god Eros are no less so. And since you mention an example that seems to have touched you, I can

426

assure you that that gentleman and his wife had never met before their wedding, which was solemnized by me in the cathedral of Toulouse. And yet, after a union of several years crowned by the birth of a son, the love they bear each other strikes even the most unobservant eye."

Anne of Austria looked grateful, and Monseigneur puffed himself up.

"Is he a hypocrite or sincere?" wondered Angélique.

The Cardinal's rather lisping voice spoke:

"I had the impression of watching a spectacle this morning. That man is ugly, crippled, disfigured, and yet when he appeared at the side of his gorgeous wife, followed by that huge Moor in white satin, I thought: 'How beautiful they are!' "

"It's a change from all those boring faces," said the King. "Is it true he has a magnificent voice?"

"That's what they say."

The gentleman who had already spoken gave a little sneer.

"It really is a most touching story, almost a fairy tale. You only hear of the likes of them down in the south."

"Oh! you're insufferable to make light of everything," protested the Queen Mother again. "Your cynicism displeases me, sir."

The courtier bowed his head and, as the conversation was resumed, he pretended to take an interest in a dog which was worrying a bone in the recess of the door. Seeing him look toward her hiding-place, Angélique quickly got up and moved away. She took a few steps through the anteroom, but her heavy cloak got caught on the drawer-handles of a pier-table. While she was bending down to disengage herself, the young man kicked the dog aside, came out and closed behind him the little door hidden by the tapestry. Having aroused the Queen Mother's displeasure, he deemed it wise to make a discreet exit.

He advanced nonchalantly, passed close to Angélique, then turned round to examine her.

"Oh! Why, it's the woman in gold!"

She gave him a haughty stare and made to continue on her way, but he barred her path.

"Not so fast! Let me contemplate this phenomenon. So you are the lady who is in love with her husband? And what a husband! An Adonis!"

She looked at him with quiet contempt. He was taller than she and very well built. His face was not without beauty, but his narrow mouth had an evil expression and his almond-shaped eyes were yellow, speckled with brown. This indeterminate, rather vulgar colour somewhat spoiled his looks. He was dressed with taste and refinement. His fair, almost white wig contrasted attractively with his youthful features.

Angélique could not help being impressed by him, but she said coldly:

"Yes indeed, you can hardly be compared to him. In my province, eyes like yours are called 'worm-eaten apples.' You see what I mean? As for your hair, my husband's is at least genuine."

An expression of hurt vanity darkened the gentleman's face.

"It's a lie," he cried, "he wears a wig."

"You can always try and pull it off, if you feel brave enough."

She had touched a sore point and she suspected him of wearing a wig because he was beginning to go bald. But he recovered his self-control very quickly. He half-closed his eyes till they were mere glowing slits.

"So you are trying to bite? This little provincial has too many talents!"

He cast a glance around, then seized her wrists and pushed her into the recess under the stairs.

"Let me go!" said Angélique.

"In a moment, my pretty one. But we have a little account to settle first."

Before she could foresee his action, he had pulled her head back and was cruelly biting her lips. Angélique gave a scream. Her hand promptly lunged forward and came down on her tormentor's cheek. Years of elegant manners had not diminished her stock of peasant violence coupled with her natural vigour. When her anger was roused, she had the same reactions as in the old days when she would go after her little peasant playmates tooth and nail. The slap echoed resoundingly and must have dazed him, for he recoiled with his hand to his cheek.

"Upon my word, a real washerwoman's slap!"

"Let me pass," repeated Angélique, "or I'll disfigure you so thoroughly you won't be able to appear before the King."

He felt she would carry out her promise and moved back a step.

"Oh! I'd like to have you in my power for a whole night," he murmured through clenched teeth. "I promise you I'd bring you to heel by dawn, you'd be a limp rag."

"That's it," she said, laughing, "ponder over your revenge . . . while holding your cheek."

She moved off and pushed her way through to the door. The crowd had thinned, for many people had gone to refresh themselves. Indignant and humiliated, Angélique was dabbing her wounded lip with her handkerchief.

"If only it does not show too much. . . . Whatever shall I say if Joffrey asks a question? I *must* prevent him from running his sword through that beast. Although he might just laugh. . . . He's the last to harbour any illusions about the manners of these fine gentlemen of the north. . . . I'm beginning to see what he means when he talks of the need of policing Court manners . . . but that's a task for which I, for one, feel little inclination. . . ."

She tried to distinguish her sedan chair and her footmen among the jostling throng in the square.

An arm slipped under hers.

"I was looking for you, my dear," said the Grande Mademoiselle, whose tall frame had loomed up next to her. "I am mortified when I think of all the nonsense I spoke this morning in your presence without knowing who you were. Alas, on a festive day, when you lack your usual comfort, your nerves get the better of you and the tongue wags carelessly."

"Your Highness has no need to worry, you said nothing that wasn't true, or else flattering. I recall only the flattery."

"You are kindness itself. I am delighted to have

you as a neighbour. . . . You will lend me your wigmaker again, won't you? Is your time free? Suppose we sit in the shade and peck at some grapes? What do you think? Those Spaniards take an unconscionable amount of time to arrive. . . ."

"I am at Your Highness's disposal," answered Angélique, with a curtsey.

The next morning, the programme called for a visit to the Pheasant Island to watch the King of Spain eat. The whole Court was jostling in the boats and wetting their fine shoes. The ladies uttered little cries as they hitched up their skirts.

Angélique, dressed in green and white satin with silver embroideries, found herself kidnapped by Péguilin and sitting between a witty-looking princess and the Marquis d'Humières. The Petit Monsieur, who was among the party, laughed a great deal, recalling the dismal face of his brother, obliged to remain on the French shore. Louis XIV was not allowed to see the Infanta before the marriage by proxy had made her Queen on the Spanish shore. Only then could he himself come to the Pheasant Island, pledge peace and carry away his fabulous conquest. The real wedding would be celebrated at Saint-Jean-de-Luz by the Bishop of Bayonne.

The boats were gliding over the calm water, laden with their sparkling charges. They touched land. While Angélique was waiting her turn to go ashore, one of the noblemen put his foot on the bench on which she was sitting and with his high wooden heel crushed her fingers. She checked a cry of pain. Looking up, she recognized the gentleman who had so wickedly molested her the previous day.

"That is the Marquis de Vardes," said the young Princess at her side. "He did it on purpose, of course."

"A real brute!" complained Angélique. "How can so gross a person be tolerated in the King's retinue?"

"He amuses the King with his impudence; besides, he pulls in his claws before His Majesty. But he has a bad name at Court. They have made a little song about him."

She hummed:

> Without in buffalo hide being clad
> One can behave like a savage,
> A beastly snout sticks out, 'tis sad,
> From handsome cloak and carriage.
> Who says: de Vardes, has said: the cad.

"Be quiet, Henriette!" cried the King's brother. "If Madame de Soissons were to hear you, she'd fly into a rage and complain to His Majesty that her favourite was being mocked."

"Pah! Madame de Soissons no longer enjoys His Majesty's favour. Now that the King takes a wife . . ."

"Where did you learn, Madame, that a wife, be she the Infanta, can have more influence over her husband than a former mistress?" asked Lauzun.

"Oh, gentlemen! Oh, ladies!" whined Madame de Motteville, "for mercy's sake! Is this a time to indulge in such talk when the grandees of Spain are advancing to meet us?"

Dark and wizened, her face seamed with wrinkles, Madame de Motteville, with her black dress and prudish airs, fitted oddly into this boatload of wigs and chattering dandies. The presence of Anne of Austria's lady-in-waiting was not, perhaps, entirely due to chance. The Queen Mother had instructed her to watch over the words of these mad young people, who were used to tearing each other to shreds and who might hurt Spanish susceptibilities.

Angélique was beginning to tire of these frivolous, scandal-mongering people, whose vices were only lightly veiled by a complicated courtesy. She heard the dark-haired Duchesse de Soissons say to one of her women-friends:

"My dear, I found two runners whom I am very proud of. I had indeed heard praise of the Basques as being lighter than the wind. They can cover at a run more than twenty miles a day. Don't you agree that to be preceded by runners who announce you and barking dogs that scatter the populace is awfully elegant?"

These words recalled to Angélique that Joffrey, who was fond of displaying luxury, still disapproved of this custom of having runners precede a carriage. As a matter of fact, where was Joffrey?

She had not seen him since the previous night. He had dropped in at their house to dress and shave, but at that moment she was still with the Grande Demoiselle. Angélique herself had had to change three or four times, in great haste and nervous irritation. She had only slept a few hours, but the liberal amount of good wine offered on all occasions was keeping her awake. She had given up worrying about Florimond; in three or four days there would be time to inquire whether the servants had given him his food instead of running off to admire the carriages or to be teased by the pages and footmen of the royal household. Anyway, Margot was keeping watch. Her Huguenot background was out of harmony with festivities and, while she was eagerly attending to every detail of her mistress's person and wardrobe, she was very strict with the servants under her command.

Angélique at last caught sight of Joffrey in the throng that was pressing inside the house situated in the middle of the island. She squeezed through to him and touched him with her fan. He looked down on her absentmindedly.

"Ah! there you are."

"I miss you awfully, Joffrey. But you don't seem very pleased to see me. Do you too bow to the prejudice that ridicules conjugal love? I believe you are ashamed of me."

He recovered his frank smile and seized her waist.

"No, my love. But you were in such princely and pleasant company. . . ."

"Oh! very pleasant," said Angélique, passing a finger over her bruised palm. "I may come out of it with my bones broken. What have you been doing since yesterday?"

"I met friends, talked of this and that. Have you seen the King of Spain?"

"No, not yet."

"Let's go into this room. They are laying the table. According to Spanish etiquette, the King of Spain must eat alone and follow a very complex ceremonial."

The room was hung with high tapestries that depicted the history of the Kingdom of Spain in pale bronze shades tinged with red and grey-blue. The place was crowded to the bursting-point.

The two courts rivalled each other in luxury and magnificence. The Spaniards outdid the French in gold and precious stones, but the latter triumphed in fashion and elegance of attire. The young men of Louis XIV's suite sported, that day, grey *moiré* coats covered with gold lace and fastened with flame-coloured studs; the lining was of gold cloth, the doublets were of gold brocade. The hats, adorned with white plumes, were turned up on one side, the brim held with a diamond pin. They laughed and pointed at the old-fashioned long moustaches of the Spanish grandees and their clothes laden with massive and outdated embroideries.

"Did you see those flat hats with their meagre little plumes?" whispered Péguilin, giggling.

"And the ladies! A row of old beanstalks with their bones sticking out under their mantillas."

"In this country, the good-looking wives remain at home behind barred windows."

"It seems the Infanta still wears a hoop-skirt with iron hoops of such dimensions that she has to go through a door sideways."

"Her corset is so tight that she seems to have no breasts at all, and yet she is supposed to have pretty ones," added Madame de Motteville, making the laces puff out over her own meagre bust.

Joffrey de Peyrac looked down at her with a caustic eye.

"The tailors of Madrid must truly be inexperienced thus to spoil what is beautiful, when our Paris tailors are so clever at making the most of what has ceased to be so."

Angélique pinched him under his velvet sleeve. He laughed, kissed her hand with an air of connivance. It occurred to her that he was hiding some secret concern from her; then, distracted by other things, she thought no more of it. There fell a sudden silence. The King of Spain had come in. Angélique, who was not very tall, managed to climb on a stool.

"He looks like a mummy," whispered Péguilin irrepressibly.

Philip IV had, indeed, a complexion of parchment colour. Thin and exhausted blood gave a pink glow to his cheeks. He walked to the table with the steps of an automaton. The big, mournful eyes did not blink. His undershot jaw supported a red lower lip which, adorned with sparse coppery hair, emphasized his sickly appearance. Imbued with his own almost divine grandeur as a sovereign, he made no movement that was not strictly required by etiquette. Paralysed by the bonds of power, lonely at his little table, he ate as if conducting a service.

A commotion in the ever-growing crowd suddenly pushed the first rows forward. The King's table was almost knocked over. The atmosphere became breathless. Philip IV was incommoded by it. He could be seen to raise his hand to his throat and fight for air by loosening his lace ruff a little.

But almost immediately he resumed his hieratic pose, like an actor conscientious to the point of martyrdom.

"Who'd think this ghost could beget with the ease of a farmyard cock," said the incorrigible Péguilin when the meal was over and they were outside again. "His natural children squeal in the corridors of his palace, and his second wife never stops giving birth to puny little things that promptly pass from the cradle to the garbage heap of the Escorial."

"The last one died during my father's embassy in Madrid, when he went there to ask for the Infanta's hand," said Louvigny, the Duc de Gramont's younger son. "Another has been born since and only has a breath of life."

The Marquis d'Humières cried, enthusiastically:

"He'll die, and then who'll be heiress to the throne of Charles V? The Infanta, our Queen."

"Your eyes are too big and you look too far ahead," protested the Duc de Bouillon pessimistically.

"How do you know this prospect was not foreseen by His Excellency the Cardinal and even by His Majesty?"

"No doubt, no doubt, but too lofty ambitions are not good for peace."

His long nose pointing towards the wind from the sea, as if he were sniffing something suspicious, the Duc de Bouillon grumbled:

"Peace! Peace! It will take less than ten years for it to topple over!"

It didn't even take two hours. Suddenly, all was

lost and there were rumours that the marriage was off.

Don Luis de Haro and Cardinal Mazarin had waited too long to settle the last details of the peace and specify the strategic villages, roads and frontiers which both of them hoped the other would give up in a fine burst of festive enthusiasm. Neither of them would yield. The war would go on. There was half a day of anguished flutters. Then the god of love was made to intervene between the betrothed who had never seen each other, and Ondedei was able to transmit a message to the Infanta in which she was told of the King's impatience to meet her. A daughter has supreme powers over her father's heart. Obedient though she was, the Infanta had no wish to return to Madrid after having been so close to "the sun. . . ." She made it clear to Philip IV that she wanted her husband, and the order of ceremonies, after a momentary upset, resumed its course.

The wedding by proxy took place on the Spanish shore at San Sebastian. The Grande Demoiselle took Angélique along with her. The daughter of Gaston d'Orléans, still mourning her father, was not supposed to attend. But she decided to appear incognito, that is to say, she tied a satin scarf over her hair and used no powder.

The procession through the streets of the town seemed a weird masquerade to the French. A hundred dancers dressed in white, with bells on their legs, advanced juggling with their swords, followed by fifty masked boys beating their Basque drums. After them came three wicker-frame giants dressed up as Moorish kings, reaching to the upper storey of the houses. There followed a giant Saint Christopher, a frightful dragon bigger than six whales and, finally, under a dais, the Holy Sacrament in a gigantic gold monstrance, before which the crowd kneeled.

These baroque pantomimes, this mystical extravaganza left the foreigners agog. Inside the church, behind the tabernacle, a staircase adorned with a million candles rose up towards the roof.

Angélique stared, dazzled, at this burning bush. The heavy smell of incense added to the unusual, Moorish atmosphere in the cathedral. In the darkness of the vaults and side-aisles there gleamed the gilt rope-moulded piers of three superimposed balconies crammed with men, on the one side, and women on the other.

They had to wait a long time. The idle priests chatted with the Frenchwomen, and Madame de Motteville was once again horrified by the words addressed to her in the propitious shelter of the shadows.

"Perdone, Déjeme pasars! (Let me pass, please),"* suddenly said a hoarse Spanish voice just behind Angélique.

She looked around, then dropped her eyes and saw a weird creature. It was a little dwarf-woman, as broad as she was tall, with an ugly but pleasant face. Her plump hand was resting on the collar of a big black greyhound. A male dwarf followed her, likewise dressed in gold braid and wide ruff, but he had a cunning expression and, looking at him, you wanted to laugh.

The crowd opened to let the midgets and the dog pass.

"That is the Infanta's dwarf and her buffoon, Tomasini," someone said. "Apparently she's taking them with her to France."

"What does she need these midgets for? There are plenty of other things to make her laugh, in France."

"She says that the dwarf is the only person who can make her cinnamon-flavoured chocolate."

Angélique saw, above her, a pale and impressive silhouette. Monseigneur de Frontenac, in mauve satin and an ermine cape, was moving towards one of the gilt-wood balconies. He was bending over the banister. His eyes were gleaming with a destructive fervour. He was talking to someone whom Angélique did not see.

Suddenly alarmed, she shouldered her way through the crowd towards him. Joffrey de Peyrac, at the foot of the stairs, was raising an ironical face towards the Archbishop.

"Remember the 'gold of Toulouse,' " the latter was saying under his breath. "When Servilius Cepion had ransacked the temples of Toulouse, he was vanquished as punishment for his impiousness. That's why the proverbial phrase, 'the gold of Toulouse,' implies misfortunes brought about by ill-gotten wealth."

The Comte de Peyrac continued to smile.

"I like you," he murmured. "I admire you. You have the candour and the cruelty of the pure. I can see the flames of the Inquisition gleam in your eyes. So you will not spare me?"

"Farewell, sir," said the Archbishop, with compressed lips.

"Farewell, Foulques de Neuilly."

The tapers illuminated the face of Joffrey de Peyrac. He was staring into the distance.

"What's happening, now?" whispered Angélique.

"Nothing, my beauty. Our eternal squabble . . ."

The King of Spain, pale as a ghost, was walking up the centre aisle, without any pomp, leading the Infanta on his left hand. Her skin was very white, so preserved by the darkness of the austere Madrid palaces, her eyes were blue, her pale silky hair puffed out by false tresses. She looked submissive and peaceful. She seemed more Flemish than Spanish.

The general opinion was that her white wool frock with almost no embroidery was awful.

The King led his daughter to the altar, where she knelt down. Don Luis de Haro, who — goodness knows why — was marrying her in the name of the King of France, stood at her side, but at a distance. When the time had come for the exchange of oaths, the Infanta and Don Luis held out their arms to each other but did not touch. With the same motion, the Infanta put her hand into that of the King and kissed him. Tears were rolling down the sovereign's ivory cheeks. The Grande Mademoiselle blew her nose noisily.

Chapter 25

"WILL you sing for us?" asked the King. Joffrey de Peyrac winced. He turned a haughty glance towards Louis XIV, staring at him as if the King were some stranger who had not been introduced to him. Angélique trembled; she gripped his hand.

"Sing for me," she whispered.

The Comte smiled and made a sign to Bernard d'Andijos, who rushed out.

The evening was drawing to its close. Near the Queen Mother, the Cardinal, the King and his brother sat the Infanta, stiff and with lowered eyes, in front of this husband to whom the ceremonies of the morrow would unite her. Her separation with Spain was consummated. Philip IV and his hidalgos were leaving, with aching hearts, for Madrid, leaving behind them the proud and pure Infanta as a token of the new peace. . . .

Giovanni, the little violinist, threaded his way through the ranks of the courtiers and handed the Comte de Peyrac his guitar and his velvet mask.

"Why do you wear a mask?" asked the King.

"The voice of love has no face," replied Peyrac, "and when the lovely eyes of ladies start to dream, no ugliness should disturb them."

He played a prelude and began to sing, mingling the ancient songs in *langue d'oc* with fashionable love couplets.

Finally, unbending his tall figure, he went to sit down by the Infanta and launched into a wild Spanish refrain, broken by hoarse Arab cries, in which burned all the passion and fire of the Iberian peninsula. The insipid face, pink and pearly, awoke at last to emotion; the Infanta's eyelids rose and her eyes sparkled. Perhaps she was re-living for the last time her cloistered existence as a small divinity, among her *camera major,* her women, her midgets who made her laugh; a slow and austere, but familiar existence where one played cards, received nuns who predicted the future, or prepared delicate meals with preserves and orange and violet-scented pastries.

There was a rather frightened expression on her face as she looked around her at all these Frenchmen.

"You have charmed us," said the King to the singer. "I desire only one thing, and that is to have frequent opportunities to hear you sing."

Joffrey de Peyrac's eyes shone strangely behind his mask.

"Nobody could wish it more than I, Sire. But it all depends on Your Majesty, does it not?"

It seemed to Angélique that the sovereign was frowning slightly.

"That is so. I am glad to hear you say it, Monsieur de Peyrac," he said a little bluntly.

When they reached their hôtel late that night, Angélique pulled her clothes off without waiting for assistance from her maid and flung herself on the bed with a sigh.

"I am exhausted, Joffrey. I believe I am not yet

broken in to life at Court. How do all these people manage to indulge in so many pleasures and still find a means of deceiving each other at night?"

The Comte lay down beside her without answering. It was so hot that the mere contact of a sheet was unpleasant. Through the open window passing torches sometimes cast a reddish light on to the bed, whose curtains they had not lowered. Saint-Jean-de-Luz was still busy with the preparations for the morrow.

"If I don't sleep a little, I shall collapse during the ceremony," said Angélique, yawning.

She stretched, then curled up against the lean, brown body of her husband. He put out his hand, caressed the round thigh which shone like alabaster in the darkness, followed the supple curve of the waist, found the high, firm little breast. His fingers quivered, became more eager, fondled the lithe body. As he risked a bolder caress, Angélique protested half-asleep:

"Oh Joffrey! I am so drowsy!"

He did not insist, and she glanced at him through her lashes to see if he was vexed. Propped on an elbow, he was looking at her with a little smile.

"Sleep, my love," he whispered.

When she awoke, she would have believed that he had not moved, for he was still looking at her. She smiled at him.

It was cool. The darkness was not yet dispelled, but the sky was assuming a greenish hue before the brightness of dawn. A transient torpor lay over the town. Still numbed with sleep, Angélique reached towards her husband, and their arms joined and carefully intertwined.

He had taught her the delights of protracting their enjoyment, the skilful joust, with its feints, its retreats, its boldnesses, the patient striving of two generous bodies, leading each other mutually to the height of rapture. When at last they broke apart, tired and sated, the sun was high in the sky.

"Would anyone think that we had an excruciating day before us?" said Angélique, laughing.

Margot knocked at the door.

"Madame, Madame, it is late. The carriages are already on their way to the cathedral, and you'll find no more room to see the procession."

The *cortège* was small. At the head walked the Cardinal-Prince de Gondi, brilliant and fiery, former hero of the *Fronde,* whose presence on this fine day confirmed the determination of both sides to let bygones be bygones.

Then came Cardinal Mazarin in flowing purple.

At a distance walked the King, dressed in gold brocade decked with abundant black lace. At either side of him were the Marquis d'Humières and Péguilin de Lauzun, captains of the two companies of the *becs-corbin* gentlemen, each holding a blue baton, emblematic of their office.

In their wake came the Infanta, the new Queen, led by Monsieur, the King's brother, on her right and by her knight-of-honour, Monsieur de Bernonville, on her left. Her dress was of silver brocade and her violet velvet coat was strewn with golden lilies. This coat, very short at the sides, had a train several feet long which was carried by the King's young cousins, the Mesdemoiselles de Valois and d'Alençon and the Princesse de Carignan. Two more ladies were holding a crown over the Queen's head. The dazzling group advanced slowly along the narrow, carpeted street which was flanked by Swiss and French guards and musketeers. The Queen Mother, draped in black veils with silver embroideries, followed the couple, surrounded by her ladies and guards.

At the tail-end came Mademoiselle de Montpensier, "the great scatterbrain of the kingdom," a cumbersome object at Court, dressed in black but with twenty rows of pearls.

It was but a short way from the royal residences to the church. There were nevertheless some moments of trouble. It was quite obvious that d'Humières was quarrelling with Péguilin. The two captains took their places in church at the King's side. Together with the Comte de Charost, captain of a company of bodyguards, and the Marquis de Vardes, captain-colonel of the Hundred Swiss, they accompanied the King for the ceremony of offering.

Louis XIV took a taper laden with twenty *louis d'or* from the hands of Monsieur who, in turn, had received it from the grand master of ceremonies, and handed it to Jean d'Olce, Bishop of Bayonne. Mademoiselle performed the same duties for the young Queen Maria-Theresa.

"Did I not carry my offering and drop my curtsey as well as anybody?" she later asked Angélique.

"Certainly. Your Highness displayed much majesty."

Mademoiselle puffed herself up.

446

"I am well suited to ceremonies, and I believe that my person adorns these occasions as effectively as my name adorns the ceremonial."

Thanks to Mademoiselle's protection, Angélique was able to observe very closely all the festivities that followed, the banquet and the ball. In the evening, she took part in the long parade of courtiers and nobles who bowed, one after the other, in front of the large bed in which the King and his young bride were lying side by side.

Angélique saw these two young people as motionless as wax dolls, stretched out between the lace sheets under the eyes of the crowd. This surfeit of etiquette deprived the consummation of their marriage of both life and warmth. How could this couple, who had met each other only yesterday and who were now posing, stiff with magnificence, starched with dignity, turn presently to each other to embrace, after the Queen Mother, according to custom, had dropped the curtains of the sumptuous bed over them? She felt pity for the impassive Infanta who had to conceal her maidenly embarrassment from curious eyes. Perhaps she was experiencing no emotion whatsoever, accustomed as she was to bowing since childhood to the demands of public display. It was just one more ceremony. One could trust Louis XIV's Bourbon blood to rise to the occasion.

As they walked down the stairs, the lords and ladies exchanged *risqué* pleasantries. Angélique thought of Joffrey, who had been so gentle and patient with her. Where *was* Joffrey? She had not seen him all day. . . .

In the hall of the royal mansion, Péguilin de

Lauzun came up to her. He was a little out of breath.

"Where is your husband?"

"Why, I too am looking for him."

"When did you last see him?"

"I left him this morning to go to the cathedral with Mademoiselle. He himself was accompanying Monsieur de Gramont."

"You have not seen him since?"

"Why no, I told you so. You seem very upset. What do you want of him?"

The short nobleman grabbed her hand and dragged her along.

"Let's go to the residence of the Duc de Gramont."

"What is happening?"

He did not answer. He was still in his beautiful uniform but his face had lost its customary gaiety.

At the Duc de Gramont's that great lord, dining among a group of friends, told them that the Comte de Peyrac had left him after Mass that morning.

"Was he alone?" inquired Lauzun.

"Alone? Alone?" muttered the Duc. "What do you mean, my boy? Is there a single person in Saint-Jean-de-Luz who can boast of being alone today? Peyrac did not inform me of his intentions, but I can tell you that his Moor was with him."

"Good. I like that better," said Lauzun.

"He's probably with the Gascons. That lot is carousing in a tavern at the port; unless he accepted an invitation from Princess Henriette of England, who intended to ask him to sing for her and her ladies."

"Come, Angélique," said Lauzun.

The English princess was that pleasant young girl next to whom Angélique had been sitting in the boat during the trip to the Pheasant Island. In answer to Péguilin's inquiry she shook her head:

"No, he is not here. I sent one of my gentlemen to look for him, but he could not find him anywhere."

"Yet his Moor, Kouassi-Ba, is a figure that hardly escapes notice."

"Nobody has seen the Moor."

At the tavern of the Golden Whale, Bernard d'Andijos got up with some difficulty from the table at which was gathered the finest flower of Gascony and Languedoc. No, nobody had seen Monsieur de Peyrac. Lord knows they had been looking for him, shouting, even hurling pebbles at the windows of his hôtel in the rue de la Rivière. They had even broken some glasspanes at Mademoiselle's. But of Peyrac, not a trace.

Lauzun stroked his chin, pondering.

"Let's find de Guiche. The Petit Monsieur was ogling your husband. Maybe he dragged him along to an intimate party at his favourite's."

Angélique followed the Duc through crowded lanes, lit by torches and coloured lanterns. They walked into houses, questioned, left again. Everywhere people were dining surrounded by the smell of cooking, the smoke of a thousand candles, the bibulous breath of servants who had been drinking at the fountains of wine all day.

449

There was dancing in the squares to the sound of tambourines and castanets. The horses neighed in the dark courtyards.

The Comte de Peyrac had vanished.

Angélique suddenly gripped Péguilin and made him face her.

"This is enough, Péguilin, speak up. Why are you so worried about my husband? You know something?"

He sighed and, discreetly lifting his wig, wiped his forehead.

"I know nothing. A gentleman of the King's suite never knows anything. It would cost him too dearly. But for some time I have been suspecting a plot against your husband."

He whispered into her ear:

"I fear they may have tried to arrest him."

"Arrest him?" repeated Angélique. "But why?"

He made a gesture of ignorance.

"You are mad," said Angélique. "Who could give the order to arrest him?"

"The King, of course."

"The King has other things to think about than having people arrested on a day like this. What you are saying doesn't hold water."

"I hope so. I had a word of warning sent to him last night. There was still time for him to jump on his horse. Madame, are you quite certain that he spent the night with you?"

"Oh yes, quite certain," she said, blushing a little.

"He didn't understand. He has gambled once more, juggled with Fate."

"Péguilin, you drive me mad," cried Angélique, shaking him. "I believe you are playing a vile joke on me."

"Hush!"

He pulled her towards him with the familiarity of a man used to women, and pressed his cheek against hers soothingly.

"I am a wicked fellow, my love, but wounding your heart is something I wouldn't be capable of. Anyway, after the King there is no man I love so much as the Comte de Peyrac. But let's not get panicky, my dear, he may have fled in time."

"But after all . . ." cried Angélique.

He silenced her peremptorily.

"But after all," she went on in a lower voice, "why should the King want to arrest him? His Majesty talked to him very graciously only last night, and I myself overheard talk in which the King did not conceal his liking for Joffrey."

"Alas! Liking . . . Reasons of state . . . Influences . . . It isn't up to us, poor courtiers, to determine the King's feelings. Remember that he was a pupil of Mazarin's, who said of him: 'He'll be late in starting but he'll go farther than the rest.' "

"Don't you think this may be some intrigue by the Archbishop of Toulouse, Monseigneur de Frontenac?"

"I don't know anything. . . . I don't know anything. . . ." repeated Péguilin.

He escorted her back to her house, told her that he would keep on inquiring and would call to see her in the morning. As she approached the hôtel, Angélique had a wild hope that her husband might be waiting for her there, but she found only Margot watching over the sleeping Florimond, and the old

451

aunt, who had been quite forgotten amid the festivities and who was trotting about the landings. The other servants had gone to a dance in the town.

Angélique flung herself fully dressed on the bed. Her brain was reeling.

"I'll be able to think tomorrow," she told herself. And she fell into a heavy sleep.

She was roused by a shout coming from the street.

"Médême! Médême!"

The moon was travelling across the flat roofs of the town. Clamouring and singing still came from the port and the main square, but the district was quiet and almost everybody had gone to sleep, broken with fatigue.

Angélique ran out on to the balcony and saw the negro, Kouassi-Ba, standing in the moonlight.

"Médême! Médême! . . ."

"Wait, I'm coming."

She rushed down, lit a candle in the vestibule and pulled the door open. The negro slipped inside with the supple grace of an animal. His eyes gleamed with a strange light; she saw he was trembling as if overcome with fright.

"Where have you been?"

"Down there," he said with a vague gesture. "I need a horse. A horse at once!"

His teeth gleamed in a savage grimace.

"They attacked my master," he whispered, "and I didn't have my big sabre. Oh! why didn't I have it with me just today!"

"What do you mean — attacked, Kouassi-Ba? Who did?"

"I don't know, Mistress. How should I know, who am a poor slave? A page brought him a piece of paper. The master went there. I followed. There weren't many people in the courtyard of that house; only a coach with black curtains. Some men got out of it and surrounded him. The master drew his sword. Other men came. They struck him. They put him in the coach. I shouted. I clung to the coach. Two footmen had mounted behind on the axle. They beat me till I fell off, but I made one of them fall, too, and strangled him."

"You strangled him?"

"With my hands, like this," said the negro, opening and closing his rosy palms like pincers. "I ran all the way. There was too much sunshine, and my tongue is bigger than my head. I am so thirsty."

"Come and drink. You can talk afterwards."

She followed him into the stables, where he picked up a pail and took a long draught.

"Now," he said, wiping his thick lips, "I shall take a horse and I'll go after them. I'll kill them all with my big sabre."

He foraged in the straw and pulled out his meagre luggage. While he was removing his torn and mud-caked satin garments to put on a simpler servant's livery, with clenched teeth Angélique went into a stall and untied the negro's horse. Wisps of straw pricked her feet, but she paid no heed. She seemed to be living through a nightmare, where everything moved slowly, too slowly. . . . She was running towards her husband, she was stretching her arms out towards him. But never again would she be able to reach him, never. . . .

She watched the black horseman dash off. The horse's hooves drew sparks from the round pebbles of the paved road. The noise of his galloping receded as another sound came alive in the limpid morning: that of the bells chiming for matins, for a thanksgiving service.

The royal wedding night was drawing to its end. The Infanta Maria-Theresa was Queen of France.

Chapter 26

THE Court returned towards Paris through the flowering orchards and countryside. Through the new wheat the long caravan trailed out its six-horse coaches, its carts carrying beds, trunks and tapestries, its laden mules, its lackeys and mounted guards.

As they approached the towns, deputations of aldermen advanced in the dust towards the King's coach, carrying the civic keys on a silver platter or on a velvet cushion. Thus Bordeaux, Saintes, Poitiers were left behind. Angélique hardly recognized the last-named town in the din and confusion.

She too was going to Paris, was following the Court.

"Since nobody has told you anything, behave as if nothing were the matter," had been Péguilin's advice. "Your husband intended to go up to Paris, so you go there too. Everything will explain itself there. After all, it may all just be a misunderstanding."

"But what do you know, Péguilin?"

"Nothing, nothing . . . I know nothing."

He hurried away, with troubled eyes, to play the fool for the King.

Eventually, after asking Andijos and Cerbalaud to escort her, Angélique had sent part of her entourage back to Toulouse. She kept with her a carriage and a cart, as well as Margot, a little maidservant who attended to Florimond's cradle, three footmen and two coachmen. At the last moment, the wigmaker Binet and the little fiddler Giovanni begged her to take them along.

"If His Lordship the Comte is waiting for us in Paris and I am not there, he will be most displeased, I assure you," said François Binet.

"To see Paris! Oh, to see Paris!" the young musician kept repeating. "If I can only meet the King's music-master, that Baptiste Lulli that one hears so much of, I am sure he'll advise me and I'll become a great artist."

"All right, get in, great artist," Angélique finally yielded.

She smiled, kept up appearances, trying to cling to Péguilin's words: "It's all a misunderstanding." Actually, barring the fact that the Comte de Peyrac had suddenly vanished into thin air, nothing seemed changed, no rumour had spread of his disgrace. The Grande Mademoiselle lost no opportunity to have friendly chats with the young woman. She could hardly be dissembling, for she seemed a very naïve person with not a trace of hypocrisy.

Everyone enquired after Monsieur de Peyrac in a very natural way. Angélique ended up by saying that he had gone ahead to Paris to prepare for her arrival. But ever since leaving Saint-Jean-de-Luz, she had been vainly trying to reach Monseigneur de Frontenac. He had, however, returned to Toulouse.

There were moments when she thought she had been dreaming, and she would buoy herself up with false hope. Joffrey, perhaps, had merely gone back to Toulouse. . . .

In the vicinity of Dax, as they were travelling through the sandy, broiling Landes country, a macabre incident brought her back with a jolt to tragic reality. The inhabitants of a village appeared and asked if some guards could not help them in a search that they were organizing to round up some terrible black monster that was putting the region to the sword.

Andijos galloped up to Angélique's coach and whispered that this no doubt referred to Kouassi-Ba. She asked to see the villagers. They were shepherds, walking on stilts to enable them to pass over the very loose downland soil.

They confirmed the young woman's fears. Yes, two days ago the shepherds had heard shouts and pistol shots on the road. They had arrived in time to see a coach assailed by a black-faced horseman, who was brandishing a curved sabre like those of the Turks. Fortunately, the people in the coach had a pistol. The black man must have been wounded and he had fled.

"Who were the people in the coach?" asked Angélique.

"We don't know," they answered. "The blinds were drawn. There was an escort of only two men. They gave us a coin to bury the one whom the monster had beheaded."

"Beheaded!" repeated Andijos, aghast.

"Oh yes, sir, and he did it so cleanly that we had to retrieve the head from the ditch into which it had rolled."

The next night, when most of the travellers were obliged to camp in the villages around Bordeaux, Angélique dreamed she was hearing again the sinister cry:

"Médême! Médême!"

She tossed and finally woke up. Her bed had been put up in the only room of a farm-house whose inhabitants were sleeping in the stable. Florimond's cradle stood near the fireplace. Margot and the little serving-maid were stretched out on the same straw pallet. Angélique saw that Margot had got up and was putting on her petticoat.

"Where are you going?"

"It's Kouassi-Ba. I'm certain of it," whispered the big woman.

Angélique had already jumped out of bed.

Cautiously the two women opened the rickety door. Happily the night was pitch-dark.

"Kouassi-Ba, come here!" they whispered.

Something moved, and a big reeling body stumbled over the threshold. They made him sit on a bench. In the light of a candle they saw that his skin was grey and hanging loose. His clothes were smeared with blood. For three days he had been roaming, wounded, over the downs. Margot

457

foraged in the trunks and made him gulp down some brandy. Only then was he able to speak.

"Only one head, Mistress. I could only cut off one head."

"That is quite enough, I assure you," said Angélique with a little laugh.

"I lost my big sabre and my horse."

"I'll give you new ones. Don't talk . . . You have found us, that's the main thing. When the master sees you, he'll say to you: 'Well done, Kouassi-Ba.' "

"Will we see the master again?"

"We'll see him again, I promise you."

While she talked, she tore some linen into strips for a bandage. She was afraid that the bullet had remained in his wound, lodged under the collar-bone. But she discovered another wound beneath his armpit, which proved that the bullet had gone through him. She poured brandy over the two wounds and bandaged them energetically.

"What are we going to do with this man, Madame?" asked Margot, frightened.

"Keep him with us, of course! He'll take his place in the cart."

"But what will they say?"

"Who — they? If you believe that all these people around us care about the exploits of my negro. . . . Good food, good horses at the relay-station and comfortable lodgings, that's all they worry about. He'll stay under cover in the cart, and in Paris, once we are established, everything will work itself out."

She repeated as if to convince herself:

"You must realize, Margot, all this is just a misunderstanding."

The carriage rolled through the forest of Rambouillet. Angélique was drowsing, for the heat was dreadful. Florimond was asleep on Margot's lap. The noise of a sharp explosion suddenly roused them all with a start. There was a violent shock. Angélique had a vision of a deep ravine. In a cloud of dust the coach turned over with an awful cracking noise. Florimond screamed, half crushed by the nurse-maid. They could hear the wild neighing of the horses, the coachman's shouts, the cracking of his whip.

The same dull report rang out again, and Angélique noticed on the coach-window a peculiar star, like frost-flowers in winter, with a tiny hole in the middle. She tried to straighten up inside the overturned carriage and take hold of Florimond. Suddenly the coach-door was wrenched open and the face of Péguilin de Lauzun bent over the aperture.

"Nobody harmed, at least?" he said, his southern accent coming to the fore under the stress of emotion.

"Everybody's screaming, so I expect everyone's alive," said Angélique.

She herself had a small scratch on her arm from broken glass splinters, but it was nothing serious.

She handed the child to the Duc. The Chevalier de Louvigny also appeared, held out his hand and helped her to extricate herself from the carriage. Out on the road, she quickly grasped Florimond again and tried to calm him. The baby's shrill cries rose above the din, and it was impossible to hear a word.

While soothing her child, Angélique saw that the Duc de Lauzun's entourage had pulled up behind her cart, as had the coach of Lauzun's sister, Charlotte, Comtesse de Nogent, and that the two carriages of the Gramont brothers, with their ladies, friends and valets, were hurrying towards the scene of the accident.

"But what happened, anyway?" asked Angélique, as soon as Florimond subsided enough to allow her to open her mouth.

The coachman looked badly frightened. He wasn't a very reliable man: a garrulous braggart, with a constant song on his lips, he had above all a penchant for the bottle.

"You were drunk and fell asleep?"

"No, Madame, I assure you. It is true I felt hot, but I was holding my horses firmly. They were moving well, when suddenly two men came out of the cover of the trees. One of them had a pistol. He fired into the air, which frightened the horses. They shied and reared back. At that moment the coach turned over into the ditch. One of the men had seized the horses' bit. I lashed him with my whip as hard as I could. The other was loading his pistol again. He came close and fired into the carriage. At that moment the luggage-cart arrived, and then those gentlemen on horseback. . . . The two fellows made off. . . ."

"That's an odd story," said Lauzun. "The forest is guarded and protected. The sergeants have tracked down all the highwaymen in anticipation of the King's passage. What did these ruffians look like?"

"I don't know, Your Highness. They weren't highwaymen, I'm sure. They looked well dressed, well shaven. The most I can say is that they looked rather like household servants."

"Two sacked footmen, up to some mischief?" suggested de Guiche.

A heavy carriage was driving up among the groups of standing people and finally came to a stop. Mademoiselle de Montpensier put her head out of the window.

"Are you Gascons making all this hubbub? Do you want to scare the birds of the Ile-de-France with your trumpeting voices?"

Lauzun ran up to her, bowing energetically. He explained the accident that had befallen Madame de Peyrac and that it would take some little time to right her coach and get it on the move again.

"But let her come in with us!" cried the Grande Mademoiselle. "Go and fetch her, my little Péguilin. Come, my dear, we have an entire banquette unoccupied. You will be quite comfortable with your baby. Poor angel! Poor treasure!"

She herself helped Angélique to get in and settle down.

"You are hurt, poor dear. As soon as we get to the relay station, I'll send for my doctor."

Angélique realized with confusion that the person sitting in the back of the carriage, next to Mademoiselle de Montpensier, was none other than the Queen Mother.

"May Your Majesty excuse me."

"There's nothing to excuse, Madame," replied Anne of Austria very graciously. "Mademoiselle

461

did well to invite you to share our carriage. The seat is quite comfortable and you'll soon recover. What bothers me is what I've been told on the subject of those armed men who attacked you."

"Good Lord, perhaps those men were out to harm the King or the Queen?" cried Mademoiselle, clasping her hands.

"Their carriage is surrounded by guards and I don't think we need fear for them. Nevertheless I'll mention it to the lieutenant of police."

Angélique now felt the reaction from the shock she had suffered. She felt she was going very pale and, closing her eyes, she leaned her head against the well-upholstered back of the seat. The man had shot point-blank into the window. It was a miracle that none of the occupants had been hurt. She was hugging Florimond against her. She realised he had got much thinner and reproached herself for it. He was tired of these interminable travels. Since he had been parted from his nurse and his little blackamoor, he was constantly whining and refusing the milk which Margot managed to obtain in the villages. He sighed in his sleep, tears hanging on the long lashes that cast a shadow over his pale cheeks. He had a very small mouth, round and red like a cherry. With her handkerchief, Angélique softly dabbed his white, round forehead on which drops of perspiration had formed.

Angélique felt alone. She could not confide in anyone. These pleasant Court relations were worthless. Everyone, greedy for protection and bounties, would turn away from her at the least hint of disgrace. Bernard d'Andijos was devoted, but so flippant! Once he was within the walls of Paris, he would disappear, would be dashing from one Court ball to another with his mistress, Mademoiselle de Montmort, on his arm, or else — in the company of fellow-Gascons — haunting the taverns and gambling-dens at night.

It did not matter, really. All that mattered was to reach Paris. There she would have solid ground under her feet. Angélique would settle down in the beautiful town house which the Comte de Peyrac owned in the Saint-Paul *quartier*. Then she would begin to make investigations to find out what had become of her husband.

Chapter 27

*A*NGÉLIQUE thought she was already in Paris when they were still driving through the suburbs. No sooner had they passed through the Gate of Saint-Honoré than she felt disappointed by the narrow, muddy streets. The noise did not have the same ringing quality as in Toulouse, it seemed to her shriller and more vociferous. The shopkeepers' and the coachmen's cries above all, the shouts of the footmen preceding the carriages and of the sedan-chair bearers rose above a dull background growl which made her think of the distant rumbles before a thunderstorm. The air was sweltering and full of foul smells.

Angélique's carriage, escorted by Bernard d'Andijos on horseback and followed by the luggage-cart and two mounted lackeys, took more than two hours to reach the Saint-Paul *quartier*. It finally reached the Rue de Beautreillis and slowed down.

They had come to a stop outside a wide carriage entrance of pale timber with wrought bronze knockers and key-locks. Beyond the white stone wall could be seen the courtyard and the large stone house, in the style of the day, with tall, clear, glass windows, and a roof adorned with dormers and covered with bright new slates that sparkled in the sun.

A lackey came to open the carriage-door.

"Here we are, Madame," said the Marquis d'Andijos.

He remained on horseback and stared at the porch with a dumbfounded expression.

Angélique alighted and ran to a little house which surely was the Swiss concierge's lodge. She rang the bell angrily. It was intolerable that nobody had yet come to open the main gate. The bell seemed to be ringing in a desert. The window-panes of the lodge were grimy. Everything seemed lifeless.

Only then did Angélique become aware of the curious aspect of the gate which Andijos kept staring at as if thunderstruck. She went up to it. Interlaced red strings were fastened on it by means of thick, coloured wax-seals. A white piece of paper, also fixed with seals, read:

The King's Chamber of Justice
Paris
1st July, 1660

464

Open-mouthed with amazement, she stared at it uncomprehendingly. At that moment the door of the lodge opened a slit, and in it appeared the perturbed face of a servant in a crumpled livery. At the sight of the carriage, he hurriedly closed the door again, then thinking better of it, opened it once more and came out with hesitant steps.

"Are you the concierge of the house?" inquired the young woman.

"Yes . . . yes, Madame, it's me, Baptiste. And I do recognize the . . . the carriage of . . . of my . . . my . . . my master."

"Stop stuttering, fool," she cried, stamping her foot. "And tell me quickly where Monsieur de Peyrac is."

The domestic looked around with alarm. The absence of any neighbour seemed to reassure him. He came even closer, raised his eyes to Angélique, and suddenly knelt down before her while continuing to throw anxious glances around him.

"Oh! my poor young mistress," he cried, "my poor master . . . oh! what a dreadful misfortune!"

"Speak up! What has happened?"

She was shaking him by the shoulders, frightened out of her wits.

"Get up, idiot! I don't understand a word you're saying. Where is my husband? Is he dead?"

The man got up with difficulty and murmured:

"They say he is in the Bastille. The house is under seals. I must answer for it with my life. And you, Madame, do try and flee while there is still time."

Mention of the famous prison fortress of the Bastille, far from shattering Angélique, almost reas-

465

sured her after the dreadful anguish she had felt. One can get out of prison. She knew that in Paris the most dreaded prison was that of the Archbishopric, situated below the level of the Seine, where you ran the risk of drowning in winter; and after that came the Châtelet and the General Hospital, which were reserved for commoners. The Bastille was the aristocratic prison. Despite some sinister legends about the strong-rooms of its eight towers, it was generally known that a stay within its walls was not a dishonour.

Angélique heaved a little sigh and tried hard to face the situation.

"I think it's better not to remain in this neighbourhood," she said to Andijos.

"Yes, yes, Madame, do leave quickly," insisted the servant.

"The problem is where to go. As a matter of fact, I have a sister who lives in Paris. I don't know her address, but her husband is a King's proctor called Maître Fallot. I even believe that since his marriage he calls himself Fallot de Sancé."

"If we go to the Palace of Justice, they'll certainly be able to direct us."

The carriage and its suite resumed their drive through Paris. Angélique did not think of looking around her. This city, which was welcoming her in such a hostile way, held no attraction for her. Florimond was crying. He was teething and vainly did Margot rub his gums with an ointment made of honey and pounded fennel.

They eventually found the address of the King's proctor who, like many magistrates, lived not far from the Palace of Justice, on the island of the Cité, in the parish of Saint-Landry. The street was called the rue de l'Enfer which, to Angélique, seemed a sinister omen. The houses were still grey and medieval, with pointed gables, sculptures, gargoyles and infrequent apertures.

The one before which the carriage stopped looked hardly less lugubrious than the rest, although each storey boasted three fairly high windows. On the ground floor was the office, and a brass plate on its door bore the words: "Maître Fallot de Sancé. King's Proctor."

Two clerks, who had been yawning on the threshold, rushed towards Angélique as soon as she had stepped out of the carriage and promptly surrounded her with a stream of words in an unintelligible jargon. She finally grasped that they were speaking in glowing terms of the merits of Maître de Sancé's office as the only place in Paris to which people anxious to win a law-suit could repair in all security.

"I haven't come for a law-suit," said Angélique, "I want to see Madame Fallot."

Disappointed, they indicated a door on the left which led towards the proctor's residence.

Angélique raised the bronze knocker and she felt something akin to excitement as she waited for the door to open. A plump servant neatly dressed and in a white bonnet showed her into the vestibule, but almost immediately Hortense appeared at the top of the staircase. She had seen the carriage through the window.

Angélique had the impression that her sister had been on the verge of falling on her neck but, seem-

467

ingly changing her mind, she affected a distant air. They kissed without warmth.

Hortense seemed even leaner and taller than in the old days.

"My poor sister!" she said.

"Why do you call me your poor sister?" asked Angélique.

Madame Fallot motioned silently towards the maid and pulled Angélique into her room. It was a spacious chamber which also served as a drawing-room, for numerous armchairs and stools as well as seats and settees were arranged around the bed with its beautiful curtains and yellow damask counterpane. Angélique wondered if her sister was in the habit of receiving her women friends lying in bed as did the *précieuses*. It was true that, formerly, Hortense had the reputation for being witty and prided herself on her conversational talents.

The room was very dark, on account of the stained-glass panes, but in this heat it was not unpleasant. The stone floor was cooled by sheaves of green grass scattered over it here and there. Angélique breathed deeply of their good country smell.

"You have a nice home," she said to Hortense.

The latter did not lose her frown.

"Don't trouble to deceive me with feigned sprightliness. I know everything."

"You are lucky, for I admit that I myself am utterly in the dark as to what is happening to me."

"How imprudent of you to show yourself ostentatiously in Paris!" said Hortense, raising her eyes to heaven.

"Listen, Hortense, don't start turning your eyes

468

to the ceiling. I don't know if your husband is like me, but I remember I could never see you pull that grimace without wanting to box your ears. Now I'll tell you what I know, and then you'll tell me what you know."

She told how, while they were at Saint-Jean-de-Luz for the King's wedding, the Comte de Peyrac had disappeared. The suppositions of certain friends led her to believe that he had been kidnapped and taken to Paris, so she too had travelled up to the capital. There she had found their town house under seal and had learned that her husband was probably in the Bastille.

Hortense said severely:

"So you can imagine how compromising your visit in full daylight is for a high official of the King? And yet you came!"

"Yes, that is strange indeed," replied Angélique, "but my first thought was that my family might be able to help me."

"It's the first time you have remembered your family, I believe! I am quite sure you would not have visited me, had you been able to preen yourself in your fine new house in the Saint-Paul *quartier*. Why didn't you go and seek help from the brilliant friends of your rich and handsome husband, all those Princes, Dukes and Marquesses, instead of creating trouble for us by your presence?"

Angélique was on the point of getting up and walking out, slamming the door behind her, but she thought she heard Florimond's cries from the street and she controlled herself.

"Hortense, I'm not nursing any illusions. As the

affectionate and devoted sister you are, you are putting me out of doors. But I have with me a fourteen-months-old baby who needs to be bathed, changed, fed. It is getting late. If I go hunting for a roof now, I may find myself having to sleep at a street-corner. Put me up for this night."

"It's one night too many for the safety of my home."

"You'd think I was bringing a scandalous reputation into your house."

Madame Fallot compressed her narrow lips, and her lively brown eyes flashed.

"Your reputation is not stainless. As for your husband's, it is atrocious."

Angélique could not help smiling.

"I can assure you that my husband is the best of men. You'd understand quickly enough if you knew him. . . ."

"God preserve me! I'd die of fright. If what people say is true, I cannot understand how you could live in his house for several years. He must have cast a spell on you."

She added after a moment's thought:

"It is a fact that, when still quite young, you already had a marked penchant for all sorts of vices."

"Your amiability confounds me, my dear! It is true that, when still quite young, *you* had a marked penchant for backbiting and spitefulness."

"This is too much! Now you come and insult me under my own roof."

"Why do you refuse to believe me? I'm telling you that my husband is in the Bastille solely because of some misunderstanding."

"If he's in the Bastille, it's because there is such a thing as justice."

"If there is such a thing as justice, he'll be released promptly."

"Allow me to intrude, ladies, since you speak so well of justice," said a deep voice behind them.

A man had just come into the room. He must have been in his thirties, though he affected a stiff and formal air. His full, clean-shaven face bore a grave, attentive expression under his brown wig. There was something clerical about him. He cocked his head slightly to one side, like someone accustomed to receiving confidences.

Angélique guessed, from his well-tailored black cloth suit with black braid and horn buttons as its only trimming, that she was facing her brother-in-law, the proctor. She dropped a curtsey. He came up to her and very solemnly kissed her on both cheeks.

"Don't use a conditional phrase, Madame. *There is* justice. In its name and thanks to its existence I welcome you in my house."

Hortense reared up like a scalded cat.

"Heavens, Gaston, you are raving mad! Ever since we married, you've kept repeating that your career comes before everything else and that it depends entirely on the King. . . ."

"And on justice, my dear," interrupted the magistrate, mildly but firmly.

"Nevertheless, for days you have been voicing your apprehension about seeing my sister come and take refuge with us. In view of what you know about her husband's arrest, such an eventuality, you said, would spell certain ruin for us."

"Be quiet, Madame, or you'll make me regret that I have betrayed a professional secret in informing you of what I learned by chance."

Angélique decided to swallow her pride.

"You have learned something? Oh sir, for mercy's sake, tell me. I have been groping for days in the most complete uncertainty."

"Alas, Madame, I shall not try to take shelter behind a sham discretion nor expatiate in soothing terms. I'll confess to you straightway that I know very little. From an official piece of information I learned, with amazement I must admit, of Monsieur de Peyrac's arrest. I must therefore ask you, in your own interest as well in your husband's, not to make use of what I'm going to tell you without my express permission. Anyhow, I repeat, it's only a small scrap of information. Here it is: your husband was arrested by a *lettre de cachet* of the third category, that is to say a sealed order issued 'on the King's behalf.' In it the incriminated officer or gentleman is *invited* by the King to proceed secretly but freely, though accompanied by a royal commissioner, to a certain place. As for your husband, he was first taken to Fort-Lévêque, whence he was transferred to the Bastille on an order countersigned: Séguier."

"I thank you for confirming what is, after all, rather reassuring news. Many people have been sent to the Bastille and have left it again as soon as light was shed on the slanders which had brought them there."

"I see you are a level-headed woman," said Maître Fallot with an approving nod of his chin, "but I would not like to delude you into believing

472

that everything will work itself out easily. For I also learned that the warrant for the arrest, signed by the King, specified that no mention should be made in the prison records of the name of the accused or of the charge brought against him."

"No doubt the King does not wish to blemish the reputation of one of his faithful subjects before he has himself examined the facts that are held against him. He wants to be able to exonerate him without creating a fuss. . . ."

"Or else forget him."

"How so, forget him?" repeated Angélique, as a cold shiver went through her.

"Many people are being forgotten in prisons," said Maître Fallot, half closing his eyes and staring into the distance, "forgotten as surely as if they were in their grave. It is certainly not dishonourable, as such, to be imprisoned in the Bastille. Nevertheless I must stress that the state of being an anonymous and secretly held prisoner is an indication that the case is particularly serious."

Angélique remained silent for a moment. She suddenly felt her tiredness, and hunger gripped her stomach. Or was it anguish? . . . She raised her eyes to the magistrate.

"Since you are kind enough to enlighten me, sir, tell me what I should do?"

"Once again, Madame, it is not a question of kindness but of justice. It is in a spirit of justice that I am receiving you under my roof, and since you ask me for advice, I shall direct you to a lawyer. For I fear any part I might take in this case would be deemed partial and interested, although our familial relations have not amounted to much in the past."

Hortense, who was champing at the bit, exclaimed in her shrill, childish voice:

"You may well say *that!* As long as she had her châteaux and the wealth of her Lame Man, she scarcely bothered about us. Don't you think that the Comte de Peyrac could have obtained some favours for you by a recommendation to some high magistrates in Paris?"

"Joffrey had few connections among the people of the capital."

"Yes, yes!" said her sister, aping her. "Just some paltry connections with the Governors of Languedoc and Béarn, with Cardinal Mazarin, the Queen Mother and the King!"

"You're exaggerating. . . ."

"Anyhow, were you invited to the King's wedding, or weren't you?"

Angélique did not answer and left the drawing-room. She could see no end to this argument. She might as well go and fetch Florimond. As she was going down the stairs, she caught herself smiling. How quickly Hortense and she had dropped again into the familiar routine of their eternal squabbles! . . . So Monteloup wasn't dead, after all. Better to pull each other's hair than to feel like strangers.

In the street, she found François Binet sitting on the step of the carriage holding the sleeping baby in his arms. The young barber told her that, seeing the child in pain, he had given him a remedy of opium and mint powder of which he had a stock, since he was, like all those of his profession, something of a surgeon and an apothecary. Angélique thanked him. She inquired after Margot and the little nurse-maid. She was told that the maid had not been able to resist the announcement of a steam-bath servant who had gone through the streets chanting:

> At the sign of Sainte Jeanne
> Go and have a bath.
> Well served you will be
> By valets and chambermaids.
> Go there now, the bath is ready. . . .

Like all Huguenots, Margot had a pronounced liking for water, which Angélique heartily approved of: "I too would gladly pay a visit to this Sainte Jeanne! . . ." she sighed.

The lackeys and the two coachmen were sitting in the shade of the coach, drinking claret wine and eating smoked herrings. Angélique looked at her dusty dress and at Florimond's face, plastered with dirt and honey to his eyebrows. What a pitiable outfit!

But it apparently still looked luxurious to a needy proctor's wife, for Hortense, who had followed her out, sneered:

"Well, my dear, for a woman who complains of being reduced to sleeping at street-corners, you are not too badly off: a carriage, a wagon, six horses, four or five lackeys, and two maids who go to have baths!"

"I have a bed," Angélique told her. "Would you like me to have it taken upstairs?"

"No need. We have enough bedding to put you

up. However, it's impossible for me to take in all your servants."

"Surely you have a garret for Margot and the girl? As for the men, they can lodge at the inn."

Hortense was looking with compressed lips and a shocked expression at those southern men who, feeling that there was no need to trouble about the wife of a proctor, went on eating while staring at her insolently out of their coal-black eyes.

"The men of your escort look like bandits," she remarked in a stifled voice.

"You attribute to them qualities they don't possess. All one can hold against them is a marked propensity for sleeping in the sun."

In the large room that had been allocated to her on the second floor, Angélique relaxed for a moment as she plunged into a tub and sprinkled herself with cold water. She even washed her hair and arranged it as best she could in front of a steel mirror above the mantelpiece. The room was dark, the furniture very ugly but sufficient. In a small bed with clean sheets, Florimond slept soundly, thanks to the wigmaker's medication.

She was at a loss as to what dress to choose. Even the plainest seemed too sumptuous next to poor Hortense, whose grey wool dress had just the merest trimmings of velvet braid and ribbons at her bodice. She eventually decided in favour of a coffee-coloured house gown with fairly modest gold embroideries, and substituted a black satin neckerchief for the dainty lace. She had almost finished dressing when Margot appeared. With an expert hand, the maid gave her mistress's hair its usual graceful waves and sprayed her with perfume.

"Be careful. I must not look too elegant. I have to inspire my brother-in-law with confidence."

"Alas! After seeing such fine noblemen at your feet, to have to see you dressing to please a proctor!"

A strident shout coming from the ground-floor interrupted them. They rushed out on to the landing. The terrified cries of a woman rose from the stair-well. Angélique raced downstairs, where she found her flustered servants huddled on the threshold. The screams continued, but were now muffled and seemed to emanate from a tall chest of imitation ebony that decorated the anteroom.

Hortense, who had come at a run too, went to the chest and managed to extricate from it the fat maid who had opened the door to Angélique, as well as two children of eight and four years who were clutching her petticoats. Madame Fallot began by boxing the girl's ears, then asked what had come over her.

"There! There!" stammered the wretched girl, pointing her finger.

Angélique's eyes followed the direction she indicated and perceived the good Kouassi-Ba, who was huddling shyly behind the servants. Hortense could not help giving a start, but she controlled herself and said curtly:

"Well, it's a black man, a Moor, that's nothing to cry about. Have you never seen a Moor?"

"N . . . no, no, Madame."

"There's not a soul in Paris who hasn't seen a Moor. You are a fool."

Coming closer to Angélique, she hissed at her:

"Congratulations, my dear! You do know how to upset my household. You even introduce an island savage! This girl will probably leave me on the spot. And I had such trouble finding her!"

"Kouassi-Ba," cried Angélique. "These small children and the young girl are afraid of you. Show them how well you can amuse them."

"Yes, Médême."

The negro bounded forward with a leap. The servant-girl let out a scream and pushed against the wall with all her might as if she wanted to burrow into it. But Kouassi-Ba, after doing a few somersaults, pulled some coloured balls from his pockets and began to juggle them with amazing skill. He seemed not to be bothered at all by his recent wound. At last, as he saw the children smile, he picked up little Giovanni's guitar and, squatting down on the floor with crossed legs, began to sing in his soft, velvety voice.

Angélique went over to the other servants.

"I'll give you money to lodge and board at the inn," she said.

The coachman of her carriage stepped forward and nervously twisted his red-plumed felt hat.

"If you please, Madame, we should like to ask you to let us have the rest of our wages, too. We are in Paris now: it's a city where one spends a lot."

The young woman, after a moment's hesitation, complied with his request. She asked Margot to bring her money-box and counted out his due to each of them. The men bowed and thanked her. Young Giovanni said he would be back the next day to inquire after her ladyship's orders. The others withdrew in silence. As they stepped out of the door, Margot, who was standing on the stairs, called after them in Languedoc dialect, but they did not answer.

"What did you say to them?" asked Angélique thoughtfully.

"That if they didn't come for your orders tomorrow, the master would cast a spell over them."

"You think they won't come back?"

"I'm afraid so."

Angélique passed her hand over her brow.

"You mustn't say the master will cast a spell on them, Margot. Such words will do him more harm than good. Here, take the money-box back to my room and see to it that Florimond's porridge is cooked so that it will be ready when he wakes up."

"Madame," said a high-pitched voice next to Angélique, "my father has told me to inform you that dinner is served and that we are waiting for you in the dining-room to say grace."

It was the little eight-year-old boy whom she had seen in the big chest a moment ago.

"You're no longer afraid of Kouassi-Ba?" she asked him.

"No, Madame. I'm very glad to know a black man. All my schoolmates will envy me."

"What is your name?"

"Martin."

The windows of the dining-room had been opened to let in a little light and save the candles. A clear, rosy dusk was lingering above the roof-tops. It was the hour when the parish bells were beginning to chime the Angelus. The deep, splendid notes boomed out and seemed to carry the very prayer of the city.

"You have very beautiful bells in your parish," remarked Angélique, to dispel the awkward silence at the start of the meal.

"They are the bells of Notre Dame," replied Maître Fallot. "Our parish is Saint-Landry, but the cathedral is quite close. If you lean out the window, you can see its two great towers and the spire of its apse."

At the far end of the table sat an old man, Maître Fallot's uncle, a retired magistrate, who was wrapped in pontifical silence. At the beginning of the meal, he and his nephew had, with the same casual gesture, dropped a piece of horn of unicorn into their glasses. This reminded Angélique that she had forgotten that morning to take the tablet of poison to which Joffrey de Peyrac wanted her to become accustomed.

The maid served the soup. The starched white tablecloth had been freshly ironed. The silverplate was of fine quality, but the Fallot family did not use forks. Joffrey had taught Angélique how to use these objects, and she remembered that, on her wedding-day in Toulouse, she had felt quite gauche with that tiny pitchfork in her hand. Several courses of fish, eggs and milk dishes were being served. Angélique suspected that her sister had sent for two or three kinds of prepared food from a *rôtisserie* to supplement the menu.

"You mustn't let my presence cause any change in your ordinary fare."

"Do you imagine that a proctor's family lives on gruel and cabbage soup?" was the acid reply.

That night, in spite of her fatigue, Angélique took a long time falling asleep. She listened to the cries of the unknown city rising from the damp, narrow lanes. A little biscuit-seller passed, shaking his dice in a horn. He was hailed from houses where the evening meal was still in progress, and merry-makers amused themselves playing dice for his entire basketful of pastries.

A little later came the tinkling bell of a corpse-crier:

Hark, all you who are asleep in bed,
Pray God for the dead. . . .

Angélique shivered and buried her face in her pillow. She longed for Joffrey's long, lean, warm body at her side. How she missed his gaiety, his eagerness, his wonderful, pleasing voice, his caressing hands! When would they find each other again? How blissfully happy they'd be! She would nestle in his arms, ask him to kiss her, to hug her tightly! . . . She fell asleep clasping the coarse linen pillow which smelled of lavender.

Chapter 28

ANGÉLIQUE removed the wooden shutter, then struggled with the leaded window of stained glass. At last she managed to open it. You had to be a native Parisian to sleep with closed windows in such heat. She inhaled the fresh morning air deeply, then stood stock-still, overcome with wonder and amazement.

Her room did not look out on the rue de l'Enfer, for it was at the back of the house. It hung over the river, smooth and shiny as a sword, speckled with gold by the rising sun and crisscrossed by small boats and heavy barges. On the opposite bank, a laundress's boat covered with a bulging white awning made a brilliant stain, like a chalkmark, on this misty pastel scene. The women's cries, the banging of their paddles, floated up to Angélique, mingling with the bargemen's calls and the neighing of the horses which the grooms were leading to the water's edge.

A penetrating, sweet-sour smell assailed her nostrils. Angélique bent forward and saw that the timbered piles that supported the old house rested in a mud-bank on which a pile of rotten fruit was surrounded by a swarm of wasps. On the right, at the corner of the island, there was a little harbour cluttered with barges. Basketfuls of oranges, cherries, grapes and pears were being unloaded. Handsome boys in rags, standing on the prows of their boats, bit lustily into oranges, scattering the peels which the wavelets washed up against the houses. They would then take off their rags and plunge into the pale water. From the dock, a wooden footbridge, painted a bright red, linked the Cité with a small island.

Just beyond the washerwomen, a long beach was crammed with trading boats. Barrels stood in serried rows, sacks were piled up, and mountains of hay were being unloaded for the stables. Armed with boat-hooks, the rivermen held back the floating timber rafts which were drifting downstream, and guided them towards the bank where lightermen rolled and stacked the logs.

Above the noise and bustle shone a sun of springlike freshness and of such extraordinary transparency that every scene was transformed into a delicate dream-picture set off by the sudden flash of a piece of linen, a white bonnet, or a shrieking seagull skimming just over the water.

"The Seine," murmured Angélique.

There was a knock at the door, and Hortense's maid came in.

"I'm bringing the milk for the baby, Madame. I went myself to the Place de la Pierre-au-Lait early this morning. The village women had only just arrived. The milk was still warm."

"It's very good of you to take so much trouble, but you should have sent my little nurse-maid upstairs with the pitcher."

"I wanted to see if the little darling was awake. I am so fond of babies, Madame. It's a pity that Madame Hortense sends hers away to be nursed. She had one six months ago which I took to the village of Chaillot. Well, every day it breaks my heart to imagine that they may come and tell me it's died. For the foster-mother had hardly any milk, and I fear above all that she may feed it with bread soaked in wine and water."

The maid was plump, with shiny cheeks and childish blue eyes. Angélique felt a sudden surge of liking for her.

"What's your name, my girl?"

"My name is Barbe, Madame, at your service."

"Well, you see, Barbe, I nursed my child myself in the beginning. I hope he'll grow to be sturdy."

"Nothing can replace a mother's care," said Barbe sententiously.

Florimond awoke. He gripped the rim of his little cradle with both hands, and sat up, fixing his lustrous black eyes on the new face.

"The beautiful treasure, the lovely darling, *bonjour*, my pet!" crooned the girl, picking him up, still damp from sleep.

She carried him to the window to show him the boats and seagulls and the baskets of oranges.

"What is this little harbour called?" asked Angélique.

"It's the port of Saint-Landry, the fruit market harbour, and beyond it is the Red Bridge which leads to the island of Saint-Louis. On the opposite bank they do a lot of unloading too. You can see the haymarket dock, the timber dock, the wheat dock and the wine dock. All that produce interests the gentlemen of the Hôtel de Ville, that beautiful building you can see over there, behind the strand."

"And the big square in front of it?"

"That's the Place de Grève."

Barbe screwed up her eyelids to see more clearly.

"I see there's a crowd on the Place de Grève this morning. They surely must have hanged someone."

"Hanged?" said Angélique, horrified.

"Why, that's where the executions take place. From my garret, which is just above, I don't miss a single one, though it's a bit far away. I like it better that way, anyhow, for I'm tender-hearted. Mostly there are hangings, but I also saw two heads cut off with the axe and a witch burned at the stake."

Angélique shivered and turned away. The view from her window suddenly seemed less cheerful to her.

After dressing with a certain elegance, since she intended to go to the Tuileries, Angélique asked Margot to take her cloak and accompany her. The little nurse-maid could look after Florimond, and Barbe would watch over them both.

"What I feared has happened, Madame," announced Margot. "Your scamps of footmen and coachmen have run away and there's no one left to drive your carriage and look after your horses."

After a moment's consternation, Angélique brightened.

"Never mind, it's just as well. I only brought four thousand *livres* with me. It's my intention to send Monsieur d'Andijos to Toulouse to bring me back some funds. But meanwhile, as we can't see into the future, it's better not to have to pay all those people. I'll sell my horses and carriage to the owner of the public stables and we'll walk. I'm very eager to have a look at the shops."

"Madame does not realize how muddy the streets are. In some places, you wade in garbage up to your ankles."

"My sister told me that if you put wooden clogs on your feet, you can walk easily. Come on, Margot, my dear, don't grumble, we're going to visit Paris, isn't it wonderful?"

Downstairs, in the vestibule, Angélique found

François Binet and the little musician.

"I thank you for being faithful," she said to them, touched, "but I'm afraid we shall have to part, for I shall not be able to keep you in my service any longer. Would you, Binet, like me to recommend you to Mademoiselle de Montpensier? In view of the success you had with her at Saint-Jean-de-Luz, I am certain she will find employment for you or will recommend you, in turn, to some nobleman."

"I thank you for your kindness, Madame, but I think I shall take employment with a master barber."

"You!" protested Angélique. "You who were the greatest barber and wigmaker in Toulouse!"

"Unfortunately, I shall not be able to find any such important post in this city, where the guilds are hard to get into."

"But at Court . . ."

"To woo the favours of the mighty, Madame, requires much patience. It's not wise to be projected into the limelight too quickly, especially when you are a modest craftsman like myself. A mere trifle — a malicious word, a venomous allusion — is enough to hurl you from the peak of honour into the blackest misery. The favour of princes is fickle."

Angélique stared at him.

"You want to give them time to forget that you were Monsieur de Peyrac's barber?"

He dropped his eyes.

"For my part, Madame, I shall never forget it. Let my master get the better of his enemies, and I shall hasten to serve him again. But I'm just a simple barber."

"You are right, Binet," said Angélique with a smile. "I like your frankness. There is no reason why we should drag you down with us into disgrace. Here are a hundred *écus*. Good luck."

The young man bowed and, taking his barber's case, retreated towards the door respectfully.

"And you, Giovanni, would you like me to try and put you in touch with Monsieur Lulli?"

"Oh yes, mistress, oh yes!"

"And you, Kouassi-Ba, what do you want to do?"

"I want to go for a walk with you, Médême."

Angélique smiled.

"All right. Well, come on, you two. We'll go to the Tuileries."

At that moment the door opened and Maître Fallot's fine brown wig appeared through the opening.

"I heard your voice, Madame, and was just waiting to ask you for a moment's talk."

Angélique motioned to the three servants to wait for her.

"I am at your disposal, sir."

She followed him into his office, where clerks and scribes were working busily. The acrid smell of ink, the creak of goose-quills, the dim light, the black suits of the down-at-heel employees did not make of this room a particularly pleasant place. On the walls hung a great number of black bags containing the files of various legal cases. Maître Fallot led Angélique into a small adjacent study, where a man was waiting. The proctor introduced him:

"Monsieur Desgrez, advocate. Monsieur Desgrez will be at your disposal to guide you in this painful affair of your husband's."

Angélique looked at the newcomer with consternation. This — the Comte de Peyrac's attorney! It would be difficult to find a more threadbare coat, a more worn-out shirt, a more faded felt hat. The proctor seemed almost luxuriously clothed next to him. The poor fellow did not even wear a wig, and his long hair seemed of the same rough, brown texture as his woollen suit. Nevertheless, despite his apparent poverty, he exuded an air of self-confidence.

"Madame," he said at once, "let's not use the future or the conditional form: I *am* at your disposal. Now tell me without fear what you know."

"Why, sir," replied Angélique rather coldly, "I know nothing, or almost nothing."

"So much the better, that way we shan't start with any false premises."

"There is one certainty though," broke in Maître Fallot, "the *lettre de cachet* signed by the King."

"Quite right, sir. The King. We must start with the King."

The young lawyer cupped his chin in his hands and frowned.

"Not very convenient. As a starting-point one could hardly begin higher up."

"I intend to go and see Mademoiselle de Montpensier, the King's cousin," said Angélique. "It seems to me that through her I might obtain more accurate information; especially if, as I suspect, it's all a matter of a Court intrigue. And through her I might perhaps be able to approach His Majesty."

"Mademoiselle de Montpensier, pooh!" said the

other with a disdainful pout. "That great gawk is a blunderer. Don't forget, Madame, that she was an insurgent and had the troops of her royal cousin fired upon. On that account she'll always be treated with suspicion at Court. Moreover, the King is somewhat jealous of her immense wealth. She'll soon understand that it is not in her interest to try to protect a nobleman who's fallen into disgrace."

"I believe, and have always heard it said, that the Grande Mademoiselle has a very kind heart."

"May it please Heaven that she use it in your behalf, Madame! As a child of Paris, I put little trust in the hearts of the mighty, who feed the people on the fruit of their discord, fruit that is as bitter and rotten as those that decompose under your house, Monsieur. But go ahead and try this move if you think it's worth while, Madame. However, I advise you to talk to Mademoiselle in a light, casual manner without dwelling on the injustice that has been done to you."

"Is a pettifogging, down-at-heel lawyer going to tell me how to talk to people at Court?" Angélique thought to herself, annoyed.

She took a few *écus* from her purse.

"Here is an advance on the expenses that your inquiries may occasion you."

"Thank you, Madame," replied the lawyer who, after glancing at the coins with satisfaction, slipped them into a remarkably flat leather purse he carried on his belt.

He bowed very courteously and left. At the corner of the house an enormous Great Dane, its white coat speckled with large brown spots, got up and followed in the lawyer's footsteps. The latter, his hands in his pockets, walked away, whistling gaily to himself.

"This man doesn't inspire me with much confidence," said Angélique to her brother-in-law. "I'd say he was a fake as well as a conceited, incapable fellow."

"He's a brilliant young man," the proctor assured her, "but he is poor . . . like many of his ilk. There's a surfeit of lawyers without cases in Paris. This one must have inherited his office from his father; he couldn't have bought one otherwise. But I recommended him to you because, for one thing, I respect his intelligence and, for another, he won't cost you much. He'll do wonders with the small sum you've given him."

"The question of money should not arise. If necessary, my husband shall have the support of the most enlightened men of law."

Maître Fallot cast a glance at Angélique that was at once haughty and shrewd.

"Have you an inexhaustible fortune at your disposal?"

"Not on my person, but I'm going to send the Marquis d'Andijos to Toulouse. He will see our banker and instruct him, if money is needed at once, to sell some of our land."

"Aren't you afraid that your Toulouse estates may have been seized and put under seal, just like your Paris house?"

Angélique looked at him dumbfounded.

"That's impossible!" she stammered. "Why should they have done that? Why should anyone be so bent on our misfortune? We haven't harmed anyone."

The lawyer spread his hands in an unctuous gesture.

"Alas, Madame, many people passing through this office utter the same words. To hear them, no one would ever do the slightest harm to anyone else. And yet there are law-suits all the time. . . ."

". . . and work for the lawyers," thought Angélique.

With this new worry on her mind, she paid little attention to their walk which took them through the rues de la Colombe, des Marmousets and de la Lanterne to the Palace of Justice. Following the Quai de l'Horloge, they reached the Pont-Neuf, at the far end of the island. The bustling activity delighted the servants. Small shops mounted on wheels were massed around the bronze statue of good King Henri IV, and innumerable cries rang out, hawking the most extraordinary variety of goods. A miraculous plaster was sold here, teeth pulled painlessly over there, elsewhere again there were flasks of a peculiar product that removed stains from clothes, books here, toys there, and tortoise-shell hoops that banished stomach-ache. Trumpets blared and music-boxes jingled. Drums rolled on a platform where acrobats were juggling with glasses. A haggard individual in a threadbare suit slipped a scrap of paper into Angélique's hand and asked her for ten *sols*. She gave them to him unthinkingly and put the sheet of paper into her pocket, then ordered her gaping suite to hurry up a little.

She did not feel in the mood for dawdling. At every step, moreover, she was stopped by beggars who suddenly loomed up in front of her, exposing an oozing wound or the stump of an arm or leg wrapped in blood-soaked bandages. Or else there were women in rags carrying children whose faces were caked with scabs and surrounded by flies. They emerged from the shadow of porches, from the corners of shops; they rose from the river-banks and spluttered appeals that were plaintive at first, but which soon turned to threats.

At last, sickened by what she saw and having spent all her small change, Angélique ordered Kouassi-Ba to chase them away. The negro promptly bared his cannibal teeth and waved his hand in the direction of an approaching cripple, who at once decamped with a surprising alacrity.

"This comes from walking on foot like peasants," Margot kept repeating with growing indignation.

Angélique heaved a sigh of relief when she at last descried the ivy-covered Tour du Bois, crumbling vestige of the ancient rampart of old Paris. Soon after they reached the Pavillon de Flore, which formed the end of a gallery and linked it at right angles with the Château des Tuileries.

The air was getting cooler. A light breeze rose from the Seine and dispelled the rank odours of the town. At last they came upon the Tuileries, a palace embellished with a thousand details, flanked by a plump dome and turrets, a summer residence of feminine grace, for it had been erected for a woman, Catharine de Medici, the pomp-loving Italian.

At the Tuileries, she was told to wait. The

Grande Demoiselle had gone to the Luxembourg Palace, in order to arrange her plans for moving. Monsieur, the King's brother, had decided to contend with her for the Tuileries, although Mademoiselle had been residing there for years. He had settled with his entire retinue in a wing of the palace. Mademoiselle had treated him as a haggler and there had been a hue and cry. Eventually, Mademoiselle yielded as she always did. She was really far too good-natured.

Left to herself, Angélique sat down beside a window and gazed at the marvellous garden. Beyond the blooming mosaics of the flower-beds glistened a vast almond-tree orchard, and beyond it the green mass of trees of the Garonne. A building along the Seine housed Louis XIII's aviary, where hunting falcons were still being bred. To the right there were the famous royal stables and the riding-school, whence came the noise of galloping and the shouts of pages and trainers.

Angélique inhaled the fresh country air and watched the little windmills turn on the distant heights of Chaillot, Passy and Le Roule. At last, towards midday, there appeared, amid much hustling and bustling, Mademoiselle de Montpensier, perspiring and fanning herself.

"My dear," she said to Angélique, "you always come at the right moment. Just when I see nothing but stupid faces whichever way I turn, your delightful little visage with its pure, clear eyes is a most . . . refreshing sight. Refreshing, that's it. Now are we or are we not going to get some lemonade and ice?"

She dropped into an armchair and recovered her breath.

"Let me tell you what happened. I almost strangled the Petit Monsieur this morning, and it certainly would not have been difficult for me. He hounds me out of this palace, where I've lived since my childhood. More than that: I can say I reigned over this palace. Look . . . here is where I sent my footman and fiddlers to cross swords with Monsieur de Mazarin's men. Mazarin wanted to flee from the people's anger but, just then, he couldn't get out of Paris. He narrowly escaped being murdered and having his body thrown into the river. . . ."

Angélique wondered how, amid this welter of gossip, she'd ever be able to broach the subject that was closest to her heart. The young lawyer's skepticism concerning the kindness of the great came back to her. Finally, taking her courage in both hands, she said:

"Your Highness will pardon me, but I know you are aware of all that's happening at Court. Has it not come to your knowledge that my husband is in the Bastille?"

The Princess seemed frankly surprised and was immediately up in arms.

"In the Bastille? Why, what crime did he commit?"

"That's precisely what I don't know. And I very much hope that you, Highness, will help me to clear up this mystery."

She related what had happened at Saint-Jean-de-Luz and the mysterious disappearance of the Comte de Peyrac. The seals affixed on their house

494

proved that the kidnapping was connected with a legal prosecution, but the secret was being well kept.

"Let's see," said Mademoiselle de Montpensier. "Let's dig into it a little. Your husband has enemies, like everyone else. Who, according to you, might be out to harm him?"

"My husband was not on very good terms with the Archbishop of Toulouse. But I do not believe the latter could have produced anything against him that would have impelled the King to intervene."

"Mayn't the Comte de Peyrac have slighted some influential person close to His Majesty? I do remember just one thing, my little one. Monsieur de Peyrac used to display a rare insolence towards my father when the latter came down to Toulouse as Governor of Languedoc. Oh, my father did not hold it against him, and he is dead, anyway. My late father was not of a jealous disposition, although he spent his time plotting. I've inherited this passion of his, I confess, and that's why I am not always in the King's favour. He is a very susceptible man. . . . Ah, now I think of it, maybe Monsieur de Peyrac slighted the King himself?"

"My husband is not in the habit of lavishing flatteries. However, he respected the King, and did he not do his best to please him when he received His Majesty in Toulouse?"

"Oh! What a wonderful pageant!" raved Mademoiselle, clasping her hands. "Those little birds that flew out of a huge rock of sweetmeat! . . . But, as a matter of fact, I have been told that it vexed the King. The same as with Monsieur

495

Fouquet at Vaux-le-Vicomte. . . . These mighty lords don't realise that when the King smiles, it means he is on edge at seeing his own subjects crush him with their splendour."

"I cannot believe that His Majesty would be so petty."

"The King seems gentle and fair, I admit. But whether you like it or not, the fact is that he always remembers the time when the Princes of the blood waged war against him. And I myself, it's true, was one of them, I no longer remember why. In short, His Majesty distrusts all those who raise their heads a little too high."

"My husband never sought to plot against the King. He always behaved as a loyal subject, and he alone paid one quarter of all the taxes of Languedoc."

Mademoiselle de Montpensier gave her visitor a friendly little tap with her fan.

"How fervently you defend him! I confess his appearance frightened me a little, but after talking to him at Saint-Jean-de-Luz, I began to understand why he had so much success with women. Don't cry, my dear. You'll get your great attractive Lame Man back even if I have to harass the Cardinal himself and, as usual, risk sticking my neck out too far!"

Chapter 29

ANGÉLIQUE parted from the Grande Mademoiselle in a more cheerful mood. It was agreed that the latter would send for her as soon as she had obtained some definite information. The Princess agreed to take charge of little Giovanni, whom she would place among her own fiddlers until she could present him to Baptiste Lulli, the King's music-master.

"In any case," she concluded, "there's nothing useful we can do until the King's entrance into Paris. Everything is being put off until after the celebrations. The Queen Mother is at the Louvre, but the King and Queen are at Vincennes. That doesn't help matters. But don't get impatient. I shan't forget you and will send for you."

Angélique strolled for a while through the corridors of the palace in the hope of meeting Péguilin de Lauzun, who she knew was in eager attendance on Mademoiselle. She did not see him but ran into Cerbalaud, who wore a rather long face. He, too, did not know what to think of the Comte de Peyrac's arrest; all he could say was that nobody spoke of it nor seemed to know anything about it.

"They'll soon know," predicted Angélique, trusting in Mademoiselle to trumpet the news abroad.

Now nothing seemed more terrible to her than this wall of silence that surrounded Joffrey's disappearance. Once people talked of it, the matter would necessarily come out into the open.

She inquired after the Marquis d'Andijos. Cerbalaud said that he had just left for the Pré-aux-Clercs for a duel.

"He's fighting a duel?" cried Angélique, horrified.

"Not he, but Lauzun and d'Humières have an affair of honour."

"Do come with me, I want to see both of them."

As she was going down the marble staircase, a woman with big black eyes approached her. She recognized Olympia, Duchesse de Soissons, one of the Mancini girls and the Cardinal's niece.

"Madame de Peyrac, I am happy to see you again," said the beautiful lady, "but what delights me even more is the sight of your ebony-black bodyguard. I had already planned to ask you for him in Saint-Jean-de-Luz. Will you let me have him? I'll pay a good price for him."

"Kouassi-Ba is not for sale," protested Angélique. "It is true that, when he was quite small, my husband bought him in Narbonne, but he never considered him a slave and he pays him wages like any other servant."

"So shall I, and very high wages, too."

"I am sorry, Madame, but I cannot give you satisfaction. Kouassi-Ba is useful to me and my husband would be grieved not to find him on his return."

"Oh well, never mind then," said Madame de Soissons with a disappointed gesture.

She cast one more admiring glance at the giant who was standing impassively behind Angélique.

"It's fantastic how such a creature can set off a woman's beauty, frailty and whiteness. Don't you think so, *mon cher?*"

Angélique thereupon noticed that the Marquis de Vardes was coming towards them. She had no wish to find herself face to face with this nobleman who had behaved so brutally and odiously with her. She still felt the smart of her lips which he had bitten so viciously. So she hastened to curtsey to Madame de Soissons and to continue on her way to the gardens.

"I have the impression that the beautiful Olympia is casting a lascivious eye on your Moor," said Cerbalaud. "Vardes, her official lover, is not enough for her. She is madly curious to know how a Moor makes love."

"Oh, do hurry instead of uttering such horrors!" said Angélique impatiently. "For my part, I am curious to know above all if Lauzun and d'Humières aren't about to run each other through."

But on the quays of the Seine a voice hailed them. A nobleman whom Angélique did not know came up to her and asked her for a moment's conversation.

"Yes, but be quick."

He pulled her aside.

"Madame, I am sent by His Royal Highness Philippe d'Orléans, the King's brother. Monsieur desires to talk to you on the subject of Monsieur de Peyrac."

"Oh, my God!" murmured Angélique, whose heart was beginning to throb.

Was she at last to have some definite news? Yet she had little liking for the King's brother, that little man with his cold, sullen eyes. But she remembered his admiring though ambiguous words about the Comte de Peyrac. What had he learned about the prisoner in the Bastille?

"His Highness will wait for you this evening at about five o'clock," continued the gentleman in a low voice. "You will enter by way of the Tuileries and proceed to the Pavillon de Flore, where Monsieur has his apartments. Don't speak of any of this to anyone."

"I shall be accompanied by my maid."

"As you wish."

He bowed and walked away, his spurs clicking.

"Who is that gentleman?" Angélique asked Cerbalaud.

"The Chevalier de Lorraine, Monsieur's new favourite. Yes, de Guiche aroused his displeasure: he did not display enough enthusiasm for perverse love and maintained too marked a fancy for the fair sex. Not that the Petit Monsieur spurns it entirely. They say that after the King's entrance he will be married, and do you know to whom? To Princess Henriette of England, the daughter of poor Charles I whom the English beheaded. . . ."

Angélique listened with only one ear. She was beginning to feel hungry. She always had a robust appetite. She felt a little ashamed of it, especially in the present circumstances. What was poor Joffrey eating in his black prison, he who was so fastidious? Nevertheless, she glanced around in the hope of perceiving a hot-pastry vendor, from whom she might buy something to fortify her.

Their present walk had taken them to the other bank of the Seine, near the old gate of Nesle flanked by its tower. For a long time the Pré-aux-Clercs — the Clerics' Field — where students in the old days used to frisk and frolic, had ceased to exist. But there still remained between the abbey of Saint-Germain-des-Prés and the ancient moats a vacant plot of waste ground planted with clumps of trees, where punctilious young men could come and expunge stains from their honour far from the indiscreet eyes of the constables of the watch.

As they neared the field, Angélique and Cerbalaud heard shouts and found Lauzun and the Marquis d'Humières, with open shirts, in duellists' attire, each about to give Andijos a joint thrashing. Both of them told how, obliged to fight it out, they had each secretly asked Andijos to come and separate them for the sake of friendship. But the traitor had hidden behind a shrub and, roaring with laughter, had watched the anguish of the two "foes," who were dragging things out as long as they could, asserting that one sword was shorter than the other, the duelling-shoes too tight.

"If we'd had the slightest courage, we'd have had ample time to cut each other's throats a hundred times!" cried little Lauzun.

Angélique joined forces with them to shower Andijos with reproaches.

"Do you think my husband has kept you for fifteen years in order to have you indulge in stupid pranks while he is in prison?" she cried. "Oh, you southerners!"

She pulled him aside, dug her nails into his arm, then ordered him to leave for Toulouse forthwith

501

in order to bring back some money as quickly as possible. Shamefacedly he confessed that he had lost all his own money gambling at Princess Henriette's the previous night. She gave him five hundred *livres* and Kouassi-Ba as an escort. When they had gone, Angélique noticed that Lauzun and d'Humières had likewise disappeared. She put her hand on her forehead.

"I must return to the Tuileries at five," she said to Margot. "Let's wait somewhere nearby in a tavern where they'll give us food and drink."

"A tavern!" repeated the maid, indignantly. "Madame, that's no place for you."

"Do you think that prison is a place for my husband? I am hungry and thirsty. So are you. Don't simper. Let's go and rest."

She took Margot's arm familiarly and leaned on her. She herself was smaller than the maid, which was probably why this woman had impressed her for so long. Now she knew her well. Quick-tempered, vehement and easily outraged, Margot had an unswerving devotion for the Peyrac family.

"Perhaps you too would like to leave?" said Angélique abruptly. "I haven't the faintest notion how all this is going to turn out. You have seen that the footmen didn't take long to show their fear, and maybe they weren't wrong."

"I never cared to follow the example of footmen," said Margot scornfully, and her eyes flashed like burning coals.

After a moment's thought she added:

"For my part, all my life revolves around a single memory. I was put together with the Comte into the basket of a Catholic peasant who took him

502

back to Toulouse to his parents. That was after the slaughter of the people of my village, among them my mother, who was his nurse. I was not even four years old, but I remember every detail. All his bones were broken and he was groaning. I was trying to wipe his blood-soaked little face, and as he was burning with thirst, I slipped a little thawed snow between his lips. No more now than at that time will I abandon him, even if I, too, should die on the straw of a dungeon. . . ."

Angélique did not answer, but she leaned more heavily on Margot and for a moment rested her cheek on the maid's shoulder.

They found a tavern near the gate of Nesle, in front of the small humpbacked bridge which passed over the ancient moat. The *patronne* cooked them a fricassee on the hearth.

It was a quiet, seldom-frequented place and the countryside was nearby. Men were pulling their boats on to the mudbank of the shores. Children were angling in the moat. . . .

When evening came, Angélique passed back over the river to reach the Tuileries. The avenues of the park were crowded, for the cool hour brought not only noblemen, but also wealthy townspeople and their families to the gardens.

At the Pavillon de Flore, the Chevalier de Lorraine himself came to meet the visitors and had them sit on a bench in the anteroom. His Highness would be coming soon. Then he left them. The corridors were full of animation. This particular passage-way served as a link between the Tuileries and the Louvre. Angélique noticed many faces she

503

had come across at Saint-Jean-de-Luz. She shrank back into the window recess, having no desire to be recognized. Anyhow, few people even noticed them. Most of them were on their way to supper at Mademoiselle's. Some were fixing after-dinner rendezvous to play at *trente-et-un* at Mademoiselle Henriette's. Others deplored being obliged to return to the Château of Vincennes, which was so uncomfortable but where the King would remain till his entrance into Paris.

Gradually, darkness invaded the corridors. Rows of lackeys appeared carrying torches which they placed on tables between the high casements.

"Madame," said Margot suddenly, "we must go. Night has blackened the window-panes. If we don't leave now, we'll never find our way out or else we'll be murdered by some ruffians."

"I shan't budge from here until I've seen Monsieur," said Angélique doggedly. "Even if I have to spend all night on this bench."

The maid did not insist. But a few moments later, she spoke again in a low voice.

"Madame, I fear that there may be an attempt on your life."

Angélique started.

"You are mad. Wherever do you get such ideas?"

"From not so far away: they tried to kill you four days ago."

"What do you mean?"

"In the forest of Rambouillet. They weren't after the King or Queen, they were out to get you, Madame. And if the coach hadn't overturned in that ditch, the bullet aimed at the window would certainly have hit you in the head."

"You're letting your imagination run away with you. Those blackguards were looking for mischief and would have attacked any coach that passed. . . ."

"Humph! Why then was the one who aimed at you your former major-domo, Clément Tonnel?"

Angélique's eyes roved over the now deserted vista of the anteroom.

"Are you certain of what you are saying?"

"I'd answer for it with my life. I recognized him all right, despite his hat pulled down over his eyes. They must have chosen him because he knows you well and they could thus be sure not to make a mistake about the person."

"Who are 'they'?"

"How do *I* know?" said the maid, shrugging her shoulders. "But there's something else I firmly believe: that man is a spy; I never trusted him. First of all, he did not come from our part of the country. Secondly, he did not know how to laugh. Finally, he always seemed to be watching something; he had a way of attending to his work with his ears too wide open. . . . Now, why he should want to kill you, that I couldn't explain any more than I know why my master is in prison. But one would have to be deaf and blind and a fool to boot, not to understand that you have enemies who've sworn your destruction."

Angélique shivered and wrapped her brown silk cape more closely around her.

"I cannot see anything that could possibly explain such relentless fury. Why should anyone want to kill me?"

In a flash, the vision of the poison-casket passed before her eyes. But she had shared that secret only with Joffrey. . . .

"Let's go, Madame," repeated Margot in a more urgent voice.

At that moment, the sound of footsteps rang out in the gallery. Angélique could not help giving a nervous start. Someone was approaching. Angélique recognized the Chevalier de Lorraine, carrying a three-branched candelabra. The flames lit his handsome face, whose affable air did not disguise, however, a shifty and slightly cruel expression.

"His Royal Highness apologizes a thousand times," he said, bowing. "He's been detained and won't be able to keep the appointment he has given you for tonight. Will you agree to postpone it till tomorrow at the same hour?"

Angélique was terribly disappointed. She agreed, however, to the new date.

The Chevalier de Lorraine told her that the gates of the Tuileries were closed; he would lead them to the other end of the long gallery. There, leaving by way of a small garden called the Infanta's Garden, they would be only a few steps away from the Pont-Neuf. He walked in front of them, holding his torch high. His wooden heels rang out ominously on the stone tiles. Angélique saw their little procession reflected in the black window-panes. She could not help thinking there was something funereal about it. From time to time they passed a guard, or a door opened, and a couple came out, laughing. She glimpsed a brilliantly lit drawing-room, where a party was gaily gambling. An orchestra of violins, behind a screen, wafted a soft, thin stream of melody to them across the deserted halls.

At last the interminable march seemed to have reached its destination. The Chevalier de Lorraine stopped.

"This is the staircase that will take you down to the gardens. Immediately on your right a small gate and a few steps, and you will be out of the palace."

Angélique did not dare to say that she was without a carriage, and the Chevalier did not inquire about it. He bowed with the formality of one who has carried out his duty, and walked away.

Angélique seized Margot's arm.

"Let's hurry, Margot, my dear. I am not timorous, but this night walk holds no pleasure at all for me."

They began to hurry down the stone steps.

What saved Angélique was her little shoe. She had walked so much all day long that the slender leather strap suddenly gave way. Letting go of her companion half-way down the stairs, she bent down to try and refasten it. Margot continued walking down the steps.

A blood-curdling shriek rose from the darkness, the scream of a woman struck to the death.

"Help, Madame! . . . I'm being murdered . . . Flee! . . . Flee!"

The voice fell silent. A horrible groan, then nothing.

Frozen with horror, Angélique peered into the

507

dark well into which Margot had disappeared. She called:

"Margot! Margot!"

Her voice echoed in a deep void. The cool night air scented by the orange-trees in the garden rose up to her, but there was no more sound. Panic-stricken, Angélique rushed upstairs again to the lights of the long gallery. An officer was passing. She ran towards him.

"Sir, help me, help! Someone's just killed my maid."

Too late she recognized the Marquis de Vardes, but in her terror he seemed sent by Providence.

"Ho! It's the woman in gold," he remarked in his sneering voice, "the woman with the nimble fingers."

"Sir, this is no time for dalliance. I am telling you again, my maid's been murdered."

"Indeed? You don't expect me to cry about it?"

Angélique wrung her hands.

"For mercy's sake, we must do something, chase the cut-throats who are hiding under the stairs. Perhaps she's only wounded!"

He kept on looking at her with a smile.

"You definitely seem less overbearing than the first time we met. But excitement is not unbecoming to you."

She was on the point of flying at his face and slapping him. But she heard the clink of his sword as he drew it and said airily:

"Let's have a look."

She followed him, trying not to tremble, and walked down the first steps at his side.

The Marquis bent over the banister.

"You can't see anything, but you can smell. You can't mistake the stench of the rabble: onion, tobacco and black tavern wine. There are at least four or five of them swarming down there."

He gripped her wrist:

"Listen."

The noise of a watery thud and a splash of spray bored through the grim silence.

"There! They've thrown the body into the Seine."

Turning towards her with half-closed eyes, he went on:

"Oh! it's a familiar spot. There's a little gate down there which they often forget to close, sometimes on purpose. It's child's play for anyone who is so inclined to post some hired killers there. The Seine is only two steps away. The thing is quickly done. Prick up your ears and you can hear them whispering. They must have noticed that they did not attack the person they were told to. You seem to have rather determined enemies, my beauty."

Angélique clenched her teeth to prevent them from chattering. Finally she managed to say:

"What are you going to do?"

"Nothing for the time being. I've no desire to test my sword against the rusty rapiers of those ruffians. But in an hour's time the Swiss guard will take up watch at this corner. The murderers will clear out, unless they get caught. In any case, you'll be able to leave without fear. In the meantime . . ."

Still holding her by her wrist, he led her back

to the gallery. She followed him mechanically, her head droning:

"Margot is dead. . . . They wanted to kill me. . . . It's the second time. . . . And I know nothing, nothing. . . . Margot is dead. . . ."

Vardes had led her into a sort of recess, furnished with a small table and some stools. He calmly put his sword back into its sheath, unfastened his belt and placed it on the table together with his weapon. Then he stepped closer to Angélique.

Abruptly she understood what he wanted and pushed him back with horror.

"What, sir, I've just seen a girl murdered to whom I was deeply attached, and you think I'd consent to . . ."

"I don't care a hang whether you consent or not. What women have in their heads is indifferent to me. I only find them interesting below the waist. Love is a formality. Don't you know that this is how lovely ladies pay their way in the corridors of the Louvre?"

She tried to put up a mocking front.

"I had forgotten: 'He who says de Vardes, says: the cad.' "

The Marquis pinched her arm till it bled.

"Little slut! If you weren't so pretty, I'd gladly leave you to the care of those good fellows who are waiting for you downstairs. But it would be a pity to see such a tender little chicken bleed. So come on, behave yourself."

She could not see him but could readily imagine the smug, slightly cruel smile on the handsome face. A dim light from the gallery gleamed on his pale blond wig.

"Don't touch me," she gasped, "or I'll scream."

"Screaming won't help. This place isn't much frequented. The only ones who might be moved by your shouts are the gentlemen with the rusty rapiers. Don't make a scene, my dear. I want you, I shall have you. I decided that a long time ago and chance has served me well. Would you rather try to get home on your own?"

"I'll seek help elsewhere."

"Who will help you in this palace, where all signs point to your destruction? Who led you to this notorious staircase?"

"The Chevalier de Lorraine."

"I say! So there's the Petit Monsieur lurking underneath? Actually, it wouldn't be the first time that he got rid of some troublesome 'rival.' So you see, it's in your interest to keep quiet. . . ."

She did not reply, but when he approached again, she no longer stirred. Unhurriedly, with insolent calm, he lifted up her long rustling taffeta petticoats, and she felt his warm hands complacently caressing her thighs.

"Charming," he said under his breath. . . .

Angélique was beside herself with humiliation and fear. Through her crazed mind swirled senseless images: the Chevalier de Lorraine and his torch, the Bastille, Margot's scream, the poison-casket. Then everything faded away, and she was jolted by the fear, the physical panic of a woman who had known only one man. This new feeling perturbed and revolted her. She writhed, trying to escape from the embrace. She wanted to shout, but no sound escaped her throat. Paralysed and shaking, she let herself be taken, hardly aware of what was happening. . . .

A flash of light suddenly dipped into their recess. A gentleman quickly turned his torch away and walked off, laughing and muttering: "I didn't see anything." This kind of thing seemed to be familiar to the inhabitants of the Louvre.

The Marquis de Vardes had not bothered to interrupt himself. In the darkness, where their hot breaths mingled, the distraught Angélique wondered when the horrible ordeal would be over. Exhausted, shattered, half swooning, she abandoned herself, against her will, to the masculine arms that were crushing her. Gradually, the novelty of the embrace, the repetition of the gestures of love for which her body was so marvellously fashioned, brought her a thrill, against which she could not defend herself. When she became conscious of it, it was too late. The spark of pleasure kindled a familiar languor in her, spread through her veins a subtle excitement which would soon change into a devouring flame.

The young man sensed it. He gave a little smothered laugh and redoubled his art and attention. Thereupon she rebelled against herself. She turned her head, groaning softly: "No, no." But the struggle merely precipitated her defeat and soon she yielded, completely vanquished. No sooner had they separated than Angélique felt an all-pervading sense of shame. She plunged her face into her hands. She wanted to die, never to see the light of day again.

Silent and still panting, the officer buckled his belt.

"The watch should be there by now," he said. "Come."

As she did not move, he took her arm and pushed her out of the recess. She disengaged herself but followed him wordlessly. Shame continued to burn her like a branding iron. Never again would she be able to look Joffrey in the face, to kiss Florimond. Vardes had destroyed everything, ravaged everything. She had lost the only thing that was left to her: the integrity of her love.

At the foot of the stairs, a Swiss guard in a white collarette and red-and-yellow panelled doublet was whistling, propped on his halberd near a lantern placed on the ground. At sight of his captain, he straightened up.

"No rogues in the neighbourhood?" asked the Marquis.

"I haven't seen anyone, sir. But before my arrival there must have been some dirty business over there."

Raising his lantern, he indicated a large puddle of blood on the ground.

"The gate to the Infanta's Garden was open towards the quays. I followed the traces of blood. I expect they chucked the fellow into the water. . . ."

"All right, Swiss. Watch well."

The night was moonless. The smell of fetid mud rose from the riverbanks. One could hear the buzz of mosquitoes, the murmur of the Seine. Angélique called out softly:

"Margot!"

She was gripped by a desire to annihilate herself in this darkness, to plunge, in her turn, into

513

this lap of liquid night.

She began to walk away, stumbling in the dust of the quayside. The night was completely black. Only a few lamps, here and there, lighted the sign of a shop, the porch of a well-to-do citizen's house. Angélique knew that the Pont-Neuf was somewhere on her right. She found its white parapet without much trouble, but as she set foot on the bridge, a sort of squatting human larva reared up before her. From the nauseous stench she guessed it was one of the beggars who had frightened her so much earlier in the day. She recoiled, uttering a strident cry. Behind her came the sound of hurrying footsteps and the voice of the Marquis de Vardes rang out:

"Back there, scoundrel, or I'll run you through."

The other remained planted across the bridge.

"Take pity, noble lord! I am a poor blind man."

"Not so blind that you can't see well enough to cut my purse!"

With the tip of his sword, he prodded the belly of the misshapen creature, who gave a start and fled wailingly.

"And now, will you tell me where you live?" said the officer harshly.

Tight-lipped, Angélique gave the address of her brother-in-law. This nocturnal Paris terrified her. She felt the teeming presence of invisible creatures, of a subterranean life like that of vermin. Through the walls seeped voices, whispers, jeers. From time to time, the open door of a tavern or a brothel shed a shaft of light onto the ground amid bellowed songs, and through the smoke of pipes could be glimpsed musketeers sprawled at tables with naked girls on their knees. Then the black lanes intertwined again in a maze of darkness.

De Vardes turned round frequently. Out of a group around a fountain, an individual had detached himself and was following them with silent, supple strides.

"Is it still far?"

"We're almost there," said Angélique, who recognized the gargoyles and gables of the houses of the rue de l'Enfer.

"Good thing, for I think I'll be forced to prick a few paunches. Listen to me, little one. Don't ever come back to the Louvre. Hide yourself, let them forget you."

"It's not by hiding myself that I'll get my husband out of prison."

He sneered.

"As you wish, oh faithful and virtuous spouse!"

Angélique felt the blood rush to her face. She felt an urge to bite, to throttle him.

A second silhouette bounded into sight from the shadows of a lane. The Marquis shoved the young woman against the wall and planted himself in front of her, his sword in hand.

In the circle of light shed by the big lantern hanging from the house of Maître Fallot de Sancé, Angélique gazed, her eyes wide with horror, at two rag-covered men. One of them had a stick in his hand, the other a kitchen-knife.

"We want your purses," said the first in a hoarse voice.

"You'll certainly get something, gentlemen, but it'll be a taste of my sword."

Angélique, gripping the bronze door-knocker,

515

hammered as hard as she could. At last the door opened a narrow chink. She dived into the house, her last vision being that of the Marquis de Vardes with his sword raised high, holding off the two blackguards, growling and greedy like wolves.

Chapter 30

IT was Hortense who had opened the door. A candle in her hand, her scrawny neck emerging from a rough linen nightgown, she followed her sister up the stairs, whispering in a hissing voice. She had always said so. A trollop, that's what Angélique had been ever since her early youth. An intriguer. An ambitious schemer who only had designs on her husband's fortune but was hypocritical enough to pretend to love him, when in fact she did not deprive herself of following libertines into the gutter of Paris.

Angélique hardly listened to her. Her ear was cocked to the noise coming up from the street; she clearly heard the clash of steel, then a cry, followed by a mad flight.

"Listen," she murmured, nervously clutching Hortense's arm.

"What?"

"That shout! Surely someone is hurt."

"What of it? The night belongs to rogues and brigands. No respectable woman would dream of going for a walk in Paris after sundown. No one except my own sister!"

She held the candle up to Angélique's face.

"If you could see yourself! Fi! You've the face of a strumpet who's just made love."

Angélique wrenched the candlestick from her sister's hand.

"And you have the face of a prim old prude who hasn't made enough love. Go and join your lawyer of a husband, who can't do anything but snore when he's in bed."

For a long time, Angélique remained sitting at the window, unable to make up her mind to go to bed. She did not cry. She relived the various stages of this dreadful day. It seemed to her that a century had elapsed since the moment when Barbe had come into the room saying: "Here's some good milk for the baby."

Since then Margot had died and she, Angélique, had been unfaithful to Joffrey.

"If only I hadn't felt so much pleasure!" she told herself over and over again, unable to stifle a recurring shiver of delight and terror.

Her body's avidity filled her with horror. As long as she had been at Joffrey's side, satisfied by his love, she had not realised how true the words were which he had so often uttered: "You are made for love." She remembered a summer afternoon, when she had lain across the bed, swooning under his caresses. Suddenly he had stopped and asked her abruptly:

"Will you be unfaithful to me?"

"No, never. I love only you."

"If you deceived me, I'd kill you!"

"Well, let him kill me!" thought Angélique. "It

517

would be good to die by his hand. He's the one I love."

Propped on the window-sill, her face turned towards the sleeping city, she repeated:

"It's you I love."

Angélique managed to sleep for an hour, but at the first rays of dawn she was up again. Tying a scarf around her hair, she crept stealthily downstairs and left the house. Mingling with maid-servants and the wives of craftsmen and shop-keepers, she went to Notre Dame to hear early Mass.

The narrow lanes, where the mist rising from the Seine was turning to gold, like a filmy fairy veil in the first rays of the sun, still exhaled the odours of the night. Vagabonds and cut-purses were repairing to their dens, while beggars, pedlars, cripples set up shop on street-corners. Rheumy eyes scowled after these prim, prudish women who went to pray to the Lord before starting their daily tasks. Craftsmen were removing the shutters from their stalls. Apprentice wigmakers, a bag of powder and a comb in their hands, were hurrying towards their bourgeois clientele to arrange the wig of a counsellor or a lawyer.

Angélique walked up the sombre aisle of the cathedral. Amid a rustle of slippers, the church-wardens were setting the chalices and cruets on the altars, filling the stoups with holy water and trimming the candles.

Angélique went into the first confessional-box. With throbbing temples, she accused herself of having committed the sin of adultery. After receiving absolution, she attended Mass, then went to order three services for the repose of the soul of her servant Margot.

When she found herself outside in the square again, she felt appeased. The hour of remorse was over. Now she would save all her courage to fight and wrest Joffrey from prison.

She bought some biscuits, still warm from the oven, from a little hawker. The bustle on the square was already at its height. Carriages were driving ladies of nobility to Mass. Outside the doors of the hospital, the Hôtel-Dieu, the nuns were lining up the night's dead, sewn up in their shrouds. A tumbrel would pick them up to carry them to the graveyard of the Saints-Innocents.

Although the Square of Notre Dame was enclosed by a low wall, it still preserved the disarray and picturesqueness which had made of it, in former times, the most popular square in Paris. Bakers still came there to sell last week's bread at low prices to needy folk. Strollers still crowded in front of the great "Faster," that enormous plaster statue coated with lead, which had stood there for centuries. Nobody knew what the monument represented: it showed a man holding a book in one hand, and in the other a stick around which intertwining snakes were coiled. He was the most famous figure in Paris. He was credited with the power of speech on days of riots, and numerous pamphlets circulated at those periods signed: "The Great Faster of Notre Dame . . ."

Listen to the voice of a preacher
Vulgarly called the Faster,

519

Because for a thousand years,
   so History says,
No food or drink he's ever had.

To the square too had come, in the course of the centuries, all the criminals, with fifteen-pound candlesticks in their hands, to make honorable amends to Our Lady before being burned or hanged. Angélique shuddered as she thought of that procession of sinister ghosts. How many had come and knelt there, amidst cruel clamourings under the unseeing eyes of the old stone saints!

She tossed her head to shake off those lugubrious thoughts and started back to the lawyer's house, when a cleric in civilian dress approached her.

"Madame de Peyrac, I present my respects to you. I was on my way to Maître Fallot's to converse with you."

"I am at your disposal, Monsieur l'Abbé, but I don't quite remember your name."

"Don't you?"

The priest lifted his wide-brimmed hat, which act also removed a short, grey horse-hair wig. Angélique recognized with amazement the lawyer Desgrez.

"You! But why this disguise?"

The young man had covered his head again. He whispered softly:

"Because yesterday, there was need of a chaplain at the Bastille."

He pulled from under his frock a small horn box full of grated tobacco, snuffed, sneezed, blew his nose and then asked Angélique:

"What do you think? Isn't it life-like?"

"Yes, indeed. I was fooled by it myself. But . . . tell me, you have been able to penetrate into the Bastille?"

"Hush! Let's go to the proctor's home. There we'll talk more freely."

On the way, Angélique was at pains to control her impatience. Did the lawyer at last know something? Had he seen Joffrey? He was walking very gravely at her side, with the dignified and modest attitude of a pious vicar.

"Do you often disguise yourself in your profession?" asked Angélique.

"In my profession, no. My sense of honour as a lawyer is much opposed to such masquerades. But one's got to live. When I'm tired of 'crowing,' that is to say of hunting for clients on the steps of the Palace of Justice in order to hook a brief that pays a miserable three *livres,* I offer my services to the police."

"Isn't it rather reckless to dress up as a cleric?" inquired Angélique. "You might be led to commit some act close to sacrilege."

"I don't present myself for the purpose of giving sacraments, but as a confidant. The frock inspires confidence. Nothing is more naïve in appearance than a substitute fresh from the seminary. People tell him everything. Oh, I admit, of course, it's nothing to be proud of. Nothing like your brother-in-law Fallot, who was a fellow-student of mine at the Sorbonne. Now there's a man who'll go far! So while I'm playing the frisky little abbé next to some charming damsel, that grave magistrate will spend the morning on his knees at the Palace, listening to Maître Talon's

521

speech in some legacy action."

"Why on his knees?"

"It's a judicial tradition come down from Henri IV. The solicitor procures, that is to say prepares the case. The advocate pleads it. He has greater prestige than the proctor, who must kneel while the other speaks. But the advocate has an empty stomach while the proctor has a bulging paunch. No wonder! He's earned his part on the twelve degrees of the procedure."

"This seems very complicated to me."

"Nevertheless, try and remember these details. They may have their importance if we ever manage to get your husband's trial started."

"Do you think we'll have to reach the trial stage?" cried Angélique.

"We'll have to," gravely affirmed the lawyer. "It's his only chance of salvation."

In Maître Fallot's small office, Desgrez removed his wig and passed his hand through his wiry hair. His face, which was naturally gay and spirited, wore an anxious mien. Angélique sat down near the small table and began to toy with one of the proctor's goose-quills. She dared not question Desgrez. At last, unable to stand it any longer, she ventured:

"You saw him?"

"Whom?"

"My husband?"

"Oh no, there's no question of it: he's kept in strict solitary confinement. The Governor of the Bastille is answerable with his head if he communicates with, or writes to, anyone."

"Is he well treated?"

"For the time being, yes. He even has a bed and two chairs, and he gets the very same meals as the Governor. I have also heard that he often sings, that he covers the walls of his cell with mathematical formulae by means of the smallest plaster pebble, and also that he has undertaken to tame two enormous spiders."

"Oh, Joffrey!" murmured Angélique with a smile. But her eyes filled with tears.

So he was alive. He had not become a blind and deaf ghost, and even the walls of the Bastille were not thick enough to stifle the echoes of his vitality. She raised her eyes towards Desgrez.

"Thank you, Maître."

The lawyer looked away moodily.

"Don't thank me. The case is extremely difficult. For these few, slender scraps of information, I must confess I have already spent all the advance you gave me."

"Money is of no importance. Ask me for whatever you deem necessary to pursue your investigations."

But the young man kept looking away as if, despite his volubility, he felt much embarrassed.

"To be quite frank," he said brusquely, "I even ask myself whether I oughtn't to try and give you your money back. I believe I was a little rash to take on this case, which now seems to me very complex."

"You'd drop my husband's defence?" exclaimed Angélique.

Only yesterday, she had not trusted this man of law who, despite his brilliant diplomas, was most

523

certainly a poor wretch who didn't eat his fill every day. But now that he spoke of dropping the case, she was seized by panic.

Nodding his head, he said:

"In order to defend him, he'd first have to be attacked."

"What is he accused of?"

"Officially, of nothing. *He does not exist.*"

"But in that case they can't do anything to him."

"They can *forget* him forever, Madame. There are people in the dungeons of the Bastille who've been there for thirty or forty years and who can no longer remember even their own names or what they've done. That's why I say his greatest chance of salvation rests in provoking a trial. But even in that case, the trial will probably be private and a lawyer's assistance refused him. So the money you are willing to spend will very likely be useless!"

She sat up straight and looked at him fixedly.

"You are afraid?"

"No, but I have been wondering. Hadn't I, for instance, better stay a caseless lawyer rather than risk being involved in a scandal? Hadn't you, on the other hand, better hide in the depth of some province with your child and the money you're left with, rather than lose your life? As for your husband, hadn't he better spend some years in prison rather than be dragged into a trial for . . . witchcraft and sacrilege?"

Angélique heaved an enormous sigh of relief.

"Witchcraft and sacrilege! . . . Is that what he's charged with?"

"That's what served as a pretext for his arrest, anyway."

"But that's not at all serious! It's merely the result of the stupidity of the Archbishop of Toulouse."

She told the young lawyer in detail the main incidents in the quarrel between the Archbishop and the Comte de Peyrac. How the latter had perfected a method of extracting gold from rock and how the Archbishop, envious of his wealth, had determined to obtain his secret, which was actually nothing more than an industrial formula.

"There is no magical action involved, just scientific research."

The lawyer pursed his lips.

"Madame, I for my part am incompetent in this matter. If this research forms the basis of the charge, we would have to produce witnesses, make a demonstration before the judges and prove to them that there is no magic or witchcraft involved."

"My husband is not a pious man, but he goes to Mass on Sundays, he fasts and receives Holy Communion on the great holidays. He is generous towards the Church. However, the Primate of Toulouse feared his influence and they have been at odds for years."

"Unfortunately, it's no small thing to be Archbishop of Toulouse. In certain respects, this prelate has more power than the Archbishop of Paris and perhaps even the Cardinal. Remember that he is the only one who still represents the Holy Office in France. Between you and me, who are modern people, such a tale doesn't seem to hold water.

The Inquisition is dying. It's kept its virulence in certain parts of the south where Protestant heresy is widespread. But actually, it isn't so much the Archbishop's sternness or the enforcement of the laws of the Holy Office that I fear in this particular case. Here, read this."

He extracted from a faded plush-bag a small square piece of paper, with the word "copy" stamped in one corner.

Angélique read:

Sentence:

Between Philibert Vénot, prosecutor-general for the Legal Office of the Episcopal Seat of Toulouse, plaintiff, in the crime of magic and sorcery, against Monsieur Joffrey de Peyrac, Comte de Morens, defendant.

Whereas the said Joffrey de Peyrac is sufficiently convicted of having renounced God and given himself up to the devil, and also of having several times invoked evil spirits and conferred with them, lastly of having resorted to several and diverse kinds of witchcraft . . .

For which cases and others he is handed over to the secular judge to be tried for his crimes.

Pronounced this 26th day of June 1660 by P. Vénot, the said de Peyrac not having protested nor appealed against it, has said that the will of God be done!

Desgrez explained:
"In less sibylline language this means that the religious tribunal, after judging your husband *in absentia* and without the accused's knowledge, and

after concluding beforehand that he is guilty, has handed him over to the King's secular justice."

"And you think the King will tolerate such nonsense? It's just the fruit of envy on the part of a bishop who would like to rule over the whole province and who lets himself be swayed by the phantasies of a benighted monk like that Bécher, who's certainly mad into the bargain."

"I can only judge the facts," remarked the lawyer. "Now this proves that the Archbishop takes great care not to appear himself in this case: you see, his name is not even mentioned in this paper although there can be no doubt that he was the instigator of the first verdict pronounced *in camera*. On the other hand, the warrant of arrest bore the King's signature as well as that of Séguier, the Président of the Court. Séguier is an upright man, but a weak one. He upholds the forms of justice, but the King's orders come first with him."

"Nonetheless, if it does come to a trial, the views of the jurors will be what counts?"

"Yes," admitted Desgrez reluctantly, "but who will select the jurors?"

"And, according to you, what are the possible risks involved in such a trial for my husband?"

"First torture, by ordinary and extraordinary question, then the stake, Madame!"

Angélique felt herself blanch, a feeling of nausea rose in her throat.

"But after all," she repeated, "you can't condemn a man of his rank on such silly gossip."

"Which, therefore, merely serves as a pretext. Do you want my opinion, Madame? The Archbishop of Toulouse never intended to deliver your husband to a secular court. He was no doubt hoping that an ecclesiastical judgment would be sufficient to bring your husband's pride to heel and make him tractable to the views of the Church. But Monseigneur, in fomenting this intrigue, found his expectations overridden, and do you know why?"

"No."

"Because there is *something else,*" said François Desgrez, raising his finger. "Most certainly, your husband must have had ill-wishers in very high places, a number of enemies who'd sworn his downfall. The intrigue of Monseigneur of Toulouse has supplied them with a marvellous springboard. Formerly one used to poison one's enemies in the dark. Now everyone loves doing it according to the rules: you accuse, try, and condemn. Thus, your conscience is at rest. If your husband's trial takes place, it will be based on this charge of witchcraft, but the *real* motive for his condemnation, we'll never know."

Angélique had a fleeting vision of the poison-casket. Should she mention it to Desgrez? She hesitated. Mention of it would mean giving form to unfounded suspicions and might even further entangle the threads that were already so hopelessly complex.

She asked in an uncertain tone:

"What kind of thing do you suspect?"

"I haven't the slightest idea. All I can say is this: that even after barely sticking my long nose into this business, I've already had time to shrink back with fright from the high personages who are mixed up in it. In short, I repeat what I said to you the other day: it starts with the King. If he signed that warrant of arrest, it means he approved it."

"When I think," murmured Angélique, "that the King asked him to sing and covered him with glowing words! He already knew that he would be arrested."

"No doubt, but our King has been to a good school for craftiness. However this may be, he alone can revoke such a summons of special and secret arrest. Neither Tellier, nor Séguier, or any other gentleman of the Gown, would do. Failing the King, you would have to try and approach the Queen Mother, who has much influence over her son, or her Jesuit confessor, or even the Cardinal."

"I saw the Grande Mademoiselle," said Angélique. "She promised to make inquiries for me. But she said that nothing could be hoped for before the celebrations for the . . . King's entry . . . into Paris."

Angélique found it hard to finish the sentence. For some moments, ever since the lawyer had mentioned the stake, she had felt a growing faintness. Drops of sweat beaded on her temples and she was afraid she might swoon. She heard Desgrez's voice:

"I share her opinion. Nothing can be done before the celebrations. The best thing for you would be to wait here patiently. For my part, I'll try and complete my inquiries."

Angélique rose in a haze and held out her hands. Her cold cheek met the severe clerical cloth.

"So you will defend him?"

The young man was silent for a moment, then said in a gruff voice:

"After all, I have never been afraid for my own skin. I've risked it no end of times in stupid tavern brawls. I may as well risk it once again for a just cause. But you'll have to give me money, for I am as poor as a church-mouse, and the old-clothes dealer who hires out costumes is an inveterate thief."

These strong words revived Angélique's spirit. The fellow was much more reliable than she had at first believed. Under an appearance of cynicism and casualness, he hid a very thorough acquaintance with legal procedure, and he devoted himself conscientiously to the tasks he was entrusted with.

Recovering her self-control, she counted out a hundred *livres*. With a quick bow, François Desgrez departed, but not before throwing an enigmatic glance at the pale face whose green eyes glowed like precious stones in the dull obscurity of this office which reeked of ink and sealing-wax.

Clutching the banister Angélique went up to her room. This faintness was surely due to her experiences of the night before. She would lie down and try to sleep a little, even if she had to put up with Hortense's sarcasm. But she had hardly reached her room when she was again overcome by nausea and barely had time to rush to the washstand.

"What is the matter with me?" she wondered, frightened.

Suppose Margot had been right? Suppose someone really was determined to kill her? The carriage accident? The attempt on her life at the Louvre?

Perhaps they were trying to poison her?

Suddenly her tense face relaxed and a smile brightened her features.

"What a fool I am! I am simply going to have a baby!"

She remembered, before leaving Toulouse, that she had already wondered whether a second child might not be on the way. Now the thing was confirmed without any possible doubt.

"How happy Joffrey will be when he comes out of prison!" she said to herself.

Chapter 31

DURING the following days, Angélique forced herself to be patient. She had to wait for the King's triumphant entry into Paris. There was talk of its taking place at the end of July; but the elaborate preparations made it necessary to postpone the date from day to day. The throng of provincials who had come to Paris for the great event began to fidget with impatience.

Angélique sold her coach and horses and some jewels. She fell into the modest existence of this bourgeois district. She lent a helping hand in the kitchen, played with Florimond who had begun to trot busily through the house, entangling himself every now and then in his long dress. His little cousins adored him. Spoiled by them, by Barbe, by the little nurse-maid from Béarn, he seemed happy and his little cheeks grew round and rosy again. Angélique embroidered a little red hood for him, under which his sweet little face framed by its black curls enraptured the whole family. Even Hortense lost her frown and remarked that for a child of that age he certainly had a lot of charm! She herself, alas, had never been able to afford a children's nurse at home, so that she only got to know her children after they had reached the age of four! After all, not everybody could marry a crippled and disfigured nobleman, grown rich by consorting with Satan, and it was better to be a lawyer's wife than lose your soul.

Angélique turned a deaf ear to all this. In order to show her good will, she went to Mass every day in the unamusing company of her brother-in-law and her sister. She began to get familiar with the peculiar character of the Cité itself. Around the Palace of Justice, Notre Dame, the parishes of Saint-Aignan and Saint-Landry, on the quays, teemed a crowd of sheriff's officers, lawyers, judges and counsellors.

Dressed in black coats and sometimes wearing the robe, they hurried to and fro, their hands fumbling with their "law-suit bags," their arms full of piles of papers which they called "useful files." They cluttered up the stairs of the Palace and the neighbouring lanes. The Inn of the Black Head was their gathering place. There one could see the glowing, bibulous faces of the magistrates behind steaming stews and round-bellied bottles.

At the other end of the island, the vociferous Pont-Neuf offered another kind of Paris which the gentlemen of the Law were most indignant to find sprouting in their shadow. Whenever one sent a lackey on an errand in those parts and asked him when he'd be back, he'd answer: "That depends on the ditties they'll be singing on the Pont-Neuf today."

Together with the songs, a swarm of poems, pamphlets and tracts were born of the continual intermingling around the shopping-booths. On the Pont-Neuf, everybody knew everything. And even the mighty had learned to fear those grimy sheets of paper which were swept along by the breeze from the Seine and which were called the *"ponts-neufs."*

One evening, after getting up from dinner at Maître Fallot's, and while everyone was sipping quince or raspberry wine, Angélique unthinkingly pulled a sheet of paper out of her pocket. She looked at it with surprise, then remembered that she had bought it for ten *sols* from a poor wretch on the Pont-Neuf, on the morning of her stroll through the Tuileries.

She read it half aloud:

> And then let's go into the *Palais*
> Where we'll find that Rabelais,
> Mocking their ways as unsavoury,
> Fell far short of their true knavery.
> Here we'll find renowned insulters
> And those who slyly mulct us,
> Let's go and see the great rush. . . .

Two indignant cries interrupted her. Maître Fallot's old uncle was choking in his glass. With a swiftness Angélique never suspected him of, her solemn brother-in-law tore the piece of paper from her hand, rolled it into a pellet and flung it out of the window.

"How shameful, my sister!" he cried. "How dare you introduce such filth into our home! I wager that you bought it from one of those half-starved pamphleteers on the Pont-Neuf!"

"Yes, indeed. It was stuffed into my hand with a demand for ten *sols*. I didn't dare to refuse."

"The impudence of those people defies belief. Their pen does not even spare the integrity of men of law. And to think they are shut up in the Bastille as if they were people of quality, when the blackest prison of the Châtelet would still be too good for them."

Hortense's husband was panting like a bull. Never would she have thought him capable of getting so excited.

"Pamphlets, lampoons, ditties, we are flooded with them. They spare no one, neither King nor Court, and blasphemy doesn't worry them."

"In my time," said the old uncle, "the race of journalists had only just begun to spread. Now they're a real vermin, the disgrace of our capital."

He rarely spoke, opening his mouth only to ask for a little glass of quince-wine or his snuff-box. This long sentence revealed how much he had been shaken by the reading of the pamphlet.

"No respectable woman ventures to set foot on the Pont-Neuf," remarked Hortense cuttingly.

Maître Fallot had gone to lean out of the window.

"The gutter has carried away this infamy. But I should have been curious to know if it was signed by the Gutter-Poet."

"No possible doubt. Such virulence is self-revealing."

"The Gutter-Poet," gloomily murmured Maître Fallot. "The man who criticizes society as a whole, the born rebel, the professional parasite! I once saw him on a platform, haranguing the crowd with goodness knows what venomous outpourings. His name is Claude Le Petit. When I think that this gaunt scarecrow with a skin like a turnip finds a means of making the Princes and even the King gnash his teeth, I find it discouraging to live in such times. When will the police at last rid us of all these mountebanks?"

The sighing continued for a few minutes, then the incident was closed.

The King's entrance into Paris occupied everyone. And it so happened that it served to draw Angélique and her sister closer together. One day, Hortense came into Angélique's room, with as engaging a smile as she was able to conjure up.

"Imagine what is happening to us," she cried. "You remember my old convent school-friend, Athénaïs de Tonnay-Charente, to whom I was so attached in Poitiers?"

"No, not at all."

"Never mind. Anyway, she is in Paris, and as she has always been a great schemer, she has already managed to get close to some important people. In fine, on the day of the King's entrance she'll be able to go to the Hôtel de Beauvais, which is right where the parade will start in the rue Saint-Antoine. Naturally, we'll have to watch from the

535

attic windows, but that won't prevent us from having a view."

"Why do you say we?"

"Because she's invited us to share this boon. She'll have her sister and brother with her, and another girl friend also from Poitiers. We'll be a whole little coachful of Poitevins. That'll be *so* nice, won't it?"

"If you were counting on my carriage, I am sorry to tell you that I sold it."

"I know, I know. Oh, the coach is of no importance. Athénaïs will bring her own. It is a little rickety, for her family is ruined. Her mother has bundled her off to Paris with a maid, a lackey and this old carriage, with orders to find a husband as quickly as possible. Oh! she'll manage it, she's trying hard enough. But the point is . . . for the King's entrance . . . she hinted to me that she was somewhat short of clothes. You see, this Mademoiselle de Beauvais who's letting us have one of her garrets, isn't just anybody. They even say that the Queen Mother, the Cardinal, and all sorts of high personages, will be dining at her house during the parade. In fact, we'll have front seats. But we mustn't be taken for chambermaids or paupers or we'll get thrown out by the lackeys."

Angélique silently went to open one of her big trunks.

"Have a look in there to see if you find something that might suit her, and something to suit you too. You are taller than I, but it's easy to lengthen a petticoat with lace or frills."

Hortense approached with shining eyes. She could not conceal her admiration while Angélique

536

was spreading out the sumptuous garments on the bed. The gold-cloth dress drew from her a cry of admiration.

"I think it would be somewhat out of place in our attic," Angélique warned her.

"Naturally, you attended the King's wedding, so you can act disdainful."

"I assure you I am very pleased. Nobody awaits the King's coming to Paris with greater impatience than I. But I mean to keep this dress in order to sell it if Andijos, as I'm beginning to fear, doesn't bring me back any money. As for the others, you can do with them whatever you like. It is only right that you should have some compensation for the expenses my presence has occasioned you."

Finally, after much wavering, Hortense decided in favour of a sky-blue satin dress for her friend. For herself she selected an apple-green ensemble which brought out her nondescript brunette colouring.

On the morning of August 26th, Angélique nodded approvingly as she looked at the skinny figure of her sister, padded out by the pannier of the mantlegown, her sallow complexion heightened by the vivid green and her sparse but soft, fine hair:

"I really do think, Hortense, that you would be almost pretty if you hadn't such a shrewish disposition."

Much to her surprise, Hortense did not get vexed. She sighed as she went on gazing at herself in the tall steel mirror.

"I think so, too," she said. "What can I do? I have never had a liking for mediocrity, and mediocrity is all I've ever known. I like to talk, to

537

see witty, well-dressed people, I adore the theatre. But it's difficult to get away from household duties. This winter, I was able to go to some parties given by a satirical writer, the poet Scarron. A horrid fellow, invalid, malicious, but what a wit, my dear! I remember those parties with delight. Unfortunately, Scarron has just died. I'll have to go back to mediocrity."

"At the moment, you don't arouse pity. I assure you, you've a lot of style."

"It's certain that on a *real* proctor's wife the same dress would not produce the same effect. Nobility can't be bought. You have it in your blood."

As they bent over the caskets to choose their jewels, they recaptured the warmth of the clan, the arrogance of their class. They forgot the gloomy room, the tasteless furniture, the insipid Bergamo tapestries which were woven in Normandy for a petty-bourgeois clientele.

At dawn on the great day, the proctor left for Vincennes, which was the assembly-point where the State representatives were to salute and address the King.

The cannons thundered in response to the pealing bells of the churches. The city militia, in gala dress, bristling with pikes, halberds and muskets, took possession of the streets, which hawkers filled with a deafening din, as they distributed booklets giving the programme of the celebrations, the route of the royal cortège, the description of the triumphal arches.

Towards eight o'clock, the somewhat shabby carriage of Mademoiselle Athénaïs de Tonnay-

Charente stopped in front of the house. She was a beautiful girl, all in glowing colours: golden hair, pink cheeks, pearly brow set off by a black patch. Her blue dress matched her sapphire eyes which, though a trifle protruding, sparkled with wit and liveliness. She hardly remembered to show her gratitude, although in addition to the dress she wore a very beautiful diamond necklace lent her by Angélique. Mademoiselle de Tonnay-Charente de Mortemart considered that everything was her due, and that one could not but feel honoured to serve her. Despite her family's impecuniousness, she considered that her ancient name was worth a fortune. Her brother and sister seemed endowed with the same conceit. All three were bursting with vitality, caustic wit, enthusiasm and ambition, which made them most attractive and redoubtable companions.

It was a merry though creaking coachful that rumbled through the packed streets, between the houses decked with flowers and tapestries. Amid the ever-denser crowd, horsemen and lines of carriages clamoured for right of way in order to proceed towards the Gate of St. Antoine, where the procession was to form up.

"We'll have to make a detour to collect poor Françoise," said Athénaïs. "It won't be an easy matter."

"Oh! the Lord preserve us from Madame Scarron-the-Cripple!" exclaimed her brother.

Seated next to Angélique, he was unceremoniously crushing her. She asked him to move over as he was stifling her.

"I promised Françoise I'd take her along," said

Athénaïs. "She is a good girl and hasn't had much entertainment since her legless cripple of a husband died. I wonder if she isn't beginning to miss him."

"After all, repulsive though he was, he earned the money for the household. The Queen Mother had given him a pension."

"Was he already an invalid when he married her?" asked Hortense. "That couple has always intrigued me."

"Of course he was. He took the girl into his house to look after him. As she was an orphan, she accepted; she was fifteen at the time."

"Do you think she took the plunge?" asked the younger sister.

"Who knows? . . . Scarron proclaimed to whoever wanted to listen that his sickness had paralyzed everything but his tongue and his you-know-what. Without any doubt, she must have learned not a few little things from him. He was always so wicked! And, upon my faith, so many people came to see them that some handsome, well-built nobleman surely must have taken it upon himself to distract her a little, too. There was a rumour about Villarceaux."

"One must admit," said Hortense, "that Madame Scarron is beautiful, but she has always behaved with great modesty. She always remained seated next to her husband's wheel chair, helped him to sit down and passed him his herb-tea. Besides which she is learned and very well-spoken."

The widow was waiting on the pavement outside a shabby-looking house.

"Good Lord, that dress!" whispered Athénaïs,

raising her hand to her lips. "Her skirt is worn to a shred."

"Why didn't you mention it to me?" asked Angélique. "I could have found her something."

"Why, it didn't occur to me. Do get in, Françoise."

The young woman sat down in a corner, after gracefully greeting the occupants of the coach. She had lovely brown eyes, which were veiled by her long eye-lids touched with mauve.

They finally reached the rue Saint-Antoine which, surprisingly, did not seem too crowded. The coaches had apparently been parked in the neighbouring lanes. The Hôtel de Beauvais was a beehive of activity. A canopy of crimson velvet, adorned with gold and silver braids and fringes, decorated the central balcony. Persian carpets embellished the façade. On the doorstep, an old one-eyed lady, decked out like an altarpiece but with her fists on her hips, was shouting directions at the upholsterers.

"What is that horrid virago doing there?" inquired Angélique, as their party was approaching the house.

Hortense motioned to her to be silent, but Athénaïs was giggling behind her fan.

"That's the mistress of the house, my dear. Catherine de Beauvais, known as One-eyed Kate. She is a former chambermaid of Anne of Austria's, who entrusted her with making a man of our young King when he was going on fifteen. That's the secret of her wealth."

Angélique could not help laughing.

"One must presume that she makes experience do for charm. . . ."

"A proverb says that there are no ugly women for adolescents and monks," the young Mortemart chimed in.

Notwithstanding their ironical sentiments, they bowed deeply to the former chambermaid. She cast a piercing glance at them out of her single eye.

"Ah! here is the Poitou lot. Don't clutter me up, my lambs. Go straight up there before my maids take the best places. But who is this one?" she said, pointing a crooked finger in Angélique's direction.

Mademoiselle de Tonnay-Charente introduced her:

"A friend, the Comtesse de Peyrac de Morens."

"Oh really! Ho, ho!" said the old lady with a kind of sneer.

"I am sure she knows something about you," whispered Hortense on the stairs. "We are childish to imagine that the scandal won't eventually be public. I should never have taken you along. You'd better go home."

"All right, but in that case give me back my dress," said Angélique, reaching a hand toward her sister's bodice.

"Keep still, little ninny," answered Hortense, struggling.

Athénaïs de Tonnay-Charente had taken by storm the window of a servant's room and was making herself comfortable together with her girl friends.

"You can see marvellously," she cried. "Look, down there, the Gate of Saint-Antoine by which the King will enter."

Angélique also leaned down. She felt herself grow pale.

What she saw under the blue sky, hazy with heat, was not the vast avenue where the crowd was milling, nor the Gate of Saint-Antoine with its triumphal arch of white stone, but a little to the right, looming like a sombre cliff, the huge bulk of a fortress.

She asked her sister in a low voice:

"What is that big stronghold near the Gate of Saint-Antoine?"

"The Bastille," whispered Hortense behind her fan.

Angélique could not take her eyes off it. Eight turrets, each topped by a watchtower, blind façades, walls, portcullises, drawbridges, moats — an island of suffering lost in the ocean of an indifferent city, a closed world untouched by life, which no joyous clamours would reach even on this day: the Bastille! . . .

The King would pass in all his glory at the foot of this fierce guardian of his authority. No sound would pierce the darkness of the jails where forgotten men had been despairing for years, for a lifetime.

The time of waiting dragged on. At last, the shouts of the impatient crowd heralded the beginning of the procession. Emerging from the shadow of the Gate of Saint-Antoine appeared the first companies. They were composed of four mendicant orders: Franciscans, Dominicans, Augustins, Carmelites, preceded by their crosses and their cradle-bearers. Their black, brown or white homespun gowns were an insult to the splendour of the sun which gleamed, in revenge, on a sea of rosy skulls. The secular clergy followed, with their crosses and banners, their priests in surplices and square bonnets.

Then the city corporations marched up, with raised trumpets whose merry bugling succeeded the pious chants. The three hundred city archers were followed by Monsieur de Burnonville, the Governor, and his guards.

After that came the provost of the merchants, riding among a magnificent escort of lackeys in green velvet, and followed, in his turn, by the city councillors, the aldermen, the masters and guards of the various guilds: drapers, spice-merchants, haberdashers, furriers and vintners, in velvet gowns of a thousand hues. The people cheered these merchant companies.

But they were cool towards the officers of the watch, who were followed by the men of the Châtelet, that is, the tipstaffs, the bailiffs and the two lieutenants — the civil and the criminal one. Recognizing their habitual tormentors, the *"grimauds"* and the *"malveillants,"* the rabble fell silent. The same hostile silence greeted the sovereign courts — the Board of Excise and the Audit Office, symbols of the hated taxes.

The first president and his principal colleagues were all resplendent in their scarlet coats with ermine trimmings, and with black velvet, gold-braided "mortar-boards" on their heads.

It was getting close to two o'clock in the afternoon. In the azure sky, small clouds formed in vain only to be dissolved by the broiling sun. The crowd sweated, steamed. They were on tenterhooks, their necks stretched towards the horizon. A roar announced that they had just seen the Queen Mother appear under the canopy of the Hôtel de Beauvais. It was the sign that the King and Queen were approaching.

Angélique had an arm over the shoulders of Madame Scarron and Athénaïs de Tonnay-Charente. All three of them were leaning out of the window of the top storey of the house. Hortense, Mortemart and the younger sister had found a place at another window.

From afar could be seen the retinue of His Eminence Monseigneur Mazarin. The Cardinal-Minister was preceded by seventy-two mules under velvet and gold sumpter-cloths; his pages and gentlemen decked in sumptuous materials escorted his coach, which was a real masterpiece of the goldsmith's art, that glittered in the sunshine.

He stopped in front of the Hôtel de Beauvais. After receiving a deep curtsey from One-eyed Kate, he went up to the balcony to join the Queen Mother and her sister-in-law, the ex-Queen of England, widow of the beheaded King Charles I.

The crowd gave an unrestrained ovation to Mazarin. He was not any better liked than at the time of the *"mazarinades,"* but he had signed the Peace of the Pyrénées, and, at the bottom of their hearts, the people of France were grateful to him for having saved them from their own folly of banishing the King whom they were now awaiting in a paroxysm of adoration.

His noblemen and their suites preceded him. Angélique could put a name to many of their faces. She pointed out to her companions the Marquis d'Humières and the Duc de Lauzun, at the head of a hundred gentlemen. Lauzun, ever impish, blew unceremonious kisses to the ladies. The crowd responded with gusts of tender-hearted laughter. How they loved these young noblemen, so brave and so brilliant! Here again, they dismissed from their minds the squandering and arrogance, the brawls and shameless tavern orgies. They only remembered their gallant deeds in bed and battle.

The throng called out their names: Saint-Aignan dressed in gold, the most pleasing figure of them all; de Guiche, with his face like a flower of the south, riding on a fiery horse; Brienne, wearing a hat with a triple tier of plumes that hovered around him like the fluttering wings of fabulous white and pink birds.

Angélique shrank back and compressed her lips as the Marquis de Vardes passed, his fine-featured, insolent head carried high under his fair wig. He led the *Cent-Suisses* guard, tightly wedged into their stiff ruffs.

A shrill outburst of trumpets shattered the rhythm of the march. The King approached, borne on the waves of thunderous acclaim.

He was there! . . . brilliant as the sun!

How grand he was, the King of France! A true King at last! Neither despicable like Charles IX or Henri III, nor too plain like Henri IV, nor too austere like Louis XIII.

Mounted on a bay horse he advanced slowly, escorted at a few steps' distance by his Great Chamberlain, his principal gentleman-in-waiting, his equerry, his captain of the guards. He had refused the canopy which the city had had embroidered for him. He wanted the people to see him.

Louis XIV rode past without suspecting the rôle that would be played in his life by the three women whom a curious stroke of chance had assembled above him: Athénaïs de Tonnay-Charente de Mortemart, Angélique de Peyrac, Françoise Scarron.

Under her hand, Angélique felt Françoise's golden-hued flesh quiver.

"Oh! how beautiful he is!" whispered the widow.

Athénaïs murmured, her blue eyes popping with enthusiasm:

"He is certainly beautiful in his silver costume. But I'm thinking that without his costume he mustn't be too bad either, and even without his shirt. The Queen is lucky to find such a man in her bed."

Angélique did not say anything.

"It is he," she thought, "who holds our destiny in his hands. God help us, he is too great, he is too mighty!"

A shout from the crowd caught her attention.

"The Prince! Long live the Prince!" they cried.

Angélique trembled.

Lean, gaunt, holding his head erect, his eyes fiery and his nose eagle-beaked, the Prince de Condé was returning to Paris. He had come back from Flanders, where his long rebellion against royal authority had led him. He did not bother about scruples or regrets, and anyway the people of Paris forgave him. The traitor was forgotten, the victor of Rocroi and Lens acclaimed.

At his side, Monsieur, the King's brother, in a cloud of lace, looked more than ever like a girl in disguise.

Finally the young Queen appeared, seated in a Roman type of chariot of sparkling silver-gilt, drawn by six horses in bejewelled caparisons embroidered with golden fleurs-de-lis and precious stones.

One-eyed Kate at the foot of the staircase seemed to be lying in wait for someone. When the modest little Poitou party appeared on the landing, she shouted to them in her raucous voice:

"Well? Were you able to watch your fill?"

They thanked her profusely, their cheeks still glowing with excitement.

"Good. Why don't you go and have some pastry over there?"

She folded her vast fan and tapped Angélique lightly on the shoulder.

"You, my pretty one, come with me for a moment."

Surprised, the young woman followed Madame de Beauvais through the rooms crammed with guests. They finally found themselves in a small, deserted boudoir.

"Ah!" sighed the old lady, fanning herself. "It's not easy to isolate oneself."

She scrutinized Angélique attentively. The half-closed eyelid over her empty socket gave her face an expression of vulgarity which was intensified by the flakes of rouge encrusted in her wrinkles and the grin of her toothless mouth.

"I think you'll do," she said after a moment's

observation. "What would you say, my beauty, to a big château near Paris, with a major-domo, footmen, lackeys, maids, six carriages, stables and a pension of a hundred thousand *livres?*"

"All this is being proposed to *me?*" asked Angélique, laughing.

"To you."

"And by whom?"

"Someone who wishes you well."

"So I imagine. But who?"

The other came closer with a conspiratorial air.

"A rich nobleman who is dying of love for your beautiful eyes."

"Listen, Madame," said Angélique, who was trying hard to keep a straight face, "I am very grateful to the nobleman whoever he may be, but I am afraid that someone is trying to make fun of my artlessness by making me such princely proposals. The gentleman doesn't know me very well if he believes that the mere mention of such munificence could sway me to belong to him."

"Are you, then, so well off in Paris that you turn up your nose so scornfully? I have been told that your possessions are under seal and that you had sold your coaches."

The sharp eye of the old shrew did not leave the young woman's face.

"I see you are well-informed, Madame, but the point is I do not yet intend to sell my body. . . ."

"Who's talking of that, little fool?" hissed the other through her black teeth.

"I thought I gathered . . ."

"Pah! You'll take a lover or you won't. You'll live like a nun, if that's what you want. You are only being asked to accept this proposal."

"But . . . in exchange for what?" inquired Angélique, taken aback.

The other came even closer and took her two hands familiarly.

"It's quite simple," she said in the reasonable tone of voice of a kindly grandmother. "You set up house in this wonderful château. You go to Court. You'll go to Saint-Germain, to Fontaine-bleau. It would amuse you, wouldn't it, to attend the Court fêtes, to be waited upon, spoiled, courted? Of course, if you are absolutely set on it, you could go on calling yourself Madame de Peyrac . . . but perhaps you would prefer to change your name. For instance, you might call yourself Madame de Sancé. . . . That sounds very pretty. . . . People would say as you passed, 'That is the lovely Madame de Sancé.' Eh, eh, doesn't that sound rather nice?"

"But really," said Angélique impatiently, "don't take me for such a fool as to think that a gentleman wants to lavish his wealth on me without asking for anything in return!"

"Ho, ho! It almost comes to that, though. All that you are asked is to give no more thought to anything but your dresses, your jewels, your amusements. Is that really so difficult for a pretty girl? You understand?" she added, gently shaking Angélique. "Do you understand?"

Angélique gazed at this witch's face whose hairy chin was plastered with blobs of white powder.

"Do you understand? Think of nothing! Forget . . ."

"I'm being asked to forget Joffrey," Angélique

said to herself. "To forget that I am his wife, to give up defending him, to erase his memory from my life, to blot out all remembrance. I'm being asked to keep silent, to forget. . . ."

The vision of the little poison-casket rose up before her. That, she was sure of it now, was the starting-point of the whole drama. Who could be interested in her silence? Some of the most highly-placed people in the kingdom: Monsieur Fouquet, the Prince de Condé, all those lords whose carefully devised treachery had for years reposed in a sandal-wood casket.

Angélique shook her head coldly.

"I am very sorry, Madame, but I must no doubt be of poor intelligence, for I do not grasp a single word of what you've been trying to tell me."

"Well, you think it over, my sweet, think it over, and then give me your answer. Don't wait too long, though. In a couple of days, shall we say? Come, come, my pretty one, don't you think that, all in all, it's better than . . ."

She leaned towards Angélique's ear and breathed into it:

". . . than losing your life?"

Chapter 32

IN your opinion, Monsieur Desgrez, why should an anonymous gentleman offer me a château and a pension of a hundred thousand *livres?*"

"My word," said the lawyer, "I suppose for the

same reason that I myself might offer you a pension of a hundred thousand *livres.*"

Angélique looked at him blankly, then blushed slightly under the young man's bold glance. She had never thought of her lawyer in this particular light. With no little agitation she noticed that his worn clothes must conceal a muscular, well-proportioned body. He was not handsome, with his big nose and uneven teeth, but his physiognomy was expressive. Maître Fallot said of him that, apart from his talent and erudition, he lacked about everything that was required to become a respectable magistrate. He did not consort much with his colleagues, but continued to haunt the taverns as in his student days. That is why he was entrusted with certain cases that called for inquiries in places where the gentlemen of the rue Saint-Landry would have hesitated to go for fear of losing their souls.

"Well, as a matter of fact," said Angélique, "it's not at all what you think. I'll put the question differently: why has someone twice tried to murder me, which is an even surer method of obtaining my silence?"

The lawyer's face suddenly darkened.

"Ah! that's what I've been waiting for," he said.

He abandoned his casual pose on the edge of the table in Maître Fallot's study, and sat down gravely opposite Angélique.

"Madame," he resumed, "I may not be a man of law who inspires you with great confidence. However, as it happens, I think your esteemed brother-in-law did not do too badly in chancing on me, for your husband's case requires the qual-

552

ities of a private sleuth, which I've become of necessity, more than a scrupulous knowledge of law and procedure. But I must tell you that I can unravel this tangle only if you supply me with all the facts. In short, here is the question I am dying to ask you . . ."

He got up, had a look behind the door, lifted the curtain that concealed boxes of files, then returned to the young woman and questioned her in a low voice:

"What is it that you and your husband know, which can scare one of the highest persons in the kingdom? I am referring to Monsieur Fouquet."

Angélique's lips went white. She stared at the lawyer with bewilderment.

"All right, I see there is something," said Desgrez. "At the moment, I am waiting for the report of a spy placed with Mazarin. But another one put me on the track of a servant called Clément Tonnel, who at one time was the handyman of the Prince de Condé. . . ."

"And major-domo at our château, in Toulouse."

"That's right. The fellow is in close touch with Monsieur Fouquet. In point of fact, he works only for him, although he rakes in substantial gratuities now and then from his former master, the Prince, probably by blackmail. Here's another question: through whom did you receive the proposal to be set up in princely fashion?"

"Through Madame de Beauvais."

"One-eyed Kate! . . . This time, it's clear as daylight. The affair has the stamp of Fouquet. He pays the old hag fat sums of money in order to know all the Court secrets. She used to be in

Mazarin's pay, but he proved less generous than the Controller-General. I might add that I've also tracked down another high personage who has sworn your husband's downfall and your own."

"And that is?"

"Monsieur, the King's brother."

Angélique uttered a cry.

"You are mad!"

The young man pulled a wry face.

"Do you think I've swindled you out of your 1,500 *livres?* I may look like a humbug, Madame, but if the information I bring back costs a lot, it's because it's always accurate. It's the King's brother who laid the trap for you at the Louvre and who tried to have you murdered. I know it from the very hoodlum who stabbed your maid Margot, and it cost me no less than ten pints of wine at The Red Cock to extract the confession from him."

Angélique passed her hand over her forehead. In a jerky voice, she related to Desgrez the curious incident of which she had been a chance witness at the Château du Plessis-Bellière some years ago.

"Do you know what has become of your relative, the Marquis du Plessis?"

"I have no idea. But he may be in Paris or else in the army."

"The civil war is bygone history," murmured the lawyer musingly, "but it wouldn't take very much to make the glowing embers flare up again. Obviously there are many people who would be afraid of such evidence of their treason being openly exposed."

With a flick of his hand he swept the table clear of its pile of papers and goose-quills.

"Let's sum up the position: Mademoiselle Angélique de Sancé, that is to say yourself, is suspected of being in possession of a formidable secret. The Prince de Condé or Monsieur Fouquet instructs the valet Clément to spy on you. He keeps a watch on you for years. At last he becomes certain about what had hitherto been no more than a suspicion: you were the one who made the casket disappear; you and your husband alone know the secret of its hiding-place. Your major-domo now goes to see Fouquet and sells his information for hard cash. From that moment, your fate is sealed. All those who've hitched their wagon to the Controller's star, all those who are afraid of losing their pensions and the Court's favour, band together against the nobleman of Toulouse who may appear before the King any day and say: 'This is what I know!'

"If we were in Italy, they'd have used a dagger or poison. But it's well known that the Comte de Peyrac is immune to poison, and, anyway, in France we like to give things a legal varnish. The stupid intrigue hatched by Monseigneur de Frontenac breaks just at the right time. The Comte is to be arrested as a sorcerer. The King is persuaded. His jealousy is kindled against this too wealthy nobleman. And there you are! The gates of the Bastille close on the Comte de Peyrac. Everyone can breathe more freely."

"No!" said Angélique fiercely. "I am not going to let them breathe freely. I shall stir Heaven and earth until justice is done. I shall go and tell the King myself exactly why we have so many enemies."

"Hush!" said Desgrez quickly. "Don't get excited. You are carrying a load of gunpowder in your hands, but take care that it doesn't blow *you* to pieces first! What guarantee have you that the King or even Mazarin doesn't know all about it? . . ."

"But surely," protested Angélique, "they were the chosen victims of the old plot: the Cardinal was to be murdered, and so, if possible, were the King and his young brother."

"I know, my beauty, I know," said the lawyer.

He collected himself with a gesture of apology:

"I concede the logic of your reasoning, Madame. But, you see, the intrigues of the mighty form a nest of vipers. You court death trying to interpret their true feelings. It is quite possible that Monsieur de Mazarin has got wind of it through some double-crossing spy in that intricate network of his. But what does Mazarin care about a past from which he emerged as the victor! The Cardinal was busy negotiating with the Spaniards about the reinstatement of Monsieur de Condé. That was hardly the moment to write one more crime on the slate which was about to be wiped clean. The Cardinal turned a deaf ear. They want to arrest the nobleman of Toulouse? Well, let them! The King is only too ready to follow the Cardinal's guidance, and he'd taken umbrage, anyhow, at your husband's wealth. It will be child's play to have him sign a *lettre de cachet* for the Bastille. . . ."

"But the King's brother?"

"The King's brother? Well, he too doesn't worry much about what Monsieur Fouquet tried to do to him when he was a child. The present alone counts for him, and for the present, Monsieur Fouquet sees that he's comfortable. He covers him with gold, goes out of his way to find him favourites. The Petit Monsieur was never much spoiled by his mother, nor by his brother. He trembles lest his protector be compromised. In short, the whole affair could have been managed neatly if only you hadn't turned up. They had been hoping that, once deprived of your husband's support, you'd disappear . . . without ado . . . no one knew where. No one would have wanted to know. Nobody ever wants to know the fate of a wife, when a nobleman falls into disgrace. Wives generally are tactful enough to vanish into thin air. Perhaps they go to a convent. Perhaps they change their name. You alone don't follow the general rule. You presume to demand justice! . . . This is the height of insolence, is it not? So, on two occasions, they try to kill you. Then, in despair, Fouquet plays the tempting demon. . . ."

Angélique heaved a deep sigh.

"It's overwhelming," she murmured. "Whichever way I turn, I see only enemies, hateful glances, envy, distrust, threats. . . ."

"Listen — perhaps all is not lost as yet," said Desgrez. "Fouquet offers you an honourable way out. They won't give you back your husband's fortune, but at least they'll set you up in comfort. What more do you want?"

"I want my husband!" shouted Angélique, rising with rage.

The lawyer looked at her ironically.

"You really are a very strange person."

"And you, you are a coward! In fact, you are shaking with fear like the rest of them."

"It is true that the life of a poor lawyer counts for little in the eyes of the mighty."

"Well, keep your little six-*sous* life! Keep it for the grocer who's robbed by his assistant, and for the disappointed heir. I don't need you."

The lawyer got up without replying, but took his time to smooth a crumpled piece of paper.

"This is the account of my expenses. You will see that I did not deduct anything for myself."

"Whether you are an honest man or a thief is a matter of indifference to me."

"One more bit of advice."

"I do not need your advice. I shall turn to my brother-in-law for what I need to know."

"Your brother-in-law is not at all keen to take sides in this affair. He has put you up in his home and recommended you to me because, if things turn out well, it'll redound to his glory. If not, he'll wash his hands of it, protesting his loyalty to the King's service. That's why I tell you one thing more: try to see the King."

He made a deep bow, put on his faded felt hat, then turned round again.

"If you need me, you can send for me at 'The Trois-Maillets' where I can be found every evening."

When he had gone, Angélique felt a sudden urge to cry. Now she was quite alone. She felt a thundering, stormy sky weighing on her, a gathering of clouds from all the corners of the horizon: Monseigneur de Frontenac's ambition, Fouquet's and Condé's fears, the Cardinal's inertia and, closer to her, the watchful misgivings of her brother-in-law and sister, ready to turn her out of their house at the least sign of trouble. . . .

In the vestibule, she met Hortense, with a white apron tied around her lean waist. The house was redolent with the smell of cooked strawberries and oranges. In September, good housewives make their preserves. It was a delicate and important operation, performed amid huge red copper basins, crushed sugar loaves and Barbe's tears. The house was upside down for three days.

Hortense, who was carrying a precious sugar-loaf, stumbled against Florimond, who was coming out of the kitchen, wildly waving his silver rattle with its three little bells and two crystal teeth. Nothing more was needed to make the thunderstorm break.

"Not only are we crowded out and compromised," gasped Hortense, "but on top of it I can't go about my work without being pushed about and deafened by an ear-splitting din. My head is bursting with migraine. And while I'm working myself to death, Madame receives her lawyer or gads about in the streets on the pretext of trying to free a dreadful husband whose fortune she's crying after."

"Don't scream so much," said Angélique. "There's nothing I'd like better than to help you make your jams. I know some very good southern recipes."

Hortense, sugar-loaf in hand, straightened herself to her full height, as if draping herself in the garments of a tragic actress.

"Never," she said fiercely, "never shall I allow you to put your hand to the food I cook for my husband and my children! I am not forgetting that you have a husband who is a devil's henchman, a spell-binder, a poison-maker. For all I know, you may have become his doomed soul. Gaston has changed since you've been here."

"Your husband? I haven't even looked at him."

"But he keeps looking at you . . . much more than is proper. You ought to understand that you are overstaying your welcome here. Originally you spoke of a single night. . . ."

"I assure you that I am trying to clear up the situation."

"All this running about will end in your attracting attention and you'll get yourself arrested as well."

"At this point, I am wondering whether I wouldn't be better off in prison. At least I'd be lodged free of charge and no fuss about it."

"You don't know what you are saying, my girl," sneered Hortense. "You have to pay ten *sols* per day, and they'd probably come to me, your only relative, to collect the money."

"That isn't so much. It's less than I am giving you. And that's taking no account of the dresses and jewels I gave you."

"With two children, it would come to thirty *sols* per day. . . ."

Angélique sighed with fatigue.

"Oh well, come on, Florimond," she said to the baby. "You can see you're tiring Aunt Hortense.

The fumes from her jam have gone to her head and make her mind wander."

The child rushed to her, waving his pretty rattle. This put the final spark to Hortense's smouldering rage.

"It's like this rattle," she cried. "Never did my children have anything like it. You keep complaining that you have no more money, and then you go and buy your son such an extravagant toy!"

"He wanted it so much. Besides, it wasn't so expensive. The cobbler's child at the corner has one just like it."

"Everybody knows that the common people don't know how to save money. They spoil their children and don't give them any education. Before you go buying extravagant stuff, don't forget that you are ruined and that I have no intention of paying your keep."

"I'm not asking you to," said Angélique, wincing. "As soon as Andijos returns, I'll go and stay at the inn."

Hortense shrugged her shoulders with a pitying laugh.

"Decidedly, you are even more stupid than I thought. You are completely ignorant of the laws and the way justice works. He won't bring you back anything, your Marquis d'Andijos."

Hortense's gloomy prediction turned out to be only too accurate. When the Marquis d'Andijos reappeared, followed by the faithful Kouassi-Ba, he informed Angélique that in Toulouse all the Comte's possessions were under seal. He had been able to bring back only a thousand *livres,* a loan made under a promise of secrecy by two of the prisoner's biggest tenant-farmers. Most of Angélique's jewelry, the gold and silver-plate, and the greater part of the valuables which the Palace of Gay Learning contained, including the gold and silver nuggets, had been seized and transported partly to Toulouse, partly to Montpellier.

Andijos seemed embarrassed. He was no longer voluble, had lost his usual geniality, and kept casting furtive glances all around. He also related that Toulouse was seething with unrest ever since the arrest of the Comte de Peyrac. Rumour having got about that the Archbishop was responsible for it, a veritable riot had broken out around the episcopal palace. The members of the Toulouse Parliament had come to see Andijos and had asked him to put himself at the head of a rebellion against the royal authority. The Marquis had had the greatest difficulties in leaving the town to get back to Paris.

"And what do you intend to do now?" asked Angélique.

"Stay in Paris for some time. My financial means, like yours, are limited, alas! I sold an old farm and a dovecot. Perhaps I'll be able to obtain a commission at Court. . . ."

His formerly bouncing accent was sagging woefully like a flag at half-mast.

"Oh! these southerners!" thought Angélique. "Great ones for swearing and laughing, but when misfortune descends on them, the fireworks fizzle out."

"I do not wish to compromise you," she said aloud. "Thank you for all your services, Monsieur d'Andijos. I wish you good luck at Court."

He kissed her hand in silence and withdrew somewhat shamefacedly. In the vestibule Angélique stared at the painted entrance-door of the proctor's house. How many servants had already left her by this door! With lowered eyes, but fleeing with relief from their disgraced mistress. . . . Kouassi-Ba squatted at her feet. She stroked his big, kinky head, and the giant gave her a child-like smile.

A thousand *livres* was something all the same. The following night, Angélique made up her mind to leave her sister's house where the atmosphere was becoming intolerable. She would take the little nurse-maid from Béarn and Kouassi-Ba with her. She would be able to find some modest inn. She still had some jewels left and her gold lamé dress. How much would she be able to get for it?

The baby she was expecting had begun to stir within her, but she hardly gave it a thought and it did not move her as Florimond had. After the first feeling of joy she had realized that the coming of a second child at such a time was almost a catastrophe. Anyhow, there was no point in looking too far ahead if she wanted to keep her courage.

The next day brought a ray of hope with the arrival from Mademoiselle de Montpensier's household of a page resplendent in a buff livery with gold and black velvet trimmings. Even Hortense was quite impressed. The Grande Mademoiselle asked Angélique to come and see her in the afternoon. The page specified that Mademoiselle was no longer at the Tuileries, but at the Louvre.

At the appointed hour, Angélique, trembling with impatience, passed over the bridge of Notre Dame. She had been on the verge of asking Hortense to lend her the wheeled chair called a *"vinaigrette"* in order to spare her last fairly expensive dress. But in view of her sister's sour attitude, she had given up the idea.

Angélique wore a two-tone dress of olive and pale green. She had wrapped herself in a plum-coloured silk cloak, for the moist wind blew forcefully in the narrow lanes and along the quays. Eventually she reached the massive palace, whose roofs and domes, topped by high, emblazoned chimneys, rose against a sultry sky.

Through the interior courtyard and up vast marble staircases, Angélique reached the apartment that had been indicated to her as Mademoiselle's. She could not help shivering as she found herself again in these long corridors, which were sinister despite their gold-encrusted ceilings, their flowered wainscoting and their precious hangings. But too much darkness stagnated in those recesses made for ambushes and foul play. A history of blood and terror loomed at every step in this old royal palace, although the Court of a very young King tried to rouse it to a little gaiety.

A Monsieur de Préfontaines informed Angélique that Mademoiselle was at her painter's studio in the great gallery and offered to lead the young woman there.

Angélique soon found herself in a sort of basement underneath the great gallery. Since Henri IV, these apartments had been reserved for artists and people exercising various crafts. Sculptors, painters, clockmakers, perfumers, engravers of precious stones, steel-swordsmiths, the most skilful gilders, damaskeeners, musical and scientific instrument-makers, upholsterers, librarians lived there with their families at the King's expense. Behind the heavy, varnished wooden doors could be heard the hammering of mauls and forges, the clatter of looms from the workshops specializing in high-warp tapestries and Turkish carpets, the dull thud of printing-presses.

The painter who was painting Mademoiselle de Montpensier's portrait was a Dutchman with a fair beard, fresh blue eyes in a face the colour of cooked ham. Van Ossel, a modest craftsman and a man of talent, parried the tantrums of the Court ladies with the fortress of a peaceful temper and a halting knowledge of French. If most of the mighty ones treated him familiarly, the way they would a servant or a workman, he nevertheless managed to make all this high society dance to his tune. Thus, he had insisted that Mademoiselle be painted with one breast bared, and actually he showed good judgment, for her bosom was the hefty spinster's best feature. Assuming that the picture was intended for some fresh suitor, one had to admit that the eloquence of this round, white, tempting object would happily complement the figure of her dowry and the nobility of her descent.

Mademoiselle was draped in opulent, dark blue velvet that fell in broken folds. She was covered with pearls and jewels, and, a rose in her fingers, she smiled at Angélique.

"I shall be with you in a moment, my pet. Van

565

Ossel, when will you at last put an end to my ordeal?"

The artist growled into his beard and, for form's sake, added a few touches of light to the single breast, object of his most tender cares. While a chambermaid was helping Mademoiselle to dress, the painter handed his brushes to a young boy who seemed to be his son and who was serving as his apprentice. He looked attentively at Angélique and her servant Kouassi-Ba. At last he removed his hat and bowed deeply.

"Would you, Madame, like me to paint your portrait? . . . Oh! Very beautiful! The luminous woman and the black Moor! The sun and the night. . . ."

Angélique declined the offer with a smile. The moment was not well chosen. But some day perhaps. . . .

She imagined the big picture that she would hang in the reception room of the hôtel in the Saint-Paul *quartier,* when she moved in victoriously with Joffrey de Peyrac. It gave her a new spurt of courage for the future.

As they were walking through the gallery on their way back to her apartments, the Grande Mademoiselle took Angélique's arm and spoke with her customary abruptness.

"My dear child, I was hoping, after some investigation, to bring you good news and to be able to tell you that it's all a misunderstanding about your husband. Some misunderstanding instigated by a soured courtier who was trying to curry favour with the King, or else some slander from an unsuccessful applicant for Monsieur de Peyrac's largesse . . . but I now fear the case may be somewhat long and complicated."

"For mercy's sake, Highness, what did you learn?"

"Let's go into my rooms, far from indiscreet ears."

When they had settled down side by side on a comfortable settee, Mademoiselle resumed:

"Actually, I learned very little, and if you discount the usual Court gossip, I must tell you that just this lack of information seems to me disquieting. People don't know anything or prefer not to."

Lowering her voice, she added with a trace of hesitation:

"Your husband is accused of witchcraft. That part is not too serious, and the matter could have been arranged without difficulty if your husband had been handed over to an ecclesiastical tribunal, as he should have been in view of the nature of the charge. I won't hide from you that I sometimes find churchmen rather annoying, but one must admit that their peculiar justice, when it comes to points that lie within their sphere, is for the most part upright and sensible. But the important fact is that despite this particular accusation, your husband has been handed over to the secular justice. Now about that justice I have no illusions. If it comes to a trial, which is not certain, the issue will depend entirely on the persons of the sworn judges."

"Do you mean to say, Highness, that the judges of the secular arm may show themselves partial?"

"It depends on those that are chosen."

"And who must choose them?"

"The King.

"Your husband must have knowledge of something. In any case, the King alone can intervene. Oh, he isn't easy to handle. He has been trained by Mazarin in Florentine diplomacy. One may see a smile on his face and even a tear in his eye, for he is soft-hearted . . . while he's preparing the dagger that will execute a friend."

Seeing Angélique go white, her protectress put an arm around her shoulder and said playfully:

"I am joking, as usual. You mustn't take me seriously. Nobody does any more. So I'll come to the point: do you want to see the King?"

And as Angélique, succumbing to the strain of this perpetual alternation of good and bad news, threw herself at the feet of the Grande Mademoiselle, they both dissolved in tears. Thereupon Mademoiselle de Montpensier informed her that the formidable appointment had already been fixed and that the King would receive Madame de Peyrac in two hours' time.

Far from being shattered by this news, Angélique felt imbued with utter calm. So this very day would be decisive.

There was no time to return to the Saint-Landry district, so she asked Mademoiselle to allow her to make use of the latter's powders and cosmetics in order to make herself presentable. Seated in front of the glass of the dressing-table, Angélique wondered whether she was still beautiful enough to influence the King in her favour. Her waist had grown bigger, but her face, which used to be childishly rounded, had grown thinner. There were dark rings round her eyes and her complexion was pale. After a stern scrutiny, she told herself that the oval curve of her face and the mauve shadows that enlarged her eyes were not unbecoming. They gave her a pathetic, touching expression which did not lack charm.

She made up very lightly, stuck a black velvet patch near her temple and let the chambermaid dress her hair. A little later, as she looked at herself in the mirror and saw her green eyes gleaming like a cat's in the night, she murmured:

"It's not me any more! But it's a beautiful woman, all the same. Oh! the King can't remain insensitive! But, alas, I am not humble enough for him. Dear God, let me be humble!"

Chapter 33

ANGÉLIQUE rose, with a throbbing heart, from her deep curtsey. The King was before her. His high heels of varnished wood made no sound on the thick woollen carpet. Angélique noticed that the door of the little study had closed again and that she was alone with the sovereign. She had a feeling of embarrassment, almost of panic. She had always seen the King amidst an innumerable throng. He had never seemed completely real and alive; he was like an actor on the stage of a theatre. Now she felt the presence of this rather husky man, who had about him the faint scent of the iris powder which he used to whiten his abundant brown hair. And this man was the King.

She forced herself to raise her eyes. Louis XIV was grave and impassive. He looked as if he were trying to remember the name of his visitor, although the Grande Demoiselle had announced her but a few moments earlier. Angélique felt paralysed by the coldness of his glance. She did not know that Louis XIV, though lacking the simplicity of his father Louis XIII, had inherited his shyness. A passionate lover of pomp and honours, he controlled as best he could a feeling of inferiority that ill-befitted the majesty of his rank. But, although married and very much of a gallant, he still could not approach a woman, and especially a lovely woman, without losing countenance.

And Angélique *was* lovely. Above all, she had a proud carriage and in her eyes, an expression that was at once reserved and bold. These eyes could at times transmit insolence, a challenge, but also the innocence of a very young and sincere person. Her smile transformed her, revealing the warmth of feeling she bore to her fellow-creatures and to life.

Just now, however, Angélique did not smile. She must wait for the King to speak and her throat contracted during this long, drawn-out silence.

At last the King spoke:

"Madame, I did not recognize you. Have you no longer the marvellous gold dress which you wore at Saint-Jean-de-Luz?"

"Unfortunately not, Sire, and I am ashamed to appear before you in such a plain and faded dress. But it's the only dress I am left with. Your Majesty is not unaware that all my possessions have been put under seal."

The King's face froze. Then, suddenly, he decided to smile.

"You come straight to the point, Madame. But, after all, you are right. You remind me that the minutes of a King are numbered and that he has no time to lose on trifling. You are, however, a little severe, Madame."

A delicate blush spread over the pale cheeks of the young woman and she smiled in confusion.

"Far be it from me to remind you, Sire, of the countless duties you are burdened with. I was merely answering your question. I would not like Your Majesty to think I was negligent in appearing before you in a worn dress and with such modest jewels."

"I did not give orders for your personal property to be seized. I even recommended that Madame de Peyrac be left free and not importuned in any way."

"I am infinitely grateful to Your Majesty for the attentions extended to my person," said Angélique, curtseying. "But I have no personal belongings, and in my haste to know what had become of my husband, I came to Paris with nothing but my clothes and a few jewels. But I have not come to complain to you of my poverty, Sire. My husband's fate is my only concern."

She fell silent, pressing her lips shut over the flood of questions she would have liked to pour out: Why have you arrested him? What do you reproach him with? When will you give him back to me?

571

Louis XIV gazed at her with unconcealed curiosity.

"Am I to understand, Madame, that you, who are so beautiful, are really in love with this crippled and repulsive husband?"

The sovereign's contemptuous tone cut Angélique to the quick. A dreadful pain filled her. Indignation made her eyes flash.

"How can you talk like that?" she cried hotly. "And yet you heard him, Sire? You heard the Golden Voice of the Kingdom!"

"It is true that his voice had a charm against which it was hard to defend oneself."

He came closer and said in an insinuating tone of voice:

"So it is true that your husband has the power of bewitching all women, even the most icy ones? I've been told this nobleman was so proud of his power that he boasted of it and even turned it into a sort of teaching, styled Courts of Love, and that the most shameless licentiousness was the rule at those fêtes."

"A good deal less shameless than what is going on right here at the Louvre," Angélique almost blurted out.

She checked herself with a great effort.

"The meaning of those fashionable parties has been wrongly interpreted to you, Your Majesty. My husband revived in his Palace of Gay Learning the medieval traditions of the southern minstrels, who had raised gallantry towards ladies to the height of an institution. The conversation, certainly, was light-hearted because it dealt with love, but decency was always preserved."

"Were you not jealous, Madame, to see your husband, whom you were so much in love with, indulge in debauchery?"

"I have never known him to indulge in debauchery in the way you mean, Sire. These traditions teach faithfulness to a single woman, wife or mistress, and I was the one he had chosen."

"It took you a long time, though, to bow to this choice. Why did your initial repugnance suddenly change into devouring love?"

"I see that Your Majesty takes an interest in the most intimate details of the life of his subjects," said Angélique, who was this time unable to check the ironical inflection of her voice.

She was seething with rage. Her mouth was bursting with scathing replies which she longed to hurl at his face. For instance: "Do the reports of your spies inform you each morning of the number of times that the lords of your kingdom have made love during the night?"

She restrained herself with difficulty and lowered her head for fear that her feelings might be read on her face.

"You did not answer my question, Madame," said the King in a freezing tone.

Angélique passed her hand over her brow.

"Why did I begin to love this man?" she murmured. "No doubt because he had all the qualities that make a woman happy to be the slave of such a man."

"So you recognize that your husband bewitched you?"

"I have lived at his side for five years, Sire. I am prepared to swear on the Gospel that he was neither a wizard nor a magician."

"You know that he is under a charge of witchcraft?"

She nodded silently.

"It is not only a question of the strange influence he exerts over women, but also of the suspicious origin of his immense wealth; it is said that he obtained the secret of the transmutation of gold by trafficking with Satan."

"Sire, may my husband be brought before a court of law and he will demonstrate with ease that he has been the victim of the erroneous conceptions of alchemists, led astray by their medieval tradition which in our days has become more harmful than useful."

The King relaxed a little.

"Admit, Madame, that neither you nor I know much about alchemy. I confess, however, that the explanations I have been given about Monsieur de Peyrac's devilish practices remain vague and call for more precision."

Angélique stifled a sigh of relief.

"I am so happy, Sire, to hear you utter words of such clemency and understanding."

The King smiled sourly and not without annoyance.

"Let us not anticipate, Madame. I merely said that I was asking for details about this tale of transmutations."

"Exactly, Sire. *There has never been any transmutation.* My husband perfected a process of dissolving the very fine gold content of certain rocks by means of molten lead, and by applying this method he made his fortune."

"If this was his fair and honest process, it would have been natural enough that he should offer its exploitation to his King, whereas in fact he never breathed a word of it to anybody."

"Sire, I am a witness that he made a complete demonstration of his process before several noblemen together with a representative of the Archbishop of Toulouse. But this process applies only to certain rocks in the Pyrénées that are called invisible gold-reefs, and it requires foreign specialists to extract them. It is not, therefore, a cabalistic formula that he can hand over, but a special science which requires a new kind of prospecting and considerable sums of money."

"He doubtless preferred to keep the working of this process for himself, since it not only made him rich but also offered him a pretext for receiving foreigners at his home — Spaniards, Germans, Englishmen, and heretics come from Switzerland. This made it very easy for him to prepare the rebellion of Languedoc."

"Sire, my husband never plotted against Your Majesty."

"He made, however, a show of arrogance and independence that were revealing, to say the least. You must admit, Madame, that for a gentleman never to ask anything of his King is not very normal to begin with. But when, in addition, he boasts that he has no need of his sovereign, that is really going too far."

Angélique felt shaken by a fever.

"Your husband wanted to create a State within the State," said the King harshly. "He had no religious faith either for, wizard or no, he claimed to rule by means of money and pageantry. Since his arrest Toulouse has been in turmoil and all Languedoc is stirring. Do not think, Madame, that I signed that warrant for his arrest without a more valid reason than a charge of witchcraft which, disturbing as it is, also carries with it other signs of disorderliness. I had convincing proof of his treason."

"Traitors see treason everywhere," said Angélique slowly, her green pupils flashing sparks. "If Your Majesty would name those who have slandered the Comte de Peyrac, I am certain I should find among them persons who, not so long ago, really did plot against the power and even the life of Your Majesty."

Louis XIV remained impassive, but his face darkened a little.

"You are very bold, Madame, to judge for me those in whom I am to place my confidence. Vicious animals that are tamed and chained are more useful to me than a distant, proud and free subject who might set himself up as my rival. Your husband's case will serve as an example to other noblemen who may be inclined to raise their heads too high. We shall see if, with all his gold, he'll be able to buy his judges, and if Satan will rescue him. It is my duty to defend the people against the pernicious influence of those great lords who want to be masters over bodies and souls and over the King himself."

"I ought to throw myself at his feet in tears," thought Angélique.

But she was incapable of it. The person of the King had lost its lustre in her eyes. All she saw

576

now was a boy of her own age — twenty-two years — whom she felt a terrible urge to seize by his lace ruffle and shake soundly like a plum-tree.

"So this is the King's justice," she said in a jerky voice that sounded strange in her ears. "You are surrounded by powdered murderers, by plumed bandits, by beggars pouring forth the basest flatteries. A Fouquet, a Condé, the Contis, Longuevilles, Beauforts . . . The man I love never betrayed you. He surmounted the most terrible adversities, he has fed the Royal Treasury with part of the wealth he earned thanks to his genius and at the cost of incessant toil and effort, and he never asked anyone for anything. And that is what he'll never be forgiven. . . ."

"That, in fact, is what he'll never be forgiven," echoed the King's voice.

He drew close to Angélique and gripped her arm with a violence that betrayed his anger despite the deliberate calm of his face.

"Madame, you will leave this room a free woman when I could easily have you arrested. Remember this in the future when you doubt the King's magnanimity. But be careful! I do not wish to hear of you again, for if I do, I'll be merciless. Your husband is my subject. Let the justice of the State be done. Farewell, Madame."

Chapter 34

"ALL is lost! . . . It's my fault! I've lost Joffrey,"
Angélique kept repeating to herself.

With a wild look, she ran through the corridors
of the Louvre. She was looking for Kouassi-Ba!
She wanted to see the Grande Mademoiselle! . . .
In vain, her anguished heart cried out for help.
The figures she passed were deaf and blind, un-
substantial puppets from another world.

Darkness fell, bringing with it an October storm
that lashed the window-panes, beat down the
flickering candle-flames, whistled under the
doors, and stirred the draperies. Colonnades,
stone-masks, the solemn shadows of giant staircases, gilt wainscots, bridges and galleries, tiled
floors, pier glasses, mouldings — Angélique
roamed through the Louvre as through a gloomy
forest, a fatal labyrinth.

In the hope of finding Kouassi-Ba, she went
downstairs and reached one of the courtyards. She
had to retreat before the rainstorm which cascaded
from the drainpipes with the roar of a mountain
torrent. Below stairs, a troupe of Italian comedians,
who were to dance before the King that night,
had taken refuge around a brazier. The red glow
of the hearth lit the gaudy-coloured costumes of
the harlequins with their black masks, the white
disguises of Pantaloon and his clowns.

Back upstairs, Angélique at last saw a familiar

face. It was Brienne. He told her that he had seen Monsieur de Préfontaines in the apartments of the young Princess Henriette of England; perhaps he might be able to tell her where she could find Mademoiselle de Montpensier.

At Princess Henriette's, gambling for high stakes was going on at all the tables in the gay, warm glow spread by the wax candles that lit the large drawing-room. Angélique noticed Andijos, Péguilin, d'Humières and de Guiche. They were absorbed in the game or else pretended not to see her. Monsieur de Préfontaines, who was sipping a glass of liqueur by the fireside, told her that Mademoiselle de Montpensier had gone to play cards with the young Queen in the apartments of Anne of Austria. Her Majesty the Queen Maria-Theresa, tired, shy and still speaking bad French, did not care to mingle with the overweening young people at Court. Every evening, Mademoiselle went to play a set with her. Mademoiselle was very kind; however, as the little Queen retired early, it was quite possible that Mademoiselle would soon be dropping in at her cousin Henriette's. In any case, she would send for Monsieur de Préfontaines since she never went to sleep without having first checked her accounts with him.

Having decided to wait for her, Angélique approached a table where the officers in charge of the royal food had set out a cold supper and pastries. She was always quite ashamed of her hearty appetite, which asserted itself even in the grimmest circumstances. Encouraged by Monsieur de Préfontaines, she sat down and ate a chicken-wing, two jellied eggs, and various tarts and jams. Then, after asking a page for a silver ewer to rinse her fingers, she joined a party of gamblers and took cards. She had a little money with her. Soon fortune smiled on her and she began to win. It comforted her. If she could line her purse, the day would not have been a total fiasco, after all. She concentrated on the game. Stacks of *écus* piled up before her. One of her neighbours who was losing, said half-jokingly, half-seriously:

"No wonder: it's the little witch."

Deftly she raked in his stakes and only grasped his meaning a few seconds later. So Joffrey's disgrace was beginning to be common knowledge. It was being whispered from ear to ear that he was accused of witchcraft. Angélique, however, resolutely stayed in her seat.

"I shall not leave the table until I begin to lose. Oh! if only I could ruin them all and have gold enough to buy the judges. . . ."

As she threw down three insolent aces, a hand slipped around her waist and pinched her.

"Why have you come back to the Louvre?" whispered the Marquis de Vardes into her ear.

"Certainly not to see you again," answered Angélique, without giving him a look.

And she freed herself brusquely.

He took up some cards and arranged them mechanically, while continuing in the same low tone:

"You are mad! Do you absolutely insist on being murdered?"

"What I want or don't want is no concern of yours."

He played, lost, put a new stake on the table.

"Listen, there is still time. Follow me. I shall give you an escort of Swiss guards to accompany you home."

This time, she looked at him with contempt.

"I have no confidence in your protection, Monsieur de Vardes, and you know why."

He threw down his cards with ill-concealed temper.

"Oh! I am a fool to worry about you."

He hesitated again, then made an ugly face and muttered:

"You're making me look ridiculous. But since there is no other way of bringing you to your senses, I'll tell you: think of your son. Leave the Louvre at once and, above all, keep away from the King's brother!"

"I shall not move from this table as long as you are about," retorted Angélique, very calmly.

The nobleman's hands clenched. But he suddenly rose from the gaming-table.

"Very well, I am leaving. Hurry and do likewise. Your life's at stake."

She saw him move away, bowing to the right and the left as he left the room.

Angélique stayed on, perturbed. She could not dispel a feeling of fright that was crawling into her like a cold serpent. Was Vardes setting a new trap for her? He was capable of anything. Yet there had been an unfamiliar note in the voice of the cynical Marquis. His mention of Florimond suddenly overwhelmed her. She had a fleeting vision of the adorable little fellow, in his red hood, toddling in his long, embroidered dress, his silver rattle in his hand. What would become of him if she should vanish?

The young woman left the game, slipping the gold pieces into her purse. She had won fifteen hundred *livres*. She picked up her coat from the back of an armchair, curtseyed to Princess Henriette who responded with an indifferent nod of her head.

Regretfully, Angélique left the room, a haven of light and warmth. A cold draught slammed the door behind her. The whistling wind prostrated the flickering candle-flames which seemed to be fluttering in a mad panic. Shadows and flames fidgeted, as if tossed by fear. Then the calm returned, as the wind went to howl farther away, and in the long silent vista of corridors nothing stirred.

After asking directions from the Swiss guard posted outside Princess Henriette's apartment, Angélique walked quickly, tightly wrapping her cloak around her. She tried hard not to be afraid, but each corner seemed to conceal suspicious forms. As she approached the angle of the corridor, she slowed down. An insurmountable anguish paralysed her.

"They're there," she told herself.

She did not see anyone, but a shadow fell across the floor. This time there could be no doubt: a man was lying in wait. . . .

Angélique stopped. Something stirred in the angle of the wall, and a figure wrapped in a dark cloak, hat pulled deep down over the eyes, slowly emerged and barred her way. She bit her lips to stifle a cry, then promptly turned round and retraced her steps. She cast a glance over her shoulder. Now there were three of them, and *they were*

582

following her. The young woman walked more quickly. But the three men were drawing closer. Then she began to run.

She had no need to turn round to know that *they* were running after her. She could hear behind her their hurrying footfalls. *They* were running on tiptoe. It was a soundless, unreal chase, a nightmare race through the empty vastness of the palace.

Suddenly, Angélique perceived a half-open door on her right. She had just passed a turning of the corridor. Her pursuers were no longer in sight. She burst into the room, closed the door behind her, slid the bolt home. Leaning against the doorpost, more dead than alive, she heard the hurrying feet of the men, their panting breath. Then silence fell again.

Reeling with emotion, Angélique went to lean against the bed. The room was empty, but someone would doubtless be coming soon. The bedsheets were turned down for the night. A fire glowed in the hearth and lit the room, as did a small oil-lamp placed on the bedside table.

With a hand over her bosom, Angélique tried to catch her breath.

"I simply must get out of this hornet's nest," she told herself.

She had been foolhardy to imagine, after escaping from one attempt on her life in the corridors of the Louvre, that she would be able to escape a second time. Naturally, in asking her to come to the Louvre, the Grande Mademoiselle had been unaware of the danger Angélique would be running. She was convinced that the King himself had no suspicion of what was being hatched inside his own palace. But Fouquet's hidden presence ruled over the Louvre. Trembling lest Angélique's secret might spell the ruin of his astounding fortune, the Controller had roused Philippe d'Orléans — the Petit Monsieur — and had thrown fear into the hearts of those who opposed him, while fawning on the King. The arrest of the Comte de Peyrac was one stage, the disappearance of Angélique completed the prudent stratagem. Only the dead don't talk.

Her eyes roved all over the room, looking for some way of escape which would not attract attention.

Suddenly her eyes bulged with terror.

The curtain just in front of her had stirred. She heard a latch creak. A concealed door opened very slowly and in the aperture appeared the three men who had pursued her.

She had no difficulty in recognizing the one who stepped forward: Monsieur, the King's brother.

He tossed away his conspirator's cloak and puffed out the lace of his ruffle with a flick of his finger. He never took his eyes off her, while a cold smile drew back his small, red-lipped mouth.

"Perfect!" he exclaimed in his falsetto voice. "The doe has fallen into the trap. But what a chase! You can boast of being light-footed, Madame."

Angélique armed herself with composure and, though her legs were giving way, she dropped a curtsey.

"So it was you, Monseigneur, who scared me so? I thought I was up against some rogues or cut-purses of the Pont-Neuf who'd managed to slip into the palace bent on mischief."

"Oh! I've had occasion to play the brigand at night on the Pont-Neuf, too," declared the little Monsieur smugly, "and nobody has to teach me how to cut a purse or pierce a citizen's paunch. Isn't that so, my dear?"

He turned towards one of his companions. The latter pushed his hat back, and revealed the features of the Chevalier de Lorraine. Without answering, the favourite stepped forward and drew his sword which gleamed with a reddish glint in the fire-light.

Angélique gazed attentively at the third, who kept a little in the background.

"Clément Tonnel," she said at last, "what are you doing here, my friend?"

The man bowed very low.

"I am at Monseigneur's command," he replied.

He added, carried away by force of habit:

"May Her Ladyship excuse me."

"I gladly excuse you," said Angélique, who felt a nervous urge to laugh, "but why are you holding a pistol in your hand?"

The major-domo glanced with embarrassment at his weapon. Nevertheless, he drew closer to the bed on which Angélique was leaning.

Philippe d'Orléans had pulled out the drawer of the little bedside table. He took out of it a glass half filled with a blackish liquid.

"Madame," he said solemnly, "you are going to die."

"Am I?" asked Angélique.

She looked at the three of them standing before

her. She had the feeling of being split into two different beings. Deep within her, a fear-crazed woman was wringing her hands and crying: "Have pity, I don't want to die!" Another woman was reflecting lucidly: "They really look ridiculous. All this is just a bad joke."

"Madame, you have flouted us," went on the Petit Monsieur, his mouth screwed up with impatience. "You are going to die, but we are generous: we leave you the choice of your death: poison, sword, or pistol."

A gust of wind shook the door violently and filled the room with acrid smoke. Angélique lifted her head hopefully.

"Oh! no one will come, no one will come!" said the King's brother with a smirk. "This bed is your death-bed, Madame. It has been prepared for you."

"But after all, what have I done to you?" cried Angélique, who began to feel the sweat of fear moistening her temples. "You talk of my death as if it were a natural, indispensable matter. Will you not allow me to share your view? The worst criminal is entitled to know what he is charged with and to defend himself."

"Even the ablest defence won't alter the verdict, Madame."

"Well, if I must die, at least tell me why," insisted the young woman vehemently.

The young Prince threw a questioning glance at his companion.

"Well, after all, since in a few moments you will have ceased to exist, I don't see why we should show ourselves unnecessarily inhuman," he said in his sugary voice. "Madame, you are not as ignorant as you pretend. You are perfectly aware at whose orders we are here."

"The King's?" cried Angélique, with a show of feigned respect.

Philippe d'Orléans shrugged his frail shoulders.

"The King is barely capable of dispatching to prison people against whom his jealousy has been roused. No, Madame. His Majesty has nothing to do with it."

"From whom, then, can the King's brother consent to receive orders?"

The Prince winced.

"I find you very bold, Madame, to talk in this way. You're insulting me!"

"And I find, for my part, that you are all rather touchy in your family!" retorted Angélique, whose anger was getting the better of her terror. "When you are being fêted or made much of, you take offence because the one who receives you seems richer than you are! When you're being offered gifts, it's insolence! When someone doesn't bow to you deeply enough, it's another! When one doesn't live like a beggar, stretching out one's hand till the State is ruined, the way your farmyard of lordlings does, it's considered rank arrogance! When one pays taxes cash down to the last farthing, it's a provocation! . . . A gang of petty pilferers, that's what you are, you, your brother, your mother, and all your treacherous cousins: Condé, Montpensier, Soissons, Guise, Lorraine, Vendôme. . . ."

She stopped, out of breath.

Rearing on his high heels like a young cock on

his hackles, Philippe d'Orléans threw an indignant glance at his favourite.

"Have you ever heard anyone talk of the royal family with such insolence?"

The Chevalier de Lorraine gave a cruel smile.

"Insults don't kill, Monseigneur. Come, let's put an end to it, Madame."

"I want to know why I am to die," said Angélique doggedly.

Determined to risk anything to gain a few minutes she quickly added:

"Is it on account of Monsieur Fouquet?"

The King's brother could not help smiling with satisfaction.

"So your memory is returning? You know, therefore, why Monsieur Fouquet has his heart set on silencing you?"

"I know only one thing, and that is that years ago I foiled a poison plot which was intended to get rid of you, Monsieur, as well as of the King and the Cardinal. And I bitterly regret that, as a result, the efforts of the Monsieur Fouquet and the Prince de Condé were not successful."

"So you confess?"

"I have nothing to confess. The treachery of this valet has fully informed you of what I knew and confided to my husband. I once saved your life, Monseigneur, and this is how you thank me!"

A fleeting emotion appeared on the effeminate face of the young man.

"Bygones are bygones," he said hesitantly. "Monsieur Fouquet has since lavished his kindness on me. It is only right that I should help him to remove a threat that is hanging over him. Truly,

Madame, I am heartbroken, but it is too late. Why did you not accept the reasonable proposal Monsieur Fouquet made to you through the intermediary of Madame de Beauvais?"

"Because I understand that I would have to abandon my husband to his sad fate."

"Naturally. You cannot silence a Comte de Peyrac except by walling him up in a prison. But a woman, surrounded by luxury and compliments, soon forgets things that have to be forgotten. At any rate, it is too late now. Come, Madame. . . ."

"And if I told you where that casket is," suggested Angélique, gripping him by the shoulders, "you, Monseigneur, you alone would then hold in your hands the formidable power of frightening, of dominating Monsieur Fouquet himself, to say nothing of the proof of the treason of so many great lords who look down upon you, who don't take you seriously. . . ."

A light gleamed in the eyes of the young Prince, and he passed his tongue over his lips. But the Chevalier de Lorraine gripped him and pulled him aside as if he wanted to wrench him from Angélique's evil power.

"Take care, Monseigneur. Don't be tempted by this woman. By lying promises she is trying to escape us, to delay her execution. It is better that she should take her secret with her to the grave. If you owned it, you would probably be very powerful, but your days would be numbered."

Leaning on his favourite's arm, Philippe d'Orléans was pondering.

"You are right, as always, dear love," he sighed. "Well, let's do our duty. Madame, which do you choose: poison, sword, or pistol?"

"Make up your mind fast!" cut in the Chevalier de Lorraine threateningly. "Or else we'll choose for you."

After a moment of flickering hope, Angélique had again fallen into a cruelly hopeless situation.

The three men stood before her. She could not make a move without being stopped by the Chevalier's sword or Clément's pistol. No bell-rope was within her reach. No sound came from outside. Only the logs sizzling in the hearth and the rain pelting against the windows broke the stifling silence. In a few seconds, her murderers would hurl themselves upon her. Angélique's eyes rested on their weapons. With the pistol or the sword, she was sure to die. But perhaps she might escape the poison? For over a year now she had absorbed each day a minute dose of the toxic products which Joffrey had prepared for her.

She held out her hand and tried to prevent it from trembling.

"The poison!" she murmured.

Lifting the glass to her lips, she noticed that a sediment of metallic brilliance had formed at the bottom. She took care not to stir up the liquid while she drank it. It had an acrid, pungent taste.

"And now leave me alone," she said, placing the glass on the table.

She felt no pain. "Probably," she told herself, "the food I took at Princess Henriette's is still protecting the walls of my stomach . . . ." She had not lost all hope of escaping from her tormentors and avoiding a horrible death.

She sank to her knees at the Prince's feet.

"Monseigneur, have pity on my soul. Send me a priest. I shall die. I am already too weak to drag myself along. You are now certain that I shall not escape you. Don't let me die unconfessed. God could never forgive you the infamy of having deprived me of the succour of religion."

She began to cry in a heart-rending voice:

"A priest! A priest! God won't forgive you."

She saw Clément Tonnel turn away and cross himself, blanching.

"She is right," said the Prince in a troubled tone of voice. "We'd gain nothing by depriving her of the consolations of religion. Calm yourself, Madame. I had foreseen your request. I shall send you a chaplain who is waiting in the next room."

"Gentlemen, withdraw," implored Angélique, exaggerating the weakness of her voice and carrying her hand to her stomach as if she were writhing in a spasm of pain. "All I wish to think of now is putting my conscience at rest. I feel too strongly that, if but one of you were to remain, here under my eyes, I'd be incapable of forgiving my enemies. Ah! how I suffer! Pity, my God!"

She flung herself backward with a horrible groan.

Philippe d'Orléans pulled the Chevalier de Lorraine away.

"Let's go quickly. She's only got a few moments more."

The major-domo had already left the room.

No sooner had they gone than Angélique rose to her feet and leaped to the window. She managed to open it, caught a gust of rain in the face, and peered into the black depth. She could not see anything at all and was unable to gauge at what distance she was from the ground, but without hesitation she climbed over the window-sill.

The fall seemed endless to her. She landed with a brutal jolt in a sort of cesspool into which she sank, but which probably saved her from breaking a limb. A shooting pain in her ankle made her think for a moment that she had broken it; but it was only a sprain.

Keeping close to the wall, Angélique took a few steps, then inserted the end of one of her curls into her throat and managed to vomit several times. She was unable to make out where she was. Groping along the walls, she was horrified to realise that she had jumped into a small interior courtyard filled with refuse and filth, where she still ran the risk of being caught.

Fortunately, her fingers came across a door that was unlocked. Inside, it was dark and damp. A smell of wine drifted towards her. She must be in the outbuildings of the Louvre near the wine-cellars. She decided to go back upstairs. She would ask for help from the first guard she happened to meet. . . . But the King would have her arrested and thrown into prison. Oh! how to get out of this mouse-trap?

Meanwhile she had reached the inhabited parts of the palace and heaved a sigh of relief. A few steps away she recognized the Swiss guard on duty outside Princess Henriette's door, the one of whom she had asked the way earlier in the evening. At the some moment, her nerves got the better of her and she uttered a shriek of terror, for at the other end of the corridor she saw the Chevalier de Lorraine and Philippe d'Orléans coming at a run, swords in hand. They must have known the only way out of the courtyard into which their victim had thrown herself, and they were trying to cut off her retreat.

Rushing past the guard on duty, Angélique dived into the drawing-room and threw herself at the feet of Princess Henriette.

"Have pity, Madame, have pity, they want to murder me!"

A cannon-ball could not have shattered that brilliant gathering more effectively. All the players rose as one, staring dumbfounded at the young woman who, dishevelled, drenched, in a mud-bespattered, torn dress, had collapsed in their midst.

Angélique, all her strength spent, cast wild, hunted eyes around her. She recognized the faces of Andijos and of Péguilin de Lauzun.

"Gentlemen, save me!" she begged. "They have just tried to poison me. They are after me to kill me."

"But who are your would-be assassins, my poor dear?" inquired the gentle voice of Henriette of England.

"There!"

Unable to say more, Angélique pointed towards the door.

Everybody turned round.

The Petit Monsieur, the King's brother, and his favourite, the Chevalier de Lorraine, were standing on the threshold. They had sheathed their swords and were affecting an air of pained compunction.

"My poor Henriette," said Philippe d'Orléans,

approaching his cousin with mincing steps, "I am so sorry about this incident. This unfortunate woman is mad."

"I am not mad. I tell you that they want to kill me."

"But surely, my dear, you must be raving," the Princess tried to appease her. "The person whom you are pointing out as your murderer, is none other than Monseigneur d'Orléans. Look at him well."

"I looked at him only too well!" cried Angélique. "I shan't forget his face as long as I live. I tell you that he wanted to poison me. Monsieur de Préfontaines, you who are an honest man, bring me some medicine, some milk, anything, so that I can counteract the effects of this horrible poison. I beg of you . . . Monsieur de Préfontaines!"

Stuttering, bemused, the poor man rushed towards a table and offered the young woman a nostrum of some kind, which she hastened to eat.

The uproar was at its height.

Monsieur was still trying to make himself heard, his little mouth pursed with annoyance.

"I assure you, my friends, that this woman has lost her wits. None of you is unaware that her husband is at present in the Bastille for a dreadful crime: the crime of witchcraft. This unfortunate woman, infatuated by this scandalous gentleman, is trying to assert his innocence and that is rather hard to prove. Vainly did His Majesty try to convince her today in the course of an interview full of kindness . . ."

"Oh! the King's kindness, The King's kindness! . . ." said Angélique, exasperated.

In another moment, her mind would begin to wander . . . that would be the end of her! She buried her face in her hands, tried to recover her calm. She heard the Petit Monsieur say in his candid adolescent voice:

"She was suddenly seized by a truly diabolical fit. She is possessed by the demon. The King immediately sent for the prior of the Augustine convent to endeavour to calm her by ritual prayers. But she managed to run away. To avoid the scandal of having to apprehend her with his own guards, His Majesty instructed me to try and find her and detain her until the friar arrives. I am so sorry, Henriette, that she should have upset your soirée. I think the wisest course would be for all of you to retire into the next room with your cards, while I discharge here the task entrusted to me by my brother."

Angélique saw, as in a fog, the serried ranks of lords and ladies dissolve around her. Impressed, and anxious not to displease the King's brother, they were all withdrawing.

Angélique raised her hands, felt the material of a dress which her fingers were powerless to clasp.

"Madame," she said in a toneless voice, "you are not going to let me die?"

The Princess wavered. She cast an anxious glance at her cousin.

"Why, Henriette," he protested sadly, "you don't trust me? When we have already exchanged pledges of mutual confidence and when we shall soon be united by sacred bonds?"

The blonde Henriette lowered her head.

"Trust in Monseigneur, my friend," she said

to Angélique. "I am convinced he wants only to help you."

And quickly she walked away.

In a sort of delirium that made her speechless with fear, Angélique, still kneeling on the carpet, turned towards the door through which the courtiers had so swiftly disappeared. She saw Bernard d'Andijos and Péguilin de Lauzun who, as pale as death, could not make up their minds to leave the room.

"Well, gentlemen," said Monseigneur d'Orléans in his shrill voice, "my orders concern you as well. Shall I report to the King that you accord more credence to the ravings of a madwoman than to the words of his own brother?"

The two men dropped their heads and slowly left the room. This supreme desertion roused Angélique's fighting spirit.

"Cowards! Cowards! Oh, cowards!" she cried, bounding to her feet and rushing behind an armchair for protection.

She only just dodged a stroke from the Chevalier de Lorraine's sword. Another stroke touched her shoulder and drew blood.

"Andijos, Péguilin, Gascons! Save me from the northerners!"

The door of the next room suddenly opened. Lauzun and the Marquis d'Andijos rushed forward with bared swords. They had been lying in wait behind the door left ajar, and now they could no longer doubt the horrible designs of the King's brother and his favourite.

D'Andijos, with a single stroke, knocked the sword out of Philippe d'Orléans's hand and slashed his wrist. Lauzun was crossing blades with the Chevalier de Lorraine.

Andijos seized Angélique's hand.

"Quickly!"

He pulled her along the corridor, running into Clément Tonnel, who did not have time to make use of his pistol. Andijos planted his blade in the other's throat. The man collapsed in a gush of blood.

Then the Marquis and the young woman raced along as fast as they could. Behind them, the Petit Monsieur's falsetto voice was alerting the Swiss guards:

"Guards! Guards! Catch them!"

The noise of running foot-steps mingling with the clatter of halberds rose in their wake.

"The great gallery . . ." panted Andijos, "to the Tuileries . . . the stables, the horses! Then, the country . . . Saved . . ."

Despite his paunch, the Gascon ran with a stamina Angélique would never have suspected. But she could keep up with him no longer. Her ankle hurt her dreadfully, her shoulder was smarting.

"I am going to fall!" she gasped, "I'm going to fall!"

At that moment, they passed before the great staircase leading into the courtyards.

"Down there," said Andijos, "and hide as best you can. I shall try and lead them as far away as possible."

In headlong flight, Angélique raced down the stone steps. The glow from a brazier made her recoil. She collapsed.

Harlequin, Columbine, Pierrot pulled her into

their shelter, concealed her as well as they could. For a long while, the big green and red lozenges of their costumes twinkled before the eyes of the young woman before she sank into a deep swoon.

Chapter 35

A green, mellow light bathed Angélique. She had just opened her eyes. She was at Monteloup, under the foliage by the river, where the sun reached her through a verdant veil. She heard her brother Gontran saying:

"The greenness of the plants is something I'll never capture. At best, by treating calamine with cobalt salt from Persia, you get an approximate shade, but it's a thick, opaque green. Nothing like the luminous emerald of the leaves above a brook. . . ."

Gontran's voice had grown thick, and hoarse, yet she recognized the sulky tone he always assumed when he talked of his paints and pictures. How many times, gazing into his sister's eyes with a kind of rancour, had he muttered: "The greenness of the plants is something I'll never capture."

A burning ache in the pit of her stomach gripped Angélique. She remembered that something terrible had happened.

"Good God!" she thought, "my little baby is dead!"

He was certainly dead! He could not have survived so many horrors. He had died when she had jumped out of the window into that black abyss. Or when she had raced through the corridors of the Louvre. . . . The panic of that mad chase still shook her limbs with fever; her heart, which had been strained to breaking-point, still seemed in pain. Summoning all her strength, she managed to move one of her hands and place it on her belly. A soft quiver responded to her pressure.

"Oh! he's still there, he's alive! What a valiant little companion!" she thought, with pride and tenderness.

The baby stirred inside her like a little frog. She felt the round head under her fingers. She was recovering her senses gradually, and realised that she was actually in a large bed with twisted columns, through whose serge curtains seeped a sea-green light that had reminded her of the banks of the river at Monteloup.

She was not at Hortense's place in the rue de l'Enfer. Where was she? Her memories remained dim; she only had the feeling of dragging with her, like a huge dark lump, she knew not what frightful drama of black poison, flashing swords, fear and clinging mud.

Gontran's voice rose again:

"Never, never will we catch the greenness of water under trees."

This time, Angélique almost uttered a cry. She must be mad, or dreadfully ill? . . .

She sat up and pulled the curtains aside. The spectacle before her eyes confirmed her conviction that she had lost her reason.

Before her on a kind of dais lay a fair, pink,

half-naked goddess holding a straw basket of luscious clusters of golden grapes whose shoots spread exuberantly over velvet cushions. A stark-naked little Cupid, adorably rounded, with a wreath of flowers sitting awry on his fair curls, was nibbling at the grapes with great gusto. Suddenly the little god sneezed several times. The goddess looked at him with concern and said a few words in a strange tongue, which was no doubt the language of Olympus.

Someone moved in the room, and a red-haired, bearded giant, dressed quite simply like a contemporary craftsman, stepped over to Eros, picked him up in his arms and wrapped him in a woollen coat. At the same moment, Angélique noticed the easel of the painter Van Ossel. Near him stood a workman in a leather apron, laden with two palettes splashed with a medley of gaudy colours. The workman, his head slightly cocked to one side, was gazing at his master's unfinished painting. Pale daylight fell on his face. He was an ordinary-looking fellow of medium size with a coarse linen shirt open on his tanned chest, brown hair carelessly cut to shoulder-length with a dishevelled fringe that half hid his dark eyes. But Angélique would have recognized that sullen lip anywhere, not to mention that rebellious nose and the jovial, heavy chin which reminded her of her father, Baron Armand.

She cried:

"Gontran!"

"The lady is awake!" exclaimed the goddess.

And the whole group, its number swollen by five or six children, promptly crowded around the bedside. The workman seemed dumbfounded. He stared amazed at Angélique who was smiling at him. Suddenly, he blushed crimson, gripped her hand in his and murmured:

"My sister!"

The opulent goddess, who was none other than Van Ossel's wife, called out to her daughter to bring an egg-nog which she had prepared in the kitchen.

"I am glad," said the Dutchman, "I am glad to have obliged not only a lady in distress but also my companion's sister."

"But why am I here?" asked Angélique.

The Dutchman related in his gruff voice how, the night before, an insistent knocking at the door of their lodgings had awakened them. In the light of a candle the Italian comedians in satin rags had held out to them an unconscious woman, blood-soaked and half-dead, and they had begged them in their excited Italian tongue to save the unfortunate creature. In the placid Dutch tongue the answer had come: "She is welcome here!"

Gontran and Angélique looked at each other now with some embarrassment. Wasn't it eight years ago that they'd parted at the approaches to Poitiers? Angélique remembered Raymond and Gontran as they disappeared on horseback along the steep lanes. Gontran, perhaps, was conjuring up the vision of the old carriage in which the three dusty little girls were closely packed.

"The last time I saw you," he said, "you were with Hortense and Madelon, and you were going to the Ursuline convent in Poitiers."

"Yes. Madelon died — you know?"

"Yes, I know."

"You remember, Gontran? You used to paint old Guillaume's portrait."

"Old Guillaume is dead."

"Yes, I know."

"I still have his portrait. I did an even better one . . . from memory. I'll show it to you."

He had sat down on the edge of the bed, his hands spread open on his leather apron — big hands stained and encrusted with red and blue, corroded by the chemical products which were used to mix the colours, and calloused by the pestle of the mortar in which, from morning to night, he ground the red lead, ochres and litharges, mixed with oils or with muriatic acid.

"But however did you come to land in this trade?" questioned Angélique with a shade of pity in her voice.

Gontran's touchy nose — the Sancé nose — quivered, and his brow clouded over.

"Fool!" he said bluntly. "If I landed in it, as you say, it's because I wanted to. Oh! my stock of Latin is complete, and the Jesuits spared no pains to turn me into a young lord, able to continue the family name, since Josselin has run away to America and Raymond has entered the famous Society. But I too had my own ideas. I fell out with our father, who wanted me to go into the army to serve the King. He told me that he wouldn't give me a *sou*. So I set out on foot like a beggar, and I became a craftsman in Paris. I am finishing my years of apprenticeship. Afterwards, I shall start my tour of France. I shall wander from town to town to instruct myself in all that's being taught about the painter's and engraver's crafts. For a livelihood, I shall hire myself out to painters or else do the portraits of the well-to-do townsfolk. And later I'll buy a mastership. I shall become a great painter, I am sure of it, Angélique! And perhaps I'll be commissioned to paint the ceilings of the Louvre . . ."

"You'll cover them with hell-fire and grimacing devils!"

"No, I'd cover them with the vaulted blue sky, with sun-touched clouds, and emerging among them the King in all his glory."

"The King in all his glory . . ." echoed Angélique in a small, tired voice.

She closed her eyes. She suddenly felt older than this young man, though he was her elder brother. He had known hunger and cold, to be sure, he had been humiliated, but he had never ceased striding towards his dream.

"And I?" she said. "You don't ask me how I landed where I am."

"I daren't question you," he said, embarrassed. "I know that, against your wish, you married a frightful and redoubtable man. Our father rejoiced in this marriage, but we all pitied you, my poor Angélique. So you've been very unhappy?"

"No. It's now that I'm unhappy."

She wavered on the brink of confiding in him. Why should she trouble this boy who was indifferent to all that wasn't his enchanted labour? How often had he dreamed of his little sister Angélique? Rarely, no doubt, and then only when he grieved at not being able to reproduce the greenness of the leaves. He had never needed anyone else.

"I am staying with Hortense here in Paris," she said.

"Hortense? What a shrew! When I arrived, I made an effort to see her, but what a litany I had to put up with! She died of shame to see me come into her home with my rough shoes. I wasn't even carrying a sword any more! There was nothing to distinguish me from a coarse craftsman! That's true. Can you see me carrying a sword with my leather apron? And if I, a nobleman, like to paint, do you think that prejudices of that sort are going to stop me? I kick them out of my way with my foot."

"I believe we are all cut out to be rebels," said Angélique with a sigh.

She took her brother's calloused hand affectionately in hers.

"You must have gone through a lot of hardship?"

"No more than I'd have gone through in the army, with a sword at my side, debts up to my ears, and usurers at my heels. I expect no pension from the good temper of a distant overlord. My master can't cheat me, for the guild protects me. When life gets a little too difficult, I sometimes nip over to the Temple, to our brother, the Jesuit, to ask him for a few *écus*."

"Raymond is in Paris?" exclaimed Angélique.

"Yes, he's living at the Temple, but he's the almoner of I know not how many converts, and I should not even be surprised if he became the confessor of some high personages at Court."

Angélique pondered. Raymond's help was what

she needed. An ecclesiastic who would, perhaps, take the matter to heart, because it was a family matter . . .

Despite the still smarting memories of the dangers she had run, despite the King's words, it never occurred to Angélique for a moment to give up. She only knew that she must act with extreme caution.

"Gontran," she said in a resolute voice, "you'll take me to the inn of 'The Trois-Maillets.' "

Gontran made no fuss about Angélique's decision. Hadn't she always been a character?

The painter Van Ossel advised waiting for nightfall, or at least till dusk. His wife lent Angélique one of her short petticoats with a dark beige bodice of simple cloth — dry rose, the colour was called. She tied over her hair a black satin kerchief, like those that the town women wore. Angélique was amused to feel the skirt, which was shorter than those of noble ladies, flap around her ankles.

When, in Gontran's company, she left the Louvre by the little portal that was called the washer-women's door, she looked more like a craftsman's sprightly little wife clinging to her husband's arm than a noble lady who, only the previous day, had talked to the King.

Beyond the Pont-Neuf the Seine shimmered in the last rays of the setting sun. The horses being led to water splashed in the river up to their breast-plates and shook their manes, neighing. Hay barges were depositing the long line of their fragrant bales along the river-banks. A ferryboat from Rouen unloaded on the mudbank its contingent of soldiers, monks and nurses.

The bells were ringing the Angelus. The pastry and biscuit-merchants ran down the streets with their napkin-covered baskets calling out to the gamblers in the taverns:

> Eh! Who calls for the biscuit-man
> When each one of you has lost?
> Buy my wafers, buy! The price
>   isn't high.

A coach passed, preceded by its runners and its dogs, and the massive, lugubrious Louvre, glowing violet at the approach of night, stretched out its interminable gallery beneath the reddening sky.

PART FOUR

The Doomed Man of
Notre Dame

Chapter 36

A thunderous roar of songs burst from the tavern, from whose enormous sign swung three wrought-iron mallets above the heads of the passers-by. Angélique and her brother Gontran walked down the few steps and found themselves in a thick haze of tobacco-smoke and fumes from sauces. At the back of the room, an open door afforded a glimpse of the kitchen where spits heavily laden with fowl were slowly turning over the glowing hearths.

The two young people sat down at a table a little away from the rest, near a window, and Gontran ordered some wine.

"Choose a good bottle," said Angélique, forcing a smile, "I'll foot the bill."

She showed him her purse, in which were the fifteen hundred *livres* she had won at the gaming-table. Gontran explained that he was not a good judge of wines. He generally made do with a good little wine from the hills of Paris. And on Sundays he would go and taste the more famous wines in the suburbs, where wines from Bordeaux and Bourgogne cost less, because no Paris toll-dues had yet been paid on them. It was customary to partake of them in *guingettes,* suburban pleasure-gardens, and these Sunday outings were his only distraction.

Angélique asked him if he usually went there with friends. He said he didn't. He had no friends, but he enjoyed sitting under an arbour, and watching the faces of the workmen and their families all around him. He found mankind pleasant and likeable.

"You are lucky," murmured Angélique, who suddenly felt the bitter tang of the poison on her tongue.

She did not feel ill, but tired and on edge.

With sparkling eyes and clasping around her the coarse woollen coat borrowed from the painter's wife, she gazed at this novel sight of a tavern in the capital.

It was a fact that, despite the absence of fresh air, one breathed a climate of freedom and familiarity here which put the regular customers very much at ease. The nobleman would come here to have a smoke and forget the etiquette of royal anterooms, the bourgeois would fill his paunch far from the suspicious eye of his crotchety spouse, the musketeer would play dice, the craftsman would drink his wages and, for a few hours, forget his worries.

Nevertheless, Angélique was getting more and more fidgety as she wondered how much longer she would have to wait in this place.

At last, the door opened once again and the enormous Great Dane belonging to Desgrez appeared. A man wrapped in an ample grey coat accompanied the lawyer. Angélique was surprised to recognize young Cerbalaud, who was concealing his pale face under a hat pulled down over his eyes. She asked Gontran to go and fetch the newcomers and bring them unobtrusively to their table.

"Merciful Lord, Madame," sighed the lawyer,

as he slipped in next to her on the bench, "since this morning I've seen you throttled ten times, drowned twenty times and buried a hundred times!"

"Once would be quite enough, Maître," she said with a laugh, but she could not help feeling pleased at finding him so moved.

"Were you afraid of seeing a client disappear who pays you so badly and who compromises you so dangerously?" she asked.

He made a piteous grimace.

"Sentimentality is a disease that is not easily cured. When a taste for adventure mingles with it, you may be sure you're fated to come to a stupid end. In short, the more complicated your case, the more it fascinates me. How is your wound?"

"You already know about it?"

"That's part of the duty of a lawyer-policeman. But this gentleman has been of great assistance to me, I must confess."

Cerbalaud, whose eyes were drooping with sleeplessness in a waxen face, related the end of the tragedy of the Louvre, in which he had found himself involved quite by chance. He had been on guard at the stables of the Tuileries that night, when a breathless man, who had lost his wig, had dashed out of the gardens. It was Bernard d'Andijos. He had raced along the great gallery, rousing the echoes of the Louvre and the Tuileries by the clatter of his wooden heels, which brought frightened faces to the doors of the rooms and apartments.

While hurriedly saddling a horse, he had explained that Madame de Peyrac had missed being murdered by a hair's breadth and that he himself had just fought with Monsieur d'Orléans. A few moments later, he was tearing away towards the Porte Saint-Honoré, shouting that he was off to rouse the Languedoc against the King.

"Oh! Poor Andijos!" said Angélique, laughing. "He'd rouse the Languedoc against the King?"

"You don't believe he'll do it?" asked Cerbalaud.

He raised his finger gravely:

"Madame, you have yet to understand the Gascon soul; laughter and rage follow hard on each other's heels, but you can never tell how the matter'll end. And when it ends in rage, *mordious!* Beware!"

"It's true that I owe my life to the Gascons. Do you know what has become of the Duc de Lauzun?"

"He is in the Bastille."

"Good God," sighed Angélique, "if only they don't forget him there for forty years!"

"He won't let himself be forgotten, never fear. I also saw the body of your former major-domo being carried off by two lackeys."

"May the devil take his soul!"

"Finally, when I could no longer doubt that you were dead, I went to your brother-in-law, Maître Fallot de Sancé. I found there Monsieur Desgrez, your lawyer. We went to the Châtelet in order to inspect the corpses of all the drowned and murdered who'd been found in Paris this morning. A wretched sight, from which I still have a queasy stomach. And here I am! Madame, what are you going to do? You must flee as soon as possible."

Angélique gazed at her two hands spread before her on the table, near the long-stemmed glass in which the wine she had not touched gleamed like a dark ruby. Her hands looked extraordinarily small and of a fragile whiteness. Mechanically she compared them with the strong, masculine hands of her companions. She felt very lonely and very weak.

Desgrez, an habitual customer of the tavern, had placed a small horn box before him and was grinding some tobacco before filling his pipe.

Gontran said abruptly:

"If I have understood correctly, you have become involved in some shady business in which you risk losing your life. That doesn't surprise me coming from you. It's just like you!"

"Monsieur de Peyrac is in the Bastille, accused of witchcraft," explained Desgrez.

"It's just like you!" repeated Gontran. "But you can still get out of it. If you are short of money, I'll lend you some. I saved some money for my tour of France, and Raymond, our Jesuit brother, will help you too, I am sure. Pick up your things, and take the public coach to Poitiers. From there you'll reach Monteloup. Once at home, you've nothing to fear!"

For a moment, Angélique conjured up a picture of the castle of Monteloup, the calm of the woods and marshes. Florimond would play with the turkeys on the drawbridge. . . .

"And Joffrey?" she said. "Who'll see to it that he obtains justice?"

There was a heavy silence, which was quickly drowned by the bawling of a tableful of drunkards

613

and by the clamours of late diners, drumming on their plates with their knives. The appearance of Maître Corbasson, the innkeeper, holding high a crisp, brown goose, appeased his noisy patrons. The din subsided and, amid the growls of satisfaction, could be heard the rattling of the cup and dice.

Suddenly, Angélique's eyes grew fixed, and her face congealed with horror. A hideous vision had just appeared in the window-pane in front of her: a nightmare face, blurred by long strands of greasy hair. The pallid cheek was marked by a violet wen. A black bandage concealed one eye; the other shone like a wolf's, and the horrible apparition was looking at Angélique, *grinning*.

"What's the matter?" asked Gontran who, with his back to the window, had seen nothing. Desgrez followed the terrified stare of the young woman and suddenly bounded towards the door, whistling to his dog.

The face disappeared from the window. A few moments later, the lawyer returned.

"He vanished like a rat in its hole."

"You know that peculiar specimen?" inquired Cerbalaud.

"I know them all. This one is Calembredaine, the notorious rascal and king of the coat-snatchers of the Pont-Neuf, as well as the biggest bandit chief in the capital."

"He's pretty bold to come like that and look at honest folk dining."

"He may have an accomplice inside whom he wanted to signal. . . ."

"He was looking at me," said Angélique, whose

teeth were chattering.

Desgrez gave her a quick look.

"Pah! Don't be frightened. We are not far from the rue de la Truanderie and the suburb of Saint-Denis. It's the headquarters of the beggars and of their prince, the Great Coesre, king of the vagabonds."

While talking, he had slipped his hand round the waist of the young woman and was pulling her firmly towards him. Angélique felt the warmth and vigour of this masculine hand. Her shattered nerves relaxed. She nestled against Desgrez unashamedly. What did it matter that he was a common, penniless lawyer? Wasn't she herself on the point of becoming an outcast, a hunted woman, without roof or protection, perhaps without even a name?

"By Jove," Desgrez broke out in a genial tone, "we don't settle down in a tavern to indulge in such lugubrious talk. Let's drink, gentlemen; afterwards we'll devise plans. Hi, there! Corbasson, you devil's roaster, are you going to let us perish from empty stomachs?"

The landlord hurried towards them.

"What can you recommend to three great lords who've only dined on thrills for the last twenty-four hours, and to a frail young lady whose appetite needs to be encouraged?"

Corbasson cupped his chin in his hands and assumed an inspired air:

"Well, for you, gentlemen, I shall recommend a big filet of beef, nicely underdone, stuck with cucumbers and gherkins, three small chickens roasted on ashes and a pan of fried cream. As for Madame, what would she say to a lighter menu? Boiled veal and salad, bone-marrow, apple jelly, a candied pear and a bag of biscuits. To finish, a little spoonful of fennel comfits, and I am convinced the roses will return to mingle with the lily whiteness of her complexion."

"Corbasson, you are the most indispensable and most lovable man in Creation. Next time I go to church, I'll pray to Saint-Honoré for you. Moreover, you are a great artist, not only as a maker of sauces, but also as a wit."

But, for almost the first time in her life, Angélique was not hungry. She merely pecked at Master Corbasson's culinary concoctions. Her body was fighting the after-effects of the poison she had absorbed the night before. Centuries seemed to have passed since that dreadful adventure. Numbed by her malaise and also, perhaps, by the coarse, unfamiliar smell of the smoke-infested den, she was overcome with drowsiness. With closed eyes, she told herself that Angélique de Peyrac was dead.

Chapter 37

WHEN she woke up, a smoky dawn was stagnating in the tavern-room.

Angélique stirred and noticed that her cheek was resting on a hard pillow, which was in fact the lawyer's knees. The rest of her body was stretched out on the bench. Above her she saw

Desgrez's face. With half-closed eyes he was still smoking with a musing air.

Angélique sat up quickly, which made her grimace with pain.

"Oh! excuse me," she stammered. "I . . . I must have been an awful nuisance."

"Did you sleep well?" he inquired in a drawling voice in which fatigue was mingled with a little drunkenness. The pitcher in front of him was almost empty.

Cerbalaud and Gontran, with their elbows on the table, presented a similar picture. The young woman glanced towards the window. She had a vague recollection of something horrible. But she saw only the reflection of a wan, rainy morning moistening the window-panes.

In the back-room could be heard Monsieur Corbasson's voice giving orders and the rumbling noise of several big barrels being rolled over the stone tiles. A man kicked the door open and came in, his hat pushed back on his head. He held a little bell in his hand and wore over his clothes a sort of faded blue overall, on which could be vaguely seen a pattern of fleurs-de-lis and the shield of St. Christopher.

"It's me, Picard, the wine-crier. Do you have need of me, taverner?"

"I do, my friend. They have just brought me from the Grève six barrels of Loire wines. Three white, three red. I broach two casks today."

Waking with a start, Cerbalaud sat up and suddenly drew his sword.

"Gentlemen, listen, all of you! I'm going to war against the King!"

617

"Be quiet, Cerbalaud," Angélique begged him, frightened.

He glanced at her suspiciously, with the eyes of a half-awake drunkard.

"You don't believe I'll do it? You don't know the Gascons, Madame. War against the King! I invite you all to join! Up and at him, rebels of the Languedoc!"

Brandishing his sword, he rose, tottered across the steps of the threshold and stumbled out. Indifferent to his ravings, the sleepers went on snoring, and the innkeeper, as well as the wine-crier, kneeling before their casks, tasted the new wine with much lip-smacking, before fixing the price. A fresh, heady smell replaced the stale odours of cold pipes, alcohol and rancid sauces.

Gontran rubbed his eyes.

"Lord," he said, yawning, "I haven't eaten so well for a long time — to be precise, not since the last banquet of the St. Luke's brotherhood, which unfortunately occurs only once a year. Isn't that the Angelus they are ringing?"

"It may well be," said Desgrez.

Gontran got up and stretched.

"I must be off, Angélique, otherwise my master will scowl at me. Listen, go and see Raymond in the Temple with Maître Desgrez. I'll drop in at Hortense's tonight, even if I get insulted by that charming sister of ours. I tell you again, leave Paris. But I know very well that you are the most stubborn mule of all those our father reared. . . ."

"Barring you," retorted Angélique.

They left together, followed by the dog who answered to the name of Sorbonne. It had rained.

The gutter in the middle of the street was carrying away a stream of muddy water. The air was still laden with moisture and a humid wind made the iron signs creak above the shops.

"Fresh from the boat! Fresh shell-fish!" cried a sprightly oyster-seller.

"A good awakening! A bellyful of sun!" shouted a brandy-seller.

Gontran stopped the fellow and emptied a goblet of alcohol in one gulp. Then he wiped his lips, paid, and after doffing his hat towards the lawyer and his sister, he disappeared in the crowd, looking like all the other workmen who, at this hour, were starting their long day.

"Look at the two of us!" thought Angélique, watching him disappear. "The de Sancé heirs have done well for themselves! I myself have got into these straits merely by the force of circumstances, but why ever did he choose to fall so low?"

A little shamefaced for her brother, she glanced at Desgrez.

"He always was an odd bird," she said. "He could have become an officer, like all young noblemen, but he only liked mixing paints. My mother used to say that, while she was expecting him, she spent a week dyeing all the family clothes black in mourning for my grandparents. Perhaps that accounts for it?"

Desgrez smiled.

"Let's go and see the Jesuit brother," he said, "the fourth specimen of this strange family."

"Oh, Raymond is quite a type."

"I hope so for your sake, Madame."

"You must not call me Madame any more," said

619

Angélique. "Look at me, Maître Desgrez."

She raised her pathetic little face with its waxen pallor. Fatigue had lightened her green eyes and given them an almost unimaginable hue, that of spring leaves.

"The King said: 'I don't want to hear of you any more.' Do you know what such an order means? That there is no longer a Madame de Peyrac. I must no longer exist. I do no longer exist. Do you understand?"

"What I understand above all is that you are ill," said Desgrez. "Do you still hold to the assertion you made the other day?"

"What assertion?"

"That you have no confidence in me?"

"At this moment you are the only one in whom I can have any confidence."

"Come, then. I shall take you to a place where they'll take care of you. You cannot approach a formidable Jesuit without being in full possession of your faculties."

He took her arm and pulled her through the throng of a Paris morning. The din was deafening. All the merchants were coming out at the same time and crying their wares.

Angélique had great difficulty in protecting her wounded shoulder from the jostling crowd, and she clenched her teeth to stifle the groans that rose to her lips.

In the rue Saint-Nicholas, Desgrez stopped in front of an enormous sign which displayed a copper basin on a royal blue background. Clouds of steam were drifting out of the first-floor windows.

Angélique realised that she was at a barber's hair-dressing and bathing establishment, and relished the thought of plunging into a tub of hot water. Maître Georges, the owner, told them to sit down and wait a few minutes. He was shaving a musketeer with wide, round movements of his arm, discoursing all the while on the misfortunes of peace, which is surely one of the worst calamities that can befall a valiant warrior.

At last, leaving the "valiant warrior" to his apprentice with orders to wash his head, which was no minor matter, Maître Georges wiped his razor on his apron and approached Angélique with an eager smile.

"Ho! Ho! I see what's the matter. Yet another victim of gallant diseases. You want me to freshen her up for you, don't you, you incorrigible skirt-chaser?"

"It's not that at all," said the lawyer very calmly. "This young person has been wounded and I would like you to give her some relief from pain. Afterwards she'll want a bath."

Angélique, who had blushed at the barber's words, felt terribly embarrassed at the thought of undressing before these two men. She had always been attended to by women and, never having been ill, was unfamiliar with medical examinations, and even less with those by shopkeeping barber-surgeons. But before she could make even a gesture of protest, Desgrez unfastened her bodice in the most natural manner and with the ease of a man for whom feminine garments hold no secret. He then untied the band that held up her chemise and let it slip down to her waist.

Maître Georges leaned forward and delicately removed the plaster of ointment and the bandage which had been placed over the long gash made by the Chevalier de Lorraine's sword.

"Hm, hm," muttered the barber. "I see what's the matter. A gallant lord who found the price too steep and paid in 'iron coin,' as we say. Don't you know, pretty one, that you must hide their swords under the bed until they've put their hand to their purse?"

"And what do you think of the wound?" Desgrez inquired phlegmatically while Angélique writhed in pain.

"It's neither good nor bad. I can see the briny ointment dispensed by an ignoramus. We'll clean the wound and replace the ointment with a cooling and regenerating pomade."

He went to fetch a jar from a row of shelves.

It was agonizing for Angélique to be sitting there, half-naked, in this shop where the smell of drugs mingled with that of soaps. A customer came in to be shaved and exclaimed on glancing at her:

"Oh! What beautiful rosebuds! Would I had them under my hand to fondle when the moon rises!"

At an imperceptible sign from Desgrez, the dog Sorbonne, which had been at his feet, rose and with one leap planted his fangs into the newcomer's calf.

"Oh! Ouch! Help! Mercy!" exclaimed the customer. "It's the man with the dog. So it's you, Desgrez, infernal roamer, who are the owner of these two divine rosy apples?"

"If you don't mind, Monsieur," said Desgrez impassively.

"In that case I've seen nothing, said nothing. Oh, Monsieur! forgive me and tell your dog to let go of my poor, threadbare hose."

With a light whistle, Desgrez called the dog off.

"Oh! I want to get away from here," said Angélique, clumsily trying to dress, her lips trembling.

Firmly, the young man forced her to sit down again. He said rudely though lowering his voice:

"Don't be a prude, little fool. Must I remind you of the soldiers' saying: war is war? You are engaged in a battle in which your husband's life and your own are at stake. You must do everything to get out of it, and this is no time for simpering."

Maître Georges returned, a small knife gleaming in his hand.

"I believe I'll have to cut into the flesh," he said. "I can see under the skin a whitish humour which has got to be extracted. Don't be afraid, little one," he added, talking to her as to a child, "no one has a lighter hand than Maître Georges."

Despite her apprehension, Angélique had to admit that he was speaking the truth, for he operated on her most skilfully. Then, after pouring over the wound a liquid which made her jump, he told her to go upstairs to the steam-baths and that he'd finish bandaging her afterwards.

The steam-baths of Maître Georges were one of the last bath-houses of the type that had existed in the Middle Ages, when the crusaders back from the East brought home, with a taste for Turkish baths, a taste for ablutions. Paris at that time teemed with steam-baths. People went there not only to sweat and rid themselves of dirt, but also for "plucking," as they called it, which meant the total depilation of the body. Their reputation, however, had quickly become suspect, for they added to their manifold specialties those which more particularly pertained to the bawdy-houses of the rue du Val d'Amour. Perturbed priests, strict Huguenots and doctors, who saw in them the cause of skin diseases, leagued together to get them suppressed. And henceforward, apart from the squalid back room of some barbershops, there was no place in Paris where you could wash. People seemed to resign themselves to it with considerable ease.

The baths themselves comprised two spacious, tiled rooms, furnished with small wooden cubicles. At one end of the rooms, an attendant was heating stone bricks in an oven.

Angélique was completely undressed by one of the maid-servants who looked after the women's room. She was shut up in one of the cubicles in which there was a bench and a small basin of water, into which the incandescent stone bricks had just been flung. The water steamed and released a searing vapour. Angélique, sitting on the bench, choked, gasped and thought she was going to die. She came out dripping with sweat.

The serving-woman then ordered her to plunge into a tub of cold water. Wrapping a towel round her, she led her into a neighbouring room where other women were already gathered. The servants, who were mostly old and rather repulsive-looking, shaved their customers or else combed their long

624

hair, while cackling like a swarm of hens. From their way of speaking and the topics of conversation Angélique guessed that most of the customers were themselves of lowly condition, servants or merchants who, after hearing Mass, dropped in at the bath-house to glean the latest gossip before running off to work.

She was told to lie down on another bench. After a moment, Maître Georges appeared, without in any way flustering the gathering. He was holding a lancet in his hand and was followed by a little girl, who was carrying a basket filled with cupping-glasses, and a stick of tinder. Angélique protested vehemently.

"You're not going to bleed me! I've already lost enough blood. Can't you see that I'm with child? You're going to kill the baby!"

The barber-surgeon imperturbably told her to turn over.

"Keep still, or I'll call your friend to spank your bottom."

Terrified at the thought, Angélique calmed down. The barber scarified three points on her back with his lancet, and applied the wet-cups.

"Just look," he said, delighted, "all this black blood flowing! How can such a white-skinned girl have such black blood?"

"For pity's sake, leave me a few drops!" begged Angélique.

"I'm dying to empty you entirely," said the barber, rolling his fierce eyes. "And afterwards I'll give you a recipe for filling your veins with a fresh, generous blood. It's this: a good glass of red wine and a night of love."

He left her alone at last, after bandaging her firmly. Two girls helped her to arrange her hair and dress. She slipped them a tip which left them goggle-eyed.

"Hey, Marquise," the younger one exclaimed, "is it your pettifogging prince with the shabby coat who gives you such fine presents?"

One of the old women jostled her and, after staring hard at Angélique, who was trying to walk down the wooden stairs on weak legs, she whispered to her colleague:

"Can't you see that she's a great lady who's come to have a change of fare from her lordly milksops?"

"They don't come in disguise as a rule," protested the other. "They put on a mask, and Maître Georges lets them in by the back door."

Down in the shop, Angélique found Desgrez, freshly shaved.

"She's done to a turn," said the barber, with a wink of connivance. "But don't be rough till the wound on her shoulder has closed up."

This time the young woman made up her mind to laugh. She felt utterly incapable of the least flicker of rebellion.

"How do you feel?" asked Desgrez, when they were out in the street again.

"As weak as a kitten," replied Angélique, "but actually it wasn't so very unpleasant. I'm viewing life very philosophically. I don't know whether the energetic treatment I've undergone is good for one's health, but it certainly does wonders for one's nerves. You may rest assured that, whatever my brother Raymond's attitude may be, he will find before him a humble and docile sister."

"That's perfect. I always fear a sudden bite from your rebellious spirit. No doubt you'll drop in at the bath-house next time you're summoned to the King!"

"Alas! Why didn't I?" sighed Angélique, utterly defeated. "There'll be no second time. Never again shall I be summoned to appear before the King."

"You mustn't say 'never again.' Life has its ups and downs, the wheel turns."

A gust of wind loosened the kerchief that held the young woman's hair. Desgrez stopped and tied it again gently. Angélique grasped the two warm brown hands, whose long fingers were not lacking in refinement.

"You are very kind, Desgrez," she murmured, raising her coaxing eyes towards him.

"You are quite mistaken, Madame. Here, have a look at this dog."

He pointed towards Sorbonne who was gambolling around them. He caught him in passing, then gripped the dog's head and bared the Dane's powerful jaws.

"What do you think of this row of fangs?"

"They are terrifying!"

"Do you know what I have trained this dog to do? Just this: when evening falls on Paris, we two go hunting. I make him sniff an old piece of smock, some object belonging to a ruffian I'm after. And we go for a walk; we go down to the banks of the Seine, we roam under the bridges and piles, we stroll through the suburbs and over the old ramparts, we walk into courtyards, we dive into holes full of that vermin of beggars and bandits. And suddenly Sorbonne bounds forward. By the time I catch up with him, he has my man by the throat, oh! very daintily, just enough to prevent the other from moving. I tell the dog *'Warte,'* which means 'Wait' in the German language, for the dog was sold to me by a German mercenary. I lean towards the fellow, question him, and then I judge him. Sometimes I let him off, sometimes I call the watchman, so they can take him to the Châtelet, and sometimes I say to myself why fill up the prisons and bother those gentlemen of the law-courts? And I say to Sorbonne *'Zang!'* which means 'Squeeze hard.' And there's one less bandit in Paris."

"And . . . you do that often?" inquired Angélique, who could not suppress a shudder.

"Fairly often. So you see I am not very kind."

After a moment's silence, she murmured:

"There are so many different elements in the same man. One can at once be very wicked and very kind. Why do you follow this dreadful profession?"

"I already told you: I am too poor. My father left me only his law office and his debts. But the way things are going, I believe I'll end up in the hardened skin of a dreadful *malveillant,* a *grimaud* of the worst type."

"What's that?"

"The name given to members of the police by the subjects of His Majesty the Great Coesre, prince of the paupers."

"They already know you?"

"They particularly know my dog."

Chapter 38

THE rue du Temple opened before Angélique and Desgrez, with its stretches of muddy slush here and there, over which planks had been thrown. A few years earlier, this district had contained nothing but kitchen-gardens, called the "Temple allotments," and in between the newly-built houses one still caught a glimpse of cabbage-patches and small herds of goats. The fortified wall, over which towered the sombre keep of the former Templars, came in sight.

Desgrez asked Angélique to wait for a moment and went into a haberdashery. A few seconds later he emerged from it adorned with an immaculate collar-band, with no lace trimmings, but tied with a violet cord. White cuffs shone on his wrists. His vest-pocket bulged peculiarly. He pulled a handkerchief from it and almost dropped a big rosary. His threadbare jacket and hose seemed to have taken on an extremely respectable air. The pious expression on his face contributed to this transformation, and Angélique felt a certain hesitation about talking to him in the same familiar way.

"You look like a devout magistrate," she said, a little put out.

"Isn't that just what a lawyer who is accompanying a young lady to visit her Jesuit brother should look like?" asked Desgrez, raising his hat with humble respect.

As they approached the high battlements of the Temple, from which rose a welter of Gothic towers dominated by the Templars' sinister dungeon, Angélique little guessed that she was penetrating into the one place in Paris where one could be most sure of living in freedom.

This fortified area, which in former times had been the stronghold of the warrior monks called Templars, and later that of the Knights of Malta, enjoyed in fact traditional privileges before which the King himself bowed: no taxes were exacted here, one could live unharassed by police or administrative measures, and insolvent debtors found here a refuge from sentences of imprisonment for debts. For several generations, the Temple had been the prerogative of the great bastards of France. The present Grand Prior, the Duc de Vendôme, was descended in direct line from Henry IV and his most famous mistress, Gabrielle d'Estrées.

Angélique, who was unfamiliar with the special jurisdiction that governed this isolated little town in the heart of the great city, experienced an uneasy feeling as she crossed the drawbridge. But she found, on the other side of the vaulted gate, a surprising calm. The Temple had lost its military traditions a long time ago. Nowadays it was merely a kind of peaceful retreat which offered its happy inmates all the advantages of a life that was both retired and fashionable. Over towards the aristocratic district, Angélique noticed several carriages stationed before the handsome mansions of the Guise, Boufflers and Boisboudran families.

In the shadow of the massive Tower of Caesar,

the Jesuits owned a comfortable residence. In it lived and came to meditate those members of the congregation, in particular, who were attached as almoners to the great persons of the Court.

Desgrez asked the seminarist who had let them in to inform the Reverend Father de Sancé that a lawyer wished to talk to him about the Comte de Peyrac.

"If your brother doesn't know all about this case, then the Jesuits might just as well close up shop," declared Desgrez to Angélique while they were waiting in the small parlour. "I have often thought that if, by any chance, I had the task of reorganizing the police, I would let myself be guided by their methods."

A moment later, Father de Sancé strode briskly into the room. He recognized Angélique at a glance.

"My dear sister!" he said.

And going up to her, he gave her a brotherly kiss.

"Oh, Raymond!" she murmured, comforted by his welcome.

He was already motioning them to sit down.

"How far have you got in this painful affair?"

Desgrez chose to answer for Angélique. He summed up the situation in a pontifical tone of voice. The Comte de Peyrac was in the Bastille on the — secret — charge of witchcraft. This was aggravated by the fact that he had displeased the King and attracted the suspicions of influential persons.

"I know! I know!" murmured the Jesuit.

He did not say how he happened to be so well

informed, but after casting a searching glance at Desgrez, he asked point-blank:

"What is your opinion, Maître, of the course we should follow to save my unfortunate brother-in-law?"

"I consider that in this case, we'd hurt our chances if we tried to obtain too much. The Comte de Peyrac is most certainly the victim of a court intrigue of which the King himself has no inkling, but which is fostered by a powerful personage. I shall mention no names."

"You do well," Father de Sancé slipped in quickly, while Angélique had a fleeting vision of the redoubtable squirrel's crafty profile.

"However, we'd be clumsy to try and foil the stratagems of people who have both money and influence in their favour. Three times, Madame de Peyrac has almost succumbed to attempts on her life. That experience should suffice. Let us bow and confine ourselves to talking of what we are allowed to discuss in broad daylight. Monsieur de Peyrac is accused of witchcraft. Well then, let him be handed over to an ecclesiastical court. That's where your help, Father, will become extremely valuable, for I won't conceal from you that my influence as a little-known lawyer would be quite unavailing. To get my remonstrances accepted as Monsieur de Peyrac's advocate would require that a trial be decided upon and legal assistance granted. Originally, I doubt that anybody even dreamed of it. But the various moves that Madame de Peyrac has instigated at Court have stirred the sovereign's conscience. I no longer doubt that the trial will take place. It is up to you, Father, to see that it takes place in the only acceptable form, and thus avoid the malpractices and falsifications of those gentlemen of the civil law."

"I see, Maître, that you harbour no illusions about your corporation."

"I harbour no illusions about anybody, Father."

"You do well," approved Raymond de Sancé.

He then promised to see certain persons whose names he did not mention and to keep the lawyer and his sister informed of the outcome.

"You are staying at Hortense's, I believe?"

"Yes," said Angélique with a sigh.

"Incidentally," Desgrez broke in, "an idea has struck me. Could you not use your connections, Father, to obtain a modest lodging in these precincts for my client, your sister? You are not unaware that her life is still threatened, but in the Temple nobody would dare run the risk of committing a crime. It is well known that his lordship the Duc de Vendôme, Grand Prior of France, does not admit rogues to this enclosure, and that he welcomes all those who ask for refuge here. A crime attempted under his jurisdiction would arouse publicity that no one desires. And, lastly, Madame de Peyrac could register under an assumed name, which would obscure the trail. I might add that she would thus enjoy some rest, of which her health stands in great need."

"It seems to me a very wise plan," approved Raymond and, after pondering for a moment, he went out and returned with a small piece of paper on which he had jotted down an address:

"Madame Cordeau, widow, lodging-house

keeper in Temple Square."

"It's a modest, even rather a poor, habitation. But you will have a large room and can have your meals with Madame Cordeau, whose duty it is to keep house and to let three or four rooms. I know that you are used to greater luxury, but I believe that this accommodation corresponds to the need of obscurity that Maître Desgrez advises for you."

"Very well, Raymond," Angélique agreed obediently, and with a little more warmth she added: "Thank you for believing in my husband's innocence and for helping us fight the injustice of which he's a victim."

The Jesuit's face grew stern.

"Angélique, I did not wish to burden you with reproaches, for your wan appearance fills me with pity. But don't think I have the least indulgence for your husband's scandalous life, into which he dragged you with him and which you are so harshly expiating today. It is natural, though, that I should offer help to a member of my family."

The young woman opened her mouth to answer. Then she thought better of it. There was no fight left in her.

Nevertheless, she was unable to curb her tongue to the end. As Raymond was leading them back through the vestibule, he informed Angélique that their youngest sister, Marie-Agnès, thanks to his intervention, had obtained one of the much sought-after posts of maid-of-honour to the Queen.

"That's splendid!" exclaimed the young woman. "Marie-Agnès at the Louvre! I am sure that she will blossom out quickly and fully there."

"Madame de Navailles is specially looking after

the maids-of-honour. She is a most amiable woman, but a wise and prudent one. I was talking a moment ago with the Queen's confessor, who told me how much Her Majesty insists on the excellent conduct of her maids-of-honour."

"Can it be that you are so naïve?"

"That's a failing which our superiors don't countenance."

"Then don't be a hypocrite," concluded Angélique.

Raymond continued to smile affably.

"I am delighted to see that you are still the same, my dear sister. I hope you will find tranquillity in the place I indicated to you. Go now, I shall pray for you."

"These Jesuits really are remarkable people," declared Desgrez a little later. "Why didn't I become a Jesuit?"

He remained plunged in thought over this question until they reached the rue Saint-Landry.

Hortense received her sister and the lawyer with a frankly hostile expression.

"Splendid! Splendid!" she said. "I notice that from each one of your escapades you return in a more lamentable state. And always accompanied, of course."

"Hortense, this is Maître Desgrez."

Hortense turned her back on the lawyer.

"Gaston!" she called, "do come and have a look at your sister-in-law. I hope that will cure you for good."

Maître Fallot de Sancé appeared, rather vexed at his wife's manner of summoning him, but at the sight of Angélique his mouth dropped open with amazement.

"My poor child, in what a state! . . ."

There was a ring at the door, and Barbe let in Gontran.

The sight of him put the final spark to Hortense's anger, and she broke out into imprecations:

"What have I done to Our Lord to be burdened with such a brother and sister? Who could now believe that my family is really of ancient lineage? A sister who comes back dressed like a rag-picker! And a brother who, falling lower and lower, is reduced to becoming a rough labourer whom noblemen and burghers can treat with contempt and trounce with their sticks! . . . They should have locked the whole lot of you up in the Bastille with that awful lame sorcerer!"

Ignoring this shouting, Angélique called her little nurse-maid to help her pack.

Hortense broke off and caught her breath.

"You can keep calling her! She's gone."

"What do you mean, gone?"

"Well, like mistress, like servant. She left yesterday with a big lout with an atrocious accent, who came for her."

Angélique was aghast. She felt responsible for this adolescent girl whom she had torn away from her native province, and she turned towards Barbe.

"You shouldn't have let her go, Barbe."

"How was I to know, Madame?" wailed the big girl. "That girl was full of the devil. She swore to me on the crucifix that the man was her brother."

"Pooh! a Gascon sort of brother. They have an expression down there, 'my country brother,' which people from the same province use among themselves. Well, can't be helped. I won't have to spend any more money on her keep. . . ."

That very night, Angélique and her little boy moved into the modest lodgings of Widow Cordeau, in Temple Square.

Temple Square was the name given to the market-place where all those who sold fowl, fish, fresh meat, garlic, honey and water-cress fore-gathered, for everyone was entitled to set up shop here, against payment of a small fee to the bailiff, and to sell his wares at whatever price he chose, free of taxes or inspection. The place was bustling and popular. The Widow Cordeau herself was just an old woman, more of a peasant than a city-dweller, who spun wool before her meagre fire. She looked rather like a witch.

Angélique found her room clean and smelling pleasantly; the bed was comfortable, and a big bundle of straw had been strewn on the floor to warm the cold, stone tiles in these early winter days. Madame Cordeau had a small cradle brought up for Florimond in addition to a stock of wood and a pot of broth.

After Desgrez and Gontran had left her, Angélique busied herself with the baby, feeding him and putting him to bed. Florimond grumbled, calling for Barbe and his little cousins. To distract him, she hummed a little song, "The Green Mill," which he loved. She barely noticed her wound any more, and looking after her child amused her. Although accustomed to being surrounded by numerous servants, her rugged childhood now stood her in good stead so that the loss of her last servant was not a shattering blow to her. And besides, hadn't the nuns who had brought her up accustomed her to hard work "in anticipation of the reverses which Heaven might decree"?

So when the child had fallen asleep and she herself lay down between the coarse but clean sheets, and the night-watchman passed under her windows crying: "Ten o'clock. The Gate's closed. Good people of the Temple, sleep in peace. . . ." she experienced a moment's feeling of well-being and relaxation.

The gate was closed. While the great city all around was awakening to the horrors of the night, with its growling taverns, prowling bandits, its murderers and burglars, the small Temple population peacefully went to sleep in the shelter of their high battlements. The imitation-jewel manufacturers, the insolvent debtors and clandestine printers closed their eyes, in the certainty of a peaceful morrow. From the Grand Prior's house, hidden in its park, came the sound of a harpsichord, and from the chapel and cloister rang out prayers in Latin, while some Knights of Malta, in black robes with white crosses, repaired to their cells.

Rain was falling. Angélique peacefully fell asleep.

Chapter 39

SHE had registered at the bailiff's Court under the name of Madame Martin. Nobody asked any questions. In the days that followed she had the novel but pleasant impression of being a young mother of the people, who mingled with her neighbours and had no cares other than those of looking after her child. She took her meals at home in the company of Madame Cordeau, her son, a boy of fifteen apprenticed in town, and a ruined old merchant who was hiding from his creditors in the Temple.

"The misfortune of my life," he was apt to say, "is that my father and mother brought me up very badly. Yes, Madame, they taught me to be honest. It's the worst defect one can have when engaged in business."

Little Florimond attracted no end of compliments, and Angélique was very proud of him. At the slightest ray of sunshine, she would go and take him for a walk through the market, and all the market-women would compare him with the Child Jesus in his crib. One of the goldsmiths, whose booth was just outside the house in which Angélique lived, presented him with a little cross in imitation rubies. Angélique was quite touched as she tied the poor trinket around the little boy's neck. Where was the six-carat diamond that Florimond had almost swallowed on the day of the King's wedding at Saint-Jean-de-Luz?

During her walks, Angélique kept away from the vicinity of the beautiful town houses, where rich and high-ranking people had chosen to take up residence within the Temple, for reasons of economy or personal taste. She was a little apprehensive of being recognized by the visitors whose carriages rumbled past the postern-gate, and above all she preferred to spare herself any regrets. A complete break with her past life was preferable from every point of view, and, anyhow, wasn't she the wife of a poor prisoner abandoned by all?

One day, however, as she was going down the stairs with Florimond in her arms, she had the impression, on passing the woman who lived in the adjoining room, that the latter's face was not unfamiliar to her. Madame Cordeau had told her that she was also housing a very poor and rather reserved young widow, who preferred to add a few *deniers* to the modest boarding fee she was paying to have her meals brought up to her room. Angélique had a fleeting glimpse of a brunette's charming face with languorous eyes, but she was unable to put a name to it although she was convinced that she had met her before.

As she was returning from her walk, the young widow seemed to be waiting for her.

"Aren't you Madame de Peyrac?" she asked.

Vexed, and a little alarmed, Angélique motioned to her to come into her room.

"You were sharing the carriage of my friend, Athénaïs de Tonnay-Charente, on the day of the

King's entry into Paris. I am Madame Scarron."

Angélique at last recognized the lovely, self-effacing person who had accompanied them in her shabby dress and had made them all feel a little embarrassed for her. Madame "Legless Scarron," as Athénaïs's brother used to say maliciously. She had hardly changed, except for her dress which was even more worn and patched. But she wore collars of immaculate whiteness and preserved an air of rather pathetic respectability.

Angélique was delighted, despite everything, to be able to chat with a fellow country-woman from Poitou, and she asked her to come and sit before the fireplace and, together with Florimond, they shared a bag of biscuits. Françoise d'Aubigné told her that she had come to live in the Temple because you could stay there for three months without paying for your lodging. She was literally down to her last *sou* and on the verge of being thrown out into the street by her creditors. She was hoping that before the three months were out she would obtain from the King or the Queen Mother the renewal of the pension of 2000 *livres* which His Majesty had granted her husband during his lifetime.

"Almost every week I go to the Louvre and take up my stand on the path leading to the chapel. You know that His Majesty, when leaving his apartments on his way to attend Mass, passes through a gallery where he allows himself to be approached by petitioners. There are lots of monks, war-orphans and pensionless old soldiers. We sometimes have to wait a very long time. At last the King appears. I confess that every time

I place my petition in the Royal hand, my heart beats so loud that I am afraid the King may hear it."

"But so far he hasn't even heard your petition!"

"No, that's true. But I don't give up hope that he will glance at it some day."

They were interrupted by a strange noise, a sort of animal growl, coming from the staircase. Madame Scarron went to open the door, then recoiled, slamming it hurriedly.

"Good God, there's a demon on the landing!"

"What do you mean?"

"At any rate, a perfectly black man."

Angélique uttered a cry and rushed out.

"Kouassi-Ba!" she called.

"Yes, it's me, Médême," replied Kouassi-Ba.

He loomed, like a sombre spectre, on the dark little staircase. He was dressed in shapeless rags held up by string. His skin was grey and flabby. But on seeing Florimond, he burst into wild laughter and, rushing towards the delighted child, he started to perform a frenzied dance. Françoise Scarron rushed out of the room with a horrified gesture and took refuge in her own room.

Angélique put her head between her hands and thought hard. When was it . . . when exactly had Kouassi-Ba disappeared? She couldn't remember. Everything was muddled. At last she recalled that he had accompanied her to the Louvre on the morning of that terrible day when she had seen the King and almost died at the hands of the Duc d'Orléans. From that moment onward, she had to admit, she had completely forgotten Kouassi-Ba's existence!

She threw a bundle of wood on to the fire so that he might dry his rain-soaked rags and offered him all the food she could find. He told her his odyssey.

In the big castle in which the King of France lived, Kouassi-Ba had waited for "Médême" for a long time. Such a long time! Passing servant-girls made fun of him. After that, night had come. After that, he had received many blows from sticks. After that, he woke up in the water, yes in the water that flows before the big castle. . . . He had swum; then he had found a beach. When he woke again, he was very happy, for he thought he was back in his own country. Three Moors were bending over him. Men like himself, not little blackamoors like ladies have as pages.

"You're sure it wasn't a dream?" Angélique asked him, much surprised. "Moors in Paris! There are very few adult Moors here."

By dint of questioning, she finally gathered that he had been sheltered by negroes who were being presented as freaks at the fair of Saint-Germain or else who acted as keepers for trained bears. But Kouassi-Ba had not felt at all inclined to stay with them. He was afraid of bears.

After finishing his story, he pulled a basket from under his rags and, squatting on his knees before Florimond, he presented him with two soft bread-rolls, called "sheep bread," whose crust was golden with egg-yolk and sprinkled with grains of wheat. They gave off a delicious aroma.

"How were you able to buy this?"

"Oh! I didn't buy. I walked into a baker's shop and did this" — he pulled a terrifying grimace

— "the lady and the young lady hid under the counter and I took the pastries to bring them to my young master."

"My God!" sighed Angélique, aghast.

"If I had my big curved sabre . . ."

"I sold it to a ragman," the young woman hastened to reply.

She was wondering whether the archers of the watch weren't after Kouassi-Ba. It seemed that even now there was much noise outside. Going over to the window, she saw a group of people massed before the house. A respectable-looking, dark-dressed man was arguing with Widow Cordeau. Angélique half-opened the window to try and hear what it was all about.

Old Widow Cordeau shouted up to her:

"It seems there's a perfectly black man up there with you?"

Angélique quickly went downstairs.

"That's true, Madame Cordeau. He's a Moor, a . . . a former servant. He's a very good fellow."

The respectable person then introduced himself as the bailiff of the Temple, in charge of high, middle and low justice on behalf of the Grand Prior within the precincts of the Temple. He said that it was impossible for a Moor to remain there, all the more so since this particular one was dressed like a beggar. After a prolonged argument, Angélique promised that Kouassi-Ba would leave the enclosure again before nightfall. She went upstairs, aggrieved.

"What am I going to do with you, my poor Kouassi-Ba? Your presence here stirs up a real fuss. And I myself have not enough money left to pay your keep. You're used to luxury, alas! . . ."

"Sell me, Médême."

And as she stared at him in surprise, he added:

"The Comte paid a high price for me, and yet I was quite small at the time. Now I am worth at least a thousand *livres*. That'll give you a lot of money to get my master out of prison."

Angélique told herself that the negro was right. Actually, Kouassi-Ba was all that was left to her of her former wealth. The thing was repugnant to her, but wasn't it the best way of finding a shelter for this poor savage, lost amid the confusion of the civilized world?

"Come back tomorrow," she told him, "I'll have thought of a solution. And be careful not to get caught by the archers of the watch."

"Oh! I know how to hide myself. I have many friends in this city. I do like this and then the friends say: 'You are one of ours.' And they take me home with them."

He showed her how he crossed his fingers in a certain way so as to be recognized by the friends in question. She gave him a blanket and watched the tall, roving hulk disappear in the rain. As soon as he had gone, she decided to ask her brother for advice. But the Reverend Father de Sancé was not to be found.

Angélique was returning, absorbed in her worries, when a young boy carrying a violin-case under his arm, passed her, skipping from puddle to puddle.

"Giovanni!"

She pulled the little musician into the shelter of the cloister of the old church and asked him how he was getting on.

"I am not yet in Monsieur Lulli's orchestra," he said, "but when Mademoiselle de Montpensier left for Saint-Fargeau, she passed me on to Madame de Soissons, who has been appointed Mistress of the Queen's household. I thus have excellent connections," he concluded self-importantly, "and thanks to them I can make a lot of extras by giving music and dancing lessons to young girls of good family. I am just on my way back from Mademoiselle de Sévigné, who's staying at the Hôtel de Boufflers."

He shyly added, after an embarrassed glance at the modest attire of his former mistress:

"And may I ask, Madame, how your affairs are progressing? When shall we see His Lordship the Comte again?"

"Soon. It's a matter of days," answered Angélique, her mind elsewhere. "Giovanni," she went on, seizing the boy by the shoulders. "I have decided to sell Kouassi-Ba. I remember that Madame de Soissons wished to acquire him, but I cannot leave the Temple, let alone go to the Tuileries. Will you act as my intermediary in this business?"

"I am always at your service, Madame," the little musician replied devotedly.

He must have hurried, for less than two hours afterwards, as Angélique was cooking Florimond's meal, there was a knock at her door. She went to open it and found herself facing a big, red-haired woman of arrogant mien, and a lackey in the cherry-red livery of the Duc de Soissons's household.

"We are sent by Giovanni," said the woman, under whose cloak could be glimpsed a very smart chambermaid's uniform.

She had the crafty, insolent manners of a great lady's favourite servant.

"We're ready to come to an arrangement," she continued, after eyeing Angélique from head to foot and casting a quick appraising glance round the room. "The question is how much is there in it for us?"

"Not so fast, young woman," Angélique cut her short in a tone of voice that promptly put the maid in her place.

She sat down and left the visitors standing before her.

"What's your name?" she asked the lackey.

"La Jacinthe, Your Ladyship."

"Very well. You at least have sharp eyes and a good memory. Why am I supposed to pay two people?"

"Well, we always work together in this sort of business."

"A partnership, I see. A good thing that His Lordship the Duc's entire household isn't in on it! Now this is what you are to do: you'll tell the Duchesse that I am prepared to sell my Moor, Kouassi-Ba. But I cannot go to the Tuileries myself. Your mistress must therefore arrange to meet me in the Temple at a house of her choice. But I insist on absolute discretion and on the fact that my name must not even be mentioned."

"That doesn't seem very difficult to arrange,"

said the maid after exchanging a glance with her companion.

"There'll be two *livres* in every ten for you in it. This means that the higher the price the better you'll be paid. It's up to you, moreover, to see that Madame de Soissons is so eager to acquire the Moor that she won't shrink from any figure."

"I'll see to that," promised the maid. "Anyway, only the other day while I was dressing her hair, Her Ladyship was still regretting not having that horrid demon in her suite! A lot of good it will do her!" she added, raising her eyes to heaven.

Angélique and Kouassi-Ba were waiting in a small room adjoining the pantry of the Hôtel de Boufflers. Laughing voices and mannered exclamations rang out from the rooms where Madame de Sévigné was at home to her friends that day. Little lackeys passed, their arms laden with trays of pastries.

Though unwilling to admit it to herself, Angélique's heart ached, for the women of her circle were leading their frivolous lives but a few steps away. She had dreamed so much of knowing Paris and its fashionable alcoves, the rendezvous of the brilliant wits of her time! . . .

By her side, Kouassi-Ba was rolling his eyes with apprehension. From a clothes-merchant in the Temple she had hired for him an old livery with faded gold braid in which he did not look very smart.

At last the door opened, to let in Madame de Soissons's maid, followed by the Duchesse herself who, closing her fan with a snap, appeared bustling amid a rustle of silk.

"Ah! this is the woman you mentioned to me, Bertille . . ."

She broke off to scan Angélique attentively.

"Heaven forgive," she exclaimed, "is that you, my dear?"

"It's I," said Angélique, laughing, "but please, don't be so amazed. You know that my husband is in the Bastille; I can hardly be better situated than he."

"Oh yes!" approved Olympe de Soissons, quick to accept the situation. "Haven't we all had our moments of disgrace? At the time when my uncle, Cardinal Mazarin, had to flee from France, my sisters and I had holes in our skirts, and the people in the street would throw stones at our carriage and call us the 'Mancini strumpets.' Yet at present, when the poor Cardinal is about to die, the people in the streets are certainly more moved than I. You see how the wheel turns! . . . But is that your Moor, my dear? He seemed more handsome when I first saw him! Plumper and blacker too."

"That's because he is cold and hungry," Angélique hastened to say. "But you'll see, once he has eaten, he'll be black as coal again."

The beautiful woman pursed her lips disappointedly. Kouassi-Ba rose with a cat-like bounce.

"I am still strong! Look!"

He tore off the shabby livery and his chest appeared, pitted with curious tattoo marks in relief. He pushed out his shoulders and, straining his muscles, lifted his arms with bent elbows like a fairground wrestler. Glimmers of light rippled on his metallic skin. Erect and motionless, he suddenly seemed to grow in height. His savage presence, although he remained impassive, filled the little room and pervaded it with a strange eeriness. Pale sunlight seeped through the latticed windows, shedding a golden glow upon this exiled son of Africa. Then his long Egyptian eyelids lowered over his ivory eye-balls and all that remained of his glance was a narrow slit resting on the Duchesse de Soissons. At last, a slow smile that was both haughty and gentle, widened the Moor's thick lips.

Never had Angélique seen Kouassi-Ba look so beautiful, nor had she ever seen him so . . . fearsome.

The negro, with his primitive power, was gauging his prey. He had sensed instinctively what this white woman, greedy for new pleasure, wanted of him. With half-open lips, Olympe de Soissons seemed utterly subjugated. Her dark eyes gleamed with an extraordinary fire. The throbbing of her lovely bosom, the avidity of her mouth betrayed her desire so shamelessly that even her maid lowered her head and Angélique felt like running away and slamming the door behind her.

The Duchesse at last seemed to recover her self-control. She began to fan herself mechanically.

"How . . . how much do you want for him?"

"Two thousand five hundred *livres*."

The maid's eyes shone.

Olympe started, quickly coming to earth.

"You are mad!"

"It's two thousand five hundred *livres*, or I'll keep him myself," Angélique declared coldly.

"My dear . . ."

"Oh! Madame," exclaimed Bertille, who had timidly placed a finger on Kouassi-Ba's arm, "how soft his skin is! One would never imagine a man could have such a soft skin; it's like a dried petal."

The Duchesse, in turn, passed her finger over the smooth arm with its tight, supple skin. A voluptuous shiver shook her. Becoming bolder, she touched the tattoos on his chest and began to laugh.

"Never mind, I'll buy him. It's sheer madness, but I already feel I can't do without him. Bertille, go and tell La Jacinthe to bring me my money-box."

As if at a given signal, the lackey entered, carrying a finely-worked leather case. While the man, who apparently acted as manager of the Duchesse's secret pleasures, was counting out the sum, the maid, at the orders of her mistress, beckoned to Kouassi-Ba to follow her.

"Goodbye, Médême, goodbye," said the Moor, going up to Angélique, "and for my young master Florimond, tell him . . ."

"That's all right. Go," she said harshly.

But like a dagger-stroke at her heart, she caught the hang-dog look which the slave cast at her before leaving the room. . . .

She nervously counted the coins and slipped them into her purse. She was now in a hurry for one thing only: to be away from there.

"Oh, my dear, all this is terribly painful, I imagine," the Duchesse de Soissons sighed, fanning herself with a much gratified air. "However, don't grieve, the wheel always turns. One gets sent to the Bastille, it's true, but one comes out of it, too.

Do you know that Péguilin de Lauzun has been restored to the King's favour?"

"Péguilin!" exclaimed Angélique, who felt suddenly cheered at hearing this name and this news. "Oh! I am delighted. How did it happen?"

"His Majesty has a fancy for the insolences of this bold nobleman. So he looked around for the first pretext that came along to call him back to favour. They say that Lauzun was sent to the Bastille, because he'd been fighting with Philippe d'Orléans. Some people even say that it was on your account that Lauzun fought a duel with Monsieur?"

Angélique shuddered at the memory of the dreadful scene. She begged Madame de Soissons once again to exercise the utmost discretion concerning her, and not to reveal her place of refuge. Madame de Soissons, who had been taught by long experience to handle with care people who had fallen into disfavour until their fate had been finally settled by the master, promised all that was asked and kissed Angélique as she left.

Chapter 40

THE business of selling Kouassi-Ba had distracted Angélique from her more immediate worries about her husband. Now that the latter's fate no longer depended on her efforts alone, she was filled with a kind of fatalism which was not unrelated to her condition. Her pregnancy, however, took its normal course, whatever she might have feared to the contrary. The child she carried was well and alive.

One morning, she was returning with Florimond from a stroll near the big keep. She was approaching the house when she heard shouting. She saw her landlady's son running home while trying to protect his head from a shower of pebbles with which he was being pelted by a crowd of boys in hot pursuit.

"Cordeau! *Corde-au-cou!* Go to it! Pull the tongue, Rope-round-the-neck!"

Without even trying to face them, the boy dived into the house.

A little later, at lunch-time, Angélique found him in the kitchen, peacefully gulping down his portion of peas and drippings. Widow Cordeau's son did not interest Angélique particularly. He was a husky boy of fifteen, square and taciturn, whose low forehead did not indicate a superior intelligence. But he was obliging towards his mother and the lodgers. His only distraction, on Sundays, seemed to be to play with Florimond, whose every whim he obeyed.

"What happened this morning, my poor Cordeau?" inquired the young woman, as she sat down before the rough bowl into which the landlady was about to pour peas and blubber. "Why didn't you give a hiding to those louts who were stoning you?"

The youngster shrugged his shoulders, and his mother explained:

"Oh, he's used to it after all this time, you know. Even I sometimes call him Rope-round-the-neck unthinkingly. And he's had stones thrown at him ever since he was quite small. He doesn't mind. What matters is that he should become a master. Later, he'll be respected all right. That I'm sure of."

And the old woman gave a smirk which made her look even more like a witch. Angélique stared at them with amazement.

"It's true, then? You don't know?" said Madame Cordeau, putting the pan back on the fire in the hearth. "Well, no need to hide it, the fact is my boy works with Maître Aubin."

And as Angélique still looked blank, she explained:

"Maître Aubin, you know, the hangman!"

The young woman felt a shudder seize her at the nape of her neck and run all the way down her spine. Silently, she began to eat the coarse food. It was the time of fasting before Christmas, and every day the same stewed whale and peas appeared, the poor man's dish of penance.

"Yes, he's an apprentice hangman," said the old woman, sitting down to table. "Ah well, it takes all sorts to make a world. Maître Aubin was my husband's brother, and he has nothing but daughters. So when my husband died, Maître Aubin wrote to me in the little hamlet where we lived, telling me he'd take care of my son and teach him his trade and, later, he'd leave him this important office. For you know, to be the Executioner of high and low justice in Paris, that's something! I'd like to live long enough to see my son wear the red hose and singlet. . . ."

Her eyes rested almost tenderly on the thick

head of her horrible offspring, who went on gulping down his stew.

"And to think that perhaps this very morning he put the rope round the neck of a doomed man," mused Angélique, horrified. "The street-urchins weren't so wrong: you can't have a name like that when you ply such a trade!"

The widow, who took her silence for attentive sympathy, continued to talk:

"My husband was a hangman, too. But it's not quite the same thing, in the country for capital executions are performed in the county capitals. Actually, apart from sometimes putting a thief to the question, he was rather what's called a 'riffler,' that is, an animal-flayer and burier of carrion. . . ."

She went on, delighted for once not to be interrupted by outcries of horror.

One would be wrong to think that a hangman's office was a simple one. The variety of methods employed to wrest confessions from patients had turned it into a difficult trade. There was no lack of work for young Rope-round-the-neck, no fear! He had to learn to sever a head with a single stroke of the sword or the axe, to handle the hot iron, pierce the tongue, hang, drown, break on the wheel, and know how to apply the tortures of quartering, water, the boot and the strappado. . . .

That day, Angélique left her plate full and went upstairs rather quickly.

Had Raymond been aware of the trade plied by Mother Cordeau's son when he had sent his sister to live with her? Surely not. Still, Angélique did not dare imagine for a moment that her husband, though a prisoner, might one day come in contact with the hangman. Joffrey de Peyrac was a nobleman! There surely was some law or privilege that forbade the torturing of gentlemen. She'd have to ask Desgrez about it. . . . The hangman was for poor people, for those who were exposed in the pillory on the market-square or whipped naked at the crossroads, or for those who were taken to be hanged in the Place de Grève, "gallows-birds" who provided the best entertainment for the populace. It had nothing to do with Joffrey de Peyrac, last descendant of the Comtes of Toulouse. . . .

From then on, Angélique was a less frequent visitor in Madame Cordeau's kitchen.

She struck up a closer friendship with Françoise Scarron and, as she had a little money from the sale of Kouassi-Ba, she bought wood to make a good fire and would often invite the young widow to her room. Madame Scarron was still hoping that the King might read her petitions some day. Hopefully she would set out for the Louvre on certain chilly mornings and would come back with her hopes dashed, but with a full stock of Court anecdotes which amused her for the rest of the day.

She left the Temple for some ten days, having found a post as housekeeper to some great lady, then returned without giving any explanation and resumed her cold, hidden life in the shadow of the enclosure. She sometimes received visits from highly-placed people who had known her when the satirical writer Scarron reigned over a little coterie of wits and wags.

One day, Angélique recognized the blaring voice

of Athénaïs de Tonnay-Charente through the wall partition. She knew that the lovely Poitevin girl was having a rather hectic career in Parisian society but had not yet hooked a handsomely titled and pensioned husband.

Another time there was a vivacious blonde who was still beautiful despite the fact that she was approaching her forties. As she was leaving, Angélique heard her say:

"Ah well, my dear, we must gather roses while we may. You pain me by living in this unheated room, with your worn-out dresses. Such poverty just isn't permissible when one has such lovely eyes."

Françoise murmured something that Angélique could not hear.

"That I grant you," replied the gay, melodious voice, "but it is up to us to see to it that a servitude, which is no more humiliating than soliciting pensions, does not become slavery. Thus the 'paying gentleman' who at the moment enables me to ride in a carriage has resigned himself quite easily to two short visits per month. 'For five hundred *livres,*' I told him, 'it's impossible for me to give more.' He bows to it for he knows quite well that if he doesn't he'll get nothing. Oh, he's a good fellow; his only quality is that he is an admirable connoisseur of meat for his grandfather was a butcher. He gives me his advice when I am entertaining. I warned him, too, that he would be ungracious to show jealousy, for I like to have my little fancies. You look shocked, my dear! I see it by the way you curl your pretty lips. Look, it's a fact, though, that there is nothing so varied in nature as the pleasures of love, even though they are always the same."

When she saw her friend again, Angélique could not refrain from asking her who the person was.

"Don't think it is to my taste to receive women of that type," answered Françoise, with embarrassment. "But one really must admit that Ninon de Lenclos is the most delightful and wittiest of women. She has helped me a great deal and does her best to find me sponsors. However, I am wondering whether her recommendation may not be less of a help than a hindrance."

"I should have loved to meet and talk to her," said Angélique. "Ninon de Lenclos . . ." she repeated dreamily, for the name of the famous courtesan was not unfamiliar to her. "When I knew that I was going to Paris, I thought: 'If I could only get myself invited to the drawing-room of Ninon de Lenclos!'"

"May an angel carry me off if I lie!" cried the young widow, with eyes shining with enthusiasm. "There's not a place in Paris where one feels more at ease. The tone is quite divine, the decency is remarkable, and you're never bored there. Ninon de Lenclos's salon is really the devil's own snare, for nobody could believe that it is being managed by a person of such reprehensible morals. You know the saying about her: 'Ninon de Lenclos went to bed with Louis XIII's reign and is getting ready to do likewise with Louis XIV's.' Which, incidentally, would not surprise me for she seems to have eternal youth."

That day, as she was entering the Jesuits' little parlour for the second time, Angélique expected to find her brother, who had sent for her, and Desgrez, whom she had not seen for some time. But the only person there was a middle-aged little man in black clothes, wearing one of those "clerk's wigs" made of horsehair, to which was sewn a small black leather cap. He rose and greeted her gauchely in an old-fashioned way, then introduced himself as the clerk of the court, at present engaged by Maître Desgrez for Monsieur de Peyrac's case.

"I have been attending to this case for only three days, but I've already had long talks with Maître Desgrez and Maître Fallot, who have briefed me and instructed me to attend to the ordinary documents and the filing of your suit."

Angélique gave a sigh of relief.

"The trial at last!" she exclaimed.

The little man gazed with a scandalized look at this client who obviously did not know the first thing about legal procedure.

"If Maître Desgrez has done me the signal honour of asking me to assist him, it's because that young man realised that, notwithstanding all the parchment awards that his great intelligence obtained for him, he needed someone who was intimately acquainted with the ins and outs of procedure. That expert on procedure, Madame, is myself."

Angélique saw him close his eyes, swallow his saliva and then watch the flecks of dust that were dancing in a ray of light. She was a little put out.

"But you gave me to understand that the plea was presented?"

"Softly, softly, beautiful lady. I merely said that I was working on the filing of the said suit and that —"

They were interrupted by the lawyer's and the Jesuit's entrance.

"What's this odd bird you brought along?" Angélique whispered to Desgrez.

"Don't be afraid, he isn't dangerous. He is a little insect that feeds on detail, but he is a minor god in his own right."

"He talks of letting my husband rot in prison!"

"Monsieur Clopot, your tongue is too long and you've annoyed Madame," said the lawyer.

The little man made himself even smaller and went to cower in a corner where he began to look like a cockroach. Angélique almost burst out laughing.

"You treat him rather harshly, your minor god of detail."

"It's the only advantage I have over him. Actually, he's a hundred times richer than I am. Now let us sit down and examine the situation."

"The trial is decided upon?"

"It is."

The young woman looked at the faces of her brother and her lawyer, which displayed some reticence.

"Monsieur Clopot's presence must already have told you so," said Raymond at last, "but we have been unsuccessful in our efforts to have your husband appear before an ecclesiastical court."

"Yet . . . since the charge is one of witchcraft?"

"We have put forward all possible arguments and used all our influence, you may believe me. But the King, I think, desires to show himself more Catholic than the Pope. In actual fact, the nearer Monsieur de Mazarin leans towards the grave, the more insistent the young monarch becomes on taking all the affairs of the kingdom into his own hands, including religious matters. Isn't it bad enough that the appointment of bishops depends on his choice, and not on a religious authority? Anyhow, all we've been able to accomplish is to set a civil court trial in motion."

"This decision is preferable to oblivion, isn't it?" said Angélique, seeking encouragement from Desgrez's eyes.

But Desgrez remained marble-like.

"It is always preferable to know one's fate once for all, rather than to entertain doubts for long years," he said.

"Let us not dwell needlessly on this failure," Raymond broke in. "The question now is to know how to exert an influence on the management of the trial. The King will name the sworn judges himself. It is our task to make him understand that he owes it to himself to act with impartiality and justice. It's a delicate task to enlighten the conscience of a King! . . ."

These words reminded Angélique of an expression she had heard the Marquis du Plessis-Bellière use a long time ago about Monsieur Vincent de Paul. He had said of him: "He is the conscience of the kingdom."

"Oh!" she exclaimed, "why haven't I thought of it before? If Monsieur Vincent could speak to the Queen or the King about Joffrey, I am sure he would shake them."

"Alas, Monsieur Vincent died last month, in his house of Saint-Lazare."

"Oh God!" sighed Angélique, whose eyes had filled with tears of disappointment "Oh! why didn't I think of him when he was still alive! He would have known how to talk to them. He would have obtained religious jurisdiction . . ."

"Don't you believe, then, that we tried every possible means to obtain this decision?" asked the Jesuit somewhat acidly.

Angélique's eyes shone.

"I do," she murmured, "but Monsieur Vincent was a saint."

There was a pause, then Father de Sancé sighed.

"You are right. Actually a saint alone could bend the King's pride. Even his most intimate courtiers don't really know the true soul of that young man who, under an apparent attitude of reserve, is devoured by a terrible urge for power. I have no doubt that he will be a great King, but. . . ."

He broke off, considering perhaps that it was not without danger to utter such views.

"We learned," he went on, "that certain scientists who live in Rome, and two of whom are members of our congregation, were perturbed by the arrest of Comte Joffrey de Peyrac and had protested against it — surreptitiously of course, since the case has been kept secret so far. It would be possible to collect their testimonies and to ask the Pope to intervene by writing to the King. That august voice, confronting him with his responsibilities and beseeching him to examine closely the case of an accused man whom all the greatest minds consider innocent of the crime of witchcraft, might shake him."

"Do you think we could obtain such a letter?" asked Angélique, without much hope. "The Church does not like scientists."

"I consider that it is not for a woman of your conduct to judge the mistakes or shortcomings of the Church," Raymond suggested mildly.

Angélique was not deceived by the blandness of his tone. She remained silent.

"I had the feeling that something was amiss between Raymond and me today," she said, while accompanying the lawyer back to the postern-gate a little later. "Why does he speak so sharply of my conduct? I think I am leading at least as exemplary a life as the hangman's wife who's lodging me."

Desgrez smiled.

"I suppose your brother must already have picked up some of those leaflets that are making the round of Paris this morning. Claude Le Petit, the notorious poet of the Pont-Neuf who, for almost six years now, has been troubling the digestion of the mighty, has got wind of your husband's trial and grasped the opportunity to dip his pen into vitriol."

"What can he have said? Did you see the pamphlets?"

The lawyer beckoned to Monsieur Clopot who was walking behind them to come closer and to hand him the bag he was holding. He pulled from it a bundle of poorly printed leaflets. They were little songs in verse. With a verve that seemed to gush spontaneously but which visibly sought the most infamous slights and the most vulgar terms, the journalist presented Joffrey de Peyrac as "the great Lame Man, the hairy one, the Grand Cuckold of Languedoc. . . ."

It was easy for him to twit the accused's physical appearance. He ended one of his lampoons with this couplet:

> And the beautiful Madame de Peyrac,
> Praying that the Bastille
>   will open nevermore
> And he remain in his cul-de-sac,
> Goes to the Louvre and plays the whore.

Angélique thought she was going to blush but, on the contrary, she went quite pale.

"Oh! that horrid Gutter-Poet!" she cried, flinging the sheets into the mud. "It's true that the filthy gutter is still too clean for him!"

"Hush! Madame, you mustn't swear," protested Desgrez, affecting a scandalized air while the clerk crossed himself. "Monsieur Clopot, will you please pick up that filth and put it back into the bag."

"I'd like to know why they don't throw these cursed gazetteers into prison instead of putting honest people there," Angélique went on, trembling with rage. "I heard that gazetteers are locked up in the Bastille, as if they were worthy of respect. Why not at the Châtelet, like the bandits they are?"

"It isn't easy to collar a gazetteer. They are the most slippery race alive. They are everywhere and nowhere. Claude Le Petit has been almost hanged ten times, and yet he always reappears and hurls his arrows at the least expected moments. He is the eye of Paris. He sees everything, knows everything and nobody ever meets him. I have never seen him myself, but I suppose his ears must be bigger than a barber's basin, for all the gossip of the capital finds room in them. He ought to be paid as a spy instead of being prosecuted."

"He ought to be hanged, once for all!"

"It is true that our dear and inefficient police classes journalist-gazetteers among the *ill-intentioned persons*. But they'll never catch the Little Poet of the Pont-Neuf, if we don't take a hand in it, my dog and I."

"Do that, I beg of you!" cried Angélique, gripping Desgrez with both her hands. "I want to see Sorbonne bring him to me in his jaws, dead or alive."

"I'd rather go and offer him to Monsieur de Mazarin, for, believe me, even more than you, he's certainly the Cardinal's worst enemy."

"How does it happen that a liar has been allowed to swagger for so long with impunity?"

"Alas! Claude Le Petit's formidable strength lies in the fact that he never lies and is rarely mistaken."

Angélique opened her mouth to protest, then remembered the Marquis de Vardes and fell silent, swallowing her rage and her shame.

Chapter 41

A few days before Christmas, snow began to
fall. The city donned festive garb. In the
churches, crèches were being set up. The banners
of the brotherhoods led long, chanting processions
through the narrow streets filled with snow and
slush.

In accordance with custom, the Augustinian friars of the Hôtel-Dieu hospital began to produce
thousands of fritters, sprinkled with lemon-juice,
which children sold throughout Paris. One was allowed to break the fast only with these fritters.
The money derived from their sale would help
to provide a Christmas celebration for the needy
and sick.

At this time Angélique, caught up in the lugubrious complications of the dreadful trial, hardly
realised that she was living through the blessed
hours of Christmas and the first days of the New
Year. To begin with, Desgrez came to see her in
the Temple one morning and brought her the information he had been able to obtain about the
nomination of the sworn judges for the trial.

"The designation of the judges was preceded
by a long investigation. We mustn't harbour any
illusions, for it seems that they were chosen not
at all for their spirit of justice, but according to
their degree of attachment to the royal cause.
Moreover, certain magistrates, though devoted to

the King, were discarded if known to be brave enough possibly to oppose royal pressure. Maître Gallemand, for instance, is one of the most famous advocates of our time. He is very much in favour for, during the civil war, he openly took the King's side even to the point of risking imprisonment. But he is a fighter who is not afraid of anybody, and his unexpected sallies make the Palace tremble. I had been hoping all along that he would be chosen, but they definitely want only safe people."

"That was to be foreseen from all I recently heard," said Angélique courageously. "Do you know the names of those who've already been appointed?"

"Séguier, the chief Président of the Court, will personally conduct the formal examination of the defendant in order to give the case the lustre it deserves as an example and as publicity."

"Président Séguier! That's more than I dared hope for!"

"Let's not be carried away," said the lawyer. "Président Séguier is paying the price of his moral independence for his lofty position. I've also heard that he's supposed to have visited the prisoner and that the interview was stormy. The Comte refused to take the oath, for the Chamber of Justice, he said, was incompetent in his eyes to try a member of the Parliament of Toulouse, the Grand Chamber of the Paris Parliament being the only court entitled to try a former *maître des requêtes,* or Special Magistrate, of a provincial parliament."

"Didn't you say that a parliamentary trial was not to be desired on account of the members' subservience to Monsieur Fouquet?"

"Quite so, Madame, and I tried to warn your husband accordingly. But either the warning did not reach him, or else his pride refuses to take advice; at any rate I can only report to you the answer he gave to the Grand Master of the King's justice."

"And what's the upshot of it?" the young woman asked anxiously.

"I suppose the King decided to ignore custom and that your husband will be tried, if necessary, 'mute of malice.' "

"Which means?"

The lawyer explained that this consisted of trying the accused as if in his absence, which would jeopardise the Comte's chances. In France an accused was always presumed guilty, whereas in England, for instance, it was the task of the prosecution to prove the guilt of an arrested person who, in the absence of a written charge, was released within twenty-four hours.

"And do you know who will be the prosecutor at the trial?"

"There will be two of them. First, there is Denis Talon, who is the King's own Attorney-General, and then, as I foresaw, there is your brother-in-law Fallot de Sancé, who's been designated as a judge. The latter made a show of withdrawing on the grounds of his family links with you, but Talon and the others must have persuaded him, for they now say in the lobbies of the Palace of Justice that it was very shrewd of him to have made his choice between his family duties and his loyalty to the King to whom he owes everything."

Angélique swallowed and her face contracted. But she controlled herself.

"There is also Massenau, a member of the Toulouse Parliament. With the Attorney-General, Massenau is the only one specifically designated by name. The others are chosen by Séguier, or by Talon himself."

"So there will be other sworn judges?"

"There'll be the president of the jury. Président Mesmon has been mentioned, and that surprises me. He's an old man, with hardly a breath of life left in him. I can't see him presiding over a hearing that has every chance of being stormy. Perhaps he's been chosen only on account of his physical weakness, for he is known to be an upright and conscientious man. If he can muster up some strength for this trial, he is one of those whom we can hope to convince. Further, there'll be Bourié, secretary of the Council of Justice, who has the reputation of being a legal forger, and a certain Delmas, a very obscure lawyer, chosen perhaps because he is an uncle of Colbert, who is himself an agent of Mazarin's, or perhaps merely because he is a Protestant and because the King wants to give his justice every appearance of legality and thereby maintain his reputation for giving the reformed religion an equal share in the performance of the kingdom's secular justice."

"I suppose," said Angélique, "that this Huguenot will be much surprised to find himself involved in a trial for witchcraft where exorcisms and possession by demons will be debated. Actually, though, it may profit us to have someone a little more open-minded among the jury, one who'll reject superstition on principle. Don't you think so?"

"No doubt," said the lawyer, nodding his head with a worried expression. "By the way, speaking of exorcism and possession, tell me if you know a monk by the name of Conan Bécher, and a nun who, before taking the veil, was called Carmencita de Mérecourt?"

"Do I know them!" exclaimed Angélique. "That Friar Bécher is a half-crazed alchemist who swore he'd wrest the secret of the Philosopher's Stone from my husband. As for Carmencita de Mérecourt, she is a volcanic person who was at one time . . . Joffrey's mistress and who won't forgive him for not letting her remain so. But what are they doing in this affair?"

"There's talk of a performance of exorcism which was presided over by Bécher and in which that lady is said to have taken part. It's all very vague. The relevant document has only just been added to the case for the prosecution and is supposed to constitute evidence of capital importance."

"You haven't read it?"

"I've read nothing of the enormous file which Councillor Bourié is busily compiling. To my mind, he'll make free use of his gifts as a forger."

"But surely, since the case is going to be heard, you, as counsel for the defence, must have cognizance of the details of the bills of indictment?"

"Unfortunately not. I have already been told several times that your husband will be refused legal assistance. So at the moment I am making every effort to obtain a statement of this refusal *in writing*."

"But that's mad!"

"Not at all. Judicial custom says that a lawyer's assistance can only be denied to a man who is accused of the crime of high treason. Such a charge is, after all, difficult to uphold in the present case. So by obtaining a written declaration of such a refusal of legal assistance, I shall be able to show that the procedure is improper, which will put me in a strong moral position. In the end, by this strategem, I think I shall compel them to name me defending counsel."

When Desgrez returned two days later, he looked satisfied and Angélique's heart jumped with hopefulness.

"The trick's come off!" he cried exultantly. "The chief President of the Chamber of Justice, Séguier, has just appointed me as counsel for the defence of Monsieur de Peyrac, accused of witchcraft. It's a victory won thanks to the tangle of procedure. Despite their overwhelming desire to please the King, those haughty flunkeys of justice found themselves too much at loggerheads with their own principles. In short, they found themselves compelled to appoint an advocate. However, I want to point out to you, Madame, that there is still time for you to choose a more famous lawyer to whom to entrust your husband's case."

Angélique was gazing out of the window. The enclosure of the Temple was almost empty and seemed to be slumbering under its quilt of snow. Madame Scarron passed, wrapped in her shabby coat, on her way to Mass in the Grand Prior's chapel. The tinkling of a little bell was muted under the grey sky.

At the foot of the house, Sorbonne was dolefully padding round in circles as he waited for his master. Angélique glanced sideways at her lawyer, who was affecting an air of gravity and composure.

"I really can't imagine a more qualified man to whom I could entrust this case," she said. "You fulfil all the desirable conditions. Indeed, when my brother-in-law Fallot recommended you to me, he told me: 'He is one of the cleverest minds in the profession and, moreover, he won't cost you much.'"

"I thank you, Madame, for holding such a good opinion of me," said Desgrez, who did not seem at all displeased.

The young woman drew patterns mechanically on the blurred window-pane with her fingers. "When I'm back in Toulouse with Joffrey," she thought, "shall I still remember Desgrez? Sometimes it'll come back to me that we were together at the bath-house and it will seem to me incredible!"

Suddenly she veered round, transfigured.

"If I'm not mistaken, you'll be able to see my husband every day. Couldn't you take me with you?"

But Desgrez dissuaded her from attempting to break the very strict orders of complete confinement that applied to the prisoner. He himself was not yet certain of being allowed to see him, but he was determined to fight for this right through the intermediary of the Bar Council. He explained that he might have a greater chance to obtain his ends than a lawyer of great renown, of whom the powers that be would have misgivings. Quick action was now essential for, since his appointment had been wrested from the royal justice only by a ruse, there was every reason to expect that the case for the prosecution would be communicated to him only very shortly before the hearing, and even then perhaps only in part.

"In this kind of case, I know that the documents frequently are just loose sheets, and the Lord Privy Seal, the Cardinal Mazarin or the King reserves the right to examine or remove or add to them at any time. Of course, this isn't common, but since this case is somewhat special . . ."

Angélique was humming that night as she cooked Florimond's porridge, and she even found Widow Cordeau's perpetual whale-stew tasty. The children from the Hôtel-Dieu hospital had passed through the Temple that day. She had bought some excellent fritters from them, and her full stomach helped her to see the future in rosier colours.

Her confidence was rewarded. The following evening, the lawyer returned with two pieces of extraordinary news: some of the documents had been shown to him, and he had obtained permission to see the prisoner. When she heard this, Angélique rushed towards Desgrez, threw her arms around his neck and kissed him fervently. For a moment she felt the clasp of two vigorous arms and she experienced a brief, intense pleasure. But she immediately shrank back in confusion and, wiping her eyes in which tears were welling, she stammered that she no longer knew what she was doing.

Desgrez, very tactfully, did not seem to attribute any importance to the incident. He said that his visit to the Bastille would take place at noon the next day. He would be able to talk to the prisoner only in the Governor's presence, but he was hoping that, later on, he could manage to see the Comte de Peyrac alone.

"I shall go with you," Angélique decided. "I shall wait outside the prison."

The lawyer then pulled from a worn plush bag a few sheets on which he had jotted down the principal counts of the indictment.

"He is charged, in the main, with witchcraft and sorcery. Stated to be an artist in making poisons and distilling drugs. Convicted of feats of magic such as seeing into the future and warding off evil spells to avoid the threat of poison. Alleged to have, by sorcery, discovered the art of bewitching many people reputed to be of sound mind and to have sent out diabolic and ludicrous invocations. He is also said to teach the use of powders and flowers to inspire love and so forth. The prosecution further asserts that one of his former . . . mistresses died and that, when her body was exhumed, it was discovered that she had in her mouth a talisman-portrait of the Comte de Peyrac. . . ."

"What a collection of arrant nonsense!" Angélique exclaimed, dumbfounded. "You surely don't mean to say that respectable judges can possibly admit such stuff as evidence at a trial?"

"They probably will and, personally, I am delighted at this very surfeit of stupidities which I

674

shall be able to demolish with ease. The rest of the indictment comprises the crime of alchemy, the quest for treasures, the transmutation of gold and — mark this! — 'the heretical presumption of having created life.' Can you enlighten me, Madame, on this last point?"

Completely at a loss, Angélique pondered for a long while and eventually placed a hand over her womb where her second child was stirring.

"Do you think they could be referring to this?" she said laughingly.

The lawyer gave a resigned and dubious gesture. He went on reading:

" '. . . has increased his fortune by means of witchcraft, not overlooking transmutation, etc.' And quite at the end I see this: 'Demanded rights that were not his due. Openly boasted of being independent of the King and Princes. Received heretical and suspect foreigners and made use of prohibited books of foreign origins.' Now," continued Desgrez with some hesitation, "I come to what seems to me the most disturbing and astonishing point in the file. It deals with the minutes of an exorcism practised on the person of your husband by three ecclesiastics, who have declared that he was proved to be possessed and to have had dealings with the devil."

"But this is inconceivable!" cried Angélique, who felt cold sweat at her temples. "Who are these priests?"

"One of them is Friar Bécher. I don't know how he was able to get into the Bastille as an official representative. But what is certain is that this ceremony actually took place and that the witnesses assert that all the Comte's reactions convincingly prove his intercourse with Satan."

"That's impossible!" repeated Angélique. "You at least don't believe it, do you?"

"I, Madame, am a libertine. I believe neither in God nor the devil."

"Be quiet," she stammered, quickly crossing herself.

She ran over to Florimond and clasped him to her bosom.

"Don't listen to what he's saying, my angel!" she murmured. "Oh! men are crazy."

After a moment's silence, Desgrez went over to the young woman.

"Don't alarm yourself," he said, "there's *certainly* something wrong here. But I emphasize the fact that this piece of evidence is very disquieting, for it's the one that may most impress the judges. The exorcism was practiced in accordance with the rites of Rome. The accused's reactions are most damning. I specially noted the reaction to diabolic spots and the casting of spells on others."

"What exactly does that refer to?"

"As for the diabolic spots, demonologists point out that certain places on the body of a possessed man are rendered sensitive to the touch of a silver probe, which has been exorcised. Now, in the course of that test, the witnesses ascertained that the accused at certain moments uttered dreadful and 'truly infernal' shrieks, when an ordinary man would have in no way been inconvenienced by the light touch of this inoffensive instrument. As for the spellbinding of others, a person was brought into his presence and manifested all the familiar signs of possession."

"If Carmencita was the person concerned, I am sure she play-acted the part to perfection," said Angélique sarcastically.

"She is probably the nun referred to, but her name isn't mentioned. At any rate, I repeat that there's some detail here that rings false. However, as I foresee that the sworn judges will allude to it at every turn, I must be in a position to knock the bottom out of this argument. Unfortunately, I do not see anything for the moment that might render it illegal."

"My husband himself may perhaps be able to enlighten you."

"Let's hope so," sighed the lawyer.

Chapter 42

WITH its thin coat of shining snow, the huge fortress of the Bastille looked even blacker and more sinister than usual. Beneath the low sky, one could see slender wisps of grey smoke rising from the platforms of the towers. Some fires had probably been lit in the Governor's and guards' rooms, but Angélique could easily imagine the icy dampness of the dungeons where the "forgotten" prisoners were cowering on their dank straw-pallets.

Desgrez had made her comfortable, until his return, in a little tavern in the Faubourg Saint-Antoine, with whose landlord, and the latter's daughter in particular, he seemed to be on friendly terms.

From her vantage-point by the window, Angélique could watch everything without being observed. She could clearly see the soldiers on the projecting bastion, who were blowing into their hands as they stamped their feet around the cannons. Occasionally, one of their comrades would call out to them from the top of the battlements, and their ringing voices echoed in the frosty air.

At last Angélique saw Desgrez coming towards her after having crossed the drawbridge. Her heart began to thump with ill-defined apprehension. She noticed that the lawyer had a curious bearing and an odd look about him. He tried to smile, then talked very fast and in a manner that seemed to Angélique falsely cheerful. He said that he had managed to see Monsieur de Peyrac without too much difficulty and that the Governor had left them alone for a few moments. They had reached an agreement about Desgrez assuring the defence of the prisoner.

The Comte at first did not want to have a lawyer, claiming that by accepting counsel he implicitly accepted the decision to be tried by an ordinary court and not by a parliamentary court, as he had demanded. He wanted to defend himself alone but, after some moments' conversation, he had accepted the assistance that he was being offered.

"I am surprised that so hot-tempered a man should have yielded so easily," Angélique marvelled. "I had expected that you would have a real battle. For when it comes to finding logical arguments to support his views, you can always count on him, you know!"

The lawyer wrinkled his forehead as if he were suffering from a violent headache, and he called out to the innkeeper's daughter to bring him a pint of beer.

He finally said in a strange tone of voice:

"Your husband gave in at the mere sight of your handwriting."

"He read my letter? Did it make him happy?"

"I read it to him."

"Why? He —"

She broke off and murmured in a toneless voice:

"You mean he wasn't in a state to read it himself? Why? Is he ill? Speak up! I have a right to know."

She had unconsciously gripped the young man's wrist and was digging her nails into his flesh. He waited until the girl who had brought the beer went away.

"Be brave," he said with unfeigned compassion. "You might as well know everything. The Governor of the Bastille did not conceal from me the fact that the Comte de Peyrac had been subjected to the preliminary question."

Angélique went ghastly pale.

"What have they done to him? Have they broken his poor limbs?"

"No. But it is a fact that the torture of the boot and the rack has much weakened him and that he is obliged to remain lying down. That's not the worst though. During the Governor's absence your husband was able to give me some details of the exorcism to which he was subjected by Friar Bécher. He said that the probe which the latter used for one of the trials was a contraption that actually, at certain moments, thrust a long needle into his flesh. In the grip of a sudden excruciating pain, he could not prevent himself from screaming several times, and this was very unfavourably interpreted by the witnesses. As for the possessed nun, he did not fully recognize her, for he had already half fainted."

"Is he in pain? Is he in desperation?"

"He has great courage, although his body is exhausted and he has had to submit to almost thirty interrogations."

After remaining thoughtful for a moment, Desgrez added:

"Shall I confess? His appearance gave me a shock. I could not fathom that you were that man's wife. And then, as soon as we had exchanged a few words, when his glowing eyes gazed into mine, I understood. . . . Oh! I forgot! The Comte de Peyrac has given me a message for his son Florimond. He wants him to know that, on his return, he'll bring his son two little spiders which he has taught to dance."

"Ugh! I hope Florimond won't touch them," said Angélique, fighting hard to suppress a sob.

"We now see more clearly," declared Father de Sancé, when he had listened to the lawyer's report of the latest events. "Do you think, Maître, that the prosecution will confine itself to the acts of alleged witchcraft and use the minutes drawn up by Friar Bécher as evidence?"

"I am convinced of it, for the rumours they tried to spread about the Comte de Peyrac's so-called treason against the King had to be dropped as baseless. So for want of a better charge, they've come back to the first accusation: he is a sorcerer whom this secular law court presumes to try."

"Good. So we have to convince the judges, on the one hand, that there is nothing supernatural about the mining research in which my brother-in-law engaged, and for this you must obtain the testimony of the workmen with whom he operated. On the other hand, it is essential to expose as valueless the exorcism on which the prosecution believes it can base its case."

"The case would be won if the judges, who are all devout believers, could be convinced that the exorcism was in fact a sham."

"We shall help you to prove it."

Raymond de Sancé struck the parlour-table with the palm of his hand and turned his fine-featured, sallow face towards the lawyer.

"For there is something you don't know, Mr. Advocate," said the Jesuit in a firm, trenchant voice, "even as many princes of the Church of France do not know it. Their religious education, it is true, is often less advanced than that of a poor, country parson. It is this: there is only one man in France authorized by the Pope to try cases of possession and manifestations of Satan. That man is a member of the Society of Jesus. Only after a long prudent life and deep and arduous studies did he receive from His Holiness the Pope the redoubtable privilege of conversing face to face with the Prince of Darkness. I am convinced, Maître Desgrez, that you will dumbfound the judges when you inform them that only a deposition of an exorcism signed by the Reverend Father Kircher, Grand Exorcist of France, is valid in the eyes of the Church."

"Indeed," exclaimed Desgrez, greatly excited, "I admit I suspected something of the sort, but this Friar Bécher acted with infernal cleverness and managed to get himself accredited by Cardinal de Gondi, the Archbishop of Paris. I shall challenge this violation of religious procedure!" cried the lawyer. "I shall challenge the unauthorized priests who, by a blasphemous mockery, cast ridicule on the Church."

"Be good enough to wait for me a few moments," said Father de Sancé, getting up.

He returned soon after, accompanied by another Jesuit whom he introduced as Father Kircher. Angélique was much impressed at meeting the Grand Exorcist of France. She did not quite know what she had expected, but she certainly had not thought she would find before her a man of such modest appearance. Without the black cassock, set off only by a copper cross on his chest, this taciturn Jesuit would easily have been taken for a peaceful peasant rather than for an ecclesiastic accustomed to conversing with the devil.

Angélique felt that Desgrez too, despite his fundamental skepticism, could not fail to be drawn by the newcomer's appearance. Raymond said that he had already apprised Father Kircher of the case and he now informed him of the latest events. The Grand Exorcist was listening with a kind, reassuring smile.

"It seems a simple matter," he said at last. "I in turn shall have to perform a regular exorcism. The report of it, which you will read at the trial and which I shall support with my own testimony, should put those gentlemen's consciences in a ticklish position."

"It's not quite so simple," said Desgrez, energetically scratching his head. "To get you into the Bastille, even as a chaplain, to see this strictly watched prisoner, seems to me quite a problem . . ."

"All the more so, since there must be three of us."

"Why?"

"The devil is too clever for a single man, even though armed with prayers, to provoke him without peril. To approach a man who is trafficking with the devil, I have to be assisted by at least two of my acolytes."

"But my husband doesn't traffic with the devil!" Angélique protested.

She quickly buried her face in her hands to hide a sudden attack of giggling. She couldn't help imagining Joffrey standing before a shop-counter and conversing with a horned and smiling devil. Oh! when they were at last back again in Toulouse, how they would laugh at all this rubbish! She imagined herself sitting on Joffrey's lap, burying her lips in his thick, violet-scented shock of hair, while his wonderful hands found again, with ardent caresses, the body he loved.

Her untimely laughter ended in a brief sob.

"Take courage, my dear sister," Raymond said gently. "The birth of Christ brings us a message of hope: peace to men of good will."

But these alternatives of hope and despair were

683

sapping the young woman's strength. When her thoughts carried her back to the last festive Christmas she had spent at Toulouse, she felt filled with horror at the long way she had come since then. Could she have imagined, a year ago, that she would find herself on this Christmas Eve, while the bells of Paris were pealing under the grey sky, with no shelter other than Widow Cordeau's hearth? Next to the old woman spinning her yarn and the apprentice hangman who was innocently playing with little Florimond, she barely felt the strength to hold out her palms to the fire. Sitting by her side on the same bench, Madame Scarron, as young and beautiful, as wretched and friendless as herself, now and then slipped her arm softly around her companion's waist and nestled against her.

The old linen-draper, also huddling by the only fire in the dismal dwelling, was drowsing in the tapestry armchair which he had moved down from his bedroom. He was muttering in his sleep and counting figures in an obstinate quest for the causes of his bankruptcy. When a crackling log woke him, he smiled and said with effort:

"Let us not forget that Jesus will be born. All the world is rejoicing. Why don't we sing a little hymn?"

And, to Florimond's delight, he sang quaveringly but with fervour:

> We were three little shepherd-lasses
> By a little brook, oh!
> Looking after our lambkins,
> Hey nonny no!
> Which were grazing in the meadow.

There was a knock at the door. A black figure could be seen saying a few words to Rope-round-the-neck.

"It's for Madame Angélique," said the boy.

Angélique rose, thinking she would find Desgrez. In the entrance, she saw a booted cavalier, wrapped in a greatcoat and whose lowered felt-hat hid his face.

"I have come to say goodbye, my dear sister."

It was Raymond.

"Where are you going?" she asked in surprise.

"To Rome . . . I cannot give you any particulars of the mission I am entrusted with, but tomorrow everybody will know that relations between the French embassy and the Vatican have taken a turn for the worse. The ambassador has refused to comply with the orders of the Holy Father, who demanded that only diplomatic personnel be admitted within the precincts of the embassy. Louis XIV replied that any attempt to impose decisions other than his own would be answered by force. We are on the eve of a break between the Church of France and the Papacy. It's a catastrophe that we must avoid at all costs. I must ride post-haste to Rome to try and negotiate an understanding."

"You are leaving!" she repeated, aghast. "You too are deserting me? And the letter for Joffrey?"

"Alas, my poor little sister, I am much afraid that under the present circumstances any plea from the Sovereign Pontiff would have a bad reception from our monarch. But you can rely on me to attend to this affair during my stay in Rome. Look, here's a little money. And now listen, I saw Desgrez less than an hour ago. Your husband has

685

been transferred to the prison of the law courts."

"What does that mean?"

"That he will be tried soon. That's not all. At the law courts, Desgrez is confident that he will be able to get Father Kircher and his acolytes admitted. This very night they hope to be with the prisoner. I have no doubt that the test will be decisive. Be confident!"

She was listening to him with a frozen heart, unable to kindle a glow of hopefulness. The priest, taking her by her slender shoulders, drew her towards him and placed a brotherly kiss on her cold cheeks.

"Be confident, my dear sister," he repeated.

She heard the receding steps of the two horses, muffled by the snowy carpet as, trotting through the postern-gate of the enclosure, they moved away into Paris.

Desgrez lived on the Petit-Pont, which links the Cité with the University district, in one of those narrow old houses with pointed gables, whose foundations had been soaking in the Seine for centuries undisturbed by floods.

Crazed with waiting, Angélique finally went to see him. She had obtained his address from the innkeeper of The Trois Maillets. When she reached the appointed place, she hesitated a little. The house really resembled Desgrez: poor, gawky, and just a trifle arrogant. Angélique climbed up the winding stairs, whose banisters of rotting timber were decorated with weird, grimacing sculptures.

On the top floor, there was only one door. She

heard the dog Sorbonne snuffle at floor-level. She knocked. The door was opened by a big wench with a painted face, whose neckerchief opened on a generous bosom. Angélique shrank back. She hadn't thought of that.

"What do you want?" asked the other.

"Does Maître Desgrez live here?"

Someone stirred inside the room, and the lawyer appeared, a goose-quill in his hand.

"Come in, Madame," he said in a very natural tone of voice.

Then he shoved the girl outside and closed the door.

"So you haven't even two *sous'*-worth of patience?" he said reproachfully. "You must come and seek me in my lair, at the risk of your life. . . ."

"I have been without news since —"

"Only six days."

"What was the outcome of the exorcism?"

"Sit down," said Desgrez, without the least pity, "and let me finish what I am about to write. Then we'll talk."

Angélique sat down on the seat he had indicated, which was nothing more than a wooden box. She glanced around, thinking to herself that she had never seen such a squalid place. The light seeped into it only through small, greenish panes of lead-framed glass. A meagre fire in the hearth did not dispel the dampness that rose from the river, which could be heard flowing below between the piles of the Petit-Pont. Books were stacked up on the floor in a corner. Desgrez himself had no table. Seated on a stool, he was writing on a plank placed on his knees. His inkstand stood on the floor beside him.

The only substantial piece of furniture was the bed, but its blue twill curtains and blankets gaped with holes. However, there were white sheets on it, worn but clean. Despite herself, Angélique's eyes constantly returned to the ruffled bed whose disarray openly betrayed the scene which, a few moments ago, must have taken place there between the lawyer and the girl whom he had so unceremoniously shown out. The young woman felt the blood rise to her cheeks.

She felt an intense desire to nestle against a masculine shoulder and forget everything in a demanding, perhaps brutal embrace. She gazed at him. She felt a little ashamed and, to conceal her confusion, she mechanically fondled the big head which the Great Dane had devotedly put on her knees.

"Phew!" exclaimed Desgrez, rising and stretching himself. "Never in my life have I talked so much about God and the Church. Do you know what these sheets represent that you see scattered over the floor?"

"No, I don't."

"The speech of Maître Desgrez, defending counsel, which he will make at the trial of Monsieur de Peyrac, accused of witchcraft, which will come up for hearing at the law court assizes on the 20th January 1661."

"The date's been fixed?" cried Angélique, who felt herself go pale. "Oh! I absolutely must be there. Disguise me as a robed man of law or as a monk. I am pregnant, it's true," she said, looking down at herself with annoyance, "but it hardly shows. Madame Cordeau assures me that I'll have a girl, because I am carrying the baby so high. At a pinch, I could be taken for a clerk with a tendency for guzzling. . . ."

Desgrez started to laugh.

"I am not sure the deception wouldn't be a little too conspicuous. I've thought up something better. There'll be a few nuns admitted to the court-room. You can disguise yourself with a wimple and rosary."

"But then I wonder if the nuns' good reputation would not be compromised by my bulging midriff!"

"Pah! under an ample gown and a good cloak it won't show. But, look: can I count on your composure?"

"I promise you that I shall be as quiet as a mouse."

"It'll be hard work," said Desgrez. "I can't tell how things will turn out. There's this to be said in favour of all law courts: they react to sensational evidence brought before them. I therefore hold in reserve the scientific demonstration of the manufacture of gold to squash the charge of alchemy, and above all, the deposition drawn up by Father Kircher, *only accredited* representative of the Church, who declares that your husband does not show any sign of possession."

"Thank God!" Angélique sighed. "We will win, won't we?"

He made a dubious gesture.

"I saw that Fritz Hauer," he said after a moment's pause. "He has arrived with all his pans and alembics. Impressive fellow, he is! A pity. Never mind! I am hiding him at the Carthusian convent in the Faubourg Saint-Jacques. As for the Moor, with whom I was able to have a talk by slipping into the Tuileries in the guise of a vinegar-merchant, we are assured of his help. Don't, above all, mention my plan to anyone. The life of these poor people may be at stake. And success may depend on these few demonstrations."

This advice seemed superfluous to the unfortunate Angélique, who felt her mouth go dry under the impact of alternate fears and hopes.

"I shall accompany you home," said the lawyer. "Paris is not a healthy place for you. Don't leave the Temple any more until the morning of the trial. A nun will come and fetch you, bring your clothes and accompany you to the Palace of Justice. I might as well tell you that this respectable nun is rather gruff. In fact, she is my elder sister. She brought me up and retired to convent life when she realised that her energetic thrashings had not prevented me from straying from the path of virtue. She prays for the remission of my sins. In short, she'd do anything for me. You can trust her implicitly."

In the street, Desgrez took Angélique's arm. As they reached the end of the Petit-Pont, Sorbonne stopped short and cocked his ears.

A few steps away, a tall, ragged athletic figure seemed to be waiting for the two strollers. Under his faded hat adorned with a feather, one could half make out a face marked with a violet wen and masked with a black bandage that hid one eye. The man was smiling almost insolently.

Sorbonne pounced upon him. The rogue jumped aside with an acrobat's nimbleness and dashed into the doorway of one of the houses on the Petit-Pont. The dog streaked after him. There was a resounding splash.

"Damn Calembredaine!" grumbled Desgrez. "He's jumped into the Seine despite the ice. I wager that at this moment he's dodging among the piles. He has real rat-holes under all the bridges of Paris. He's one of the boldest bandits in town."

Sorbonne came slinking back, his tail between his legs.

Angélique tried to control her fright, but she could not rid herself of a fearful apprehension. It seemed to her that this wretch suddenly looming in their path was a symbol of a dreadful destiny.

Chapter 43

DAY was just breaking as Angélique, accompanied by the nun, passed over the Pont-au-Change and found herself in the Cité.

The cold was biting. The Seine was jammed with big blocks of ice that produced sinister cracking sounds in the piles under the old wooden bridges. Snow decked the roofs, edged the cornices of the houses, and transformed the spire of the Sainte-Chapelle into a blossoming branch planted in the heart of the serried mass of the law courts.

Had it not been for her pious disguise, Angélique would gladly have stopped the brandy-merchant. The red-nosed vendor was hurrying past to rouse the unskilled workers, the poor clerks and apprentices, all those who had to rise first to open workshop, stall or study. Six o'clock sounded from the big clock on the corner tower. The clock-face on a background of azure and golden fleurs-de-lis had been a rare novelty in King Henri III's time. The clock was the jewel of the Palace of Justice. Its coloured clay figures, its dove representing the Holy Ghost, sheltering under its wings Justice and Piety, were gleaming with their red, white and blue enamels in the grey morning.

After passing through the big courtyard and mounting a flight of steps, Angélique and her companion were at last approached by a lawyer whom Angélique recognized with surprise as Desgrez. He intimidated her in his ample black robe, his immaculate neck-band, his wig with its white rolls carefully topping one another under his square doctor's cap. He was holding in his hand a brand-new brief-bag bulging with documents. Very gravely, he told them that he had just seen the prisoner in the cells of the Palace of the Conciergerie.

"Does he know that I shall be in the court-room?" inquired Angélique.

"No! It might unsettle him. What about you? You promise to remain cool and collected?"

"I promise."

"He is . . . he is in a bad way," said Desgrez hoarsely. "He's been horribly tortured. But the obviously flagrant abuses of those who rigged this trial may impress the judges. Whatever happens, you'll be strong?"

With a constricted throat, she nodded.

At the entrance to the court-room, the King's

guards asked for signed tickets of admission. It hardly surprised Angélique when the nun handed them one, murmuring almost inaudibly as she did so:

"In the service of His Excellency the Cardinal Mazarin."

A court-usher then guided them to the centre of an already packed room, where the black robes of the legal practitioners mingled with the frocks and cassocks of priests and monks. A somewhat sparse gathering of noblemen filled the second row of the semi-circle. Angélique recognized none of them. She could only presume that the Court gentry weren't admitted or knew nothing of this trial which was being held virtually *in camera,* or else that they did not wish to compromise themselves.

The Comtesse de Peyrac and her neighbour sat a little apart, but in seats from which they could see and hear everything. Angélique was surprised to find herself sitting next to a string of nuns of various orders, whom a high-ranking chaplain seemed to be watching over discreetly. Angélique wondered what these nuns could be doing at a trial for alchemy and witchcraft.

The court-room, which was situated in one of the oldest parts of the Palace of Justice, had a vaulted, arched dome, from which carved pendants held masses of acanthus leaves suspended over the heads of the public. It was dark on account of the stained-glass windows, and a few candles added to the lugubrious atmosphere. Two or three big German stoves, with gleaming glazed earthenware, spread a little warmth.

Vainly she searched the crowd for familiar faces.

Neither the lawyer, nor the prisoner, nor the jury, had yet arrived. The court-room, however, was full by now, and many people were crammed in the passages despite the early hour. It was obvious that some of them had come here as if to a spectacle, or rather as if to a public class in law, for a great part of the audience was composed of young law clerks. In front of Angélique was a group that seemed particularly noisy. In an undertone, they were making comments that were doubtless intended for some inexperienced listeners nearby.

"What are they waiting for?" a young lawyer, with profusely powdered hair, was clamouring impatiently.

His neighbour, whose pimply face was wedged in a tight fur collar, answered with a yawn:

"They are waiting for the doors of the court to be closed, whereupon the accused will be brought in and put on the stool of repentance."

"The stool is that isolated bench down there?"

A grinning clerk, as dirty as they come, turned round towards the group and protested:

"You surely wouldn't want them to prepare an armchair for a devil's henchman!"

"Apparently a wizard can stand upright on a pin-point or a flame," said the powdered lawyer.

His plump companion answered gravely:

"They won't ask him to do that, but he will have to remain kneeling on that stool, under a crucifix placed at the foot of the president of the jury's desk."

"That's still too much luxury for such monsters!" cried the clerk with the dirty hair.

Angélique shivered. If the general feeling of a crowd, carefully chosen and composed of the cream of the judicature, was already so biased and hostile, what was to be expected of the judges, who had been handpicked by the King and his servitors? But the deep voice of the lawyer in the fur tippet spoke up:

"As far as I am concerned, all this is a trumped-up charge. This man is no more a wizard than you or I, but he must have got in the way of some vast intrigue of those in power, who'd like to have a legal pretext for suppressing him."

Angélique bent forward to get a better look at the face of this man who dared to give such frank expression to a dangerous opinion. She was dying to ask his name. Her companion lightly touched her hand to remind her to be more discreet. The neighbour of the man in the fur collar whispered, after glancing all around:

"If they really want to suppress him, the nobles don't usually, I believe, trouble to obtain a judgment."

"One's got to satisfy the people and prove to them now and again that the King occasionally punishes some mighty ones."

"If your theory that they want to throw a bone to the public, as Nero used to do, were correct, they would have ordered a vast public hearing, Maître Gallemand, and not an almost secret trial," opined the impatient young man.

"One can see that you are still a greenhorn in this confounded profession," said the famous advocate, of whom Desgrez had said that his sallies made the Palace tremble. "At a public hearing,

695

you run the risk of real popular riots, for the people are sentimental and not as stupid as they look. Now the King is already an old hand at legal procedure, and he fears more than anything that matters might take the same turn as in England, where the people knew full well how to place a King's head on the block. So over here, people with ideas of their own or who are considered a nuisance are suppressed quietly and without fuss. Afterwards, their still twitching carcasses are offered as food to the basest instincts of the rabble. The latter are promptly accused of bestiality. The priests perorate on the need to control our vilest passions, and Mass is said, of course, before and after."

"The Church has nothing to do with such excesses," protested the chaplain, leaning forward. "I would even point out, gentlemen, that too often nowadays laymen who are completely ignorant of canon law presume to substitute themselves for divine law. And I think I can assure you that most of the clerics whom you see here are perturbed by this encroachment on religious law by the secular power. Thus I, who have come from Rome, have seen our embassy at the Vatican gradually being transformed into a refuge for all the riff-raff of the worst type. The Holy Father himself is no longer master in his own home, for our King, to settle this argument, did not hesitate to send troops of reinforcement, French military forces, to his embassy with orders to shoot at the Pope's regiments if the latter laid hands on the Italian and Swiss thieves and bandits, who have taken refuge at the embassy of France."

"But any embassy in foreign territory must remain inviolable," suggested a prudent-looking old burgher.

"No doubt. But it mustn't give shelter to all the rabble of Rome and help to undermine the unity of the Church."

"But the Church, in turn, mustn't undermine the unity of the French State, whose defender is the King," replied the old burgher, with a dogged look on his face.

People stared at him and seemed to wonder what he was doing there. Most of them assumed a suspicious air and turned away, visibly regretting that they had pronounced such daring words before a stranger, who might be a spy of His Majesty's State Council.

Only Maître Gallemand retorted, glaring at him:

"Well, watch this trial attentively, Monsieur. You will no doubt be seeing a minor aspect of the great and very real conflict which already exists between the King and the Church of Rome."

Angélique was following this exchange of words with a feeling of terror. She now had a better understanding of the Jesuits' reluctance and the failure of the Pope's letter in which she had put all her hope for so long. So the King no longer recognized any master. There was, then, but one chance left for Joffrey de Peyrac: that the judges' conscience would be stronger than their servility.

A vast silence spread across the amphitheatre and brought the young woman back to reality. Her heart missed a beat.

She had just caught sight of Joffrey.

He was coming in, walking with difficulty and supporting himself on two sticks; his limp was more marked, and at every step she had the impression that he was going to lose his balance. He seemed to her at once very tall, very bent and horribly thin. She had a dreadful shock. After those long months of separation which had blurred in her memory the outline of the dear figure, she saw him now through the eyes of the public and was terrified to discover his unusual, even disquieting appearance. Joffrey's abundant black hair framing a ravaged face of ghostly pallor, on which the scars drew red furrows, his shabby clothes, his gauntness — they all contributed to impress the crowd.

When he raised his head and his glowing black eyes slowly glanced around the semicircular courtroom with a sort of mocking self-assurance, the pity which some of them had felt disappeared and a hostile murmur ran through the audience. The sight before them exceeded even their wildest hopes. This really was a sorcerer!

Flanked by guards, the Comte de Peyrac remained standing before the stool of repentance, on which he was unable to kneel.

At this moment, a score of armed Royal guards entered through two doors and took up positions at various points in the vast room.

The trial was about to begin. A voice announced: "Gentlemen, the Court!"

The entire audience rose, and through the platform door came the halberdier-ushers in sixteenth-century costume, with frilled ruffs and plumed caps. They preceded a procession of eight judges in gown and ermine collar, wearing the square doctor's cap. In front of Angélique, Maître Gallemand was commenting in an undertone:

"The old man in black at the head is the principal Président of the Court, Séguier. The man in red is Denis Talon, Attorney-General of the King's Council and chief prosecutor. The red cape belongs to Massenau, a parliamentarian from Toulouse, who has been named president of the jury for this trial. The youngest among the judges of the jury is the solicitor Fallot, who calls himself Baron de Sancé, and who doesn't hesitate to curry the Court's favour by consenting to try the accused who is said to be a close relative of his by marriage."

"A drama out of Corneille, in short: heroic devotion to duty," suggested the greenhorn with the powdered hair.

"I see, my friend, that like most flighty young men of your generation you go to those theatrical performances, which no self-respecting man of law can attend without finding frivolous. But believe me, you'll never hear in a theatre a finer comedy than the one you'll be attending today. . . ."

Amid the hubbub, Angélique could not hear the rest. She would have liked to know who the other judges were. Desgrez had not mentioned that there would be so many. Not that it mattered, anyhow, since she did not know any of them, except Massenau and Fallot.

Where *was* her lawyer?

She saw him come in through the same door as the jurors. He was followed by several unknown monks, most of whom sat down in the first row of official spectators, where seats had evidently been reserved for them. Angélique was perturbed not to recognize Father Kircher among them. But Friar Bécher wasn't there either, and the young woman sighed with relief.

The silence was now complete. One of the priests recited a blessing, then tendered the crucifix to the accused, who kissed it and crossed himself. At this gesture of submission and piety, a wave of disappointment passed through the court-room. Were they going to be deprived of a spectacle of wizardry and offered only the plain judgment of a quarrel among gentlemen?

A shrill voice cried:

"Show us Lucifer's exploits!"

This produced a commotion in the ranks: the guards pounced on the irreverent spectator. The young man was rudely seized and immediately dragged outside.

"Accused, take the oath!" said Président Séguier, unfolding a sheet of paper which a clerk on his knees had handed him.

Angélique closed her eyes. Joffrey was going to speak. She expected his voice to be broken, feeble, as did all the spectators apparently, for when the deep, clear voice rang out, there was a stir of surprise. Shaken to the core, Angélique recognized the alluring voice which had murmured so many words of love to her on hot nights in Toulouse.

"I swear to speak the whole truth. I know, however, gentlemen, that the law authorizes me to challenge the competence of this court for, in my capacity as a *maître des requêtes* and a member of Parliament, I maintain that I must be tried by the Grand Court of Parliament. . . ."

The Grand Master of Justice seemed to hesitate,

then said with some haste:

"The law does not permit of restrictive oaths: just swear, and the court will then be empowered to try you. If you do not take the oath, you will be tried as standing mute of malice, that is to say as if you were absent."

"I see, Monsieur le Président, that the dice are loaded. That is why, to facilitate your task, I relinquish the advantage of resorting to legal technicalities. Instead, I shall put my trust in this court's spirit of justice and I confirm my oath."

Crafty old Séguier did not conceal his satisfaction.

"The court will value at its merit the limited honour you apparently do it by accepting its competence. Before you, the King himself decided to trust in its sound justice, and that's all that matters. As for you, gentlemen of the court, do not for a moment lose sight of the confidence which His Majesty has placed in you. Remember, gentlemen of the jury, that you have the great honour of representing here the sword which our monarch holds in his august hands. Now, there are two kinds of justice: one which applies to the deeds of ordinary mortals, the other which applies to the decisions of a King who rules by divine right. Do not let the gravity of this relationship escape you, gentlemen. By judging in the name of the King, you bear the responsibility of his greatness. But by honouring the King, you will also honour the foremost defender of religion in this kingdom."

After this somewhat confusing speech, Séguier withdrew majestically with an effort to conceal his haste. When he had left, everybody sat down. The

701

candles that were still burning on the desks were snuffed. A crypt-like light now invested the courtroom, and when the pale winter sun seeped through the stained glass, the blue and red gleams suddenly gave some faces a rather eerie appearance.

Maître Gallemand, his hand cupped before his mouth, was whispering to his neighbours:

"The old fox doesn't even want to shoulder the responsibility for presenting the bill of indictment himself. He acts just like Pontius Pilate and, in case of a condemnation, he won't hesitate to throw the blame on the Inquisition or the Jesuits."

"But he can't, since it is a secular trial."

"Pooh! Courtly justice must be at its master's orders but it must also send the people to sleep as regards its motives."

Angélique heard these seditious conversations about the King in a state of semi-consciousness. It did not seem to her for a single moment that any of this could be real. It was a waking dream, or perhaps, yes, a stage-play. . . . She had eyes for her husband only, who was standing, stooping and heavily leaning on his sticks. A still vague idea was beginning to form in her mind. "I shall avenge him. All that his tormentors have made him suffer, I shall make them suffer, and if the devil exists, as religion teaches, I would like to see Satan carry off their pseudo-Christian souls."

After the not very dignified departure of Séguier, the Attorney-General, Denis Talon, tall, lean and solemn, climbed into the pulpit and broke the seals of a large envelope. In an acid voice, he set about reading the "charges, or bill of indictment":

"Sieur Joffrey Peyrac, who has already forfeited his rights to all his titles and possessions by judgment in the King's Privy Council, has been handed over to this court of justice to be tried for acts of witchcraft and magic and other acts offending both religion and the security of State and Church by practising the alchemistic manufacture of precious metals. For all these deeds and other kindred ones which the case for the prosecution holds against him, I demand that he and any possible accomplices be burned at the stake on the Place de Grève, and their ashes scattered, as is fit for magicians convicted of dealing with the devil. I demand further that he be previously subjected to the ordinary and extraordinary question so that he will reveal his other accomplices. . . ."

The blood throbbed so loudly in Angélique's ears that she could not hear the end of the reading. She recovered her senses when the ringing voice of the accused sounded for the second time:

"I swear that all this is false and biased, and that I am in a position to prove it here and now to all men of good faith."

The royal prosecutor compressed his narrow lips and folded his paper, as if the rest of the ceremony did not concern him. He, in turn, made as if to withdraw, when defending counsel Desgrez sprang up and cried:

"Gentlemen of the court, the King and you yourselves have done me the great honour of appointing me to defend the accused. I therefore take the liberty of putting a question to you before the departure of the Attorney-General: how is it that the bill of indictment was drawn up beforehand and thus presented ready and even sealed, when nothing of the sort is provided for by lawful procedure?"

Stern Denis Talon stared down at the young lawyer from his full height and said with lofty contempt:

"I see, young Maître, that with your lack of experience, you did not trouble to be informed of the vicissitudes of this prosecution. Learn, then, that it was Président de Mesmon first, and not Monsieur de Massenau, who was charged by the King to make the preliminary investigations and preside over this trial. . . ."

"According to the rules, Président de Mesmon ought to be here to present the indictment himself!"

"You seem to be unaware that Président de Mesmon died suddenly yesterday. He had time, however, to draw up this bill of indictment which, in a way, is his last will and testament. You may see in this, gentlemen, a very fine example of the spirit of duty of a great magistrate of the kingdom!"

The entire court-room rose to honour the memory of Mesmon. But some shouts could be heard coming from the public:

"Stinks of devilry, this sudden death!"

"Murder by poison!"

"It starts well!"

The guards intervened again.

Président Massenau rose to speak and reminded the audience that this was not a public hearing. At the slightest demonstration the hall would be cleared of all those who had no part to play in the trial.

Order returned to the court-room. On his part, Maître Desgrez contented himself with adding that he accepted the terms of the indictment on the understanding that his client be tried strictly on that basis. After a few words exchanged in an undertone, agreement was reached. Denis Talon introduced Massenau as Président of the Court of Justice and solemnly left the hall.

Président Massenau promptly proceeded to question the prisoner.

"Do you admit the acts of witchcraft and magic that you are charged with?"

"I deny them one and all!"

"You have no right to. You will have to answer each question contained in the case for the prosecution. Besides, this is in your own interest since there are points which cannot be denied and which you had better admit, since you have sworn to speak the whole truth. Thus: do you admit having manufactured poisons?"

"I admit that I occasionally manufactured chemical products, some of which would be harmful if consumed. But in fact I never meant them to be consumed, or sold, nor did I use them to poison anyone."

"So you admit that you utilised and manufactured poisons such as green and Roman vitriol?"

"I do. But for this to be a crime, it would have to be proved that I actually poisoned someone."

"For the time being, it is enough to establish the fact that you do not deny having manufactured venomous products by engaging in alchemy. We shall establish the purpose later."

Massenau pored over the thick file before him and began to turn the sheets. Angélique trembled lest a charge of poisoning be put forward. She remembered that Desgrez had spoken of a certain Bourié who had been appointed as sworn judge in this trial because he was renowned as a skilful forger. Angélique leaned forward to try to recognize him among the magistrates.

Massenau kept on leafing through the file. At last he coughed and seemed to be taking his courage in both hands. He began by mumbling, then his voice cleared and became quite audible as he finished:

". . . With a view to showing, if it were necessary, the high degree of equity of the King's justice and the safeguards that it adopts to ensure the utmost impartiality; and before going on to enumerate the various charges which each judge commissioned by the King has before his eyes, I wish to state and inform the court how difficult our preliminary investigation has been and how beset with pitfalls."

"And with activities in behalf of a rich and noble defendant!" said a mocking voice in the audience.

Angélique expected the ushers to seize the trouble-maker. To her great surprise, she saw a sergeant, posted nearby, give a sound kick to a police constable.

"The police must have men in the court-room who are paid to provoke hostile incidents against Joffrey," she thought.

The Président's voice went on as if he had not heard the interruption:

". . . To show, therefore, to all that the King's justice is not only unbiased but generous, I think I may reveal that, out of the very numerous documents in the case for the prosecution, presented and compiled from various sources and after prolonged investigations, I had to *set aside* a great many after mature thought and much inner debate."

He stopped, seemed to take a breath and resumed in a somewhat muffled voice:

". . . Exactly thirty-four documents were set aside by me as doubtful and apparently forged, probably to satisfy some personal vengeance against the accused."

This statement produced a commotion, not only among the public, but also among the judges, who doubtless had not expected such a sign of courage and leniency on the part of the Président of the Court. Among them, a little man with a crafty face and a hooked nose could not restrain himself and cried:

"The dignity of the court, and even more its independent judgment, is set at nought, if the Président considers himself free to keep evidence for the prosecution, which may include principal charges, from the scrutiny of all the commissioners. . . ."

"Monsieur Bourié, in my capacity as Président, I call you to order and leave you to choose whether you will disqualify yourself as a member of the jury."

A considerable hubbub ensued.

"The Président is bribed by the accused! We know all about the gold of Toulouse!" yelled a spectator.

The greasy-haired clerk in front of Angélique added his voice:

"When for once a rich notable is brought to justice for his misdeeds . . ."

"Gentlemen, the hearing is adjourned, and if this disorder continues, I shall have the court-room cleared!" Président Massenau managed to cry.

Indignantly, he put his cap on his wig and left, followed by the Bench. Angélique thought that all these solemn judges looked like puppets that walked in, did their little turn and walked out again. If only they'd never come back! . . .

Chapter 44

THE noise subsided and the court-room made an effort to behave in order to bring about the return of the judges and to ensure, with calm restored, the continuation of the spectacle. All rose when they heard the Swiss guards' halberds thumping on the stone flags, as they preceded the return of the court.

Amidst a religious silence, Massenau resumed his seat.

"Gentlemen, the incident is closed. The documents which I judged to be suspect are enclosed with the file which each commissioner can study at leisure. I marked them with a red cross, and every juryman can form his own idea of my judgment."

"Those documents mainly concern acts that

challenge the Holy Scriptures," declared Bourié, who did not hide his satisfaction. "They deal in particular with the manufacture, by alchemical processes, of pygmies and other creatures of diabolical essence."

The crowd wriggled with restrained mirth.

"Will we see any as exhibits?" a voice shouted.

The interrupter was immediately expelled by the guards, and the hearing continued. Desgrez then rose:

"Speaking as counsel for the defence, I consent to *all* the exhibits being produced!" he said.

The Président resumed the examination.

"Now, to finish with this matter of the poisons which you admit you have manufactured, how is it, if you had no intention of using them against other people, that you publicly boasted of absorbing some daily 'in order to avoid any threat of poison'?"

"That is perfectly correct, and what I said then still holds good today: I am boasting that I cannot be poisoned by either vitriol or arsenic, because I have taken such quantities of them that I run no risk of even a slight sickness were someone to try to dispatch me to the next world by this means."

"And you still maintain today this claim to immunity against poisons?"

"If that were all that is needed to satisfy the King's court, I am perfectly willing, as a faithful subject, to swallow one of these drugs in your presence."

"But then, you yourself admit that you have some magic safeguard against all poisons?"

"There's no magic about it, it's the very basis of the science of antidotes. What *is*, however, a belief in magic and witchcraft is the use of toadstone and other harmless nonsense, which I believe, gentlemen, almost all of you in this room indulge in, fondly imagining that it protects you against poisons."

"Accused, it is very wrong of you to taunt and mock respectable customs. However, in the interests of justice which requires that everything should come to light, I shall not linger over these details. All I shall keep in mind, if you agree, is that you admit to being, in fact, an expert in poisons."

"I am no more an expert on poisons than on anything else. Besides, I am only protected against certain current poisons, such as the ones already mentioned: arsenic and vitriol. But what does this infinitesimal knowledge amount to compared with those thousands of vegetable and animal poisons, exotic Florentine or Chinese poisons, which none of the most illustrious surgeons of the kingdom would know how to combat, or even detect?"

"And you have knowledge of some of those poisons?"

"I have arrows which the Indians in America use for hunting the bison. And also arrow-heads, used by the pygmies of Africa, a wound from which is enough to kill an animal as gigantic as the elephant."

"In fact, you more than admit the charge of being an expert on poisons?"

"Not at all, Monsieur le Président, but I am explaining this to you in order to prove that, if

I'd ever intended to get rid of some poor wretches who'd looked at me askance, I wouldn't have troubled to manufacture such common and easily recognized products as arsenic and vitriol."

"Why, then, did you manufacture them?"

"For scientific purposes in the course of chemical experiments on metal-ore which sometimes entail the formation of these products."

"Let us not stray from the point. It is enough that you yourself agreed that you are extremely versed in matters of poison and alchemy. So, according to what you said, you'd be in a position to kill someone without anybody being able to realise it or find you out. How do we know that you have not done so already?"

"It would have to be proved!"

"You are also held accountable for two suspect deaths, though I hasten to add, only incidentally: the first is the death of the nephew of Monseigneur de Frontenac, Archbishop of Toulouse."

"Does a duel after provocation and in the presence of witnesses nowadays become an act of witchcraft?"

"Monsieur de Peyrac, I urge you not to persist in your ironical attitude towards a court which is only seeking to shed light on all the facts. As for the second death laid at your hands, it is alleged to have resulted either from your invisible poisons or from your magic spells. For, on the exhumed body of one of your former mistresses, this medallion, representing a half-length portrait of yourself, was found before witnesses. Do you recognize it?"

Angélique could see that Président Massenau

711

was handing a small object to a Swiss guard, which the latter held out to the Comte de Peyrac, who was still leaning on his two sticks before the stool intended for him.

"I do indeed recognize the miniature which the poor, over-wrought girl had painted of me."

"This poor, over-wrought girl, as you say, was also one of your countless mistresses, Mademoiselle de . . ."

Joffrey de Peyrac raised his hand in a peremptory gesture.

"For pity's sake, do not publicly profane her name, Monsieur. The unfortunate woman is dead!"

"She died from a slow decline which we are beginning to suspect you of having caused and fostered by black magic."

"That is untrue, Monsieur le Président."

"Why, then, was your medallion found in the mouth of the deceased, and as if pierced by a pin at the heart?"

"I have no idea. But from what you say, I should rather guess that it was she who, being very superstitious, had sought to cast a spell on me in this manner. So here, instead of a spellbinder, I become spellbound, for a change! That is really very funny, Monsieur le Président."

And suddenly the long spectre shaking on his sticks laughed heartily.

The court-room, at first nonplussed, relaxed and there were outbursts of laughter. But Massenau never lost his frown.

"Don't you know, accused, that the fact of finding a medallion in the mouth of a corpse is a definite sign of spellbinding?"

"From what I can gather, I am much less conversant with these superstitions than you, Monsieur le Président."

The magistrate overlooked the insinuation.

"Swear, then, that you have never practised them."

"I swear on my wife, my child and the King that I never engaged in this kind of tomfoolery, at least as it is understood in this kingdom."

"Explain what you mean by the restriction you have applied to your oath."

"I mean that, after travelling a great deal, I saw for myself, in China and in India, strange phenomena which prove that magic and witchcraft really do exist, but have nothing to do with the charlatanism generally practised under this name in European countries."

"In fact, you admit that you believe in them?"

"In genuine witchcraft, yes . . . And that, incidentally, comprises a good many natural phenomena which future centuries will no doubt explain. But when it comes to following blissfully the fairground performers or the so-called learned alchemists. . . ."

"Ah, so you have led up to alchemy yourself! According to you, there is, I expect, just as for witchcraft, a true and a false alchemy?"

"Yes, indeed. Certain Arabs and Spaniards are beginning to call true alchemy by a separate name, chemistry, which is an experimental science in which all exchanges of substances can be reproduced and are, therefore, independent of the operator, provided, of course, that the latter has learned his craft. But a convinced alchemist, on the other hand, is worse than a sorcerer!"

"I am happy to hear you say so, for you thus make our task easier. But what can be worse than a sorcerer, according to you?"

". . . a fool and a fanatic, Monsieur."

For the first time during this solemn hearing, Président Massenau seemed to be losing his self-control.

"Accused, I entreat you to show the deference which is, moreover, in your own interest. It is quite enough that in your oath a moment ago you had the insolence to invoke His Majesty after the names of your wife and your child. If you persist in displaying such arrogance, the court may refuse to listen to you. . . ."

Angélique saw Desgrez leap towards her husband as if trying to say something to him, but the guards restrained him.

"My remarks, Monsieur le Président, were by no means aimed at you or any other of these gentlemen," the Comte de Peyrac went on after the hubbub had subsided a little. "As a scientist, I was attacking the practitioners of that baneful science which is called alchemy, and I do not believe that any one among you, who are burdened with such serious occupations, is secretly engaged in it. . . ."

This little speech pleased the magistrates, who nodded gravely.

The examination was resumed in a more serene atmosphere. Massenau, who had foraged in a mountain of papers, managed to extract another sheet from it.

"You are accused of having used pieces of skeleton in your mysterious practices which, to clear yourself, you call by the new word of chemistry. How do you explain so un-Christian a practise?"

"Monsieur le Président, it is important not to confuse occult practice with chemical practice. I use animal bones merely to make ashes, for bone-ash has special properties for absorbing the dross of molten lead while leaving the gold and silver content free."

"And do human bones possess the same property?" Massenau asked insidiously.

"Probably, Monsieur le Président, but I confess that animal bones give me full satisfaction and I content myself with them."

"In order to suit your purposes, must those animals be burned alive?"

"Why, no, Monsieur le Président. Do you cook your chickens alive?"

The magistrate's face contracted, but he controlled himself and remarked that it was surprising, to say the least, that in this kingdom bone-ash was being used by only one person, and for purposes which a "sensible man" could only consider extravagant, not to say sacrilegious. And as Peyrac scornfully shrugged his shoulders, Massenau added that a charge of sacrilege and impiety had been brought forward and was not based on the use of animal bones alone, but that it would be examined at its proper time and place.

He continued:

"Was not the real purpose of using bone-ash the occult one of regenerating base matter such as lead in order to bring it back to life by transforming it into precious metal, such as gold or silver?"

"This view is rather closely related to the specious dialectics of the alchemists, who claim to operate by obscure symbols, when actually one cannot create matter."

"Accused, you admit, though, the fact of having manufactured gold and silver otherwise than by removing them from river-sand?"

"I never *manufactured* gold nor silver. I only *extracted* them."

"Nevertheless, people who know something about it say that those rocks from which you claim you extracted those metals cannot yield a trace of either gold or silver, however much you may grind the rock, even after washing."

"That is true. But molten lead attracts and mingles with noble metals that are contained therein, but which are invisible."

"So you claim you can produce gold and silver from any rock?"

"Not at all. Most rocks don't contain any, or only very little. Besides, despite difficult and protracted trials, it is difficult to recognize these rocks which are very rare in France."

"If it is so difficult to find out, how is it, then, that you are the *only* man in the kingdom who can do it?"

The Comte replied, exasperated:

"I might say that it is a talent, Monsieur le Président, or rather a science and an arduous profession. I might also take the liberty to ask you, in turn, why Lulli is at the moment the only man in France to write operas, and why you do not write some, too, since anyone can study music."

The Président looked annoyed, but did not answer. The juryman with the crafty face raised his hand.

"You may speak, Councillor Bourié."

"I would like to ask the accused this, Monsieur le Président: if it is true that Monsieur de Peyrac discovered a secret process concerning gold and silver, for what reason did this high nobleman, who protests his loyalty to the King, not think it fit to communicate his secret to the sovereign master of this country, I mean His Majesty the King? Not only was this his duty, but also a means of relieving the people, and even the gentry, of so many crushing though indispensable burdens which the taxes represent, and which even the tax-exempted legal profession pays, at least in the form of diverse charges."

An approving murmur ran through the audience. Angélique felt the hatred of the public surge against the man, broken by torture, who was beginning to sway with fatigue on his sticks.

For the first time, Peyrac turned his eyes towards the audience. But it seemed to the young woman that his glance was distant and that he did not see anyone. "Doesn't he feel that I am here and suffering with him?" she thought.

The Comte seemed to hesitate. He said slowly:

"I have sworn to speak the whole truth. The truth is that, in this kingdom, personal enterprise is not only not encouraged, but is exploited by a horde of courtiers, whose only concern is their own interests, their ambitions or else their quarrels. Under these circumstances, the best thing for a man who really wants to create something is to hide himself and protect his work by silence. For 'you don't cast pearls before swine.' "

"What you are saying is very grave. You are doing the King and . . . yourself a great disservice," Massenau said mildly.

Bourié jumped up.

"Monsieur le Président, as a juryman I protest against the too indulgent fashion in which you seem to receive what should, to my mind, be recorded as proof of the crime of *lèse-majesté*."

"Monsieur, if you continue, I should be obliged if you would request that I be relieved of the presidency of this court, a request which I have already made to our King and which was not granted, which seems to show that I have his confidence."

Bourié flushed and sat down, while the Comte explained in a tired but composed voice that everyone understood his duty after his own fashion. Not being a courtier, he did not feel strong enough to make his views triumph in the teeth of unanimous opposition. Wasn't it enough that, from his own distant province, he had managed to pay into the Royal Treasury every year more than a quarter of what the whole of Languedoc was paying to France; and wasn't it understandable, if he thus laboured for the common good, even though it was to his own benefit as well, that he preferred to give no publicity to his discoveries, for fear of being compelled to exile himself, as many misunderstood scientists and inventors had had to do?

"In short, you admit that you were in a bitter and disparaging frame of mind with regard to the kingdom," the Président remarked with the same mildness.

Angélique shuddered again. Desgrez raised his arm.

"Monsieur le Président, forgive me. I know the time has not yet come for me to plead, but I would like to remind you that the defendant is one of the most loyal subjects of His Majesty, who honoured him by paying him a visit in Toulouse and afterwards personally invited him to his wedding. You cannot, without yourself discrediting His Majesty, suggest that the Comte de Peyrac worked against him and against the kingdom."

"Silence, Maître. I have been very indulgent to let you say all this, and believe me that we are taking note of it. But do not interrupt what is still a direct examination, which will enlighten all the jury about the accused and his affairs."

Desgrez sat down. The Président reminded the court that the King's desire for justice demanded that everything should be given a hearing, including justified criticisms, but that it was up to the King alone to judge his own conduct.

"But there's the crime of *lèse-majesté* . . ." Bourié cried again.

"I am not entertaining the charge of *lèse-majesté*," said Massenau firmly.

Massenau continued the interrogation by saying that apart from the transmutation of gold, which the accused himself did not deny but claimed to be a natural and in no way diabolical phenomenon, there was abundant testimony to the effect that he had the power of fascinating people and, more particularly, very young women. And that the impious and dissolute gatherings organised by him were generally attended by a great majority of women, "which was a certain sign of satanic intervention for, at witches' sabbaths, the number of women always exceeded that of men."

And as Peyrac remained silent and seemingly lost in reverie, Massenau became impatient.

"What is your answer to this precise question which is suggested by a scrutiny of the cases that have come up before the Church authorities, and which seems to embarrass you greatly?"

Joffrey gave a start, as if he was waking up.

"Since you insist, Monsieur le Président, I shall answer two things. First, I am not certain that you are so very familiar with the proceedings of the official court of Rome, the details of which cannot be communicated outside ecclesiastical tribunals; secondly, your knowledge of these singular facts can only have been acquired by personal experience, which is to say that you must at least have attended one of those satanic sabbaths which I for my part, I confess, have never yet come across in all my life, rich in adventures though it has been."

The Président leaped with rage. He remained speechless for a long while, then spoke with a threatening calmness:

"Accused, I could turn this circumstance to account and stop listening to you, try you in your absence and even deprive you of all means of defence by a third party. But I do not wish that, in the eyes of some ill-intentioned persons, you should pass for a martyr of I don't know what sombre cause. That is why I shall let other sworn judges pursue this questioning, in the hope that you may not discourage them from listening to you. I call upon you, Councillor of the Protestants!"

A tall, stern-faced man rose.

The Président of the jury exhorted him:

"You are here as a judge, Monsieur Delmas. You owe it to the majesty of justice to listen to the accused seated."

Delmas sat down again.

"Before starting to question the accused," he said, "I would like to make a request of the court; a request which is prompted by no biased leniency towards the accused, but merely by a humane concern. It is common knowledge that the defendant has been an invalid since childhood. As the hearing has every chance of being protracted, I would ask the court to authorize the accused to sit down, for he may succumb to faintness."

"It is out of the question!" Bourié broke in. "The accused must attend the hearing, kneeling, under the crucifix, as formally required by tradition. The court is already lenient in allowing him to remain standing."

"I repeat my request," the Councillor for the Protestants persisted.

"Of course," yelped Bourié, "it's no secret that you consider the condemned man almost as a co-religionist, because he was suckled by a Huguenot nurse and alleges he was molested by Catholics in his infancy."

"I repeat that it's a matter of humanity and wisdom. The crimes this man is accused of horrify me as much as they do you, Monsieur Bourié, but if he falls in a swoon, we'll never finish with this trial."

"I shall not swoon and I thank you, Monsieur Delmas. Let us continue, if you please." The accused cut short the argument in so authoritative a tone that the court, after some wavering, complied.

"Monsieur de Peyrac," Delmas resumed, "I accept in good faith your oath to speak the truth, and also your affirmation that you had no contacts with the evil spirit. However, there remain too many obscure points for your good faith to be strikingly obvious in the eyes of justice. That's why I ask you to reply to the questions I am going to put to you without seeing in them anything but a desire on my part to dispel the dreadful doubts that hang over your deeds. You claim to have extracted gold from rocks which, according to qualified people, do not contain any. Let us grant it. But *why* did you engage in such odd, laborious work for which you were not intended by your noble rank?"

"In the first place, I wished to gather riches by working and putting to use the intellectual gifts I had received. Others solicit pensions or live at their neighbours' expense, or else remain paupers. As none of these three solutions suited me, I sought to make the most of myself and my few estates. By doing so, I do not think I ran counter to the teachings of God himself, for He has said: 'Thou shalt not bury thy talents.' This means, I take it, that if we have a gift or a talent, we haven't the *option* to use it or not, but a divine obligation to make it fructify."

The magistrate's face became stony.

"It's not up to you, Monsieur, to speak to us of divine obligations. But let us proceed. . . . Why did you surround yourself either with libertines, or with bizarre people from abroad who, without actually being convicted of espionage against our country, are not exactly friends of France or even of Rome from what I have been told?"

"Those whom you consider bizarre are in fact mostly foreign scientists, Swiss, Italian or German, with whose research I would compare my own. Arguing about the gravitation of the earth and the universe is an inoffensive pastime. As for the licentiousness I am reproached with, what happened at my palace was no more scandalous than was customary at a time when chivalrous love, according to learned men, 'was civilizing society,' and certainly much less scandalous than what is happening every night at Court and in all the taverns of the capital."

This daring declaration made the court frown. But Joffrey de Peyrac, raising his hand, cried:

"You, gentlemen — magistrates and gentlemen of the robe who form part of this gathering — I am well aware that by your pure morals and prudent life you represent one of the soundest elements of society. Do not take offence at a statement which is aimed against a way of life other than yours, and at words which you yourselves have often murmured in your heart."

This adroit sincerity disconcerted and flattered the judges and the clerics. Delmas coughed and pretended he was turning the pages of the file.

"You are said to be familiar with a dozen languages."

"Pic de la Mirandole, in the last century, spoke eighteen, and nobody suggested at the time that Satan himself had gone to the trouble of teaching them to him."

"Anyway, it is a recognized fact that you bewitched women. I do not want needlessly to humiliate a man already stricken with misfortunes and disfavours, but looking at you it is hard to believe that your physique alone attracted women to such a point that they killed themselves and went into raptures at the mere sight of you."

"We mustn't exaggerate," the Comte retorted with a modest smile. "Those who let themselves be bewitched, as you say, were the ones who wanted to be; as for a few highly-strung girls, we all have come across some of their kind. The convent, or rather the hospital, are the only places suited for them, and we mustn't judge women by the example of a few mad ones."

Delmas made a show of even greater solemnity.

"It is of public notoriety, and borne out by numerous reports, that in your Courts of Love at Toulouse — which is an impious institution in its very principle, for God said: 'Thou shalt love in order to procreate' — you publicly glorified the carnal act."

"The Lord never said: 'Thou shalt procreate like a dog or a bitch,' and I don't see in what respect the teaching of the science of love is diabolical."

"What is diabolical is the magic you practised!"

"If I were as skilled in magic as all that, I shouldn't be here."

Bourié got up and roared:

"In your Courts of Love you preached disrespect for the laws of the Church; you said that the institution of marriage was an obstacle to feelings of love, and that there was no merit in being devout."

"I may indeed have said that merit does not consist simply in displaying devoutness if on the other hand one is mean and heartless, but that the true merit which pleases women consists in being merry, a good rhymester, a skilful and a generous lover. And if I also said that marriage is an obstacle to feelings of love, I was referring to it not as an institution blessed by God, but to what in our day has become a positive trade of interests, a shameful barter, in which parents negotiate lands and dowry, and young people frequently are united by force or threats without their ever having set eyes on each other. It's methods of this kind that have ruined the sacred principle of marriage, for couples linked by such chains can only seek release from them in sin."

"You are again insolent enough to preach at us!" protested Delmas, at a loss.

"Alas, we Gascons all have a somewhat teasing disposition and a tendency to criticize," the Comte admitted. "And this turn of mind has led me to war against the absurdities of my century. In this I have imitated a famous hidalgo, Don Quixote de la Mancha, who tilted at windmills, and I am much afraid that I have proved as foolish as he."

Another hour passed, during which various

judges put a series of most incongruous questions to the accused. He was asked what method he used to render flowers "bewitching," so that the mere sending of a bouquet entranced the person who received it; the formula of the aphrodisiacs which he poured out for the guests of the Courts of Love and which sent them into "lewd trances"; and finally, with how many women he was able to make love simultaneously.

The Comte de Peyrac answered these abstruse questions either with a shrug of disdain or an ironical smile. It was obvious that nobody believed him when he asserted that in love he made do with one woman at a time. Bourié, whom the other judges allowed to pursue this delicate subject, remarked with a smirk:

"Your amorous capacity is so renowned that we weren't surprised to learn that you practised so many shameful amusements."

"If your experience were as great as my amorous capacity," the Comte de Peyrac replied with a caustic smile, "you would know that the search for such amusements derives from impotence, which seeks the excitement it needs in abnormal pleasures. As for me, gentlemen, I confess that one woman at a time, met in the discreet solitude of night, is all I need to fulfil my desires. I would even add this," he added in a graver tone of voice, "I challenge all the malicious tongues of Toulouse and Languedoc to prove that, since my marriage, I was ever considered the lover of any woman other than my wife."

"The investigations do indeed bear out this detail," Judge Delmas approved.

"Oh! a very minor detail!" said Joffrey, laughing.

The court fidgeted with embarrassment. Massenau motioned to Bourié to drop the matter, but the latter, who had not forgiven the systematic rejection of the documents he had so carefully forged, did not consider himself beaten.

"You did not answer the charge brought against you of having poured into the drinks of your guests exciting products which led them to commit odious sins against the Seventh Commandment."

"I know that there are products intended for this, such as cantharides. But I have never been in favour of provoking artificially an excitement which should be generated solely by the pulsations of a generous life and the natural inspirations of desire."

"It has been reported, however, that you gave a good deal of attention to the food and drink supplied to your guests."

"Wasn't that natural? Wouldn't any man, desirous to please those whom he invites, do likewise?"

"You claimed that what one ate and drank had an influence on seducing the man or woman whom one wished to conquer. You taught charms. . . ."

"Not at all. I taught that we should savour the gifts which the earth bestows on us, but that in all things, to arrive at the desired ends we must learn the rules that lead up to them."

"Give us some details of your teaching."

Joffrey looked around and Angélique saw the flash of his smile.

"I notice that these questions fascinate you, gen-

727

tlemen of the court, just as they do less aged adolescents. Whether we be a schoolboy or a magistrate, don't we all dream of conquering our lady-love? Alas, gentlemen, I fear I shall much disappoint you. I have no magic formula. What I teach is human wisdom. Thus, Monsieur le Président, when as a young clerk you first set foot in these solemn precincts, did you not think it natural to instruct yourself in all that might some day enable you to reach the position that you occupy today? You would have considered it mad to mount the bench and start to speak without a prolonged study of your case. For many years you took care to avoid all the obstacles that might rise in your path. Why should we not bring the same care to matters of love? Ignorance, in all things, is harmful, not to say blameworthy. There was nothing occult about my teaching. And since Monsieur Bourié asks me to define it, I would advise him, for instance, when he is on his way home in a gay mood and well-disposed to caress his wife, not to stop at a tavern and down several tankards of light beer. He might well find himself a little later in a sorry plight in his featherbed, while his disappointed spouse would be tempted to respond to the gallant ogling of some friendly musketeer she might meet the next day. . . ."

Some bursts of laughter rang out and there was a ripple of applause.

"I certainly admit," Joffrey's melodious voice continued, "that I am in a wretched state to speak in this way. But since I must reply to an accusation, I would conclude by repeating this: if you wish to devote yourself to the service of Venus, there is, I hold, no better stimulant than a pretty girl whose healthy complexion stirs you not to spurn carnal love."

"Accused," Massenau said severely, "I must once again recall you to decency. Remember that there are holy women in this court-room who have dedicated their maidenhood to God."

"Monsieur le Président, may I point out that it wasn't I who led the . . . conversation, if I may call it thus, to this slippery and . . . charming ground."

There was more laughter. Delmas remarked that this part of the examination should have been conducted in Latin, but Fallot de Sancé, speaking up for the first time, objected not unreasonably that, since everybody in the audience, which was composed of lawyers, priests and nuns, understood Latin, there would have been no point in putting oneself out merely for the chaste ears of the military, archers and halberdiers.

Angélique had the impression that, though the hearing on the whole had been confused, the argument boiled down to the sole charge of witchcraft, diabolic spells over women, and "the power of making real gold" obtained by alchemic and satanic means.

She sighed with relief: with this single charge of trafficking with Satan, her husband stood a chance of extricating himself from the claws of royal justice. Desgrez could call on the evidence of the faked probe to show up the vice of procedure in the bogus exorcism to which Joffrey had been subjected. And finally, to show in what consisted "the increase of gold," the demonstration to be given by the old Saxon Hauer would perhaps convince the judges.

Angélique then let herself relax for a moment and closed her eyes.

Chapter 45

WHEN she opened them again, she thought she was having a nightmare: Friar Bécher had appeared on the rostrum.

He took the oath on the crucifix which another monk held up to him. Then he began to tell, in a jerky, muffled voice, how he had been devilishly deceived by the great magician, Joffrey de Peyrac, who, before his eyes, had made real gold spurt from molten rock, by using a Philosopher's Stone brought back no doubt from the country of Cimmerian Darkness which the Comte had, in any case, described to him complacently as an absolutely virgin, glacial region, where the thunder rumbles day and night, wind and hailstorms alternate, and where a mountain of fire permanently spits molten lava which falls constantly on the eternal ice which never melts despite the heat.

"This last detail is a visionary's invention," remarked the Comte de Peyrac.

"Do not interrupt the witness," the Président ordered.

The monk continued his preposterous tale. He confirmed that the Comte had manufactured in his presence an ingot of more than two pounds of pure gold which, when later assayed by specialists, had been found good and genuine.

"You haven't mentioned that I made a present of it to Monseigneur de Toulouse for his pious charities," the accused again broke in.

"That is true," the monk confirmed gloomily. "That gold even resisted thirty-three exorcisms. This does not prevent the magician from conserving the power to make it vanish, whenever he so desires, in a roll of thunder. Monseigneur de Toulouse was himself a witness to that frightful phenomenon which greatly upset him. The magician boasted of it, referring to fulminant gold. He glories in his ability to transmute mercury in the same way. All these facts are reported in a written statement which is in your possession."

Massenau tried to adopt a jocular tone:

"Listening to you, Father, one would expect the defendant to have the power of making this great Palace of Justice collapse, just as Samson made the columns of the Temple crumble."

Angélique felt a wave of sympathy towards the parliamentarian from Toulouse. Bécher rolled his eyes like marbles and quickly crossed himself.

"Oh! do not provoke the magician! He is certainly as strong as Samson."

The Comte's mocking voice rose again:

"If I had the power with which this torturing friar credits me, rather than make him and his likes disappear by magic, I should first use a magic formula to abolish the greatest stronghold in the world: human stupidity and credulity. Descartes was wrong to say that the infinite is not humanly conceivable: for the stupidity of man provides a

731

very good example."

"Do not forget, accused, that you are not here to discourse on philosophy, and you have nothing to gain by getting round us with mental acrobatics."

"Let us continue to listen, then, to this worthy representative of the Middle Ages," said Peyrac, ironically.

Judge Bourié asked:

"Father Bécher, you who were present at those alchemical operations on gold and who are yourself a well-known scientist, what was, according to you, the purpose of the accused in delivering himself up to Satan? Wealth? Love? Or what?"

Bécher pulled himself up to his unimpressive height, and to Angélique he looked like an angel of hell taking wing. She quickly crossed herself and was promptly imitated by the whole row of nuns, who were beginning to be positively fascinated by the atmosphere of the scene.

Bécher exclaimed in a toneless voice:

"I know his purpose. Wealth and love? No! . . . Power and conspiracy against the State or the King? Not that either. But he wants to become as strong as God Himself. I am certain that he knows how to create Life, that is to say, that he is trying to challenge the very Creator."

"Father," said Delmas, the Protestant, with deference, "have you proof to support these extraordinary allegations?"

"I have, with my own eyes, seen dwarfs leave his laboratory, as well as gnomes, chimeras, dragons. Numerous peasants, whose names I have, also saw them, on certain stormy nights, prowl and leave their lair, this famous laboratory which one day was almost completely destroyed by an explosion of what the Comte calls fulminant gold, and what I call unstable or Satanic gold."

The entire audience sat panting, oppressed. A nun swooned and had to be carried outside.

The Président turned to the witness with solemn insistence. He affirmed that he wished to know the whole truth, but that called upon to judge of such unbelievable magic as that of breathing life into beings that he had hitherto considered as purely legendary, he asked the witness to recollect himself and weigh his words. He further asked him, as a man conversant with hermetic sciences and as the author of well-known books authorized by the Church, how such a thing could be possible and, above all, whether he knew of any precedents in such matters.

Friar Bécher again pulled himself up and seemed to stretch even higher. One almost expected to see him soar up in his wide, black gown, like a baleful raven. He cried in an inspired voice:

"There is no lack of famous writings on this subject. Paracelsus already affirmed, in his *De Rerum Natura*, that pygmies, fauns, nymphs and satyrs are engendered by chemistry! Other writings say that homunculi, or little men, often no bigger than a thumb, can be found in children's urine. The homunculus is invisible at first, and he feeds on wine and rose-water: a little cry announces his true birth. Only magicians of the first order can produce such a diabolic birth, and the Comte de Peyrac was one of these supremely powerful magicians, for he himself asserted that he had no need of a Philosopher's Stone to cause the transmutation of gold. Unless he had at his disposal that seed of life and noble metals which, according to his own words, he went to look for at the ends of the earth."

Judge Bourié got up, much excited, and stammered with spiteful glee:

"What have you to say in answer to this accusation?"

Peyrac shrugged with impatience and finally said, fatigued:

"How can you refute the ravings of a fellow who is obviously mad!"

"You have no right to dodge a reply, accused," calmly intervened Massenau. "Do you admit to having given life, as this priest says, to those monstrous creatures he referred to?"

"Of course not, and even if the thing had been possible, I don't see how it could possibly have interested me."

"You consider it possible, then, to engender life artificially?"

"How am I to know, Monsieur? Science hasn't said its last word and doesn't Nature offer disconcerting examples? When I was in the Orient, I saw the transformation of certain fish into newts. I even brought some specimens back to Toulouse, but this mutation never recurred."

"In other words," Massenau said with a dramatic tremolo in his voice, "you give no credit to the Lord in the creation of living beings?"

"I never said that, Monsieur," the Comte replied quietly. "Not only do I know my *credo*, but I believe that God created everything. Only I don't see why you should forbid him to have provided certain intermediate stages between vegetables and animals, or from tadpole to frog. However, I personally have never 'manufactured' those beings that you call homunculi."

Conan Bécher then pulled out of the vast folds of his gown a small bottle which he held out to the Président. The bottle passed through the hands of the jury. From where she was sitting, Angélique could not make out what it contained, but she saw that most of the robed men crossed themselves and she heard one of the judges call a little clerk and send him to fetch holy water from the chapel.

All the members of the court assumed a horrified air. Judge Bourié was rubbing his hands ceaselessly — there was no knowing whether with satisfaction or to wipe off the traces of sacrilegious pollution. Peyrac alone, with averted head, did not seem to take any interest in this ceremony.

The bottle returned to Président Massenau. To examine it, he put on his thick, horn-rimmed glasses, then finally broke the silence.

"This kind of monster looks rather like a shrivelled lizard," he declared in a disappointed tone of voice.

"I discovered two of these wizened homunculi which probably served as charms, by creeping into the Comte's alchemical laboratory at the risk of my life," Friar Bécher explained modestly.

Massenau turned to the accused:

"Do you recognize this . . . this thing? Guard, take the bottle to the accused!"

The colossus in uniform whom he had addressed was trembling like a leaf. He stammered, hesitated, at last gripped the bottle resolutely, then let it drop so clumsily that it broke.

An "oh!" of disappointment passed through the crowd, which thereupon felt a desire to take a closer look and surged forward.

But the archers had formed a barrier before the first row and pushed back the curious. At last, a halberdier advanced and impaled on his weapon an indistinguishable little object which he poked under the nose of the Comte de Peyrac.

"It's probably one of the newts I brought back from China," the latter said calmly. "They must have slipped out of their aquarium in which I used to dip my alembic in order to keep the water constantly lukewarm. Poor little things! . . ."

Angélique had the impression that of all these explanations about exotic lizards the audience had retained only the word "alembic," and an anguished "ah!" escaped from them again.

"Now this is one of the last questions in the examination," Massenau went on. "Accused, do you recognize this sheet I am holding? On it is enumerated a list of heretical and alchemical works, and this is said to be a faithful copy of one of the shelves of your library which you most frequently consulted. I see in this list, in particular, the *De Rerum Natura* by Paracelsus, where the passage concerning the satanic manufacture of monstrous beings such as the homunculus, whose existence the learned Father Bécher has revealed to me, is underlined in red with a few words in your handwriting."

The Comte replied in a voice that was becoming hoarse with fatigue.

"That is correct. I remember thus underlining a certain number of absurdities."

"I also note in this list books which do not deal with alchemy but are nonetheless prohibited. I quote: *Gallant France Has Turned Italian, Love Intrigues at the Court of France*, etc. These books were printed in The Hague or in Liège, where we know that the most dangerous pamphleteers and journalists driven out of the kingdom have taken refuge. These writings are clandestinely introduced into France, and those who acquire them are greatly guilty. I also draw attention in this list to names of authors such as Galileo and Copernicus, of whose scientific theories the Church disapproves."

"I presume that this list was communicated to you by a major-domo of the name of Clément, a spy in the pay of I know not which important person, and who stayed with me for some years. The list is correct. But I should like to point out, gentlemen, that two motives may prompt an amateur to put such or such a book into his library. Either he wishes to possess a testimony to human intelligence, and that is the case when he has works by Copernicus and Galileo, or else he wishes to gauge by the scale of human foolishness the progress already accomplished by science since the Middle Ages as well as the progress which still remains to be made. That is the case when he skims through the lucubrations of Paracelsus or Conan Bécher. Believe me, gentlemen, the reading of such works is in itself a great penance."

"Do you disapprove of the lawful condemnation by the Church of Rome of the impious theories of Copernicus and Galileo?"

"I do, for the Church was obviously mistaken. Which does not mean that I accuse the Church on other counts. I would have much preferred to put my trust in her knowledge of exorcisms and witchcraft to finding myself involved in a trial which is straying into sophistical discussions. . . ."

The Président made a theatrical gesture as if to show that it was impossible to make an accused of such bad faith see reason. He then consulted his colleagues and announced that the examination was concluded and that they would now proceed to call upon some witnesses for the prosecution.

There now walked into the court-room two monks in white, followed by four nuns and finally two Franciscan friars in brown frocks. The group lined up in front of the jury's box.

Président Massenau rose.

"Gentlemen, we now come to the most awkward part of this trial. Called upon by the King, defender of the Church of God, to try a case of witchcraft, we had to seek testimonies which, according to the ritual of Rome, would prove conclusively that Monsieur Peyrac had dealings with the devil. Principally, as regards the third point of the ritual, which says that —"

He bent forward to read the text.

"— which says that a person engaged in trafficking with the devil, and who is traditionally called a true demoniac, possesses 'supernatural strength of body' and 'power over the mind and body of others,' we have ascertained the following facts."

Despite the rather keen cold in the court-room,

738

Massenau discreetly wiped his brow, then continued reading with an occasional stammer:

". . . We have received complaints from the prioress of the women's convent of Saint-Léandre in Auvergne. The latter has declared that one of her novices, only recently received into the community and who had hitherto given full satisfaction, has shown signs of demoniac possession, of which she accused the Comte de Peyrac. She did not conceal the fact that the Comte had formerly drawn her into guilty licentiousness and that the remorse that she had felt for her faults had led her to withdraw to a convent. But she found no peace there, for this man continued to tempt her from afar and had certainly bewitched her. Shortly after, she brought to the prioress a bunch of roses which she claimed had been flung to her over the convent wall by a stranger, whose figure resembled that of the Comte de Peyrac, but who must doubtless be a demon, for it was proved that at that time the gentleman in question was in Toulouse. That bouquet promptly caused strange disturbances throughout the community. Other nuns were seized by extraordinary and obscene ravings. When they recovered their senses, they spoke of a lame devil, whose mere appearance filled them with a superhuman joy and kindled an inextinguishable fire in their flesh. Naturally, the novice who had caused all this disorder remained almost permanently in a state of trance. Alarmed, the prioress of Saint-Léandre eventually appealed to her superiors. Just at that time the preliminary investigations started for the trial of Monsieur Peyrac, so the

Cardinal-Archbishop of Paris communicated the dossier to me. The witnesses we shall now hear are the nuns of that convent."

Bending over his desk, Massenau respectfully addressed one of the lowered wimples.

"Sister Carmencita de Mérecourt, do you recognize in this man the one who pursues you from afar and who has 'cast a diabolic and pernicious spell' over you?"

A pathetic contralto voice rang out:

"I recognize my one and only master!"

Dumbfounded, Angélique discovered beneath the austere veils the sensual, warm-tinted face of the beautiful Spaniard. Massenau cleared his voice and pronounced with obvious difficulty:

"But, Sister, did you not take the veil to devote yourself exclusively to the Lord?"

"I wanted to escape from the face of my spell-binder. In vain. He pursues me even to divine service."

"And you, Sister Louise de Rennefonds, do you recognize him who appeared to you during scenes of delirium to which you fell a prey?"

A young, tremulous voice answered feebly:

"Yes, I . . . I think so. But the one I saw had horns. . . ."

A roar of laughter shook the court-room and a clerk cried:

"Ay! he may well have grown some while he was in the Bastille!"

Angélique was crimson with rage and humiliation. Her companion took her hand to remind her that she had to keep cool, and she checked herself.

Massenau continued, turning to the abbess of the convent:

"Madame, although this hearing is very painful for you, I am obliged to ask you to confirm your statements before this court."

The aged nun, who did not seem much upset but merely indignant, did not need much pressing, and declared in a clear voice:

"What's been going on, these last few months, in the convent whose prioress I have been for thirty years, is a real disgrace. One has to be cloistered, gentlemen, to realize to what grotesque pranks the devil stoops when he has a chance to manifest himself through a sorcerer. I won't conceal that the duty which falls on me today is a very unpleasant one, for it pains me to have to disclose actions that are so injurious to the Church before a secular court, but His Excellency the Cardinal-Archbishop has ordered me to do so. I shall demand, however, to be heard in private."

The Président granted her request, to the great satisfaction of the abbess and the disappointment of the audience. The Court retired, followed by the abbess and the other nuns into a back room.

Carmencita alone remained, under the watch of two Swiss guards and of the four monks who had brought her. Angélique now had a look at her ex-rival. The Spanish woman had lost none of her beauty. Convent life had perhaps added refinement to her face, in which the big black eyes seemed to pursue some ecstatic dream. The public too seemed to revel in the sight of the beautiful possessed woman.

Angélique heard Maître Gallemand's mocking voice say:

"The Great Lame One is rising in my esteem!"

The young woman saw that her husband had not deigned even to glance at this spectacular scene. Now that the court had left, he was no doubt trying to rest a little. He sought to settle down as well as he could on the bench of infamy, which was the stool of penance. He managed it while contorting all his features. The standing position on his crutches and, above all, the torture of the needle that had been inflicted on him at the Bastille, had turned every move into an ordeal.

Angélique's heart ached with heaviness as if it had turned to stone. Her husband so far had shown superhuman courage. He had managed to speak calmly, though not always without restraining his customary irony which, unfortunately, did not seem to have made a favourable impression on the court or even on the public. At present Joffrey was ostensibly turning his back on his former mistress. Had he even seen her?

Sister Carmencita, after a moment's apathy, suddenly took a few steps in the direction of the accused. The guards came between them and made her retreat. All of a sudden, the magnificent Spanish madonna-like face was transformed completely. In a moment it had turned into a vision of hell. Her mouth opened and closed, like that of a fish out of water. Then the nun suddenly raised her hand to her lips. Her teeth clenched, her eyeballs rolled up, a white froth appeared at the corners of her lips.

Desgrez leapt up, livid.

"Look! There we are: the big soap-bubbles scene!"

But he was roughly seized and dragged out of the court-room. His solitary shout had produced no echo from the panting crowd who were craning towards the spectacle with spellbound faces.

A convulsive tremor shook the nun's whole body. She tottered a few steps towards the accused. The monks once again blocked her way. She stopped, raised her hands to her wimple and began to tear it off with frantic gestures. And in doing so, she spun around violently. The four monks threw themselves upon her and tried to control her. Either because they did not dare to apply strength or because they really could not manage to subdue her, she slipped out of their grip like an eel.

She threw herself on the ground and, crawling and contorting herself with snake-like ease, she managed several times to slide under the priests' legs and robes, tripping them up. She then made obscene gestures, trying to lift the monks' cassocks. Twice or three times, the poor friars rolled on the floor in as undignified postures as can be imagined. The archers, gaping at this spectacle of tangled robes and rosaries, did not dare to intervene. Finally, the possessed woman, spinning and writhing in all directions, managed to undo her string of beads, then her dress, and suddenly stood up, magnificent and stark-naked, in the sombre light of the court-room.

The pandemonium was indescribable. People screamed. Some wanted to rush out, others wanted to have a look. A respectable magistrate, seated

743

in the front row, got up, tore off his own robe and, bounding on to the scene in singlet and hose, flung his gown over Carmencita's head and managed to veil the shameless madwoman.

The nuns next to whom Angélique was sitting hastily rose under the guidance of their superior. Room was made for them, for they had been recognized as the nuns of the General Hospital. They surrounded Carmencita and with cords, which they produced from one knew not where, they tied her up like a sausage. Then they walked out, almost in procession, carrying away their foaming captive.

Then a shrill shout rose from the frantic crowd: "Look! The devil is laughing!"

Outstretched arms pointed towards the accused.

Indeed, Joffrey de Peyrac, only a few steps away from where the scene had taken place, was giving free vent to his hilarity. Angélique recognized in his ringing laughter the outburst of natural, spontaneous gaiety that had enchanted her life. But the frantic minds saw in it hell's own provocation.

A wave of indignation and horror made the audience surge forward. The guards rushed up and crossed their halberds. Without them, the accused would certainly have been torn to pieces.

"Come with me," Angélique's companion whispered.

And as the young woman wavered, stupefied, she insisted:

"Anyhow, the court will be cleared. We must know what has become of Maître Desgrez. He will tell us if the hearing will be continued this afternoon."

Chapter 46

THEY found the lawyer in the Palace courtyard, in a small tavern kept by the hangman's
son-in-law and daughter.

The lawyer, with his wig awry, seemed very
nervous.

"You saw how they put me out, taking advantage of the court's absence! . . . I assure you, if
I'd been there, I'd have made that demented creature spit out the piece of soap that she had put
into her mouth! But never mind. The very excesses
of those two witnesses will serve my case for the
defence! . . . If only Father Kircher weren't keeping us waiting so long, it would put my mind at
rest. Well, come and sit at this table near the fire,
ladies. I ordered eggs and chitterlings from the
hangman's little wench. You didn't put the juice
of any dead man's head into the gravy, I hope,
my beauty?"

"No, sir," the young woman replied brightly,
"we only use that in the soup for the poor."

Angélique, her elbows propped on the table, had
buried her head in her hands. Desgrez was glancing
at her in perplexity. Then he noticed that she was
shaking with nervous laughter.

"Oh, that Carmencita!" she gurgled, her eyes
bright with unshed tears. "What an actress! I never
saw anything so funny! Do you think she did it
on purpose?"

"You never can tell with women!" growled the lawyer.

At a nearby table, a clerk was commenting on the scene for his colleagues.

"If it was an act that nun was playing, well, it was a good act. When I was young, I attended the trial of Abbé Grandier, who was burned for bewitching the nuns of Loudun. Things happened just like that. There weren't enough cloaks in the hall to cover all the pretty girls who kept stripping as soon as they set eyes on Grandier. You didn't even have time to turn round! What we saw today was nothing. At the hearings in Loudun, some of them, stark naked, rolled on the ground and . . ."

He bent forward to whisper some particularly scurrilous details.

Angélique regained control of herself gradually.

"Forgive me for laughing. I am all done in."

"Laugh, poor girl, laugh," Desgrez muttered gloomily. "There's always time to weep. If only Father Kircher were here! What the devil has happened to him? . . ."

Hearing the cry of an ink-seller, who was roving through the courtyard with his barrel slung over his shoulder and goose-quills in his hand, he called him and, scribbling a message on a table-corner, he summoned a clerk to carry it at once to the police lieutenant, Monsieur Aubray.

"This Aubray is a friend of my father's. I've told him that I'll pay whatever necessary if he gets his watchmen on the move and brings Father Kircher here to the Palace, by hook or by crook."

"Did you send to the Temple for him?"

"Twice already I have sent young Rope-round-the-neck with a note. He came back empty-handed. The Jesuits he saw say the Father left for the Palace this morning."

"What are you afraid of?" Angélique inquired, alarmed.

"Oh, nothing. I'd rather he were here, that's all. In principle, the scientific demonstration of gold extraction ought to convince the magistrates, narrow-minded though they are. But convincing them isn't everything, we've got to defeat them. Only Father Kircher's voice has enough authority to sway them to override the . . . royal preferences. Come on, now, for the hearing will be resumed and you might find the doors closed."

The afternoon session opened with a declaration by Président Massenau. He said that the judges' conviction, after hearing the various witnesses for the prosecution, had been sufficiently enlightened on the diverse aspects of this difficult case, as well as on the peculiar character of the accused, and that the witnesses for the defence would now be heard.

Desgrez motioned to one of the guards, and a little Parisian ragamuffin with a smart face appeared. He gave his name as Robert Davesne and said he was a locksmith's apprentice, in the rue de la Ferronnerie, at Maître Dasron's at the sign of the Copper Key. In a clear voice, he swore to speak the whole truth, invoking the name of Saint Eloi, patron of the locksmiths' brotherhood. He then stepped towards Président Massenau and passed him a small object at which the latter peered with surprise.

"Now what may this be?"

"It's a needle with a spring, Monsieur," the child replied, unruffled. "As I am clever with my hands, my master ordered me to make an object just like it, which a monk had ordered from him."

"What *is* this rigmarole?" the magistrate inquired, turning towards Desgrez.

"Monsieur le Président, the prosecution has laid at the defendant's charge his reactions to the exorcism performed in the prison of the Bastille by Conan Bécher, to whom I refuse, out of respect for the Church, to give his ecclesiastical rank. Conan Bécher has told us that the defendant reacted to the test of the 'diabolical spots' in a way that leaves no doubt of his relations with Satan. At each of the crucial points foreseen in the ritual of Rome, the defendant is said to have uttered such screams that the wardens themselves trembled. Now, I wish to point out that the probe with which the test was performed was manufactured on the same model as the one you are holding in your hands. Gentlemen, that bogus 'exorcism' on which this court of justice is in danger of basing its verdict, was conducted with a *faked* probe. That is to say, under its harmless appearance, this probe hides a long spring-operated needle which, when released by an imperceptible pressure of the finger-nail, plunges into the flesh. I defy any self-possessed man to stand this test without screaming like a madman at times. Is any one of you, gentlemen of the jury, brave enough to offer himself up to the refined torture to which the defendant was subjected, and which now serves to accuse him of being possessed by the devil? . . ."

Fallot de Sancé got up, very stiff and pale, and held out his arm.

But Massenau intervened impatiently.

"Enough play-acting! Is this probe the very one which was used for the exorcism?"

"It is an exact copy. The original was taken three weeks ago to the Bastille by this very apprentice, and handed to Bécher. The apprentice can bear witness to the fact."

At that moment, the youngster roguishly released the instrument, and the needle shot out under the nose of Massenau, who jumped back.

"As Président of this court, I object to this last-minute witness who does not even figure on the list of the registry. Moreover, he is a child, and his testimony is therefore unreliable. And lastly, this is most certainly not a disinterested testimony. However much were you paid for coming here?"

"Nothing yet, sir. But I was promised double what the monk already gave me, that is to say twenty *livres*."

Massenau turned to the lawyer in a towering rage.

"I warn you that, if you insist on having such testimony recorded, I shall be obliged to forego hearing the other witnesses for the defence."

Desgrez lowered his head in token of submission, and the boy streaked through the door of the record-office as if the devil were after him.

"Have the other witnesses brought in," the Président ordered curtly.

There was a noise like the trampling of a strong team of furniture removers. Preceded by two sergeants, a curious procession filed in. First there came several porters from the central market, sweating and unkempt, who were carrying odd-shaped parcels, from which iron pipes, forge bellows and other odd contraptions could be seen sticking out. They were followed by two little street arabs, dragging baskets of charcoal and earthen jars with strange labels on them.

And finally, behind two guards, a misshapen gnome came in, whom the huge negro Kouassi-Ba seemed to push before him. The Moor, stripped to the waist, had daubed himself with stripes of white clay. Angélique recalled that he used do this on festive days in Toulouse. But his appearance, like that of the whole weird procession, drew from the crowd a gasp, in which astonishment mingled with terror.

Angélique, however, heaved a sigh of relief. Tears welled up in her eyes.

"Oh! what good people," she thought, looking at Fritz Hauer and Kouassi-Ba. "And yet they know what a risk they run by coming in aid of their master."

As soon as they had put their parcels down, the porters left. The old Saxon and the Moor alone remained. They proceeded to unpack and set up the portable forge as well as the foot-worked bellows. They also installed two crucibles and a big bone-ash cupel. Then the Saxon opened two sacks. From one of them he extracted a heavy black slab that looked like slag; from the other an ingot of what seemed to be lead.

Desgrez's voice explained:

"In accordance with the court's unanimously expressed desire to see and hear everything that concerns the charge of magical transmutation of gold, here are the witnesses and — in the terms of our justice — 'accomplices' of this allegedly magical operation. I would like you to note that their presence here is entirely voluntary. They have come in aid of their former master and not at all because their names were wrested by torture from the defendant, the Comte de Peyrac. . . . Now, Monsieur le Président, will you allow the accused to demonstrate before you, with his customary helpers, the experiment which the bill of indictment calls 'black magic' but which, according to the defendant, is but the extraction of invisible gold, revealed by a scientific process?"

Maître Gallemand whispered to his neighbour:

"Those gentlemen are torn between their curiosity, the attraction of the forbidden fruit, and the stern orders from on high. If they were really astute, they'd refuse to let themselves be swayed."

The young woman shivered, fearing lest the only visible evidence of her husband's innocence be ruled out at the last moment. But curiosity or, perhaps, the spirit of justice, carried the day. Joffrey de Peyrac was invited by Massenau to direct the operation and answer all necessary questions.

"But before that, can you swear, Comte, that with all this business of fulminant gold, neither the Palace nor the persons in it are in any way endangered?"

With her ever-present sense of irony, Angélique did not fail to remark that, under the stress of their fear of the mystery in preparation, these infallible judges rendered his rank to the man who had so high-handedly been deprived of it.

Joffrey assured them that there was no danger whatsoever. Judge Bourié asked that Father Bécher be called back so as to be confronted with the accused during the alleged experiment and thus to avoid any trickery. Massenau gravely nodded his wig, and Angélique could not check a nervous tremor which always seized her at the sight of that monk, who was not only the principal tool of this trial, but who must also have been the inventor of the torturing needle and probably the instigator of Carmencita's play-acting. Was he really monstrously lucid and merely trying to avenge his smarting failure in alchemy? Or was he a dim-witted visionary who, like certain madmen, had occasional moments of lucidity? Not that it really mattered. One way or the other, he was Friar Bécher!

He represented everything that Joffrey de Peyrac had fought against, the flotsam, the residue of a bygone world, of those Middle Ages which had rolled like a formidable ocean over Europe but which, as they receded, left in the hollow of the new century the stagnant scum of sophistry and dialectics.

His hands in the ample sleeves of his robe, with craning neck and glaring eyes, Bécher was watching the Saxon and Kouassi-Ba who, after putting up the forge and "luting" the joints of the pipes with clay, were beginning to stir up the fire.

Behind Angélique, a priest was saying to one of his colleagues:

"It is a fact that such a collection of human monsters, and in particular this Moor, smeared as if for a magical ceremony, are not designed to re-assure faint hearts. Fortunately, our Lord will always be able to recognize His own. I have heard that a secret but regular exorcism, undertaken on orders of the Paris diocese, resulted in the conclusion that there was nothing diabolical about the accusation unjustly brought against this gentleman who, perhaps, is being punished for his lack of piety. . . ."

Distress and comfort were contending in Angélique's aching heart. The clergyman was surely right. But why did poor Fritz Hauer have to be hump-backed and blue-faced, and why did Kouassi-Ba have to look so terrifying? And when Joffrey de Peyrac stretched out his long, broken body and limped over to the glowing forge, he only added to the sinister picture.

The accused asked one of the sergeants to pick up the black, porous-looking block of dross and present it first to the Président and then to the jury. Another sergeant handed them a strong magnifying-glass so that they might be able to examine the stone very closely.

"You see, gentlemen, this is the matte of molten gold-bearing pyrite, extracted from my mine at Salsigne," Peyrac remarked.

Bécher confirmed:

"It's the same black stuff which I ground and washed and in which I found no gold."

"Well, Father," the accused went on with a deference that Angélique admired, "you will be able to display once more your gold-washing talents. Kouassi-Ba, pass me a pestle."

The monk turned up his wide sleeves and eagerly began to crush and pound the black stone which was fairly easily reduced to powder.

"Monsieur le Président, will you be good enough to send now for a big tub of water and a tin basin, well cleaned and scrubbed with sand."

While two guards went to fetch what he required, the prisoner proceeded to show the judges a metal ingot.

"This is lead for making bullets or water-pipes, 'poor' lead, as specialists call it, for it contains practically no gold or silver."

"How can we be sure of it?" the Protestant Delmas remarked judiciously.

"I can prove it to you by assaying."

The Saxon handed his former master a big tallow candle and two small white cubes. With a penknife, Joffrey dug a small cavity out of the face of one of the cubes.

"What is this white stuff? Is it porcelain clay?" inquired Massenau.

"It's a cupel of bone-ash, those ashes that impressed you so much at the beginning of this hearing. Actually, you will see that this white stuff merely serves to absorb the scum of the lead when the latter is being heated by the flame of a tallow candle. . . ."

The candle was lit, and Fritz Hauer brought a small tube curved to form a right angle, into which the Comte began to blow in such a way that the candle-flame was directed on to the piece of lead inserted in the bone-cupel.

The flickering flame curved, touched the lead, which began to melt and give forth a greyish-blue smoke.

Conan Bécher raised his finger with a pontifical air.

"Authorized scientists call this 'blowing the Philosopher's Stone,' " he commented in a croaking voice.

The Comte interrupted his operation for a moment.

"If one listened to this fool, all chimney flues would soon pass for Satan's exhalation!"

The monk assumed a martyr's face, and the Président called the defendant to order.

Joffrey de Peyrac began to blow. In the falling dusk, the molten lead could be seen to seethe at red heat, then cool, and finally darken, while the prisoner stopped blowing into his tube. Suddenly, the small wisp of acrid smoke dissipated, and it could be seen that the molten lead had completely disappeared.

"It's a piece of sleight-of-hand that proves nothing at all," Massenau remarked.

"It merely shows that the bone-ash has absorbed or, if you like, *imbibed* all the oxydized poor lead. And this indicates that this lead contains no precious ore, which is what I wanted to show you by this operation which the Saxon metal-workers call 'blank assaying.' I shall now ask Father Bécher to finish washing this black powder which I say is gold-bearing, and we shall then proceed to extract the gold."

The two guards were back with a tub of water and a basin. After washing by gyration the powder he had pounded, the monk triumphantly showed the court the very feeble residue of heavy elements that had formed at the bottom of the basin.

"It's just as I contended," he said. "Not the minutest trace of gold. You cannot produce any from it except by magic."

"The gold is invisible," Joffrey repeated. "My assistants will extract it from this pounded stone with the sole aid of lead and fire. I shall take no part in the operation. You can thus convince yourselves that I shall add no fresh element to it, nor accompany the process by any cabalistic formulae, and that it is in fact an almost artisanal process, performed by workers who are as far removed from sorcery as any blacksmith or boiler-maker."

Maître Gallemand murmured:

"He talks too simply and too well. Presently they'll accuse him of bewitching the jury and the entire audience."

Kouassi-Ba and Fritz Hauer once again got busy. Bécher, who was obviously reticent, but enthralled by his "mission" and the leading rôle he was gradually taking in this trial, followed without interference the preparations of loading the furnace with charcoal.

The Saxon put the lead into a big terracotta crucible, then added the black powder of the crushed dross. He covered all this with a white salt which presumably was borax. Finally, some more charcoal was heaped on top, and Kouassi-Ba began to work the pedals of the two bellows.

Angélique admired the patience with which her husband, who had only a few moments ago been so proud and haughty, now lent himself to this comedy. He kept resolutely away from the furnace, near the stool of repentance, but the glow of the fire lit his lean, gaunt face buried under its heavy mane.

In the big fire in the furnace, the lump of lead and dross was melting. The air was permeated with smoke and an acrid smell of sulphur. Some people in the front rows began to cough and sneeze.

The entire court at times disappeared behind a screen of dark smoke. Angélique told herself that the judges had some merit after all in thus exposing themselves, if not to magic, at least to a most unpleasant ordeal.

Judge Bourié rose to ask permission to step closer. Massenau granted the request. He took up a position between the furnace, on which he turned his back, and the accused whom he kept watching unrelenting. The fumes of the forge occasionally blew down on Bourié and made him cough, but he remained in this uncomfortable and exposed position without taking his eyes off the Comte.

Judge Fallot, known as de Sancé, seemed to be on tenterhooks. He avoided his colleagues' eyes and kept nervously fidgeting in his big red velvet armchair.

"Poor Gaston!" Angélique thought. Then she stopped taking an interest in him.

The crucible, in the heat of the fire which a guard was constantly feeding with charcoal, was already turning red, then almost white.

"Halt!" the Saxon miner ordered. Covered with soot, sweat and bone-ash, he was looking more and more like some monster risen from hell.

He advanced towards one of the sacks and pulled from it a pair of big, bulging tongs with which he seized the heavy crucible amidst the flames.

With arched back and propped solidly on his bow-legs, he raised the crucible with no apparent effort. Kouassi-Ba held out a sand-cast. A brilliant, silver-like jet spurted and poured into the ingot-mould.

Comte Joffrey seemed to come out of his lethargy and commented in a tired voice:

"Here, then, we have the lead casting which has collected the precious ore of the gold-bearing matte. We shall break the mould and forthwith assay this lead on a 'bed-plate' of ashes placed at the bottom of the furnace."

Fritz Hauer held out this bed-plate, which was a big white brick in which a cavity had been dug. He put it on the fire, then, to remove the ingot from the crucible, he had to use an anvil, and the august Palace resounded with ringing hammer-blows for some moments. At last, the lead was carefully deposited in the cavity and the fire was stirred up. When the brick and the lead were red-hot, Fritz stopped the bellows and Kouassi-Ba removed all the remaining charcoal from the furnace.

All that remained was the glowing brick filled with incandescent, molten lead which seethed and grew ever brighter. Kouassi-Ba seized a small pair of hand-bellows and directed them towards the lead. The cold air, far from extinguishing the incandescence, revived it and the bath became dazzlingly bright.

"Look at the magic!" Bécher yapped. "There's no more coal, but hell-fire is beginning to produce the Philosopher's Stone! Look! The three colours appear!"

The Moor and the Saxon took it in turns to go on blowing on the molten bath, which writhed and was seized by whirls and tremors like a will-o'-the-wisp. An egg of fire formed in the seething mass. Then, as the negro withdrew the bellows, the egg stood up on its large axis and, spinning like a top, began to lose its brightness and darken gradually.

But, suddenly, the egg fiercely lit up again, became white, quivered, slipped out of the cavity and, with a soft thud, rolled on to the ground, at the Comte's feet.

"Satan's egg has joined its creator!" Bécher shouted. "It's lightning! It's fulminant gold! It'll explode over us!"

The audience screamed. In the semi-darkness in which they found themselves, Massenau called for candles. Amidst this pandemonium, Friar Bécher kept babbling of the "Philosopher's Egg" and the "Sage's Chicken," so much so that a facetious clerk climbed on to a bench and gave vent to a ringing "Cock-a-doodle-do!"

"Oh, my God, they don't understand anything!" thought Angélique, wringing her hands.

At last, police constables appeared at various points of the hall with three-branched candelabra, and the tumult gradually died down. The Comte, who had not moved, touched the piece of metal with the tip of his crutch.

"Pick up that nugget, Kouassi-Ba, and take it to the Judge."

Unhesitatingly, the negro jumped to pick up the metallic egg and presented it, gleaming on his black palm.

"It is gold!" Judge Bourié gasped, and he stood as if turned to stone.

He wanted to grab it, but no sooner had he touched it when he gave a dreadful scream and jerked his burned hand away.

"How is it, Comte," Massenau asked, trying to steady his voice, "that the heat of this gold does not burn your black servant?"

"It is common knowledge that Moors can bear glowing embers in their hands, just like the charcoal-burners of the Auvergne."

Bécher appeared with bulging eyes and, uninvited, emptied a bottle of holy water over the incriminating piece of metal.

"Gentlemen of the court, what you have seen here is the manufacture, against all ritual exorcisms, of the devil's gold. Judge for yourselves the immense power of this magic!"

"Do you think this gold is real?" Massenau asked.

The monk grimaced and pulled from his inexhaustible pocket another little bottle which he unstoppered with care.

"This is an acid, which attacks not only brass and bronze, but also gold-silver alloys. However, I am convinced beforehand that this is *purum aurum.*"

"Actually," the Comte broke in, "the gold extracted from the rock before you is not absolutely pure. Otherwise the ore wouldn't have produced the flash which lit up the metal at the end of the assay and which, accompanying a sudden change of state, produced that other phenomenon which made the nugget jump. Berzelius was the first scientist to describe this strange effect."

Judge Bourié's sullen voice asked:

"Is this Berzelius at least a Roman Catholic?"

"No doubt," Peyrac replied placidly, "for he was a Swede who lived in the Middle Ages."

Bourié gave a sarcastic laugh.

"The court will judge the value of so remote a testimony."

There was a moment's indecision, while the judges, leaning towards one another, debated the need of continuing the hearing or adjourning it to the next day. It was getting late. The audience was both tired and over-excited. But nobody wanted to leave.

Angélique felt no fatigue whatsoever. She was as if detached from herself. At the back of her mind, a small feverish argument was in progress: she could only follow its meanderings without being able to direct it. It was not possible that the demonstration of gold extraction would be un-favourably interpreted for the accused . . . Hadn't Friar Bécher's very excesses displeased the judges? Massenau might affirm his neutrality as much as he liked, but it was obvious that he favoured his Gascon compatriot at heart. But, against this, wasn't the whole court composed of rough, stiff men of the north? And in the audience it was only the truculent Maître Gallemand who dared to dis-play feelings of the least hostility towards the King's decisions. As for the nun who was accom-panying Angélique, she was certainly helpful, but the way a block of ice is when placed on the burn-ing brow of a sick person.

Ah! if this had taken place at Toulouse! . . .

And this lawyer of hers, himself a child of the streets of Paris, unknown and poor into the bargain, when would they let him speak at last? . . . Wasn't he trying to slink away? Why did he no longer speak up? And where was Father Kircher? Angélique vainly tried to distinguish, among the front-row spectators, the sly peasant face of the Grand Exorcist of France.

Hostile murmurs buzzed all around her.

"It seems that Bourié was promised possession of three dioceses if he obtains this man's condemnation. Peyrac's only fault is to be in advance of his century. You'll see he'll be sentenced. . . ."

Président Massenau coughed.

"Gentlemen," he said, "the hearing continues. Accused, have you anything to add to what we have seen and heard?"

The Great Lame Man of Languedoc drew himself up on his crutches, and his voice rang out, full and sonorous, and vibrant with a sincerity that made a quiver run through the ranks of the public.

"I swear before God, and on the blessed heads of my wife and my child, that I know neither the devil nor his magic, that I never performed the transmutation of gold nor created life according to satanic counsels, and that I have never sought to harm any fellow-creature by the effect of spells or charms."

For the first time during this endless hearing, Angélique noticed a feeling of sympathy for the man who had just spoken. A clear, childish voice from the heart of the crowd cried:

"We believe you."

Judge Bourié rose, waving his sleeves.

762

"Take care! This is the effect of a charm that we have not mentioned enough. Do not forget: the Golden Voice of the Kingdom . . . the redoubtable voice that enticed woman. . . ."

The same childish voice rose:

"Let him sing! Let him sing!"

This time, Président Massenau's southern blood rushed to his face and he began to pound his desk with his fist.

"Silence! Or I'll have the court-room cleared! Guards, remove the trouble-makers! . . . Monsieur Bourié, sit down. There've been enough interruptions. Let's get it over! Maître Desgrez, where are you?"

"I am here, Monsieur le Président," the lawyer replied.

Massenau stopped for breath and made an effort to control himself. He continued more calmly:

"Gentlemen, the King's justice owes it to itself to take everything into consideration. Therefore, although the case is being heard in private, the King, in his magnanimity, did not wish to deprive the accused of all means of defence. It is in this spirit that I considered it my duty to consent to the accused's producing even dangerous demonstrations, in order to throw light on the magical processes which he is accused of possessing. Finally — as supreme proof of princely clemency — he has obtained the assistance of a lawyer, whom I now call upon to speak."

Chapter 47

DESGREZ rose, bowed to the court, thanked the King in the defendant's behalf, then climbed up two steps to a small rostrum to address the court.

Seeing him so straight and grave, Angélique found it hard to imagine that this black-robed man was the same tall young fellow with a ferret's nose who, round-backed under his threadbare jacket, would stroll through the streets of Paris, whistling to his dog.

The wizened little records clerk, Clopot, who had procured the documents for the case, went to kneel before him, according to custom. The lawyer looked at the court, then at the audience. He seemed to be looking for someone in the crowd. Was it on account of the yellow candlelight? Angélique had the impression that he was pale as a ghost.

However, when he spoke, his voice was clear and composed.

"Gentlemen.

"After the display of so many efforts by the prosecution and the jury, in the course of which your knowledge of the law vied with the height of your classical erudition — and this, let us firmly repeat it, for the *sole purpose* of enlightening the King's justice and making *truth* shine brightly — you have, gentlemen of the jury, already exhausted all the light of the sun and the stars to hear this trial. How can an obscure lawyer who is defending his first great cause hope to find a few slender rays of light to illuminate a truth deeply buried in the bottomless well of the most dreadful accusation? This truth appears to me, alas, so distant and so dangerous that I tremble within myself and almost wish that this poor flame would go out and leave me in the quiet obscurity in which I was before. But it is too late! My eyes have seen, and I must speak. And I must cry: Take care, gentlemen! Take care lest the choice you will make render you accountable to future centuries. Do not be among those men whose faults will make our children's children cry as they look back on our century: 'It was an era of hypocrites and ignoramuses. For there was a great and noble gentleman in those days, who was accused of witchcraft for the sole reason that he was a great scientist.' "

The lawyer paused. Then he went on in a more subdued voice:

"Imagine, gentlemen, a scene of bygone days, of that dark period when our ancestors used but the clumsiest stone weapons. And now suppose that, among them, one man has the idea of collecting the mud of a certain soil, puts it into the fire and extracts from it a keen, hard material which had been unknown. His companions cry 'It's witchcraft!' and condemn him. And yet, a few centuries later, our weapons will be made out of this unknown material — *iron*. I shall go further. If in our day, gentlemen, you enter the laboratory of some perfume-manufacturer, will you recoil in horror and talk of witchcraft before the display of retorts and philters which release fumes which are not always sweet-smelling? No, you'd consider this ridiculous. And yet, what mystery is being concocted in that craftsman's lair! He materializes in liquid form that most invisible thing of all: scent. Do not be among those to whom could be applied the terrible words of the Gospel: 'They have eyes to see and see not. They have ears to hear and hear not.' I do not doubt, gentlemen, that the mere charge of engaging in unusual research would not have sufficed to trouble your minds, which profound study has opened to all sorts of perspectives. But disquieting circumstances, a strange reputation surround the defendant's personality. Let us analyse, gentlemen, on what facts this reputation is based, and let us see if each fact by itself, divorced from all others, can reasonably support a charge of witchcraft. Joffrey de Peyrac, a Catholic child entrusted to a Huguenot nurse, is dashed out of a window into a courtyard by fanatics at the age of four. He is crippled and disfigured. Should we accuse of witchcraft, gentlemen, all the cripples and all whose sight is fear-inspiring? However, although disfavoured by nature, the Comte possesses a marvellous voice, which he trains with Italian masters. Should we accuse of witchcraft, gentlemen, all those golden-voiced singers who make noble ladies, and even our wives, swoon with pleasure? From his voyages, the Comte has brought back a thousand fascinating tales. He has studied new customs, delved into foreign philosophies. Should we sentence all travellers and philosophers? Yes, I know: all this does not make for a very simple personality. And I come to the most surprising phenomenon: this man who has acquired a profound science and grown rich thanks to his knowledge, this man who speaks and even sings superbly well, this man has managed, despite his physique, to be attractive to women. He likes women and does not hide the fact. He glorified love and has numerous liaisons. That among the women who are in love with him there are a few over-excited or shameless ones is a normal occurrence in a life of licence which the Church certainly frowns upon but which is nonetheless extremely wide-spread. If, gentlemen, we were to burn all the noble lords who love women and all those who are pursued by disappointed mistresses, I do believe, in faith, that the Place de Grève would not be vast enough to contain their stakes. . . ."

There was a stir of approval. Angélique marvelled at Desgrez's skill. How tactfully he had avoided dwelling on Joffrey's wealth which had aroused so much envy, while on the other hand, stressing as a regrettable fact, but one which sober-minded burghers were helpless to alter, the licentious life that was the privilege of noblemen.

He gradually whittled down the charges, reduced them to the proportion of provincial gossip so that his listeners would soon feel surprised at having made so much ado about nothing.

"He is attractive to women!" softly repeated Desgrez, "and we, members of the strong sex, are amazed that, with his unprepossessing physique, he should inspire so much passion in southern ladies. Oh, gentlemen, let us not be overbold! Ever since the world began, who has been able to fathom the heart of women, and the why and wherefore of their passions? Let us remain respectfully on the edge of this mystery. For if we don't, we might be compelled to burn all women at the stake! . . ."

The laughter and applause were cut short by Bourié, who jumped up from his armchair.

"Stop the comedy!" the Judge shouted, and his face turned increasingly yellow. "You are mocking the court and the Church. Are you forgetting that the charge of witchcraft was originally brought by an archbishop? Are you forgetting that the chief witness for the prosecution is a monk, and that a regular exorcism was performed on the accused, showing him to be a henchman of Satan? . . ."

"I'm not forgetting anything, Monsieur Bourié," Desgrez gravely retorted, "and I shall answer you. It is quite true that the Archbishop of Toulouse was the first to bring a charge of witchcraft against Monsieur de Peyrac, to whom he had been opposed by a rivalry of long standing. Did this prelate regret a gesture to which, for reasons of personal grievance, he had not given enough thought? That is what I like to think, for I have here abundant documents, in which Monseigneur de Frontenac repeatedly demands that the accused be handed over to an ecclesiastical court and refuses to be a party to any decisions that may be taken by a civil court on the subject. He also refuses to support — I have his letter, gentlemen, and can read it to you — the facts and words of the man whom you call the chief witness for the prosecution, Conan Bécher, a monk. As for the latter, whose frenzy might well seem suspect to any person of sound mind, I remind you that he is responsible for the single exorcism on which the prosecution

768

seems to base its case. That exorcism took place in the prison of the Bastille on the fourth December last, in the presence of Fathers Frêlat and Jonathan, who are in the court. I do not contest the authenticity of this deposition inasmuch as it was actually drawn up by this monk and his acolytes, about whom I shall say nothing, not knowing whether they are credulous, ignorant or whether they are accomplices. But I do contest the authenticity of the exorcism!" Desgrez cried in a thundering voice. "I do not wish to enter into the details of the incongruities of that sinister ceremony, but I shall stress just two points: the first is that the nun who, incidentally, simulated the symptoms of possession in the presence of the accused, is the same woman Carmencita de Mérecourt, who, a little while ago, gave us a sample of her talent as an actress, and concerning whom a clerk of the record-office can testify that he saw her, as she left the hall, spitting out the piece of soap by means of which she simulated the froth of an epileptic fit, a trick well known to those shammers who try to rouse public pity in the streets. Second point: I revert to the faked probe, that infernal needle which you ruled out as being supported by insufficient evidence. And yet, gentlemen, what if it were true, what if a madman of fiendish cruelty really did subject a man to such a torture with the aim of misleading your judgment and burdening your conscience with the death of an innocent man? . . . I have here the statement made by the physician of the Bastille a few days after that abominable experiment."

In a jerky voice, Desgrez proceeded to read a

report by Maître Malinton, prison doctor at the Bastille who, having been called to the bedside of a prisoner whose name he did not know, but who had scars on his face, had found the latter to have all over his body small festering wounds which appeared to have been caused by deep needle-pricks.

In the profound silence which followed this reading the lawyer went on in a slow, grave voice:

"And now, gentlemen, the time has come for you to listen to a solemn voice, whose unworthy spokesman I am, a voice which, beyond all human turpitudes, has always sought to exhort the faithful to prudence. The hour has come for me, humble clerk that I am, to make the voice of the Church heard at this trial. It says this."

Desgrez unfolded a large piece of paper and read:

" 'On this night of 25th December 1660, in the prison of the Palace of Justice in Paris, a ceremony of exorcism was performed on the person of Joffrey de Peyrac de Morens, accused of intelligence of and trafficking with Satan. Whereas, according to the ritual of the Church of Rome, genuine demoniacs must possess *three extraordinary powers*, to wit one: knowledge of languages they have not learned; two: the power of divining and knowing secret matters; and three: preternatural powers of the body; we, in our capacity as the sole Exorcist lawfully empowered by the Church of Rome for the whole diocese of Paris, but nevertheless assisted in this by two other priests of our holy congregation, have subjected the prisoner Comte Joffrey de Peyrac to the exercises and examinations provided by the ritual on this night of the 25th December 1660. From which it was made evident that the exorcised had knowledge only of such languages as he had learned and in particular was unconversant with Hebrew and Chaldean, with which two of us are familiar; that this man appears to be very learned but in no way a divine; displayed no preternatural strength of body, but only wounds provoked by deep, festering punctures and infirmities of long standing; therefore we declare that the examined Joffrey de Peyrac is in no wise possessed by the devil. . . .' There follow the signatures of the Reverend Father Kircher, of the Society of Jesus, Grand Exorcist of the diocese of Paris, and those of the Reverend Fathers de Marsan and de Montaignat, assisting."

The stupefaction and uneasiness of the audience was almost tangible, and yet nobody stirred or spoke.

Desgrez looked at the court.

"What can I add to this testimony? Gentlemen of the jury, you will consider your verdict. But you will at least do so fully cognizant of one certainty: that the Church, in whose name you are asked to condemn this man, has found him innocent of the crime of witchcraft for which he has been brought here. . . . Gentlemen, I leave you face to face with your conscience."

Desgrez composedly picked up his cap, put it on his head and walked down the steps from the rostrum.

Judge Bourié then rose and his shrill voice rang out in the silence:

"Let him come! Why doesn't he come in person?

It is for Father Kircher to testify on this secret ceremony, which is suspect on more than one count, having been held secretly and without the knowledge of the judicial authorities."

"Father Kircher will come," Desgrez asserted very quietly. "He should be here now. I have sent for him."

"Well, I tell you he won't come," Bourié exclaimed, "for you lied, you have trumped up this whole fantastic rigmarole of a secret exorcism in order to impress the judges. You have hidden behind the names of important churchmen in order to sway the verdict. . . . Your deceit would have been discovered, but too late. . . ."

With his customary agility, the lawyer bounded towards Bourié.

"You insult me, Monsieur. I am not a forger, as you are. I remember the oath I took before the King's Council of the Bar when I was invested as a lawyer."

The audience was in an uproar. Massenau, standing up, tried to restore order. Desgrez's voice still rose above the din:

"I demand . . . I demand the adjournment of the hearing till tomorrow. The Reverend Father Kircher will ratify his statement. I swear it."

At this moment a door flew open. A cold draught mingled with snow-flakes blew from one of the court-entrances that gave on to the yard. Everybody turned towards this opening in which two snow-covered archers had appeared. They stepped aside to make room for a small, stocky, swarthy man, who was smartly dressed and whose wig and cloak were almost dry.

"Monsieur le Président," he said in a gruff voice, "I learned that the court was still in session despite the late hour. I therefore felt it my duty to bring you without delay some news which I believe to be important."

"We are listening," answered Massenau, surprised at this intrusion by the Lieutenant of Police.

Monsieur d'Aubray turned towards the lawyer.

"Maître Desgrez asked me to search throughout the capital for a Reverend Jesuit Father by the name of Kircher. After dispatching several constables to the various places where he might have been and where nobody had seen him, I was advised that the body of a drowned man, found amid the ice on the Seine, had been transported to the morgue of the Châtelet. I went there, accompanied by a Jesuit Father of the Temple convent. The latter formally identified his colleague, Father Kircher, whose death must have occurred in the first hours of the morning. . . ."

"So you do not even shrink from murder!" yelled Bourié, flinging his arm out towards the lawyer.

The other judges became restless, too. The crowd shouted: "Enough! Have done with it!" . . .

Angélique, more dead than alive, could not even make out whom this hooting was directed at. She covered her ears with her hands.

She saw Massenau rise and make an effort to be heard.

"Gentlemen, the hearing continues. The chief witness for the defence summoned by Council at the last minute, the Reverend Father Kircher, having been found dead, and in view of the fact that the lieutenant of police in person was evidently unable to discover upon him any document which, from beyond the grave, would testify to the truth of Maître Desgrez's statements, having regard also to the fact that the personality of the Reverend Father alone could have lent weight to an alleged deed drawn up in secrecy, the court in its wisdom . . . declares that deed as null and void and the incident as non-existent. The court will now retire to consider its verdict."

"Don't do this!" cried Desgrez's desperate voice. "Adjourn the verdict! I shall find witnesses. Father Kircher has been murdered."

"By you!" Bourié flung at him.

"Calm yourself, Maître," said Massenau, "and trust the judges!"

Had the jury been out for a few minutes or several hours?

It seemed to Angélique that the judges had never moved, that they'd always been there with their square caps and their red and black robes, that they would stay there for all eternity. But now they were standing. Président Massenau's lips were moving. They were articulating, in a trembling voice:

"I require for the King that Joffrey de Peyrac de Morens be declared guilty and convicted of the crimes of abduction, enticement, impiety, magic, witchcraft and other abominations mentioned at this trial, and in reparation of which he shall be delivered into the hands of the executioner of high justice, taken and led to the square of Notre Dame, shall there ask pardon of God, bare-headed and barefoot, with a rope around his neck and a fifteen-pound taper in his hand. Whereupon he shall be taken to the Place de Grève, tied to a stake set up for this purpose and burned alive until his body and bones be consumed and reduced to ashes, which shall then be dispersed and scattered to the four winds. And each and all of his possessions shall be forfeited to and confiscated by the King. And, before being executed, he shall be subjected to the question ordinary and extraordinary. I require that the Saxon Fritz Hauer be declared his accomplice and, in reparation, be sentenced to be hanged and strangled until death ensues, on a gallows to be set up for this purpose on the Place de Grève. I require that the Moor Kouassi-Ba be declared his accomplice and, in reparation, be sentenced to the galleys for life."

By the bench of infamy, the tall figure, supported on crutches, was swaying. Joffrey de Peyrac raised a ghastly face towards the court.

"I am innocent!"

His shout echoed in a deathlike silence.

He then went on in a calm, toneless voice:

"Your lordship Baron Massenau de Pouillac, I understand that it is too late for me to protest my innocence. I therefore keep silent. But, before being taken away, I wish to pay public tribute to the concern for equity which you have sought to maintain throughout this trial, whose presidency was forced upon you, as was its conclusion. Receive the assurance of a nobleman of old lineage that you are worthier to carry the blazon than those who govern you."

The ruddy face of the Toulouse parliamentarian

contracted. Suddenly, he raised his hand to his eyes and shouted in that *langue d'oc* which Angélique and the condemned man alone could understand:

"Farewell! Farewell! Brother countryman."

Chapter 48

OUTSIDE, in the night that was still black though dawn was approaching, the snow was falling and the wind swept enormous flakes before it. Stumbling in the thick, white carpet, the court-room audience left the Palace of Justice. Lanterns swayed at the carriage-doors.

Angélique, a solitary figure, walked away through the dark streets of Paris. At the moment of leaving the Palace, a commotion had separated her from the nun.

Mechanically she took the way that led to the enclosure of the Temple. Her mind was blank; she longed only to be back in her little room near Florimond's little cradle.

How long did it last, that stumbling walk? . . . The streets were deserted. In this frightful weather, even the rogues kept underground. Hardly any noise came from the taverns, for the night was drawing to a close, and the drunkards who had not gone home to their lodgings were snoring under the tables or confiding their misfortunes to some drowsing trollop. The snow decked the city in a gloomy silence.

As she approached the fortified walls of the Temple, Angélique remembered that the gates must be closed. But she heard the muffled sounds of the clock of Notre Dame and counted five strokes. The bailiff would open in an hour. She passed the drawbridge and went to cower under the vault of the postern-gate. Thawing snow-flakes ran along her face. Fortunately, the ample thick woollen gown of the religious dress with its many petticoats, vast wimple and hooded cloak, had protected her well. But her feet were icy.

The baby stirred inside her. She put her hand over her body and pressed it with sudden rage. Why should that child live when Joffrey was going to die? . . .

At that moment, the moving curtain of snow was torn asunder, and a monstrous, panting shape came bounding under the vault.

After a first movement of fright, Angélique recognized the dog Sorbonne. He had put his paws on her shoulders and was licking her face with his rough tongue. Angélique fondled him, scanning the darkness where the snowflakes were still falling in a tight swirl. Sorbonne meant Desgrez. Desgrez would come, and with him, hope. He would have an idea. He would tell her what more she could do to save Joffrey.

She heard the young man's step on the wooden bridge. He was advancing cautiously.

"Are you there?" he whispered.

"Yes."

He came closer. She could not see him, but he was talking to her from so nearby that the tobacco smell on his breath reminded her dreadfully of Joffrey's kisses.

"They tried to arrest me as I was leaving the Palace. Sorbonne throttled one of the constables. I was able to get away. The dog followed your track and led me here. You must disappear now. Do you understand? You will no longer use your name, you will attempt no more moves, nothing. Otherwise you will find yourself in the Seine some morning, like Father Kircher, and your son will be an orphan twice over. As for me, I had foreseen this atrocious outcome. A horse is waiting for me at the Gate of Saint-Martin. In a few hours, I'll be far away."

Angélique clutched at the lawyer's soaked jacket. Her teeth were chattering.

"You aren't leaving? . . . You aren't abandoning me?"

He gripped the young woman's slender wrists and loosened the clenched fingers.

"I staked everything for you, and I have lost everything, except my skin."

"But tell me . . . tell me what I can do for my husband?"

"All that you can do for him . . ."

He faltered, then spoke fast:

"Go and see the hangman and bribe him so that he'll strangle him . . . before the fire. That way he won't suffer. Here, take these thirty *écus*."

She felt a purse being slipped into her hand. Without another word, he walked away. The dog hesitated to follow his master. He came back to Angélique and lifted towards her his good, friendly eyes. Desgrez whistled. The dog pricked his ears and bounded away into the night.

The hangman, Maître Aubin, lived in Pillory Square facing the fish market. He had to lodge there and nowhere else. The letters of investiture of the executioners of Paris had stipulated this detail since time immemorial. All the shops and stands on the square belonged to him and he rented them to small shopkeepers. Moreover, he had the right to levy from each stand on the market one handful of the displayed green vegetable or corn, one freshwater-fish, one sea-fish, and one truss of hay.

If the fishwives were the queens of the market, the hangman was its secret, despised lord.

Angélique went to see him at nightfall. Young Rope-round-the-neck was her guide. Even at this late hour, the district was still bustling with activity. Through the rue de la Poterie and the rue de la Fromagerie, Angélique penetrated into this colourful quarter which rang with the strident shouts of the ladies of the fish market who, famed for their ruddy faces and their picturesque language, formed a privileged guild of traders. Dogs were fighting for refuse in the gutters. Carts of hay and timber blocked the streets. Over all hung a smell of fresh fish.

A nauseous stench coming from the nearby graveyard of Saints-Innocents and its horrible charnel-houses, where the bones of Parisians had been piling up for five hundred years, mingled with these strong odours and with those of meats and cheeses.

The pillory stood in the middle of the square.

It was a kind of octagonal tower with a pointed roof. The construction comprised a ground floor and a single storey above with high, vaulted windows, through which one caught a glimpse of the big iron wheel which was situated in the centre of the tower.

A thief was on view there tonight, his head and hands passed through the holes which ran all around the wheel. Now and then, the wheel was set in motion by one of the hangman's assistants. The thief's face, blue with cold, and his dangling hands emerged alternately in the windows like the macabre figure of a mechanical clock, and the assembled spectators laughed at his grimaces.

"It's Jactance," someone said, "the biggest cut-purse in the market."

"Oh! now we'll know him!"

"Let him show his face in the neighbourhood, and servants and dealers will shout: 'Beware the cut-purse!' "

"You can pack up your scissors, my friend, they'll be of no more use!"

There was quite a big crowd at the foot of the pillory. But if there was a throng at this place, it was not so much in order to gaze at the exposed thief as to make a deal with the hangman's assistants.

"See, Madame," said Rope-round-the-neck with a certain pride, "they are people who want to have tickets for tomorrow's execution. It's sure there won't be enough to go round."

He showed her the notice that the criers had been trumpeting at all the street-corners that very morning:

"Maître Aubin, executioner ordinary of high and low justice of the city and suburbs of Paris, announces that he will rent seats on his scaffold at a reasonable price, for watching the fire that will be lit on the Place de Grève for a sorcerer. Tickets can be obtained at the pillory from his assistants. The seats will be marked with a fleur-de-lis and the tickets with a Cross of Saint André."

"Would you like me to get you a ticket, if you have the wherewithal?" the hangman's apprentice suggested obligingly.

"Oh no!" said Angélique, horrified.

"You have a right to it," said the other philosophically, "because without a ticket, you won't be able to get near. Hardly anybody comes for hangings: people are used to them. But the stake's a rarity. There'll be a press of people, you can take my word for it; Maître Aubin says he's all hot and bothered at the thought of it. He doesn't like it when there's too much of a crowd yelling all around him. He says you never know what may come over them. Well, here we are, Madame. Do walk in."

The room into which Rope-round-the-neck had shown her was clean and well-kept. The candles had been lit. Around the table, three little neatly-dressed girls, with fair curls under their woollen bonnets, were eating gruel out of wooden bowls. By the fireplace, the hangman's wife mended her husband's scarlet singlet.

"Greetings, Maîtresse," said the apprentice. "I brought this woman here. She wants to talk to the old man."

"He's at the Palace of Justice. He won't be long.

Sit down, my dear."

Angélique sat down on a bench against the wall. The woman glanced at her out of the corner of her eye but did not ask any questions, as any other housewife would have done. How many haggard-faced women she had seen — distraught mothers, desperate daughters — seated on that bench waiting to beg the hangman to render a last favour, to relieve a beloved one from pain . . . ! How many had come to this peaceful home, with hands full of gold or threats on their lips, to plead for the executioner's help in a supreme, impossible escape!

Hearing a footfall on the threshold, Angélique half rose. The newcomer was a young priest who carefully wiped his thick, mud-covered boots before coming in.

"Maître Aubin isn't in?"

"He won't be long. Do come in, Monsieur l'Abbé, and make yourself comfortable by the fireside."

"It's very kind of you, Madame. I am a mission priest and I've been appointed to assist the condemned man tomorrow. I've come to see Maître Aubin to show him my credentials signed by the lieutenant of police, and to ask him to let me see that poor man. A night of prayer isn't too much to prepare yourself for death."

"Certainly," said the hangman's wife. "Sit down, Monsieur l'Abbé, and dry your coat. Rope-round-the-neck, throw a log on the fire."

She dropped the red singlet and took up her distaff.

"You are a brave man," she went on. "You

aren't afraid of a sorcerer?"

"All God's creatures, even the guiltiest ones, deserve our pity when the hour of death has come. But this man isn't guilty. He is innocent of the hideous crime he is accused of."

"They all say that!" said the hangman's wife philosophically.

"If Monsieur Vincent were alive, there wouldn't be a stake tomorrow. I heard him speak with anxiety, a few hours before his death, of the injustice that was about to be done to a nobleman of the kingdom. Were he alive, he'd have climbed on to the stake himself next to the condemned man to shout to the people to burn him rather than an innocent man."

"Ah! that's just what's torturing my poor husband," the woman cried. "You can't imagine, Monsieur l'Abbé, how much he's worried about tomorrow's execution. He's had six Masses read at Saint-Eustache, one in each side-chapel. And he'll have another read at the high altar."

"If Monsieur Vincent were still here . . ."

". . . there'd be no more thieves and witches, and we'd be left without work."

"You'd sell herrings in the market, or flowers on the Pont-Neuf, and you'd be no worse off."

"Why, no. . . ." said the woman, laughing.

Angélique gazed at the priest. He was young, but the fire of Monsieur Vincent glowed in him; he had big hands and the plain, simple ways of a man of the people. He'd have had the same attitude before the King. But Angélique did not move. For two days now, her eyes had been smarting with all the tears she had shed in her lonely little room. She had no tears left now; her heart was numb. No balm could soothe the gaping wound. Out of her despair an evil flower had been born: hatred. "What they make him suffer, I shall pay back to them a hundredfold." She had drawn from this resolution a purpose in living. Could one forgive someone like Bécher? . . .

She remained motionless, stiff, her hands clenched under her cape around the purse that Desgrez had given her.

"Believe it or not, Monsieur l'Abbé," the hangman's wife was saying, "but my greatest sin is pride."

"Now there you astound me!" the priest exclaimed, smacking his hands on his knees. "I don't wish to lack in charity, my daughter, but you who are loathed by all on account of your husband's profession, you whose very neighbours turn away muttering when you pass, I wonder where you can possibly find cause for pride and conceit."

"Yes, that's a fact," sighed the poor woman. "And yet, when I see my man, well planted on his legs, lift his big axe and, bang! lop off a head with a single stroke, I can't help being proud of him. It's not so easy, you know, Monsieur l'Abbé, to manage it with a single stroke."

"You make me shudder, my daughter," said the priest.

He added pensively:

"One cannot sound the human heart."

Just then the door opened. A square-shouldered giant walked in with a calm, heavy stride. He growled a greeting and glanced around with the imperious air of someone who is always within his rights. His fleshy face, pitted by pock-marks, had coarse, impassive features. He did not look a wicked man, but cold and hard like a stone mask. He had the face of a man who must neither laugh nor weep, an undertaker's face . . . or a king's, thought Angélique, who suddenly found that, despite his coarse craftsman's jacket, he bore a resemblance to Louis XIV.

This was the hangman.

She got up, and so did the priest, who wordlessly held out his letter of introduction.

Maître Aubin stepped over to a candle to read it.

"Very well," he said. "Tomorrow at dawn I'll take you along with me."

"Couldn't I be admitted tonight?"

"Impossible. Everything's closed. I'm the only one who can take you into the condemned man and, frankly speaking, Monsieur le Curé, I want to have a bite. All the other workmen are forbidden to work after curfew. But for me, day or night is all one. When it comes over them to make a patient confess, those gentlemen of the high courts get themselves into such a state, they'd all but go and sleep there! They gave him everything today: water, the boot, and the rack."

The priest wrung his hands.

"The unfortunate man! Alone in the darkness of a dungeon with his pain, his anguish at approaching death! Oh God, help him!"

The hangman cast a suspicious glance at him.

"You aren't going to make any trouble, are you? I've quite enough with that Friar Bécher at my heels, who never thinks I'm doing enough. By

Saint-Côme and Saint-Eloi, I think if anyone's possessed by the devil, it's he rather than the other!"

While talking, Maître Aubin was emptying the vast pockets of his jacket. He flung a few objects on the table and, suddenly, the little girls gave a cry of admiration. A cry of horror answered them.

With dilated eyes, Angélique had recognized, among a few gold pieces, the little pearl-inlaid case in which Joffrey used to keep the small tobacco-sticks he liked to smoke. With a swift gesture she could not check, she grasped it and pressed it against her. Without any sign of annoyance, the hangman opened her fingers and retrieved the case.

"Gently, my girl. What I find in the pockets of a condemned man is mine by rights."

"You're a thief!" she gasped, "an infamous ghoul, a despoiler of corpses!"

The man composedly went and took from the mantelpiece a chiselled silver casket and stored his booty away in it without answering. The woman went on spinning, nodding her head. She murmured in an apologetic tone, looking at the priest:

"They always say that, you know. You mustn't mind them. Yet surely, this one ought to realise that we don't get much out of it when they burn a fellow. I can't even recover the body to make a little extra with the fat, which the apothecaries ask for, and the bones which —"

"Oh, for pity's sake, my daughter!" said the priest, putting his hands to his ears.

He stared at Angélique with eyes that were brimming over with compassion. But she was not looking at him. She was trembling and biting her lips. She had insulted the hangman! He would now refuse the grim plea she had come to make.

With the same heavy, rolling gait, Maître Aubin walked round the table and went up to her. With his thumbs in his wide belt, he calmly looked her up and down.

"Apart from that, what can I do for you?"

Trembling and unable to utter a word, she held out the purse. He took it, weighed it in his hand, then stared again at Angélique with his inexpressive eyes.

"You want him to be strangled? . . ."

She nodded.

The man opened the purse, let a few crowns slip into his big palm and said:

"All right, it'll be done."

Noticing the horrified gaze of the young priest who had followed this conversation, he frowned.

"You won't talk, Father, will you? I'm risking a packet, you see. If I were caught, I'd have no end of troubles. I have to manage it at the very last moment when the smoke's hiding the stake from the public. It's to do a favour, you see?"

"Yes . . . I shan't talk," the abbé said with an effort. "I . . . you can rely on me."

"I scare you, eh?" said the hangman. "It's the first time you'll be assisting a condemned man?"

"During the wars when I used to bring the troops the comforts collected by Monsieur Vincent, many a time I went to accompany the poor fellows to be hanged, to the very foot of the tree. But that was war, the horrors and fever of war . . . whereas here . . ."

His helpless gesture motioned towards the fair-haired little girls sitting before their bowls.

"Here, it's the law," the hangman said, not without grandeur.

He leaned over the table familiarly, like a man eager for a chat.

"I like you, Father. You remind me of a prison chaplain whom I worked with for a long time. I can say this for him, that all the condemned men whom the two of us led died kissing the crucifix. When it was all over, he used to weep as if he'd lost his own child, and he'd be so white that many a time I had to force him to have a glass of wine to recover. I always have a pitcher of good wine with me. You never can tell what may happen, especially with apprentices. My father was a hangman's assistant when they quartered Ravaillac the regicide in the Place de Grève. He told me . . . ah well, perhaps you wouldn't enjoy this sort of story. I'll tell you later when you are more used to them. Anyhow, I used to say to that chaplain sometimes: 'Father, d'you think I'll be damned?' And he'd say: 'Hangman, if you're damned, I'll ask God to damn me with you. . . .' Look, Father, I'll show you something that'll help to put your mind at rest."

After foraging again in his numerous pockets, Maître Aubin displayed a small flask.

"It's a recipe I have from my father, who himself had it from his uncle, who was a hangman under Henri IV. It's made up for me in great secrecy by an apothecary who is a friend of mine, and whom I supply, in exchange, with human skulls for the manufacture of his magistral powder. He says that magistral powder is a sovereign remedy for gravel and apoplexy, but it needs the skull of a young man who's died a violent death. That's his business, after all. . . . I supply him with a skull or two, and he concocts my potion without breathing a word. When I give a few drops of this to a condemned man, he becomes quite cheerful and he suffers less. I only give it to those who've families that pay. But, still, it's doing them a good turn, isn't it, Monsieur l'Abbé?"

Angélique was listening open-mouthed. The hangman turned towards her.

"You want me to give him some tomorrow morning?"

She managed to utter through white lips:

"I . . . I have no more money."

"There'll be no extra charge," said Maître Aubin, bouncing the purse in his hand.

He pulled the small silver casket towards him again and put the purse inside. Mumbling a vague farewell, Angélique walked towards the door and left.

She felt like vomiting. Her whole body pained her. Yet the bustling square, still ringing with shouts and laughter, seemed to her less unbearable than the sinister atmosphere of the hangman's house. The shop doors were open despite the cold. It was the hour of day when neighbours were chatting on the porches. The archers were conducting the thief who had been taken down from the pillory to the Châtelet prison; a swarm of ragamuffins pursued them with snow-balls.

Angélique heard a hurrying tread behind her. The little abbé appeared, out of breath.

"My sister . . . my poor sister," he stammered. "I couldn't let you go away like that!"

She shrank back with a sudden movement. In the semi-darkness, faintly lit by a dim shop-lantern, the frightened churchman saw a face of translucent whiteness in which two eyes glowed with an almost phosphorescent glint.

"Leave me," Angélique said in a metallic voice. "You can't do anything for me."

"My sister, pray to God. . . ."

"It's in the name of God that my innocent husband will be burned tomorrow."

"My sister, do not aggravate your sorrows by revolting against Heaven. Remember that it was in the name of God that Our Lord was crucified."

"Your prattle drives me mad!" Angélique shouted in a shrill voice which seemed to her to come from far away. "I shan't stop until I in turn have struck one of your kind, until I've made him perish in the same tortures. . . ."

She leaned against the wall, put her hands to her face and a dreadful sob shook her.

"Since you will see him . . . tell him that I love him, that I love him . . . Tell him . . . ah! that he made me happy. And then . . . ask him what name I shall give the child that will be born."

"I shall do so, my sister."

He wanted to take her hand, but she avoided him and continued on her way.

The priest gave up following her. Bowed by the weight of human sorrows, he walked away through the narrow streets.

Angélique hastened towards the Temple. It

e monsters arrived below,
ok with fright
adful sight,
r beauty,
uded,
f was duly awarded.

s ran on to the signature:
e Gutter-Poet."
her mouth, she crumpled the

ll!" she thought.

her husband," Angélique said
un rose and a sparkling pure
spires of the city.
he would follow him to the
would have to take care not
he was still running the risk
sted. But perhaps he would
cognize her. . . .
e stairs with the sleeping
ns and knocked at Madame

th you for a few hours, Ma-

ned her sad witch-like face

bed, I'll mind him for you.

seemed to her that her ears were booming, for she suddenly heard shouts around her:

"Peyrac! Peyrac!"

She finally stopped. This time it wasn't a dream.

". . . but Peyrac, all agree . . . to Satan himself . . ."

Perched on one of the milestones that riders used to hoist themselves into the saddle, a skinny little scamp was bellowing at the top of his hoarse voice the last verses of a song, of which he had a bundle of copies under his arm.

The young woman came back and asked for a leaflet. The coarse paper still smelled of fresh printer's ink. Angélique could not read the words in the dark lane. She folded it and walked on. As she was approaching the Temple, the thought of Florimond grew uppermost in her mind. She was always worried to leave him alone now that he toddled about so much. You almost had to tie him up in his cradle, and this was not at all to the child's liking. Usually, he would cry during all the time of his mother's absence, and she'd find him coughing and feverish on her return. She did not dare to ask Madame Scarron to look after him for, ever since her husband had come to trial, the cripple's widow avoided her and almost crossed herself when she passed.

On the staircase, Angélique heard the baby's sobs and she hurried upstairs.

"Here I am, my treasure, my little prince. What a big boy you are."

She quickly threw a log into the hearth and put the pan with the child's food on the andirons. Florimond screamed even more lustily and flung out his arms. She released him from his prison at last, and he shut up as if by magic, deigning even to smile most engagingly.

"You are a little bandit," said Angélique, wiping his tear-stained little face. Her heart melted. She raised Florimond in her arms, and gazed at him in the light of the fire that made a red spark twinkle in the child's black eyes.

"Little king! Adorable little god! You are all that's left. How beautiful you are!"

Florimond seemed to understand what she was saying. He arched his little waist and smiled with a kind of innocent, self-assured pride. His attitude loudly proclaimed that he knew he was the centre of the world. She caressed him and played with him. He chatted like a little bird. Madame Cordeau often said that he was much in advance of his age as far as talking went. His syntax was far from perfect, but he knew very well how to make himself understood. When his mother had given him a bath and put him to bed, he demanded that she sing him a cradle-song, the one about the Green Mill.

Angélique tried hard to stop her voice breaking.

"Again! Again!" clamoured Florimond.

Then he put his thumb back into his mouth with a blissful air. She did not mind his being so tyrannical and thoughtless. She feared the moment when she would find herself alone again, waiting for the night to end. When Florimond had fallen asleep, she gazed at him deeply, then rose and stretched her aching body. Were the tortures that had broken Joffrey thus reverberating in her? The hangman's words came back to her with unbearable pain: "They gave him everything today:

792

wat
exa
she
lov

S
"
at

co
rea

fu
h
n
o
t

That when thes
Hell itself sho
At such a dre
And the prize f
while all appl
To Satan himse

Angélique's eye
"Claude le Petit, th
With bitterness in
sheet.
"Him, too, I'll ki

Chapter 49

A wife must follow
to herself, as the
sky spread over the
So she would go.
very last stage. She
to betray herself for
of getting herself arr
notice her, would re
She went down t
Florimond in her arr
Cordeau's door.
"Can I leave him w
dame Cordeau?"
The old woman tu
towards her.
"Put him into my

It's as it should be, poor lamb! The hangman looks after the father, the hangman's widow will look after the son. Go, my child, and pray to Our Lady of the Seven Sorrows that she may help you in your grief."

Like a sleep-walker, the young woman crossed the Temple Gate and headed in the direction of the Place de Grève. The mist over the Seine was just rising and disclosed the fine buildings of the Hôtel de Ville on the edge of the vast square. It was very cold, but the blue sky held promise of a sunny day.

In the foreground of the square, a high cross had been set up on a stone base near the gallows from which the body of a hanged man was swaying. A substantial crowd had begun to collect and was clustering around the gibbet.

"It's the Moor," someone said.

"No, it's the other one. They strung him up when it was still dark. The sorcerer will see him when he arrives on his tumbrel."

"But his face is quite black."

"That's because of the hanging. His face was already blue before. You know the song? . . ."

Someone started humming:

> The first man's face was coloured blue,
> The second man's had a jet-black hue.
>> But Peyrac, all agree,
>> Was ugliest of the three. . . .
> And the prize for beauty,
>> while all applauded,
> To Satan himself was duly awarded.

Angélique put her hand to her mouth to stifle a cry. She had just recognized in the misshapen body with its bloated face and swollen tongue, the Saxon Fritz Hauer.

A youngster in rags looked at her and laughed:
"The wench here is already swooning. What'll she do when they roast the sorcerer!"

"It seems that women stuck to him like flies to honey."

"No wonder: he was richer than the King, that's why!"

"He made all that gold by devil's work."

Shivering, the young woman clasped her cloak about her. A fat pork-butcher, standing on the doorstep of his shop, said to her good-naturedly:

"You should go away from here, my girl. What's going on here isn't a sight for an expectant mother."

Angélique stubbornly shook her head. After scrutinizing her wan face and her wild, staring eyes, the butcher shrugged his shoulders. He knew the dismal figures that came roaming around the gallows and the scaffold.

"Is this the place of the execution?" Angélique asked in a toneless voice.

"It depends on which one you've come for. I know they're hanging a journalist at the Châtelet this morning. But if it's for the sorcerer, it's here all right, on the Grève. See, there's the stake over there."

The stake had been put up some distance away, almost at the river's edge. It was an enormous platform of stacked faggots, at the top of which was a post. A small ladder was required to reach the top of it. A few yards away, the scaffold which served for decapitations was fitted out with stools on which the first ticket-holders of booked seats were beginning to take their places.

A dry wind rose and lashed the reddened faces with a fine snow-dust. A little old woman came to take shelter under the pork-butcher's porch.

"It's chilly this morning. I wouldn't have minded staying snugly round my brazier selling my fish in the market. But I promised my sister I'd bring her back a piece of the wizard's bone for her rheumatism."

"It seems it's effective."

"Yes. The barber of the rue de la Savonnerie told me he'd pound it for me with a little poppy-seed oil. There's nothing better for pain, he says."

"It won't be easy to get hold of some. Maître Aubin, the hangman, has asked for a double guard of archers."

"Of course, he wants to keep the choicest bits for himself, that flesh-eating devil's handyman! But hangman or no, everyone will have his share," said the old woman, baring her rotten teeth.

"At Notre Dame, you might have more luck in getting hold of a piece of his shirt."

Angélique felt a cold sweat dampening her spine. She had forgotten the first part of the ghastly programme: the public apology at Notre Dame. Hurriedly she began to run towards the rue de la Coutellerie, but the stream of people pouring into the square like teeming ants blocked her way and pushed her back. Never, never would she be able

797

to reach Notre Dame in time!

The fat pork-butcher left his door-step and came up to her.

"You want to go to Notre Dame?" he asked under his breath in a compassionate voice.

"Yes," she stammered. "I didn't remember . . . I . . ."

"Listen, this is what you do. Cross the square and go down to the wine-docks. There you ask a boatman to take you across to Saint-Landry. You'll be at Notre Dame in five minutes."

She thanked him and broke into a run again. The pork-butcher had given her good advice. For a few *sols*, a boatman took her in his boat and, with three strokes of his oars, landed her at the jetty of Saint-Landry. Looking at the tall, timbered houses standing in the mire of rotting fruit, she vaguely remembered that bright morning when Barbe had told her: "Down there, before the Hôtel de Ville is the Place de Grève. I saw a witch being burned. . . ."

Angélique was running. The street she had taken was behind the chapter-houses at the back of Notre Dame and it was almost empty. But the rumbling noise of the crowd reached her, punctuated by the deep, sinister notes of the knell. Angélique was running. She never knew by what superhuman strength she managed to fight her way through the serried ranks of spectators, and by what miracle she found herself in the front row, just outside the cathedral.

Just then, a long roar announced the arrival of the condemned man. The crowd was so tightly packed that the procession could hardly move forward. The hangman's assistants were trying to thrust the people aside with mighty lashes of their great whips. At last a small wooden tumbrel appeared. It was one of the rough-hewn vehicles in which the city's garbage was collected. Traces of mud and straw still clung to it.

Towering over this ignominious equipage, Maître Aubin, upright, with his fists on his hips, in scarlet hose and singlet and his chest emblazoned with the city arms, gazed sombrely down at the roaring populace. The priest was sitting on the edge of the cart. The mob clamoured for the wizard who could not be seen.

"He must be lying on the bottom," said a woman next to Angélique. "They say he is half dead."

"I hope not," her neighbour exclaimed spontaneously — a pretty girl with fresh cheeks.

The tumbrel meanwhile had come to a stop by the statue of the Great Faster. Archers on horseback, their halberds pointed horizontally, were holding the populace at a distance. Some policemen, surrounded by a crowd of monks of various brotherhoods, were moving across the square.

A sudden surge threw Angélique back. She screamed and clawed her way back to the front row like a fury.

The knell continued to toll over a crowd that had suddenly become silent. In an open space, a ghostlike apparition had emerged and was climbing the steps. Angélique's blurred eyes saw nothing but this silhouette of shimmering whiteness. Then she suddenly noticed that the condemned man had one arm over the hangman's shoulder, the other over the chaplain's, and that he was actually being dragged; he was unable to use his legs. His head with its long black hair was hanging down.

He was preceded by a monk who was carrying an enormous taper, the flame of which swayed in the wind. Angélique recognized Conan Bécher, his face contorted with ecstasy and spiteful glee. Around his neck, an enormous white crucifix hung down to his knees and made him stumble. He seemed to be performing a grotesque dance of death in front of the condemned man.

The procession advanced with nightmarish slowness. When they had reached the pavement outside the cathedral, the group stopped before the porch of the Last Judgment. A rope was dangling from the condemned man's neck. A bare foot beneath the white shirt was poised on the icy stone flags.

"That isn't Joffrey," Angélique thought.

It wasn't the man she had known, so fastidious and elegant, enjoying all the pleasures of life. It was some wretch, like all the wretches who had come here before him, barefooted, in a shirt, the rope round the neck.

At that moment, Joffrey de Peyrac raised his head. In the shrunken, colourless, deformed face, the immense eyes alone shone with a sombre glow.

A woman gave a piercing scream:

"He's looking at me. He'll bewitch me!"

But the Comte de Peyrac was not looking at the public. He was gazing straight ahead at the assembled old stone saints on the grey front of Notre Dame. What prayer was he addressing to them? What promise did he receive? Did he see them at all?

A court clerk had stepped up on his left and read out the sentence in a nasal voice. The tolling knell had stopped. But the words could hardly be heard.

". . . for the crime of abduction, enticement, impiety . . . magic . . . be delivered into the hands of high justice . . . taken bare-headed and barefoot . . . ask public pardon . . . a burning taper in his hand, and kneeling."

Conan Bécher then pronounced the words of *"amende honorable,"* the public apology.

"I admit the crimes of which I am accused. I ask pardon of God. I accept my punishment in expiation of my faults."

The chaplain had taken the taper which the condemned man was unable to hold. The people waited for the guilty man's voice to rise and they were growing impatient.

"Speak up, devil's henchman!"

"So you want to burn in hell with your master?"

Angélique had the impression that her husband was gathering up his last bit of strength. A wave of life coursed through his livid face. He pulled himself up on the hangman's and the priest's shoulders. He seemed to grow till his head towered over Maître Aubin. A second before he opened his mouth, Angélique had guessed, with love's intuition, what he was going to do.

And suddenly, in the frosty air, a deep, vibrant, extraordinary voice rang out.

The Golden Voice of the Kingdom was to be heard for the last time.

It sang, in the *langue d'oc,* a Béarnais refrain which Angélique recognized:

Les genols flexez am lo cap encli
A vos reclam la regina plazent
Flor de las flors,
  nou Jhésus prés nayssença
Vulhatz guarda la cientat de Tholoza. . . .

Angélique alone understood the meaning:

> . . . With knees bent and bowing head
> I commend myself to you, gentle queen,
> Flower of flowers in whom
>   Jesus had his birth
> Kindly watch over the city
>   of Toulouse . . .
> Most gentle flower in which
>   we take shelter . . .
> Most gentle flower
>   where everything blooms . . .
> Keep Toulouse always flowering. . . .

Angélique felt a pain like a dagger-stroke shoot through her, and she uttered a cry.

The cry rose alone in a sudden, terrible silence. For the singer's voice had stopped. Friar Bécher had lifted his ivory crucifix and had struck the mouth of the condemned man, whose head fell forward while a red saliva spilled from his lips to the ground. But almost at once Joffrey pulled himself up again.

"Conan Bécher," he cried in the same clear, ringing voice, "I shall meet you before God's tribunal ere the month is out."

A shudder of fright seemed to run through the populace, and there was an outburst of furious yells which stifled the Comte de Peyrac's voice. The spectators were convulsed with rage, in the grip of a delirious indignation. But what had provoked this outburst was not so much the friar's gesture as the condemned man's arrogance. Never had there been such an outrage on the square of Notre Dame! To sing! . . . He had dared to sing! If he had at least intoned a hymn! But the condemned man had sung in a foreign tongue, a diabolical tongue. . . .

Like some monstrous wave the stampeding crowd lifted Angélique up. Carried, crushed, trampled on, she found herself at last in the recess of a porch. She pushed open a door. The darkness of the empty cathedral received her, gasping and panting.

She tried to control herself, to control the pain that gripped her. The baby had stirred violently inside her while Joffrey sang.

The shouts outside were muffled as they reached her. For several minutes the clamour rose to a kind of paroxysm, then it gradually subsided.

"I must leave, I must go to the Place de Grève," Angélique told herself.

And she left the shelter of the sanctuary. On the square outside, a group of men and women was fighting on the spot where Bécher had hit the Count de Peyrac.

"I've got it, the wizard's tooth," one of them cried.

And he ran away, pursued by the others. A woman was waving a white rag.

"I managed to cut off a piece of his shirt. Who wants it? It brings luck."

Angélique was running. Beyond the bridge of Notre Dame she came again upon the throng that was escorting the tumbrel. But in the rue de la Vannerie and in the rue de la Coutellerie, it became almost impossible to advance. She begged people to let her pass. Nobody listened. They seemed delirious. Under the warm rays of sunshine, the snow was slipping from the roofs and falling in heavy lumps on their heads and shoulders. But nobody paid any heed.

At last Angélique managed to reach the corner of the square. At that very moment she saw a huge flame spring up from the stake. With her arms flung up, she heard herself shrieking like a madwoman:

"He's burning! He's burning! . . ."

Wildly she fought her way through to the stake. The heat of the blaze reached her. Stirred up by the wind, the fire roared.

There was a thunder-like, hail-like crackling. What were those human shapes that fidgeted in the yellow blaze of the flames. Who was that man, clad in scarlet, who was moving around the stake, plunging his flaming torch into the bottom layers of faggots?

Who was that man in the black cassock, clutching the stepladder, with seared eyebrows, who, with a crucifix held in his outstretched arm, was crying:

"Hope! Hope!"

Who was that man caught inside that blazing furnace? Oh God! could there be a living being inside that blaze? No, it wasn't alive, since the hangman had strangled him!

"Hear how he screams!" people were saying.

"No, no, he doesn't scream, he's dead," Angélique kept repeating.

And she put her hands to her ears, thinking she heard from that fiery curtain she knew not what heart-rending clamour.

"How he screams! How he screams!" the crowd was saying.

And others complained:

"Why did they put a hood over his head? We want to see his grimaces!"

A shower of white leaves blown about by a whirlwind escaped from the brazier and scattered in ashes over people's heads.

"They are the books of devilry that are burning with him. . . ."

The wind suddenly beat down the flames. Angélique saw, in a flash, the stack of books from the library of the Gay Learning and, behind it, the post to which a black, motionless form was tied, its head covered by a dark hood.

She fainted.

Chapter 50

SHE came to herself in the pork-butcher's shop on the Place de Grève.

"Oh! I've such a pain," she thought as she sat up.

Had she gone blind? Why was it so dark? A

woman with a candlestick in her hand was bending over her.

"You're better now, dear! I was afraid you might be dead. A doctor came and gave you a blood-letting. But it's my idea, if you want to know, that you are in labour."

"Oh no!" said Angélique, putting her hand on her belly. "I am not expecting for another three weeks. Why is it so dark?"

"Faith, it's getting late. They have rung the Angelus."

"And the stake?"

"It's all over," said the pork-butcher's wife, lowering her voice. "But it lasted a long time. What a day, my friend! The body wasn't entirely burnt till two hours after noon. And when the ashes were being scattered, there was a real battle. Everybody wanted some. They almost tore the hangman to pieces!"

She added after a moment's silence:

"You knew the wizard?"

"No," said Angélique with an effort, "I don't know what came over me. It's the first time I've seen anything like this."

"Yes, it gives you a turn. We shopkeepers of the Place de Grève, we see so much, it no longer impresses us. We even feel as if we've missed something when there isn't a hanged man on the gibbet."

Angélique would have liked to thank these good people. But she only had some small change on her. She said she would come back and repay them for the doctor's visit.

In the blue twilight, the belfry of the Hôtel de Ville was ringing the close of work. The cold was sharp with the falling dusk. At the far end of the square, the wind was kindling a huge red flower of glowing embers: these were the last remnants of the stake.

As Angélique was prowling around it, a humble figure moved out of the shadow of the scaffold. It was the chaplain. He came closer. She recoiled with horror, for he was bringing with him, in the folds of his cassock, an unbearable smell of burnt wood and roasted flesh.

"I knew you would come, my sister," he said. "I was waiting for you. I wanted to tell you that your husband died like a Christian. He was ready and unrebellious. He regretted leaving this life, but he had no fear of death. He told me several times that he was looking forward to coming face to face with the Master of all things. I believe he drew great comfort from the certainty that he would know at last . . ."

The abbé's voice expressed hesitation and a certain astonishment.

"That he would know at last whether or not the earth revolves."

"Oh!" Angélique exclaimed, revived by a sudden anger. "Isn't that just like him! Men are all alike. He doesn't care whether he leaves me on this earth, revolving or not, in misery and despair!"

"No, my sister! He repeated to me over and over again: 'Tell her that I love her. She filled my life with happiness. Alas, I shall have been but a passing stage in hers but I trust her to chart her own course.' He also said that he wished the name of Cantor to be given to the child to be born, if it is a boy, and Clémence, if it is a girl."

Cantor de Marmont, the troubadour of Languedoc, Clémence Isaure, the muse of the Floral Games of Toulouse . . .

How distant all this was! How unreal it all was in the face of the lurid hours that Angélique was living. She was now endeavouring to reach the Temple, but she walked with great difficulty. For a few moments she prodded her grievance against Joffrey. This grievance sustained her. Of course, Joffrey had not cared whether she was eaten up with pain and tears. What's the worth of a woman's thoughts? . . . Provided he, on the yonder side of life, would at last find an answer to the questions that had been haunting his scientific mind! . . .

Suddenly, a flood of tears streamed over Angélique's face and she had to lean against a wall to prevent herself from falling.

"Oh, Joffrey, my love," she murmured. "You know at last whether the earth revolves or not! . . . Be happy in all eternity!"

The pain in her body became racking and unbearable. She felt her whole being break asunder. Then she understood that she was going to give birth.

She was far from the Temple. In her aimless walk she had lost her way. She saw she was near the Bridge of Notre Dame. A cart was rumbling over it. Angélique hailed the driver:

"I am ill. Can you take me to the Hôtel-Dieu?"

"I'm on my way there," the man replied. "I'm going to collect a load there for the graveyard.

I am the fellow who drives the dead. Climb in, pretty lady."

"What name will you give him, my daughter?"
"Cantor."
"Cantor! That's not a Christian name."
"I don't care," said Angélique. "Give me my child."
She took the red, still damp little thing from the arms of the midwife. The virago who had welcomed him on this sorrowful earth had bundled him up in a rag of dirty linen.

The day was not over: midnight had not yet sounded from the lilied clock of the Palace of Justice, and the doomed man's child was born.

Angélique's heart was broken. Her body had been racked, her bowels torn. Angélique had died at the same time as Joffrey. With the little Cantor, a new Angélique was born, a new woman in whom there scarcely survived a trace of the strange sweetness and ingenuousness of the former Angélique. The wildness and harshness that had vibrated in the undisciplined girl of Monteloup came to the fore again, rushed like a black river through the open breach of her distress and her terror.

With one hand she pushed away her neighbour, a frail, burning creature who was softly raving in a delirium. A third woman, shoved against the edge of the bed, protested. She was suffering from a slow haemorrhage which had not stopped since morning. The sweetish smell of blood which impregnated the straw-pallet was nauseating. Angélique pulled a second rug towards her. The third occupant of the bed again protested feebly.

"Those two are here to die," thought the young mother. "So my baby and I might as well try to keep warm and get out of here alive."

With wide-open, wild eyes, she saw in the stinking darkness the yellow light of tallow-lamps shine through the torn curtains of the bed.

"What an odd thing!" she thought. For Joffrey had died, but Angélique was the one to be in hell.

In this nauseous den, where the foul smell of filth and blood hovered thick as fog, she heard sobs, wails and groans as if she were deep in a nightmare. The shrill screams of babies never ceased. It was like an endless singsong which mounted, then subsided, then rose again at another end of the ward.

It was icy cold despite the wheeled braziers put at the intersection of the corridors, for the draught dispelled their warmth. Angélique learned in what far-reaching experience the poor people's fear of hospitals was rooted. Wasn't it the anteroom of death?

How could they survive this accumulation of disease and filth, where convalescents mingled with contagious patients, where surgeons operated on soiled tables with razors which, a few hours earlier, had served to shave the beards of the local customers in their shops?

Dawn approached. The bells could be heard ringing for Mass. Angélique remembered the dead of the Hôtel-Dieu whom the nuns lined up before the porch at this hour and whom a tumbrel would take to the graveyard of Saints-Innocents. A tepid wintry sun might light the Gothic façade of the ancient hospital, but the limbs of the poor dead, sewn in their shrouds, would never come to life again.

A hand pulled back the curtains of the bed. Three male nurses in grimy smocks cast a glance at the three women on the pallet, then seized the last one, the woman with the haemorrhage, and put her on a stretcher. Angélique saw that the poor woman was dead. There was also the body of a child on the stretcher.

Angélique looked again at her baby whom she held pressed against her. Why wasn't he crying? Was he dead too? No, he was asleep, with clenched fists and a peaceful expression on his face, a funny one for a new-born baby. He did not seem to have the slightest inkling that he was a child of sorrow and disgrace. His face looked like a rosebud, and his skull was covered with a fine, fair down. But Angélique kept shaking him, afraid lest he might be dead or dying. Then he would lift his eyelids over blue, filmy eyes, and fall asleep again.

In the ward, nuns bent over the beds of other women in confinement. They certainly were devoted and displayed a courage which could find sustenance in God alone. But they were to cope with insoluble problems.

Clutching at her ardent wish to live, Angélique forced herself to drink the contents of a bowl that was handed to her. Then, in order to forget her feverish neighbour and the blood-soaked mattress, she sought strength in sleep. Ill-defined visions passed before her closed eyelids. She thought of Gontran. He was walking somewhere on the roads of France; he would stop by a bridge to pay the toll and, to spare his purse, would make a portrait of the toll-keeper. . . .

Why did she think of Gontran, who had become a poor wanderer on his tour of France but who at least was wandering under a pure sky? Gontran was like those surgeons who were there bending over an aching body imbued with the fervent determination to discover the secret of life and death. In the half-sleep in which she hovered detached from earthly contingencies, Angélique discovered that Gontran was one of the most precious men in the world . . . just like those surgeons. . . . But why were they no more than poor barbers, shopkeepers held in low esteem, when their rôle was so important? . . . Why was Gontran, who carried a world inside him and the power to rouse the enthusiasm even of kings, only a poor, needy, lowly craftsman? . . . Why think of such useless things when you had to gather up all your bodily strength to escape from hell? . . .

Angélique stayed only four days at the Hôtel-Dieu. Fierce and hard, she demanded the best blankets for herself, forbade the midwife to touch her or her baby with her dirty fingers. She would take from the proffered trays two bowls of food instead of one. One morning, she tore off the clean apron which a nun had just put over her dress, and before the poor novice could run to call her superior, she had torn the apron up into bandages to swaddle the baby and bind herself.

She countered all remonstrances with a fierce silence and gazed at her interlocutors out of scornful, implacable eyes. There was a gypsy in the ward who declared to her companions: "This green-eyed girl is a soothsayer!"

She spoke only once, when one of the administrators of the Hôtel-Dieu came in person to reproach her, holding a scented handkerchief to his nose.

"I have been notified, my daughter, that you object to another sick person sharing this bed which has kindly been granted to you by public charity. It even appears that you have already thrown down on the floor two women, who were too weak to defend themselves. Aren't you ashamed of this attitude? The Hôtel-Dieu owes it to itself to receive all the sick who are brought here, and there are not enough beds to go round."

"In that case, you would do better to sew up at once in shrouds the sick that are sent to you!" Angélique replied bluntly. "In the hospitals founded by Monsieur Vincent, each patient has a bed to himself! But you did not want anyone to come and reform your unworthy methods, because you would have had to render accounts. What happens to all those gifts of public charity you mention, and to the monies contributed by the State? People's hearts must be very ungenerous and the State very poor if you can't buy enough bundles of straw to change the bedding every day for those poor wretches who soil themselves and whom you let rot in their filth! Oh! I am sure that if Monsieur Vincent's ghost comes back to roam the Hôtel-Dieu, it must weep with sorrow!"

The administrator's eyes, behind his handkerchief, bulged with amazement. In the fifteen years that he had been managing the Hôtel-Dieu, he had certainly had to cope at times with unruly individuals, vociferating fishwives, foul-spoken prostitutes. But never had there risen, from those miserable couches, so blunt an answer in such polished language.

"Woman," he said, drawing himself up in all his dignity, "I can see from your words that you are strong enough to return to your home. You can leave this place where you do not appreciate the kindness shown to you."

"I shall be only too glad to," Angélique retorted bitingly, "but before doing so I demand that the clothes which were taken away from me when I arrived here and were piled up with all the rags of the sufferers from smallpox, venereal disease and the plague, be washed in front of me in clean water. If not, I shall walk out of this hospital in a shift and shout in the square of Notre Dame that the donations from the wealthy and from the public funds are lining the pockets of the administrators of the Hôtel-Dieu. I'll appeal to Monsieur Vincent, the conscience of the kingdom. I'll cry so loud that the King himself will ask to check the accounts of your establishment."

"If you do that," he said, bending forward with a cruel expression, "I'll have you seized and locked up with the lunatics."

She trembled but did not give ground. The reputation the gypsy had given her crossed her mind. . . .

"Then let me warn you that if you perpetrate this fresh infamy, all your family will die in the coming year."

"There's no risk in making such a statement," she thought, stretching out again on her squalid straw-mattress. "Men are so stupid! . . ."

The air in the streets of Paris, which she had formerly found so evil-smelling, seemed pure and delicious when she found herself free at last, alive and dressed in clean clothes outside the repulsive building.

She was walking almost gaily, holding her baby in her arms. Only one thing worried her: she had very little milk, and Cantor, who had so far behaved like a model child, was beginning to complain. He had cried all night long, pulling avidly at her empty breast.

"At the Temple there are herds of goats," she thought. "I shall bring up my child on goat-milk. Never mind if he grows up to be a romping young goat."

And what had become of Florimond? Widow Cordeau surely hadn't abandoned him. She was a kind woman. But Angélique felt as if she had left her firstborn years ago!

People passed her with tapers in their hands. A smell of hot pancakes came drifting from the houses. She told herself that this must be the second of February. People were celebrating the presentation of the Child Jesus at the Temple and the Purification of the Virgin Mary by exchanging gifts of candles, according to a tradition that had given this day the name of Candlemas.

"Poor little Jesus!" Angélique thought, kissing Cantor's brow, as she passed through the gate of the Temple.

As she was approaching Widow Cordeau's house, she heard a child crying. Her heart jumped, for she had the intuition that it was Florimond. Stumbling in the snow, a little figure appeared, pursued by ragamuffins, pelting him with snow-balls.

"Sorcerer! Hey, little Sorcerer! Show us your horns!"

Angélique rushed forward with a scream, seized the child in her arms and, hugging him against her, plunged into the kitchen, where the old woman was peeling onions in front of the hearth.

"How can you let those ruffians torment him?"

Widow Cordeau passed the back of her hand over her eyes.

"Ho, ho, my daughter, don't shout so much! I looked after your little one all right while you were gone, though I wasn't so sure I'd ever see you again. But I can't have him on my hands all day long, after all. I put him out so that he'd have some fresh air. What do you expect me to do when the kids call him 'Sorcerer'? It's a fact, isn't it, that his father was burned in the Place de Grève? He'll just have to get used to it. My boy was not much bigger than he, when they started flinging pebbles after him and calling him 'Rope-round-the-neck.' Oh! the little darling!" the old woman exclaimed, dropping her knife and coming towards her with an ecstatic face to admire Cantor.

In her poor little room, which she entered again with a sense of well-being, Angélique placed her two children on the bed and hastened to make a fire.

"I am so happy," declared Florimond over and over again, looking at her with his sparkling black eyes.

He clung to her.

"You won't leave me again, Maman?"

"No, my treasure. Just look at the pretty baby I brought back for you."

"I don't like him," Florimond promptly declared, snuggling up to her with a jealous air.

Angélique unswaddled Cantor and took him over to the fire. He stretched his little limbs and yawned. Heavens! By what miracle had she been able to give birth to such a fat baby amidst such torments!

For a few days longer, Angélique lived peacefully enough in the enclosure. She had a little money and was hoping for Raymond's return. But one afternoon, she was summoned by the bailiff of the Temple, who was in charge of the private police of this so-called privileged district.

"My daughter," he said unceremoniously, "I have to notify you on behalf of the Grand Prior that you will have to leave the enclosure. As you know, he extends his protection only to those whose reputation cannot in any way harm the good name of his little principality. You will have to go."

Angélique opened her mouth to ask what they were holding against her. Then she thought of throwing herself at the feet of the Duc de Vendôme, the Grand Prior. But she remembered the King's words: "I don't ever want to hear of you again!"

So they knew who she was! They were still afraid

of her, perhaps. . . . She understood that it was useless to ask the Jesuits to support her. They had loyally helped her as long as there had been something to defend. But now that the die was cast, they would keep all those in the background who, like Raymond, had been compromised in this painful affair.

"Very well," she said through clenched teeth. "I shall leave the enclosure before nightfall."

Back in her room, she packed all her belongings into a small leather trunk, wrapped up her two children warmly, and loaded the lot on a barrow. Widow Cordeau was out at the market. Angélique left a little purse on the table.

"When I am a little better off, I shall come back and be more generous," she promised herself.

"Are we going for a walk, Maman?" inquired Florimond.

"We are going back to Aunt Hortense."

"We'll see Baba?"

It was the name he had given to Barbe.

"Yes."

He clapped his hands. He gazed all around him with delight.

Pushing her wheel-barrow through the streets, slushy with mud and thawed snow, Angélique kept looking at the two little faces of the children who were closely pressed to each other under the blanket. The fate of these frail creatures weighed like lead upon her.

Above the roofs, the sky was clear and swept clean of clouds. There would be no frost tonight, for the weather had been warming up for the last few days, and the poor felt hope stir in their breasts again as they sat by their fireless hearths.

In the rue Saint-Landry, Barbe gave a great cry as she recognized Florimond. The child stretched his arms out to her and kissed her delightedly.

"Oh God, my little angel!" the servant stammered.

Her lips trembled, her eyes were filled with tears. She was staring fixedly at Angélique as if she were a ghost risen from the grave. Was she comparing this thin, hard-faced woman, more poorly dressed than herself, with the woman who had rung at the same door only a few months ago?

Angélique wondered curiously whether, from her attic-window, Barbe had watched the fire in the Place de Grève. . . .

A stifled exclamation from the staircase made her turn round. Hortense, holding a torch in her hand, seemed transfixed with horror. Behind her, on the landing, Maître Fallot de Sancé appeared. He was wigless, clothed in a dressing-gown, with an embroidered bonnet on his head. His lips dropped open with fright at the sight of his sister-in-law.

At last, after an interminable silence, Hortense managed to raise a stiff, trembling arm.

"Go away!" she said tonelessly. "My roof has sheltered an accursed family for too long already."

"Shut up, you fool!" Angélique replied, with a shrug.

She walked up to the foot of the staircase and raised her eyes towards her sister.

"I am going," she said. "But I ask you to take

in these innocent little mites who cannot do you any harm."

"Go away!" Hortense repeated.

Angélique turned towards Barbe, who was hugging Florimond and Cantor in her arms.

"I entrust them to you, Barbe, my girl. Look, here's all the money I have left, to buy milk for them. Cantor doesn't need a nurse, he likes goat's milk. . . ."

"Go away! Go away! Go away!" screamed Hortense in a shrill crescendo.

And she began to stamp her foot.

Angélique walked towards the door. Her last backward glance was not for her children, but for her sister.

The candle in Hortense's hand flickered and cast frightful shadows on her contorted face.

"And yet," thought Angélique, "didn't the two of us watch the little lady of Monteloup, the ghost with outstretched hands that used to pass through our rooms? . . . And we'd nestle close to each other with fright in our big bed. . . ."

She shut the door behind her. For a moment, she stopped to look at one of the clerks who, perched on a stepladder, was lighting the big lantern before Maître Fallot de Sancé's office.

Then, turning away, she plunged into Paris.

seemed to her that her ears were booming, for she suddenly heard shouts around her:

"Peyrac! Peyrac!"

She finally stopped. This time it wasn't a dream.

". . . but Peyrac, all agree . . . to Satan himself . . ."

Perched on one of the milestones that riders used to hoist themselves into the saddle, a skinny little scamp was bellowing at the top of his hoarse voice the last verses of a song, of which he had a bundle of copies under his arm.

The young woman came back and asked for a leaflet. The coarse paper still smelled of fresh printer's ink. Angélique could not read the words in the dark lane. She folded it and walked on. As she was approaching the Temple, the thought of Florimond grew uppermost in her mind. She was always worried to leave him alone now that he toddled about so much. You almost had to tie him up in his cradle, and this was not at all to the child's liking. Usually, he would cry during all the time of his mother's absence, and she'd find him coughing and feverish on her return. She did not dare to ask Madame Scarron to look after him for, ever since her husband had come to trial, the cripple's widow avoided her and almost crossed herself when she passed.

On the staircase, Angélique heard the baby's sobs and she hurried upstairs.

"Here I am, my treasure, my little prince. What a big boy you are."

She quickly threw a log into the hearth and put the pan with the child's food on the andirons. Florimond screamed even more lustily and flung out his arms. She released him from his prison at last, and he shut up as if by magic, deigning even to smile most engagingly.

"You are a little bandit," said Angélique, wiping his tear-stained little face. Her heart melted. She raised Florimond in her arms, and gazed at him in the light of the fire that made a red spark twinkle in the child's black eyes.

"Little king! Adorable little god! You are all that's left. How beautiful you are!"

Florimond seemed to understand what she was saying. He arched his little waist and smiled with a kind of innocent, self-assured pride. His attitude loudly proclaimed that he knew he was the centre of the world. She caressed him and played with him. He chatted like a little bird. Madame Cordeau often said that he was much in advance of his age as far as talking went. His syntax was far from perfect, but he knew very well how to make himself understood. When his mother had given him a bath and put him to bed, he demanded that she sing him a cradle-song, the one about the Green Mill.

Angélique tried hard to stop her voice breaking.

"Again! Again!" clamoured Florimond.

Then he put his thumb back into his mouth with a blissful air. She did not mind his being so tyrannical and thoughtless. She feared the moment when she would find herself alone again, waiting for the night to end. When Florimond had fallen asleep, she gazed at him deeply, then rose and stretched her aching body. Were the tortures that had broken Joffrey thus reverberating in her? The hangman's words came back to her with unbearable pain: "They gave him everything today:

water, the boot and the rack." She did not know exactly what horrors those words concealed, but she knew that they had tormented the man she loved. Oh! let it be over soon!

She said aloud:

"Tomorrow you'll be at peace, my love. You'll at last be freed from ignorant men. . . ."

On the table, the song-sheet she had bought had come unfolded. She took the candle over to it and read:

> Far below in his bottomless pit,
> Satan in front of his mirror would sit
> And think men were perfidious
> To say his face was hideous.

The poem went on to describe in sometimes funny, frequently foul terms Satan's perplexity as he wondered whether, all told, his face, so much maligned by the image-makers of cathedrals, could not honourably stand comparison with the faces of mankind. Hell offered to organize a beauty contest with the next arrivals from Earth.

> Just then, three rogues in
>   the fire were thrown,
> Wicked magicians, every one.
>   And soon as they were roasted
>   To hell the three were posted.
> The first man's face was coloured blue,
> The second man's had a jet-black hue.
>   But Peyrac, all agree,
>   Was ugliest of the three.
> No one will be surprised to know

That when these monsters arrived below,
  Hell itself shook with fright
  At such a dreadful sight,
And the prize for beauty,
  while all applauded,
To Satan himself was duly awarded.

Angélique's eyes ran on to the signature:
"Claude le Petit, the Gutter-Poet."

With bitterness in her mouth, she crumpled the sheet.

"Him, too, I'll kill!" she thought.

Chapter 49

"A wife must follow her husband," Angélique said to herself, as the sun rose and a sparkling pure sky spread over the spires of the city.

So she would go. She would follow him to the very last stage. She would have to take care not to betray herself for she was still running the risk of getting herself arrested. But perhaps he would notice her, would recognize her. . . .

She went down the stairs with the sleeping Florimond in her arms and knocked at Madame Cordeau's door.

"Can I leave him with you for a few hours, Madame Cordeau?"

The old woman turned her sad witch-like face towards her.

"Put him into my bed, I'll mind him for you.